MEET EUGENIA PRICE'S CHARMING HEROINE AND THOSE WHO TOUCH HER LIFE . . .

Anne Couper

She trusted love, endured heartbreak and found that nothing could keep her from the man she loved.

James Hamilton Couper

For Anne's strict, yet affectionate brother, honor was a simple matter of right and wrong. Would his demand for family loyalty end her chance for happiness?

Eve

The daughter of a slave and a vicious overseer, she cared for Anne more than any living creature . . . until the love for the slave called Ebo June awakened the woman in her.

Ebo June

Abducted from his native land, he chose life over death. Now that he had won Eve's heart, would the proud slave choose freedom over love?

Lieutenant John Fraser

Beautiful Anne Couper, planter's daughter and slave owner, represented all the abolitionist Royal Marine loathed, yet he loved her with all his heart.

SHARE ANNE'S TRIALS, FAITH AND DESIRE

St. Martin's Paperbacks Titles
by Eugenia Price

Bright Captivity
Where Shadows Go
Beauty from Ashes

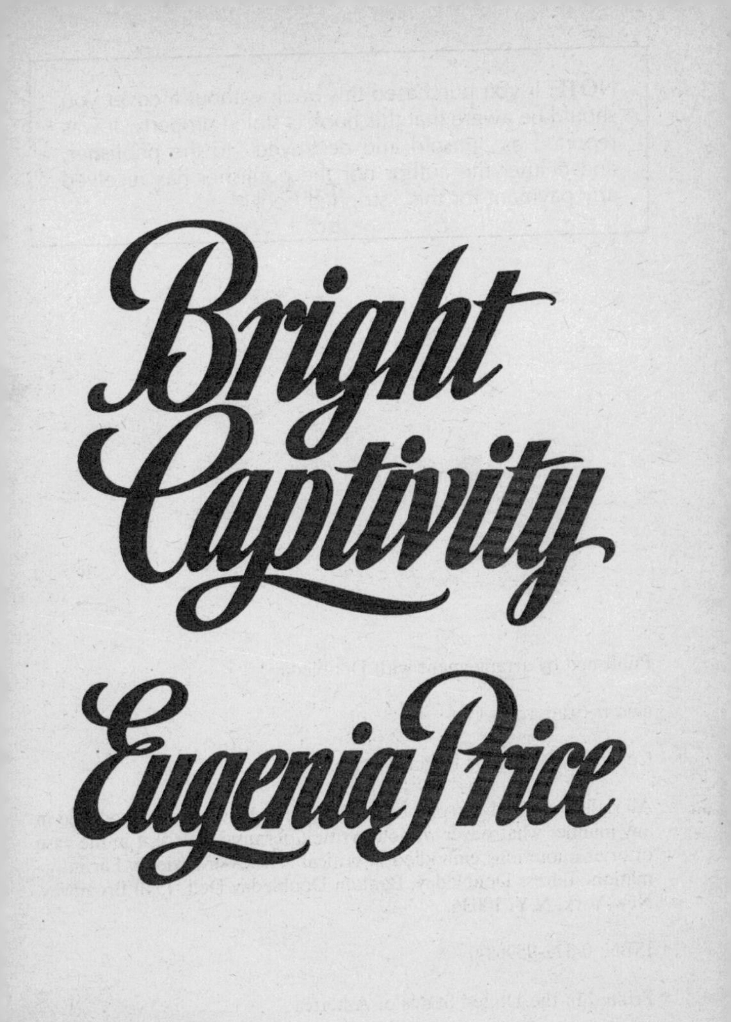

St. Martin's Paperbacks

Published by arrangement with Doubleday

BRIGHT CAPTIVITY

ISBN: 0-312-95968-0

Printed in the United States of America

Doubleday hardcover edition/May 1991
Bantam paperback edition/April 1992
St. Martin's Paperbacks edition/July 1996

St. Martin's Paperbacks are published by St. Martin's Press, 175 Fifth Avenue, New York, NY 10010.

10 9 8 7 6 5 4 3 2 1

FOR
JO COUPER
CAUTHORN

Bright Captivity

Prologue

May 1803

Some mornings six-year-old Anne Couper felt herself lifted slowly, happily, into a new day by birdsong outside. Today, though, it wasn't melody she heard. It was a loud, steady banging, as if someone was pounding. She came awake so fast she thought it must be the comical, huge red-crested woodpecker, which Papa's people called the Lord God Bird, chopping away on the old live oak at the corner of the cottage where the Coupers were living until Papa's fine new house could be finished.

Being waked up by what Papa called bird business, of any kind, was certainly nothing new or strange, but a sort of prickly chill ran through her at what she'd heard and, eyes wide open, she sat bolt upright in bed. Something was different! There was no sunlight between the slats of the wooden shutters. It wasn't morning at all. It was still nighttime, and hurrying herself out of sleep, she realized that the darkness outside was clattering and roaring with rain and thunder and wind. What was the Lord God Bird doing hunting breakfast in the middle of a stormy night?

Then she knew. That wasn't a bird. Someone was pounding hard on the cottage door downstairs.

An anxious, half-whispered conversation from her parents' room across the hall, then the quick shuffle of Papa's slippered feet on the steep stair that led down to the front door, told her Papa was on his way to investigate. She hated her door closed at night, so knew for sure when the yellow flare of the lighted candle he carried threw a shadow across her ceiling.

Anne rubbed her eyes to be absolutely certain she wasn't dreaming and thought crazily that maybe she'd imagined the knocking and that Papa was just giving in to their shared, special urge to march back and forth on the front porch because it was storming outside. Neither of them had ever been able *not* to march in a rainstorm, no matter how foolish her picky, brainy brother, James Hamilton, and Mama thought it was. "Your brother, James Hamilton, don't forget, is the Old Gentleman in our family," Papa always said laughingly in the private, secret way father and only daughter shared a joke, but she felt sure now that Papa wasn't marching tonight. Someone had been beating on the door and although storms never scared her a bit, her whole body felt goose-bumpy and cold—like winter instead of May.

Anne had no idea what time it was, but the bond that seemed always to tie her to Papa tugged and when another splitting clap of thunder followed a flash of lightning, she was out of bed feeling for her slippers, then tiptoeing toward the hall. Someone was downstairs with Papa and she meant to find out who. If Papa doesn't take him into the parlor and close the door, she thought, I'll be able to hear what they say. Mama had ears like a deer. Anne would have to be sure not to step on a squeaky board or she'd be caught. Her heart was pounding, but she didn't know why because Papa could settle anything that might have gone wrong out at the quarters. And back when she was very young and wanted to keep a candle burning in her room to push away the dark, he'd always told her that the dead of night on the north end of St. Simons Island was a very safe place to be. Maybe the safest place anywhere on the whole earth.

Whoever was down there with Papa sounded a lot like Mr. Roswell King, Major Pierce Butler's manager at nearby Hampton Plantation, but what was he doing crossing Jones Creek to their house in the black of night in a rainstorm?

Her mother's tall clock downstairs struck four times. Four in the morning! Anne hadn't heard Papa shut the parlor door and she also hadn't heard him say one word that she could make out. The man with him was dreadfully upset, talking fast, sounding out of breath. . . . Something terrible had happened, but even though she was sure now that their visitor was Mr. Roswell King, she hadn't yet been able to tell exactly what he was saying. I'll just have to wait, she thought, and wished that James Hamilton wasn't such a sound sleeper and could be there to listen with her.

Finally, she heard Papa's voice. "Slow down, King! You roused me from a sound sleep with a tale I'd have trouble following at high noon. I gather I've lost some of the new Africans I bought from Mein and Mackay in Savannah and that young Spalding has lost part of the cargo he ordered too. But what I want to know is, why did it take my overseer, Patterson, three whole weeks to get his cargo from Skidaway Island to St. Simons? The secret African holding camp at Skidaway is on this side of Savannah—to the south. What took so long?"

Mr. King was speaking more slowly now, so Anne could hear every word. "First a week's wait for your children's new British tutor to reach Savannah. Browne, I think his name is."

"That's right," she heard Papa say. "Is William Browne here on St. Simons now? Did he come from Savannah in the schooner with the Negro cargo?"

"That's right, and as far as I know, the young man is still down at Major Page's at Retreat. Likely scared half out of his wits. But safe."

"Good, but even so, what did take the *York* all that time to get here?" Papa demanded.

"Bad weather all the way, Mr. Couper, plus those infernal winding rivers and creeks between here and there. Long layovers when the tide or the wind didn't suit. Poor Patterson was not entirely to blame. A month or so ago, when I went up to bring back the first boatload of slaves for Major Butler's rice plantation, we were nearly two weeks on the way. One ripped sail when a squall hits can use up two days to mend. I guarantee you nobody meant to take so long, to risk keeping that untamed cargo of niggers penned up a minute more than necessary. Ebos aren't known for being exactly mild."

"Has Thomas Spalding heard about the uprising yet?"

"I thought to ride here first, sir, cross the creek to my own bed for what's left of the night, let the storm blow over. Anyway, Mr. Spalding's not due back from the senate in Louisville until day after tomorrow. I'll make my way then up to Sapelo Island to tell him."

For what seemed a long time, neither man said a word and Anne tried to hold her breath so that she could stay absolutely quiet. Papa had mentioned an uprising. What, she wondered, was that?

Then Mr. King blurted, "To tell the truth, I all but lied to you just now, Mr. Couper."

"Lied?"

"I didn't tell you the half of how fierce the uprising was. Grizzly. Glad I left my boy at home. Those niggers leaped up out of the ship's hold, chains and all, and if your man Patterson and the two white crew members hadn't jumped overboard, they'd have been murdered on the spot. Your fancy British tutor hid under the tarpaulin of a lifeboat. That saved him."

"You saw it all, King?"

"Saw it plain as day. Wasn't even twilight yet. I was standing right down there on that Dunbar Creek bluff when those black savages came roaring out. God knows I don't have an overdose of sympathy for any nigger, essential as they are to us. After this, I know I'll never have an ounce of sympathy for any Ebo—certainly not them that took their own lives at your expense. Yours and Spalding's. It was hideous! I well could have lifelong nightmares at what I seen." Mr. King made an ugly shuddering sound. "What I seen with my own two eyes, I'll never forget."

"I—I'm not quite sure why *you* were there tonight, King," Anne's father said, his voice husky. "You'd already met the other schooner with Major Butler's Ebos aboard. Why were you down at Dunbar Creek when the *York* brought our cargo?"

"I'm overseeing the building of Spalding's new house for one thing. You were always a good neighbor to my employer, the major, when he lived here. He's called headstrong by most men, but Major Butler's a gentleman. I knew he'd want me to be of any help I could to you *and* Spalding. Yet, as God is my witness, it was a fearsome sight. Saw it all happen. Saw it *all* happen."

Anne wondered why Mr. King kept telling her father that he saw it all happen. She'd always thought Major Butler's manager didn't talk much, but he seemed not to be able to help himself now. "I not only saw it all take place, sir, I heard that wild, keening noise the Ebos made when they jumped overboard—those throat-splitting yells when they came screamin' up out of the *York*'s hold. I reckon they'd call it some kind of singin'—savage! There were sixty or seventy altogether, I guess. I saw their pink mouths open, gasping for air, black arms reaching when it was too late.

One Ebo let out an unmerciful cry, slapped both hands together in the air, and sank in his chains down into the brackish tide. All but a handful seemed bent on killing poor Patterson and the crew. The nine or ten niggers not outright attacking the white men just stood there as though they were waiting for something or somebody to come help them. Then I saw some try to jump like scared rabbits out onto the creek bank. They didn't make it. You know, sir, Dunbar Creek is infested with man-eating 'gators. Before another big Ebo went under, he thrashed around in the water with the bloody stump of one leg jerking in the air. It was all hours ago and I can still see your poor overseer, Patterson. I kept thinking it could have been me. The charge of those Ebos scared him so bad, he leaped overboard, fought the water till the current caught him. He screamed like a woman—just once. And then with my own eyes, I seen him go under. Two sailors drowned too. Three innocent white men. Nightmare, Couper, nightmare. . . ."

By now Anne felt sick, but she kept listening hard. After another long silence, Mr. King said, "You know I would have saved your overseer if any man could have saved him. But I was fifty feet away on the bluff, the wind was roaring, the creek raging, it was high tide, and—"

"Save your breath, King." Papa's voice was cross. "I'm sure you'd have saved my overseer had you been able to do it. But did anyone, anyone at all try to help a single Ebo who drowned? Was no one there from Brunswick who could have lent the poor devils a hand?"

"Only the two men I hired and they were waitin' on the bluff with me. One of the reasons Patterson picked out that spot on Dunbar Creek to unload 'em was that Hawkins Island shields it from the river traffic. Even so I have to say I hear criticism in your voice, Mr. Couper, and I'm hurt by it. My feelings are hurt. Those Ebos jumped overboard on their own—screamin' their wild songs. Yellin' in their savage tongue. They *meant* to kill. I take your remark as an unkind cut, sir. After all, they were *your property.* Any white man would have done all a man can do to save property. I tell you the niggers were out of control—wild beasts—ready to kill! *They* killed Patterson."

Anne caught her breath. Had those Ebos really caused nice Mr. Patterson to drown? Papa had always called his overseer "the kindest young bumbler anywhere," but Anne liked him a lot because he'd been willing to stop his work anytime to put a wheel back on her cart and one day he showed her how to wrap a corncob doll. Now Mr. Patterson was dead somewhere out there in the black, stormy night. She shuddered. Was he still under the waters of Dunbar Creek, his lean young body bumping around on the bottom in the mud?

"Any white man but that bookish tutor would have tried to save your property, sir," Mr. King said again, struggling to keep his voice low. "Your property and Spalding's. Never mind that Spalding thinks he doesn't approve of owning slaves. He imported his share of illegal Ebos right along with you because he's got a big house to build too. He's got to have more hands to work for him. You both suffered an enormous loss. Five hundred dollars a head. Between you and Spalding, you lost ten or twelve head. That's big money. To say nothing of the fact that you'll both pay ten dollars for each nigger salvaged."

Anne tried to think what *salvage* meant, but the almost hard tone of Papa's voice when he spoke again caused her to forget.

"Hang the money!"

"Hang the money, Mr. Couper?"

"Aye, hang it from the near-r-rest t-r-ree limb." Papa was rolling his Scottish *r*'s as he always did when he was upset. Anne wondered exactly what Mr. King had said to make him so angry. "You've spoken, mon, like any good, pr-practical overseer and perhaps in a day or so, I can discuss such matters as my financial loss more calmly. I just can't do it now."

The silence Papa fell into suddenly grew so long Anne began to worry. Especially when he finally said that he was just too stricken tonight for more talk and that he'd thank Mr. King properly tomorrow for coming in such weather to report the tragedy. Then, offering Mr. King one of the Couper skiffs to take across narrow Jones Creek to his own cottage at Hampton's Point, Papa bid their neighbor good night and closed the door softly. In a minute, Anne heard him jerk it open again and yell over the storm for Mr. King to come back.

"In the name of heaven, what *did* happen, King? What made my man Patterson jump overboard in the first place? You were there. Was he trying to save the Ebos? Did they really scare him so much he lost his head? Or—or are you trying to tell me the Ebos chose *death* over working for me here at Cannon's Point?"

Anne strained to hear Mr. King's answer from the front porch, but the rain was beating hard on the roof and windows, the wind too loud through the trees for her to catch one word. Shaking all over from the unfamiliar fear she'd felt every minute since she'd been wakened, she was comforted but not a bit surprised when her mother, carrying a flickering candle, slipped an arm around her and pulled Anne down beside her on the top step.

Even Papa's voice was mostly lost in the storm when he spoke again to Mr. King, but Anne did hear him say he'd go along when Mr. King went to tell Mr. Spalding what had happened.

She heard the door close but still sat close to Mama on the stair, peering wide-eyed down into the gloomy cottage hallway at her father's anxious, upturned face. "Papa?" she whispered. "What happened? Why did Mr. Patterson get drowned?"

"Anne! Mr. Patterson didn't get drowned, dear," Mama almost scolded. "Did he, Jock? Tell the child our overseer is just fine. Anne is acting so strangely, almost as if she's in the throes of a bad dream."

"She is, Becca," Papa said as he came slowly up to where they sat side by side on the stair. "The gir-rl must have heard the whole ugly story. It's like a hideous, never-to-be-forgotten nightmare."

"But Papa's here with us now, darling," Mama whispered. "He's right here with us. He'll explain everything."

Before Papa could say another word, James Hamilton, sleepy-eyed, dark hair tousled, came down the upstairs hall in his nightshirt. "I heard Mr. King's voice out in the yard just now. What's wrong?"

"A lot, son," Papa answered on a deep sigh. "Along with Thomas Spalding, I—I ordered a boatload of Africans early this year through the Savannah firm of Mein and Mackay. Did it when you and I were up there."

"I know," James Hamilton said. "I remember. You told me then."

"I also told you, I'm sure, son, that to do what we did was against Georgia law."

"Yes, sir," the boy answered. "A Georgia law forbids the

importation of slaves from foreign countries. A law written into the state constitution, which you signed. You and Mr. Spalding both."

"Aye, James. Just five years ago at the State Constitutional Convention at the capitol in Louisville. You might as well know—all of you—that good, br-rainy, well-intentioned Thomas Spalding and I br-roke the law."

"You told me that in Savannah, too, Papa," James Hamilton said. "But we break the law every time we teach one of our people to read."

Papa's heavy sigh sounded so wretched, Anne longed to hug him. "Well, evidently, from what King just reported tonight, the Lord is passing judgment. Some time yesterday, at least ten or twelve of those Africans committed suicide—*because* we broke the law."

"John, should you be saying such things before Anne? The child is so young!"

Mama didn't call Papa by his real name, John, unless she was worried. Anne glanced at her mother's troubled face, then right back at Papa towering above them on the steps in the moving shadows the candlelight made. He looked sad and scared. Because she'd never seen him this way before, she clung harder than ever to her mother's hand.

"Anne's got to learn sometime, Becca, that no matter how hard a man tries to be considerate of his people, no matter how necessary is the evil of slaver-ry, how totally a planter's livelihood depends on it, God's punishment can blow through the cracks of the best intentions with the fury of a hurricane. I—I was even forewarned of trouble. The poor wretches who drowned themselves were Ebos."

"Ebos, Papa?"

The word *Ebo,* which Anne had never heard until tonight, seemed to have some special, grown-up meaning for her awfully grown-up nine-year-old brother.

"Aye, Ebos, son," Papa said in a flat voice. "Back in late January while you and I were still in Savannah, I told Robert Mackay of Mein and Mackay that since Spalding and I had such urgent need for extra people to build our new homes, we'd settle for the spirited, freedom-loving, therefore often troublesome Ebos because they had already been loaded aboard a ship on the Gulf of Guinea and could get here sooner."

"John, does Eliza Mackay know her adored husband,

Robert, deals—on the side—in illegal importation of slaves?" Anne heard her mother draw in her breath. "Oh dear, Anne, forget I ever said such a stupid thing, please?"

"I'll try, Mama."

"Papa," her brother broke in, "I'm sure I heard Mr. King say Mr. Patterson drowned too. What caused him and the Ebos to drown? Where did it happen?"

"Down at Dunbar Creek, here on St. Simons. And to me, the cause is the hard part. Evidently Patterson knew the shape they were in, so was afraid to open the hold when the *York* passed Spalding's place on Sapelo. Poor Patterson lost his head and jumped overboard because the Ebos evidently came to the end of their endurance. They chose to die rather than live in bondage. When Patterson opened up below deck to transfer them out, onto shore, they str-ruck!"

"Struck, Papa?" James asked.

"Rose up against Patterson and two crew members. They'd been shut up in the cramped hold of the schooner *York* for nearly thr-ree weeks just getting from Skidaway Island to here. The white men were seized with panic, jumped for their lives into the r-roiling water, and dr-rowned. Except the new English tutor, Browne, a passenger on the *York*. Seems he hid in a lifeboat. I'll know more later, but there were at least sixty Ebos all told. Ten or twelve are now dead." Anne saw Papa look up toward the dark hall ceiling. "What will haunt me forever is that the Ebos chose to die rather than work for me."

"But our people here at Cannon's Point have good lives," Mama said weakly. "If only they'd waited to find out."

As though he hadn't heard Mama at all, Papa said, "I may learn what actually happened. Or I may never really know unless the new tutor can tell me, and because the English hate slavery so much, no one may ever know the whole truth."

"I guess nobody was able to tell the Ebos that you're such a kind master, Papa," James Hamilton said. "I guess being primitive, they couldn't understand what anybody might try to tell them—about anything."

Anne herself didn't understand much of what she'd just heard, but she had never seen such a dark look on Papa's face as when he plodded past them and headed in silence toward his room. Squeezing the fingers of her mother's hand, she longed to be able to understand all of what had made Papa feel so sad and hopeless.

Right then and there, though, she vowed to hope and pray and try terribly hard to feel happy again. But what if she could never forget the look on Papa's face or what happened to those Ebos and her poor friend Mr. Patterson, no matter how long she lived? Worse yet, what would it be like having the Ebos who didn't drown living right there with them all at Cannon's Point? Would the Ebos be mean? Or dangerous? Or just awfully scared and strange? She had been so excited that Mr. William Browne from Oxford was coming to be their new tutor, but why did Papa seem to think he might not tell them the truth about what happened?

All the next day while he waited for Thomas Spalding to return from his senate session in Louisville, John Couper did his level best to act as though things were normal at Cannon's Point. He did remain behind the closed door of his tiny plantation office longer than usual, though not working, as he hoped his family would believe, on his records. Mostly he sat staring at the yellowed water stain on the old cottage wall, thinking, because he couldn't help it, of the blow it would be to young Thomas Spalding when King told him the details of the Ebo tragedy.

More of a blow than it was to me? He wondered and decided that yes, it would be. After all, Thomas Spalding was the grandson of John Mohr McIntosh, who had, some sixty years ago, before slavery was allowed in the colony of Georgia, not only signed but composed the petition to the colonial governor-general begging that the urgent request by Savannahians to permit slavery in the colony be flatly denied. Eighteen liberty-loving Highlanders from Darien had signed McIntosh's antislavery petition, and the ultimate rightness of it still infected young Thomas Spalding.

Infected? Was *infected* the word? Aye, it was. Of course, the Scots' petition had been turned down. The few planters then on St. Simons Island had agreed with the Savannahians that in order to prosper, they must all own slaves and therefore had remained silent. Twenty-nine-year-old Thomas was himself now a large slaveholder, but his hereditary disapproval of the dark evil he had felt forced by circumstances to embrace kept him struggling against his own dislike of one race's owning the very lives of another.

Through the years of their friendship, John Couper had learned a certain tactful, noncommittal response when Thomas fretted over it aloud even as both men went on trying to lighten the burdens of the people they already owned. Couper had learned to give Thomas a safe, understanding smile that he hoped had long ago convinced the younger man that he, too, deep in his heart, wished there were another way for a man to succeed at planting.

Only alone with his thoughts could John Couper face and confess his own deep-down belief that slavery's evil was no less simply because the so-called free laboring classes in other parts of the world also lived horribly burdensome lives. He knew only that one man's total mastery over another—any other—was dead wrong. Yet, it was also absolutely necessary to the planter's system in this year 1803. Necessary and dangerous. More dangerous in the long run, he was sure, to the white man's soul than to the African's. Much of the time he avoided thinking about it, but he was dwelling on it today, and today in particular, he chafed more than usual at being forced to face the ugly fact. Life was far more pleasant at Cannon's Point when he lived on the edges of what he knew to be true, treating his own people well though firmly—for everyone's sake. He needed his people in order to provide for both his children and his beloved Rebecca, to give them the good, secure life they deserved.

Did his intelligent, thoughtful wife ever find herself troubled over the peculiar institution? So far as he honestly knew, she did not. She had grown up in a happy family in the Midway district, just beyond Darien, on the orderly plantation of her Scottish father, James Maxwell. John truly doubted that Rebecca had ever given much thought to the question of slavery. He hoped not. More than anything on earth, he wanted her happiness. Part of his reason for being so considerate with his people had to do with creating the right kind of untroubled atmosphere around Rebecca, his son, James Hamilton, and his adored daughter, Anne. The hundred or so people he owned were as much a normal part of Anne's daily life as the river flowing by, as the subtle coastal change from spring to summer, as the tiny bright bird he and Anne insisted on calling a nonpareil and *not* a painted bunting as scientific-minded James Hamilton urged.

Would James be forced to defend their way of life at the North when some day he attended Yale College? Couper smiled to himself. Every thought of his unusual son always made him want to smile with the kind of pride only a father could feel in such a capable, mature boy. If Northern classmates at Yale should taunt him because his father was a slave owner, Couper had no doubt that James Hamilton could stand his ground with courteous aplomb. Unruffled was the word for precocious, already composed James Hamilton Couper, the family's Old Gentleman. Far more unruffled than his father, heaven knew. Problems to James had always seemed to present only challenges, never guilt or anger or worry. With all his heart, today John Couper wished that his cherished young friend Thomas Spalding felt as adequate to all of life as nine-year-old James seemed. Thomas tended to brood, though, carried the scars of owning slaves, was tormented to find a way to move them out of serfdom into a kind of spiritually oriented community where each African would labor on Sapelo Island as Spalding himself did, for sheer love of the land.

Never one to wear his faith on his coat sleeve, Couper's thoughts went to the one Person anywhere able to steady him now. As a boy back in Scotland, he had rebelled some at his minister father's strict religion, but the kernel of Papa's faith had taken root in him. Worrying, squirming over the tragedy, was getting him nowhere, so from habit he took up a conversation with God as though they hadn't left off talking: "Can a man care properly for his loved ones, Almighty God, with no thought of profit at all? Can a helpless mortal protect and provide for his family with no means but good intentions and a show of love? I render my own sinful heart and my beloved family to Thee on this scarred day after the mysterious tragedy of yesterday down on Dunbar Creek. But I see no way *not* to render also unto Caesar! Hold up my weak hands when I go with Roswell King tomorrow to tell young Thomas what happened. Help me accept the death of my own overseer. I pray for the soul of poor, terrified Patterson. Strengthen *my* limp soul so that I may, for Thomas's sake, for the sake of my family, at least appear to be making the best of a necessary evil."

Slowly, he pulled his tall, middle-aged frame out of his chair, made himself straighten his shoulders, stood there motionless for a moment. Then, stalling the inevitable, he went to the small cottage window open to the still-overcast but mild May morning. Because it never failed to lift his spirits, he leaned out for a look at the well-proportioned shape of his unfinished new home about to be attached to the old cottage. Did God answer a man's prayer for strength by showing him a sign of his own material success? Probably not, but he felt sure the good Lord didn't particularly object that forty-four-year-old John Couper felt a sense of accomplishment. By next year he could move his little family out of the cramped Cannon cottage into the new Cannon's Point mansion. "In my Father's house are many mansions," he whispered. The Scripture referred to heaven, he knew, but he saw no point in being ashamed of the mansion he was building here on earth.

By ten the next morning, John Couper sat facing Roswell King in one of the Butler cypress dugouts, relieved that King had left his cocky young son at home. The four Butler oarsmen, who had brought King across Jones Creek from Hampton Plantation to get Couper for the trip to Spalding's place up on Sapelo Island, would normally be singing by now to the rhythm of their oars. They were not singing on this bright, blue-clear day, though, even after rowing as far north as Doboy Sound. The water was calm after a windy, overcast sky yesterday, but the boatmen were silent. Only the regular clunk of heavy oars in the oarlocks and the occasional cry of a gull broke the quiet. So far, Couper and King had spoken little, to each other or to the oarsmen. Africans, usually loquacious, seemed almost to need no communication when something untoward happened. They seldom even needed to be told. They knew. He would have sworn that these four Hampton slaves already knew about the Ebo drownings, even though Major Butler's earlier cargo of Ebos had been safely deposited at his other vast holding on Butler's Island, some sixteen miles away.

"Don't fret about how I'll get back to Cannon's Point, King," Couper said because he needed to say something. "Spalding will see that I'm delivered to my own dock before my Ebos can possibly be brought there from Dunbar Creek. With the new Ebos already at Major Butler's rice island place, you need to be over there, I'm sure. Every man among them must be in turmoil."

With no change on his gaunt face, Roswell King said,

"You're right. I should be there. Taming time with any gang of savages is never a simple matter."

"I'm not talking only about 'taming time'!" Couper heard the edge in his own voice. "Don't much like that word *taming* anyway. I just know you need to be there to handle things." When King only nodded, Couper, unable to bear the sullen silence, went on. "Still seems strange I can't ask young Patterson why this all happened. I need to know if the Ebos I ordered were properly fed, had enough water down in that ship's hold for such a long voyage. I haven't quite realized I can't even ask my poor overseer one single question."

"It's unfair to criticize the dead," King said, "but the one surviving crew member off the *York* blamed Patterson's bad management for at least part of the cause of the uprising. Good overseeing is everything to an owner. You deserved proper management, Mr. Couper."

Not even trying to avoid the note of sarcasm in his voice, John said, "Every plantation owner isn't fortunate enough to have an overseer with your extreme talent for *tough* management, Mr. King."

"The major seems satisfied," Roswell King said in the way he had of sounding humble even while boasting. "Look here, sir, no need to avoid the subject with me as though I'm not aware that you and Spalding are on one side of the slavery question, while I, from sheer loyalty to my employer in Philadelphia, stand firmly on the other. Major Butler and I both know you and Mr. Spalding are against owning slaves."

Despite the exhaustion he felt from two nearly sleepless nights, Couper's blue eyes twinkled with a half-smile. "Am I that obvious? Of course young Spalding makes no secret of his own revulsion at our peculiar institution. He inherited it straight from his Scottish ancestor, John Mohr McIntosh, but I thought I managed to mask my own feelings rather well. Still, I want you to tell me while we're on the hateful subject, King, have you ever heard Cannon's Point called 'nigger heaven'?"

"Not exactly, sir. Only Spalding's place. I am your closest neighbor, though, Mr. Couper, with my main residence just across the creek from your land. I know how easy you are on your people."

Believing it past time to end such talk, John said in what

he hoped was good humor, "Be that as it may, Spalding and I both earn a splendid profit most years, in spite of the way we choose to handle our people. Furthermore, we've been conversing, you and I, as though we're alone in this good cypress dugout of the major's. Four of his quite human people are here rowing us. We're not alone in spite of the odd silence of our oarsmen. I feel downright discourteous."

Totally ignoring what Couper had said, King muttered, "Spalding owns slaves now, no matter how strong his inherited convictions. He also owns four thousand acres of land on the south end of Sapelo, plans to buy more, and so, his Scottish grandfather notwithstanding, young Spalding will always be a slave owner. A big slave owner. And with all his nobility, a bit of a hypocrite in my eyes."

Couper took a deep breath in an effort, he supposed, to dislodge that word *hypocrite.* "I think I'll let that pass, sir. Without doubt, Thomas will always be a slave owner, as will I. At the moment, I hope you'll feel free to urge the major's oarsmen to sing. They row better singing, and by nature, I thr-rive on it!"

Half an hour later, the wide expanse of Doboy Sound behind them, the Hampton dugout scraped along the sandy landing at the mouth of the Duplin River, which wound through the marshes of Sapelo Island. Almost all the way from Cannon's Point, a few gulls had followed the wake of their boat, and as Couper and King made their way ashore and along the dim, tree-canopied, moss-draped road that led to the modest cottage where the Spalding family lived, the air around them seemed in motion with marsh birds—clapper rails, egrets, herons, redwings, ospreys, kingfishers.

"There's a mystery about Sapelo, I always felt," Couper said as they trudged along. "As though the ghosts of its former occupants—Indians, Spanish priests, the English, the French—could still be haunting these gloomy, dense woods. Still, in such a definite way this is young Thomas's place now. In a special sense, his very own." As though speaking aloud to himself, certainly not expecting the practical King to respond, Couper added with a chuckle, " 'Twould ease my foolish heart some if I thought my friend Spalding possessed even a slight sense of humor, though. Do you know the young man sees nothing funny about the way a seagull waddles on land? Do you realize he actually despises music of all kinds? Dancing, singing? How on earth does he keep his people from breaking into song while they work? I thought we got here just as Major Butler's oarsmen were getting tuned up."

"They sing all right, I'll wager, when Spalding is out of hearing," King said. "By the way, Mr. Couper, it wasn't my fault the oarsmen were silent earlier. Some days when one pouts, they all seem to. Today was one of those days. I let 'em sing at will. They work better."

For the first half hour or so, once welcomed by Spalding himself into the small, well-furnished parlor of his temporary cottage, Couper said little as he listened to King's retelling of the Ebo uprising. His own heart ached this time even more than before. Watching Spalding's sensitive, handsome face closely, the ache grew. His young friend was receiving the news with enormous pain and sorrow. Except for the expected questions as to the number of Ebos drowned, what might have gone wrong, Thomas Spalding spoke little. There was an almost cold detachment in King's retelling, as though he'd found a way during the intervening time to handle his earlier sense of property waste as well as his own horror. When King finished, an awkward silence fell around the three men.

Finally, Spalding said, "Thank you, Mr. King. I hope you'll feel at liberty to be on your way now to the major's rice plantation on Butler's Island. Am I correct that you've already engaged the same schooner, the *York*, to deliver the remaining Ebos? Back up to me here and to Mr. Couper's place?"

Standing now, King rubbed his hands in what John Couper saw as entire self-satisfaction. "Oh, the niggers'll be safely brought in the *York* here to you, sir—in chains. The other part of the cargo in small numbers in dugouts, guarded well, to Cannon's Point. All was arranged for by Major Page at Retreat. The major will also bring the new Couper tutor to Cannon's Point in his own boat. I worked that out with him before I even rode to tell Mr. Couper the stormy night it happened. There won't be another uprising. I can guarantee you that—both of you."

"And when can I expect my Ebos to arrive?" Spalding asked.

"Before noon tomorrow the *York* should reach Sapelo.

Late this afternoon the dugouts, Major Page, and the English teacher should be arriving at Cannon's Point, I should think." Then King stood and bowed elaborately. "Until then, good day, gentlemen."

For a long time after Spalding had seen King to the door and rejoined John Couper in the pleasant parlor, the two close friends sat without speaking. Spalding's adored wife, Sarah, brought tea and left, wisely asking no questions.

"She's eerily sensitive at times," Thomas said at last. "I marvel that the good Lord brought her my way, Couper."

As they sipped their tea in another lengthy, heavy silence, broken only by the ticking of a mantel clock and a wren calling outside the open parlor windows, John Couper waited for his young friend to speak again.

"We broke the law, Jock," Spalding said just above a whisper.

"Aye."

"Is that all you can say—'aye'? Every fiber of my body is at this minute so filled with revulsion and shame, I could—I could wish my life would end!"

After a time, Couper said softly, "You could wish your life would end were it not for your beautiful wife, your little girls, this lovely island—and God."

Both hands extended helplessly, Spalding groaned, "God is punishing us both—justly. Buying on the Savannah market is legal. Importing slaves is not."

"Aye."

"You have the same Scottish way of my blessed late father. You include everything—everything good and bad—in one 'aye.' "

"Is there much else to add, Thomas?"

"Only that we bear an intolerable burden by being what we've chosen to be—slave owners." Then, in his usual solemn manner, the younger man added, "God's punishment will go on too. When the remaining Ebos reach us, whatever kindness and consideration we both try to show may not work out so well—with them. It will take them months to learn any English." He struck the arm of his chair. "I hate it! I hate all of it. In spite of how we try, these fiftysome surviving black men will go right on here on Sapelo and at your place being shut up—cut off from life, from all that's familiar—as surely as they were in the stinking hold of the ship that brought them from their homes and families in Africa."

"A slave ship brought many of our people at one time or another away from Africa, Thomas."

Looking straight at Couper, the younger man said, "This is worse somehow. Dozens of our other people were born in this country. We feel stronger guilt now only because the earlier ones were delivered to us without tragedy. Until this shipment of Ebos, we didn't get caught breaking the law. We got by, Jock. Except for our own consciences, we'll get by this time too. Mark my word. Every one of the other island planters will choose to forget about our Ebo cargo."

What Thomas said was so true, John decided to add nothing. What could be added to a whole truth?

Part One

January 1815–May 1815

Chapter 1

On the morning of January 7 of the new year 1815, first light had just begun to push the dark from the sky outside the window of Anne's room on the third floor of the Couper mansion when Eve opened the shutters and blew out one stand of candles.

"You did that too soon," Anne complained, pent-up excitement and nervousness showing in her voice. "It isn't even light enough yet to see the bare outline of the trees over on Little St. Simons!" Oddly, her personal maid, Eve, said nothing. "I'm having enough trouble getting this bulky shawl into this box," Anne said. "I need to see what I'm doing. The last thing Papa said yesterday was that the *Lady Love* would need to be moving out into the river away from our dock the minute the sun appears. You know he never allows his oarsmen to be pushed for time. It's fortysome miles down to Cumberland Island. Eve!"

"Yes'm."

"You've acted funny ever since you helped serve breakfast. The rude way you banged that big tray of pancakes and ham down on the buffet in the dining room certainly proves you aren't sick. You're peeved at something and this is no time for one of your big acts! Light those candles again, do you hear me? And then come help me with this stubborn shawl."

For the first time, Anne realized that they'd been packing for at least half an hour without one word from Eve beyond the toneless "Yes'm," which usually meant the slender, bright-skinned girl was pouting.

Anne walked around the bed, still strewn with unpacked clothing, so that she faced her servant, who stood like a rock, back turned, head down, refusing to meet Anne's eyes. As always in difficult moments, Eve gave her the eerie feeling that inside the tawny, startlingly beautiful girl, deep, wise, even frightening things were going on. Anne had never tried to explain it to anyone, even to herself, because it was too mysterious, too puzzling, too unnerving. Eve could not know anything Anne didn't know. She was a whole year younger than Anne, whose eighteenth birthday would finally come while she and the family and Anna Matilda Page, her best friend, were at the eagerly anticipated house party at Dungeness on Cumberland Island. Eve was not even seventeen yet, wouldn't be until after Anne returned later in January. So, how could Eve know anything or be any way that would cause Anne to feel helpless with her? To feel, in a way, less than Eve?

"You know how I've been longing to go to Mrs. Shaw's house party at Dungeness," Anne almost pleaded. "You know how long I've waited for this very morning. It's finally here and it's the very worst time for one of your pouts. If you care about me half as much as you pretend, you'll help me find a place for this aggravating shawl and stop acting so, so weird." When Eve, untypically, again said nothing, Anne snapped, "Look at me! Nobody at Cannon's Point talks as much as you most of the time, and there you stand, head down with—" What sounded like a sob caught in Eve's throat. "Look at me!" Anne repeated. "I want to see the condition of your eyes." Her instinct told her they were dry.

She reached her hand to lift Eve's chin. It was firmly locked. Eve was fully in charge by the weight and force of her silence. Mama knew how to be convincingly firm at a time like this with any servant in the house. Anne longed for even a shred of her mother's way with their people, her calm and composure. Instead, more like Papa, she found herself struggling not to laugh in case something was really wrong with Eve. Devoted as she knew Eve to be, good at her work, the dark-skinned sixteen-year-old with the strikingly lovely features and perfect form could, at the slightest whim, be utterly ridiculous. Anne and her father always laughed at the ridiculous.

She decided to try reason. "I'll be back from Cumberland in plenty of time for your birthday, Eve. I know you're making a present for me, but I promise to be home again for your seventeenth. We can exchange presents then. Won't that satisfy you?"

"No, ma'am. It sure won't. An' that ain't the reason I'm heartbroke anyway."

Plainly, Eve meant to maneuver her into asking the reason for her sullen behavior. Well, Anne could be stubborn, too. She tried more logic and ended up talking too much. "Not only should we have all these things ready for June to carry down to the dock, I should be down there too, right now. Papa won't allow his people to be overworked at rowing a boat or at anything else. You know perfectly well how long it will probably take for us to stop at Retreat Plantation to pick up Anna Matilda Page. If her parents are still there, that will take more time while James Hamilton and Papa and Major Page discuss the dumb British and the stupid war. Do you want us to reach Cumberland way after dark?"

"Effen you take me along, I'd see to you," Eve muttered, "even in the black dark."

"I know you would, but there isn't room in Papa's boat. That's been settled and I think you're dreadfully selfish to send me off on such a happy occasion with my nerves on edge. I know you're still young, but you look like a grown woman. A capable, mature woman."

How Eve happened to be so much more beautiful than the other women on the plantation Anne didn't know, but nowhere among the house servants or any of those down at the quarters was there a female of any age as downright attractive as Eve. There was a kind of elegance about her. Mama had argued that Eve was too young and headstrong to have been allowed to look after Anne during her final year at Miss Datty's boarding school in Charleston, but Anne and Papa had won. Mama had been right, Anne and Papa wrong. Eve went along and now she couldn't get over feeling superior because of it. It was certainly Eve's nature to feel superior anyway. She knew she was pretty. Some of Papa's people had dull, very dark skin. Eve was a vibrant color; the skin on her arms, neck, and remarkably even-featured face literally glowed.

As Anne and Eve were growing up, Mama had helped Anne learn patience with Eve's often smart-aleck ways, had explained at length that the years would temper her. She'd just about convinced Anne that it was only natural for a servant as quick and lovely as Eve to feel a notch or two above the other house people. Eve was independent, even with the older, respected servants such as statuesque Rhyna, who much of the time took complete charge and acted as though she, not Papa, owned them all.

"I know what I look like," Eve said, after another silence. "I can see in your lookin' glass too. What's more, I know why I look the way I do. An' I hate it!"

"You hate the way you look?"

"No, I likes it! But I hate the reason I look like this." Eve whirled to glare at her. "You strainin' not to laugh at me."

"No, I'm not! But I am puzzled. You're one of the few people even at Cannon's Point, certainly one of the few on St. Simons Island, who can read a book. You can write. You can do anything you really want to do except control your selfish disposition. I'd think you'd be happy that I'm so looking forward to going to Louisa Shaw's party."

Staring down at Anne's bed, strewn with packing boxes, Eve spit out her words: "She oughta be 'shamed to be givin' a party just two month arter her ma died!"

"Mrs. Shaw's mother's been dead four months," Anne corrected. "Anyway, everyone knows her mother, Mrs. Catherine Miller, believed in parties."

"Them rich folks on Cumb'land so high 'n' mighty they give you a servan' girl you like more'n you like me. They got thousands!"

"The Shaws have plenty of servants, but not thousands, and I'll never be satisfied with anyone but you, Eve. Not ever."

Now Eve turned from folding scarves on the bed to look at her, the arresting features alight with joy. "You don' eber lie to me, does you? Least I ain' neber caught you lyin' to me. Ain' nobody look arter you but me. Nobody as good as me."

"The word is *after,* not *arter,* but you're right. I couldn't possibly get along without you." Anne was smiling back at her now with real affection. The moment hung there shimmering, bright with meaning, both hearts in it. "You're naughty, Eve. You're also stubborn and spoiled and self-willed, but with me, you're always going to be first."

Without actually touching her, Eve gave a little wave in Anne's direction. "You whip me good if they's one wrinkle in your purty, new velvet dress when some fumblin' nigger way down there on Cumb'land take it outa that box, you hear?"

"Pooh! I hear you, but I'm as likely to whip you *ever* as I am to, to grow polka dots on my face! Here," she ordered, handing Eve the thick shawl. "If you're so good, squeeze this in too."

"Lay it down," Eve said, expertly making room in the box.

"Papa's going to be calling me any minute, so hurry!"

"Mos' likely it be you brother, Mausa James," Eve grumbled, poking at the shawl's long fringe. "I declare he done got tall an' bossy since he been up North to dat fancy college place. You know he keep track even of hisself ebry minute—by his watch?"

"Eve, you're stalling with all this nonsensical prattle about my brother. Finish that box so I can ask you something very important. So important, I need your full attention."

"What you wanna axe?"

"Finish that last box first. June will be up here to take all my luggage down any minute."

For an instant, Eve's sly smile struck Anne as more playing, stalling for time just to keep her from going. But when Eve went on grinning in her most knowing manner, Anne began to feel curious. "What's so funny?"

"Ain't nothin' funny. You sure June be the one comin' up to carry all this?"

"That's what James Hamilton told me. Why?"

Eve stacked the bulging portmanteau on top of a well-packed box and then just stood there, hands on hips.

"What are you waiting for?" Anne asked.

"For you to axe me. Do it hab anything to do wif you take me to Cumb'land? You play one of your games?"

"No! You can't go to Cumberland unless you swim along beside the *Lady Love* because there's no place in it for you to sit down. But I would like to find out—straight from you—if what Rhyna told me yesterday is true. She told me you have your heart set on one of Papa's best oarsmen. If that's true, which one?"

Eve's eyes blazed. "Ol' Rhyna tell you? That rattlemouth ol' woman!"

"She isn't a rattlemouth and she's no older than my father and you're not allowed to keep anything secret from me."

"Where dat down in plantation law?"

"Don't act smart just when I have to leave, please! It isn't written into any law anywhere. I—I'm a whole year older than you but I don't know anything about—falling in love with a man, and I either want to be sure you don't or find out for certain if you do! *And* his name."

"You call his name, just a while ago." A look so impish and delighted lit Eve's eyes, Anne could have flounced angrily from the room if she hadn't been so curious, so in need of learning about love. Even from Eve. After all, Anna Matilda Page was far too sheltered and innocent to discuss such things even though she was rich and an heiress who would surely marry someday.

"You are in love, aren't you, Eve? With whom? What's his name? Stop teasing and tell me."

"He be here any minute you say."

Anne's mouth fell open. "June? *Ebo June?*"

"You know June long as I know him."

She certainly did know June and for an instant she felt frozen where she stood by the same, half-forgotten panic of that stormy night back when she was only six. The ugly, still-unexplained panic she'd felt when she overheard Mr. Roswell King tell Papa that five or six of his Ebos had drowned themselves in Dunbar Creek. The early years, growing up in Papa's new big house, had been too good, too filled with sun and laughter and fun and love to remember the terrifying night very often, even to have the same nightmare over it very often, but she was remembering it right now, of all times: the night her child-mind had experienced its first nameless dread. Dread of what? To this day she didn't know, and all these years, her reserved tutor, Mr. Browne, had refused to talk about it, even to Papa. But the dread loomed huge and dark between her and Eve this minute because one of the young Ebos brought in chains, still alive, two days later to Cannon's Point, had eventually given himself the name *June.*

"Ebo June?" she gasped. "Of course I know him! I remember when he came. But isn't—isn't June awfully old for you? He must be past thirty by now."

Not a muscle moved in Eve's face. Only her eyes changed. Without a word, Eve was giving to her, from those dark, knowing eyes, Anne's first glimpse of what it might be like when at long, long last, Anne Couper fell in love too. The dark-skinned girl was her personal maid. In a very real sense, Anne had always owned her, had always had every right and reason to command her, and yet at this moment, she again felt the lesser of the two. With all her being, standing there under Eve's wise, piercing gaze, Anne longed to beg Eve to explain, to give her some small hint of what actually happens inside a woman when one man out of the whole world appears to fill her horizon. Eve had not put it into words, but Anne knew that Eve and June loved in a way few white people ever dreamed their Negroes could love.

"How old June is don't matter none to me or to him," Eve said after the long, almost scary silence in which she had looked back at Anne with that strange, grown-up, secret knowledge *about a man.* "The *way* June love me counts. The way I love him back." With an abruptness that took Anne completely off guard, Eve fell to her knees, a torrent of words tumbling out—tumbling and tumbling. "You don't reckon Mausa Couper sell June away! You don't reckon he keep me *eber* some way from June's arms. Me an' June, we meets by dat big oak tree off by the riber. Dere June show me how old he be don' make no diff'rence—how young I be. June show me how a man an' woman kin be jus' one pusson. Only June then. Only me. . . ."

Anne made herself ask how June showed Eve and if she didn't feel ashamed of herself for letting him.

Jumping to her feet, Eve dropped the poignant, pleading tone. "Shamed?" She laughed, and then some inner, dark thought twisted her face. "I don' feel no shame to love June. I does feel bitter, though, fo' my mama. Bitter an' sad for my good mama!"

"Why? Why on earth would you feel bitter or sad for your mother, Fanny? I'd think you'd feel ashamed of loving June in secret because Fanny's so honest and gentle and good."

"Hush, Miss Anne!"

Aghast, Anne whispered, "Hush? Did you tell me to hush?"

"I did 'cause I ain' done. Long before he was Major Butler's white overseer, ol' Roswell King, he done come here to do timber bi'ness with your papa. Way back then, either him or his timber helper *force* my mama an' den I come along. Mama won't say, but I b'lieve it was King. He done threaten to tell Mausa Couper she steal!" Eve's voice was all defiance. "Nobody tell me sure, but I know *he be my papa,* ol' King!"

So overwhelmed by what Eve had just told her, Anne could only gasp, "Fanny—steal? Never Fanny!"

"Co'se not! She too godly. *I hate dat man,* but it don' matter no more, 'cause Mausa Couper own my mama *an'* me now." Eve's superior smile flashed. "An' anyway, ol' King give me a straight nose an' thin lips like you, an' since he come to work for Major Butler he don't cause us no bother. He don' even know me, so I win. 'Cept since June, I feel sad ain't nobody eber show my mama what heaven it be —what it really be between one man an' one woman."

Eve's expression had turned so soft now, so dreamlike, Anne almost forgot about hurrying, almost forgot her own shock at learning that Roswell King may be Eve's father. Even if Eve was wrong, she would never, never forget what the girl had just shown her about the sheer wonder of one man and one woman.

"I speck I did tell you to hush," Eve said. Not apologizing, smiling, dreamlike, speaking just above a whisper: "Oh, Miss Anne, my heart done set forever on June."

In a sudden rush of feeling, Anne embraced her. "Thank you, Eve! I was prying. I'm sorry. I hate nosy people. I—I just long to know so much that I don't know. . . ."

As though Anne were by far the younger of the two, Eve promised, "Some day when you need to know, Eve splain *all* you don' know. I tell you this much now—Eve already know you longs for the time when *you* find only one man to love you back."

Anne's heart raced. What on earth would this loyal, impulsive, strong-minded girl dare say to her next? How could Eve know her so well? Suddenly, nothing seemed fair. Her own maid, at sixteen, had already found her one true love, while Anne still longed, still hoped, still searched. Oh, there had been the clumsy attentions of the fat, sweating son of the Macks who lived in the run-down cottage on Frederica Road. There had also been well-off, pimply, fast-talking Bubba Crawford, down the island, who vowed undying love for Anne *and* her best friend, Anna Matilda Page—both vows, they later discovered, uttered not one full day apart. Neither young man counted for anything.

There was no more time to talk now, but Eve continued to stand there, glowing with love for her tall, lithe, smooth-muscled Ebo. June was a good worker, an excellent cooper and boatman, Papa always said, but so spirited and proud he required firm handling, even by gentle, generous Papa.

Just then, the crisp, authoritative voice of James Hamilton called from downstairs. It was past time to go. "You're already fourteen minutes late, Sister! The *Lady Love*'s loaded except for your things. Come on, this minute. June's on his way to carry down for you."

At the front window, Eve almost hissed, "Look! Here *she* comes! Here come ol' Miz King just a hightailin' it up to where your mama waitin' down at our dock. What she doin' cross Jones Creek on our side?"

Rushing to the window, Anne could see Mrs. Roswell King, wife of Major Butler's manager, and from the look on the woman's face, something was very wrong. "I'm going on down," Anne said, wrapping herself in her heavy winter travel cape. "You know what to tell June to bring, Eve. See to it."

From the hall outside her bedroom, Anne could hear and then see June mounting the steps toward her two at a time. Then she remembered that she had not said a proper good-bye to Eve, so hurried back to her room.

I'd give almost anything to be here when June lopes in, she thought, teasingly admonishing Eve to behave while she was gone, to keep Anne's birthday present safe and sound until her return. Even with June on his way upstairs, Eve would surely have begun to pout again, had Anne neglected a special good-bye.

"Eve up here ready to give me orders?" June asked a moment later, standing aside on the wide stair landing for Anne to pass, his strong, dark face eager, and quite handsome, Anne noticed for the first time.

"You know she is, June, and you do exactly what she says."

He laughed his low, velvety laugh. "Dat depends, Miss Anne. Even with Eve, dat depends."

"But Mrs. King," Rebecca Couper argued as the two women stood together out of the way of the oarsmen stowing the last of Mr. Couper's boxes into the bow of the forty-foot plantation boat, "I'd hate going all the way to Cumberland without my husband! Are you quite sure there's real danger here? Aren't the British still way up north? Tell me exactly what your husband told you."

"He doesn't have to *tell* me anything! The anxiety I feel for his safety is so great, I can't sleep a wink. He's already seen two British warships right here in our waters! I hadn't laid eyes on my husband or our son, Roswell, Jr., in almost two days until they came ashore an hour ago to find Mr. Couper. My poor husband stays on the water, keeping a faithful watch. You know his respect for all of you at Cannon's Point. And, of course, his life turns around Major Butler's interests at both his plantations. My poor worried Roswell is not only exposing himself to the evil British enemy but to the cold weather, too. Our son is only eighteen! Mr. Couper just must not run off to a house party and leave my husband here in such danger! Our husbands are both needed here to protect *property.* The British really are stealing slaves, luring them away, setting them free."

"Where is your husband now, Mrs. King?"

"Down at your stables trying to convince Mr. Couper not to leave Cannon's Point. Night and day, he's been out on the water in that penetrating wind. He has an awning over his boat, but that's cold comfort in January weather like we're having now. Roswell never allows himself to lose sight of those British ships at anchor. I beg you to urge your husband to listen to him, help at least to protect his own property, not to leave!"

Anne had reached the dock in time to hear only part of Mrs. King's frantic appeal. Setting aside courtesy, she butted right into the conversation between her elders. "Papa *has* to go with us! Half the fun will be spoiled if he stays here."

"But, Anne, your brother is certainly old enough to escort us to Cumberland." Her mother turned to Mrs. King. "Oh, dear, Rhyna and Liz and I packed some of Mr. Couper's clothing in the same boxes with mine. Think of the rowing time we'll lose if we have to unpack now. We're late as it is. Still, it can be done if my husband thinks he's needed here."

Anne's heart sank. If Papa didn't go, Mama might decide they all had to stay, and for weeks, since the December day when Louisa Shaw's invitation came, Anne, for a reason even she didn't quite fathom, had *lived* for the Cumberland house party. Her burning desire to attend had nothing to do with her family's being among the select few invited to holiday festivities at such a grand house as Dungeness. Of course, there was a stupid war going on with the British—

something about their stealing American sailors and now slaves—but Anne *had* to be at that house party on Cumberland Island. She had to be.

"Mama, I'm sure the British are still somewhere up near Washington City. I don't think Louisa Shaw would give a party at all if she thought there'd be any kind of trouble."

Before her mother could quiet her for offering an opinion on a subject that only gentlemen understood, Anne heard her father call from the wide porch of their house to tell them that he and James Hamilton were on their way to the dock. As the two came trotting down the path, James warned his mother and sister not to board the *Lady Love* yet.

"I don't like the sound of any of this," Anne grumbled.

"If you think any of us likes the danger we're in," Mrs. King said, "think again long and hard, Miss Anne. You know full well that beast, British Admiral Cockburn, and his barbaric forces burned our national capitol in Washington! They say that Cockburn stood on top of the statehouse speaker's desk in muddy boots and ordered even the president's house burned so bad one part of it's crumbling. And at least two British ships are already right out there in our waters. He's comin' for us any day!"

Just then Papa and James Hamilton hurried up and before Papa said one word to Mama or Anne, he ordered the oarsmen to begin unloading certain boxes from the *Lady Love,* leaving only the portmanteau he knew held nothing but Mama's things.

"Jock," Mama asked, "does this mean we're going without you?"

"Aye, Becca. And you and Anne and James are going to have a splendid, merry time. I just had a quick talk with Mrs. King's husband, which made me see that I must forgo the pleasure. Two British men-of-the-line are nearby and although King is sure Major Butler's people are going to remain loyal, as I hope will ours, I find I can't bring myself to traipse off to a party leaving our home and fortune in the hands of poor King and my temporary overseer."

"Papa's right," James Hamilton said, reminding June, who had just come down with Anne's boxes, that he could fit her luggage into the space left open by Master Couper's small trunk. "It may be better this way," James Hamilton said, addressing his remarks—and they were always, to

Anne, carefully formed "remarks" anytime her brother spoke—to her and Mama. "You two ladies have nothing to fear with me along."

He's more the Old Gentleman now than ever, Anne thought, with his diploma from Yale and his ripe old age of nearly twenty-one. But then James Hamilton smiled at her and she melted. Her brother's smile had always softened any resistance rising in her when he became too proper, too dictatorial. She and Mama would be fine with him along to look after them, but oh, how she would miss Papa's jokes and good humor! Her own unexplained compulsion to go was still there, but nothing would be half as much fun without Papa.

After a quick shifting of boxes and trunks and bundles, they climbed into Papa's favorite plantation boat, the *Lady Love,* its brass trim gleaming in the clear winter sun. They began shouted good-byes and endless waving to dear Papa standing on the dock in his inverness cape, arms and shoulders draped in the just unpacked extra pairs of knee breeches and fancy vests, not one but two cocked hats stacked on his head, and several white stocks hanging around his neck. He was waving, too, determined, Anne knew, to see them off in a reassuring, cheery manner.

"Poor, poor Jock," Mama said softly, waving from her seat beside James Hamilton. "He'll miss us. He'll be so lonely here without his family."

"Papa wouldn't have stayed back if he didn't think it important," James said firmly.

"You have to admit it's sad, though," Anne said. "Even you must know, Brother, how he loves parties. Mama, you certainly know it's breaking Papa's heart."

"I know it's breaking mine," her mother answered. "Unlike other planters, your papa seldom leaves Cannon's Point. I'm just not accustomed to being without him at all."

"Of course, the whole British scare may come to absolutely nothing," James Hamilton declared. Anne could sense his launching into a lecture and worked at keeping her face straight. Papa had to shoulder some of the blame for her snickering. Her intellectual brother had always made her and Papa smile, no matter how much they admired him. "We haven't the foggiest idea how next to anticipate British plans," James went on earnestly. "Actual military action so far has been distant from us down here. I hear there *is* movement toward a peace treaty, but it's possible that Papa acted wisely. On the other hand, his decision was rather abrupt. Personally, I would weigh carefully every alarm sounded by Mr. Roswell King."

"Both the Kings do tend to exaggerate," Mama said, still looking back now and then toward their dock as the strong Couper oarsmen, June right in front of where Mama and James sat, pulled the heavy dugout slowly, steadily, up the Hampton River toward Buttermilk Sound. From there they'd take the Frederica River down the leeward side of St. Simons to Major Page's Retreat. Anna Matilda would be dressed and waiting, no doubt breathless with excitement.

"I'm so glad the Pages agreed to go on to their safe haven in Darien without Anna Matilda," Mama said from the seat in front of Anne. Sitting alone for now was good. There was so much to think through since Eve had fired her bombshell about June. Mama went on musing that the Pages too must be quite worried about the British enticing away their slaves, because they were actually moving for a time away from their comfortable home at Retreat all the way to Darien, taking along many of their best people for safekeeping.

What Anne had to think about had nothing to do with the British danger, so she left it up to James Hamilton to respond to their mother, which he would surely do at length. Worrying and thinking about such things as the dangers of war and damage to property were a man's domain. Loss of property, she knew, meant mainly the loss of slaves, but after what Eve had just told her, she could concentrate only on June's wide shoulders the way they looked now—long muscles moving rhythmically under his heavy brown work coat as he and the other Couper oarsmen moved as one man to propel them through the roughening gray water. The loaded *Lady Love,* riding low, made their work hard—the boat heavier and harder to row with each mile, Papa always said, because cypress soaked up so much water.

When the big plantation boat was easing out into Buttermilk Sound, Anne was still thinking about Eve and June alone under their big oak tree by the river, Eve's long-fingered, slim hands moving up and across June's wide back.

By the time they had reached the full expanse of the sound, June and the other oarsmen began, as though it was the most natural thing in the world, one of their familiar Sea Island songs. A song that was, to Anne, utterly natural, far more familiar and pleasing and filled with happy memories of her childhood than was any composed, staid Episcopalian hymn she joined in singing with the tiny congregation that met in various planters' homes each Sunday to hear Rev. Matthews preach.

Papa had been chosen to be one of the first vestrymen as soon as Christ Church was organized seven or eight years ago, and some day they'd have a real little church. Along with everyone else, she'd like that—especially the singing if the vestry did manage to buy an organ—but her musical home, because it had been a daily part of growing up, was in the African songs Papa's people sang. Try as she surely had, Anne sensed she could never quite get the rhythms right, but the surprising beat and the musical "trimmin's" certainly *felt* natural to her, were as much a part of her life as was the familiar, pungent smell of marsh mud. Mama always said that what made their people's songs sound so different was that they were hummed or sung in tones "not in our scale at all." Well, to Anne, they seemed to be in *her* scale, almost as much as they were in Eve's—or in June's.

The oarsmen were singing an old rowing song now that Anne knew so well she could follow the intricate pattern with the smallest part of her mind while her gloved hand beat the tricky time on the brass trim of the big, varnished, wall-sided boat, rocking heavily along through Buttermilk Sound.

Her thoughts still whirled about the startling fact that her very own Eve loved Ebo June! Taming time for Papa's share of the Ebo cargo when they reached Cannon's Point had, so far as she remembered, gone fairly well. As with all new shipments of Africans, the Ebos had been held together in a special pen for a month, fed extremely well, and made to do no work at all. Anne had grown up with the practice and so, after all these years, didn't remember it too clearly, but she did remember that Papa had seemed pleased and had told Mama that Spalding also was quite satisfied with the taming of his Ebos. "The pen is to protect them, keep them in touch with each other," she'd heard Papa explain to the new, green overseer he'd made the mistake of hiring soon after poor Mr. Patterson drowned. "It also gives them a chance to look out, see how the other workers fare at their assigned tasks. Gets them familiar slowly, with as little stress as possible, to the new scenery around them, the strange species of trees and bushes and flowers." June, Anne thought, had been held in that Ebo pen nearly twelve years ago.

When the oarsmen switched playfully into a made-up song comparing Anne herself to a "pretty redbird," she smiled and gave them her full attention, then clapped her hands in appreciation. As soon as they began singing another familiar song, her thoughts flew back to the peculiarly disturbing but fascinating idea that her own Eve was probably going to be allowed to marry Ebo June. One of her favorites, Papa's fisherman, Big Boy, was steering behind where she sat. No one could see her face. She felt free to frown her way through the brand new, strange idea with which Eve had hit her right between the eyes—only minutes before she had to leave. That was like Eve, though, and at least she knew now that Eve wasn't pretending to pout only because Anne was going away without her. Eve had wanted to go because Ebo June was going too. If only Anna Matilda weren't so naive, it would help a lot to be able to tell her, but—but what? What if she is young-acting and an only child, Anne asked herself. If I can get used to the idea of Eve's being married long before I am, why should it trouble or confuse Anna Matilda? She already knows I'm desperate to find the one person I can love with all my heart. Anne smiled to herself. Papa says I don't really *have* to be so sure I always know ahead of time what's best for everyone else or for myself. I don't care whether I have to know or not. I *want* to.

She gave a quick, short laugh. No one noticed, because the people were singing a loud song, but a flash of realization that her serious, brilliant, careful brother might someday fall in love had suddenly struck her funny. James Hamilton, she decided, would undoubtedly make a careful list—maybe even a chart—of which characteristics he does and does not want in a wife!

Dismissing such an idea simply because James's sense of orderliness was so foreign to her, Anne followed the pattern of the curious, twisting rhythms of a shout song called "Kneebone," each beat of which she seemed to see now in the rippling muscles of June's broad, powerful back.

The *Lady Love* had left Buttermilk Sound and was moving with a steady, rocking motion, water slapping its sides, down the leeward shore of St. Simons on the Frederica River, past the ruins of old Fort Frederica. Being rowed in one of Papa's sturdy plantation boats had always made Anne feel almost one with the water, with every mullet that might at any minute jump into a silvery arc above the sun-speckled surface of any island river or creek. Hearing a gull cry or the cracked squawks of red-winged blackbirds from the marshes bordering the salt waterways never seemed like an interruption. She and the gulls and redwings and soaring hawks and wide-winged buzzards had always been too much a part of one another for any of them to strike her as noise or distraction. In the most daily, friendly fashion, Anne and snowy egrets and boat-tailed grackles and pelicans and blue kingfishers belonged together. They would all be on Cumberland, too, because they, like Anne and almost everyone she knew, were coastal. Even at school in Charleston, she had missed living close to her wild friends, although at night in her room she could hear an occasional owl and with the early sun, the gulls. A clapper rail, out of sight in the tall marsh grass along the river, let loose its long, sustained clucking call. She smiled to herself. The rail sounded always like a scared yard chicken, but Anne knew better. Usually, that frantic burst did not mean the rail was afraid at all.

What if she, Anne Couper, opened her own mouth now and attempted to sound a call that might make plain everything glorious and scary inside her? Mama might jump out of the boat with alarm and James Hamilton would begin at once to diagnose what ailed her. What, she wondered, would June do if she released her own kind of wild, excited, expectant call? She giggled to herself. June was still singing with the others, his rich, deep-mossy voice easily singled out. Did he sing to Eve? Anne's blood tingled. She felt almost light-headed with the thought of Eve and June, with the even more disrupting thought that something truly big and overwhelming might be about to happen to *her.* Anna Matilda must be excited, too, at her family's Retreat, watching the lemon winter sun rise higher and higher in the sky.

Anne loved her best friend. They had certainly known each other most of their lives. For the years just before they both left for school in Charleston, Anna Matilda had actually lived at Cannon's Point on weekdays. The Pages had sent their sweet-mannered daughter first to the Floyds in Camden County to study with the Floyd children, because they wanted Anna, since she was an only child, to learn how to be with others her age. Then, later, Papa and Major Page worked it out so that Anna Matilda could stay all week at Cannon's Point and be taken home every weekend. Along with Anne and James Hamilton, Anne's friend had been carefully tutored by gentle, Oxford-trained Mr. William Browne. The reserved, devoted teacher still lived at Cannon's Point because Papa liked his company so much and encouraged Anne and Anna Matilda to follow the careful guidance of William Browne in their personal reading. Just this morning, in fact, before he left to tutor the Gould children for the winter, he had handed Anne her copy of Walter Scott's *Lady of the Lake* to pack with her party dresses—hoping, she knew, that she and Anna would make room amid the festivities at Dungeness to read something that might nourish their minds. She had thanked Mr. Browne politely, because she loved Scott's imagery, but tucked the book in a box of daytime dresses and wished for Papa so that they could make one of their jokes about how odd and unnecessary they both thought Walter Scott's ancient and fierce Scottish clan wars really were to modern life in the United States. Dear Papa was a full-blooded Scot, but that, as he said, only by a "happy accident of birth." He had, from a fully believing heart, chosen to be an American Patriot, and in all ways he certainly lived his life in the quickening tempo of the nineteenth century.

A line of white ibises flew above them against the graying winter sky and because they were moving south, she wondered where the fish-eating big birds might be headed—Jekyll Island, or maybe all the way to Cumberland with her! She thought of asking June where he thought they were going but decided against it because after what Eve told her this morning, Ebo June had come to be somehow different from the other, ordinary oarsmen.

A lot of reading she and Anna Matilda would get done on Cumberland, she thought with a secret smile, remembering that just before Christmas when they were together last, most of what they did was dream and talk of their own future romances, all but ignoring the poetry of poor Mr. Scott. Anne considered the Scottish poet and novelist great because she had been taught to think of him that way, but she did wish he would write a lot more romantic books, since William Browne regarded him so highly.

Both Anne and Anna Matilda certainly hoped they might find at least one eligible young man at Louisa Shaw's house party, although neither could think of who it would be, since their families knew all the Camden County people who might have an attractive son. The two had talked only in generalities, because Anne could not be sure her friend would ever believe that Anne *knew,* sensed in her very heart, that something earth-shaking lay ahead for one or both of them. She did know, though, and knew she would surely tell Anna Matilda, about Eve and June. Anna's father had been a big help to Papa and Mr. Spalding after the Ebo uprising, so Anna Matilda probably knew about the Ebos. Major Page, who saw to rounding them up that terrible night, had come along in one of the dugouts that had brought June and the others finally to Cannon's Point. June's name wasn't June back then. Anne supposed that even Papa didn't know his Ebo name, but Papa had told her later why the young man had chosen the name *June.*

All those years ago, June had been one of the Ebos who had hung back, sulked longer in the taming pen. All of them had sulked for a time, some scampering to the rear of the pen every time a white person came near. Mr. Spalding told Papa, if she recalled rightly now, that Ebos feared white men might eat them. In those days, Mama scolded Papa some because she was convinced that he had always told Anne too much.

Did Eve know how June got his name? Anne would have to ask her as soon as she got home again. Did she know that June had been, if Anne's memory served, practically the first of the Ebos to take a new name because he was smart enough to learn some English between May 1803, when he first came, and the very next month, June? There was so much to ask Eve now and it was just too bad, she thought, that she always had to be careful not to give her maid the upper hand.

The overloaded plantation boat scraped sand at the Retreat landing and even as she waved wildly to petite, dark-haired Anna Matilda standing on the dock, portmanteaus and boxes stacked around her, both parents hurrying down the tree-lined lane, Anne wondered how anyone ever managed to capture June and the other rioting Ebos that night. Had June been salvaged "at ten dollars a head" from the roiling waters?

Anne and Mama went with Anna Matilda and portly Mrs. Page up to the Retreat house to refresh themselves quickly so that they could be on their way to Cumberland as soon as possible, while James Hamilton stayed on the dock, explaining at length to Major Page, Anne knew, why Papa had not come.

With the help of the efficient Page house people, the ladies were on their way back in no time and when Anna Matilda demanded of her father why he suddenly looked so worried, Anne's mother came to the rescue.

"Mr. Couper is worried too, my dear," she explained in her calming voice, "but you and Anne are *not* to worry. Mr. Couper didn't come with us, although he was all packed, because a British ship or two have already been sighted up near Cannon's Point. There's some danger apparently that should they land anywhere nearby, they might try to entice some of our people to leave with them."

"But why?" Anna Matilda wanted to know. "Why would any of our people want to leave any of us? I don't believe a single one of them would even think of going away, do you, Mama?"

"We hope not, my dear girl," Mrs. Page said—a bit shakily, Anne thought—"but we can never be sure. You already know that's why your father and I are taking so many of our best people with us to Darien."

"She knows that, Mrs. Page," Anne said quickly and felt very adult. "Anna Matilda and I are just so excited about Mrs. Shaw's party, we're not thinking straight. We do understand, though. After all, we're women now." Then, to Anna Matilda, she exclaimed, "Just wait, my friend, until I tell you *who,* at only sixteen, has already found the one man in all the world for her!"

A cold west wind was rising and the *Lady Love* had crossed the somewhat choppier waters of St. Simons Sound, passed Jekyll Island, and moved into the open water at the south end before James Hamilton ordered the oarsmen to hoist the sail and rest from their labors. Because soon, Anne knew, the men would have to row through the always tricky waters of St. Andrew Sound, where the shoals made sailing difficult, it was high time her brother took pity on them.

Anne's mother, who for some reason always seemed to be hungry lately, pointed to the wide, white beach known as High Point, at the north end of Cumberland Island, and called over her shoulder to Big Boy, ordering him to steer the boat toward land.

"But, Mama," Anne complained, "if we stop for a picnic, we could be another hour and a half reaching the Dungeness dock!"

"I know you girls are fidgeting to get there, but our long boat ride has made me ravenous! Besides, Sans Foix will want to know the moment we get home how we liked his splendid luncheon."

Of course, James Hamilton obeyed their mother, even to opening the baskets of fried chicken and deviled eggs himself, piling Mama's plate extra full. "If Louisa Shaw still has the same expert cook, I'll be so fat by the time we get home again, your father may not like me anymore," Anne's mother said, her thoughts obviously still on poor Papa left by himself at Cannon's Point.

Both far too excited to eat, the two girls only nibbled at the food on their own plates. The first thing Anna Matilda said, once they were all back in the boat, gave Anne a little hope that her friend had finally stopped fretting over her parents, who were escaping the British by going all the way up to Darien, some eighteen miles from St. Simons.

"There just might be hope for us, Anne," Anna Matilda whispered, "if Eve is really already in love. I've been thinking about what you told me during our picnic. Mama says Eve has white blood by someone, which makes her so pretty, but if one of our people can be that lucky, we should certainly be. Do you know who Eve's white father was?"

Not wanting to get off the subject of their own possible romantic futures, Anne answered in her vaguest manner. "I guess no one's sure. And you know how Eve's mother, Fanny, is. She seems so sweet and friendly, but stubborn as a mule and she won't say. Eve thinks it was Roswell King, or at least a young man who came to Cannon's Point to help Mr. King back when he was in the timbering business. Who cares?"

"Anne, do you really think there'll be any eligible young men at the Dungeness house party we don't already know and make fun of?"

"No, but with all my heart, I'm hoping." Then, leaning close to Anna Matilda's ear, she whispered: "I meant to tell you when June and the others were off by themselves while we were eating, but I don't want Mama and James Hamilton to hear."

With her brother expounding to Mama on the nesting habits of brown pelicans and the oarsmen singing again softly, Anne told her the true identity of Eve's lover—Ebo June. Anna Matilda seemed to be listening but plainly not sharing the extent of Anne's own excitement that if such a thing could happen for a servant girl, who could tell what wonders might be waiting for the two of them at Dungeness? "Mrs. Louisa Shaw has just been married to her Scotsman, Mr. Shaw, something like a year," Anne went on. "I'm sure, even though she may still be grieving over her mother's death, she must, at past thirty herself, be well disposed toward helping girls like us find husbands too. But, Anna Matilda, you and I, if we're to stand a chance, must put ourselves in a—a Romeo and Juliet mood and stay there! I truly think we can block beautiful events by refusing to expect them to happen. You know neither of us cares a fig for any boy on St. Simons."

After a silence, Anna Matilda said wonderingly, "I believe you're really serious about all this, Anne."

"I am quite serious!"

"But I wonder if we should get our hopes too high, especially in the middle of a war."

"What can the war possibly have to do with it?"

Anna Matilda only shrugged. She didn't really know and plainly hadn't even guessed about Anne's own compelling, mysterious, powerful hunch that something new and glorious could be just up ahead. Right then, Anne decided, it would be better not even to try to get Anna more involved in any of it. From now on, she would simply hold it all deep within her own heart. If romance didn't come at the party, she could still dream for the future. And she *was* dreaming —dreaming hard.

Chapter 2

A few days later, long before he heard his butler, Johnson, sound four long blasts on the big conch shell to rouse the people from sleep, John Couper was bathed and dressed, red hair combed and retied into a queue, and waiting—alone at the tall front window in the high-ceilinged downstairs parlor. For what was he waiting? Certainly not to rejoin Roswell King for yet another futile freezing day out on the waters around Cannon's Point and Butler's Hampton Plantation. He'd had more than enough of that. More than enough of King himself, actually. What earthly good did it do for two men to expose themselves to the bitter January chill and icy rain just to be rowed about looking at two British ships anchored off Little St. Simons Island? Except for a skiff or two let down for fishing each of the three days his little family had been gone, the ships stayed put. Jock saw no sense whatever in exposing himself or his boatmen to any more discomfort. Of course, he could easily imagine the endless, brave-sounding detail in each of Roswell King's weekly letters to his employer, Major Pierce Butler, in Philadelphia: "I can assure you, honored sir, that not one skiff is lowered into the waters near those enemy ships that is not duly recorded by me in your behalf."

Jock Couper, surely today the loneliest man in the entire state of Georgia, rather enjoyed admitting to God and himself that he simply didn't much like Roswell King. He was a hard worker, utterly responsible, intelligent, but the man bored Couper stiff. King not only had an irritating way of boasting while appearing to act humble, he could almost match Will Shakespeare at creating drama. Even a self-assured, wealthy, arrogant man like Major Butler must often find himself annoyed by King in his perpetual endeavor to prove himself the world's most conscientious overseer and manager.

True, Roswell King did turn an enormous profit from the rice plantation over on Butler's Island and from the cotton fields at Hampton, separated from Cannon's Point only by Jones Creek. But after all, Butler paid King, housed him, kept him supplied with everything a manager needs—food, the best Sea Island cotton seed, the best seed rice, and hundreds of slaves to work the land. Couper felt certain that King had lately filled pages of reports to Butler concerning his own infinite care in protecting his employer's property. Valuable cattle not needed for daily milk had been driven as far as possible from the Butler mansion and other plantation buildings, out of reach of the British, as had the horses, pigs, hogs, sheep, and even the chickens, guineas, and ducks. "I've assured him to the best of my ability, though," King repeated to Couper ad infinitum, "that because of my firm but kind treatment of his slaves, not one will relent to the enticements of the British should they capture St. Simons Island. Slaves, Couper, are what they're after and I know for a fact, since my recent trip down to Fernandina in Spanish Florida, that the British rascals are filling coastal niggers with unmitigated hogwash. They're promising freedom, whatever that means—lives of leisure in Jamaica, Nova Scotia, or another British colony where the poor devils might be taken if they choose to believe the hogwash; plenty to eat, good clothes, and no work; also full British citizenship; and one lying British Artillery officer even spread the ludicrous rumor down there in Florida that the Queen herself is a nigger! Told the slaves that British gentlemen prefer nigger wives! That British ladies choose nigger husbands without fail when one is available."

Couper didn't doubt any of that, not only because he had kept as current as possible with British activity since this second war with England began over two and a half years ago, but because he was a Scot. No full-blooded Scot could be surprised at any overbearing act or false rumor spread by anyone connected with the throne of Great Britain. During the American Revolution, he had found it pragmatic to accompany his Loyalist employer from Savannah to what was then British Florida. It had been the sensible thing to do. Jock prided himself on good sense in most things, but he'd come to America about the same time as had his best island friend, James Hamilton, and America had been good, good to them both.

They had reached the new land as very young men. Now that John was almost 56 and James Hamilton 57, each had ample reason to be loyal citizens of the United States. Each was the owner of a vast, productive cotton plantation on St. Simons Island; jointly, they owned an even larger property called Hopeton on the mainland near Brunswick, plus other scattered acreages near it. Couper also owned Lawrence, the tract adjoining Cannon's Point to the south, and another oceanfront tract at the far south end of the island. Therefore his reasons for becoming an adopted citizen of America made excellent sense: he was a truly prosperous, happy man because of the opportunity to succeed offered by his adopted land. In his native Scotland, under the power of the British throne, he'd never have prospered. Unless a man was born a British lord, he lived his life being lorded over by the throne. So, none of what Roswell King vowed the British were doing now to entice coastal slaves away from their owners surprised him. In fact, he was deeply worried himself. Worried and lonely. Lonely in his bones and blood for Rebecca, for the companionship and counsel of his wise son, and for his beloved Anne, the very apple of his eye.

The handsome mahogany bed he'd had made and shipped down from Philadelphia had never seemed so enormous or so empty. Becca never forced her opinions on him, but with all his heart and mind, he respected her every thought on any subject. Daily, they seemed to think more and more alike. Rebecca Maxwell Couper was also now a true American Patriot, but still kept alive enough of her odd fascination for the typical Scottish worship of ancestral valor in battle so that he loved to josh about it. The Almighty knew Scots had been born and bred to battle in the old days when her feudal family, the Maxwells of Dumfriesshire, had ruled the area north of the English border from their great and fabled castle, Caerlaverock, on the Firth of Solway. Couper never tired of teasing Becca because she'd married a common Scot, a poor parson's son from the country, forced by lack of funds to come to America indentured to an established British merchant. He also never tired of joking every time she called for her blooded mount for a ride in the

Cannon's Point woods: "Ah, there goes my Druid, stealing off to worship!"

Rebecca was a true aristocrat but reminded no one of her famed ancestry. She was, when they'd met and married nearly twenty-three years ago at Sunbury, Georgia, just comely Rebecca Maxwell—tall, slender, bonnier than any other girl on the entire coast, gracious, playful, a little reserved, but never offended by John Couper's tireless love of filling the house with people and his equally tireless enjoyment in entertaining them with his stories and often ludicrous humor.

Although Rebecca was sixteen years younger than he, her innate wisdom often put his to shame, and this morning he missed her to near distraction. Today he was far more lonely for her than worried over what the British might do. No woman ever handled servants as skillfully as Becca. He himself had surely learned from her. The house people must feel as lost as he without her to guide them. He could think of nothing better on this cold, rainy morning than knowing what she thought about how their people might react to the farfetched British enticements should Admiral Cockburn's men actually capture St. Simons Island as Roswell King was sure they meant to do.

First light had now broken across the low, cloud-scudded rainy sky above Cannon's Point. He could see swirls of white mist above the river, and Anne's Lord God Bird was hacking away already at the old dead live oak she'd persuaded him to let stand just for the convenience of the comical, handsome woodpecker. "I love that big bird, Papa," Anne had insisted. "He not only makes us laugh because he's so huge and awkward, he has a red crest just like yours. Don't argue with me. Leave the tree. Every fancy, rare kind of tree or bush you plant grows and thrives. It won't hurt one bit for my Lord God Bird to have one fine dead one for bugs." The tree stood, of course. Whatever Anne wanted, her father wanted too. Even her foolish, quirky desires made him happy because he certainly could be as foolish and odd as anyone on earth. Anne, he was quite sure, had inherited her love of laughter and the unexpected from him. James Hamilton, his only son, whose brilliance of mind and common sense had all but overwhelmed his fun-loving father since James had been a small boy, was another matter. The tall, well-built, utterly sane, serious young man came by his proper solemnity straight from Jock's Papa, a strict Scottish parson who had, Jock always claimed, sent the mischievous young son to America at an early age "for the good of Scotland."

A small clatter at the wide parlor doorway caused him to turn around and offer young Eve, Anne's personal servant, a cheerful good morning as she came bearing his breakfast on a huge silver tray. Eve wished him a good morning, too, her even-featured face an enigma to him as she herself had always been. Oh, he knew the rumors about the identity of Eve's white father. His own man, Johnson, had told him years ago that before the century turned, Roswell King, in the timbering business at Darien then, while spending three days cutting trees at Cannon's Point, had spied Couper's mild, obedient Fanny, the seamstress, and probably sired Eve. Not an unheard-of act, he knew, and despite his own frequent annoyance with the man, King had undoubtedly given Eve a streak of good blood. Roswell King wasn't going to remain Butler's overseer forever. His abilities and ambitions ran too high. King was a good neighbor, too, just too obsequious and unimaginative to suit Jock.

How an old man's thoughts do jumble themselves, he mused, cutting into a thick, pink slice of the cured ham no one knew how to prepare as did his own superior cook, Sans Foix.

"I'm lonely," he said aloud and realized that he didn't really feel hungry. "I'm too—worried. Worried enough to be talking to myself and feeling a fool for doing it," he mumbled, hoping Eve wasn't lingering outside in the downstairs hall, because being Eve, she'd likely come right back into the parlor, demanding to know what was wrong. Eve's a handful, he thought. Only my daughter really understands the girl. But then, Anne, although more outspoken and far more apt to laugh at the wrong time than her mother, was also going to know how to handle servants. Anyone who could get along so well with the enigmatic mulatto must have been born knowing.

Anne and Eve, he felt certain, were close. Sometimes a mistress and her maidservant became fast friends. And then he knew what he himself needed to do at that very minute! Hauling his tall, lean frame up out of his easy chair, he set the breakfast tray on a nearby table, took one last sip of coffee, put on his inverness cape, and headed in the rain for butler Johnson's good, tight cabin—the largest of the quarters houses—built of wood and floored with plank. No one, not the Almighty Himself, could ever doubt that he, John Couper, and his favorite, the Cannon's Point butler and fiddler, Johnny, were friends—deep-down, trusting friends. Mutually trusting, because he felt certain that Johnson trusted him as wholly as he trusted his longtime servant.

If Roswell King's claim that the British were offering outlandishly false enticements to coastal slaves was true, Johnson would know, if anyone knew, just how loyal the Cannon's Point people might be in the face of such temptation, should the thieving British really capture St. Simons Island and attempt to take property.

This troubled morning, more than usual, he needed Johnson.

"You soakin' wet, Mausa Couper," Johnson said as he swung open his cabin door and removed Couper's dripping cape. "Come in, come inside by my fire an' warm yo'self."

Standing, his back to the live oak logs blazing on Johnson's wing-shaped hearth, Couper gave his man a smile. "You're one of a kind, aren't you, Johnny?" he asked after a moment in which the two stood looking at each other in silence. "Any other man on the place would either be scared or mouthing a streak of dumb questions about why I'm here in your cabin at this hour. Not you."

"I figure you tell me when you ready, sir." Johnson's smile was the truest mirror of his heart. "You got some reason to come. I speck ol' Aunt Emma done seen you cuttin' this way, knockin' on my door. She fumin' 'roun' inside her cabin right now, trying to think up why Mausa Couper bother to come to *me.*"

A quick frown furrowed Jock's brow as he eased himself into one of Johnson's carefully hand-built rocking chairs. "Aye. But don't you suppose by now all the people know I'm likely to do quick, sudden, impulsive things? I'm sure they all know we're—friends."

"Oh, they do know that, Mausa. They do." The soft, low laugh came. "I pays up for that friendship most eber day."

"I'm sure. I almost said I was sorry, but I'm not. Whatever our friendship costs either of us is worth it. Do the others pester you for favors from me still? Don't answer. I don't think I really want to find out. I'm sure they do, knowing how I depend on you. But I'm not here only for a social call today."

"No, sir."

Of course Johnson already knew that. A master seldom if ever set foot inside a quarters cabin. The mistress, yes. Certainly Becca, who watched over the people and their children with infinite care, visited the cabins often.

"You and Liz have your place fixed up nice, as I'd expect," Couper said. "Liz is a born mother, even without any children of her own. My offspring couldn't have had a better nurse. Does she still tend your dead baby's grave down in the orange grove?"

"Yes, *sir.* Reg'lar, eben after all these years."

"You and I aren't exactly young anymore, are we, Johnny?"

"We bof still good, strong men, though, sir." After a moment's wait, Johnson asked, "You troubled 'cause of Mistah Rozell King takin' you out in the cold on that water for two days, Mausa Couper?"

Jock smiled, amused again that Johnson had always called Roswell King by a woman's name, *Rozell.* Mostly though, he was relieved that his man did understand why he had come this morning. Knew he needed help, guidance.

"What will our people do if the British take over St. Simons Island and hold out their tempting offers of the good life to them? How worried should I be?"

"I don't reckon some of 'em even knows they's such a thing as a British war goin' on."

"That's no answer and you know it. I grant you there are times when ol' mausa needs you to be careful with him, my friend. This is not one of those times. I want a straight answer—man to man. Friend to friend."

For a long, slow-moving moment, his butler stood by the fire, studying the scrubbed plank floor of his spotlessly kept cabin. Finally, when he knew he'd be nudged if he didn't say something, Johnson spoke in his most careful manner: "How many of us you reckon you got at Cannon's Point now, Mausa Couper?"

"How many people? I'm sure my son knows exactly. I'd say between a hundred and a hundred twenty or thirty. I'm not interested in a survey. I want your opinion. How loyal will my people be to me?"

"Some wouldn't leave for love nor money."

"But others would, is that it?"

Johnson nodded.

"Major Butler's overseer, Mr. King, is dead sure none of Butler's people would be disloyal. But I can't afford to lose anybody. I haven't caught up financially after the loss of those five Ebos the year before we had our devastating damage from the hurricane in 1804. And after that poor crop last year, I might be nearly bankrupt if even two or three dozen of my people went off with the British. I know King's a fine manager, but how in the name of heaven can he be so sure the major's people would all stay?"

"He can't be, sir. Mistah Rozell King shootin' off his mouth effen he say that!"

"I didn't come here to get you to say something just to make me feel good. I merely hoped you'd help me feel a little less worried."

"I'm remindin' you ob the creek, Mausa."

"Jones Creek?"

"Jones Creek. Major Butler and Mistah King not gonna git no loyalty outa' the people that they won't even let cross that narrow ol' creek to our side. Hampton folks got hard lives. They might could *all* run off wif de British, I say."

Couper leaned forward. "I know for a fact a few of them slip across the creek anyway, Johnny. What do they tell you when they do?"

Another silence filled the cabin so that only the crackle of the good hot fire could be heard. Johnson's eyes were on the floor again.

"You're not tattling on any of them when you let me know what I already know perfectly well," Couper said firmly. "I don't appreciate your silence. I understand it, God knows, but I don't appreciate it. You know what I think of that Hampton rule! Keeping his people penned up within his own boundary lines is probably the cruelest, most ridiculous thing I ever heard of and you *know* I feel that way about it. It's wrong, dead wrong, stupid. It's treating them as if they were animals who needed to be penned up or they'd run wild. I'm sure I've told you that I don't approve, haven't I?"

"No, sir, you didn't tell me."

"But you knew, didn't you?"

Again Johnson only nodded his head that yes, he did know.

"I can see you aren't going to give me much of an answer

to my question, but would you consider telling me if I'm right to believe that any kind of forbidden boundary is not only foreign, but downright silly, to the African way of seeing things? Poor little old Jones Creek couldn't keep you and the others here at Cannon's Point from visiting, so isn't such a rule as silly to the African mind as to my own?"

Johnson's slow, wise smile told him what he needed to know, but today even Johnson seemed unwilling to offer the kind of comfort, freedom from worry, which Couper wanted. Unwilling? More to the point, he knew, Johnson simply was unable to assure him that *all* the Cannon's Point people would, under the persuasion of Johnson or Couper's reliable, intelligent Muslim driver, Tom, choose to stay. Roswell King had spoken of a talk he'd had at Fernandina with an aide to a British officer who declared that although the British had come to conquer, they would take no slave who chose to stay with his master. King had shipped most of the Butler rice and cotton, had driven even the Hampton oxen deep into the woods, but he had only his own skewed self-confidence that Butler's slaves—the most valuable property—wouldn't jump at the chance for freedom if the British came.

"My Liz, she cross the creek eber few days to visit ol' Flora ober at Hampton," Johnson said. "Major Butler a hard mausa. Flora too ol' to work, but he order her to graze a goose on a string eben on a rainy day."

Johnson knew perfectly well Couper was aware that what he'd just said had nothing to do with any of the potential trouble the British might make for *him* at Cannon's Point. For Butler, for that matter. For any St. Simons planter or farmer who owned only a few slaves. Johnson also knew that losing numbers of the Cannon's Point people could spell fresh, possibly insurmountable, financial problems. Johnson was anything but dumb. Plainly, he took the kind of pride Couper wanted his people to have in the prosperity of their homeplace. No butler ever polished silver with more care than did Johnson. No butler ever served the excellent food Sans Foix prepared with more obvious pleasure and self-esteem. To please his owner, Johnson had gone as far as to tackle and master playing the bagpipes! With all his foolish heart—at least he knew Roswell King thought it foolish—Jock wanted his people to take pride in the beauty of the cotton fields when the bloom was pink, pride in the rich oil pressed from his prize olive grove—the first two hundred trees of which President Jefferson himself had recommended he buy.

Back before the turn of the century, when the lighthouse builder, Jock's close friend James Gould, had come to St. Simons as a young man from the North in search of just the right timber for the building of the U.S. frigate *Constitution,* Couper had glowed at the pleasure on the faces of Johnny and all the others when they found out Mr. Gould had chosen one of the Cannon's Point live oaks as a stern post for the great ship. Couper wanted, needed, willing hard work from each of his people, but he also enjoyed their feeling privileged to have had a part in the lavish, gracious hospitality of his big house, in the fruits of his vast array of imported and domestic trees, in all of the Cannon's Point beauty. If he were totally honest, he cared deeply that his people like and respect its master, John Couper.

Although he believed that Africans, even those born in this country as was Johnson, needed a strong, considerate, firm-minded "chieftain" on whom they could depend not only for food, clothing, and shelter but for guidance, he had never found it easy to be such a chieftain to them. Kindness and laughter came naturally. Discipline and firmness did not.

As the two men sat together in another of their long, easy silences, Couper seemed better able to think clearly. There were certainly rules at Cannon's Point. Rules made to be obeyed for the smooth operation of the place, but rules made also for the protection of his people. He truly knew of no stupid, cruel restrictions such as Butler's forbidding his people to cross over Jones Creek. Only last night, miserably lonely in his fine big house, Jock had been forced to make himself stay on his side of the creek in order not to interfere when he heard a Butler slave screaming from a bullwhip laid again and again across his bare back. "That be young Robert," his cook, Sans Foix, had explained. "He slip across the creek to see if I had any of my plum tart left over. I did an' I give him some. I feel that lash on my own back, Mausa Couper. I feel it for Robert. He like my plum tart that much! I warn him what might happen to him. He swear he could swim the creek without anybody noticin'."

Roswell King, Couper was sure, had stayed out on the water again all night, playing his martyr role. Mrs. King must have caught Robert and ordered the whipping. One firmly held rule at Cannon's Point barred all whippings for any reason. Whippings or brandings. He doubted that James Gould would whip his people either when he finally got his big house built at New St. Clair. Gould was a New Englander who had only one or two house servants down at the lighthouse where he was still keeper. He'd bought them long ago to save them from a worse fate at a legal slave auction in Savannah. Of course, in the future Gould would have to buy many more. He was going to plant cotton. He would have no choice, but Couper would have wagered there'd be no laying on of whips, no searing branding irons. He'd never thought about it, but he also doubted that such was allowed down at Major Page's Retreat. He knew for certain that his revered friend James Hamilton was a good master. And never, never was there cruelty at Thomas Spalding's "nigger heaven" on Sapelo.

He looked across at Johnson now, still standing out of deference, allowing him needed silence, still facing his master out of courtesy, although he felt sure the man's backside must be scorched by the fire. "Sit down, Johnny." Couper smiled.

The dark-skinned, dignified man smiled back. "I be fine this way, sir."

Johnson had said all he dared to say for reasons perhaps even Johnson sensed but undoubtedly didn't fully understand.

"I may ride down to the south end of the island tomorrow if this rain lets up," Couper said, getting to his feet to go. "I need to see my old friend James Hamilton. He keeps talking about moving to Philadelphia and I couldn't do without him here, especially till the British trouble's settled. I also think I'll visit James Gould. I might even stay in his snug keeper's cottage if they'll have me for a day or so. I suppose in this thick weather, a man can't see much even from the top of Gould's good light tower, but if it lifts a little, we'd be able to see any additional British ships from there."

"You want I should ride down with you, Mausa Couper? Keep you company?"

"You're welcome to go along, but Gould's people, Larney and her John, have a wee cabin. I doubt there'd be a place for you to sleep."

"I speck you right, sir."

"I believe the rain's lightened a bit now. I don't hear it on your roof much anymore."

"My roof don't leak a drop these days. Me an' Liz, we thanks you for gettin' your carpenters to fix it up."

For a few seconds, the two men stood looking at each other.

"Oh, Johnny, a mon's got so many weights bear-rin' down on his mind these days. 'Tis good, 'tis ver-ry good to have such a friend as you. You do your best for me always, don't you?"

Solemnly, slowly, they shared a rare handshake.

"I wish wif all my heart, I could do more, Mausa Couper. Lots more than I *kin* do."

Chapter 3

About midmorning on her longed-for eighteenth birthday—another rain-soaked, gloomy, heavy-skied day—Anne sat alone in the spacious third-floor Dungeness bedchamber she shared with Anna Matilda. Not only was she eighteen today, January 11, 1815, it was also the fourth day of poor Louisa Shaw's dreary house party. Having been reared to be a lady under all circumstances, Anne still tried desperately not to admit even to herself that she was bitterly disappointed that no one, not even Mama, had mentioned her birthday. Not one good wish during breakfast or after, when the guests had labored through still another boring attempt at small talk over coffee in the magnificently furnished Dungeness front parlor. Sweet Anna Matilda Page was still downstairs struggling, she supposed, to be amenable. Well, it wasn't *her* birthday. Anne, not bothering this time to guard against her bent to let annoyances show, had simply flounced out of the parlor, her cup of after-breakfast coffee untouched, up the stairs to her room and sat now in one of Miss Louisa's graceful rockers, feeling hurt and quite neglected.

"You're an attractive young lady, Anne," Mama had reminded her off and on over the past few years, "and people find you excellent company when you're not pouting. We all have bad times for one reason or another, but that gives us no right to inflict them on others. We're responsible for the kind of atmosphere we create around us."

She could never quite bring herself to say that Mama gave the impression that she thought herself always right, because she didn't. She could be firm, but one of Papa's most repeated compliments when speaking of his tall, slender, intelligent wife was that when she turned out to be wrong about something, "Becca will be the first to admit it. The lady keeps short accounts with the Almighty. She never permits unforgiven sins to pile up!"

All right, Anne thought, I'm allowing my sins to pile up and today I don't care! Birthdays are special days and when one's own mother fails to remember a birthday so important as an eighteenth, I have every right to feel ignored and sorry for myself.

Rocking fast in the little armless chair, she pushed aside the fact that she did feel genuine sympathy for Mrs. Shaw at the obvious failure of her long-planned house party. After all, being a hostess was hard work at best and Louisa Shaw made dozens of trips daily up and down the elaborate stairs of her mansion, attempting to give of herself to both her ill husband and her restless guests. Never mind that most of those attending the party pretended to be enjoying themselves. Anne considered such behavior hypocritical at best. She was bored and let-down and had no intention of pretending that she wasn't.

Late yesterday she had even given up on her favorite author, Walter Scott. Her copy of *Lady of the Lake* lay untouched on the night table beside the big, heavily carved bed where she and Anna Matilda slept. What had Anne really expected? In the *Lady Love* on the way down to Cumberland, her soaring hopes had made the long, cramped boat trip seem actually short. She had been so sure something *big* was going to take place at the Shaw party. She was going to turn eighteen at last and somehow her life, because of what she *knew* was going to happen, would never again be the same. Rocking hard now, the foolish hope once more swept her body, her mind, her heart. It was somehow far better up here in her room alone, safe, at least, from one more endless backgammon game—indoors because of the steady rain—and all that forced small talk she and Papa loathed. If her life depended on it, she still could not have put the reason for her rush of fresh hope into words, but it was there and it didn't matter that she felt young and giddy because of it. Even with the dreary rain still falling, the damp, airless room tingled with excitement.

What had she expected? What was she expecting now?

The guest list, at least of those who actually attended the

party, could not have been more pathetic. Only three lackluster young men were there aside from her own brother, and although one from St. Marys was a superb dancer, he was only that. Anne had said not one more word to Anna Matilda about her sure sense that an event of supreme importance was going to take place. What good would that have done when her friend appeared to be satisfied with nothing more than the prospect of an elaborate house party? For a supposedly spoiled only child, it seemed to her that Anna puddled along under very low expectations, content without a hint of suspense or hope. Even last night, her friend had fallen asleep still worrying aloud about possible danger from the British to her parents during their temporary stay in Darien. The way Anna Matilda fretted about the operation of Retreat Plantation, one would think she'd already inherited it!

All the older people at the party talked a lot about the British ships sighted in the waters around the nearby town of St. Marys and Cumberland Island and wondered and stewed about the weakness of the American defenses that far south on the Georgia coast. If the danger was so great, where were the United States troops who had for a time been bivouacked right at Dungeness? Papa had told her that they had all been sent to protect Savannah, and they certainly were all gone. She had struggled through four long, rainy, stuffy days without a glimpse of one handsome officer on either side of this dreary war. The whole war with Britain was stupid anyway. It had gone on for more than two and a half years, and along coastal Georgia most of the confusion so far had been just talk and dread.

At breakfast though, everyone, including her mother, had seemed peculiar. Too calm, too casual, and on Anne's birthday, too. Even her hostess, Louisa Shaw, had acted more preoccupied than usual. Anne knew well that Mrs. Shaw's thoughts stayed split between living up to her famous mother Caty Greene Miller's reputation as a hostess and the needs of her poor husband sick in his bed upstairs, but today, the woman's nervousness was acute. They all knew, of course, that Mrs. Shaw still grieved over her mother's death, still seemed anxious about pleasing her in everything she undertook. Miss Louisa worried, according to Mama, that someone might criticize her for having had the party so soon after her mother died. Giving a party at any time, Anne knew, would only have delighted Caty Greene Miller, a far more beautiful, attractive, and sought-after lady than any of her three daughters. Adored by men and gossiped about by women, Miss Caty, the widow of Revolutionary War hero General Nathanael Greene, and also the widow of her children's tutor, quiet, intellectual Mr. Phineas Miller, had not endowed Louisa Shaw with her own social aplomb and almost careless charm. Louisa Shaw seemed to work hourly at pleasing everyone. It hadn't been at all like her not to have wished Anne a happy birthday, because Mama had surely told her. Or had she? They both behaved strangely at breakfast. Did they all know something frightening about the war that they were, for some unexplainably crazy reason, keeping from Anne?

Because she had to do something or explode, she jumped up from the rocking chair and looked for the third or fourth time through her party dresses Eve had so carefully packed. Even if no one else knew it was her birthday, she meant to dress in her elegant best for dinner! Holding the bottle-green embroidered silk up to what dull light was finding its way through the window that looked out over the planted garden enclosed within its high tabby wall, she felt sick that she'd chosen the dress. What if the sun didn't come out again once during this dreary, endless house party? The dress, breathtaking as it had been back home, looked drab and dull under the low coastal sky outside Dungeness. Beyond the lush garden—all green on this January day except for red and white blooms on the camellia bushes—she could see Spanish Florida dimly across Cumberland's southern marsh, its breadth rolling with the thick mist that hung gloomily over all of Dungeness's beauty.

Their arrival had been so promising the day they docked under a magical island sunset, and she remembered someone's telling her that the Dungeness gardens were planted in terraces made of old oyster mounds built by the Creek Indians long ago. Her eyes followed the terraces now along a little tongue of dry land running from the gardens into the nearest stretch of marsh. The slight elevation of high land stood thick with great live oaks, their moss banners, green-gray from the rain, waving in what appeared to be a rising breeze off the waters around Cumberland. She was looking across what Louisa Shaw had said was an expanse of three thousand acres of salt marsh spread from the Spanish East Florida town of Fernandina all the way west to the city of St. Marys, Georgia, her gaze following a seemingly endless strip of wide, white beach bordering the vast Atlantic.

Despite her odd mood, the view refreshed her. It was still true that no one, not even Mama, had mentioned her birthday, but for her, something dark was lifting. Lifting slowly, but lifting. Why? Nothing had happened to cause her spirits to rise. Absolutely nothing except that she had, still holding her party dress, walked across the room to look out a window.

The bottle-green dress, which had looked so dull and sedate a minute ago, shimmered now almost as it had shimmered under the St. Simons sun the morning Eve had packed it four days ago. Moving closer to the window, she spread the graceful folds over her arm, eyes wide with delight at the transformation that only rising light could make. There *was* light that seemed already to be clearing the marsh and sky and sea and beach! All her life, she had seen the abrupt, swift, coastal sun turn radiant the heavy, cloudy air around her home at Cannon's Point, but today it was harder to believe what she was seeing. As though an unseen hand were dropping flames down on one, then two, then three, then numberless tall candles, the woods outside were lighting up!

Tossing the party gown in a heap on a chair, she threw wide a casement window and leaned out. Rain was no longer falling and the sun was breaking through nearby intertwining branches of live oak trees she hadn't even noticed until now.

Even with a fire roaring in the fireplace and wrapped in two thick shawls, a moment ago she had been shivering. Now, she threw off both shawls and held her arms out the window as though reaching for what could really be her revived dream.

She laughed aloud and seemed to hear Papa's laughter too. "The clouds come fast, the light turns up even faster along our beloved coast, Annie. Dinna' look so surpr-rised!" Papa, laughing with her, lapsing merrily into his Scottish brogue.

Hurrying to still another window, she jerked it open to

the rain-sparkled ivy and leaf-dappled sharpness of shadows that never failed on an island to make the sun seem to glow more brightly. She no longer believed that nothing was likely to happen. Something had happened. Best of all, something else light-filled and glorious was going to happen any minute. She had no idea what, but it was her eighteenth birthday and *it was time.*

A bright-green lizard raced into her line of vision on the thick, shell-pocked tabby sill outside the open window, stopped suddenly and blew out his pink throat bubble into the carefree, hopeful sunlight. A glance at the crumpled heap she'd made of her green silk party dress showed its color gleaming, too.

"Happy birthday to me," she whispered and hugged herself, for what reason she didn't know. The house was still occupied only by the same lumps plus Mama and James Hamilton and Anna. But it was time for something else bright. It was past time.

Clustered in the wide, gracious doorway of the Dungeness dining room downstairs, girls giggling, boys shuffling, none as quiet as Louisa Shaw had urged, all the guests—faces turned upward—stood waiting.

"We'll never surprise my daughter if they don't keep quiet," Rebecca Couper whispered to Louisa. "I know this special birthday dinner is being a dreadful strain on you, my dear, with your poor husband so ill. Do you really think we should go through with it? Couldn't we all assemble quietly in the dining room without your fiddler playing and with no singing?"

Her plain but intelligent face taut with strain, Louisa Shaw said, "No. Absolutely not, Mrs. Couper. My darling mother would never agree. I feel her so close to me today. I'm sure she's daring me to succeed. We've done the hard part. We all managed to keep mum before Anne at breakfast. Help me. Don't try to talk me out of it!"

"I do apologize for my daughter's sulkiness earlier, but I'm sure she thought we'd all forgotten what day it is. Anne's usually sunny and cheerful, far more like her father than like me. It just isn't like her to go off alone to her room and sulk. I do apologize. And I will help you all I can, my dear Louisa."

On a signal from his mistress, the Shaws' skinny, dark-skinned fiddler struck up a tune and with the first stroke of his bow, the entire group of guests—young and not so young —began to shout, "Happy Birthday, Anne! Happy eighteenth birthday, Anne Couper! Come down! Come down! Come down, Anne Couper!"

Rebecca's face clouded as she wondered how gruff, grumbling Mr. Shaw would survive the yelling and laughing and loud, shrill fiddle playing. She quickly began to smile, though, when she glimpsed Anne in her bottle-green gown at the top of the stair, looking taller than usual and even more slender. Her daughter's face, glum at breakfast, shone beneath her dark, thick curls with the contagious, heart-stopping smile that could so easily rule all of Cannon's Point and everyone who lived there—in the big house and at the quarters.

The dinner party was such a happy success, Anne looked so radiant and delighted, that Rebecca thought even the worry lines on Louisa's face seemed to lessen. Her people served the gleaming table well. The first two courses, clear soup and then baked sea trout, were so deliciously seasoned, Rebecca felt sure the Coupers' longtime friend, the superb Miss Caty, knew it and was applauding the triumph of her favorite among her three daughters. The long-awaited house party, which even Rebecca had until now found flat, had ignited with laughter, good talk, and an unexplainable excitement—the odd, suspense-filled excitement Rebecca had tried to ignore in Anne from the moment they'd received Louisa's invitation. For a reason she simply had not understood, Anne had seemed to anticipate this particular party more than any other in her eighteen years, during which their own home on St. Simons had been the lively scene of countless such affairs.

While the young people chatted with each other at table as though the party had only just begun, Rebecca Couper's thoughts raced back to the day of Anne's birth in the cramped, former owner's cottage at Cannon's Point. To the relief of the young guests, the rain had finally stopped and talk of their first chance for long walks in the glowing woods and picturesque gardens left Rebecca free to dwell in her thoughts. Every remembered moment, even her own pain and discomfort as the then young Rhyna showed her early skills at midwifery, seemed now to light the brightening afternoon. She recalled the quiet pride she and Jock had felt in their only daughter, even as a small girl. They had always been proud of Anne's obvious intelligence, shown both in her studies and in her quick wit, but also in the events about which the child had cared deeply. When a new calf died, Anne had grieved, and her mother could still see her tender agony of disbelief the day she'd found one of her cherished painted buntings dead, its bright blue and coral and gold-green feathers still and crumpled on the path at the foot of the wide front steps that led to the big porches around which Anne and Jock marched during every storm.

Rebecca smiled, remembering that she had somehow felt forced to agree with their serious-minded son, James, when he questioned the sanity of two people who seemed to love being soaked in a rainstorm just for the sheer fun of it. She had never really understood James Hamilton well enough to know for sure why he was so solemn and his father so jovial, but she did know that secretly she thoroughly enjoyed Jock and Anne on parade each time the thunder roared and the lightning flashed. Even now, in all the noise and talking, she smiled at the memory.

Then, trying to listen above the chatter, Rebecca thought she heard a quick rap on the massive front door of Dungeness. The center hall lay between the dining room and the door, but she was certain now that she had heard sharp, repeated knocking.

"Louisa!" Rebecca called, but her hostess was totally caught up in the unexpected triumph of her dinner party.

And then there was no need to try for Louisa's attention. Another knock, this time the arresting, somehow frightening clank of metal on wood. Repeated once, then again with more insistence. Gradually, an odd silence spread from one end of the long, glistening table to the other. Anne jumped to her feet and stood staring in the direction of the front door, her face an indecipherable picture of contradictions—even to her own mother. She was surely half-smiling, as though at long last the moment for which she'd waited had come. But there was also a look of fear that she might miss it altogether or somehow not be able to bear it.

Still at her place at the head of the table, Louisa Shaw was rigid in her chair. Oh dear, Rebecca thought, what should Louisa do? The odd, insistent knocking should be answered by a man—the man of the house—but Mr. Shaw was upstairs sick in his bed.

Seconds after Anne jumped up, the four young men, upon realizing that a lady was standing, got quickly to their feet, James Hamilton with them. Almost at once, Rebecca saw her son stride resolutely out of the dining room, heard his boots along the wide, spacious center hall, and with the metal object beating hard now on the front door, she heard an impatient male voice shout from outside: "Open up! Open up, I say!"

James Hamilton's heart pounded as he lifted the wrought-iron latch, turned the brass knob, and threw open the door. The glaring sunlight startled him as much as what he saw. "We're at dinner, gentlemen," he managed, nervousness plain in his normally controlled voice. "The master of the house is quite ill in his bed. I'll thank you to make less racket."

When a rumble of rough laughter greeted his admonition, he felt his own anger rise. There was no doubt about the identity of the intruders. James Hamilton stood in the doorway alone facing a contingent of British marines!

The shorter officer heading the group of ten or fifteen other officers and aides stepped brazenly inside the great hall. A tall, wide-shouldered, younger officer stepped in protectively to stand with his superior.

"May I present myself, sir," the first officer said in a clipped British accent. "I am Lieutenant Colonel Richard Williams in command of this contingent of Royal Marines." Nodding in the direction of the taller, more imposing younger officer, he added, "And this is Lieutenant John Fraser, Third Battalion, Royal Marines. We intend no harm to you or to anyone present, providing you obey our commands."

"Obey your *commands,* sir?" James heard his voice squeak as though he were far younger. "I am only a guest here at the Shaws' home, but I must inquire your reason for expecting to be obeyed."

Not even trying to analyze why, James Hamilton, while addressing the superior officer, kept his eyes on the impressive, arrogant face of Lieutenant Fraser, the younger marine. Actually, they exchanged looks—eye to eye—because the lieutenant was every bit as tall as James and had the arresting look of a tightly reined, thoroughbred horse. How inappropriate that he goes on smiling, James thought, but said nothing. After all, his own unanswered question still hung there: *By what authority did either man expect obedience?*

"We expect to be obeyed because you are all under arrest," Colonel Williams said in a brusque, though not unpleasant voice. "You and every person in the house, which we know is called Dungeness, are under arrest from this moment—prisoners of His Majesty's forces. The British, sir, have, at the command of Admiral Cockburn, captured, as of last night, the entirety of Cumberland Island."

"I'm sure, young sir, as your rather awed countenance suggests, that you are taken aback, to put it mildly." This from the handsome, dark-haired, pleasant young lieutenant who had only now spoken his first words to James. "The ways of war are not always courteous. We apologize, after a fashion, for the intrusion, but Colonel Williams is correct, of course. As he is the officer now in command until Admiral Cockburn arrives, you have no choice but to obey his orders."

"And what, may I ask, might those orders be, sir?" James felt a bit proud of his own flippancy.

"That you and every guest and servant not needed to supply our needs," Colonel Williams said, "go at once to the upper floors of this mansion and remain there until further orders from me."

With that both officers pushed past James, strode briskly along the hall and straight into the now almost silent dining room where sat or stood Louisa Shaw's perplexed, frightened houseguests.

James Hamilton, following the marines, rushed first to his mother, touched her reassuringly, then marched straight up to where Anne stood staring into the still-smiling gray eyes of the taller junior officer, Lieutenant John Fraser. James simply stared back at his sister, who looked as though she'd been caught and was being held at the most helpless moment of a startling dream.

Helpless? The look on Anne's face, her wide, pale blue eyes locked with those of the tall, pleasant enemy named Fraser, showed no outward sign of needing help. But what *did* her look show? James, still watching Anne closely, moved back toward his own chair at the table, hating as always any feeling of inadequacy about his own ability to understand causes and effects. For once he could think of nothing to say.

After clearing his throat rather awkwardly, the superior officer, Colonel Williams, proclaimed to the roomful of guests: "You are each one under arrest and the captive of His Royal Highness King George Third!"

James glanced briefly at Louisa Shaw, who looked as though she might faint, then back at Anne. If, when he first entered the room, he'd thought Anne appeared clamped in a dream, he had no words to describe her face now. *They were all under arrest.* They were all miles from home, captives of British forces, and there stood his sister, resembling nothing more than an impish angel.

"James?" His mother spoke his name questioningly, softly.

"We're—captives, Mother."

"Well, you seem to have understood at last, sir," Colonel Williams said politely. "But from now on, I make all announcements and explanations and give all orders. Is that clear, Mr.— Mr.—?"

"Couper," James said. "My name is James Hamilton Couper of St. Simons Island, Georgia."

"Ah, St. Simons Island, eh?" Fraser, the handsome junior officer, addressed James but kept his eyes fixed on Anne's face. "We hope to visit your island one day quite soon, Mr. Couper. We hear 'tis a beautiful spot. It would have to be to equal the beauty we've seen on our march this morning along Cumberland, though."

To James's orderly mind, nothing fit together. Courteous, conversational pleasantries did not match captivity by enemy forces. He called on every ounce of control to keep from hitting the disarmingly pleasant Lieutenant Fraser in his still-smiling mouth. If only there was a way to let Papa know the British were heading for St. Simons! His very blood seethed with fury and—for him, worse—frustration. He could think of no plausible response to Fraser's comment. The frustration only mounted when he looked again at his sister's animated expression. Best, he thought, to say nothing at all.

"Sorry to disturb your meal, ladies and gentlemen," Colonel Williams said, "but you will all kindly retire now to the upper floors of Dungeness and remain there until I notify you further." When no one moved, he snapped, "Now! I order all of you upstairs—all dinner guests, all poor benighted slaves except those required to serve our needs. Go! Now!"

If ever in his life James had known anyone who flared, rebelled at being ordered, it was Anne. She would surely flare now at what the commanding officer had just said. In case she did, James took a step toward her.

Anne was still looking at Lieutenant Fraser. Finally she spoke. "And—when do you think you'll be going to St. Simons Island, sir?"

"When, Miss?" Fraser repeated her question eagerly. "Now, that, I believe, is a military secret—for the moment, at least."

James could scarcely believe what he had heard in both their voices, what he was seeing with his own eyes. They were each—his own sister and this oddly disturbing, oddly appealing British marauder—exchanging looks of what could only be genuine *recognition*! How could it be? How in the name of common sense could they recognize each other?

All he was able to muster by way of an answer to his own unspoken question was that the looks that passed between them had nothing whatever to do with common sense.

Climbing the long stairs to the guest chambers, Anna Matilda Page tried her best to stay close to Anne. It wasn't easy. The others kept crowding in, everyone scared and confused. Her best friend was there nearby, but Anna might as well have been climbing alone. Not one word had passed Anne Couper's lips since they'd all left the dining room. Even though the sun was shining outside, shadows filled the elegant, crowded staircase. It was hard to tell for sure, but Anna Matilda felt certain that Anne, for some irrational reason, was not as frightened as she. James Hamilton was supposed to be in charge of them, but his firm insistence that they all be allowed to finish their dinner had not made a dent in British Colonel Williams. "You're captives," he'd reminded them, and as though they were cattle or slaves, he and Lieutenant Fraser had gone on herding them toward the stairway. "You're captives and under our command. Until further orders, you will all remain upstairs in your rooms with absolutely no contact room to room."

Anna Matilda surprised herself by daring to ask Colonel Williams what they were supposed to do up there. Miss Rebecca Couper silenced her with a finger to her lips. Anna needed an answer. She felt lost because someone had always gone ahead of her to plan or fix things for her comfort, her amusement, her pleasure. She knew she wasn't spoiled because Mama kept telling her she wasn't. She was just plain scared.

It was a relief when she and Anne were alone inside their room, where she could really see Anne's face, gather some idea of what she thought might happen to them. The door safely closed, Anna rushed into Anne's arms.

"I'm terrified!" she whispered. "How can you be so calm? What do you think they'll do with us? How will we get food? Do you think they'll starve us to death shut away up here?"

After a brief hug, Anne said with the same faraway, peculiar look on her face she'd had downstairs when the British had arrested them, "We won't starve and you're certainly not acting as though you'll be the mistress of a large plantation—ever, Anna Matilda! Aren't you ashamed?"

"No, I'm afraid. Aren't you one bit scared?"

For a long moment, Anne said nothing. "I'm not sure," she said finally. "I don't know any more than you know, except—"

"Except what?"

"Except that somehow I'm sure we're going to be all right."

"But you've never been captured by an enemy before! How can you be so brave? I don't like you this way. I wish you'd act—human with me. We're under arrest!"

Anna's frantic, altogether superfluous announcement went unanswered while her friend walked slowly to a tall window and stood looking out.

"What do you see out there? Are there thousands of British marines in the garden outside, Anne? Do they have swords and guns?"

"Of course they have swords and guns. They're soldiers. And no, there aren't thousands. I'd say only about fifteen or twenty. The two officers we met downstairs are talking to the others."

"Do they seem angry? Excited?"

"They seem serious, that's all. Are you such a child you're afraid to come look for yourself?"

"Yes."

"Then you'll have to wait, as will I, to find out what's next."

Chapter 4

On Wednesday, January 11, his adored Anne's eighteenth birthday, John Couper, in need of comfort, conversation, and advice, rode to the southwestern end of St. Simons Island to visit his longtime friend James Hamilton.

For more than an hour the two men had been talking together before a crackling fire in the Hamilton Plantation parlor, which overlooked the Frederica River and its marshes, cloud-shadowed now by the welcome return of island light. Time spent with his boyhood Scottish friend had always eased Couper's mind of whatever problem he faced. For over a quarter of a century, the two had been intimate, trusting friends. Hamilton, still a bachelor, spent a lot of time away from St. Simons these days and was insistent now on moving permanently to Philadelphia. Still, neither distance nor disagreement had ever truly come between them.

Today, though, when John had come for comfort and counsel in his loneliness for his family, his deep concern over what the British might do, he had found neither. Oh, their talk had helped, although again he'd failed to convince Hamilton to remain on St. Simons.

Mostly, Couper realized as he got to his feet to leave, Hamilton was as worried as he about what the next British move might be.

"I'm truly sorry, Jock," James Hamilton said as they shook hands in the entrance hall before he opened the front door to the icy wind off the river. "I'm sure you're disappointed that I, once more, have no answer for either of us. You flatter me, always expecting me to have one. You and Roswell King have at least seen the British schooners up at your end of St. Simons. I didn't even know that much. We both have fortunes to lose, but we just have to wait and see, old friend."

"Aye," Jock said, forcing a smile. "War wouldn't be war if both sides knew what the other was about. I—I think I came today mainly because it's Anne's eighteenth birthday and I miss my family shamefully. I thought if I could persuade you to go on living near me here on St. Simons, it might lift me old heart."

"We've never allowed business to come between us," James said, his voice tender. "We won't this time. It is business interests that are taking me to the North."

"Aye. Business and despair at ever finding a wife good enough for you here. One word of advice. Remember a real Scot tries, at least, to choose a *very young* girl. That way a man can train her to his ways. It makes for peace on both sides."

Hamilton laughed. "So you've told me at least a hundred times. Pull up your cape collar, Jock, and don't hurry on your ride to Gould's. You tend to gallop too hard. You're in fine shape, but neither of us is any longer a broth of a lad."

"I thought I might spend a day or so watching the surrounding waters from James Gould's light tower. Probably futile, but there's no better vantage point. The two ships-of-the-line at the north end seem only to be patrolling and that half-heartedly. King vows that if the British come for us and our people, they'll be moving up from somewhere south of here. I'm not sure of that, but if he's right, I'd have time to ride home before they could land, should Gould and I spot them coming." He sighed heavily. "Poor Gould is worn out with waiting and worrying about the British capture of his only brother, Horace, up in Maine."

"War is far more than killing. It's also waiting," Hamilton said. "By the by, Jock, this may seem an offhand way to tell you, and I know you'll keep my secret until I've told your son, but I've come to a decision about my place here. In fact, the decision has to do with my belief I've made the right choice about leaving St. Simons. I plan to give Hamilton Plantation and all its people to young James, if at the end of his first year of operation, he's as successful running it as I expect him to be."

A slow smile lit Couper's face. "You seemed to have no answers for my troubled state of mind when I came here today, old friend. But, as always, you've rallied my hope. I'll try to think of a way to let you know what that generous gesture means to me as soon as I've had a chance to digest it. For now, because I'm so eager to scan the waters from Gould's tower, suffice it to say that your decision has reminded me that life will go on someday after the trouble with Britain is past." He embraced his friend. "Gr-ratitude at this moment is a weak word."

Returning the embrace, Hamilton said, "Be grateful, too, that James is on Cumberland to see to the welfare of Anne and Rebecca. The boy has a remarkably level head."

Now Jock laughed a bit. "Too level for his father's comfort at times. But after all, beloved friend, he *is* named for you."

Both girls afraid to open the door to their room, Anne and Anna Matilda spent the next hour or so listening, ears pressed to a crack around the wide wooden frame, trying to catch a few words from the British guards posted outside in the hall. More men had assembled downstairs, Anne felt sure. The noise and confusion seemed to grow by the minute. Plainly, the British had taken shelter from the cold right in Louisa Shaw's fine mansion.

"From the sound of their voices, they're helping themselves to the Shaws' superb wine cellar," Anne whispered. "Miss Caty was famous for her brandy. Papa always said Miss Caty's rare old stock was what made brandy in a home the mark of the coastal elite. Isn't that silly?"

Anna Matilda, too worried to joke, kept silent.

Giving up on a response from her friend, Anne wondered where poor Miss Louisa was now. In the sickroom with her husband, she supposed, trying to pretend for his sake that things weren't as crazy and strange as they were downstairs, out in the gardens, probably all over Cumberland Island. She wasn't about to add fuel to the fire of Anna Matilda's fear, but there well could be thousands of British troops moving from plantation to plantation, from small farm to farm, enticing slaves to desert their owners and board British ships to freedom. James Hamilton, in a whispered conversation with Anne right after they were all ordered upstairs and before the guards stood duty in the hall, had told her that stealing slaves was the main reason the British were on Cumberland. She already knew it was the reason

Papa stayed back at Cannon's Point. As kind as Papa was to his people, he still feared losing numbers of them. Anna Matilda, of course, was sure not one of Major Page's Retreat people would leave. Well, Major Page was no kinder than Papa was to the Cannon's Point people! Anna Matilda was definitely very young.

A heavy roar of laughter and a shouted huzzah! from downstairs caused her young friend to grab Anne's arm and cling to it. Then an excited male voice shouted above the others from downstairs: "I say we invite them down! After all, if they refuse, Colonel Williams can always *order* them to join us."

"That's—*his* voice," Anne whispered.

"Whose? Whose voice?" Anna Matilda wanted to know.

"Never mind. Just never mind."

More than one pair of heavy boots began at once to pound up the stairs. Anna Matilda was gripping Anne's arm so hard, she had to pull to disengage her friend's hand. "You'll leave a bruise," she scolded, no longer bothering to whisper since the marines were in the upstairs hall, now beating on first one and then another closed chamber door.

Still whispering, Anna Matilda gasped, "What will they do to us downstairs?"

"How do I know? Just listen a minute."

What surely sounded like an argument was coming from the end of the hall in the direction of James Hamilton's room. Anne knew one voice was unmistakably her brother's, and for one of the few times in his orderly life, he was shouting:

"You can order all you want, sir, but I forbid Mrs. Shaw's guests to join you downstairs! Do you hear me? I forbid it!"

Her brother's fury was met with a hearty laugh—*his* laugh. To Anne, there was no mistaking it—sheer music, altogether pleasant, easy, natural. There was no anger; it was exactly what real laughter should be. Her heart racing, she knew that no matter what James Hamilton said, she was going to accept the British order. Gladly.

Again clutching Anne's arm, Anna Matilda breathed, "James Hamilton is very wise, Anne. He forbids us to join those scary men downstairs. What will we do?"

"I do not obey my brother. Only my parents. Mama's still in her room up the hall, so I'm going to try to fix my curls, retie this sash, and go downstairs. That's the handsome lieutenant my brother's shouting at and he isn't dangerous at all! The British officers have simply changed their minds. Instead of forcing us to stay shut away up here, they now want us to join them downstairs. Let go of my arm, so I can be ready as quickly as possible."

Before Anna could say another word, they were both startled by a brisk knock. "Who is it?" Anne called out.

"It's I, Sister, James Hamilton. Open to us, please."

"Who's with you?"

"Just—open the door." Her brother's frenzy and frustration were so evident, Anne stifled a giggle. Papa probably would have laughed, she thought, throwing open the door as Anna Matilda leapt behind it out of sight.

There, with James, stood the stylish, smiling lieutenant, in full-dress uniform—red jacket, white breeches, black Hessian boots—his long, elegantly handsome face glowing with what she could only think was eager anticipation.

"We've been *ordered* to—to join the party, Anne," James spluttered. "This—this British officer has ordered us to join what *was* your birthday dinner in the dining room downstairs!"

"Your birthday, eh?" The lieutenant looked pleased. "I say, what could be more perfect, Miss— Miss—"

"Couper," she answered quickly, calmly, she hoped. "My name, sir, is Anne Couper."

He bowed. "And I'm Lieutenant John Fraser. Will you do me the honor of allowing me to escort you back to your own birthday party, Miss Anne Couper? But, are you alone in this room?"

Stepping uneasily out from behind the half-open door, Anna Matilda let herself be seen, obviously still as nervous as a cat. "No, sir," she said. "I'm here, too. What are you going to do with us?"

"We simply plan to enjoy your company, if you agree to do us this honor," he said in his wonderful voice with its clipped accent, the accent that Anne was not at all sure was English after all. The cadence sounded quite like Papa.

"Are you Scottish, sir?" Anne asked.

"Aye, that I am," he answered, still smiling. "Does it matter?"

"Oh, yes. It matters a lot! To your credit, I might add."

"Then I congratulate myself and hope you'll agree to my acting as your attentive escort."

"Anne Couper," James said sternly, "you're being downright brazen!"

"Shall we ignore your suspicious brother, Miss Couper?" John Fraser asked lightly.

"Oh, always," Anne said, returning his smile. "I'll be honored to have you escort me, Lieutenant Fraser, just as soon as I'm quite prepared."

"Anne," James tried again, "this man is our enemy! He means us harm. He and his superior have dared to place us under arrest and heaven knows what other mischief, what other devilment they may have in store in the way of thieving and plundering the homes and quarters of the Shaws here at Dungeness and their neighbors all over Cumberland."

John Fraser delighted Anne still more with his decidedly amused response. "I fully expect you will all be shot at dawn, Mr. Couper," he joked, "but I *order* you, sir, to come with me, until these lovely ladies are ready." He turned again to Anne. "I fail to understand, however, how I will bear up under yet more—beauty than that which has me reeling now."

With James still forbidding her and Anna Matilda to go, vowing that *he* surely intended to remain upstairs, Anne gave Lieutenant Fraser the merest knowing smile as he took James by the arm and moved him firmly out into the hall.

"Half an hour, Miss Couper?" Fraser asked.

"Half an hour, sir."

Couper recognized his children's tutor, William Browne, before he reached the beach beside Gould's light tower. There was no mistaking the slight, skinny fellow, stooping in the sand beside Gould's oldest boy, Jim, about seven or eight now, he supposed. He knew from having tried in vain half a dozen times that there was little use in attempting to learn anything about what British intentions might be from young Browne, but the boy *was* English and he did read bundles of British papers sent over by his widowed mother in Crewkherne, England. The rub was getting such a scholarly gentleman, who figuratively *lived* between the covers of a book, to give any credence to anything so mundane as British or American military intentions. Browne was a fine teacher. Both Anne and James Hamilton were devoted to him and ever since Major Page began allowing Anna Matilda to live at Cannon's Point during the week to study under William Browne, his splendid reputation had been growing. One thing Couper knew: if his own son, James Hamilton, respected the man, he must have a brilliant mind. He simply lived and breathed teaching.

Couper spurred his horse and pulled up on the hard-packed beach beside the tutor and his plainly uninterested pupil, Jim Gould.

"Hello, Mr. Couper!" the boy shouted, far more pleased than a boy had reason to be at the sight of an older visitor. On his feet, a big smile on his face, Jim said, with almost ridiculous enthusiasm, "I'll run get my papa. I know he'll be tickled to see you!" And with that, young Gould ran like a rabbit toward the small keeper's house.

Still holding the empty shell of a horseshoe crab, Browne greeted him with his vague smile. "I wouldn't exactly say I'd riveted my pupil's attention on what seemed to me one way of keeping him quiet long enough to concentrate."

Couper leaned down to shake hands with William Browne. "Lessons not going too well, sir?"

"With young Mary Gould, marvelously well, but I can't say the same for her older brother. What brings you all the way to this end of the island, Mr. Couper? I hope nothing's wrong at Cannon's Point."

"Nothing beyond my ignorance of what your countrymen might be planning by way of thievery, William. I'm here to find out if Mr. Gould has noticed any British activity down this way." He chuckled. "I don't suppose there's any point in asking you if you've seen or heard anything that might be of help."

"I know only that Mr. Gould is worried, too, sir. I—I had my narrow escape when I first landed on St. Simons Island some twelve years ago. I'm sure you know my lips are not only sealed on the subject of slavery—and now the ultimate fate of those poor benighted people at the hands of the British—I simply think it's far wiser to keep my peace." As though just realizing he still held it, Browne tossed away the crab shell. "I'm not of a governmental or political turn, as you must also know."

"This chilly day is no time to ask, but I can't help wondering if they taught you no history—military or otherwise—at Oxford."

"Yes, sir. I was an honors student in world history, but my

interest in it has waned. I find my own singular kind of happiness in literature. And languages."

Couper grinned down at him. "So you do and I must say my son and daughter—and Miss Anna Matilda—are doing well with their French these days."

"Have you any word of them from Cumberland?"

"Nothing. And I've kept you standing here in this cold wind long enough. Are you quite comfortable staying with the Goulds, William?"

William Browne came as close to a real laugh as Couper had ever heard. "If sharing a room with my obstreperous pupil, Jim Gould, can be called comfort, yes. I do find his parents most considerate and kind. But I trust I'm not being rude to say I'll be glad to end this period of tutoring and return to the privacy of my own quarters at your spacious home, sir."

"Not rude at all. You were generous to offer to help out my friend Gould and his sweet lady until they can find someone else suitable. I think I envy your being able to stay so snug and unperturbed inside your own world of literature, though." He tipped his riding cap. "I'll be off to find Gould now. I don't mind confessing to some considerable worry over what your more intrusive countrymen might be hatching up to plague us."

Gould met Jock outside and together the two friends climbed to the top of the light tower, both shaking their heads at the odd, seemingly contented isolation in which William Browne lived.

"As far as he's concerned," Gould said, "there is no war, nothing amiss anywhere in his world—except the inattention of my son Jim."

In the small, neatly kept room at the top of the St. Simons light tower, they scanned the now bright waters of St. Simons Sound, their long glasses trained on two British ships. Both lay at anchor not far off Jekyll, the neighboring barrier island to the south between St. Simons and Cumberland.

"I felt a bit foolish at first," Couper said, "riding all the way here because of sheer nerves over what the infernal British might be up to, James. No longer. I see I had reason to worry! I wish I'd come to you before I stopped at Hamilton's place. He knows nothing of those two ships out there."

"I was just wishing there was some way for me to get word to you and Hamilton," Gould said. "My one man, John, has a strained back. I've known since late yesterday they were out there. I'd like to warn every planter on St. Simons, but especially you, Jock. You've been my good friend ever since I first came here hunting timber for the U.S. Navy." Couper noticed that Gould had lowered his long glass to give him a rare, warm smile. "After all, it was you who sold this land where my lighthouse stands to the government for a dollar."

"Best dollar I ever made," Couper said, sounding as cheerful as possible for his friend's sake. Gould had reason to be anxious. Should the enemy actually invade St. Simons, they could well take aim at his beloved light tower. Such an action would, of course, make no sense. Their vessels needed Gould's light the same as other ships did, but he'd never been one to put any fool thing past the British. "Tell me, James, did you see from which direction those two ships-of-the-line approached our waters?"

"I did. They came up from the south."

"I was afraid of that. I'd hoped the schooners Roswell King and I saw near Cannon's Point had just moved down here from up north, but I see the sails do differ." He sighed deeply. "I did a thoroughly dumb and dangerous thing, I'm afraid, when I allowed my beloved family to attend that Cumberland house party. They're down there now. Knowing there were already two British vessels in my waters, I still let them go! Even my far wiser son seemed not to give a thought to the now obvious fact, if those ships out there tell us anything, that the scoundrels might well be assembled today on or near Cumberland Island."

"But active as they've been to the north, how in blazes could you or James Hamilton be expected to know or even suspect they'd go south of us before attempting to invade St. Simons?"

"Go on and say it, Gould. Where my daughter, Anne, is concerned, I'm a tenderhearted fool. The girl had her heart set on Mrs. Shaw's house party, longed to be there when she reached her eighteenth birthday, which she did—today. James, may I stay for a while here with you? I know your wife already has young Browne on her hands. I'll sleep little at best, but none if I can't climb this tower and look for myself at what might be threatening us."

"You're more than welcome," Gould said quickly. "I did

have foresight enough to put an extra bed in the parlor of that cramped little keeper's cottage. My Janie and I would be happy if you stayed."

"Much obliged to you. If more ships heave into sight out there, I'd have time to ride back home before they could land. Roswell King vows the British are promising all sorts of outlandish rewards besides freedom to all coastal slaves. I don't like the system any better than you, a New Englander, do, but I've yet to hear anyone explain how a man can operate a plantation without his people."

"I know, Jock. I dread the day I have to go into the Savannah or Charleston markets but I love St. Simons Island. I've built my light. It's time now for me to think about providing for my wife and children. On St. Simons, that means acres and acres of planting." Silence had always fallen comfortably between Couper and his thoughtful friend James Gould. For a time, neither spoke. Finally, James said, "Try not to worry about your family down there on Cumberland. My wife, Janie, is already praying for them. Now, don't let that trouble you. It's just that Janie is Janie, up to her lifelong habit of reminding the Almighty what's needed. Like you and me, Janie doesn't put anything past the British."

Chapter 5

When Lieutenant Fraser escorted her and Anna Matilda downstairs at Dungeness, Anne saw other young officers already partaking of her surprise birthday dinner so carefully planned by Louisa Shaw, and, of course, some of the marines had drunk too much. Even Colonel Williams, the short, stocky officer in command, had helped himself freely to the Shaws' brandy. Lieutenant John Fraser danced like a god, though, could not have been better company, and the entire evening was, for Anne, without doubt the high point of the house party. Mama, although weary, smiled often and even danced once gracefully with an officer. Just before midnight, Anne tumbled into bed in an excited state of anxious but soaring happiness.

Anna Matilda had seemed to allow herself to enter into the laughter, too, and the dancing and the glorious unexpectedness of it all. Oh, she did act quite young, especially when she complained aloud right at the table that her lips had been burned as she drank scalding tea from one of the invaders' own silver cups. For some reason, which Anne couldn't now remember because there was far too much else to be remembered, one of the officers had unpacked a handsome box containing silver service that belonged to the still-absent Admiral Cockburn. Anne could not have cared less, but she did pretend to listen intently as Lieutenant John Fraser explained that the admiral had been detained in a boat off Charleston, South Carolina, by the endless days of bad weather.

James Hamilton had deigned to eat with them. After all, Anne thought, snuggling wide-awake under Mrs. Shaw's warm down comforters, even her proper brother got hungry along with the rest of the human race. Of course, James had sharply informed Colonel Williams that no one had better continue laughing at Anna Matilda's childlike pout because the silver cup was too hot. "I feel impelled to let you know, sir," he'd said, "that this young lady will some day be the mistress of one of St. Simons Island's largest, most productive plantations. She's the only daughter of Major William Page of Retreat. In case your ugly plans include any idea of enticing away even one Retreat slave, I advise you to ignore such a plan. It seems the least you could do to compensate for having poked fun at the major's only daughter."

The British officers who had overheard James laughed uproariously. Anne smiled to herself now, cozy in her bed, when she remembered that one officer did make a solemn, ridiculous promise that Anna Matilda's charm would surely guarantee Retreat's complete protection. Then, she tried to remember exactly what John Fraser had said on the subject. Had he laughed? Probably. The almost frighteningly good-looking young man with the attractive cleft in his chin laughed easily and often. If she never laid eyes on him again, she would think of him always laughing, not at anyone or anything but for the sheer joy of it.

"Anna Matilda?" She whispered her friend's name more to find out if she was awake than to say anything special. The sleeping girl didn't budge. Good. Anne felt freer somehow, safer, knowing she was alone with her own special thoughts.

I don't even want to answer myself during these strangely blessed minutes, she thought, and didn't understand at all what that meant. I only want to lie here and know that I—exist.

Would she ever see Lieutenant John Fraser of the British Royal Marines again? Where was he now, this minute? Asleep somewhere on a lower floor, she supposed. Did he think even once of Anne Couper from St. Simons Island before falling asleep tonight? Did he remember the way he held her as they waltzed to Louisa Shaw's fiddler's music around the cleared dining room and parlor of Dungeness? Or were his seemingly sincere, openhearted attentions merely a way for any Royal Marine officer to pass an evening in the midst of what was probably the most peculiar war ever? Had John Fraser already forgotten her?

No. That simply could not be! She fully intended to tell

Eve the moment she could go home again that Eve wasn't the only woman in the world who had found the *one* man.

But would there be a way to meet him again—ever? He had escorted her and Anna Matilda back upstairs to their shared room when his superior officer ordered the dancing to end an hour or so ago, but not one word about another meeting had passed between them. He had merely handed Anna Matilda politely through the door of their bedchamber, then looked down at Anne for one pulsating moment. He had bowed over her hand but made no sign that he even thought about kissing it, which, of course, would have been perfectly acceptable.

He was not in command. Like Anne, John, too, was subject to the orders of his superior. She gathered that they were all under the ultimate authority of the fabled, cruel Admiral Cockburn, who was supposed to be arriving on Cumberland any day. Any day. How long were she and Anna Matilda and Mama and James and the others to be held in captivity? They *were* captives! They were all captives, not free even to go downstairs in Mrs. Shaw's house without permission.

She was really perplexed at what had taken place. At their capture and at her own excitement in the midst of it all. The evening that had been so gay, so full of light, still glowed brightly in her mind and heart. She honestly hadn't considered until now that they could be in real danger. After all, Papa stayed at home because of the danger of losing some of his people to the British who were sailing around coastal waters in their noble-sounding efforts to grant freedom to the slaves owned by kind and considerate planters like Papa and Major Page and Mr. Spalding on Sapelo. Of course, she'd heard that all slave owners weren't considerate of their people, but how many Negroes, even the mistreated among them, would take the risk of leaving the familiar shelter of their cabins to board strange ships manned by armed British monsters?

Monsters?

One was surely not a monster. After all, Lieutenant Fraser had told her he was even Scottish, like Papa. True, he was an officer in the hated British Royal Marines, but maybe he couldn't help that. Some of the officers present at what had turned into the most surprisingly overwhelming birthday party anyone ever had, did drink too much, were loudmouthed and smart-aleck. Lieutenant Fraser couldn't help that, either. With her, through the shining hours in which they'd danced and danced, he'd been a perfect, light-hearted, graceful gentleman.

"Anna Matilda?" She tested her friend again, then whispered to herself, "I am a captive. I should be scared. I really don't know what's going to happen—even tomorrow. But what an odd kind of bright captivity this is! I miss Papa terribly. I would surely die if I never saw him again, but I wasn't really living before I was captured either. Not like this minute. *Never* like this minute!"

Well into the third day of captivity, Anne and Anna Matilda were kept in their room alone, except when one of the two house servants the British left to Mrs. Shaw trudged upstairs with their meals on trays.

"Do you ever see my brother or my mother?" Anne asked creaky old Phebe when she shuffled into their room about ten o'clock in the morning. "Do you take meals to my mother, Mrs. John Couper of St. Simons Island, Phebe? I haven't laid eyes on her in almost three days! I'm worried. About Mrs. Shaw, too, and her poor sick husband."

Laboriously, as though her pipestem legs might not hold her up, Phebe lugged the heavy tray to a table and set it down with a clatter. "I see 'em, ma'am," she said, her dim, milky eyes peering at Anne as though she were seeing her for the first time. "I see 'em. I see you be somepin' like your ma too, now that I got a look. She fine as a lady could be wif the house swarmin' wif strange mens. Mr. Shaw, he be up some now. Feelin' better. They all scared, though. Ever'body scared but me an' the other niggers. Dem British gonna set us free!"

"When, Phebe? Who told you that?"

"Dem British gent'mens. Dey claim the Queen ob England be as black as me!"

"That's a lot of nonsense," Anna Matilda said, her voice seething with scorn.

"We've seen pictures of the Queen of England," Anne snapped. "She's as white as I am!"

"Yes'm."

"What do you mean, yes'm? Do you believe me or do you believe them, Phebe?"

Whether from sheer exhaustion at being left alone in the

house with only one of Mrs. Shaw's young servants to help her with all the cooking, or from genuine confusion, old Phebe moaned, "Lawd Jesus, I don't know what I mean, Miss! I tell you the truf, I—don't know nomore."

"But you're sure my mother is all right?" Anne pressed her own question, wishing she knew how, or even if she dared try, to comfort Phebe.

"She eat like she be all right. She wanta know 'bout you too. So do your brother. I tell 'em you bof eat Phebe's cookin' good."

When the woman banged the door too hard behind her, Anne said uneasily, "I don't think that faithful old thing meant to slam the door so hard, Anna. You know Mrs. Shaw's trained her better."

"She's just so tired, I guess. Her biscuits look wonderful, though. Come on, Anne. Let's have some breakfast. I'm starved."

Cutting into a fat sausage, Anne tried her best to eat with the relish Anna Matilda showed. She couldn't. It was some relief to know that Mama seemed all right. James, too, though he was probably angry. How Anne hated the British! All but one, of course, and he was blessedly a Scot. But it did seem ridiculously cruel to keep harmless women penned in their rooms—mother apart from daughter. Sister from brother. Where *was* Lieutenant Fraser today? Hour after hour she'd watched from their third-floor windows, hoping —even praying—for a glimpse of him among the other enlisted marines and officers moving freely around outside as though they owned Mrs. Shaw's beautiful gardens, coming and going with boxes and crates and barrels from the Dungeness dock, where Papa's *Lady Love,* she supposed, was still tied.

Where were the Couper oarsmen? *Where was June?* What if the pompous, thieving British were trying to entice June to go aboard one of their ships and leave for a life of what they were calling freedom? What would Eve do if June decided to leave?

"Oh dear!" The thought was so horrible, Anne had unintentionally spoken aloud and, of course, Anna wanted to know what was wrong.

"Nothing. Nothing's wrong that wasn't wrong already. I—I just thought about Papa's oarsmen. Where do you suppose they are? Do you think the British will try to steal them, too? You know if they do, we have no way to get home."

"I'm scared, Anne! I'm just terribly scared. Some of them are truly polite, even charming, and I've tried so hard to be grown-up so you wouldn't tease me for acting young. But I'm exactly the way I am and that's so scared, I'm eating far more than I even want."

Anne was just about to ask her friend how soon she thought they might be allowed to see Mama or James when the clear morning air was split by a series of sharp crackling sounds—*shots*—then a thunderous roaring. Anna Matilda dropped her heavy silver fork so abruptly it clattered onto Mrs. Shaw's good china plate and off onto the floor.

For a frozen moment the girls sat staring at each other; then Anne ran to a window.

"What's that horrible noise?" Anna Matilda gasped. "Can you see anything?"

"Nothing different," Anne said. "Our room faces south. It just looks quiet down toward Florida. But I'm sure there's a battle going on somewhere. I'm positive that ghastly noise is *firing.*"

"Oh, Anne, if only we could go to your mother's room! It faces north. I'm sure she can see what it is. Do you think we dare?"

"No, I don't. There are three guards in the hall, but if I ever get a chance to confront my brother again in this life, I'm surely going to let him know what I think of him for not keeping us posted."

"How can he? He's shut in his room, too, with that pimply St. Marys boy."

"But he's a man and men are supposed to help ladies at a time like this no matter what!"

At that moment, there was a quick knock on their door and Anne recognized James Hamilton's whisper from the hall outside. He was calling her.

Easing open the door, she threw both arms around him. "James! You did come to rescue us after all. Have you seen Mama?"

"Quiet, Sister," he ordered as he stepped into their room and closed the door. "Just listen to me. I've already tried to calm Mother by telling her all I managed to learn."

"What, James?" Anna Matilda begged. "What did you learn? What's all that shooting? Are we going to be killed?"

In as quiet a stream of words as he could manage, James told them he felt sure the few Americans from the battery at Point Peter across the Cumberland River east of St. Marys were right now meeting the British. "I overheard the guard at my end of the hall when he was ordered to go outside to help carry in fresh supplies for the British, who've already made Dungeness their headquarters." As always, James explained in too much detail for the girls to take in, and Anne only half-listened as he said something about protecting Savannah and also that there was a short supply of food on Cumberland. "Far too little to feed and care for fifteen hundred British troops in the dead of winter in an area where each farm and plantation depends solely on slave labor to feed and clothe itself."

"But where are the Cumberland slaves, James?" Anne asked.

"Stolen! Haven't you realized that the brutes have left Mrs. Shaw only two women to help out here?"

"But can't the Americans defend us at Point Peter?"

"Anne, you're not listening! I told you there's only a remnant there. Most went up to protect Savannah. Our remaining men evidently went out to meet the marauders, but—" he stopped. "Sh! I'd say the battle's almost over already. The firing's slowed. And, I overheard correctly. The marine who came to take my guard downstairs seemed to think the British would completely wipe out the few American troops at Point Peter. The capture of St. Marys is only a matter of time. The enemy is running out of water, thank heaven. Many are falling ill. That might help us some, but I must be truthful with you and trust you two to stay strong. You both have good blood. Now prove it."

"But how long will we be here?" Anna Matilda asked.

"Who can possibly predict the British?" James Hamilton snapped. "Mama is being brave, Anne. She expects the same of you."

Anne drew on every shred of self-control in order not to ask James if he just might have some word of Lieutenant John Fraser. The way James felt about all British, she dared not. She simply stood there in silence, looking at the carpet.

As though he had read her mind, James sneered, "I'm sure you wouldn't care to float about the parlor *now* in the arms of your attentive enemy lieutenant as you so shamelessly did the night of your birthday, Anne."

James had risked his own safety to inform them and Anne felt grateful, but panic was rising in her. "Lieutenant Fraser could be among those—fighting near Point Peter right now," she gasped. "Dear God! *Dear God. . . .*"

When she glanced at James and Anna, both were staring at her in such a puzzled way she felt almost sorry for them, but there was just no room now for pity in behalf of two persons like James and Anna who were, at the moment anyway, perfectly safe. Cold fear for the very life of vibrant, laughing John Fraser was filling her whole being. It must show on her face. Well, let it show. Only finding out about *him* mattered now. He could, at this very moment, be wounded—be needing all the strength she could muster.

After a long silence, with all three just standing there, James exclaimed, "Listen! The firing's stopped altogether."

"Is that a hopeful sign, James?" Anna Matilda whispered.

"Probably not. It could well mean the few Americans at Point Peter have surrendered. The town of St. Marys will be next. For their sakes, I hope the citizens will surrender quietly. It could save some lives and property."

James, of course, was being his usual analytical self, Anne thought, but now her annoyance with him was gone. She was too weak. Still too filled with fear for John Fraser because if anything had happened to *him,* it had also happened to her.

Chapter 6

For two more endless days, Anne sat through every waking hour by the window from which she could watch at least some of the British activity in and around Dungeness. Yesterday her mother had been allowed to visit her and Anna Matilda, but then for no more than twenty minutes during which a freckled-faced British enlisted man stood guard just inside the bedroom door, listening to every word they said. Most of each precious minute Mama had spent trying to calm Anna Matilda's fears for her parents "way up there in Darien."

"We just have to trust our menfolk, my dear," Mama kept reminding Anna. "It was your father's idea to take refuge in Darien. I'm sure he knows exactly what he's doing."

"I know, Mrs. Couper, but do you think they'll be back on St. Simons when we're allowed to go home again?"

"No one can answer that, Anna. The British officers, at least, are so courteous to us here, I feel strongly that one of them would tell us when we can leave if he knew." Then Anne saw her mother glance warily at the young guard before she whispered, "I—I have a feeling my son, James, may have some word for us later today."

"How, Mama?" Anne demanded. "How can he find out anything?"

"I'm not free to say one more word, Anne, but I beg you both to wait and try to be patient."

Mama dropped just that one maddening hint and nothing more. That was yesterday. Anne was still waiting, but not patiently. From her window lookout, she grew restive watching nothing more exciting than the almost steady procession of British soldiers hard at work carrying loads of lumber and supplies from the Dungeness dock, while others were erecting some kind of fortification. Along with the tireless gull cries, now and then she could hear a shouted command, even occasional laughter from the garden below, but such ordinary behavior told her nothing of what might have happened during all that shooting over by Point Peter day before yesterday. Hardest of all, nothing she saw gave her one clue of John Fraser's whereabouts.

Anna Matilda only added to Anne's jittery state by her constant quill scratching as she wrote in her diary. Never one to keep current with her own half-empty daybook, Anne had hours ago given up trying to persuade her friend to stop scribbling away in hers. Anna Matilda seemed to be almost obsessed with setting down every word, every footstep in the hallway. Normally quite submissive and sweet, she showed a stubborn streak by refusing point-blank to stop writing, even when Anne begged.

A sudden, light tap at their door startled them both. Anne jumped to her feet. Anna Matilda actually dropped her quill. Was Mama being allowed to pay them another visit? It couldn't be Phebe. She'd already brought a breakfast tray, informing them that they could thank the British for their food, much of which came straight from them because food on Cumberland was in such short supply. Eating British food had angered Anna Matilda, but Phebe's admiration for the enemy was plainly growing. In her secret heart, Anne was so worn down with anxiety over Lieutenant Fraser, she still had trouble eating. Then, the knock came again, not careful and quiet now, but brisk.

"Come in," Anne called, sounding as nervous as she felt.

"And do you think that would be quite proper, Miss Couper?" a man's voice asked pleasantly from the hall outside.

She'd heard people declare that at certain moments their heart stopped. She would never doubt again that such a thing could happen. Her own heart stopped beating, and when it began again, she could feel the pounding in her ears.

"Who's *that?*" Anna Matilda gasped, rushing to where Anne still sat by the window staring across the room at the closed door.

"I'll go," Anne whispered and hurried to open the door to —*him.*

"Good day, Miss Couper." The incredibly handsome

face, which Anne had decided would look terribly arrogant without the twinkle and the cleft chin and the smile, was beaming calmly at her now as he invited her to step out into the hall, where they could speak more privately. He even added courteous, gentlemanly apologies to Anna Matilda.

"Don't leave me," Anna choked out. "Please don't leave me here alone, Anne!"

Touching her elbow as they walked together toward the far end of the hall, John Fraser said, "I'm sorry to see your pretty friend so frightened. There's really no reason for it, you know."

He was there, standing at a hall window beside her, but she couldn't speak. He hadn't been killed or even wounded in the Point Peter fighting. Best of all, he had come to talk privately with her of his own volition. Her thumping heart would surely interfere with anything she might try to say in response to his aggravating contention that there was really no reason for her to be afraid. What could she say anyway to such an absurd assurance in the face of the long days of imprisonment?

"I've thought about you almost constantly, Miss Couper, since last we met. Every thought of you convinced me of many things, high among them that you somehow—trusted *me* from the start."

"Trusted you?" she gasped. "Did you think I wouldn't be frightened at being shut in my room, just because I trusted *you*?" She had flared at him and felt relieved. "I'm not one bit sorry I said that, either," she added, then surprised herself by suddenly smiling up at him. Really smiling. For some peculiar reason that she didn't have sense enough to think through, her own quick smile in the face of the flare-up made her recall a thousand moments when she and Papa might also have flared at each other had not one of them smiled—or laughed outright.

"I think it was the Frenchman Voltaire who wrote that 'a sense of humor is the only thing that keeps intelligent people from hanging themselves,' " he said. "Do you agree?"

"Do I agree that Voltaire said that or that what he said is true?"

She had asked the flip question as a diversion, purposely, but it had done more than that. Lieutenant Fraser seemed so pleased, he tossed back his gorgeous head and laughed the musical laugh she had honestly been afraid she'd never hear again. Her joy brimmed so dangerously, Anne wondered how she was able to go on standing there, but she was standing there not a foot away from him—within easy arm's reach—and she was smiling her most practiced, most flirtatious smile, dead sure that he had no idea how her heart was misbehaving.

His smile abruptly gone, the rich, musical voice turned husky and John Fraser breathed, "I don't really care how you interpreted my pathetic comment, Miss Couper. I missed you—painfully. Dare I hope you thought of me at all these past few days?"

In some desperation, she reminded herself that she needed to keep the upper hand. "They may have seemed but a few days to you, Lieutenant. The time was endless for me shut up in that room like—like an ordinary prisoner."

For a long time he stood there looking down at her. When he spoke at last, Anne would have staked her life that he meant every word.

"I'm deeply sorry for the bad time you must have had. You and your little friend, Miss Page, and your charming, very likable mother. Even your somewhat contentious brother."

Being sincerely sorry for their captivity seemed somehow to fall short of what Anne was reading in his eyes. They were masking laughter again.

"I find nothing laughable about being a captive, sir!"

"I do deeply regret your inconvenience, but because you are a captive, I knew you would still be here where I could find you once I returned from our little skirmish near Point Peter. Knowing that definitely gave me a light heart."

Before she could stop herself, Anne asked, almost pleadingly, "It—did, sir?"

"Yes. In fact, I begged to be relieved of the rewarding duty in the actual capture of St. Marys because I was so eager to get back here and talk with you again."

"Did your—forces take St. Marys?"

He nodded. "Capture of the little town was one of our main goals in this breathtakingly beautiful spot. We do need to block navigation. In order to create as much economic loss as possible for your 'Jonathans,' we had to effect the capture of St. Marys." He was smiling again. "I hope you aren't too offended that I used our somewhat derogatory term *Jonathans* for your American forces."

She decided to ignore that. "Did the people of St. Marys really surrender?"

"They had no choice. I'm sure the Royal Marines occupy it even now. Miss Anne, our headquarters will be here, though, at Dungeness. Does that please you?"

"How do I know?"

"You don't seem to mind that I'm near enough now for us to talk."

He wasn't flippant. It might have been much easier if he were. "I'm—I'm relieved, Lieutenant, that you weren't—wounded."

He laid one wide hand on her forearm. "You are?"

"You'll find I don't say things I don't mean."

"Then, will you honor us—you and your friend and family—by sharing meals downstairs? In the company of my fellow officers? And in my company, Miss Anne?"

Unable not to return his hopeful smile, Anne asked, "Would it matter if I refused?"

"Yes, greatly. But, you're my captive. I could order you to join me."

Left with no appropriate response, she decided to ask exactly what she longed to find out. "Could you—would it be against your military orders to tell me if you'll—still be here at Dungeness tomorrow?"

"Admiral Cockburn has just arrived and will settle in at once, so I'll definitely be here. Does that make you happy at all?"

In case she found no other chance to speak to him alone, Anne was determined to say only what she truly meant. "Yes, it relieves me and makes me quite happy."

She could feel her heart sink when she realized that their conversation was coming to an end. Try as she might, she could think of no other reason to detain him.

"I'm due to take over down at the dock. In fact, I'm sure I'm overdue, but I'll escort you to dinner in a short while, if you still agree. Miss Page, too, of course."

"Will you let my mother and brother know about—meals?"

"I will indeed, if you'll answer one question for me."

"What?"

"On the night we met, do you remember asking outright if we had plans to take over St. Simons Island any time soon?"

"Of course, I remember."

"Are you a spy for the 'Jonathans'? Or did you ask because *you* wanted to know?"

"I'm not a spy for anyone but my father! Someone promised Anna Matilda Page you'd leave her father's Retreat Plantation alone. Will you promise me not to steal my father's people, should you capture St. Simons?"

"We *are* going to take St. Simons, but I'm a loyal marine. I can't promise anything beyond my best effort to protect your father's property. A military man operates under orders. I don't always approve of my orders, but I'm obedient to my superiors. Actually, although I don't like slavery, my experience to the north along your coast showed me that planters could not farm without their slaves. I wish I could promise to protect your father's property. All I can say is—I'll try."

"My father treats his people far better than England treats its working classes!"

She had flared at him again, and again he was smiling down at her. "I have no argument with that whatever. In fact, I'm known in London as a reasonable Radical. I'd actually fight, if I could, for our poor working people."

He was going to leave her now for sure. Because it just *had* to be a good parting, Anne managed a smile too, fighting both her own excitement and her weakness. "I like it that you're a 'reasonable Radical,' sir," she said, her hand out to him.

He grasped it in both of his. "I—like *you,* Miss Anne Couper. I find I undoubtedly like you more than even I know. So much that I'm going to tell you something I should not be telling you. Your belligerent brother, just this morning, marched himself down to the dock bearing a white flag and demanded to be assured that all property, including slaves, be held sacred, left untouched by our forces."

Anne stared at him. "James Hamilton did that? What was he told?"

"I'm afraid he was lied to by one of our officers. He was told that indeed all property would be held sacred, left alone. I am not at liberty to tell him, Miss Anne, but I am telling you. That's not true. Every slave who agrees to come aboard a British ship will be taken—every slave here and on St. Simons Island."

Chapter 7

Rebecca Couper, dreading another long day of imprisonment alone in her room at the far end of the third-floor hall from where Anne and Anna Matilda slept, was relieved when she heard a knock at her door soon after Phebe had brought breakfast one morning toward the end of January.

"Come in, please," she called out, not surprised that it was Louisa Shaw, who had tried hard each day to spend at least a few minutes with her and to whom the British granted liberty to move about her now dusty, neglected mansion.

Feeling unusually queasy today, Rebecca did not leave her chair to greet her troubled friend. She had told her hostess a week ago about her own belief that she was carrying Jock's child. No one else knew. She had not been positive when they left St. Simons earlier in the month and saw no reason yet to trouble Anne. There was enough troubling everyone already.

Nothing could have made Rebecca as happy as the thought of giving Jock another baby, *if* she'd been safely at home under the care of Dr. Tunno and the Coupers' own capable Rhyna. But here, in a strange place, a prisoner in the home of a woman with more than enough to worry about, the possibility had been almost too much to bear.

"I've always rather prided myself on my own strength," she heard herself telling Louisa, who had taken the rocker beside her own. "Common courtesy to you as my hostess, Louisa, should keep my mouth shut about me today and it will. I had some morning sickness again, but it's better now. You have more than enough on your poor overburdened mind. How is Mr. Shaw this morning? Is he still feeling stronger?"

"Blessedly, yes," Louisa said nervously, the deep crease in her smooth, high forehead belying her words. "He's up and about again and giving me all sorts of problems. Rebecca, one would think he actually wished me harm the way he criticizes the Americans and praises those uncouth British marines who have made themselves at home in *my* house! I know you don't feel well enough to listen to my complaints, but when my otherwise kind husband begins to spout about his scorn for anything not British, I feel so alone, so lost, so helpless. Are you sure you feel better? You're quite pale. You need the care of a doctor. A midwife." She covered her face with her hands. "My Myrtle has gone with all my other people—to the British. You know I have only eleven-year-old Sallie to look after me and try to help poor exhausted Phebe. I honestly think Phebe would have left me too had Admiral Cockburn not decided to keep her on as *their* cook!"

Her head swimming, Rebecca fought a sickening wave of nausea and blurted, "Louisa, one of the most hurtful things about all this difficulty we're in is seeing our people turn against us." Tears stung her eyes, but she had to tell someone. "It will break my poor husband's heart if even one of his people chooses to go with the British. Jock is the kindest of masters, the sweetest, gentlest husband any woman ever had, but if he has a fault, it's pride in his workers' regard for him. They *are* going to capture St. Simons. Anne told me two days ago. She had it straight from her British lieutenant. And I won't be there to help Jock!"

"That's why I came so early this morning, Rebecca," Louisa said, her face stricken. "I can't bear to see you go. I do feel so cut off from everyone dear to me, close to me—everyone who is a real part of my familiar world. But you are leaving Cumberland, you and Anne and James Hamilton and the Page girl. All my houseguests. That quite civilized Lieutenant John Fraser told me not ten minutes ago. It's been decided by the admiral himself that our food supply is too low to keep you here any longer. Oh my dear, are you up to such a long boat ride?"

Rebecca felt strength drain away. "No. No, I'm not up to anything this minute, but I'll—manage. When are we going?"

"Tomorrow. First thing tomorrow morning—the worst time for you. Shall I let Anne know? Or do you want to tell her now that you're allowed to visit your own daughter once a day. Or perhaps your son should be the one to break the news."

"Yes," Rebecca said weakly. "Would you ask him to tell the girls to be packed? Oh, Louisa! I just thought of something. Where are our oarsmen? I hope you're not going to tell me they've all deserted to the British!"

"Two have. You'll be short two oarsmen. My husband told me two of Mr. Couper's younger people fled to join the enemy's West India Regiment."

Some of the nausea was passing. Rebecca pulled herself out of the low rocker and went to a window. "Well, the weather's clear. I suppose we'll manage with only six oarsmen, although their work will be very hard. I wonder which two left us. Poor, poor Jock. . . ."

"I don't believe a word of what you're saying, James," Anne almost shouted at her brother when he informed her and Anna Matilda that they were to leave so soon for St. Simons. "And don't stand there looking as though your eyes could be scraped off your face! Of course, I want to go home—of course, I long to see Papa. But—but until I hear it from—someone else, someone who *knows,* I won't believe it!"

"I know who you mean," Anna Matilda said, "but you haven't laid eyes on your precious lieutenant in almost three days! He's a kind, charming man in a lot of ways, but he is the enemy and there's no way to be sure all the attention he's been paying you hasn't just been a pleasant way to pass his time here."

James Hamilton seemed so amused and delighted by what Anna Matilda had just dared to say, Anne could have smacked him.

"You surprise me, Miss Page," James said. "Good for you! It takes a mature woman to see through a man like Fraser. I commend you for being far more perceptive than my poor sister."

Standing motionless in the middle of their bedroom, Anne's thoughts whirled in confusion. At any minute she thought she might cry. James had to be wrong! Anna Matilda had taken complete leave of her senses. True, it had been almost three days since she'd seen John, but he was a busy officer in the Royal Marines. She didn't need to understand how he could love his unit so deeply. That he did was enough for her. He not only loved being in the military, he obeyed orders. For over two entire days, she'd been struggling to convince herself that he'd been sent off on some mission and would come to her the instant he got back. He'd even hinted, the last time they walked together at sundown out under Mrs. Shaw's spreading live oak trees, that an American merchant vessel called the *Countess of Harcourt* had been hidden from the British some distance up the St. Marys River. The Royal Marines had taken everything from the town of St. Marys and loaded it onto British warships—including quantities of cotton, furniture from people's houses, foodstuffs, machinery.

"But Admiral Cockburn isn't considering leaving that heavily loaded merchant ship and its cargo safely up the St. Marys River. When we'll capture it I don't know, but we will," John had declared with a twinkle. He'd said no more, but this minute, reeling before the unkind attacks from both her best friend and her only brother, she clung to what she'd already decided—that Lieutenant Fraser had been sent to capture the prize from the Americans. Except for the scary time when he helped fight in the capture of the feeble battery near Point Peter, he hadn't missed a day seeing her until now, had he?

When anyone criticized John, Anne felt herself criticized. Under the guise of being courteous to a lady, James would, she knew, wait for her to speak next. "I know what I know," she said uncertainly. "And what I know is entirely my own business."

"And mine, so long as you're under my guidance," James said, his voice abruptly kind and gentle. "Papa sent you three ladies in my care and I intend to look after you until you're safely back at Cannon's Point."

"I didn't mean to hurt your feelings, Anne, by what I said." Anna Matilda spoke just above a whisper. "I'm truly sorry. You will let me go home to Cannon's Point with you until my parents come back from Darien, won't you?"

"You're always more than welcome, Anna Matilda, as are all our friends, at Cannon's Point. Now, if you'll deign to give me a hand, we'd better begin packing." Her strength was returning because real anger was welling in her. "But both of you remember one thing—Lieutenant Fraser will be back in plenty of time to see us off tomorrow morning!" Quickly, Anne crossed the room to the ornate, mahogany armoire that held her party dresses. How had she dared make such a claim? John could at this very minute be on his way in a British warship to St. Simons! Or up the St. Marys River—or anywhere!

At the door, James Hamilton, as though reading her thoughts, asked, "How do you dare say a thing like that, Sister? How do you dare claim he'll be here?"

Well, she had dared and she was glad. Scared, more scared than at any other moment of their captivity, but all the way through, she was glad she'd said it.

"Does Mrs. Couper know we're going home?" Anna Matilda asked.

"Yes," James Hamilton said as he opened the bedroom door. "Mama knows and I'm very concerned about her health."

Anne whirled to face him. "Is Mama ill?"

"She vows not, just tired, but as soon as we're home, Papa must have Dr. Tunno examine her. One would think the *Royal* British Marines would have a doctor available to see to her before we leave, but no. Their one surgeon—your mighty lieutenant's own brother, Anne—is nowhere around. Dr. William Fraser is as remote when needed as is his handsome brother."

Anne turned her back. What James Hamilton had just said could not be true! If the British doctor—wherever he kept himself—was John's brother, *why hadn't John told her?* Why had he told her nothing about his family? She had chattered on and on about the Coupers and her mother's family, the Maxwells, whose ancient castle still stood near Dumfries, Scotland. John wasn't British; he was a Scot and right from Dumfries! Why had he kept her so in the dark about his own roots? Did he plan to tell her all that later when the British captured St. Simons Island? Had he known before their last meeting that she and Anna Matilda and her family were to be sent home? In the confusion that swept her, she grabbed one and then another party dress, balled them up shamelessly and began stuffing them into her packing box. Had she allowed James and Anna Matilda to plant a seed of real doubt in her about John?

Without another word, James left, closing the door behind him.

After a long, awkward silence during which Anne raked a row of dress shoes off a shelf and dumped them into the same box with her party dresses, Anna Matilda asked, "Do you think you can ever forgive me, Anne, for what I said about Lieutenant Fraser staying away so long—without a word?"

"I don't know. Yes. Yes, I do know. I guess I forgive you. You're still too young and inexperienced to understand—much of anything." And then she turned to face her friend. "But whether or not you really understand, I want you to remember that before we leave the Dungeness dock tomorrow morning and head for home, Lieutenant Fraser will have made an appearance." The relief, when she felt her own painful doubt begin to diminish, was immense. "He will not allow me to leave Cumberland without saying good-bye. You'll see—he will not, he will not, *he will not.*"

Mama looked so pale and miserable when James Hamilton helped her into the *Lady Love* just after dawn the next morning, Anne thought she might die of shame. Something was obviously wrong with her mother, and all Anne had thought of when James Hamilton told her yesterday was her own hurt feelings that John Fraser hadn't mentioned having a doctor brother. For the whole time of their captivity at Dungeness, she'd felt off to one side from her own family, had thought almost every minute only of John. Oh, she'd tried to be cheerful during the few visits she'd been permitted with her mother—so cheerful, in fact, that Mama had laughingly asked her once to stop trying so hard and to cry on her shoulder if she needed to. Anne had felt no such need, even knowing, as she certainly did, how mothers enjoy being necessary.

"I'll sit beside Mama, James," she said now as her brother gave Anne a hand into the big plantation boat.

"I think not," her brother said calmly, so calmly it infuriated her. "Mama may need a strong arm to support her if the water is as rough as usual when we cross St. Andrew Sound. You'd better sit by Anna Matilda, Sister, as you did when we came down."

Not trusting herself to answer James in a civilized way, all Anne could do was hear over and over in her mind what he had just said: ". . . when we came down, when we came down." Nothing would ever again be as it had been when they came down to Cumberland. Nothing—ever. John had *not* come to tell her good-bye. For all she knew, he could be expecting to find her still at Dungeness when he finally returned from wherever he had gone. Or their next meeting, if there was ever to be one, could be on St. Simons. Her faith in him today was still only partly intact. Through the long night hours, she had struggled to convince herself that somehow in all that was taking place, John, too, was an innocent, helpless bystander as she felt herself to be.

Two lovers torn apart by the ridiculous fortunes of war!

Lovers? Yes. Yes, they were and although much of the joy had been blotted out by his sudden disappearance, by Mama's odd illness, Anne held firmly to her belief that indeed John Fraser *was* her lover. Somehow he would always be.

Settled in the big plantation boat beside Anna Matilda, for the first time Anne noticed that again, in the seat directly in front of where her mother sat, June was laboring with the remaining Couper oarsmen to move them toward the risky St. Andrew Sound at the northern end of Cumberland Island. *June had not run away!* No matter how much persuasion, how many false promises the British had offered, June had remained true to Eve. Ebo June, at least, would not be breaking Papa's heart by deserting him.

"I find I take quite a bit of comfort," James was saying to their mother, "in what that rather gentlemanly British officer told me several days ago. He vowed that unless a slave begged to leave with them, all property would be held sacred."

Poor, misled James, Anne thought. Poor Mama if she happened to believe him, which she was sure was the case because they all thought of James Hamilton as though he were Aristotle. John had told her in confidence that the officer lied, that no property would be considered safe or sacred. Only Anne knew that even when they reached St. Simons again, June could, as soon as the British captured their island, still decide to go with them. For that matter, he could take Eve too!

"What's wrong, Anne?" her friend wanted to know. "You're sitting there practically wringing your hands. Are you so sad that Lieutenant Fraser didn't appear to tell you good-bye?"

She was sad, crushed to the depths of her being, frantic because who knew how long she'd have to wait for him to reach St. Simons Island and capture her again—along with maybe dozens of Papa's people, bales of their cotton, and heaven knew what else? How did she, the only Couper daughter, *dare* to sit there tingling with anticipation of the moment the enemy might come to steal her own father blind?

Would June think of leaving Cannon's Point? If he did, would Eve go with him? What on earth would Anne do without Eve, who had always been there to take care of her every need? Eve belonged to her! Surely Eve, so smart, so quick, knew that when someone *belonged,* that meant forever. But what could stop Eve from jumping over a broom to marry June and then running away with him to Bermuda or Nova Scotia or wherever the British were promising to send entire slave families? Was June up there now laboring at his oars through the dangerous, tricky shoals of St. Andrew Sound only because he meant to return for Eve and then take her away? Until the frightening thought struck, Anne had taken for granted that June's loyalty to Papa prompted him to resist the fiendish British offers in order to help take the Couper family safely home again.

Beneath grunts as he pulled the heavy oars, was June laughing that devilish, private laugh of his? Laughing at her and Anna Matilda and James and Mama? Poor Mama. It was so unlike her to sit there with her head on James's shoulder, saying nothing in the way of encouragement either to the oarsmen or to her family.

"Mama? Mama, are you all right?"

"Yes, Anne, I'm feeling much better now, thank you."

"She needs her strength, Sister," James Hamilton said over his shoulder. "I don't believe you should try to engage her in conversation."

"Oh, you don't! Well, she's my mother too, Mr. Yale Graduate, and I'll thank you not to butt in."

"Anne, please!"

"Now, you see, Sister? You've upset her," James Hamilton scolded. "Would it be all right if I told Anne why you don't feel well, Mama? She really does have a right to know."

Anne caught her breath. Was something seriously wrong with Mama? Had she told only James just because he was older and grown-up and making such a big thing of looking after them all?

"Just as soon as we're safely across St. Andrew Sound, my dear, I'll tell you—everything, and until then, please don't feel hurt because your brother knew first. I—I don't need that kind of family bickering right now."

Anne's own mind had been in such turmoil over so much, she had only this minute realized that the Couper oarsmen had not been singing. Had Mama felt so poorly she'd asked them not to? Something must be terribly wrong for the people to be silent, and because Anne felt so scared and worried and confused, she reached for Anna Matilda's hand and held it tight all the remaining distance across the rough sound.

When her mother finally lifted her head from James's shoulder and turned around on the wide seat to look at Anne, she was smiling.

All Anne could say was, "Mama? What is it that's made you ill, Mama?"

"It's something beautiful and right, but very difficult for me, dear."

"Please don't make me wait—you're not going to die, are you?"

Her mother tried a small laugh. "No. And I'm not really ill at all. Even for a nearly forty-year-old woman like me, everything's perfectly normal. I'm—going to have a baby."

Anne's eyes opened wide. "After all this time—with James and me so grown-up—a baby?"

"That's right, darling."

Anne reached forward to put both arms around her mother. "Well, is there anything I can do—right now to help?"

"Just pray we'll somehow eventually get all the way back to our dock so I can tell your blessed father!"

A heavy swell struck the loaded boat so that icy cold water flowed over the wall side nearest Anne and soaked her feet.

Looking quickly over her shoulder at Anne's wet slippers and the drenched hem of her long skirt, her mother smiled helplessly and repeated her own words. "Yes, yes, you can pray, Anne, that we'll eventually get all the way back to our dock so I can tell your blessed father—and you can get into some dry shoes."

Chapter 8

To Rebecca's great relief, the bedraggled, travel-worn little party reached the Cannon's Point dock just as darkness was falling that evening, January 28. Both Jock and Johnson had spotted the loaded boat coming down the Hampton River and, along with two or three dozen of their other people, were out to greet them. For the first few minutes, it seemed to Rebecca that everyone was talking at once. Even normally quiet Anna Matilda just kept on exclaiming in amazement because Mr. Couper and Johnson had learned only yesterday from Mr. Roswell King that Cumberland Island *and* St. Marys had been captured by the British.

With every ounce of energy left to her, Rebecca tried to act normally, tried not to show Jock how upset she'd been, how exhausted, how frustrated, that for over two weeks, while confined to their rooms, they had also surprisingly been treated as almost social guests by the British invaders. Time enough to talk freely about it all to her husband once they could be alone.

Leaning heavily on Jock's arm as he led her up the path to their welcoming, brightly lighted house, she felt her heart had never been more torn by contradictions: joy at the news she ached to tell Jock about the baby she now knew they could expect in the early fall; relief that in the confusion he hadn't seemed to notice the two missing oarsmen; painful anxiety that the British could any day land on St. Simons and rob them of more people and other property. There was also anxiety of another kind over what must be utter chaos in Anne's own heart because her beloved Lieutenant John Fraser had not appeared to say good-bye. Beloved? Rebecca knew Anne had fallen deeply in love. Mother instinct was plainer than words this time. Anne had told her almost nothing, but in the fortnight they'd been at Dungeness, Rebecca sensed that the girl had turned into a woman whose every moment was driven by her heart. She would talk it all over with Jock, of course, and clinging to his strong arm as they climbed the gentle path to their blessed front steps, she thanked God that he was a man of understanding.

Even Louisa Shaw had seen Anne's romance flourish. Worried as their hostess had been throughout their captivity over her husband's illness and the loss of so many people, Louisa had fretted that Mr. Couper might object to his only daughter's falling in love with the enemy. "You're wrong, Louisa," Rebecca had assured her. "Jock isn't like that. He'll be as angry as the next one to lose any of his property, but he'll understand about Anne and her young man. It may take a little time, but I'd stake my life on that."

Eve had come running down the path almost as soon as Jock helped Rebecca from the boat, and it puzzled Rebecca some that Anne was deep in secret talk with Eve this minute instead of with her father or Anna Matilda. Poor Anna Matilda trudged alone beside Rhyna, who had always been partial to the Page girl and had long ago extracted a promise from Rebecca that she would be allowed to go down to Retreat to "help with the birthin' " of Anna's first child some day.

"What have you heard from Anna Matilda's parents, Jock?"

"Not one word, Becca," he said, and she knew his cheerfulness was strained. Many dreadful burdens lay quite near the surface, she was sure. A fortnight wasn't a very long time, but so much had happened, she almost dreaded all they would both have to say to each other tonight before she could sleep.

"June!" her husband called out, stopping to look behind them for his oarsman. "I want you to see to my daughter's luggage, do you hear? Mrs. Couper's too. Be sure that Miss Page is cared for. I'll be with my wife."

"Yes, sir, Mausa Couper," June said, moving past them on the path, his arms loaded with boxes and portmanteaus. "That's one thing you can forget about. June in charge of everything!"

June wasn't smart-aleck, Rebecca thought, just confident.

Confident, strong, outspoken, and, as he'd always been to her, mysterious. Not once had she felt at ease with June. Not afraid of him in any way, but uneasy, because she'd never been able to be sure of what he was thinking.

Her tenderhearted husband had wept for joy when she told him about the child she carried and when he began to report to her on conditions on St. Simons Island, she was glad she'd told him about the baby first. His happiness, she knew, moderated some of his deep worry that indeed the British might be coming to take over their beloved island.

"I'm afraid I've become a nuisance to the poor Goulds," he told her. "Twice I've ridden down to their place to keep watch with James from his tower. Stayed two days once, three the next. I followed a hunch yesterday, Becca, or I'd have stayed there tonight and missed all this."

Later, lying beside her in their bed, he held her weary body close to his dear, warm, strong self—the clear, uncluttered self where Rebecca had always found complete safety and rest.

"I must thank the Goulds for their kindness to you, my dear Jock. What does Mr. Gould think might happen next to us here?"

"He knows no more than I," he said on a deep sigh. "Nor do the other planters. Hamilton knows nothing, Wylly knows nothing, Demere knows nothing, Abbott knows nothing. Roswell King, as usual, expects the worst, except for his crazy conviction that not one of Major Butler's people will desert him should the enemy capture us."

"Jock, they just may come here, but I'm sure none of our people will desert you."

His voice quavered when he said softly, "I—pray not, Becca. With all my heart, I pray not. I'm still short of funds from the bad hurricane the year we moved into this house, but it's more than the possibility of another financial loss. When I face the idea that my people might not feel about me the way I have to believe they do, I die a little inside. You know I'm not one to mention it often, but some of the sin of being a slave owner dims for a man if he thinks his people respect him."

She took his hand and held it to her cheek, postponing the moment he would find out that two oarsmen were already gone. "Jock, you're a kind master. Your people have good lives."

Somehow he managed a chuckle. "Come now, my beautiful Becca, you're far too weary to force yourself to cheer your puny, fretting husband. It's time to sleep."

"Not until I've told you one more thing. Our Anne has fallen in love with a—British officer named Lieutenant John Fraser."

He jerked himself upright in the bed. *"What?* Anne in love with—the enemy? I must be hearing things, woman!"

"No, you heard only what I said. And I beg you to try hard to understand. Not knowing where he is or even if he's safe right now is hard enough on the girl. She all but worships you. Anne needs you to understand. Her mother *begs* you to understand."

For a few seconds he just sat there, saying nothing. Then, his voice gentle, almost teasing, he whispered, "And did the gir-rl put you up to this? Did she beg you to try to pacify her one hundred percent *American* father?"

"No. Anne hasn't even told me herself, and that's very hard on a mother's pride. But I know she'll tell you. He's a handsome, gentlemanly, well-bred young man, Jock. All the officers stationed at Dungeness were gentlemen. Oh, a few drank too much at Anne's surprise birthday dinner, but—"

"At Anne's surprise birthday dinner? What manner of captivity was it, Becca? Did the enemy throw a surprise birthday party for our daughter?"

"No, Louisa Shaw gave the party, bless her, but they captured us right after we started eating. They herded us all upstairs first, then changed their minds and invited us back down. The young people danced until midnight!"

"And our high-spirited, independent daughter fell in love that first night, I suppose."

"She did indeed and I—I already know you do understand and will accept her young man into the family."

"Accept him into the family? They're getting married and she hasn't even mentioned a word of it to her own mother? Becca, are you sure you're all right?"

"I'm very sure and I want your promise before I go to sleep this night that you will not make any more discomfort for Anne."

He sank back onto the pillows, pulled up the covers, and took her again into his arms.

"Jock?"

"Hm?"

"Are you—happy for Anne?"

He nuzzled her neck and murmured. "Aye. Aye, if her invading lieutenant ever shows his face again, which I doubt, I'll be happy for her, Becca. I'll find a way. The gir-rl has always had her poor father wrapped around her little finger. No one is likely to change that."

In her own room across the upstairs hall, Anne stopped Eve from unpacking one single box until she'd told her everything. Not only that she, too, had at long last found the one man in all the world for her, wherever John might be right now, but that she'd actually prayed June wouldn't be fooled by a single wild British promise made to him and all the other servants on Cumberland.

"What you pray for?" Eve wanted to know. "That June come back here to get me?"

"No! I didn't pray for that. I prayed he'd have enough sense not to believe their outlandish promises!"

"Just so you didn't think June eber leave me behind."

Anne was puzzled. Eve didn't say what she had been so sure she would say. Compelled to discover why, Anne asked, "If they come here—and I'm positive they're coming, because Lieutenant Fraser told me they were going to capture St. Simons too—*you* wouldn't even think of leaving me, would you, Eve?"

"Whatever June say, I do."

"But June wouldn't betray my father, would he?"

Through the entire time they'd been alone together, Eve had been standing as usual. Now, Anne ordered her to sit down.

"You want I should—sit down in your bedroom, Miss Anne?"

"Yes, I want you to sit down in my bedroom. We're two women in love now, don't you realize that? I feel funny with you standing there like a lump in the middle of the floor."

"I ain't no lump."

"Eve, sit down. Do you hear me?"

"Where you want I should sit?"

"Anywhere! That other rocker will be fine. What difference does it make?" When Eve pulled the small chair a little to one side and sat down uneasily, Anne couldn't believe her own eyes because there were real tears in Eve's. "Are those tears?" she demanded.

"Yes'm, I reckon."

"But, why? June came back to you. I'm home safely in time for your birthday tomorrow. I've fallen in love, too. What's left to cry about?" Eve said nothing. She kept her eyes on the carpet, but Anne could see tears drip off her cheeks. "Eve! If anyone should cry, I should! I—I don't even know where Lieutenant Fraser is!"

Eve looked straight at her, the even features crumpled with love and pity. "Miss Anne, you know how sorry I be for you!"

"How sorry you—what for me?" Anne corrected her grammar.

"Ain't no time for tellin' me how to talk an' not talk when I feel so much pain for you. How you *live* all the way here in dat boat not knowin' when or if you eber see him again?"

Anne felt tears sting her own eyes. What a dumb thing for her to lose control now after forcing herself to stay strong hour after hour while June and the others rowed them mile after mile through those ugly, cold, gray, pounding waters. It was Eve's fault. With no warning whatever, Eve had dropped her familiar sassy ways and was actually feeling Anne's pain and fear of never seeing John again. Anna Matilda should be doing exactly what Eve was doing this minute—feeling with her—but she was probably already asleep.

"What your mama say 'bout you lovin' her enemy?"

For the first time Anne felt a pang of guilt. Her mother had confided her secret about her new baby, but Anne had said not one word about her love for John. "My—my mother doesn't know."

"She don't see what happen right in front ob her own eyes?"

"I don't think so. I mean, maybe she did. She's awfully smart. Awfully hard to fool, but honestly, I didn't try to fool anyone. I just—I just lived inside my own thoughts, I guess. Mama seemed to be quite comfortable around John. He even danced with her one night. I think she found him extremely pleasant. She'd have to! He's—oh, Eve, he's—wonderful! Tall, handsome, beautiful manners, and he has the most musical laugh I've ever heard in my whole life."

"Do he sing good?"

"Sing? I—why, I don't know about that."

"He not sing to you? June sing to me a lot."

When Anne got up from her rocker, Eve jumped quickly to her feet, too. "Eve, will you pray—pray hard that he'll come to St. Simons soon? I know that sounds crazy, because when they do get here, they're going to steal from Papa and his planter friends. They'll even try to take all his people, but—" She pulled Eve closer so she could look right into her eyes. "But—*you* won't leave, will you? I couldn't get along without you. Not only the way you help me with everything, but we're friends now and—and only you know how terribly in love I am. Promise? Eve, will you promise me you won't be enticed away by the British? June won't leave if you stay. Do you promise—a solemn oath?"

For an instant, the expression on Eve's face was that of a trapped animal. "Where—they take us to, the British?"

"Oh, dreadful places like Bermuda, where it's even hotter than it gets here, or Nova Scotia, where you'd freeze in winter."

Without saying one word, Eve turned away, turned all the way around, her back to Anne. A wave of desperation caused Anne to shudder. She barely managed to speak. "You—can't promise, can you?"

Eve's back was still turned, but Anne could see that she was shaking her head no.

Of course she couldn't promise anything. She was already promised to June. If June went away, Eve would go too.

Anne sank again into her little rocker. How could life be two opposing ways at once? How could she know so much bliss and joy in loving John, how could she hope so fervently that even tomorrow he might appear right there on St. Simons Island, when his appearance could easily mean ruin for poor Papa? Her own loss of Eve? Such deep-down helplessness was the one trouble Anne couldn't endure. This minute, she was helpless in all ways. As helpless as her father, the only person who could always fix everything for her.

Without another word, Eve quickly hung up Anne's clothes and hurried out of the room, leaving her alone.

By the time Anne joined James, Anna Matilda, and Mama at breakfast the next morning, Papa had already left for Mr. Gould's lighthouse at the south end of the island.

"He hated to leave us all on our first day home," Mama explained, looking wan and pale, "but he's so worried about —everything, he felt he just had to go. The light tower is a marvelous place to keep watch."

"How are things going for Mr. Browne down there?" Anne asked.

"Your father didn't mention him to me. All right, I'm sure."

"My deductions tell me," James said as he sank his fork into a steaming stack of Sans Foix's griddle cakes, swimming in butter and cane syrup, "that when and if the British capture St. Simons, they'll take Frederica first. That is, if they know its location."

"What's to capture over at Old Town?" Anna Matilda wanted to know. "There's nothing left there but a crumbling part of Oglethorpe's fort and some ruins of the old houses." She took a deep breath. "I'm surely glad that officer promised he wouldn't touch anything at my father's place."

James scoffed. "If any British officer can be believed."

"One can." Anne sounded firm and in control, she thought, then turned to her mother. "Are you feeling well enough for a shock, Mama? I hope so and I apologize for not having told you before, but it wouldn't surprise me if you already knew."

"I do know, Anne. Your brother and I both know you've been devoted to British Lieutenant John Fraser since the night they took us captive."

Anna Matilda gasped audibly but said nothing, for which Anne was grateful. "I am sorry, Mama. I guess I just thought you had enough to worry about down on Cumberland, and —no! The truth is I was selfish. This is the first time I've ever loved a man and I just found myself keeping everything inside me."

"I really don't see anything so unusual about that, my dear."

"Do you mean that, Mama? Wasn't I selfish?"

"Yes, perhaps you were, but we change when we believe ourselves to have found an entirely new life, Anne."

She leaned eagerly toward her mother. "We do, don't we? Yes! We really change. Oh, Mama, thank you for knowing that! When do you think Papa might be home? I was so hoping to tell him this morning."

"If he thinks there's a chance the British aren't coming this way today, he'll stay the night again. He's been doing that while we were gone. But, he already knows about Lieutenant Fraser, Anne."

"Who told him?"

"I did. Last night."

"What did he say? Did Papa object the way James does that I've—I've fallen in love with an officer in the Royal Marines?"

"No. He was surprised, but he didn't actually object. And this seems as good a time as any, James Hamilton, for me to tell you that your father and I expect you too to suspend all your verbal objections. Anne must be left to follow her own heart in such matters. Is that clear?"

Anne felt her brother looking at her before she turned to look at him. For once, he didn't say a word. He was just giving her his rare, melting smile and even though she didn't know for sure she'd ever see John Fraser again on this earth, she felt almost happy because the Couper family was her family and no one else's. For an instant, she'd had the childlike impulse to jump up and throw both arms around Mama. Instead, she smiled at her and said, "Mothers, especially mine, are very necessary persons."

"What about brothers?" James Hamilton asked, still grinning at her.

"Brothers, too," Anne said. "But just wait until *you* find the one girl you want to marry!"

"I fully intend to wait *and* to weigh it all very, very carefully, Sister. At Cumberland I was simply fulfilling my obligation to Papa to attempt, at least, to look after you and Mama and Anna Matilda."

His griddle cakes finished, James got to his feet, bowed to them all, and excused himself. "With Papa down at the lighthouse, my duty lies in giving driver Tom his orders for the day. Johnson may need me, too."

After James stooped to kiss Mama's hair, he couldn't resist making one of his proper little speeches about his hope that something he might say to the people would assure their continued loyalty to Papa should the British come. "I believe we have strong allies in Johnson and Tom, also in Liz and Rhyna. Sans Foix, of course, is already a free person of color."

Almost afraid of what the answer might be, Anne heard

herself ask, "And what about Ebo June, James? Do you think June will remain loyal to Papa?"

"I fail to see how anyone could tell for certain about June," Mama said softly.

"Nor I," her brother agreed. "Nor I."

Chapter 9

Before John Couper had ridden halfway down Frederica Road toward Gould's lighthouse at the south end of the island, rain had begun to fall. A stiff, cold wind blew so hard it was like physical labor to gallop under the ancient oak and gum and hickory limbs that formed an almost unbroken canopy above the narrow, shell lane.

Despite his relief that Rebecca and the children had reached home safely and his deep-down joy in anticipation of another child in his house, he rode this morning with an uncustomarily heavy heart. After learning that two of his young oarsmen had deserted on Cumberland, nothing short of the impending loss of even one more of his people could have driven him out into such a dark, ominous day, especially when he so longed to spend time with his wife. As always, Rebecca had urged him gently not to make the long ride, but also, as always, she had sent him off with words to lift his heart: "We've come through hard periods before, Jock. We will come through this. The British really are quite gentlemanly. If they come here, you'll see."

So "gentlemanly," he thought, that his beloved Anne had fallen in love with one of them! Just having Rebecca beside him again last night had made a sound sleep possible, in spite of the nagging worry that this unknown British officer may not be good enough for Anne, may indeed break her heart by sailing away when the war finally ended and never show his handsome face again.

He would not, he could not, object openly if his girl had decided that young Fraser is the man she truly loves. How could he stand in Anne's way when he and Becca had spent their entire married lives living love before the child? Had they been wise to do this so conscientiously? He had always believed so, but having grown up in a loving family surely made Anne more vulnerable to heartbreak now, more vulnerable to being hurt. Believing that this enemy officer truly loved her would not, because of what she'd always believed about love, be at all hard for Anne. She had never been given one single reason to doubt that her mother and father loved each other wholly. Her every day had pushed her toward the one day when she, too, would find her own heart's love and welcome it without question.

Rain was falling harder now. He could feel the cold, winter dampness across his broad back through the thick wool of his inverness cape. A glance at blowing strands of Spanish moss waving from the branches above his head could still bring a half-smile of gratification. John Couper loved those wide-spreading, live oak branches, their twisted lengths cushioned now with fresh, rain-revived resurrection ferns. The banners of moss, gray on a dry day, were sage green and alive-looking now that the rain was really coming down. Even the bare branches of gum and hickory seemed friendly. How he loved St. Simons Island! And the predictable springing up of its resurrection ferns—curled, dry, and dead-looking if the rain stayed away too long—was as vital a part of his attachment to the island as the certainty that the moss would turn greenish gray when wet through. There was no time of the year when he didn't live surrounded by some form of God's greenery. Even today, at almost the end of January, he rode in the sunless magic of pine and cedar and oak and magnolia green.

Let his back get wet. Who cared? Gould would loan him a change of clothes, and wonder of wonders, Gould's legs were as long as his. The borrowed dry clothing would fit.

What *did* he expect to find out after this long, soaking gallop down the island? Lightly, he spurred his mare, Bonnie. He was eager to learn if Gould had sighted more than the two British ships that had lain at anchor in St. Simons Sound to the south for over two weeks. Roswell King had done him the courtesy of reporting early this morning that the same schooners still lay in the Atlantic off the north end of St. Simons. He did find King uninteresting but freely admitted—reminded himself often, in fact—that the humorless, hard man was a thoughtful neighbor. If Jock was honest, what annoyed him most about King was the strict, cruel insistence that no Butler slave ever be permitted to cross Jones Creek, the narrow, gentle boundary between their plantations. Jones Creek was a meandering, harmless stream, but Couper at times almost hated it because of what it stood for, because of what it stood against. The threat of a flogging held Major Butler's people on the Hampton side of the creek, guaranteeing profit to King and to the major because it kept their people everlastingly at work.

Surely part of today's anxiety lay in uneasiness because of Rebecca's condition *and* Anne's sudden romance, but his deepest pain came from uncertainty about the faithfulness of his Cannon's Point people should the British offer them freedom. He had no worries about Johnson, his favorite man, or his Muslim driver, Tom. Sans Foix had come to him as a freeman and was noticeably proud of being the Couper chef. Johnson had undoubtedly been right when he said some would remain loyal, some would not. The British had allowed his family to return home mainly, he gathered from Rebecca last night, because food on Cumberland was too scarce to feed them along with fifteen hundred or two thousand British invaders. Time was running out. If the British planned to capture St. Simons Island, they'd be doing it any day now.

How much *did* the Cannon's Point people respect John Couper, their master? How much of their good humor with him was real, how much feigned for their own well-being? The questions plagued him.

Later, in sight of Gould's sturdy, octagonal light tower, he forced back a sharp, fresh worry: What if Anne's British officer wanted to marry her? Would he take her away from Cannon's Point to live in England? He could only push aside such a wrenching prospect. Throughout Anne's eighteen years of life, she had laughed and danced and played her pianoforte, charming her father to the very core of his being. He didn't want to block her happiness, but neither could he bear even the thought that Anne might ever be taken away from St. Simons Island.

For nearly four hours Couper had stood beside James Gould in his light tower, keeping watch. Only the same two British ships lay at anchor out in the St. Simons Sound, and as the pale, rainy-day light of the sun began to fade above the misty stretch of roiling gray water, Jock found that in his efforts to lift James's spirits, he'd also raised his own.

"We've both much to be thankful for, James," he said, laying aside his long glass. "Your family's no longer being held by the enemy to the north, mine's safely home from Cumberland, there are only two enemy ships out there—so shouldn't we give thanks? And be hopeful that perhaps something will be worked out between our country and Britain at the Ghent peace conference?"

"We've heard rumors of a peace treaty coming out of Ghent since before Christmas, Jock, but evidently the British are still headed our way."

Couper held only warm, affectionate feelings for James Gould, but the man's New England caution sometimes irritated him. It irritated him now as he pulled up a nail barrel and sank down onto it, unable not to try one more time to break Gould out of his gloomy mood. "Well, now, we do know the British took a real trouncing at New Orleans, such a trouncing, I understand from the *National Intelligencer,* we could well suffer only a boastful, not too unpleasant occupation should they really invade us here. Perhaps only enough of an occupation to make old Cockburn's military reports look better. Our charming 'spy,' my daughter, Anne, seemed convinced that her new suitor, Lieutenant Fraser, rather looked forward to their visit here. I know for a fact my family was courteously treated on Cumberland."

As was his habit, Gould made no further comment but focused his own long glass suddenly on the cloud-hung water. "Jock! I see 'em! They're coming in from the south! Look, *look!*"

Darkness was coming fast now, so John had trouble focusing his own glass.

A bloom of bloodred, smoky flame burst into the darkening sky above neighboring Jekyll Island. "Dear God," Couper breathed, "that's duBignon's place. They're burning it down!"

"That means they'll be here tomorrow," James said in a hoarse whisper.

Next morning they agreed just before dawn broke that when the British did land, James Gould would give correct directions for their thieving forays among St. Simons plantations. Then Jock mounted Bonnie for the ride home.

"I see no point in trying to confuse them, James. Our roads are few but well kept, our island relatively small. They'll find us anyway if they've a mind to. At least we're having a golden sunrise today. Let's take that as a good omen. Oh, and it might be better if young Browne stays here for the time being."

"Whatever you say, Jock. Ride carefully and give my regards and my Janie's regards to your family. Come again as soon as possible. If they land here, they'll find me protecting my tower with my own gun, believe me. I don't expect much help from the professor."

"Your tower's safe I'm sure. They need its light." He reached down to shake Gould's hand. "We'll get through whatever comes to us, old friend. I'm sure they'll want directions to Hamilton's plantation or Retreat first. They'll need to steal horses and wagons to get around the island to pay respects to the rest of us. See you again as soon as possible."

With that, he rode off across the packed stretch of sandy beach that led to his favorite shortcut over to Frederica Road. As he galloped along through the breaking light, his mind raced from one troubling question to another. Would Lieutenant Fraser actually be among those who were about to invade his home island? Was the young man out there aboard one of those British ships right now, about to sail in to the pier just below Gould's tower? Had his son, James, managed to convince the Couper people to remain loyal? Would any but Johnny and Tom tell the truth about what they meant to do? Did his people really know themselves how each would act when the British actually offered them freedom? Had Ebo June and the other oarsmen spread the word of what they saw and heard on Cumberland?

Galloping through the sun-and-shadow streaks in the now soft, windless St. Simons dawn, he wondered if indeed he knew what he himself would do should Anne's young man dare to propose marriage while in the very act of stealing property from her father.

Chapter 10

At her insistence and because he'd always taken Anne around the plantation with him any time she wanted to go, John Couper crossed Jones Creek in a small skiff on a foggy early February morning with Anne beside him, two of his oarsmen rowing. Cheeks flushed, eyes bright with a mixture of anxiety and excitement, she held tight to his hand with her one free hand and smiled up at him often during the short row to the Hampton Point side of the creek.

"You're holding on to that basket on your lap as though it were full of gold, Anne," he teased, hoping to hide his own worry that for nearly a week there hadn't been one word of any kind about what the enemy was up to on St. Simons. Not a word since the day he'd galloped home from Gould's tower the morning after six additional British warships appeared in the sound.

"I'm taking a load of Sans Foix's pastries to some of my elderly friends and to Robert at Major Butler's plantation," she explained as though it were any normal, happy, carefree day. "It's past time young Robert may try to sneak across Jones Creek again, hoping to find Sans Foix's plum tarts, and you know what happened to him the last time he tried."

"I do," her father answered grimly. "He got the lash. Annie, I try hard never to worry you or your mother about anything that might be bothering me, but you were on Cumberland with the British scoundrels. Are you—fearful of what they might do to us now that they're really here?"

He saw a tiny frown. "Fearful, Papa? If you mean that they'll free some St. Simons slaves, yes. They did that all over Cumberland. They took cotton and all the other supplies they could find, too, both at Cumberland and at St.

Marys, but they'll be courteous to *us.* Mr. Hamilton and Major Butler, even the Pages, will lose some slaves, I'm sure, and I know they're valuable property but I don't think they'll take any who don't want to leave. Your people will be loyal to you!"

He sighed heavily. "I'm not that sure." Then, forcing a smile, he added, "I am sure you're eager for them to reach Cannon's Point no matter what they plan to do to harm my property." She said nothing, but when she glanced up at him again, he saw tears standing in her eyes. "You—love this young man, don't you, Annie?" For years, it had been his habit to call her Annie in intimate moments. "You hate to see your old papa robbed of property, but you can't wait for him to rob me of you."

"Oh, Papa, he hasn't asked me to marry him."

"But he will if you have anything to say about it."

"Yes. Yes!"

"Then, the young lieutenant doesn't stand a chance of escaping." Giving her an impulsive hug, he added, "Whatever makes my girl happy, even if I don't like it, I pray will come to pass."

"Papa, I love you."

"I love you, Daughter, and I'm glad you wanted to cross Jones Creek with me today." He sighed again. "Although why I'm going I'm not exactly sure. It's no secret, within our family anyway, that I'm not exactly fond of Roswell King, but the man stays informed. I thought he may have heard something we don't know. May be aware of just where they are now on the island."

"John Fraser is coming to St. Simons," she said almost commandingly. "I'll die if he doesn't!"

The light skiff bumped the muddy shore on the Hampton side of Jones Creek just as they both stiffened in their seats to listen. Thunderous pounding from what must be the hard galloping of more than a dozen horses came from the direction of the lane that branched off Couper Road toward Hampton Plantation.

"Papa?"

"I think so, aye," he spoke grimly. "That must be the British just reaching Hampton, undoubtedly astride my friend Hamilton's fine, stolen horses. It's been nearly a week since Gould and I first saw them enter the sound. They've been working their way—stealing their way—up the island since, I'd wager."

The galloping horses slowed and a quick succession of shouts and yells, commands, then cheers filled the chilly February air.

"Papa, listen! Are they—stealing slaves now? Already?"

"This is an odd time to bring it up, but you know full well, Anne, your mother and I don't use the word *slaves.* They're people!"

"I know," she said absently. "I must have gotten used to hearing it on Cumberland." Still clutching her basket, she gripped his hand hard. "Papa, do you—do you suppose Lieutenant Fraser is—actually here at Major Butler's plantation? Right here at Hampton across Jones Creek from us?"

"He could well be, but you and I must get right back home, Anne."

"No! I've waited too long! I didn't see John for days before we left Cumberland. I can't breathe if I have to wait five minutes more."

Shouting at his two oarsmen in a voice louder and sharper than necessary, Jock ordered the boat turned around and rowed straight back to Cannon's Point. Halfway across the creek again, he reached to pat Anne's hand. "Forgive me, my dear, but I am the master of Cannon's Point. I do have to do whatever I can to protect my property."

"I know you do," she said in a shaky voice. "Anyway, I'm sure they'll cross over to our place as soon as they're finished at Hampton." When he didn't answer, she asked, "Don't you think I'm right?"

"Aye, Daughter. In fact, I'm sure of it."

"Do you think they'll take my dear elderly friends from Hampton? The ones too old to work any longer?"

"If anyone can take an Englishman's word for anything, they claim to be offering freedom to them all. But, according to your brother, only to those who go willingly."

"Do you believe that, Papa?"

"Aye. I have to believe it."

"Well, don't. John himself told me that whoever said that to James was lying! They use all kinds of tricks."

He stared at her. "And you didn't tell your mother that? Or James?"

"No. I was pretty closemouthed on Cumberland about—

too much. But I am telling you now, Papa. You mustn't feel heartbroken if some of our people who seem so loyal—go too. I love John Fraser with all my heart, but the British are taking everyone and everything possible!"

Eve, her mother, Fanny, and her sharp-tongued grandmother, Sofy, stood listening at the paneless window in the kitchen corner of their one-room Cannon's Point cabin, all three trying to decide why there was such a ruckus across the creek at Hampton.

"I reckon ain't none of our business what's goin' on," Fanny said. "What can we do about it anyway?"

"Hush up, Fan," Gran'maum hissed. "How we gonna hear wif you mumblin'? Move some, Eve, an' give me room to listen."

"I need to hear, too," Eve said firmly. "I got to hear 'cause I think I know what's goin' on ober there. I think the British have come to free us all!"

"You talkin' crazy, Eve," Fanny said. "What you know?"

"I know what June tol' me an' don't forget June just got back from British headquarters on Cumb'land Islan'. June seen it all take place down there an' he tell me the English Queen be a black woman an' that if us niggers go of our own free will wif the British, we never have to work again."

"Shoot! Ain't no such thing as a nigger not workin'—wif dem Britishers or nobody else."

Gran'maum, Eve thought, was being her usual aggravating self, spouting off so's nobody knew what she was really thinkin' inside her. Did the old woman mean the British were lyin' to June 'bout no more work? "What chu sayin', Gran'maum? You know?"

"Co'se I knows! I the one done said it." With a quick, rough jerk, she whirled Eve around so they stood face-to-face. "You an' June turnin' tail on Mausa Couper, Eve?"

"Don' you two git in no fight now," Fanny pleaded. "You bof so much alike!"

"We ain' fightin', we talkin', Fan. Hush up an' listen."

"Nothing to hear if she do listen, 'cause I don't know if me an' June go or not."

"I don't mean listen to us, Evie," her grandmother said. "I mean listen 'cross the creek to what's goin' on ober dere 'mongst them po' Butler niggers. Eber one of *dem* oughta turn tail an' run off, if you axe me!"

"Nobody's axin' you, Maum," Fanny said. "But, I know one nigger gonna git in hot water an' her name's Eve! You done supposed to be tendin' to Miss Anne a whole hour ago."

"She gone wif her papa to Hampton 'cross the creek," Eve said in her surliest voice. "But you done give me an idea. Miss Anne might be back by now. I'm goin' straight to the big house! Your turn to move over, Gran'maum, so's I can squeeze by to get out."

Eve heard Miss Anne calling for her the minute she rushed through the back door and toward the front hall of the Couper house. "I'm comin', Miss Anne," she muttered. "Hold your horses!"

From the bottom of the wide stair that led to the second floor, she could see her mistress leaning over the banister. The funny look on her face was one she had never seen before. Eve was in no mood for puzzles.

"Hurry on up here, Eve. I've got to talk to you!"

Inside Miss Anne's room, door closed, they stood facing each other.

"I demand to know this minute if you and June are going to run away with the British! I've just come back from crossing the creek with Papa and then recrossing it because they've already come. The British are over at Hampton right now!"

"Yes'm, I know they be over there."

"How do you know? And you used *be* again instead of *are.*"

"What diff'rence that make today, Miss Anne?"

"It makes a difference every day because you're smarter than most people and I want you to speak plainly."

"The way I talk *is* plain—to me."

"Hold your tongue and let's start over. There's enough wrong and confusing already. I refuse to argue with you. I—I don't even want to. I think *he*'s here, Eve! I'm all but sure Lieutenant Fraser is over at Hampton Point right now."

"You didn't see him ober there?"

"No. My father and I didn't get out of our skiff. But we could tell the British were there trying to talk Major Butler's people into turning against him."

Eve laughed. "They don't need to waste their brefs on that. They already against him *and* his—overseer."

"Don't smart-mouth me. Not now, please. I need you. I need you to tell me what you and June plan to do. I'm too excited and upset to wonder or care what Major Butler's people might think. I need to know how you and June mean to treat my father, whether or not *you* have any idea of how mixed up and scared I am this minute."

Eve smiled at her. "You scared your new man might not still love you the way June love me?"

"I don't know! I don't know why I'm scared except that to have Papa's people turn against him, along with wondering if I'll ever really see John again, would be more than I could bear. Doesn't that bother you? Don't you care that I'm—so worried?" When Eve said nothing, Anne pressed her question. "Eve, tell me the truth. Have you been pretending we're friends all this time because you want to stay on the good side of me just because I own you? Don't you care if my heart breaks?"

For a long time, Eve could only stand there, honestly not knowing what she felt or thought. Belonging to Miss Anne had been a part of life for as long as she'd been on earth. She'd never had a choice. Everybody knew Couper people lived better than most niggers, but that didn't help Eve, because she both hated and liked being part white. She hated it because she knew Major Butler's overseer was a hard, cruel man and even if her mama wouldn't tell, she knew he'd sired her. She liked it in a way, because somehow it made her feel she *deserved* to be treated the best of any Couper nigger. Miss Anne, she realized only this minute, had no choice any more than Eve had in how she was born! No more than she'd had in who was *her* papa or *her* mama. What a woman did decide for herself unless she happened to be Fanny, Eve's weak-spined mother, was which man she belonged to. Well, Eve knew that for sure. She belonged to June because he was strong and soft at the same time and he knew his own mind. He had picked her out and she him and that was more than enough. Together, they would decide about what happened from now on. They both *were* better than most other niggers and they had a chance now for getting free of belonging to anyone on earth but each other. She hoped the best for Miss Anne, but if June said they would go off with the British, Miss Anne wouldn't matter much.

"Eve? Don't you know whether or not you care if my heart breaks?"

"Yes'm, I know. Right now I don't know zactly how much, but I know. I hope it don't break, Miss Anne."

"That isn't very convincing! I don't think you really know how you feel about me."

"If your new man know how he feel about you, why it make any difference how I feel?" When Miss Anne didn't answer right away, Eve asked, "He know, don't he?"

Her mistress turned away. "Yes. As far as I could tell the last time I saw him, he knows. But what's wrong with my needing to know you'll be loyal to me? After all these years, doesn't it make any difference that my father has been such a good master?"

Eve's head whirled. Every new question of Miss Anne's, even every new thought of her own, was, to Eve, just that. New. Untried. Until this morning she'd never had to wonder about her own loyalty to anyone but June. She'd simply belonged to Master Couper and because of that, to Miss Anne.

Her mistress repeated her concern. "Does anyone in the Couper family mean *anything* to you, Eve?"

Eve felt as though she were taking a shortcut through a thick patch of woods. Anybody knew there'd be no path, that clumps of sticky brambles could trip her with almost every step, if she didn't watch. Of course, there was nothing to cutting *around* a prickly berry hoop to keep from gettin' scratched. She did that now.

"Look here, Miss Anne, it seem to me we bof worryin' 'bout crossin' a riber that ain't there yet. Ain't no British officer handin' me no freedom *yet.* Me an' June ain't had a chance to make up our minds what we might do. Whatever June decide, I decide too. Look like I be lyin' to you if I tell you I stay because of you, when whatever I do, is because of June. If we go, he tell me he build me a good house way off in a place called Halifax."

"Then you *have* talked about it! Halifax is in Nova Scotia, Eve, and it's bitter, freezing cold up there. Anyway, neither you nor June can know for sure that the British are really offering you freedom. I was on Cumberland Island, too. I also know what I heard. The British might just as easily be going to sell all of you into slavery. Use your good brain, Eve. *Think!*"

"What you s'pose I'm doin'?"

Miss Anne turned abruptly to face her. Tears brimmed in the pale blue eyes. "I—I'd give almost anything to know what it is you're thinking, Eve."

Eve frowned. Her mother's mother, Gran'maum, was a good, trusty woman, but she sometimes talked in riddles and Eve hated it when she did. The last thing she wanted was to be like Gran'maum! The last thing she meant to do right now was to make Miss Anne cry. That didn't happen often enough for her to know how to act. When there was fussin' and spattin' in their cabin, her gran'maum made Eve feel she'd like to drain out every drop of the old woman's blood from her own veins. There had been times when she thought she disliked having her grandmother's blood as much as old King's blood flowing through her body, but all she could really think right now was that she didn't want to behave stubborn, like Gran'maum, with Miss Anne.

Seeing tears in her mistress's eyes made her hurt. Made her want to tell Miss Anne exactly what she was thinking, not to act one bit like her grandmother. But she found that she could say now only what she knew was the truth: "I was thinkin' 'bout my blood," she said softly. "About not wantin' to hab a drop of *his* white blood—or either hab all of it."

"Oh, Eve! Poor Eve. . . ."

"Don't you pity me none."

"All right. But—it just came to me like a flash of lightning that you and I might not be as close as I need us to be. Why do you think God made some of us with white skin and some of us—with dark?"

More than once in their years together, a grin had gotten her and Miss Anne past a bramble patch and so Eve grinned now. "I be purty smart, Miss Anne," she said, "but not that smart."

Anne reached the wide front porch just in time to see her brother, James, ride off down the lane that would take him to Couper Road, her father waving him good-bye.

"Where's he going, Papa?"

Deep distress in his voice, he said, "Any other plantation between here and Hamilton's where he might find out something that will help me."

Both arms around her father's neck, Anne said, "Let me

help, too! Isn't there something a—woman can do at a time like this?"

He gave her a half-smile. "As our people say, just 'stay sweet,' Anne."

"What will our people do, Papa? Will they refuse to leave us or will they believe the hogwash the British are trying to tell them?"

Gently, he removed her arms from around his neck so that he could straighten up. Papa's so worried, she thought, he doesn't even look as tall as usual.

"Have you seen your mother since we came back from over Hampton way?" he asked.

"No, but she didn't feel well at all before we left."

"I'd better go to her, Anne."

"Could you tell me first when you think they might be coming over here?"

Now he smiled broadly. "Your pretty head must be a very crowded place today, lovey. Full of tossing thoughts—concern for Mama, for what the British might do to us, for your lieutenant. I wish I had some way of finding out for you if he came up to St. Simons from Cumberland with the others. Your old father is helpless though. Helpless in all ways right now, I'm afraid. We're all helpless."

"That's not true!" Anne heard the rock-solid certainty in her own voice. "I can do this much for you anyway. I can promise you that unless he was ordered not to come, John Fraser's over there at Hampton right now. I can also promise you, Papa, that *he* will not lift a finger to try to persuade one single person to leave us!"

That afternoon, at his home on the south end of St. Simons, James Hamilton hurried along the pinestraw walkway to his bridle path, up which his namesake, James Hamilton Couper, galloped. Young Couper slowed his frothing black mount and grasped Hamilton's hand the instant he swung to the ground.

"I doubt I've ever been so glad to see anyone, son," Hamilton said. "Have the British reached Cannon's Point yet?"

"Probably by now, sir. I'm sure they took Frederica easily. They were just across Jones Creek at Hampton when I rode off. Are there losses here?"

Leading the way to his front porch, Hamilton sighed. "I know that's why you've come and yes, there are losses. Only about fifty people so far, but over a hundred British are bivouacked around the place and they're still using every imaginable pressure on my poor deluded Negroes."

"Do they give you any chance at all to do your own persuading, Mr. Hamilton?"

"Yes, I will admit they do, except for a few smart-aleck enlisted men who promise the moon with a bejeweled fence around it to the poor devils. Some are staying loyal and so far, at least, I haven't heard of any of my people being taken against their will." Hamilton opened his front door and the two went inside. "Sit down, James. You must be stiff with cold from that long ride."

"I can't stay, sir. I've been to the Caters and the Wyllys. No British at either place yet. I promised Father I'd come here, then find out on my way back what's happening at Major Page's Retreat, the Abbotts, the Demeres—anything else I can learn. I know he'll be impatient for me to return. I'll want to do whatever I can to help Papa convince our people to stay. Could I ask what means you use?"

"Oh, the obvious persuasion," Hamilton said, standing beside James as they warmed their backsides before the huge fire. "I try to convince the more sensible among them not to be so foolish as to leave their homes here and risk separation from their families by going into a strange country where they probably will not live out the year. I must say I found none of my Negroes insolent. Most appeared genuinely sorry, quite solemn; some even wept. The determined ones, though, seemed to be infatuated with the British promises almost to the degree of madness. Some were quite intoxicated. The British saw to that. Some vowed they had to follow their wives, others their sons and daughters. Others acted as though they were in a delirium over the happy days to come with freedom. I fear the fifty or so who have already boarded British ships, either here at my wharf or down by Gould's lighthouse, are but the beginning."

"Oh, sir, what can we do?"

"No more than any other captives are able to do, son. The enemy is in possession of St. Simons Island. We're all prisoners of war. And yet, rumors keep circulating that a treaty has been signed at Ghent. That the war's over. But don't let me keep you talking, James. I don't want to add anxiety over you to your dear father's already burdened heart."

"He did seem almost old to me this morning," James said,

shaking his head. "You know the man seldom grumbles or even frowns. I'm sure losing you so soon only adds to his concern. He vows that knowing I'll be in charge of your plantation helps him a lot, but Papa will miss you when you move to Philadelphia, more than any of us can know."

Hamilton's laugh was halfhearted. "I am leaving, but not as soon as I might have were I not a British prisoner of war. Tell your father he'll be saddled with me at least until we all know more of what lies ahead."

Chapter 11

Anne sat with her mother in the dining room. The two women were eating midafternoon dinner alone because James Hamilton was still off learning what he could of British damage on the island, while Papa, a biscuit and a piece of fish in hand, was outdoors pacing up and down on the Cannon's Point side of Jones Creek, keeping watch over at Hampton.

"I don't know what he's looking for," Anne's mother said, plainly struggling to eat a few bites of Sans Foix's flaky baked trout and corn soufflé. "Poor Jock. I feel so helpless where he's concerned."

"Papa feels helpless, too," Anne said, "even though I've promised him Lieutenant Fraser will do all he can to keep our people from running away with the British."

Mama frowned. "You promised your father that?"

"Yes."

"How could you? How can you know such a thing, Anne? I'm sure your lieutenant obeys orders. We both know the British are after every single Negro who will agree to go with them—our Negroes, our cotton, horses, cattle, and heaven knows what else."

"I could promise that because John promised me!"

"Oh my dear, don't add that to the worries we already have!"

"Don't add *what?*" Anne demanded.

"Such a chance of disillusionment for yourself. Did your British officer also promise you he'd disobey an outright order?"

Anne waited. "No. He told me he obeyed orders at all

times but that he didn't always approve of the orders in the first place."

"Well, that was at least an honest confession. I—I want a miracle for you, Anne. So does your father, but we don't want you hurt. It will be a miracle if anything permanent comes of this feeling you and Lieutenant Fraser share, you know."

"It's already a miracle, Mama. Please don't worry. I know it sounds crazy. It's just that the miracle has already happened."

"I'm afraid I can't follow that."

"We love each other. Isn't that a miracle in itself?"

"Falling in love—always seems like a miracle, dear girl."

"Well, isn't it?"

"Yes. Certainly for your father and me. And, every day the miracle seems to be made new."

The quick, familiar, playful knock at their front door brought Anne to her feet, still holding her fork in one hand, her damask napkin falling unnoticed to the floor. "That's John! That's his knock. *He's here!*" She was running down the hall to swing wide the door before she remembered to call, "Excuse me, please, Mama?"

With her free hand, she grabbed the big brass knob and twisted. The knob didn't budge. Without noticing that she still held her fork, she shifted it to her left hand and tried the knob again. It turned this time and there he stood, beaming his radiant smile, his red-cockaded officer's hat in one hand, the other reaching toward her.

"I said I'd be here, didn't I?"

"Yes! Yes, you did, John. You did say you'd come."

"I did my best to land first at the Couper dock. My superior had all those Negroes at Major Butler's place on his mind, though. I crossed the creek as soon as I found a free minute. Did you actually call me—John?"

"I don't know. Did I?"

"It's been a very long time, hasn't it?"

"Yes, yes! Too long. Far too long."

He stepped inside, grinned down at the silver fork she was still clutching. "Dare I—ask for a kiss, Miss Couper? Or did you come purposely armed? You *are* my captive once more, you know."

Staring at the fork, Anne gasped, "Yes. I'm your—captive again and yes, you may ask for a—kiss, sir."

"With you still holding on to that weapon?"

It was as though they hadn't been apart for one minute. He was there, as he had been on Cumberland, only this time he was close, his lips kissing hers so tenderly, so naturally, she was enabled by that one kiss to forget every seemingly endless, uncertain, anxious hour since she'd seen him last.

The kiss wasn't the rough, hungry kiss of a man merely pursuing a woman because he needed diversion from a hard life spent mainly in the company of men. It was the natural, unavoidable gentle kiss of the other half of Anne herself. The kiss of a friend? Yes, but far more. With it, there flowed into her an entirely new sense that as long as John was there, she would be forever safe and certain of everything. An even stronger certainty than Papa could give, an even safer place to be than her own familiar room at Cannon's Point. The wild fluttering in her heart stopped. A new, steady beat took its place. Her heart was beating now as though eternal life had, for the first time, invaded her.

Every move he made was right. Even when he freed her and stepped back as though to seal forever, with his deep gray eyes, the way he felt about her, about the two of them together.

Now that he had come, Cannon's Point was dearer, somehow more familiar. She glanced outside the open door beyond where he stood and smiled. On the thick, gray trunk of a big old oak, the Lord God Bird landed sideways, gave one comical blast from what had always sounded to Anne like a rusty tin horn, and flew off.

Anne laughed softly. "Do you know what a Lord God Bird is?" she asked.

"No, should I?"

"Yes. That's just one more discovery still up ahead for you, Lieutenant Fraser."

"How can I wait?"

Suddenly—without thinking—Anne threw her arms around him. "If only we both didn't have to wait," she breathed. "If only everything weren't so upside down—this war, everything!"

His arms were around her, too, and she could feel her own longing in him. "Even if the war were over," he whispered, "you would still be my captive."

Her arms tightened. "You're my captive, too, Lieutenant."

Again, at exactly the right time, John stepped back to look down at her. "I am that, Miss Couper. It's as though we've suddenly leaped ahead of even the end of the war, the probable loss of some of your father's property, my return to Cumberland—eventually to England, for that matter. It is as though we've made a mighty leap. Do you agree?"

She could only nod vigorously and rush back into his arms. "I don't want you to go—ever! Not ever. . . ."

"I've just come from Butler's place at Hampton across the creek, Jock," Thomas Spalding told Couper the next morning when he arrived by boat at Cannon's Point. "Major Butler has lost dozens of his people. His overseer, King, is as angry as I've ever seen a man."

"I know," Couper said, his voice heavy. "He was over here at dawn to find out if the enemy had landed at my place first. They didn't. I guess the major's wealth is widely known, along with his American patriotism, even to the British. They went to Hampton first yesterday. Some are still there making outlandish promises to the Butler Negroes. You're right. Roswell King is fuming. He may cool down later on, but right now he blames all the trouble on the major's poor people. Vows God cursed the Negro by making him black. King claims to curse the man who first brought the Negro from Africa. Swears the Negro has neither honor nor gratitude."

"I know you hold your tongue on the slavery issue, Jock," Spalding said, a deep frown furrowing his brow, "but I fail to see how King or Butler could blame the Negroes at Hampton for wanting to leave. All they have to do is look at that creek that divides the major's property from yours. One look at that little creek I just crossed and they know how unfairly they're treated over there."

"What you're really telling me, Thomas," Couper said with a wry smile, "is that your people and mine, because of our Christian kindness, would be without honor or gratitude should *they* choose to leave. You're no hypocrite. Dinna' speak like one."

"But, Jock, at least you and I *try* to be reasonable."

"Any sign of the British on Sapelo yet?" Couper asked as the friends took chairs in the Cannon's Point parlor.

"No. I flatter myself that I took precautions against that. I wrote the governor and asked for weapons to arm my people."

Couper stared at him. "You *armed* your people, Thomas? You weren't afraid they might turn on you with those guns?"

"If I've been a reasonable master, I knew they wouldn't. The British have a good spying operation. Evidently they know we're all armed on Sapelo."

"But who's in charge while you're here today?"

"My good Bul-ali." Spalding smiled a little. "Of course, he made his intentions plain to me. Said he'd guard every Muhammadan with his own life against the British, but not one Christian dog among them would he lift a finger to protect."

Jock grinned too. "If every communicant of Christ Church were as faithful to the Lord as Bul-ali is to Muhammad, we'd have more money than we need to build a real church building. Can you stay to eat with us, Thomas?"

"Thank you, no. I feel we're all safe on Sapelo, but I also feel my duty to be there. And I'm sure I'm keeping you." The men shook hands. "Your only hope now is your considerable power of persuasion, Jock. You need to be talking hard and fast to your people. You haven't lost any yet, have you?"

Couper looked at the wide boards of his parlor floor. "Yes. Yes, I have. There's no way I can know exactly, but as of early this morning, including the two who left me on Cumberland, the word is I've lost at least twenty-seven. My Johnson is making the rounds of the cabins now. Sans Foix is helping him, along with Tom, my driver. I can't do as well, I figure, unless I lie and promise them all freedom. I can't afford to do that. The most I can hope for is that my losses won't be as big as the major's are already. King told me there are only six fieldhands left at Hampton! Not one shoemaker, not one tanner, stayed loyal. Only three blacksmiths and I believe two bricklayers, Jimmy and Sancho, are still over there. It seems young Sancho is King's one ray of hope right now. Sancho's family all went. His mother even took most of his clothes and his one blanket. The faithful boy is still there. King and his overgrown son seem to find solace today in reminding Sancho how smart he is to stay, to show appreciation for twelve years of comfort and care. Roswell told me half a dozen times if he told me once that to treat Negroes with humanity is like tossing pearls to swine, throwing away value and getting insult and ingratitude in return. I could almost write his letter this week to the major in Philadelphia after the bombast I heard from Roswell King today." As Spalding stood to go, Couper clasped his friend's hand. "I'm grateful for your interest, Thomas. I pray you and all your people will remain intact on Sapelo. As for me, tomorrow could reveal how many of my servants think *me* humane."

"I should have given you the idea earlier, Jock," Spalding said, returning the handclasp. "Had the British known Cannon's Point people were armed, they might well have stayed on the other side of Jones Creek this morning."

Couper looked squarely at his young friend and said in the voice that inevitably showed to those who knew him well the immensity of his secret conflict. "I'm not as trusting as you, Thomas. Not all my people will desert me, but some will. Some have. I try to be humane and just with them, but I'm not as sure as you are that they all consider me so. I might as well admit to you that even had you made the suggestion, I would have been afraid to arm one single man."

Chapter 12

With every slave owner on St. Simons Island a prisoner of the invaders, neither Couper nor his son, James, had dared visit their neighbors again once the British took over Cannon's Point as their headquarters on the north end of the island. Couper was a caged lion—sleepless at night, restless, pacing, prowling about through the chilly winter days into the middle of February.

"Are you trying with all your might, Jock, to trust God in this?" Rebecca asked him at breakfast on Tuesday morning. "The good Lord knows what's happening to us here at Cannon's Point. You know He does. He knows the British are taking our people just to populate their far-flung Empire."

"Aye, Becca, but some days when I try to talk to Him, even the Almighty appears deaf as a post. We have only two or three dozen British encamped out there under my fine orange trees and in my storehouses. I try to thank Him for that when poor Hamilton has a hundred or more swarming over his place." His smile was feeble. "I also try to give thanks that at least being a prisoner of war is keeping my friend Hamilton here on St. Simons—away from his dirty, crowded, beloved Philadelphia. My gratitude goes no higher than the ceiling, though. Rumors persist that the war is over, the Treaty of Ghent already signed. Wouldn't you think some member of the vaunted Royal Marines would know for sure one way or the other?"

"One of them or *someone* on our side," she agreed. "I'd so hoped when we won in that dreadful fighting at New Orleans, it might all end. Our daughter vows that her lieutenant knows nothing for sure."

"Would he tell her if he did?"

"Why don't you ask Lieutenant Fraser yourself, Jock?"

"I'll swallow my pride and talk to the young man soon, I promise, Becca. I—I just haven't found enough grace or courtesy to bring myself to do it yet. We've lost too much, we still stand to lose too much! I want Anne's happiness with all my heart, but—"

"I understand, my dear. And I may be such a romantic myself that I only imagine he'd tell Anne if he knew."

On his feet now, Couper strode to a dining room window, looked out, and came right back to stand beside her. "If only I thought it safe to pay a visit to Hamilton or even to James Gould! I guess poor William Browne's trapped down there, but Gould would know at least if any of the British ships have sailed back to Cumberland yet. It's knowing absolutely nothing that sends a man out of his mind. I'm the master of this place. I'm accustomed to knowing!"

"Yes, Jock. Yes."

"Yes, what? How is it we find out that the Wyllys are actually entertaining the invaders in their home? That Raymond Demere gave a dinner for them last week but I can learn nothing?"

"Our people's grapevine is still working," she said. "The Negroes always know when there is entertaining—anywhere. No family on St. Simons has a nicer house than the Coupers do, Jock. Can't you bring yourself to enter in just a little?"

"Entertain the enemy in my own house?"

"We entered in on Cumberland. Poor Louisa Shaw, even with her husband so ill, did her best to take part in what must be the oddest possible kind of hospitality! Her latest letter tells me she's actually grown to like her captors. You have to admit that the officers, at least, are gentlemen. Of course, I can't say as much for those of lower rank. They seem to be the ones promising our confused people a life they can never give them. Certainly, though, you have to admit that Johnson has told you of no occasion when Lieutenant Fraser has made even one attempt to steal any of our people. Neither Lieutenant Fraser nor any of his fellow officers staying here. You gentlemen don't seem to feel free to travel as you'd like, but women do. Mrs. Abbott drove here in her buggy only yesterday. Some of our neighbors are furious with the British, but others are giving parties for them!"

He sank back into his chair. "And I haven't even agreed to talk with Anne's young man in a proper fashion. I sense your disappointment in me. For over a week, I've sensed it, Becca. And I'm ashamed of myself. One would think that if our neighbors can entertain them, then so can John Couper. Wouldn't one think that?"

She smiled at him. "Yes, Jock. One would. Anne told me only yesterday that she prays every day for you two to meet somewhere alone, even if only by accident. I think her young man has been obligingly trying not to embarrass you."

"I don't like your being so far ahead of me, Becca! I don't like lagging behind like this. Where d'ye think young Fraser might be this minute?"

"He and Anne take a walk every morning. Otherwise, don't you know she'd be here eating breakfast with us?"

"Who knows where anyone is these troubled days? But I will meet the boy, dear Becca. We will also give a dinner if you're up to it. I—I haven't even asked how you are this morning, have I? How do you feel?"

"Better than usual, or we couldn't have had such a successful, difficult talk. I'm going to be fine, Jock. I am fine."

"I'll meet the boy," he repeated. "Forgive me for being so slow. I will meet him. I just need a bit of time alone first—out in my blessed garden—if that's possible with enemy troops in command of it."

"Thank you," she said, "but there's nothing to forgive. You're just very human, Jock Couper. Don't be too hard on yourself. And don't blame yourself if—even more of our people go. You're a genuine Christian gentleman, my love. There isn't a more compassionate master anywhere in the South than my husband. Our people are human, too, though. So, you must promise me not to blame yourself because some choose to leave us. You haven't failed or even faltered. There's a war and that changes everything."

On his feet again, he almost growled, "But *is* there still a war, Becca? For all we know here, it could be over. If only some mail would get through! If only I could lay my hands on a copy of the *National Intelligencer*! Even a copy of the *Republican* or the *Savannah Evening Ledger*!" He banged his silver napkin ring on the table, then bent to kiss her dark hair. "I'm going outside, my dear. Should you lie down? And do you agree that surely we'll know something about the end of this rotten, peculiar war at least by the time our new little one joins us?"

Because he looked so earnest, Rebecca tried to stifle a smile. "I don't feel like lying down, Jock, and yes, we'll know that the war is somehow ended long before our little one comes this fall." She clung for a moment to his hand, then kissed the curling red hair on his long fingers. "I know you met him briefly, but please do make an effort to introduce yourself properly to Lieutenant Fraser if you happen to meet up with him somewhere outside."

"You really cotton to the boy, don't you?"

"I've no reason not to. With me, he's always been a perfect gentleman and, Jock, his sense of humor is very much like yours."

It was too pat, as though Rebecca or Anne had somehow planned it. He had met Lieutenant Fraser only briefly the first day the British crossed Jones Creek to Cannon's Point, but Couper knew him at once when he saw the tall, impressive figure swinging toward him along the path from the quarters.

"Good morning, Mr. Couper," Fraser said pleasantly, his hand out. "I fail to see how we could have a more beautiful February day. Did you order it, sir?"

"Plantation owners have a certain amount of power, Lieutenant, but circumstances can and do diminish it at times. No, I did not order the high blue sky or this brisk air. Both come with the territory."

After a handshake, the two men stood looking out over the bright, almost glasslike waters of the Hampton River toward Little St. Simons Island and the ocean beyond. A somewhat awkward silence was broken abruptly when a Lord God Bird in a pine above them sounded what Anne called his tin horn—three short toots.

"That's a pileated woodpecker," Couper said lamely. "My son insists that I call him by his correct name."

"Miss Anne's Lord God Bird," Fraser said warmly.

Despite the tense, clumsy circumstances, Couper liked him. He liked him despite being a victim of his flagrant robbery.

"My daughter has educated you concerning the big red-crested bird, I see."

Fraser laughed and Couper welcomed the laughter because it erased at once what otherwise simply had to be called the pompousness of the lean, handsome face. "Aye, Miss Anne has educated me about Cannon's Point in more than the habits of her beloved Lord God Bird, sir."

Taking his time, determined not to be thrown off guard by this unusual young man, Jock stood unashamedly looking him over, cockaded hat to freshly polished black boots.

John Fraser laughed again. "Go ahead and inspect me, sir. I don't blame you a far-rthing. You must know by now that I'm as taken with your daughter as you seem to suspect Anne is taken with me. She's a bonnie lass if ever these Dumfr-ries eyes beheld one!"

"Oh ho!"

"Oh ho, sir?"

"You're a Scot! Why hasn't someone told me? Even after all your British associations, your tongue can still r-roll an *r*, eh?"

"Aye, Mr. Couper, and my tongue is far-r more at home doing it than not. Anne, of course, has told me both her parents are Scottish. Where in Scotland is your family?"

"In the sad and poor and lonely country town of Lochwinnoch."

"Aye, Lochwinnoch! I know it well, although I'm a Dumfries lad. My father, as a young man in Glasgow, used to visit in Lochwinnoch."

Couper eyed him suspiciously. "Did my daughter put you up to saying that, Lieutenant?"

"Nothing of the kind. I haven't had a chance to tell Miss Anne much about my family. Mostly, I've tried to let her speak of the esteem and happiness she feels in her own family. You, in particular, sir. Your daughter all but worships the ground you walk on, but I'm sure you know that."

Feeling his face flush with pleasure, along with the uneasy sense of being bested in the conversation, Jock said, "Anne and I have always been close, but I'm glad you said she 'all but worships' me. She's eighteen now. I comfort myself that the girl knows it's not safe to worship any mere man."

"Mr. Couper, sir, I need to ask a question."

Couper nodded assent.

"Are you misguided, too, as I found your fine son to be today, in thinking that you are literally a prisoner of the Royal Marines?"

"I'm *not* a prisoner?"

"Not in the usual sense, no, most certainly not. We have taken over your lovely island, every slave who agrees to leave with us we will take—some cattle and horses and, of course, cotton and other provisions—but we didn't sail up to St. Simons to take citizens prisoners of war. You and young Couper are as free as the ladies of the island to come and go as you please. All gentlemen can move about freely. Anne's poor tutor can come home anytime he likes."

For a moment, Couper studied the strong, now almost eager young face. Then, at the point when he sensed that Fraser would be unable to wait much longer for a response of some sort, he asked, "And what of the war itself, Lieutenant? There are strong rumors, you know, that a treaty was signed at Ghent in Belgium late last year. Your capture of our waters prevents us from receiving mail and newspapers. I have no way to learn anything except by rumor. Can you shed any light for me? Have you heard that a treaty was signed?"

"A rumor only. I know Admiral Cockburn fairly well, know how despised he is by Americans for having ordered the burnings in Washington City. I also know Admiral Cockburn to be fair as I know his superior, Vice Admiral Cochrane, to be. Cochrane ordered us to burn public buildings in your national capital because the Americans had already burned York in Canada last year, pressing their belief that Britain was infringing on American rights at sea. Both sides need to begin to make room for each other, sir."

Again, Couper took his time responding. Fraser had thrown no light on the ending of the war, but if ever truth were spoken, Anne's young lieutenant had just spoken it about both sides needing by now to make room for the other. Today, though, with perhaps a half dozen of Fraser's fellow marines doing their level best at this moment to persuade his valuable human property to desert him, Couper was not ready to make room for anything British. Still, Anne's officer was Scottish by blood. . . . Her young man did strike him as being honest and straightforward. A man of integrity, in spite of the uniform of the despised Royal Marines. He could—would—make room for him, for Anne's sake, but there was no space left for Admiral Cockburn standing in his muddy boots on the Speaker's desk in the Hall of Representatives in Washington!

Seeming to sense the difficulty the older man was having,

John Fraser said—not apologetically, just candidly—that he hadn't intended to preach a moment ago when he'd suggested both sides needed to make room for each other. "I simply know, sir, that when the war is over, all our lives—American and British—will go on. If I have anything to say about it, I never mean to lose Miss Anne. I haven't anything more definite now, because I truly don't know what lies in my future, but I do know I love your daughter."

"And does she know that?"

"Aye, she knows it. Mr. Couper?"

"Yes, Lieutenant?"

"I need a friend right now. I need to tell someone I can trust that—"

"That what?"

"May I confide in you?" The smile came again. "In you, sir, of all people?"

"That depends on what it is you consider telling me. I'm like an angry bear protecting a cub where Anne is concerned. I feel this must have to do with Anne, since you refuse to answer my question about the end of the war."

"I don't refuse, Mr. Couper. *I don't know.* But my confidence does have to do with her. My loyalty to the Royal Marines runs deeper in me than even I realize. I can't explain that because I am a Scot, but I believe that you and I must find a meeting of *our* minds and a mutual trust. No two men anywhere love Anne Couper as we love her."

"What is it you want to tell me in confidence, sir?"

"That I love her with all my heart and hold only one dream for the remainder of my life aside from working in the service of His Highness, and that is to make Anne my wife."

One of Couper's reddish eyebrows shot up. "And does my daughter know this?"

"I haven't told her outright, but I think she knows, yes."

"And do you know why you felt compelled to tell me?"

"Yes, sir. I know."

"Am I allowed in on that secret too?"

"I'd pictured our having this talk in comfortable chairs, perhaps in the Cannon's Point parlor some evening after dinner. Since this is where we finally met, I feel a bit awkward, but after the trouncing we took at New Orleans, the war, I believe, will end soon. It well may be that once it's ended, I'll be mustered out because His Majesty will have no further use for such a large contingent of marines. Napoleon hasn't been fighting for a principle, only for self-aggrandizement, and I fully expect to learn of his final defeat before this year is over. With that war behind them too, the British won't need a large military force. I've simply always been in service. I have no idea how I would support a wife and family outside the military, but I'll know when the time comes. Right now, I am grateful from my heart for a friend in whom I can confide." The cheerful smile flashed again and it was only that—not clever, not manipulative—cheerful. "My own father has always preferred my younger brother to me. I needed to tell someone about the uncertainty of my future."

All John Couper could think of was another question. "You have only one brother, young man?"

"Yes. He's bivouacked down at Hamilton Plantation. William's our Royal Marine surgeon."

"And do you get along well together?"

"Oh yes, splendidly. He's a fine fellow, a brilliant medical man. A bachelor too."

"And will he stay in service?"

"I doubt he'll be needed either, once both wars are over."

Couper took a deep breath of clean island air. "Wouldn't it be the mercy of God if everything were peaceful—everywhere on a beautiful day such as this one?"

"Aye, it would be. But, sir, do you think me foolish to want you to know just a little about my two dreams? Of remaining in the service in some capacity and—of marrying Anne?"

"Are you asking for her hand?"

"No. I have no right yet. That's the customary reason, I know, for telling her father such a deep secret. I'm not altogether certain why I needed to confide in you. Perhaps I thought I'd make the right decisions at the right time if someone like you, who loves her too, knew a bit more about me."

Couper smiled back at the boy now, his hand out. "I haven't been very gracious keeping you standing outside like this and I'm sorry. Let me make it up to you at dinner today, Lieutenant? You and any of your fellow officers you may care to bring along." They clasped hands, Jock, perplexed, shaking his head. "Very little appears to be customary right now, does it, Lieutenant? You, my captor, tell me

I'm free to come and go as I please. I, the captive, invite you to dinner. I've never much liked conformity, though, now that I think of it. You'll learn that conformity is exclusively my son's specialty. See you at dinner, young man."

Chapter 13

When a lone British officer trotted his horse up the lane to the Cannon's Point house on an unusually mild early afternoon of the following week, Anne and Anna Matilda were watching from Anne's bedroom window. Neither knew the identity of the slightly built, graceful officer, but Anne was sure that she could guess.

"Who is that, Anne? He isn't one of the officers staying here. Did we meet him on Cumberland?"

"No," Anne answered, tight-lipped, "and I don't think I like it much that we didn't. More than that, I still don't understand why we didn't."

"Stop being so mysterious! Just because you know Lieutenant Fraser so well doesn't mean you also know every other officer in the Royal Marines, does it?"

"Obviously not, but I'm guessing that's John's brother, William. He finally told me yesterday that his brother is right here on St. Simons Island, down at Hamilton. But if that is William Fraser, he's certainly not half the man John is!"

"How can you possibly know that? Just because he's shorter, slightly built, and has light hair doesn't mean anything. I know to most people my mother is far too fat. To me, she's lovely because I see inside. Mama says it's a sign of maturity when we don't judge by appearance only." Anna Matilda giggled as she turned absently away from the window. "I *must* be growing up."

"Maybe so, maybe not," Anne said, "but I was right! That *is* William Fraser, because John just ran up to embrace him!"

* * *

After William handed his horse over to a Couper groom, the two brothers walked arm in arm toward a large outbuilding south of Couper's orange grove.

"I'm surprised to see you bivouacked in a cotton storehouse, John," William said as they went inside the sturdy, whitewashed frame structure. "We're cared for right in Hamilton's own home. I even have a room of my own. I thought surely you'd be treated here at Miss Anne's father's place with equal respect."

"It was either sleep here or share a room with her brother, the elite James Hamilton Couper. I chose the storehouse and the snores and good humor of my fellow officers."

William laughed. "Ah, yes, I remember you told me about the self-esteem of young Couper while we were still on Cumberland. I heard he came down to the dock with his white flag to extract a promise from Colonel Williams that we'd honor all American property as sacred."

"Colonel Williams seems to have promised we'd do exactly as young Couper demanded," John said, "and I have to admit I almost enjoyed that lie. Not that I don't like Anne's brother. Actually, I've come to respect him, to hold him in the high regard his family feels where his intellect is concerned. Unlike his sister, he's just a bit stuffy. She and her altogether likable father, it seems, have always called him the Old Gentleman. That appeals to me."

"I take it you still like Miss Anne."

"You must come to know her not one minute later than today, William."

"Does she know yet that I even exist?"

"Aye, she knows it now and you almost came between us when I told her. She's a reasonable lass in most ways, but she seemed to think I was—keeping you a secret." John grew solemn. "And truthfully, maybe I was. You see, Brother, I love Miss Anne Couper. She isn't just a pleasant wartime interlude. You know I've never been very sure of my own charms when my scholarly brother is on the scene."

John watched as William removed his officer's bonnet and hung it carefully on a wall hook. "You don't still think that after all these years!" William exclaimed, turning to look straight at John. "Isn't it past time you accept our dear father as the opinionated, biased man he is? I admit he seemed always to favor me. I confess to taking full advantage of it when we were boys. We both know that even when he's been proved wrong, the old bear can't admit to it. You're a far superior man now that we're grown, Brother—lithe of limb, nearly a foot taller, broader of shoulder—you're downright manly, John. And you sing like a cello in the hands of a master. Any woman would gravitate to you first and you're as pigheaded as our father if you don't agree. True, we're both officers in the best branch of His Majesty's service, but I'm still only a boring scholar at heart. You revel in all this military activity."

John's face flushed, but he gave his brother a big smile. "I don't revel in stealing men's property any more than you do. That is beside the point, though. You'll always be the golden-haired boy to our father—as you are to me, William. But I do know now that Miss Anne cares for *me.* I wasn't too sure last month when we first took Cumberland, so I kept you a secret. I don't mind a bit introducing you now. It really wasn't convenient down there."

As always, William's teasing remained gentle. "And you also saw no merit in wasting even one of your precious minutes alone with her by speaking about your bookish brother."

"That lady talks so constantly of her own family, there really wasn't time. By the way, she's quite interested in the writing of your literary hero, Walter Scott," John added proudly.

"And you're not yet?"

"Well, thanks to Anne's insistence, I have read a bit more of him. She does have the knack of insistence. And she knows her own mind."

Perched on the foot of John's makeshift cot, William grinned. "Just so she knows her mind and favors my excellent brother."

"I plan to marry her someday, William."

Frowning thoughtfully, though not in disagreement, William asked, "You plan to take her back to England to live? And does she agree to leaving this beautiful island and her family?"

"I don't know the answer to either question."

"You mean you haven't asked her yet? Shame on you, John. You and Miss Anne have been seeing each other at every possible moment ever since we captured Dungeness!"

"I did tell her father, Mr. John Couper."

"You *told* him? I'm not experienced at these things, but isn't it customary for the suitor to *ask* a father's permission?"

Hatless now, too, John ran one hand through his dark, thick, short-cropped hair. "I told Mr. Couper because I needed to tell someone I respect. You see, up until last week, he'd avoided talking to me. The man's become an American 'Jonathan' all the way, even though he was born not far from Glasgow. He takes his American citizenship with the utmost solemnity and we are *stealing his property.* Planters live on the fruits of slave labor. He'll recover from what livestock and cotton we take, but so far I think our men have gotten several of Couper's slaves to go with us and we could be placing him in financial trouble if we take more. I understand his suspicion of me, but—I needed him. From my first meeting with him, I felt drawn to the man."

"Tell me, how do you cope with your duty up here at Cannon's Point feeling about Couper as you do? Are you working at convincing his human property that the Queen is black, that if they will only come with us, life will be free and easy?"

John definitely did not find that funny. "I'm being a good marine. I handle my routine duties, but I'm *not* working at persuading any Negro to leave any master on St. Simons." He sighed. "Here, while I'm still stationed at Cannon's Point, I'm simply clinging to every treasured moment. I know the time I have left with Anne is almost over. In fact, I'm sure you came here today to tell me—when." He tried to smile. "I'm not sure I want to know."

"You and Miss Couper have one more week to plan your future together. Admiral Cockburn has ordered us to be back at headquarters on Cumberland no later than March 1."

John began to pace the room. Then he asked, "Will we be discharged when we get back to England, William? The only life I've known since age sixteen is the military. But will we be needed any longer if the rumors about a peace treaty with the Americans are true? What have you heard?"

"Only rumors, but they're flying thick and fast on St. Simons, at least. A peace treaty could well have been signed, even before our ghastly defeat at New Orleans, but Captain Ramsey's aide stationed at Frederica told me he'd heard that Admiral Cockburn has no intention of ordering our coastal conquest to end until he's learned of the peace directly from Vice Admiral Cochrane. There's no way we can know any time soon, dear brother, what our future will be with the Royal Marines. If Napoleon is eventually defeated and if the American war is over, I've no doubt we'll both be discharged on half pay. Not good medicine for the heart of a man in love, is it?"

"The worst." John's characteristic smile returned. "Well, not quite the worst. The worst would be finding out that Anne isn't interested in me as a husband."

"But you already know that she is, don't you?"

"When I'm with her I have no doubts. At night, alone with my cornshuck pillow and blanket there on that pallet, doubts nearly smother me."

John felt relieved when his brother lapsed into their lifelong habit of teasing. "Well, don't fret. Once you've witnessed her meeting with me, you'll see the extent of your good standing in her eyes. What color are her eyes, by the way?"

A look of wonder crossed John's face. "I honestly don't know," he said just above a whisper. "They're light—very light and usually they seem blue. A clear sort of ice blue, but far from cold. You'll meet her at dinner today, William. The officers dine with the Coupers now. Once he and I managed an almost accidental conversation alone, Mr. Couper seemed to lose his aloofness with me completely. Oh, he still resents what our forces are doing. He wouldn't be human otherwise. I'd feel as he does, I'm sure, were I in his position. But, he must be the most charming host on St. Simons. The man works sincerely at staying buoyant for the sake of his beloved family. You'll see."

William got quickly to his feet and laid a hand on his brother's arm, then said quite tenderly, "I want you to know that *I* know how hard it's going to be for you to leave her in a week. Maybe harder than either of us can imagine now. I wish I could be here with you when you tell her good-bye. My orders are to ride back to Hamilton Plantation early tomorrow."

"I—I honestly don't know how to prepare myself for our good-bye," John said. "I wish you *could* be here. Did you say Anne and I have a week?"

"Yes. One week from today."

Their mood was broken by the rattle and rumble outside

of what was unmistakably a large wagon, a team pulling it. John looked out. "Oh-h," he groaned, "unless I'm mistaken, poor Mr. Couper's losing still more people! There must be ten or fifteen piled in that wagon!"

At the door beside John, William gave his brother a curious look. "Do you care that much about Couper's fortunes? I can understand liking his daughter, but are you obeying our orders at all here on his place? Have you made any effort to persuade even one of his slaves to accept our offer of freedom?"

"No, not one. Have you?"

Again, William waited to answer. Finally, with a wry smile, he said, "I don't think either of us has been missed in that capacity. Our regulars, it appears, have worked very hard at it. Made a kind of game of talking the poor wretches into leaving when we leave. I was told down at Hamilton that not even one officer up here has joined with the Regulars in lying about the Queen of England being black, that an easy life with carriages and bountiful food and free housing and clothing awaits any slave who comes with us, especially those who enlist in the West Indian Company, and hundreds have. I know of a few of Mr. Hamilton's slaves who believed a British marine's vow that should a slave die on a British ship at sea, he'd go straight to heaven because he would die free."

John stared at him. "They're telling them that if they don't go as free men when we go, they'll die here on St. Simons someday and head straight for Hell?"

William nodded. "That's right. I've heard it myself. I've *seen* the lie turn the trick with at least three Negroes."

"What in the name of the Almighty does that have to do with honorably fighting a war?" John demanded.

William only shrugged.

The wagon had stopped some distance from the storehouse door where they were watching. Tall, spare, broad-shouldered John Couper had stopped the team, was speaking rapidly, both hands out beseeching the Negroes. Some among the wagon's human cargo hid their faces, two wept openly, the others merely turned away. Then, on a command from the Regular seated beside the Negro driver up front, the team lurched forward at the crack of a whip and left John Couper running alongside, dropping behind the rickety wagon as it clattered away around a bend out of sight. If even one fleeing Negro looked back, his last sight of his old home was of the master who must himself be feeling the helplessness of a slave.

"We're Royal Marines, John," William said, once the wagon was gone. "British Royal Marines. We're supposed to be freeing slaves from their bondage, but—are they worse off really than the ordinary British working blokes?"

John took a deep breath and exhaled noisily. "I don't know. I honestly don't know. Across the creek over there, at Major Butler's Hampton Plantation, my answer to that question would be yes. Still, I believe even they receive some kind of care in their old age. As for Mr. Couper's people, I'd have to say no, they're probably not worse off. He's an honorable gentleman. I'm convinced from what I've seen for myself that he does his very best under the hateful system to be considerate of his people. They earn his living. He must surely believe he owes them real consideration. Something tells me Couper's simply allowed himself to be trapped into owning slaves because he loves agriculture and is totally determined to give his family a good life."

"Couper didn't tell you that himself?"

"No. He's a proud Scot. Too proud, I'm sure, to make apologies for himself to anyone. It's just something I sense about the man. You may be able to decide for yourself today when we dine with the family. I'm not sure about the extent of our welcome from all of Couper's neighbors, but Royal Marine officers stationed here at Cannon's Point have been courteously received."

Smiling a little, William said, "Undoubtedly an only daughter gets her way most of the time with a gentleman like Couper."

"I want you to watch Anne at dinner," John said, boyish exuberance back on his expressive face. "I want you to learn for yourself that this dream of mine isn't all mine. That Anne and I have truly found each other. Most of the time, I'm convinced that she loves me, too."

"And what of that wagon full of slaves who just turned against her father? To Couper, we represent thieves. Property thieves. Will this new loss today make trouble between you and your lady, John?"

A quick frown came, then vanished. "A difficult moment or so perhaps. Anne adores her father. Anything that causes him heartache hurts her, but—" He looked at William.

"You'll just have to find out for yourself, Brother, that between Anne and me, there is far more than moonlight and romance. We're also friends. What we have found is—forever. I think you'll see."

Chapter 14

When her father called from downstairs just before dinnertime, Anne sent Eve to tell him she'd be there in a minute. "Say I'm not quite finished with my hair."

"You mean *I'm* not done wif your hair," Eve said over her shoulder as she hurried out of the room.

All right, Eve, Anne thought, pulling at one dark curl because it seemed a touch too tight. Eve always wanted credit, but nothing could be more important these days than that her hair be combed just so. The crown of dark curls had to perch evenly on her head, with no more than three or four smaller, longer ones falling over each ear. Did John really notice such things? If she noticed that his close-cropped Brutus haircut allowed the exact perfect dip of dark bangs across his dear forehead, he surely wouldn't miss the jauntiness of her curls. It was also vital that she make a good impression today because John's brother would dine with them.

Both Papa and Mama—even James Hamilton—seemed to be going out of their way to be gracious to John. Not true, she'd heard, of every island family since the British had stolen so many slaves all over St. Simons. She and Anna Matilda had called on the Wyllys yesterday at their St. Clair Plantation and they were also entertaining British officers, but the Wyllys and the Armstrongs were known to be deeply pro-British, unlike other islanders. Once Anna Matilda's parents returned from Darien, they would, of course, show every courtesy simply because they were genteel folk. Oh well, what really mattered was that the Coupers were also genteel and were proving it daily. Dear Papa had lost only some of his people. None since last week, so far as she knew, and Papa always confided in her about things like that.

Wrapping a stray crown curl around one finger, Anne caught herself smiling in the looking glass at the mere idea that the Roswell Kings might lift a finger to entertain even one British officer. Of course, the marine officers she'd met wouldn't be too happy to sit at table with glum Mr. King or his lippy son *or* his bossy, pudgy wife. Anyway, Roswell King was an overseer, in full charge of Major Butler's vast holdings, but still an overseer.

The smile she'd caught in the looking glass turned to a fleeting frown when, out of the blue, she tried to imagine quiet, submissive Fanny, Eve's mother, in the arms of skinny, beard-shadowed Roswell King! Of course, no one knew for certain, but it was true that Eve had inherited some white features from someone, although they certainly looked better on her. She'd evidently inherited some of his glum, stubborn moodiness, too, so sometimes it wasn't too hard to realize that he might be Eve's natural father. But Anne was feeling her first genuine pity for poor Fanny, who had been given no choice.

Where in the world was Eve now? How long could it take her to call down to Papa that Anne would be there just as soon as possible?

Eve didn't call to her master down the curving stair. She hurried down herself the minute she saw him standing alone in the big hall, his head buried in both hands.

"You need something, Mausa Couper?" she asked as she reached the bottom step.

She'd obviously startled him. The stricken look on his face was one Eve had never seen there before.

"Where's my daughter?" His voice sounded hollow, as if it came out of a big, empty shell. "I need my daughter. I don't want to disturb her mother. I need to see Anne before dinner. Where is she?"

"She be in her room. We're not quite done wif her hair. She say I should tell you she be down soon."

"I need her now."

"Somepin' wrong, Mausa Couper?"

"Wrong?" He rubbed his forehead. "I'm not sick, if that's what you mean. Wait. Maybe you can tell me what I need to know. Yes. You'd be able to tell me. You'd be far more apt to know than Miss Anne. Was—was June among those in the wagon who just left me a while ago? I was too upset to tell. Did—June leave me?"

The question stunned Eve. Had Miss Anne told her father about her and June? Cautiously, head cocked to one side, she asked, "What made you axe if June be in that wagon, Mausa?"

"Because I need to know!" His usual pleasant way was not there, Eve thought. He sounded cross, like maybe he was fighting himself not to break down. "I—I have a special reason for needing to know if June went too."

"What reason?"

"When I ask you a question, Eve, don't I have a right to expect an answer? Or do you normally answer a question with another question?"

"No, sir, that ain't my way. I just wonder why you pick out June and not some of the other niggers?"

"I see. Well, I'm very worried, Eve. Upset. You see, I just thought that if—if June had refused to turn against me, perhaps none of the remainder of my people will swallow the enemy's lies. June's a leader. They listen to him, don't you agree?"

"I listen to him, if that's what you mean, sir."

The merest smile flickered at the corners of his mouth. "Yes, well, I'm not surprised. Are you and June still planning to ask my permission to marry?"

"Miss Anne done tol' you!"

"That's right, she did. Soon after she and June got back from Cumberland, but I wouldn't hold that against her if I were you. She was merely preparing me to give my consent. My daughter is quite skillful at preparing her father for whatever she feels is important, you know."

Eve smiled a little too now. "Yes, sir. I knows that!"

"Did June go?"

Her head very high, Eve said firmly, "No, Mausa Couper, June be here. If you don't believe me, go to my mama's cabin and look for yourself. June smart. He know they don't want no more women niggers. He decide to hide in our cabin where the British thinks only three womens live. Go see. You find June there with my gran'maum."

Eve had never seen a man look more relieved and for a reason she didn't quite understand, his relief made her feel proud. Maybe because Mausa Couper, one of the best-thought-of St. Simons masters, plainly thought a lot of June. Just the way Miss Anne thought a lot of her. She would have to talk to June about why she felt proud that the Coupers were their people and that they would both stay at Cannon's Point. June would know. She and June *were* better than most niggers. Eve could never doubt that now.

" 'Scuse me, sir, Miss Anne she be needin' me. She gonna be riled anyway that I stay so long with her hair not fixed."

"Then you'd better run back upstairs and make her perfect," he said, looking again almost like his usual self. "You've put my mind at ease over June, Eve. Thank you. But I still need to tell Miss Anne a little secret I think she should know before we have dinner."

His blue eyes were actually almost twinkling with mischief now, Eve thought. "Yes, Mausa Couper. I tell her," she said, starting up the stair. "You sure can change from glooms to grins fast, sir."

She heard his good laugh. "I guess I've learned with the years. No one likes a grumpy face. Tell my daughter what I have to say to her has to do with her friend Lieutenant Fraser."

Halfway up the stair, Eve stopped. "You got a secret 'bout —*him*?"

"I guess it would be more accurate to say I just found out something about him a few minutes ago when I met his brother, Dr. William Fraser. Don't look so perplexed, Eve. It's something splendid. And Anne should know before dinner."

Hidden, she hoped, behind one of the partly open sliding doors into the dining room, Eve tried to hear what her master was whispering to Miss Anne, who looked prettier than ever this minute, wearing her yellow Chinese silk high-waisted dress, eyes popping most out of her head at whatever Mausa Couper was telling her. Eve couldn't make out a word, though, and vowed to offer to help Johnson serve the meal in case something special might take place. If today turned out like the other days the British mens come to Cannon's Point to eat, they'd be ten or twelve officers in uniforms with yellow braid and bright gold buttons. She certainly had no intention of missing a thing that might have to do with Miss Anne and her man. Whatever it was Mausa Couper had whispered sure made Miss Anne happy. She didn't always let her mistress know, but anything that pleased her also pleased Eve down inside.

I'm supposed to obey Miss Anne, Eve thought, but me and her got a lot in us these days that's mostly alike. Miss Anne's got her John. I got my June. Down deep, what's the real difference between us?

Unlike other afternoons since the British had taken over Cannon's Point, only two officers, the Fraser brothers, were on hand to dine with the Couper family and Anna Matilda, whose parents were still in Darien. John Couper was both relieved and concerned about the absent officers—not sure what they might be doing and not daring to ask either Fraser. Probably, he thought, seating his wife, he didn't feel free to ask either Fraser for fear of learning the truth: that the other normally social minded officers might at this moment be transporting still more Couper people who had decided in the past hour to run away. There had been at least fifteen in that one wagon!

Even so, Couper meant to act in a pleasant manner at dinner. Later would be time enough to face further loss and the possible need to borrow still more money from his factor. He meant to allow nothing in his own demeanor to spoil this occasion. Anne appeared too eager, too expectant, had seemed too delighted at what he had just whispered to her. For today, at least, he could protect her. Heaven only knew the heartache and suffering she might be facing in the months and years ahead after her beloved John left.

Couper had never felt himself more drawn to anyone in so short a time as to Marine Artillery Surgeon William Fraser. Not a bit like his brother, John, either in build or personality. John was ebullient, with a ready smile that lighted up the place. William was quiet, gentle of humor, thoughtful. More Scottish in his speech and manner than John was but quite "un-Scotified," as old Ben Jonson used to put it, in his ready laughter and quick wit. That the brothers were close Jock had no doubt. It had seemed extremely important to William that someone at the Couper residence learn that John possessed a remarkably fine singing voice. Couper had met Dr. Fraser only minutes after the shattering blow of seeing the wagonload of his people leave him—at the moment when his spirit most needed buoying. He had actually felt his spirits lift somehow when William first told him that

Anne's young man could truly sing. He loved the sound of music in his house. Anne shone at the keyboard of her much-loved pianoforte. Between them, perhaps the two could help keep his spirits out of the doldrums.

Seated at Couper's right in the place of honor since this was his first visit to Cannon's Point, William Fraser seemed not to be much involved in the noisy chatter taking place among Rebecca, John, Anne, James Hamilton, and Anna Matilda, so Jock felt free to talk with him. "And did you say that 'Drink to Me Only with Thine Eyes' is your brother's favorite song, Dr. Fraser?"

"Aye," William said. "I hope you remembered to tell Miss Anne."

Couper chuckled. "On the contrary. I purposely didn't tell her. You see, it's her favorite too! What do you say we make a small wager that she'll strike up that very tune right off—even without knowing it's a favorite of John's? What kind of wager shall we make?"

"Personally I like the idea of exchanged handshakes," William said.

Couper, puzzled, rubbed his long, patrician nose. "You mean if I lose, I give you a handshake, and if you lose, you offer your hand to me?"

"Exactly, sir. That way neither one of us can be a loser."

"Excellent, excellent! After all, such an odd wager is no more peculiar than that I, your captive, have welcomed you, my captor, to my table to break bread."

The warm smile faded from William's face. "This is a—strange conquest, isn't it, sir? Cheerful, pleasantly courteous, while at the same time, tragic."

"Aye," Couper said, his mind flying again to the people who had deserted him. "To tell the truth, the loss of my Negroes may bankrupt me, Fraser, but the worst part of it all is the loss of my self-respect. My people took much of that with them, you know."

"Your self-respect, sir?"

"Aye, and my honor. Until now, I hadn't given it much thought, but the owner of a plantation like Cannon's Point comes, after a time, to depend on his people, not only for their help to him in his business but for what he sometimes deludes himself into believing is their respect. I see by your expression that hadn't occurred to you."

"No, no, it hadn't," Fraser said. "But I think I understand.

What your people think of you in a measure, at least, defines what you think of yourself."

"Yes. You see, my people and I generally laugh easily together. I'm sure you've discovered I'm not your typical dour Scot. I like to laugh. When one of my feeble jokes makes them laugh, I take what I need to take from their seeming appreciation of what I've just said. From their ready humor—and most of them have it—I begin to fancy myself quite a fellow, pleasant, likable, respected. A kind, well-thought-of master. Oh, there are some among them who never try to fool me by overlaughing at my jokes, by too readily agreeing with my orders. There are others who overdo everything in order to better their own lives. I understand that. It's just that seeing such a number of them go at one time somehow took too much of the respect I'd grown accustomed to believing I possessed." He sighed. "In a definite way, a slave owner is just about as dependent on his slaves as they on him."

"And I'm sure that in your position here at Cannon's Point, it's important for other planters on this island to consider you a benevolent master, well loved by your people."

When Eve served puffy hot rolls from a silver-mesh basket, Couper took one eagerly. "Try one of these, young man. Take two. My cook, Sans Foix, is a genius with bread dough."

Both men busied themselves for a time buttering their rolls. Then Jock said as though he hadn't a care in the world, "Now, Dr. Fraser, I'm all but positive that my daughter will, of her own accord, play the well-loved melody set to old Ben Jonson's poem once we've had our dessert, but your acute understanding of a moment ago makes me want to shake your hand—complete our wager—right now. You're an extraordinarily perceptive young man!"

"Thank you, Mr. Couper. Even if Miss Anne weren't so charming in her own right, I'd have to say my brother is altogether fortunate that she's your daughter."

Lieutenant John Fraser was still praising Sans Foix's rich, creamy flan when it was decided by the entire group that they would all—men and women—retire immediately to the parlor for coffee and Couper's much vaunted 1796 cognac.

"We won't stand on formality," Couper announced as the party took seats in the large, comfortably furnished room, warmed by a blazing fire. "No one, after all, can term this merely another social event. I have always intended that my house be known for its warmth and hospitality to invited guests"—Jock stopped midsentence and beamed on each person—"and that welcome has been extended lately to what one might term 'surprise' guests. This afternoon, I hope we can all forget for a few enjoyable moments that the Fraser brothers are among the latter. At times, there is good sanity in a measure of well-intended pretense. This day we will all pretend we have known one another a lifetime, that there is no war between our countries, that peace reigns in our troubled world as indeed I feel it does in this room. Our new friend, Dr. William Fraser, and I seem to have directed our full attentions to each other as we all partook of Sans Foix's excellent food. We beg your forgiveness. Now is the moment for general enjoyment among us all, so I lift the first glass to our welcome guests."

Couper had delivered his little speech from his favorite leather armchair, his blue eyes moving as he spoke from one face to another. Eyes hinting, he turned to Anne. "And I can think of no more enjoyable way to spend some of these valued moments together than listening as my daughter, Anne, favors us with what I have already wagered is her own *favorite song.*" He exchanged sly smiles with William Fraser, then got up to escort Anne to her pianoforte in the corner of the parlor.

"Thank you, Papa," she said, beaming up at him after a small, playful curtsy. "I doubt that I could play a single note if you didn't oblige by escorting me. How long have we done this?"

"Since you first learned to play six notes that actually went together," he joked. "And I hope you'll select whatever *you* like best to play for us now, my dear."

Seated again in his big chair, Couper glanced at William Fraser, who was still wearing an amused, knowing smile as the two waited to find out who would actually win their wager. Then he looked over at young John, who sat on the very edge of his own chair, his eyes riveted on Anne.

"What shall I play, Mama?" Anne asked.

Rebecca laughed a little. "My advice is to obey your father, who seems to be performing at his best as host, my dear." Since she had taken her own dainty rocker near her husband, Rebecca reached to pat his hand.

"Splendid advice, Becca," he said. "Splendid!"

Anne touched a few random notes, then played a quiet introduction and went at once into "Drink to Me Only with Thine Eyes."

John Couper sat watching the young lieutenant's always expressive face. There was now no hint of the near arrogance he'd noticed in the lean, strikingly handsome features. As though his own heart were reading both the young people's hearts, Couper saw again that they truly loved each other. He also saw deep suffering ahead for Anne, because whether or not it could be confirmed that the war had ended, John would be leaving St. Simons soon. The British had surely done most of their damage by now.

Heaven knew there was personal as well as financial suffering ahead for Couper, too, in the loss of his people. He was enduring it now. Even as his daughter played, thoughts of each of the people who had deserted him kept flooding over his best intentions to remain a gracious host. Person by person, he tried to imagine what each might be doing right now, where each might be. All of them, he felt sure, were either already aboard a British warship or scrambling this minute up a rope ladder onto an enemy schooner at anchor somewhere down near Gould's light tower.

Put them out of mind, he ordered himself. This time, in a special way, belongs to Anne. Dr. William Fraser had told Couper that the British would probably all be gone from St. Simons in a week. He felt sure Anne hadn't heard that yet. This could well be her last evening of unqualified joy. From now on, her dear, tender heart would grow heavier with the passing of each day.

Anne had almost finished the lovely song once through. Couper smiled at William Fraser when, unbidden, Lieutenant John got to his feet and strode eagerly toward the pianoforte to stand beside her. The tall young man stood gazing down into Anne's soft eyes until the final notes of the tune ended. Then, without looking away, John began to sing:

"Drink to me only with thine eyes,
And I will pledge with mine;
Or leave a kiss within the cup,
And I'll not ask for wine;
The thirst that from the soul doth rise,
Doth ask a drink divine;

But might I of Jove's nectar sip,
I would not change for thine, for thine. . . ."

For what seemed a full minute or more after the last golden note had died, there was only the ticking of Becca's mantel clock and the crackle and snap of blazing logs. Anne still sat, hands resting on the keyboard, looking up at John in what struck her father as an expression of sheer wonder. A sense of wonder pervaded the entire room because there was no one there who had ever heard John Fraser's heart-melting, golden tenor but his brother, William. Perhaps, Couper thought, even William had never heard John sing as he did just now.

Breaking the long, wordless silence, Anna Matilda breathed to no one in particular that she never again expected to hear such a voice.

Finally there followed a polite smattering of applause. Couper joined in, but applause was out of place, as though they had all intruded on a private world that belonged only to Anne and John. The taut moment was eased a bit when William came over, smiling, to shake Jock's hand—the gentle culmination of their wager. But for everyone in the room, there was nothing at all to say. It was actually a relief when John took Anne's arm, offered a courteous, brief apology, led her out the front door across the wide veranda and into the rich, coppery glow of the February sunset.

They had been outside in the changing color long enough to walk beside the river all the way to what Anne felt sure must be the big oak tree where June met Eve. Still neither had spoken.

Under the sheltering branches of the great tree, its bark and moss banners rose-gold in the sunset, Anne stopped walking and looked up at him. "Why didn't you tell me you could sing like that?" she asked, her face a mask of both anxiety and awe. Anxiety because she had made up her mind to ask outright when he would be leaving St. Simons, awe because she loved him so much and he was still with her, still within reach.

"I didn't tell you because—"

"Because what?"

"Oh, Anne," he groaned, taking her roughly into his arms, "there hasn't been time enough for anything except to fall hopelessly in love with you! I am in love with you, Anne Couper, from my very heart. Do you believe me?"

"As soon as you explain why you're so secretive, I'll tell you."

"Don't act coy—don't flirt, don't tease me! We don't have time for that." He was holding her so hard against him, the buttons on his officer's jacket hurt.

"I'm not teasing! I'm certainly not being coy. I hate that. I know there hasn't been enough time. I've changed my mind. Don't explain anything. Just tell me—how much time do we have left? When do you have to go?"

"A week from today," he said hoarsely, "I'll be—gone."

She tightened her arms and clung to him. "What if I can't let you go?"

"I have to go."

"Why didn't you tell me when we first met that you had a brother?"

"You didn't stop talking about your family long enough for me to get in a word edgewise."

"That's not true!"

"No, not quite. The truth is, I was making absolutely sure of how I felt."

"I've known from the first dance at Dungeness that I—love you," she said, surprising herself by such forwardness. "I know that's a terrible thing for me to say, but didn't you know how *you* felt?"

He held her away from him for a better look into her eyes. "I know now that I've cared hopelessly for you from the start, but the world, our world, is so unstable, the future is so uncertain. Anne, doesn't it make sense that I had to curb myself? My dearest, I care about you inside, where you live. I care about the way you feel. I want to give you joy, not pain."

"The only pain you could give me is—not to be here."

"There! You see? I will be giving you pain because the war is still going on so far as any of us knows and what I've done is allow you to care enough about me so that there's no possible way *not* to give you pain."

"What makes you think you *allowed* me to fall in love with you? Only I could have controlled that."

"I wonder."

"You wonder what, John?"

"If either of us can—help ourselves. Does heaven create a love like this, Anne? Or is it all our doing?"

"What difference does it make?" she demanded and grabbed one of his hands in both hers. "I'm going to put a kiss in your hand," she whispered, pressing her lips against his wide palm. "It's right there. Don't forget. Right there where you can hold it always. Where it will go on haunting you if you're tempted to be untrue to me." Both arms around his neck now, she held him to her. "I fully intend to hold you like this—forever, John Fraser. Even when you're gone out of my sight, I'll—find a way to hold you when you need to be held. Then you'll have to come back to me!"

"Yes! Oh, yes, my beloved girl. I have to leave you, but I also have to find a way to come back to you. And Anne, I will. I—will!"

Chapter 15

The days of what Rebecca had come to think of as Anne's bright-dark final week sailed by so fast her own heart felt squeezed, trapped, even frightened. Jock's silent torment, palpable to her at this moment as they sat together on their porch, after breakfast on John's last day at Cannon's Point, tightened her sense of entrapment. By now sixty of his people had gone with the British, were either at the south end of St. Simons awaiting passage or already on Cumberland Island. Again and again she pled with God to keep even one more Negro from leaving. Of course, their loss would make Jock's financial standing shaky, their future uncertain, but the state of her husband's dear heart was her main concern.

Why even one of their people had chosen to leave the security and benevolence of Cannon's Point she had no idea. More than a hundred had fled Major Butler's place. A tragedy, too, but in a way, she could understand that. One of the most productive and successful overseers on St. Simons Island, Roswell King had never seemed to make much effort to understand the feelings of the Hampton people. The paradox was that he considered himself a benevolent overseer. But as long as he could make his weekly written report to Major Butler in Philadelphia, outlining foodstuffs and clothing and shelter for the Hampton Negroes and, most important of all, large profits from their labors, King was more than satisfied with himself and his work in behalf of the absent Butler. It was certainly true that Roswell King and his wife were reliable, conscientious workers. She would never have thought of asking Jock, but Rebecca felt sure that acre for acre, in spite of her husband's genius for agriculture, Hampton Point was somewhat more productive than were the Couper holdings. So be it. She much preferred Jock's endearing humanity. They had never discussed it, but even though she idolized her own father, Rebecca knew his strictness as a master far exceeded Jock's.

In colonial days coastal Scotsmen were strongly opposed to all slavery, in fact, but until she'd seen with her own eyes as John Couper's wife that his unusual benevolence actually worked with his people—caused most of them to work better—she had actually felt uneasy at what had appeared to her, as a bride, a dangerously light master's hand. Jock Couper *was* a compassionate master. To Rebecca it was no mystery at all that his dear heart ached now at the sight of sixty Negroes turning against him.

She looked over at him, bundled, as she was, in a heavy cloak, both outside because they loved the fresh, mildly chilly late February air on their wide porch facing the river. Jock had been abnormally silent for a long time. Even now, he only returned her smile, then leaned his head against the high wooden back of his chair. That his heart ached for Anne, too, she had no doubt. From the moment he first saw their only daughter, minutes after her birth in the old Cannon cottage, Jock had been captivated by Anne. The years had only increased his attachment to her. The two were fast, fast friends. That Anne would even now be perfectly capable of running Cannon's Point plantation Rebecca had no doubt. The girl had followed her adored father everywhere, had shown a unique fascination for everything that had to do with the operation of a huge, successful agricultural enterprise. As a tiny girl, Anne had toddled about the vast gardens alongside her papa, clutching her own tiny trowel and shovel Jock had instructed Cuffy, the blacksmith, to make for a child's small hands. Always devoted to their people, Anne could sing the African songs almost as though her skin were black, and she loved their peculiar rhythms—so compelling but forever strange to most white listeners. Not to Anne, who was also grieving over their tragic loss.

"I'll miss them all too," Anne had told her mother only last night. "How could they do that to Papa—to all of us?"

When the song "Drink to Me Only with Thine Eyes" began now from the parlor inside, Jock sat up in his chair and turned to Rebecca.

"Listen, Becca! There it is again."

"Yes," she breathed. "Doesn't it break your heart?"

"Aye, that is, if my old heart can be broken any more than it is already," he said, giving her a determined half-smile. "Their time together is even shorter than we thought. John told me this morning. I'm sure he's told Anne by now. He's to report with all the other enemy forces here down at Hamilton a day sooner—today."

Rebecca nodded. "That nice Dr. Fraser told me last night."

"And you kept it from me to protect my poor heart."

"I did, because I love your heart."

"You do, don't you? I'm an ingrate to act so down-in-the-mouth about anything with a wife like you." He listened for a few seconds to John's smooth, silken voice as he sang, "Or leave a kiss within the cup, and I'll not ask for wine. . . ."

"Jock, will Anne ever be able to play that song—once he's gone? I couldn't if you were leaving me. What can we do for her? How can we find a means to help her?"

"We can't. In a very definite way, in spite of the loyalty and devotion she has for us both, our girl has, by a natural act of God—by falling so much in love—moved a bit to one side of us now. In a way I can't quite put my finger on, she's already cleaving to Lieutenant John Fraser."

"I agree. Except for my own certainty that you were the one man for me, I've never seen the beginnings of real love so marked as in Anne. And although she seems even more loving to us, she is, as you say, to one side of us now. Still affectionate and warm, but in a special world of her own—of *their* own."

The music stopped. Rebecca reached to touch her husband's hand.

"He has to leave her so soon. They need time alone now," she said, almost to herself. "They'll be going for a walk, I'm sure. Are you chilly, my dear? Should we go inside before they cross the veranda to head for the river path? We can spare them having to make small talk with us."

Abruptly, Jock got to his feet. "Do I hear voices down at our dock?" he asked, peering out toward the river. "Is that Thomas Spalding's boat? We don't have any warning when he's coming because the man doesn't like his people to sing!"

"He's one of the best friends you have, Jock, even though he doesn't like music. You'd better go down to meet him. It *is* Mr. Spalding and remember not to chide him because we couldn't tell who was coming by the oarsmen's songs."

"I'll remember," he said and headed down the high front steps. "I'm too deep in gloom today to chide about anything." From the yard he called softly up to her. "You miss the people who left us, too, don't you, Becca?"

At the sight of what could only be called grief on his face, tears filled her eyes. "Yes! Oh yes, Jock, I miss them too."

After a brief, warm greeting at the dock, Thomas Spalding handed Jock a copy of the *National Intelligencer* in which was printed not only a copy of the Treaty of Ghent but an article explaining that the peace treaty had indeed been signed on Christmas Eve last and unanimously ratified by the Senate on February 17, over a week ago!

As Couper scanned the story, Spalding announced that he was leaving tomorrow for Savannah. "Don't insist that I go up to the house because there isn't time. I do want to keep you apprised of my every step in this endeavor, though. That's why I'm here today."

"Why are you going to Savannah, Thomas? For what reason?"

"I've written to both United States General Thomas Pinckney and General John Floyd asking for authority to go down to Cumberland for the express purpose of negotiating with Admiral Cockburn for the return of American public and private property. This newspaper proves the war ended Christmas Eve of last year!"

"But the British haven't touched one Negro or one bale of cotton at your place on Sapelo! Would you go to all that trouble for the rest of us who have lost so much?"

"I would. And there's no doubt I'll get the authority the minute I can talk directly to Floyd or Pinckney. I've asked that young, bright Captain Thomas Newell of the U.S. Sea Fencibles be allowed to go with me. He's more than willing."

"I honestly don't know what to say, neighbor." Jock's voice was thick with emotion. "How we need someone to shoulder the burdens! I can think of no one better equipped. I promise we'll try to find a way to show our gratitude."

"Wait until I've succeeded," Spalding said. "Birdsey Norton from Darien was down at St. Marys last week. He tells me the admiral is a courteous but stiff-necked gentleman, who refuses even to discuss the fact that a treaty has been ratified—that the war is really over."

"Did Norton actually speak with Admiral Cockburn?"

"No. The admiral's a haughty, lofty presence, at least in his own eyes, but Birdsey talked to two St. Marys men who had addressed him. He learned firsthand that Cockburn is still loading and sending off American goods, still receiving American Negroes, even a few white refugees. He's also still training recruits. Norton claims that Cockburn will go on refusing to abide by the terms of the peace treaty, refusing point-blank to return all property taken since its ratification on February 17, *until* he receives his orders directly from his superior, Vice Admiral Cochrane. I declare there are no greater scoundrels on God's earth than the British!"

"Can't you at least come in for a bracing cup of tea?"

"Sorry. But I'll be back to report on my efforts on Cumberland sometime in mid-March if all goes well." He held out his hand. "I have real hope, Jock, of being able to retrieve at least some of your people."

Walking slowly back up his path after Spalding's oarsmen moved out into the Hampton River, Couper wondered if he had ever experienced so many contradictory emotions. As did everyone else, he longed for it to be true that the war was actually over. He would be forced to face the possibility of financial collapse if none of his people could be returned, and yet, there was Anne, his very heart. Her loss was even greater. If indeed a peace treaty had been ratified, there would be no hope that she would see her John again for a long, long time. Maybe never.

Halfway up the path, he stopped to look at the imposing, welcoming shape of the Cannon's Point house in its leafy, prosperous setting by the river. The shape of John Couper's dream. The sight that had, until now, always lifted his spirit.

A glimpse of Anne and John, arms entwined, walking north along the river path, brought almost unbearable pain. As much as a man could love a place, he loved Cannon's Point, felt gratified with what he'd achieved there, experienced a ray of hope that Spalding might indeed negotiate the return of some of his people, but nothing could ever be right again if Anne were caused to suffer.

* * *

They had walked in silence along the river toward what Anne was calling "our tree," arms about each other until they reached the great oak. In all his nearly twenty-four years, John Fraser had never felt so helpless. Even in the thick of the fighting with the Americans up in Virginia at Farnham Church late last year, he had experienced no desperation like this.

These minutes passing now were his last to be alone with Anne. The remainder of this day would be spent at Frederica, where he'd been ordered to supervise the loading of the cotton bales taken from both Cannon's Point and Hampton. Being with her for the last time was choking him with dread, with a terror the roar of gunfire and cannonfire had never brought. In battle there were other men in the same danger, drawing courage from one another, pretending together, at least, not to be afraid.

Now, he stood alone with the one woman he would ever love, with whom he'd spent so little time, whose young, lithe body caused him a kind of strange joy and an equally strange pain. Except for the fighting in Virginia, near Washington, the American war, for John, had been mainly a lark, an adventure, despite his conscientious attention to duty. This agony was unlike any other because Anne was unlike anyone else. Her compelling, fresh, intelligent beauty was only hers. The graceful set of her shoulders was unlike that of any other woman. There was spirit in the very set of her head on those shoulders—an independent spirit. In her love for him, he had found more to reinforce his own self-esteem than in any commendation he'd received for any act of valor even after the fighting in Virginia. His sense that from their first meeting Anne felt drawn to him, too, had lifted his opinion of himself. In his heart, he now knew that in spite of the differences in personalities, he was, in his own way, equal to his revered, scholarly brother, William. In Anne, he had found new confidence. Enough, he felt sure, to face any hardship.

Not so. Standing beside her now under the shadowy, sheltering branches of the great oak, he could find no strength to help himself. Certainly none to help Anne, whose own dread was causing her to tremble in his arms. It was a man's place to give strength. John had none to give. There was nothing in him to offer any clue whatever to how he would be able to mount a horse later today and ride away. His breeding, his manhood, prodded him to do something, to say something that might reassure Anne. He found nothing. There were no words for such helpless pain. He could only take her in his arms and hold her to him. She was holding him, too, her body still trembling, her dear voice whispering, "John—oh, John, what are we going to do?"

"We're going to love, Anne. We're going to go on loving each other just the way we love right now. . . ." He could feel sobs rising in her, could feel her struggle against them. "We—we can write lots of letters," he said lamely. "And I will. I will. You must write often to me, too."

"Don't go!"

"I have to go. You know that. Anne, it's—it's bloody hard being a man. I'm suffering exactly the way you are now, but I can't beg you not to leave me. I'm the one who has to leave because—I'm a man. I'm supposed to be strong. I'm not. I'm weak and frightened and—"

Her arms tightened still more around him. "And dear. Oh, John, you're so dear to me! And you're not weak. You're just—unfair because life is unfair. The war is over! Everyone knows now a treaty was signed last December. Being a man isn't any harder than being a woman, except that men are pigheaded. You're pigheaded to insist on leaving me."

Panic gripped him. Panic matched only by the helplessness. She blamed him for leaving! He was the one under orders. What she had just said was unreasonable. Not at all like her. "I'm not pigheaded. I *have* to go. A man has to obey orders. None of what you said seems a bit like you!"

"I've never been this way before! Neither have you. You don't know what you're saying any more than I do."

He felt a welcome loosening inside. What she had just admitted *was* like her. Honest. Direct. And she was right. He *didn't* know what he was saying. Neither did she. How could they know? Everything was so new. In the military a man was trained to live with danger, with chaos—to develop a means of keeping his head when even the next minute was uncertain. Still, in battle someone else had given the order to move, someone higher up told a military man how to take risks. Loving Anne, which now seemed the greatest risk of all, was his doing. Loving her was John Fraser's first total responsibility. Seeing how sheltered a life she'd lived at Cannon's Point made it clear that bearing her part of their separation would also be her first real responsibility, her first real burden.

"I don't want to be a burden, Anne."

For what seemed a long time, she said nothing and his panic mounted. If loving him was a burden, could she go on loving him once a vast ocean lay between them?

An acorn, still clinging to the gnarled live oak that seemed now to be spreading darkness above them, let go and fell to the ground beside where they stood. The sound was like a shot.

Anne's body stiffened. Then she laughed—more a nervous little squeak than a real laugh. "Acorns dropping don't make that much noise! The way we both jumped," she said, "you'd think we'd been hit by a bullet."

Her blessed humor. How to respond? Humor was the last thing John felt now. What he said lay like a rock between them: "No, Anne. A bullet—doesn't feel like that."

She jerked quickly away and glared up at him. "Don't you dare say such a thing to me again!"

"I know how stupid it sounded."

"Not stupid—terrifying!" Her proud chin lifted. "It's going to be official any day now that the rumors are true—that the war *is* over. There will be no more bullets." As suddenly as she'd pulled away, Anne threw herself back into his arms. "Have you ever been—hit by a bullet, my darling?"

"No, no, Anne. Grazed, but only once. Don't tremble. What I said was—stupid."

Still clinging to him, she whispered, "Everything's stupid. Dumb. This beautiful island winter day is dumb. It doesn't match anything. Even the sunshine is making fun of us."

"The truth is, we're the luckiest two people on the face of the earth," he said weakly.

"That's certainly dumb! Why did you even think it?"

What he heard himself say next surprised him. "Because I suddenly seem to see clearly for the first time the kind of dark trouble your father could be causing for us this minute."

"Papa?"

"He has every reason to resent me bitterly. I pray he knows I've done nothing to persuade one single slave to leave him, but I certainly stand for the cause of his tragic losses. We are lucky—downright blessed, Anne—because Mr. John Couper is such a fair-minded, openhearted gentleman. He could be making the prospect of our wretched separation far worse, you know. He isn't. If the man doesn't genuinely like me, I'm more mistaken than ever before in my nearly twenty-four years."

"Twenty-four. I think you told me on Cumberland you're almost twenty-four, but I don't even know when your birthday is!" Her light, troubled eyes brimmed with tears. "How do we know we love so much when we know so little about each other?" She took a step away from him. "Do you think you'll still love me once you've really gotten to know me?"

He looked up into the gnarled branches. "I love you more right now than when we reached our tree just minutes ago."

Because there seemed so little left to say, they just held each other and kept on holding. Two more acorns fell. A squirrel barked. They went on holding.

When Anne spoke again, he sensed a new quiet in her. "When I play or even think of our song, I'll come very close to you, no matter how many miles there are between."

"You will, won't you?"

She tried a brave little smile. "I did more, don't forget, than merely 'leave a kiss within the cup.' I left a kiss right there in your hand." She left another.

The pain would come. He would ride away. They would be apart for some empty, indefinable length of time. But just now, under the stretching, enfolding branches of their great tree, they had somehow found their way. Together, they had moved somewhere safely beyond the total desperation. The pain of leaving her would be no less, but by some means, he could go now.

Chapter 16

For over an hour Anne had been in her room struggling to write an acceptable letter to John, back on Cumberland. The British were still holding residents captive there, although Papa knew the war was really over.

Concentration seemed next to impossible with noisy young Polly clattering around her room—cleaning, changing linens, and, as usual, dropping things. The letter had to be right, with nothing that might in any way worry John should he read it a hundred times as she had read the two perfect letters he'd already found a way to send since he left eight days ago.

In the first paragraph, she had told him of her sadness for Papa because his longtime friend Mr. James Hamilton felt certain enough about the end of hostilities to be leaving any day to live forever in Philadelphia. John would care too about Papa's pain at the loss of his friend. Beyond that one paragraph, she felt too rattled, too nervous, to form a decent sentence. Her own pain simply was too sharp for ordinary words, even if there had been time today to think straight. Her brother was taking some business papers down to Mr. Hamilton for Papa, and James's rigid schedule never allowed any leeway for anything. He had promised to ride first to Frederica with her letter, to hand it directly to the postmaster, George Abbott, but only if it was finished at the exact moment he intended to ride out.

John's letters had been warm and eager, filled with declarations of love and his determination to find a way to come back to her as soon as he knew something definite about his future with the Royal Marines. That he longed to stay in the military she did not doubt and she hated the thought of it.

Hated the whole idea of his being any part of fighting and killing. At the same time, she wanted his happiness above everything else. If he did stay in the service, in order to be with him she would surely have to leave St. Simons and her family.

In one letter, now torn up, she had begged John shamelessly to leave his unit, his own land, and move to Georgia. To be with her forever in the only place where she could ever feel at home. The letter was shameless. Cruel and selfish-sounding. Why did everything she wrote sound so stiff and proper or downright unladylike and testy?

After ordering Polly to come back later to finish dusting, she tried again: "My brother is in such a hurry that I have but a few minutes to devote to you, blessed John," she wrote, "when I long to devote every minute of the remainder of my life. Believe me, your dear letters are far from an imposition! They are a source of unaffected pleasure and joy to me. In spite of a recurring headache, which struck as soon as you left me, I certainly should have written to you by Mr. Spalding, but I knew nothing of the exact date of his departure. I cannot answer for some of our neighbors rejoicing in your leaving, but in our family there is no such feeling. You are so kind and such excellent company, we are all deeply sorry you have gone. How could I have spent over a fortnight with you and not experience dreadful regret at separation?"

Fingering her quill, she scanned the page. "Dumb! It all sounds just plain dumb," she said aloud to herself, unmindful now that Polly had sneaked back in, bent on dusting the mahogany wardrobe. "Dumb, dumb."

"What I do dumb now, Miss Anne?" Polly asked, not sounding as though she cared much one way or another.

"Nothing, Polly. I was just muttering to myself. Be quiet. I'm having a dreadful time writing this letter and my brother is probably waiting now—champing at the bit."

"You want I should go tell him to hold still?"

"No! I have to keep writing. So don't bother me anymore about anything."

"Yes'm."

Polly wasn't actually bothering her that much. Anne was bothering herself by feeling so rushed and helpless. "You must know that I have had a few sly whispers from Dame Prudence," she wrote, "who is not a little offended at my giving my heart and receiving the gift of yours in such a short length of time. I have tried hard to silence the Dame by reminding her that this is the first time I have in any manner violated her rules, but it is in vain since every now and then—though not often because she knows I am not listening—she takes it into her head to reproach me."

Then, even though her windows were closed against the quiet, chilly March morning, she heard a lone rider gallop up outside and James Hamilton's voice greet someone. She didn't care who it was but felt even more nervous because hearing her brother's voice from outside, down on the road, meant he was ready to leave. Scribbling as fast as she could, she wrote: "My father is certain, as is Mr. Spalding, that President Madison and the Congress have already ratified the peace treaty and so I hope and constantly pray that in a very short space of time, we shall see you again back on our island under totally unwarlike conditions. I hold your promise to come back to me as I hold to my very life."

When her father called from downstairs, she slopped a blot of ink across the page in her frantic effort to finish the awkward letter before James Hamilton left without it. "My father and mother desire to be remembered to you," she wrote swiftly, trying to keep her sleeve out of the wet ink. "Don't judge my pen scribbling too harshly and know that this letter does not say anything that comes close to the way I miss you and long to see you—night and day. Adieu, Your loving and sincere friend, Anne Couper."

As she was folding and sealing the letter, Papa called again, more urgently this time. Downstairs, after she had raced without a cloak outdoors to hand it to James, Anne rushed back inside and was surprised to see Mr. James Gould, the lighthouse builder, standing in the parlor with her father. Both men looked disturbed.

"Good day, Mr. Gould," she said. "You called me, Papa?"

"Repeatedly, Daughter. Mr. Gould thought we should know that through connections from his old days in the timber business some miles up the St. Marys River, he's learned what will surely be upsetting news. My way would be to keep it from you until we knew more, but Mr. Gould thinks—"

Her mouth went dry. "What? Is it about John?"

"Aye. Brace yourself, dear girl. Cockburn sent John and a

handful of others up the St. Marys to capture a prize ship the Americans believed safely hidden upriver. There was a fairly savage—fight."

"Papa, you're stalling!"

"Lieutenant John Fraser is not dead, Miss Anne," James Gould said in his maddeningly calm voice. "But he is severely wounded."

"Severely, but not mortally wounded. It's his arm," Papa said. "That means he'll get well. Evidently he's safely back on Cumberland under his brother's medical care."

Head whirling, Anne thanked Mr. Gould, then ran from the parlor, up the stairs, and locked herself in her room.

Across the upstairs hall, Anna Matilda laid down her quill to listen. The letter she was writing to her parents could wait. No one was going to Darien anyway who might deliver it for her. And something must be terribly wrong for Anne to run so fast up the stair, bang her door, and turn the lock.

Standing in the hallway, Anna Matilda, suddenly nervous about knocking on her best friend's door, finally tapped and waited, heart thumping. After what must have been a full minute, she heard Anne's slippers cross the stretch of bare floor beyond the pretty carpet with peacocks in its border. From inside, the lock turned slowly. Anne hadn't actually opened the door. She had only unlocked it. When Anna stepped hesitantly inside, Anne Couper was standing in the middle of the floor, looking like a ghost. There was almost no expression on her face, no color.

"What's wrong?" Anna Matilda breathed. "Something terrible has happened, hasn't it?"

At first, Anne only nodded. Then she whispered, "Yes. John. They must have sent him right into battle almost as soon as he wrote my second letter from Cumberland."

"Was he killed?"

"No. Severely wounded, Mr. Gould said. He's back on Cumberland now. Mr. Gould rode up to tell Papa. I guess he's still downstairs." Burying her face in her hands, Anne spoke brokenly, "Oh, Anna Matilda, it's one of his dear arms that's—hurt. I'm not sure I can—bear that!"

Anna Matilda struggled to take it all in, to understand some of what Anne must be suffering at this minute that caused her friend to seem so far away. Never before had she felt so young, so inexperienced, in meeting adult troubles.

Never before had she rebelled at the prospect that one day she, too, might well endure pain of the kind Anne was enduring now. If only her parents were back at Retreat, so that she could ask Mr. Couper to send her home in one of his buggies. What a dreadful time for them to be in Darien, still protecting their best people from the British—especially since Mr. Couper vowed the war was really over. If she could only ask Mama what to say or to think in this terrifying moment!

There stood Anne—older, so much older—agonizing for love's sake and there she stood—so young—not knowing about love and afraid to find out.

"They were sent to capture a hidden American prize ship," Anne was explaining numbly. "Of course, Admiral Cockburn sent a select few of his bravest, best marines."

How mature Anne's voice sounded, speaking words that normally only older people ever thought about. Anne had grown away from her almost overnight. As familiar as Cannon's Point was, she felt isolated enough to cry. She felt downright scared of not being young anymore.

"Papa did me great honor by telling me point-blank what had happened," Anne said. "I'll always be grateful to him for that. It—it hurts more knowing, especially when I'm too far away to comfort John, to try to ease his pain. But I'm glad I know. Being separated is too ghastly to have to endure not knowing, too. Papa truly honored me."

"I don't think I'd want to be honored like that," Anna Matilda blurted. "Oh, Anne, is it—is it just dreadful to be a grown woman?"

Anne turned to look directly at her and Anna Matilda thought her friend had never been so beautiful. "Yes," Anne answered, "it's dreadful and marvelous. I wouldn't be anyone else in all the world—but me. Even with John, my tender, strong John, so wounded."

"The further tragedy of all this," James Gould said as Couper went with him to the door, "is that we all know the war is over. My old neighbor from St. Marys, who brought up my lumber order, told me Cockburn himself has known for weeks, too. He knew weeks before his own officers found a British newspaper on that American prize up the St. Marys. It carried the whole story, including the ratification last month."

"Do you mean Cockburn knew all along? Even before he saw the text of the treaty in that British paper?"

Gould nodded. "Miss Anne's friend was wounded for nothing. You lost your people for nothing. They were stolen from you *after* Cockburn knew perfectly well that it was all over!"

"Roswell King's right. He told me he wrote Major Butler that he should do all he could as a prominent man in our federal government to demolish the British once and for all. If not, they'll just keep on making trouble for us here in the United States." Couper rubbed both hands over his face. "Oh, Gould, I'm finding it very hard to wait for Thomas Spalding to get back from Cumberland. Whether or not he negotiates the return of any St. Simons Negroes, at least he'll know some facts."

"When do you look for him to be home?"

"He should be on his way down there now. He had to go to Savannah first for an official commission to represent planters along our coast. I'd say he could be back before the middle of March. Just when the weather is getting blustery."

As Couper had predicted, the weather during the second week in March was bitter cold, the wind blowing a steady, chilling gale. The first few days Spalding and Captain Newell spent on Cumberland Island were made more intolerable by Admiral Cockburn's flaring temper and stubborn refusal to admit that the war indeed had ended.

Thomas Spalding could only call the first meeting with the admiral tempestuous. He and Newell entered Cockburn's private quarters at Dungeness armed with a copy of the *National Intelligencer* in which the full story of both the signing of the Treaty of Ghent on December 24, 1814, and its ratification on February 17 appeared in detail. Furious that Spalding and young Captain Newell had dared to confront him with their demands that according to the treaty, coastal slaves be immediately returned, Cockburn had insisted that until he received *direct orders* from his superior, Vice Admiral Cochrane, who had not yet reached Cumberland, no Negro would be released from British control.

Back on St. Simons by the third week in March, Spalding reported to John Couper that his mission had failed. Cochrane did not arrive.

"If you can believe me, Jock," Spalding said, pacing the

parlor of the Cannon's Point house, "the rascal Cockburn, stalling for time, demanded that we copy the wording of the entire treaty by hand from the *Intelligencer* account! Of course, he vowed that then he would allow all Negroes stolen since ratification to be returned. He reneged on his word."

Couper's only response was to remind him that by now, Spalding should know better than to expect anything but tricks from the British.

"I will say," Thomas went on, "that Newell and I were allowed to board the *Regulus,* on which were still stashed most of the Negroes stolen from St. Simons, and allowed to plead with them to return."

Couper stared at him. "You actually *saw*—my people who left me, Thomas?"

"I did, and Jock, I only stopped short of falling on my knees. I begged them to come home. I failed almost entirely, although five of your people will be brought back, six are returning to Wylly, one only to Hampton across Jones Creek, and one to your close friend Hamilton. Thirteen in all stepped forward when I'd finished my plea. Thirteen out of over two hundred Negroes packed onto that ship!"

When Couper got to his feet without a word and walked slowly to a window, Spalding went to stand beside him.

"Don't feel too bad, Thomas," Jock said. "At least, we know the war is over. The killing and the stealing will stop now. No more young men will be wounded."

"I should have reported on Miss Anne's young man first thing," Spalding said. "I know his wounds are a cause of heartache to you right along with the loss of your people and of your old friend Hamilton to Philadelphia."

"I've already heard the latest about young Fraser. The boy's getting well. Gaining strength even after all the blood he lost. The wound was in his left arm. The worst part was so much bleeding. Anne's heard from him—" He chuckled slightly. "She'd have been right here demanding news from you otherwise, you can be sure. Fraser was able to write a few lines while he was still on Cumberland. Sent the letter up by Alexander Wylly while you were still down there."

Spalding looked surprised. "Alexander went to Cumberland?"

"Foolishly, as it turned out. The weather was so bad, he couldn't even get as far as Dungeness. In the midst of a violent gale, he and his Negro were received aboard the hospital ship. John's brother, Dr. William Fraser, handed him a letter for Anne. The girl's suffering these days, but at least she knows now that her lieutenant is going to be all right. When will my five people be back, Thomas? Or do I have to send for them?"

"You have to send a boat down, Jock. By the way, Mrs. Shaw at Dungeness seems now to consider even Admiral Cockburn a gentleman," Spalding sneered. "He returned all *her* people and she appears to be in full charge again of her mansion. It seems she and Cockburn got along famously. His courtesy doesn't extend to returning all *your* stolen property, though." He held out his hand. "I did my best, Jock. It's important to me that you believe that. Five Negroes out of sixty is not good, I know."

Couper gave him a big smile. "Better than none, surely. I'm glad you lost no people, and don't worry about me. Tragedies like this are simply a part of the *glory* of being a slave owner. It helps that I know Anne's worry over her young man is lessened. There for a while, after I knew Hamilton was really leaving for good, my old heart came to be overcrowded. It comforts me a lot that Anne isn't quite so worried now."

"It must be rather serious between those two, Jock. I know you think highly of British Lieutenant Fraser, but isn't it all a bit awkward here on the island under the circumstances?"

"Not yet. At least, very few repercussions so far. But, Thomas, I need to ask a big favor."

"Anything."

"We have been careful not to talk about the deep regard in which Anne holds young Fraser. Except for you, only the Page girl, Wylly, Gould, and our immediate family know the extent of it. For the time being, it just seems better that way."

"You have my word, Jock. And you must know that since you evidently give your blessing, I wish only the best for them."

"Thank you. They do have my blessing. Whatever makes Anne happy, makes me happy, too. I—I seem even to feel her torment, the missing, the longing just to look at the boy again. It could well be, in this tangled world we live in, though, that the separation is forever. If that's true, Anne will need me as never before. Her mother, too. I'm ripped in far too many directions today, though, to face any of that." He sighed. "Right now, I'd give almost anything if the Almighty would show me the exact route to being both a slave owner *and* a slave to the attachment I feel for my only daughter."

Chapter 17

Couper was sitting beside his valued chef, Cassamene Sans Foix, on the kitchen steps at Cannon's Point when they saw Roswell King clamber stiffly out of a small Butler skiff on their side of Jones Creek.

"Mr. King, he hobbles these days like an old man, sir," Sans Foix said in his slight Domingan accent, a grin on his full, dark face. "Beside him, you are like a young man and you are much older."

Couper laughed. "Flattery will take you far, my friend. Just as your cooking has taken me far as a host. Still, I manage to feel pity for Roswell King at times, so crippled with rheumatism, yet having to carry the responsibility of running two plantations for an owner as watchful as Major Pierce Butler. I wonder what King's doing over here on our side of the creek today. You usually have a theory, Cassamene. Why do you think he came across?"

The intelligent, confident Sans Foix shrugged. "Something is on his mind. Not often is he here these days. Back in Santo Domingo, I was taught to expect trouble in the unexpected."

"Whatever King has on his mind is very apt to be troublesome. I try my best to like the man. The Almighty knows how often I fail," Couper said, getting up to greet King, who had begun to limp slowly up the long path from Jones Creek. "By the way, I had a reason for calling you out of your kitchen, Sans Foix. One of my foolish, old-man notions. Do you think we could safely pack and send Lieutenant Fraser a canister of your superb sugar-nut cakes? Would they keep long enough to make an Atlantic crossing?"

Standing too, now, Sans Foix beamed. "Sir, I guarantee it!

But, where do they go? Does Miss Anne know where her gentleman is at this time?"

"Not for sure yet. Somewhere in England. She believes his ship will dock in Portsmouth. We're only sure that the British flag was finally struck at Dungeness on the thirteenth of this month—last week. I'm certain he's on the ocean now, so the canister of sugar cakes is nothing we have to do at once. I—I just wanted to be able to tell Anne that you and I had it in mind."

"Very well, sir. Tell her I start the newly returned, no-good boy, Guy, to crack nuts this very week in preparation." Sans Foix snorted. "He deserves only to be allowed to crack nuts after what he did to you!"

Couper grinned. "You're a sly one. You know Guy can go right back to making wheels if I say so. I don't intend to punish any Negro who chose to leave me. But I happen to know Guy *likes* to crack hickory nuts in your kitchen." He laid a hand on his chef's shoulder. "Now, I must begin something far less pleasant than talking to you, Cassamene. Mr. King has almost made his way up that path. I'll see what he has on his mind today."

The two neighbors greeted each other, and as usual, Roswell King launched right into his plan: "On my way back here from the rice plantation on Butler Island late yesterday, I stopped briefly at Spalding's on Sapelo. I'd heard Spalding was being sent to Bermuda in still another attempt to obtain release of our stolen niggers."

"Thomas is going to Bermuda? Who's sending him?" Couper interrupted, surprised.

"President James Madison. He'll be going on purely official business, but what's to stop you and me from making the trip too? I've thought it through, Mr. Couper. We can take Major Butler's carpenter, Abraham. That faithful fellow did more to influence the Butler slaves when the British were here than any other single nigger on the place did. Those who left showed their savage ignorance in going, but they all respect Abraham. His influence could help us."

"But would Abraham make the long ocean voyage to Bermuda? You know that any Negro who reached this country by ship in the first place is terrified of a sea voyage. Abraham, if I recall, was brought years ago from the Gold Coast."

"He'll go if I order him to go."

Couper sighed. "Of course."

"Crippled up as I am," King went on, "I can be ready to leave when Spalding goes in three days. I assume you can do that, too."

"I don't recall having agreed to go at all," Jock said, struggling as always, when King pressured him, to control himself.

"You lost sixty niggers, sir! Only five came back. Are you so rich you can't make one last effort to reclaim so much valuable property?"

"I'm far from rich, but I do pride myself on a modicum of common sense. What guarantee do we have that any will agree to come home with us? Those in Bermuda now, according to Cockburn's narrow interpretation of the treaty, are legally free. Anyway, Spalding is my good friend. He'll be there in an official capacity, on presidential business. I can count on him to make every effort to retrieve property of mine."

"But will any persuasion of his be as telling with those ingrates who benefited from *your* coddling before they fled? Word is that they're sickening and dying like flies right now under the care of their new British masters. Once they see you, I have no doubt that your niggers will leap at the chance to return to Cannon's Point, where they will never have to run the dangerous risks of freedom again."

Jock looked off up the winding, tree-shaded creek that separated his land from Butler's. "Some days, King, I admit I miss them all. Some days more than others, but not a day passes that I don't think at least a few times of each one who left me. A man doesn't try to take care of his people for all the years some of them were here and just forget them. I wonder in my bed at night who's sick, who's dead. You're right." He paused. "I should make the effort. Not, however, without first discussing such a journey with Mrs. Couper and both my children. You know perfectly well there can be dangerous storms in those waters at any time of year. Mrs. Couper's with child. I'd hate adding to her trials."

"Anne, can't you sit still long enough for me to read Louisa Shaw's letter aloud to you?" her mother asked when she and Anne had excused Jock and James Hamilton from the table after breakfast the April morning before Jock was to leave. "I know your father and brother have work to do even out in this drizzle, so neither would be willing to listen, but Louisa has made a real effort to tell us what actually took place in her mind during the weeks Dungeness and all in it were captured. You were a captive, too, Anne. Aren't you the least bit interested?"

"I am, Mama! And I'm sorry I'm fidgety. But I—I dreamed about John last night. I just hope it doesn't mean anything more is wrong for him."

"Was it a bad dream, dear? A nightmare?"

"No," she said uncertainly. "Not really. Not the kind I still have sometimes about the scary night the Ebos jumped overboard."

"Do you still have that old nightmare?"

"Not as often as I did, but yes. Sometimes. I think just knowing Eve and Ebo June are married now has helped a lot. I was actually afraid of Ebos that night when I overheard Mr. King and Papa talking about what happened to them."

"You're not still afraid, are you?"

"No! Not of anything but losing John. In my dream last night, foolish as it sounds, I heard him singing to me."

"With a voice like his, how could that have been a worrisome dream, dear?"

Frowning, Anne said, "I don't know."

"Was John happy in the dream?"

"Don't ask me any more questions, please! His voice sounded like his voice, but—read Mrs. Shaw's letter, Mama. I'm just so restless until I know he's safely back in England. Until I hear *something* from him."

"And it would be unnatural if you weren't."

"Read, please. I'll listen. I promise."

"Very well, if you're sure."

Because the spring day was dark, a light rain falling, her mother moved her chair closer to the piecrust table, where two candles burned, and began to read: " 'It is good to have the house to ourselves again and yet, dear Rebecca, James, my pro-British husband, seems still to miss our captors. He became extremely fond of Admiral Cockburn and his officers. I can join James in honest admiration for the kindness and liberty granted us during the British occupation—the oddly social, pleasant period when they were all still here. I can't help wondering about the gossip on St. Simons. *All* my slaves were returned to me and so perhaps I may find myself an unwelcome visitor—resented in future visits to your lovely home. I've heard Mr. Couper's losses were heavy and I regret this. As you know, I was bitter at first, but time is a healer. I have also heard that your daughter, Anne, is now very much in love with Lieutenant John Fraser of the Royal Marine Light Artillery. How circumstances in our chaotic world will treat the prospects of their future no one can know, but please tell the enchanting Anne that I wish her well from my heart.' " Her mother looked up. "There, my dear Anne, aren't you glad you settled down to listen?"

"Yes. Yes, I am." She sighed deeply. "But, Mama, what *will* happen in our world? What will happen to John and me? I—I sometimes think I can't bear another moment's waiting to find out. To find out about *something.*"

"It's far too early to lose patience, darling. I know how old that sounds, how beyond your understanding now."

"Everything's beyond my understanding. I don't even understand how I came to love him so much!"

"Shall I finish Louisa's letter? There's only a bit more. Or would you rather just talk?"

"No. Read. I don't really have anything to say."

Her mother hunted for her place. "Let's see. 'The last British ship, *Albion,* sailed out of our sight in Cumberland Sound at two-thirty in the afternoon, 18 March—sailed away from Cumberland forever, carrying Rear Admiral Sir George Cockburn, a gentleman we now consider our friend. He is, of course, a "wretch in human form" to many of our neighbors in Camden County. To the Negroes, I suppose, he is their liberator.' "

When her mother stopped reading, Anne sat in silence, hands clenched. Then she said, "John could have been on the *Albion* that day, too, if he had recovered enough by then to leave the hospital ship. At least now I know about when he sailed." She took a deep breath. "March 18. This is April 12. He couldn't possibly be in Portsmouth yet. The Atlantic, Papa says, can be very rough now. Oh, Mama! I'll be a lot better company once I've had time to hear from him! Just one line telling me he survived the long, hard voyage after being wounded would turn me into a new woman. Aren't you just frantic that Papa is going willy-nilly all the way to Bermuda? I am. I'm dying inside over both John and Papa!"

Chapter 18

Alone in her room at first light, the late-April day outside so dismal and foggy she couldn't see nearby Hampton River, Anne struggled against still another bout of guilt because she knew Mama needed her to be at least a little brave. She wasn't being brave at all. Last night, when her mother had all but begged for her to have faith that both John and Papa would be safe, Anne's own agony was too painful to help anyone. She couldn't even help herself.

I'm suddenly growing backward into childhood, she thought. I pile all my worries onto Mama, who needs me to be her friend now as much as I need her to be mine. Even Anna Matilda, if Anne's last visit to Retreat was any indication, is being more helpful with poor Mrs. Page. Poor, fat Mrs. Page, who hadn't even written Anna Matilda that she had been ill much of the time she and her husband had taken refuge from the British in Darien.

Now that the Pages were home and Anna Matilda no longer at Cannon's Point, Anne missed her terribly. Twice in the short time Papa had been gone, Anne had ridden her own horse, Gentleman, all the way to the south end of the island, desperate for the companionship of someone her own age. Not that Mama didn't try. She did, constantly. She tried too hard, actually, and anyway, Anne and her mother were consumed with the same worry over Papa's safety. For her sake, Mama was anxious about John, too, of course, but last night she had turned to Anne in what seemed a deep, helpless way.

She turned to me and I failed her, Anne thought. But how could I help Mama when both my rocks—John and Papa—are undoubtedly still somewhere on the Atlantic? Papa could be in Bermuda by now, of course, but they are both out of sight, both in danger.

On one visit to Retreat, Anna Matilda had acted stubbornly grown-up, to the extent of asking Anne if faith in God didn't come into the picture somewhere. Her friend's reminder only infuriated her. Even when Anna Matilda shared her own worry because Dr. Tunno had declared that all that fat could kill Mrs. Page, Anne had trouble sympathizing.

"I'm afraid," Mama had told Anne last night in a frighteningly weary voice, "that you're very like my paternal grandmother. I always heard Grandmother Maxwell was given to dark, gloomy moods. Until now, all your life you've been only cheerful, good-spirited like your dear father."

A briar of resentment that her mother had said such a thing still pricked this morning. Standing at her front window, she remembered something else Mama had said, which also still rankled. Like Anna Matilda, Mama had mounted a spiritual pedestal. "Doesn't faith come into the picture, Daughter? We both know that wherever John and your father might be—this minute—they're *in God's hands.*"

From babyhood, Anne had been taught that. And, of course, she prayed. She prayed now—morning, noon, night, and in between—but God didn't answer in any way that really helped. She'd had no word at all that John had reached England safely. Now Papa was off on a dangerous wild-goose chase in one final, desperate effort to see British Vice Admiral Cochrane, believing, in the childlike way Papa believed things, that he might get more of his people back. What if he failed? Mr. Spalding had all but failed when he went to Cumberland. Anne shuddered at the thought of Papa's making the long return voyage knowing the trip had been for nothing.

Still at the window, thoughts and spirit as thick and foggy as the day trying to break outside, she struggled to make sense of what Mama had said last night. Anne simply did not want to be like her great-grandmother Maxwell—prone to despondent days, to making life miserable for everyone around her. She wouldn't be if only John were still where she could see his face, feel his arms, talk to him, hear his dear voice answer.

What good, she wondered, would it do for Papa to appeal

directly to Vice Admiral Cochrane when it was he who gave the order that every Negro taken before the Treaty of Ghent had been ratified now legally belonged to the British? John had told her that Cochrane was a courteous man, but the Negroes were gone because Cochrane ordered it. How could even Papa change that?

Dark thoughts, dark thoughts. Mama would accuse her of being Great-grandmother Maxwell. She turned from the window wondering what to do next, thinking she might stop breathing any moment because she was so lonely.

Aloud, she said, "I can at least begin a letter to him."

She spoke the words to herself, alone in her room, as though writing to John hadn't been possible through all the eternity he'd been gone. The truth was it hadn't. He'd given her a tentative address in Portsmouth, England, where he was to report sometime before the end of May, but her mood had been too shadowy, too morose, to inflict on him. What kind of love letter could anyone write from such a hollow heart?

She hurried to her desk, grabbed a piece of writing paper. She would make the effort at least, because whatever she wrote could always be torn up.

26 April 1815
Cannon's Point, St. Simons Island

Beloved John,

If a few words do not find their way to this paper from my heart to yours, I think I might die! It is barely 7 A.M., and I have slept so little—last night or any night since you rode away from me—I would believe myself to be going blind if I didn't know how thick the fog is outside my window. I looked and looked, trying desperately to see our big oak tree. I couldn't find it. It is blotted out except in my empty, lonely heart. My poor trusting father is away on what will undoubtedly turn out to be a fruitless chase to Bermuda, hoping to convince Vice Admiral Cochrane to return at least some of his people. I am bereft without him. I am bereft without you. My dear friend, you will learn, if Providence permits us time to learn, that at certain periods I have begun to experience unbearable times of dark, thick gloom due to a heavy heart over both you and Papa. Perhaps it is because I have never known such times before in my eighteen years and that I am unable to write cheerfully—unable even to think straight. Why I am writing this down I cannot say, because I am so fogged in with bad thoughts today that I have decided, out of deep regard for you, to tear this half-filled sheet into tiny, tiny pieces!

Distraught at what she had written, she crossed the room to the fire, ripping as she walked. As though to vent her disgust with herself, she ripped and ripped until the handful of white fragments tossed into the embers was so fine it disappeared almost before it flamed.

Chapter 19

Had it been a normally mild, soft May afternoon when the familiar, always welcome song of the Cannon's Point oarsmen came floating through Anne's open bedroom window, she would have shrieked with joy and pulled Eve along in a happy flight downstairs, across the yard, and down the path to the Couper dock. Instead, when she heard the song, she caught her breath and grabbed Eve's hand. "Stop! Eve, stop brushing my hair and listen. . . ."

Her face shining, Eve gasped, "I hear, Miss Anne! That be June singin'! I can tell him over all the rest. That be June!"

"And it could be my father with him! Unless something else terrible has happened, Papa should be here."

"Course he be here," Eve scolded. "You so grumpy an' down-in-the-mouth these days, you always think bad things goin' on. Lemme quick get your hair pinned."

"No! You go on down to meet June. I look a mess after all that brushing, but I can just stick in a comb. I'll be right down." Eve was already out the bedroom door when Anne called, "Tell Mama Papa's coming, do you hear?"

Anne's hands trembled as she pulled up her thick, dark hair and haphazardly pinned it with one, then two tortoise-shell combs. What if Papa wasn't in the boat with June and the others? Dear God, what if the oarsmen had waited for two days on Sapelo at Mr. Spalding's only to learn that Papa had been in a shipwreck or was too ill to make the long voyage back from Bermuda? The people wouldn't be singing though if Papa wasn't with them, would they?

I don't even know myself anymore, she thought, hurrying down the stairs. I do always expect bad things these days. And I've always felt so happy down inside. I don't want to be like Great-grandmother Maxwell! I want to be me. What makes me even think Papa isn't right out there at our dock this minute?

When she heard the shouts and laughter of the house people running across the yard from all directions to greet their master, she knew he wasn't ill or dead. He was safe and Mama was coming, too, as fast as she could right behind Anne, warning her to be careful not to run too fast in her thin-soled house slippers.

Without even waiting for her mother, she rushed out onto the dock and threw herself into Papa's outstretched arms, weeping, crying out, "You came home! Oh, Papa, you came home!"

"Aye, little Annie. Didn't you expect me?" He was laughing, holding her away from him, trying to look at her face, obviously puzzled at her tears and panic.

"Papa, oh Papa, at least I have one of you back," she said, struggling to control her weeping.

"No letter yet from your lieutenant, lovey?" he asked.

"No, nothing. Nothing. He's certainly in Portsmouth by now, isn't he? I've been so frantic about you both!"

"She has been," her mother said, standing close by now. "I've missed you terribly, too, dearest Jock, but I'm here to tell you our daughter is just like my grandmother Maxwell. When she's separated from her loved ones, she's hopeless."

Anne gave her mother a tearful, apologetic look. "I'm sorry, Mama. Here I am hugging Papa and you feel the way I'd feel if—if John had just stepped onto our dock."

Giving Anne a big kiss, her father joked, "Papas love to be hugged, Daughter. But if you don't mind too much, I would like to put my arms around my wife."

While her parents held one another in a long, affectionate embrace, James Hamilton ran down the path shouting, "Papa, Papa! How did it all go? Did any of our people come back with you? Did you see Admiral Cochrane? What manner of man is he? As bullheaded as Cockburn?"

Father and son shook hands, then hugged each other. Anne could tell by the look on Papa's face that there was a lot he hadn't told her and Mama before his trip to Bermuda. A lot of man things, and her sixth sense let her know that none of it was good.

"I saw Vice Admiral Cochrane," Papa told James. "The man impressed me greatly, but you and I can discuss all that later. Right now, only two things need to be said before I bathe and eat. Cochrane treated me with enormous courtesy, but the other thing I must tell all here assembled is that I failed to bring back even one of our people." An indefinable mumble went through the cluster of house people still waiting to one side of the dock to give a proper welcome to their master. "I wasn't allowed one moment to speak with any of my people still in Bermuda. Admiral Cochrane was gracious in his refusal, but he did refuse me. In fact, most of them had already been shipped to Nova Scotia. Worse than all that, I learned that five from right here at Cannon's Point either died en route north or from the bitter cold up there."

Another wave of low, stunned comment went through the Negroes still standing there. Some gasped, "Lord, have mercy!" Others just made keening noises.

"Ebo June wanted to know during our trip here from Sapelo," Papa went on, "which of our people died. I could find out the names of only two. One was frail, old Aunt Sally, the other was my good blacksmith Cuffy's fine son." Anne saw her father scan the group of silent Negroes. "I'm glad Cuffy isn't here. I'd rather tell him alone that his boy is gone."

While Papa made the rounds shaking hands with each of the house people and William Browne, back at his studies now at Cannon's Point, Anne looked around for Eve. She was alone with June, standing to one side of the path that led away from the Coupers' house to the quarters. The two were just standing side by side, not feeling free, Anne knew, to touch each other before their white folk. June had been waiting at Sapelo for only two days, but Anne could feel Eve's longing for his arms around her. Eve had never told her they didn't feel free to show affection before the Coupers, but suddenly Anne knew. It troubled her, but in a way she didn't understand, so she quickly put it to one side. There had already been too much troubling her. This was not the time to worry about that. This was the time to be glad that at least half of her worries had vanished. Papa was home. She breathed a prayer of thanks and promised God to do a better job of trusting Him.

When her parents began to walk together toward the house, arms linked, Anne welcomed her brother's arm around her. Relieved as she was to have Papa home, she was still frighteningly alone.

Chapter 20

Galloping hard down Frederica Road from George Abbott's house in the old town of Frederica, young James Hamilton's handsome black mount rounded the bend that led into Couper Road. His thoughts were galloping, too, because James's own future looked so promising. His diploma from Yale was neatly framed and hung on the wall of his room at Cannon's Point, and within days he would be in full charge of vast, fertile Hopeton Plantation on the mainland as well as of Hamilton Plantation. Hopeton was still owned jointly by his father and the now absent James Hamilton, but one of his principal goals was to own Hopeton and Hamilton himself. Goals, already set down in his neatly kept journal, spurred him to action. The orderly, logical life he planned for himself would be structured by basic, attainable goals, one already achieved: a week ago, when his father's close friend Hamilton had sailed north, full responsibility for Hamilton Plantation on St. Simons had become his. From now on, James would be running it. Because he meant to succeed, in a year he would own it outright. He lacked words to sympathize properly with Papa's loss when Hamilton left. He would, however, do his best to take the man's place in his father's esteem and trust. Would help him plan how to divide Hopeton and Hamilton slaves in order to compensate for those who had left Cannon's Point.

Even at twenty-one, James lacked his father's natural ebullience, but riding now, the very blood coursing in his veins exhilarated him and he permitted himself a rare measure of conscious celebration because the mid-May day itself was so invigorating. The feeling of celebration would last, of course, only while the occupation of riding prevented his doing anything more profitable with the time. Cantering in and out of sharp black-and-white shadows along the narrow road, he glimpsed an osprey's nest atop a dead pine tree, and he made a careful mental note to examine it more closely later when time allowed.

He was urging the horse now for Sister's sake. In the pocket of his riding jacket he carried the Couper mail picked up at George Abbott's place at Frederica, and although he often had to stifle his own amusement at Anne's highly romantic bent, his heart quickened. He was carrying her longed-for letter right in his pocket. No mistaking it, since it came from Portsmouth, England, where he knew the British Royal Marines who had pillaged Georgia's coastal area had been headed now that the war was finally over.

Not once had it occurred to James Hamilton Couper that he would ever experience emotion toward anyone of the kind his sister showed for her lieutenant. Still, he had set down the goal of marriage for himself someday, being careful, of course, to follow his father's advice in seeking out a suitable, intelligent, but quite young woman. The approximate date beside his goal marked *marriage* was, if he recalled correctly, sometime in the mid-1820s. Certainly no sooner. If need be, even later. A gentleman had to reach a known state of maturity before taking such a serious step. All that could wait for at least another decade or longer.

What was urgent now was to learn all he could of the complex management of Hamilton Plantation on the Frederica River along the southwestern side of St. Simons. That he was born to privilege he never doubted, and unlike some young men his age, he certainly had no intention of allowing his good fortune to corrupt him, make him lazy. His father had struggled for everything he now owned, had worked his way up from a mere indentured clerk to one of the most prosperous planters on the coast. James Hamilton would sooner squander a dollar of his own than a penny of Papa's, and he felt proud that his revered father and Hamilton trusted him with at least the management of Hopeton Plantation on the mainland along with Hamilton's own productive place on St. Simons. He wouldn't allow himself to fail.

I feel satisfied, he thought, even eager to put my talents to such a test.

Galloping around the bend in Couper Road toward the big house, he smiled from sheer pleasure and anticipation. The legal documents had been drawn up and signed before

Mr. Hamilton left—documents that, once he had mastered the intricacies of operating the vast acreage, had come to understand how to handle the Hamilton people, guaranteed James full ownership of the entire holding as a gift from his godfather: "In gratitude and affection for the signal honor of knowing young James Hamilton Couper, son of my treasured friend John and my namesake." James knew that line from the document word for word, but if there was a "signal honor," that honor belonged to him.

In sight of the Cannon's Point house, he slowed the sweating horse, his own mind racing in anticipation of so much to be learned and accomplished as the only son of his greathearted, generous father.

As he walked the horse toward the wide front veranda beside which his groomsman, Jasper, was already waiting, he gave thanks that he, James Hamilton Couper, was but twenty-one. His tenderhearted, somewhat impractical father would have a levelheaded son to watch out for his interests for as long as he lived.

He had no sooner turned the horse over to Jasper when his sister's maid, Eve, appeared on the porch.

"You bring any letters, sir?" she called. "Miss Anne send me to find out."

For an instant James considered a bit of teasing, then thought better of it. Anne *had* been suffering. "You may tell my sister that I did indeed bring letters and unless I'm mightily mistaken, the one she's been waiting for is among them."

The flash of joy on Eve's pretty, bright-skinned face was almost blinding. "Do that mean she hear from—*him*?"

"I would say that's very close to the truth. Now, go!"

Forgetting or just plain ignoring the manners she'd been taught, Eve grabbed the book Anne was reading, jerked her mistress up from the parlor rocker, and shoved her toward the front door.

"Eve! For heaven's sake, what's got into you?" Anne demanded, stopping in the front hall, hands on hips.

"Nothin' got into me," Eve answered, grinning from ear to ear. "You find out once you keep goin' out to the front yard and see your brother, Mausa James."

Anne stiffened. Trying not to think what she so longed to think, she just stood there staring at Eve.

"Lordy, Miss Anne," Eve murmured, her grin gone, "Lordy, I worries 'bout you. 'Fore you even know the good news, you lookin' scared. It be a letter for you from *him*!"

"Please come outside with me, Eve! It could be something terrible. You know, not every letter means good news."

"No, ma'am, I don't know. I never got no letter, but I be right behind you. Go on, see if it be good or bad."

When they reached the porch, James stood halfway up the front steps holding the letter. Anne, trembling all over, clutched Eve's arm, suddenly more frightened, more a stranger to herself than ever. Then she grabbed the letter, pushed Eve away, and, without thanking James, hurried down the steps, across the yard, and ran as hard as she could run toward *their* big tree.

By the time she reached the giant oak, her head had begun to throb, the pain so bad she sank down on a thick, smooth root. Through the weeks of loneliness, she had often run to sit on that same root, seeking safety and shelter, a familiar touch. A familiar touch that was somehow a part of John. Everyone had an occasional headache, she told herself, and as much as this one hurt, it was nothing like the pain in her heart.

"But it's here!" She spoke aloud, kissing the dark-red blob of sealing wax he'd actually touched.

Because of her trembling hands, she ripped too hard, tearing a piece of his dear, strong script. Then, the letter open at last, one sheet fell to the ground and was blown a short distance away by a breeze off the river. When she reached for it, she crushed some tiny star flowers. All her life, Anne had carefully, painstakingly, tried to avoid stepping on even one tender clump of white star flowers. They went almost unnoticed now as she smoothed the two-page letter and began to read.

Wednesday, 5 April 1815
Royal Marine Headquarters
8 Thomas Street
Portsmouth, England

My Beautiful Anne,

If I can contain my troubled thoughts of you, I mean to set down at least a few lines so that Captain

Maddon, in whose care you must write, can oblige me by posting this before noon today. If you are half as disturbed as I at not being able to read one line from you in more than a month, I pity you indeed. After my bad luck up the St. Marys, blood loss caused my mind to wander some, but I believed firmly that I had told you my exact Portsmouth address.

"You did not, John!" she said aloud. "Do you think I wouldn't have had several letters waiting if you'd told me? I didn't have your address until right now. I didn't even know for certain that you were still alive."

She turned the page, hoping, praying that he had told her more about being hurt.

Right after I left you, I was ordered, as you know, to a fracas up the St. Marys and was clipped in my left wing. At least, I think I managed a scrawl to you from Cumberland telling you I was not at death's door. William gave me preferred medical treatment and except for a jagged, red scar, I am now quite recovered. I assume Anna Matilda's parents, upon learning of the peace, brought their slaves back to St. Simons and that our little friend is once more at home at Retreat.

"Yes, John, she is, but is that all you're going to tell me about you? About your poor arm? You didn't even say whether the bullet struck you in your forearm or your dear upper arm."

The second page held his clear, large script on only one side.

Events look promising for the eventual surrender of the rascal Napoleon. I wait daily for word of whether or not my services will any longer be needed now that the war with America is ended. I wait, beloved Anne, with sharply mixed feelings. As surely as I love you, I love the Royal Marines and long to remain an officer for the rest of my life. Equally, I long to return to America and take you once more into my arms.

My kindest regards to your parents and brother and to Miss Page as well. Also to the other friends I flatter myself to have found on that most enchanting isle.

With all my heart, I pray you know in your heart that in me you have indeed found a friend forever. You have found more than a friend and you must never cast away one who loves you wholly. I live my days believing that you care for me within the bonds of true friendship and far, far beyond. My heart is enclosed. Please keep it safely. Do not forget our song. I drink to you only and forever with my eyes. I beg you to give my eyes a letter to devour.

Yrs Affectionately and always,
John Fraser

Still holding the pages, she looked closely for the first time at the trampled star flowers and felt the old sadness at having crushed them. At least, she was feeling again. The pain in her head was worse, but she welcomed even that. Until this moment, she had experienced only despair—flat, hard desolation. Papa's return had helped for a day or two, then she had sunk again into an airless agony, had pushed through her days as though through the stagnant waters of a pond where nothing recognizable lived.

And then, she heard the familiar magic sound: the singular, almost secret call of her favorite songbird. A few times through the years, she had actually seen him singing, his throat seeming to burst with gladness, but more often the bird hid himself when he felt like making music. Now, as usual, he had Anne peering high into the leafy branches above her head, searching, searching for a glimpse of her dear painted bunting, which she and Papa insisted on calling—to James Hamilton's scientific horror—a nonpareil. The highly colored little finch was up there somewhere, his scarlet breast, bright blue cap, and chartreuse shawl as glorious as his song. Why, she wondered, did he always have to hide when the notion struck him to sing in the tip-top of a tree—almost always out of sight? The notion had struck now, though, and this time he was in *their* tree, just above her because the shining, silver bars he pushed out into the soft air hung there, revived her spirit, and began a kind of healing in her heart.

Through her thoughts, other silver melody bars were running too—lessening the desolation. The nonpareil's song wasn't the only music in the universe today. The melody of *their* song, the song John had sung to her, sounded in her memory, bringing her slowly back to being Anne Couper again . . . Anne Couper with a skull-splitting headache, but Anne Couper, woman.

"She's still lying down in her room with the shutters closed, Jock," Rebecca said as the two dined alone the next day. He sat beside her where their hands could touch at will.

"Poor child," he said, spooning the last of Sans Foix's diamondback terrapin soup into his mouth. "Poor, lovesick child."

"I agree she's lovesick, my dear, but Anne is no longer a child. She is more herself, though, since John's letter. Even with the violent headache she complains of, she seemed to be reaching toward me this morning at breakfast." Rebecca smiled. "She had to work at it, but bless her, she made the effort to be her usual, happy self with me."

For a time Jock said nothing as they waited for Johnson to serve the crisp, fried trout Big Boy had caught that very morning. "Our fish course should be especially delicious," he said at last.

"I'm sure it will be, my dear. It has to be if Sans Foix prepares it, and if it isn't the best we've ever tasted, Big Boy will get those huge tears in his eyes."

"I hope you'll make a point of complimenting him should you see the big fellow this afternoon, Becca."

"Do you think for a minute I'd forget a thing like that?"

"I miss Anne!"

Rebecca looked up at him, frowning. "You miss her, Jock?"

"Every hour of every day. She's still here where we can see her and talk to her, thank heaven, but our little girl has, in a way perhaps only a father understands, already left us."

His wife reached to touch his hand. "That's perfectly ridiculous and you know it. Anne just has a beastly headache. Not surprising after all the anxious waiting she's endured, but it will be a long, long time—if ever—before it's necessary to miss her." She shook her head. "Those two may never get together again. Anyway, our daughter's roots are right here at Cannon's Point, planted as deep as roots can be in our skimpy layer of sandy St. Simons soil. We haven't lost her, Jock. We haven't lost Anne at all. You'll see. She's become a woman, but she's still Anne."

Part Two

January 1816–February 1816

Chapter 21

On a mild, overcast January morning right after the start of the new year 1816, Anne rose even earlier than usual, her plans for the day completely made. Dawn came late and darkness fell early, so it was necessary that the daylight hours be laid out ahead of time. Her parents seemed pleased that she wanted to visit Anna Matilda again, so Papa would see that horses were ready and his giant Ebo, Big Boy, free to ride alongside.

Since the still strange, shocking afternoon last September when their new baby, Isabella, had been born to Mama—an exciting but frightening day for Anne—she had stayed close to Cannon's Point in what to her seemed a thoroughly helpless attempt at taking Mama's place in the household. The actual day of Isabella's birth had scared her because, even though Papa declared that their new baby came quite easily, it was Anne's only firsthand experience with the physical suffering women had to endure in order to give babies to their husbands. She had also been excited by the irrevocable fact that the event had deepened her own longing for John. To the personal pain of nearly ten months of separation had now been added a uniquely personal yearning to endure for his sake, as Mama had endured.

The contradiction had made little sense to her then. It made no more sense now as she rode her own horse, Gentleman, through the gentle winter morning down the one island road toward Retreat Plantation. Since the Sunday before Christmas of last year, she had held a shining secret close to her heart, telling no one. Yesterday she realized that could not go on. She absolutely had to tell someone and only Anna Matilda seemed right.

For as long as Anne could remember, even when they were little girls and the Pages, newly arrived on St. Simons, were still staying with Major Butler at Hampton across Jones Creek, the two had cottoned to each other. It had certainly taken Anna Matilda a long time to begin to grow up, but when the Pages visited Cannon's Point just after Christmas, Anne thought she sensed a great change in her. As always, Anne had begun the visit by talking to Anna Matilda as though she were still a mere girl, but in no time, she had been able to tell her a few things about John that she'd never have considered telling her before.

Today Anne was bringing, tucked inside her reticule, not only John's long-hidden, secret gifts—the tiny gold brooch and a single carnelian stone—but what she had begun to think of as his "golden letter"—the one she received in December—with the idea of actually letting Anna Matilda read it. Of course, there was still time to change her mind. She and mostly silent Big Boy, who more and more often rode with her, had a way to go before they even came in sight of Retreat. Big Boy did seem never to speak except when spoken to, but Anne liked him and felt safe with him along because he was so mountainous a man he could probably fend off with his bare hands all three panthers said to roam St. Simons.

As usual, Big Boy rode a little to one side, astride Papa's unruly Buck, because he was the only rider who could keep the horse from bucking at will or jumping over every ditch he passed. Buck still snorted and pranced a lot and had to be reined in firmly during a ride, but he trusted Big Boy, who now and then waved his enormous hand at Anne as though to reassure her that all was well. She was careful each time to give him a smile in return. At almost seven feet and nearly 300 pounds, all muscle, Big Boy had feelings fragile as a young girl's. Without Eve's June, Papa always said that Big Boy, who had come at the same disturbing time when the other Ebos committed suicide, might have been impossible to handle. As enormous as Big Boy was even back then, June, although a stranger too, had taken him in hand and had patiently guided him as though he were a child into the unfamiliar new life in a foreign land. Big Boy was still childlike, but he seemed mostly content now, was utterly dependable and an expert fisherman. He was waving again. Anne smiled and nodded her thanks. The dark giant never failed to respond to a smile.

"I'm so glad you're along today, Big Boy," she called. She was, because he wouldn't mind a bit how long she kept him waiting to see her safely home again this afternoon. With or without one of the Page people, he would simply go fishing.

By now, this day with Anna Matilda had become extremely important. It was urgent in all ways. The days were passing, it was almost her birthday again, but even more crucial, she had to be convinced of Anna Matilda's new, almost sudden maturity. Was life about to change abruptly, magically, for Anna Matilda too? Had Anne and her childhood friend both slipped into womanhood within the space of one year? The still-glowing night at Dungeness almost a year ago when her surprise eighteenth birthday party had been broken into by the British—and by John—had begun such a dizzying change in everything for Anne, her need to share it today was like an Independence Day firecracker waiting to explode.

Never before had she kept anything so vital from Mama and Papa. Telling them every single thing that even mildly interested her had always been completely natural, but since her realization that women do have a sixth sense, she had vowed to follow hers and so had held what John had written totally to herself. An occasional prick of guilt had been quickly dispelled by rationalizing that it was far better not to tell her parents because they would surely worry and fret over the whole glorious prospect. Both would think it all too uncertain, too risky—only a foolish dream. But it wasn't a dream. It was real.

"Of course, it's risky," she said to herself over the steady beat of the two horses as they trotted into the lane that led to the inviting Page cottage and its beautiful gardens stretching all the way to the St. Simons Sound. "Of course, it's uncertain. All of it is uncertain as parents see life, but so be it. That's the way it is."

Trotting Gentleman into the clean, well-kept yard at Retreat, Anne saw exactly what she expected to see—Anna Matilda in her new, bright blue Christmas cape, Mrs. Page standing with her on the front porch of their roomy, eighteenth-century English-style cottage, both waving. They had seen her coming. From her own girlhood, Anne had loved

Mrs. Page and always had to push aside fears shared by her own mother that the poor woman, whose face was so pretty even with its full chin and pudgy cheeks, could easily die young from sheer overweight. She isn't very young now, though, Anne thought, as she and Big Boy checked their horses. Mrs. Page was almost Papa's age, quite a few years older than Major Page. Neither she nor Anna Matilda must ever lose their mothers!

We're too young for that, Anne thought, as Sam, the Pages' eager, dependable boy, held Gentleman's bridle while Big Boy helped Anne dismount. She and her parents and James Hamilton had been making the pleasant trip down to Retreat since Anne and Anna Matilda were children. Suddenly she began to think that everything *wasn't* good about their both having become grown women so fast! There had been such cozy comfort in being little girls, with loving, well-off parents to see to their every want. Being a woman was far more complicated than even Anne had expected. For an instant, she stood in the yard just looking at the welcoming, endearing sight of sweet Mrs. Page dressed in spotless white, a cap like snow on her dark head, its familiar three blue gauze bows in front. A truly beloved woman. Beloved by everyone and, along with intelligent, striking Major Page, so intent on seeing to it that their one child not grow up to be spoiled because of her high station in life.

"We've been watching you ride up," Mrs. Page called, as Anne and Anna embraced in the yard. "We're waiting breakfast for you, dear child!"

"You shouldn't have," Anne said, both arms out to Mrs. Page, "but I'm certainly glad you did." After the always comfortable, ample, warm embrace, Anne gave her a sly smile. "Dare I hope? Dare I?"

"You certainly may hope, my dear," Mrs. Page chuckled, "because I've already ordered them made. Joan's fluffy pancakes first and then for dessert at dinner you shall have all my arrowroot pudding you can possibly eat."

Anne hugged her again. "With that light-as-a-feather vanilla sauce?"

"Mama always sees to the best meals on earth," Anna Matilda said, "but somehow, even with Papa in Darien, when it's you, Anne, she fusses even more over everything, especially your favorite dessert."

Just then, Lady, the Pages' superb housekeeper—the head, as she called herself—appeared in the front door to announce breakfast. Behind her, also to greet Anne, stood Joan, the cook, Old Betty, Polly and Lilla, Haynie, Anna Matilda's nurse, Minerva, Rutty, and a gathering knot of other servants.

Feeling almost as though she were bidding a bittersweet farewell to her own childhood, Anne smiled to herself when, as always, Lady stood carefully to one side of the others. In all ways Lady *was* "the head." No wonder their parents invariably commented, each time island families visited each other, on how good it was to see everything still the same. There was something very like longing connected to being older, Anne thought, realizing that this time next year she'd be—twenty!

Chapter 22

Breakfast over, Anna Matilda could stand the suspense no longer. From her first sight today of Anne Couper, she knew something was about to happen—something momentous. As deftly as she could manage, she gained her mother's permission for the two of them to be excused to take a second cup of coffee in Anna Matilda's room upstairs. As always, Mama made it easy and now they sat—Anne on the four-poster bed, Anna in her favorite little cherry rocker—just looking at each other.

"What, Anne?" she demanded. "What is it? I thought we'd never finish breakfast, but you know Joan and Lady are both cross for days if everyone doesn't stuff to the eyeballs on Joan's pancakes. I can tell you're here for an important reason, so what is it?"

In answer, Anne jumped up, hurried across the room to the sewing table where she'd laid her reticule, took out a little blue velvet box and handed it to Anna Matilda. "Open it," Anne said, "and you'll know everything!"

Lifting the tightly sprung lid, she looked at the delicate, flawlessly twisted gold brooch and a quite ordinary piece of reddish carnelian beside it on the white satin liner of the box. The brooch certainly was lovely, although it needed some polishing, but what did Anne mean when she said Anna Matilda would know everything once she'd seen inside the box?

She looked at her friend, who was perched eagerly on the edge of the bed, obviously expecting an exclamatory response of some kind, but what? "I'm—I'm growing up, I think," Anna Matilda said hesitantly, "but maybe not as fast as you believe, Anne. What is it I'm supposed to know?

Please tell me! I—I really am longing to find out. I can tell something very—*mature* is in the wind."

"It's John, silly," Anne said in her most condescending manner. "The brooch and that breathtaking piece of carnelian are gifts from John! I couldn't keep my secret any longer. Not a minute longer than it took to ride down here today. But you'd just better be grown up enough to trust. You'd better be!"

"Trust with what? Did you just get these gifts from John?"

"No, I've had them a long time. He sent them as soon as he had a chance to visit his father's house in London, late last year."

"I keep forgetting his father lives in London."

"Well, he does. He's been a wine merchant there since before John's mother died and I think that was about ten years ago."

"He sent these gifts to you from London?"

"I just told you he did. They belonged to his mother and were at the family home in London."

For a long time Anna Matilda just looked at her. "All right, Anne, you can stop giving me your withering look." She had surprised herself by saying it because she'd always felt rather submissive with Anne Couper. "I'll be eighteen this year and you'll be nineteen in just a few days. I think it's time we begin to converse the way your mother and mine talk to each other. I'm only a year younger and it might be a lot more comfortable if I looked *at* you instead of *up* to you the way I always have. So, tell me without acting as though I should have known all along why you've kept the brooch and that piece of carnelian a secret for so long. Surely your parents know. Surely you showed your dear mother!"

"No one but you has laid eyes on them, I swear."

"Because your parents would have made you return the gifts?"

Anne's quick, warm smile made Anna Matilda want to hug her friend. She hurried to sit on the bed beside Anne.

"This is just like old times, isn't it? We're having secrets again! Maybe growing more mature also includes knowing exactly how old *and* how young we really are. Do you think that could be true?"

The look on Anne's face seemed both relieved and embarrassed. "Sometimes lately," she said, "I think you may be outgrowing me, Anna Matilda Page. That was a wise thing you just said. It is hard to pin oneself down exactly as to years. Except, of course, when it comes to falling in love forever and ever and ever!"

Anna Matilda felt her eyes prickle with tears. "Yes," she whispered. "And sometimes I despair of that ever happening to me. The days just keep going by with only fat or skinny or pockmarked island boys trooping around and I worry a lot that—" She looked down at the still-open blue velvet box and saw suddenly why the fairly common-looking piece of carnelian looked so breathtakingly beautiful to Anne. "I worry that no one truly important will ever give me treasures of love like these."

"What's happened to me should prove to you that's just not true," Anne said sternly. "Who would have thought only days before we stopped at your dock here one year ago to take you with us to the Dungeness house party that such a miracle was about to happen for me?"

"I remember you did believe something would happen. We both longed to attend Mrs. Shaw's party, but you always felt you had an unknown reason. I'm sure I remember that. And even if I do find someone to love who wants to marry me one day, none of it could be as romantic, as downright amazing as Lieutenant John Fraser—literally capturing you."

Anne looked dreamily past her friend, out the window toward the sound and the vast ocean blurring into the gray, misty winter sky. "He did capture me," she mused.

"And you also captured him!"

"Yes. I also captured him. And Anna Matilda, it's all settled!"

Anna literally jumped. "It's all *settled*? What on earth do you mean? You've always had something new and exciting to tell me all our lives—every time we've been together—but are you telling me now that you and John are going to get married? When? How? With John all the way across the ocean in England, how can you possibly do that?"

Again, instead of the expected response, Anne walked almost sedately back to the table where her reticule lay, took out a letter, returned slowly to where Anna Matilda sat, and then just stood there holding John's letter without saying a word.

"What, Anne, what? You're acting so funny. As though you can't say what you mean to say."

Anne nodded, her pale blue eyes growing darker as though they mirrored the depths of her feeling. "I thought I'd be so full of joy I'd have trouble keeping my voice down so that no one else could hear," she said weakly. "It—it isn't like that at all. You're right. I can't say it!" She held out the letter. "I have to trust you to read it for yourself." When Anna Matilda reached for the letter, Anne drew it back. "I can trust you not to tell a single soul, can't I? Not your mother—not anyone?"

"Cross my heart," she said, but not too convincingly.

Once more Anne held out the letter. This time, Anna Matilda made no move to take it. Not because she didn't long to find out, but suddenly she wondered if she would be able to hold back something so important from her mother. The most natural thing on earth had always been to tell Mama first of all. Telling Mama about anything that troubled her had always been the same as telling God. Now, this minute, without warning, she felt divided, as though she were two persons. As though she herself were still a young girl who stood on one side of a high wall, while on the other side stood a woman, calmly thinking things through. They were the same person and they were not the same person. The wall was, she knew, too high for her to scale and one person in her seemed unable to communicate with the other. In a funny way, the young girl longed to speak to the older woman, who definitely knew the right solution. Right now Anna Matilda felt irrevocably drawn to the woman she was becoming, who seemed less and less a stranger.

"Can't you be a little more convincing when you promise not to tell anyone?" Anne asked.

And then, the wall was gone. The young girl named Anna Matilda Page *was* the same person as the thoughtful, calm woman who had, only seconds ago, been standing out of reach on the other side of that wall. "Yes," she said. "I can be more convincing. After all, you and I have been best friends for most of our lives. Friends keep confidences. You're not asking me to shut out my mother, just to keep a confidence for you."

The anxiety left Anne's face, and once more she held out the letter. "It took me a long time to decide to ride down here today," Anne said. "I came mainly to let you read what John wrote. You want to read it, don't you? Aren't you just dying to know?"

"Yes! Oh, yes, and I think I'm maturing, or I'd have grabbed it out of your hand right off." She handed the blue velvet box to Anne. "Another thing I just realized is that while I'm reading the letter, *you* should be holding this box of treasures from John. Even before I find someone for myself, I seem to know—really to understand—that you own this little box in some quite special, eternal way. Oh, Anne, you can trust me. It scared me some at first when you asked me not to tell even Mama, but now I promise."

The two rushed into each other's arms—both laughing.

"It isn't a very long letter," Anne said in an excited whisper. "Oh, read, read! Please read. . . ."

Eagerly, Anna Matilda unfolded the letter.

20 November 1815
Liverpool

My Beautiful Anne,

This will be brief since a fellow officer waits to post it himself on the first boat to Savannah. And, Anne, my beloved, in just two days, I'll be on my way to you! I have been discharged from my much valued unit, am now on half pay and free to come to you.

"Anne! John will be here any day!"

Anne could only nod yes, yes, still clutching the box and beaming pure joy.

I pray you are deeply affected by the news that I will be, as you read this, bounding toward you on the high seas. My heart is broken that my services with the Royal Marines are no longer needed, and I will certainly keep trying to rejoin, but I find I cannot endure one more day away from you. Now, my sailing date is as definite as any can be. On November 22, I will set sail. Some five or six weeks beyond that date, you will know everything because my arms will tell you. Blessedly, peace has come to my country. Even Napoleon is in exile on his Elba Island and I am also about to get out of exile and back in your arms. My brother, who has his heart set on being present at my wedding, will sail with me. Wait for me, Anne, and please be ready to marry me.

Yr adoring John Fraser

The girls were embracing again because neither knew what else to do. Finally, Anna Matilda asked, "How long have you had this letter?"

"Since Sunday services at Mr. Beck's house on Christmas Eve."

"How did you do it? How have you kept all this a secret from everybody?"

"I don't know! I don't even know how I kept breathing. How will I keep breathing until he gets here? Do you suppose he's hoping to be at Cannon's Point on my birthday? Do you realize that's this week? Isn't this the eighth of January?"

"Don't you even know what day it is?" Anna Matilda hugged her again. "Anne! If you haven't even told your parents he's coming, your wedding plans won't be finished. Your father has to engage the Reverend Matthews to marry you. It takes weeks to prepare food and decorate the house for a big wedding. Won't your parents be furious? At least, hurt?"

"No."

"No?"

"There won't be a big wedding. You know how some people on St. Simons still are. Mama said they were talking something terrible because poor, skinny Suzy Mack's parents had the bad taste to make a big social event out of her wedding over two weeks ago."

"It certainly wasn't what could be called a big wedding."

"Only because her parents aren't particularly well liked, but people are still just so upset, Papa says, over what the British did to us. And after all, John was a British Royal Marine."

Anna Matilda looked perplexed. "But no one anywhere on the island thinks John Fraser had anything to do with persuading a single Negro to desert. He really must be a strange man. Have you thought of that?"

"He is not! He simply promised me he would do all he could to keep Papa's people from leaving. And he did. He didn't make a single enemy the whole time the British were here. That's not strange, that's wholly admirable."

"Since we're being so grown-up and forthright today, maybe I'd better tell you something. Papa told us yesterday that one of our Retreat people heard on the grapevine that Lieutenant Fraser even called a meeting of Cannon's Point people and urged them *not* to believe what the British Regulars had been telling them about the good life they'd live if they deserted your father. Did you know he did that?"

Wide-eyed, Anne said, "No, I didn't. But isn't that just like him? Isn't that just like something John would do?"

"I—I guess so, but—"

"What do you mean, you guess so? It's just like him!"

"But," Anna Matilda said, genuinely puzzled, "sometimes I get so mixed up."

"About what?"

"If John loves his military unit so much, how is it he could call that meeting to convince the Negroes *not* to do what the British Army so wanted them to do—desert? Doesn't that bother you at all, Anne?"

"Of course not." She lifted her chin. "He simply promised me he'd try to protect my father's property. He kept that promise even more truly than he let me know. I didn't hear a thing about the meeting he called, which proves he's not only true to his word, he's humble. And no smart remarks about the fact that because he's so handsome, he doesn't look very humble." Abruptly, Anne sank down on the bed. "What really bothers me is that I hate the whole idea of his loving the military in the first place. I don't want him to be a part of killing! Not ever again."

"But he's discharged now."

"You didn't read his letter very carefully. He also said he'll go on trying to get back in. I hate that!" A slightly defiant smile lit her face. "If I'm his wife, though, he'll have me to—to contend with if he does try."

"He will, Anne? You'd actually argue with him for doing what he most wants to do?"

"I won't argue. I just intend to make him so happy while he's here on St. Simons Island, he'll forget all about his old unit."

Deciding she'd better not pursue such a ticklish subject, Anna Matilda asked, "Do you think he'll look very different out of his elegant uniform?"

Anne shrugged. "Maybe, but he'll still be John, and to me, the very sight of him will always be—beautiful." She kissed the little velvet box. "Oh, how can I wait? How can I possibly wait? It could be another whole week before his ship docks in Savannah."

"Do you really think your parents will agree to let you get married so soon? And do you really think you won't be sorry someday that you missed having a big, elegant wedding at Cannon's Point?"

"Yes, they'll agree and no, I won't be sorry. What matters —all that matters is that we will be *married.*" Anne got to her feet and stood looking down at Anna Matilda, almost comically assuming her mature woman manner. "I must tell you, dear friend," she said, "that I've really enjoyed our talk today. I believed you were ready for it. I was right. I'm deeply grateful that I was."

Anna Matilda had to stifle a giggle. How like Anne, she thought. Nothing makes her so happy as being proved right. She felt happy too, though, because she did look up to Anne Couper and still needed her approval. A wave of surprising helplessness swept over her before she could think of anything adequate to say. Growing up required a kind of courage she hadn't expected it to require. With all her heart, she wanted Anne always to be as happy as she was this minute, but for the first time she realized that Anne's happiness could mean that she would go away to England to live. The thought struck terror.

"What is it?" Anne asked. "You look almost stricken. Dearest friend, your day will come. I know how lonely you've been this year past since your parents came back from Darien. I've even written to John about it. I tell him everything, even that I pictured you down here at Retreat without me to talk to, taking solitary walks by the water, longing, wondering if the day will ever come when someone else is there to walk with you."

"Anne Couper, that isn't why my eyes kind of filled up at all! I just realized that when you're married, you'll probably have to move all the way to London or some other faraway place and I'll never see you again."

On impulse, Anne embraced her. "Oh, you can't know that for sure. I'll have something to say about it all, don't forget. And nothing matters now except that John's coming soon, and wherever we live, we'll never, never be apart again."

"I'm as happy as anyone can be that he's coming and that you'll be married, Anne, but I need some time to face up to the idea that I'll probably lose you forever. And if I feel this sad, how will your dear parents feel when the time comes for you to leave?"

Chapter 23

Never faithful at keeping a diary, Anne was determined to take it up again this morning, Wednesday, 10 January 1816, the day before her nineteenth birthday. Mama had urged her to write daily in the pretty, silk-bound journal. "It's good for a woman," she'd said again at breakfast. "There are thoughts that one needs to articulate, but which all of us at times find hard to talk about to another person. So many things we say, even in a close family like ours, are worded in a way that almost forces a certain response. That isn't necessary in a diary. There we can feel perfectly free. Please go back to it. You'll be glad someday."

I will be glad, Anne thought, reaching for the small book with all its neglected blank pages. I'd give almost anything if I'd kept it all along because I honestly don't know now how I lived through almost a whole year without him. What did I do? How did I pass the hours, the days, the weeks—the endless waits between his letters?

She had kept all his letters, had read and reread them, could fill some of the time today by reading them again, but there wasn't any way to do it without stirring up the nagging worry that seemed to be growing in her. It had helped to tell Anna Matilda that John was coming to marry her *and* that she had begun to despise the thought of his ever returning to the military. But rereading his dear sentences, each one of which ignored her pleas that he never return to his or any other branch of the military, would only worry her more. Nowhere in any letter had John argued for, or even defended his attachment to, his life in the Royal Marine Artillery. To Anne, he had done the worst thing he could do—ignore the whole subject. More than anything she hated being ignored. Didn't he know her better than that? Maybe not. How could either of them know the other well in such a short time? Still, John had become her life. No longer did she have any doubt that she had also become his. There would be time, years of time ahead, to learn each other. Maybe writing in the diary today would help keep her worry in perspective. Today was not the time for nagging doubts, only the time for happy anticipation, for joy too engulfing to contain. He was coming back to her! At this very moment he was surely on the ocean, his ship splitting huge waves, plowing, plowing toward Georgia.

Dipping her quill, she recorded the date and began to write:

> In just a matter of days my life will begin, and no matter how old I am when I reread these lines, I will know the eternal meaning of what I have just written. My beloved John is coming back to me. Soon he will actually be here, close enough to touch, close enough so that I can hear his voice, his laughter. So that I can see his dear eyes so full of love, so deep and gray. If only writing this will help me hold that thought, perhaps the *worry* will lessen. He has written that with Britain no longer at war with Napoleon or my own country, he is now discharged from the military at half pay. My silly heart should be only singing and yet there is the worry. I am truly relieved that he is no longer an actor in such scenes of misery and death as come with any war, but is he bereft away from his beloved unit? If he is, how can I be so glad of something that causes him sadness?

Unable to sit there a minute longer, she threw down the quill and went to look out over the dear, familiar yard of Cannon's Point from the house to the river, seeking quiet and solace and security in the nourishing sight of Papa's lovingly tended gardens and groves—the winter sun glancing off dark-green orange and magnolia leaves. She looked away toward the soft, usually restful gray of the olive grove, beyond the green-black, rounded silhouettes of tall longleaf pines over on Little St. Simons, and beyond that, to the sea. The same sea that was bringing John back where he belonged—to her arms. The olive grove did not rest her today.

Even the thought of rest was maddening. She needed to dance, to sing, to cry, to climb a tree. . . .

"I'm going to be married," she whispered. "Soon, probably in less than a month, I'll be Mrs. John Fraser!" She knew her parents would never stand in the way of her happiness and she meant to tell them any time now that John was on his way to her. As perceptive as they were, Mama and Papa would both know why he was coming back, coming back to *her* even though his heart ached for the life's work he loved above all others. She shuddered. John's sadness at leaving the military could not last. It must not. It would be up to her to find a way to fill his empty place, to pack it so full of joy and laughter and music and love that he would want to lift his beautiful voice for more reasons than just to please her.

She looked again out over the familiar sweep of Cannon's Point land and marsh to the sea. In his letters John had written all that she needed to know about everything *but* his willingness to try to live a regular life, to try working at something else—anything else but being a Royal Marine.

A new thought seized her: Maybe he wasn't really ignoring her dread of his going back to the military. Maybe he knew deep in his heart that the British wars were over, that there was little or no chance of his ever being able to get back in his unit, and so, because his loss was so great, he simply considered silence the safest way to handle the whole subject until they could be together again.

Still, loving her as he did, how could he not know that for Anne, response meant everything? Even if the response was the wrong one, some response was better than silence from anyone she loved. Now and then, Mama fell silent, never Papa. Papa always answered, always smiled back at her, made a joke, or at least frowned if he disagreed with what she wanted.

Had she remained silent with both parents because she'd thought it unfair to tell Papa she would be marrying John and not tell Mama? Why not Mama? Had she feared Mama's falling into one of her silent spells until Anne and John had a chance to get to know each other better? She refused the whole idea. She had kept her secret from her parents for one reason and one only—the warmth and excitement of holding it all to herself. It had helped to tell Anna Matilda, to find her so grown-up and understanding. Anne didn't know exactly why it had helped so much except that she knew herself not to be really secretive. Sharing with those she loved had always defined her very life. Could her continued silence with her parents, both of whom she adored, be part of the reason she found herself troubled now? She also rejected that. Her one worry was John's missing his life in the Royal Marines. No point in making things more complicated than they were.

Undoubtedly, she thought, I'm still in the process of learning how to be a woman in love.

Over an hour ago, Eve had fixed her hair. She was dressed in a freshly ironed flower-sprigged day dress, but because she didn't know what else to do, she sat down at her dressing table and toyed with her curls.

I could get out some needlepoint, she thought, knowing full well that she wouldn't. "Why?" she asked aloud. Why didn't he ever write one single thing about his future plans? How he intends to earn our living once we're married? John Fraser's the most gregarious, outgoing, talkative man I know outside of Papa, she thought. He loves to talk to all kinds of people and he can converse so charmingly, so intelligently, about anything he chooses. Of course, it's true, he didn't mention having a brother for what seemed to her a very long time, but he had explained that.

Looking around to be sure Eve hadn't slipped into the room, she began studying her own face in the looking glass, wondering if she was truly beautiful. Not really, she decided, even though Papa had always declared her so and even though John always began his letters with "My Beautiful Anne." She did have good cheekbones and wide-set, light, light blue eyes. Her medium-sized, straight, fairly good nose came, Mama said, from the Maxwells. James Hamilton had a prominent nose, something like Papa's. Actually, Papa and her John resembled each other a lot. To her, they looked enough alike to be father and son. Both had somewhat long faces. Except that John had that arresting cleft in his chin, and only John had John's perfect mouth and elegantly arched dark eyebrows. And only John's arms knew how to hold her. Her face must have a certain kind of beauty, she thought, wetting her finger to smooth her own brows.

The new, still-unfamiliar ache deep inside had pushed through her with this kind of intensity for the first time only a few days ago. It was there again.

Once, John had actually told her of his own aching body,

the urgency of it when he held her in his arms. She had only felt those arms, the deep, strong chest, from outside his gold-buttoned, red officer's jacket. This minute, she dared to imagine the agony and the bliss when John's body would no longer be covered by thick, scratchy wool and braid.

"You fussin' wif your hair without me to see to it, Miss Anne?" Eve scolded from the doorway.

Anne whirled on her. "Eve! You've got to stop barging into my room like that. Don't you care that you frightened me half to death?"

When Eve laughed at her, Anne felt like crawling under the carpet, but she made herself laugh a little too.

"What I should do—bang two pots together to warn you? I know what you been doin', though. You don' fool me none."

"What do you mean you know what I was doing when you hurtled through that doorway?"

"You dreamin' 'bout *him.* 'Bout havin' his arms round you."

"Eve!"

"He comin' back soon, ain't he?" Eve laughed again. "You keepin' it all secret, but I knows."

"What do you know?"

"That your man be comin' back to Georgia."

There was no way Eve could know that! She and Anne had been together every day with no mention of her secret. Except for that weird practice the people called their grapevine, she simply could not know. Anyway, someone had to put the word out on the grapevine in the first place, and only Anna Matilda knew.

Anne jumped to her feet. She needed to stand face-to-face with Eve if there was to be an encounter. "Did you come up here for something special?" Anne asked. "Or just to plague me?"

"You happy tomorrow be your birthday?" Eve wanted to know, tucking a stray curl back in place behind Anne's ear. "Seem to me like Mausa Couper an' Miss Becca be happier than usual 'bout it."

"You're imagining again."

"I am not! Miss Becca an' Mausa Couper, they want you should come down to the front parlor—*now.* They axed me to see you come."

A shiver of anxiety ran through Anne and for want of something better, she asked, "Now?"

"Now. Mausa Couper, he say not to leave him for to fleech."

This made Anne laugh. *"Fleech,* Eve? Do you know the meaning of the word?"

"No, ma'am. But I keep it in my mind til I git up here."

"It's one of Papa's Scottish words. What he meant was for me not to make him *coax* me downstairs. *Fleech* is Scottish for coax." She frowned. "Don't you have any idea what they want to talk to me about?"

Eve's sly grin was worse than no response at all. She knew something Anne didn't know and that not only infuriated Anne, it made her ashamed. Ashamed to the marrow of her bones for keeping such an important secret from Mama and Papa. She had known for weeks that John was on his way back to St. Simons to marry her. Not one word had she told her parents. Other girls she knew kept things from their mothers and fathers for various good reasons, but Anne had no good reason at all. Her parents had never once been really unfair with her. Even when they disciplined her, they made sure she understood fully why she must never repeat the behavior. So seldom had she dreaded a talk with either of them, this moment of shame seemed almost too hard to live through.

"Mausa Couper gonna *fleech* if you don't git downstairs," Eve said, then clapped her hands in a way that was intended to make Anne feel like a bad child—and did.

"You asked quite a lot of Eve, Jock," Rebecca said after Eve hurried upstairs to Anne's room. "I'd like to have heard how your instructions were really carried out up there."

"You mean when I told her to tell Anne that I said, 'dinna' make me fleech'?" He chuckled. "I'd also like to know how Eve delivered my message. But this is a wonderful plan we've concocted, wife, *if* you're quite sure Baby Isabella will be all right in Liz's care."

"Of course, she'll be all right. Liz is nursing her anyway. I'll miss the dear child, but she'll be fine without me." She smiled. "After all, her mother's quite out of practice caring for an infant. Nearly nineteen years is a long time!"

"Very well, if you say so. I admit I'll enjoy the whole adventure far more with you along. And remember now, not one word to Anne when she gets here that I knew of John Fraser's arrival even before she did or that we feel the least bit slighted that she's kept the big secret all to herself."

"You know perfectly well that you're the one who has to be careful. I did not feel hurt or the least bit slighted. I understood. That's why I urged her to begin keeping her diary again. I knew she was a bundle of nerves inside. But, Jock, are you sure we're doing the right thing to agree so quickly to Anne's marrying a gentleman who has no idea how he's going to support her?"

"No, I'm far from sure we're doing the right thing, but John did the honorable, straightforward thing to have let me know even before he wrote Anne that he himself was unsure of his future. Such honesty goes a long way with me. Perhaps because I didn't know how I'd support you, either, Becca. There are times when a young person needs the faith of his elders."

"I'm willing," Rebecca said firmly. "Our daughter's life revolves around John Fraser. I may have appeared far more strict with her than you, but I love her as much, although I do think she might have told us about her letter from the lieutenant. I'm sure she got one. Not a word to her own parents that they plan to be married. John told you in his earlier letter that he was waiting only a few days to write Anne of his plans to come back to marry her."

"Now, Becca, Anne only meant to keep us from worrying."

"Worry! How on earth can a mother plan a daughter's wedding without talking to her about it?"

"There can be no big wedding, Rebecca. Even though you and I accept John, trust him, we also have to live among radical American Patriots, island neighbors who matter to us and who would strongly disapprove of our taking so recent an enemy into our family. Granted, the Wyllys would be delighted to honor a groom late of the British Royal Marines, but there must be no big social wedding on St. Simons anytime soon."

Rebecca got up from her chair by the parlor fire and went to kiss his red hair. Even pulled back into its queue, it felt thick, the hair of a young man. "Calm yourself, Mr. Couper. I'm not even considering an elaborate wedding, as much as I've longed for one. So, don't fret about my inviting any of our neighbors who might harbor ill feelings toward John.

From now on, we're going to think of the boy as simply Scottish, like us."

"Aye and your old husband has a thought or two concerning his future work now that he's no longer a Royal Marine." A finger to his lips, he whispered, "Listen! I hear her lovesick highness descending the stair. She sounds a bit hesitant, perhaps, but she's on her way down."

"Anne, dear," Rebecca called as their daughter came slowly across the downstairs hall. "Come in! Your father and I have a surprise for you!" Whispering, too, now, she added, "*You* tell her, Jock."

Anne spoke almost timidly from the doorway. "You wanted to see me?"

"Aye, Daughter," Couper said. "Sit down, sit down. Unlike a certain exceedingly pretty member of this household, your mother and I dislike keeping secrets. Especially do we dislike keeping one when it directly concerns our elder daughter, who, tomorrow, if memory serves, will celebrate her nineteenth birthday."

Rebecca thought Anne's relieved giggle sounded much more like twelve than nearly nineteen, but she too felt relief when Anne ran to hug her father.

"I love you, Papa." Hugging Rebecca, too, she added, "I love you, Mama. And I've been dreadful!"

"You have?" Jock teased. "We thought you were acting normally for an eighteen-year-old whose heart was deeply pierced by Cupid's dart."

"You know you just made a dreadful poem, don't you, Papa?"

"Aye, Annie, I know that, but we do have a glorious plan. A birthday surprise for you."

Rebecca watched Anne closely, studied her young, vulnerable face for every sign of pleasure or resistance. After all, the girl had been locked within her own world for days, undoubtedly making her own plans for John's arrival. Poor child didn't even know yet that John Fraser had already asked for her hand in a warmly personal letter to Jock.

"Now, my dear girl," Jock was saying. "Are you all ears to know what's afoot?"

His boyish excitement seemed to put Anne on guard. "I—I guess so, Papa."

"As a special birthday present, you, your mother, and I

will leave tomorrow morning for Darien and from there, I've arranged passage on a Spalding schooner to Savannah."

"Savannah, Papa? We can't do that!"

"And why can't we?"

"Uh—little Belle needs Mama!"

"You know perfectly well that Liz is splendid with infants. Besides, your mother and I want you to shop in the city for some new gowns and anything else you need or want. We'd thought to spend a few days with our friends the Mackays, but your mother just heard from dear Mrs. Eliza Mackay and—well, you tell her, Becca."

"Mrs. Mackay begged to be excused," Rebecca explained. "She feels so sorry, but she has a brand new baby and with Mr. Mackay still recovering from his recent heart attack, she's arranged for us to stay nearby at the Minises. Eliza Mackay says we must not stop at any Savannah hotel unless we want a harvest of bedbugs."

When Anne buried her face in her hands, Rebecca went to her.

"Did I say something wrong, Becca?" Her husband's voice sounded so startled and helpless, she knew it was time for her to take charge.

"Listen to me, Anne. I wanted your father to have the pleasure of telling you of our surprise, but I sense you're even more upset with the idea of a trip to Savannah than either of us suspected. John wrote to your father days ago—before he wrote to you—asking for your hand in marriage. We mistakenly thought you'd tell us when your letter came. But we believe you had every right to hold it to yourself for a few days. We only meant to surprise you. With the best intentions, we did a very insensitive thing. Neither of us wanted John Fraser to reach Savannah without a proper welcome from the Coupers."

Jock was standing now, looking at Anne with such adoration and expectancy, Rebecca longed to embrace him.

For a moment, no one said anything. Then Anne dropped her hands from her face and gave them both a warm smile. "I—I have been dreadful, haven't I?"

"Not dreadful at all, my dear," Rebecca said. "Just too much alone. In a family like ours, it isn't good to be alone for such long periods of time. Your father and I wish John had more definite plans for your future, but we—we want so much to do the right thing for all concerned."

Giving the girl his warmest smile, Jock said, "We've missed you, Daughter."

"I've missed both of you, too," Anne said more brightly than Rebecca had dared hope. "So—so much has changed. I know it seems as though I've been away. I haven't." She looked beseechingly at her mother. "Oh, Mama, I've missed John so much!"

"But, my dear, we all know he's on the high seas somewhere right now on a ship called the *Neptune.* Don't you see that's why we have to go to Savannah?"

A flicker of anger flared in Anne's eyes. "He didn't tell me in my letter that he'd be sailing on a boat called the *Neptune.*"

When she saw the girl rush abruptly into her father's outstretched arms, Rebecca felt herself swept unexpectedly into a roaring sea of uncertainty and dread over Anne's future. That they had made Anne happy for now she had no doubts. She would simply have to settle for that. She and Jock must leave Anne's uncertain future, even where their daughter might be living, in God's hands.

There were times, after all, when that was the only thing sensitive, loving parents could do for a child.

Chapter 24

Anne's birthday picnic took place on Thomas Spalding's family schooner along the waterway between Darien and Savannah, which they reached just as darkness was falling across the city. Sans Foix, of course, had filled boxes and hampers with specially prepared food for the occasion—tender ham slices, roast chicken, shrimp remoulade, more of Anne's favorite deviled eggs than even she could manage, and a high, multilayered spice cake swirled with foamy caramel icing. Far too excited to eat, she did her level best to pretend she was hungry and stuffed herself so that the thought of still more food at the Minises, where they would be staying, was more than she could face.

To please Mama, she went along for a visit to the Mackay house on East Broughton Street and by eight o'clock the night they arrived, she sat with the two older ladies in Miss Eliza Mackay's parlor, entering into the pleasant conversation as little as possible, lost in her own leaping thoughts of John's arrival. Her father was with Miss Eliza's husband, Robert, talking, she was sure, about the effects of the recent war on coastal planters with Mr. Mackay and the strikingly handsome young Mark Browning from Philadelphia, who now lived with the Mackays.

Had John not filled her thoughts, she would have been paying more attention to what Miss Eliza and Mama were saying, in case they discussed the tall, elegant young Mark Browning. Any unattached girl would have listened closely. Not Anne. She did think about Mark Browning and Anna Matilda, who had found no one so far, but not for long, because it was actually possible that John could be in Savannah by tomorrow. Papa had promised to inquire first thing in the morning about the expected docking time of the *Neptune.* What she already knew was that she meant to get married almost the minute they got back to Cannon's Point. If James Hamilton was down at Hamilton Plantation still busily designing a new drainage system, one of Papa's people would have to ride to Retreat to inform Anna Matilda that she was to be Anne's maid of honor, then to Pike's Bluff to notify the Reverend Matthews, who would perform the wedding ceremony.

On the schooner from Darien, she and Mama had decided that except for Anna Matilda and her parents, the Spaldings, the Goulds, and the British Wyllys, only family would be present. Family, of course, to Anne, included Eve, Mr. Browne, and all the house people. She had been Eve's attendant when, in the Cannon's Point parlor, Eve had jumped over a broom the day she married June. For the first time, she realized how perfectly sensible it was that Negroes took time only to adorn a hat with flowers and then, amid laughter and singing, to jump over a broom. As a little girl, she'd listened, enraptured, when Mama told her of the splendid, huge wedding Anne would have someday, the big house filled with flowers and guests. Such a waste of time and energy now seemed utterly ridiculous. John had changed all that. John had changed everything.

Just as she was struggling to imagine how she could possibly sleep a wink tonight, a question her mother asked Miss Eliza caught her attention.

"Oh, my dear," Mama was saying, "how did you get any rest at night out there at your Savannah River plantation with your husband so ill? Weren't you beside yourself with worry and fear—alone in the house except for a woman servant and your children?"

Miss Eliza's soft, half-laugh seemed to pierce Anne's heart. She began to listen.

"Of course, I lived with fear the whole time, Mrs. Couper," Eliza Mackay said. "And I don't think I did rest much, but I wasn't alone, you know. Our wonderful young friend Mark Browning was there with us. The boy was almost as torn up as I was. Mark sat beside Robert hour after hour while I rested. By day, he kept the children occupied. He was always there when I needed him. I wasn't brave at all." Miss Eliza took a deep breath. "I don't know how I managed to live through Robert's heart attack. Each time I even tried to face the fact that I might have to—live the remainder of my life without him, I almost suffocated."

Anne's own thoughts took over again when her mother began to tell Mrs. Mackay that she had no idea how she would ever manage without Papa. *John is young,* Anne kept thinking—thinking hard—repeating the words to herself. John is young. Mr. Mackay, handsome as he is, isn't young. He's in his forties, I'm sure. She squelched the thought that Papa was almost fifty-seven. But Papa was strong—tall and strong and healthy. And it would be years and years and years before John would be old enough to fall deathly ill.

When Miss Eliza began to tell Mama that their Savannah doctor thought an ocean voyage might help her husband recover fully and that later this summer, he and young Mr. Browning would be taking their two sons north to place them in a good school, Anne began to wonder when Mama would ever say it was time for them to get back to their rooms at the Minises down the street.

She only half heard Miss Eliza tell her mother that she was thirty-eight. Nineteen years Anne's senior. Old. With children and a husband who wasn't at all well. Thousands, millions of minutes had passed already for Eliza Mackay. Time, Anne had heard, didn't drag by for older people as it dragged for those who were still young. She could vouch for that. For her, a plague of hours tonight, then tomorrow, would drag and drag and drag. As every minute away from John would always drag. . . .

In one of the Minises' comfortable guest rooms that night, her head on his shoulder, Rebecca asked Jock if Robert Mackay had thought it strange that Anne had fallen in love with the enemy. "I know the British mostly left them alone here in Savannah, but for months they did live in fear of an attack."

"Aye, they did, but Mackay thought Anne's romance splendid. He's far too much in love with his own wife to be surprised at any path real love might take. Anne's John is no longer the enemy anyway, my dear. The war is over. He isn't even a member of the hated Royal Marines these days."

"Is Mr. Mackay still dealing in the illegal importation of slaves?"

"Not that I've heard. It was never a big part of his business, but even if he is, your husband will not be a client of

Mein and Mackay again in that regard. I learned my lesson when I broke the law by buying that tragic load of Ebos back when Anne was just a little girl. Heaven knows, though, after our losses I need a dozen or so new fieldhands, especially with the interesting plans I'm hatching for John Fraser once he's here among us."

"What on earth are you talking about?"

"The boy's future, of course. Have you given no thought to what he'll do? How he'll earn a living for Anne and the family I'm sure they'll both want?"

"Yes, but I try to leave all that to you."

"Well, I do have plans. The boy can take over the adjoining Lawrence land and operate it for me. Or I may just give it to him. I've let that fertile land lie fallow since I bought it from A. D. Lawrence way back in 1801. Fifteen years of wasted time and money simply because I didn't have quite enough people or a manager. In my younger days, I could have operated it myself. I'm not quite sure how, but with John Fraser here to take it over, I plan to shift my people around and give it a try. It's small compared with what our son's looking after at Hamilton and Hopeton, but after all, James grew up observing me at Cannon's Point and—" he chuckled, "he *is* James Hamilton Couper, scientific, managerial, general genius. He'll be a big help to young John at Lawrence and, of course, I'll be right next door. I think I can teach him well, Becca, even though managing a plantation will be totally foreign to the lad." When she fell into one of her careful silences, which he and Anne had never quite understood, Jock asked, "Is something wrong, my dear? Have I taken the wrong road? In my 'humble dogmatic' opinion, I'm only guaranteeing a good life for our Annie. You don't agree?"

She pressed her head reassuringly against his shoulder. "Oh, Jock, I certainly don't disagree. I just hadn't dreamed you'd gone so far with your plans. What if the idea of operating a plantation doesn't appeal to John Fraser? What if he has plans of his own to—to rejoin his regiment? Plans for them to—to live in England or Scotland?"

She felt him stiffen. "I won't hear of such a thing!"

"You what, my dear?"

"I would find life intolerable with Anne so far away! So would you. I don't deserve to have my grandchildren born across the ocean, so far away I might never even see them.

As far as I know, John Fraser has little or nothing beyond half pay as a Royal Marine lieutenant. I certainly don't intend to allow my beloved daughter to live a life of want so long as I'm alive on this earth."

Rebecca slipped her arm across his chest. "Beloved Jock, they aren't even married yet! I'm sure they probably will be, but not tonight. I—I rather resent them both right now, actually, coming between us like this. Of course, you have to enter into their future plans, but doesn't kissing me appeal to you a bit more this minute?"

When he turned and took her in his arms, laughing, pulling her close, she felt drowned in their oneness. "Oh, Jock," she breathed, "was there ever a man on earth to equal you? Who else could make such love to a woman while laughing at himself?"

At first light the next morning, Jock and Rebecca were wakened from a sound sleep by a soft but urgent knock on their bedroom door and Anne's muffled voice from the Minis upstairs hall, calling, "Papa, Papa, could you come out here for just a minute, please?"

"Something must be very wrong," Rebecca whispered. "Find out, Jock, but don't forget your slippers. The room's like ice."

He roused himself as fast as possible, rubbed his eyes, ran his fingers through his long, tousled hair, freed of its binding queue, found his slippers, and hurried into the hall, where one stub of a candle still flickered.

"Thank you, Papa," Anne whispered hoarsely. "Will you close the door, please? I won't keep you but a minute and I don't want to wake Mama."

Closing the door softly, he mumbled, "Do you imagine for one minute, gir-rl, that your mother is still asleep? She had to get me moving when we heard you out here. What's the matter, child?"

"I am a child and I'm ever so sorry to disturb you, Papa, but I had that dream again! I must have just come to from having it because I was so scared, I just had to run to you as though—as though I were still a stupid child."

"You were never a stupid child. But don't tell me you're still having that nightmare, Annie?"

"Not for a long time, but I just did." She threw both arms around him. "June told Eve those Ebos honestly believed the water would take them home again. It didn't! They drowned! Hold me, Papa. White people still drown in shipwrecks. You don't think my dream means something ghastly has happened to John, do you? The water will bring him home to me, won't it?"

Hugging her, he murmured, "Yes, Annie, that water just could bring John right here to the Savannah dock this very morning. It must be nearly morning now. I'm sure I can see light breaking down there at the shadowy end of this hall. In no time, I'll be able to find out when he might arrive. Tides can suit, you know, as well as hold boats back. Today could well be the day."

"Thank you, Papa," she whispered, more in control. "I'm ashamed of myself for acting like such a baby. I know it was only a bad dream. I'm sorry you and Mama had to be wakened this way."

"Don't be sorry. Be glad. Your mother and I are so, so glad we still have you with us. Wake us up anytime!"

"Papa?"

"What is it, lass?"

"I could go with you wherever it is you go to find out if there's been any word of the *Neptune,* couldn't I?"

"If the day isn't too chilly."

"Even if it is, I'm sure nice Mrs. Minis would see that her driver took us in their carriage. I'm really ashamed of waking you because of a silly dream." She kissed him on his ample nose. "I love you, Papa, and I am going with you once daylight has come. Please don't waste your breath refusing me."

Giving her one more hug, he asked, "Have I ever refused you?"

John Couper had just closed the front door of Robert Mackay's countinghouse behind him, delighted for Anne at the news he'd just heard about the immediate docking of the *Neptune,* when he saw a familiar, tall young man in a dark-gray cloak run along the wharf below and grab Anne in his arms. For a moment, Couper stopped where he stood, heart still pounding, but now with a kind of pain he would have been hard-pressed to explain. He also felt consuming gladness, relief for Anne. The pain was for himself. At that moment, in a way never before realized, he had lost his beloved daughter to another man.

Lost her only *now*? he asked himself. What in the name of heaven have I been thinking since the first moment she returned from Dungeness a year ago? Was I pretending through all those months watching her pine away over John Fraser that it wasn't real? That she was merely caught up in a romantic haze that would clear away with the first stiff wind that blew up? Haven't I gone so far as to make plans to give the young man my own Lawrence Plantation? Why the heartache now?

And then he knew. He knew because of what he could see from where he stood on the iron walkway a full story above Mackay's own wharf, where the *Neptune* lay at anchor, its graceful bow extended out over the crowd of well-wishers, the stacks of boxes and barrels on the wharf. What he saw was more than a young couple who had just rushed into each other's arms. What he saw was far more final than that. Oh, they were still clinging to each other, but they were not merely two handsome people desperately in love. He saw *their future*—with or without the young woman's father, John Couper. He saw Mr. and Mrs. John Fraser—together as husband and wife forever. Oh, Anne would not stop loving her parents. Blinking now in the windy, winter sun, he could almost see her leading one and then another of John Fraser's children up the path to Cannon's Point to visit their grandparents. But she would be bringing them from her own home—somewhere—to his and Rebecca's home. Cannon's Point would never again be the one spot on earth that beautiful, spirited Anne Couper loved above all others.

"Mr. Couper?"

He turned woodenly to see who might be calling to him from Mackay's front door. Mark Browning, the charming young Philadelphian who now all but ran Mackay's mercantile firm, had followed him outside to make sure he had no trouble locating the berthing place of the *Neptune.*

"She's at anchor, sir," Browning said, coming to stand beside him. "I was watching from our balcony on the river side and saw the two find each other. They certainly looked overjoyed to be together at last."

"Aye," Jock said. "They did, didn't they? Thank you, Browning. You're indeed kind." He took a deep breath.

"Aren't you going down? You can take a shortcut by that flight of wooden steps to River Street."

"I know. I know. I—I just thought to give them a bit more

time alone. But I am grateful to you. Don't let me keep you from your work, young man. It's chilly out here in the wind."

"Excuse me for butting in." The dark-haired, slender young man laughed apologetically. "I'll go inside, then."

"Good idea," Couper said, his eyes on Anne and John standing together below him on the crowded wharf. People arriving and people meeting other passengers milled around them. They were aware only of each other. How long should he wait, he wondered, before interrupting? Had he been rude to young Browning? He sincerely hoped not.

Then he laughed at himself and felt far less sorry for John Couper than he had five minutes ago. Down there clinging to her lieutenant's arm, Anne had once more bested him. They had ridden over in the carriage together, but obviously the girl had charmed the Minises' driver into taking her straight to the wharf while Couper had expected her to wait for him to return with good or bad news about the *Neptune.* He liked Anne's independence. Since the day she was born, the girl's spirit had been lifting his.

His spirit was high again now and before he put her to the bother of having to look for her father, he bounded down the flight of wooden steps to join them—to welcome his future son-in-law, handsome as ever even without his fancy, high-fashioned British officer's uniform.

When he reached the waterfront, a wave of relief swept over him because there, too, was Dr. William Fraser, also in civilian clothes, making his way slowly along the wharf alone. For the moment, Jock had completely forgotten that John's letter had informed him his brother was coming to act as groomsman, should Couper agree to the marriage. At least, he wouldn't be stranded alone with the two lovers. At least, he would not be the only one who would have to be tolerated in their bedazzled state. He could return to the carriage with gentle, amiable Dr. William Fraser. The two might even decide to walk back to the Minis house together, allowing the lovers to ride alone in peace and bliss.

He would agree to the marriage, of course, but all the time praying that young Fraser would agree to settle in Georgia. At the moment, Couper felt totally convinced that uppermost in his mind was his daughter's happiness. In spite of his losses, he would gladly pay for a wedding trip to England and Scotland, but Anne could never be content away from St. Simons. His son would help find a way to redistribute his people among his holdings. Walking briskly toward Dr. William Fraser, hand out, he felt fresh gratitude. Age and experience and success did give a man confidence in his own rightness.

"I'm sure my husband has tried, Mrs. Couper, to tell your husband how deeply we here in Savannah felt your losses when the British captured St. Simons. We lived in fear for months, you know," Mrs. Minis said as the two ladies took coffee before the parlor fire.

"Oh, our greatest loss was our people," Rebecca said. "I don't think Mr. Couper has recovered emotionally from the fact that sixty of them chose to leave him. Five did return, but while we got to know some of the British officers—actually enjoyed them socially—poor Jock has carried a heavy burden."

"Word has gotten all the way up here that at least the enemy lieutenant your daughter fancies so did his best to persuade your people to stay with you. I've hesitated to ask bluntly, but I gather that you both like Anne's choice."

"We do indeed," Rebecca said, glad for a talk with warm-hearted, gracious Dinah Minis. "John Fraser certainly captured my daughter in all ways. He's a disarming young man. A charmer, and yes, evidently he did try to convince my husband's people that they simply could not believe all that the British enlisted men were telling them."

"Is he handsome enough for Anne? I hadn't seen her, you know, since she was a little girl. She's a remarkably attractive young lady now. So intelligent, so high-spirited. Both my daughters are literally at her feet."

"You've all made us so welcome," Rebecca said. "Anne feels as though she's really inconvenienced Henrietta by taking her room, forcing her to double up with her little sister, Sarah. We're ever so grateful."

Mrs. Isaac Minis replaced her cup on the silver tray. "I'm really not prying, Mrs. Couper, but is there something worrying you? Something you'd like to talk about? If not, do forgive me for asking."

Until now Rebecca had kept it buried, even from herself. She knew the Minises to be an upper-class, prominent Jewish family in Savannah, well liked by every Savannahian of importance. Surely, they had all been more than gracious to take in the Coupers when Eliza Mackay could not, but until this minute she hadn't thought of confiding in Dinah Minis.

"Yes," she blurted. "Yes, I am worried and I hadn't even admitted it in my own most secret thoughts until you asked." She tried to smile. "You see, my husband has his heart quite set on young John Fraser's taking over the management of an unused plantation he owns adjoining our property at Cannon's Point. And we, none of us—not even Anne—so far as we know, has any idea what Mr. Fraser himself is planning for his future."

"They *are* going to be married?"

"I would certainly assume so, yes. My daughter's life centers around him. It seems to be one of those rare instant romances. John Fraser wrote to Mr. Couper asking for Anne's hand even before he let her know he was coming back so soon."

"But said nothing about where they might live or what he plans to do now that he's no longer in British service?"

"Nothing. My husband let me read the letter. Both young people appear to believe that everything will fall into place if only they can be together."

Dinah Minis laughed a little. "I remember the feeling well, don't you?"

"Yes. And I'm afraid that after all these years of marriage, I tend to believe still that if only Jock and I can look at each other, any trouble or difficulty can be settled, made right."

"I know. I'm happy to say, in spite of his often reserved manner, I feel the same with my Isaac. He doesn't talk much, but when we're together, we can solve a lot, as you say, just by looking at each other." She paused. "Are you worried about how John Fraser will support Anne now that he's no longer a Royal Marine?"

"Yes. My husband is too."

"Mr. Couper certainly doesn't act worried."

"Jock's way is always to act as though he and everyone else in the world are fine and successful and happy. The man simply can't bear a glum face." She thought a minute. "Actually, Anne's John is rather like him, I'd guess. He also talks freely, charms those around him without even trying, and makes everyone feel important."

"That's a gift, isn't it? But is it always quite the way things really are?"

"No," Rebecca answered. "Sometimes it just papers over, much the way wallpaper covers a crack in a wall. But how does a woman go about telling her husband what he should do with a piece of his own property? Mr. Couper has lost numbers of people. I find I wonder how, in the face of such loss, anyone could operate an additional three-hundred-acre plantation. I'm sure my husband has a plan. I'm not sure Anne's intended will go along with it. Can you think of anything I can do except—wait?"

Dinah Minis smiled warmly. "No, I can't, of course. I can agree, though, that waiting won't be easy and I do sympathize."

Chapter 25

Late that afternoon, after dining with the Minises, John and William registered and left their luggage at the City Hotel. As the Exchange clock struck four, Anne and John were walking arm in arm along Bay Street, the buildings of Factor's Walk and Commerce Row turning pink-gold now from the vivid winter sun setting behind them to the west.

John brushed at a fleck on the lapel of his new dark-gray cloak. "How do you like me without the adornment of my uniform and polished Hessian boots, Miss Couper?" he asked, smiling down at her.

"I don't miss the uniform at all," she said. "Oh, John, I do have you, don't I?"

Falling into his teasing manner, he said as though deep in thought, "I'll have to ponder that some, lass. I'm still trying to recover from the shock of finding you running toward me down that bustling, noisy wharf this morning. A man's heart can stand just so much, you know. I had myself prepared for another long sail in some sort of contraption all the way to St. Simons Island before I found you. By the way, it was most gracious of Mr. and Mrs. Minis to invite William and me to dinner, never having met either of us. Do you think I thanked them properly?"

"What a silly question! Of course you did," she said sharply, obviously annoyed. He had come to expect quixotic changes in her and thought he'd schooled himself to be ready for them during the long months of separation. She'd caught him off guard again now, though, and surprised him even more when she asked, "After all this time apart, is that all you can think of to talk about? *Dinner?*"

He chose to laugh. "No, ma'am, it isn't. What would you think if I said I love you?"

"Say it!"

"I love you with all my heart, Anne Couper, and I mean to marry you just as soon as we can escape from Savannah, Georgia."

"Tomorrow!"

"But don't you have to shop for those fancy new gowns your father keeps talking about?"

"I do not. I've already told Papa that all I really want is to go home, send for Anna Matilda and Reverend Matthews, and marry you."

"I like that very much," he said, beaming. "I like *you* very much, especially when you're irritated."

"What would make you say a thing like that? I'm just boxed in up here in front of all these people. There are too many people in Savannah! Look at them milling up and down Bay Street. We can't even take a walk and know we'll be alone. Women can't go in the City Tavern and sit at a private table the way men can. If we'd stayed at the Minis house, there would be all that chatter and all those servants and people. If we called on the Mackays, there would be children and more servants and more chatter. What would we do today—this minute—if it happened to be storming? Or even colder and windier? I've waited almost eleven long months to be alone with you and here we stand in a throng of nosy people interrupting us. I want to be under our tree *—alone.*"

He stopped walking and stood looking down at her. "Anne, will you feel boxed in *anywhere* except on St. Simons Island?"

He studied her amazing eyes, watched them narrow, saw the tiny crease mar her perfect forehead when she frowned. Then as her laughter came, the hooded, pale blue eyes opened wide again. "I always thought wedding trips were for seeing new places," she said. "They're not, are they? Wedding trips are to let two people in love out of a box. Where can we go and not have to see one single human being but each other?"

"Did you answer my question about St. Simons?" he asked as they began walking again.

She took his arm. "No, I didn't—purposely."

"Is ignoring a question another of your charming habits?"

"I certainly hope not," she said. "I hate it when someone does that to me. I didn't give you an answer about living anywhere else but St. Simons Island because I smell a problem in the whole thing. I think my father's afraid you'll want to take me back to England or Scotland."

"Oh, I'm sure he is."

"He's told you? When have you had time alone with Papa?"

"I haven't and he hasn't said one word to me about it."

"Then, how do you know he's worried that you might want us to live in some faraway place?"

"Because anyone would hate losing sight of you, even for a day."

"Don't tease. And put your question aside for—oh, for a long time after we're married. Please?"

He waited while an empty dray rattled past.

"You don't think we need to make a few plans?" he added. "I intend to have a long talk with Mr. Couper." She gave him the look again, the look that always made him think of a highly intelligent, almost awesome bird. Her perfect dark head sat in a singular way on her elegant long neck when she gave him that look. John was sure she did use it only at certain times for certain reasons. He'd make a point of finding out, without actually asking her, why and when she used "the look." Already, he knew she hated being pinned down. He was sure of that because so did he. So, he merely smiled down at her and asked, "Shouldn't I arrange for a long talk with your father? Isn't that rather expected of me?"

"Yes, but not until after we're married."

His good, free laughter exploded. "I'm so hopelessly in love with you, it's too late to do anything about it, but are you as clever, as tricky as you sometimes seem?"

"I'm not tricky at all! I just happen to be the only person alive on this earth who knows how I suffered without you and I don't intend to allow anything to keep us from being married almost the minute we get back to the island."

"Anne, I adore you, but I can't follow all you're saying."

"Then, don't try. I have the world's most wonderful, most understanding parents, but they are—parents. Papa is going to have everything all worked out for us both. It may or may not be what you want, so where we live and what you do for a living must *not* be discussed yet."

She was giving him "the look" again, but John decided not to pursue it or to mince words. "Anne, my sweet, adorable girl, I have already written to you exactly what I want to do with my future. You didn't like it one bit. You made no bones about letting me know, but my dream is to return somehow, by some means, to my regiment. I will have to go back to England in order to do that. There are no strings to be pulled here in America. That hasn't changed. Surely you haven't forgotten that I'm like a fish out of water away from the Royal Marines!"

She stopped walking. "No, I haven't forgotten, but there's nothing you can do about it today, so why do you have to spoil everything by even bringing it up?" With no warning, her expressive blue, blue eyes filled with tears. "I—I think I'm going to cry, John, and here we are on this public thoroughfare with no place to go where I can bury my weepy face in your shoulder. You can't even put your arms around me out here on Bay Street and hold me."

"But I can hold your hand, dear one." He *was* holding it. "Please don't cry! Tears are good sometimes, but this is not one of those times."

"Do you think I don't know that? I'm ashamed. I'm so ashamed of myself. It's—it's almost harder being so close to you and not being able really to touch you. Is that terribly brazen?"

"No, it's human. When we're back with your parents again, should I agree with their longing to buy you some new gowns or help you urge them to go back to St. Simons?"

"Don't you think everything will be lots better when we're back there—free to be the way we've been almost from the first day we met? Away from these prying eyes?"

"Yes, yes!"

"Then why did you even ask about agreeing with me or with Mama and Papa?"

"Because I know how much they mean to you. Your father has always—well, almost always—been kind and accepting of me, even as his enemy. It took a few days at the outset, when we first captured St. Simons, if you remember, but I deeply value my relationship with him now. It's important to me as a man and it's all important as a man about to become his son-in-law!" When she just stood there looking vulnerable and almost too beautiful to bear, he whispered,

"You *have* suffered, haven't you, my darling? You're all worn out from being away from me."

Her quick smile came. "Did you just realize that this minute?" she asked. "Come on, John," she said, taking charge. "Let's go back to the Minis house and settle this now. I've always been able to depend on Papa to understand me. He understands me sometimes when Mama doesn't, but we can count on both of them to help us by agreeing to go right back to Cannon's Point. I can think straight there. Anybody could think better away from all this noise and clatter."

Arms locked again, they began walking toward the corner where Abercorn intersects Bay. For a few minutes neither spoke. They just clung together and hurried along.

Finally, nearing Broughton on Abercorn, John said, "I've learned one important thing about you today, my beautiful Anne. You're not a city girl, are you?"

"I don't know what I am. Certainly not today when all I want is to be alone with you."

"Are you terribly disappointed, Jock," Rebecca asked as they were packing the next morning, "that Anne didn't accept your generous offer of new gowns? Were you looking forward to spending more time here in Savannah?"

Still wearing a nightshirt, arms loaded with his silk dressing gown and two clawhammer tailcoats—one gray blue, one green—he stood smiling at her before dumping the clothing onto the bed for a Minis servant to pack. "Disappointed, my dear? We made this trip for Annie, didn't we? If she doesn't want to fling awhile in Savannah society, then neither do I."

Rebecca took down the four extra sacque gowns she'd brought for possible formal events and laid them carefully beside his coats. "Don't forget your knee breeches, my dear, and your collars and cravats."

"And my white dress shirts," he chuckled, catching her in his arms.

"It's a marvel Anne isn't spoiled rotten the way you pamper her," she said. "She's headstrong but not spoiled, and it's rather a miracle."

Still holding her, his voice almost solemn, he said, "Rebecca, our daughter, like me, really isn't happy away from Cannon's Point. We'll take her home as soon as it's humanly possible."

She kissed his chin. "And her doting father feels quite triumphant that she seems actually to need to be at home. Promise you won't put too much pressure on John to accept your offer to manage Lawrence?"

"Do I ever insist? Aren't I always amenable and reasonable, Becca?"

"In your altogether charming, irresistible way, I suppose so."

"I think Anne was quite reasonable, too, in the end. She did agree to wait until February for the wedding. To please her mother."

"For a girl so much in love, I've chosen to take that as a good sign. We compromised. We agreed to miss services and to sail on Sunday and she agreed to wait two whole weeks and two days for the wedding. I tried for later in February because spring will be doing its own decorating by then. I lost. February first was as long as she'd wait. There will be camellias blooming, though."

He went back to the wardrobe for his vests. "Two weeks will give me plenty of time to convince John that the smartest thing he can do is agree to manage Lawrence."

"With your powers of persuasion, I'd say it should be plenty of time, but his heart seems set on getting back into the marines. Try not to allow your hopes to soar too high, my dear."

"Too late, Becca. They're already soaring and our Annie will be my strongest ally. You'll see."

Chapter 26

Poor planning and a shortage of stevedores to load the Spalding schooner at the Savannah waterfront delayed their sailing. Their departure for Sapelo Island, where they would reload everything into the *Lady Love,* was late. Late enough so that darkness lay over Cannon's Point when finally they reached home. Anne knew Big Boy, as usual, had been the one to light the pine flares on the Cannon's Point dock.

In her own bed at last after the tedious but joyful journey, during which she held on to John's hand most of the way, Anne felt amazingly fresh and full of energy. Had they been able to sail on time, she and John could have slipped off alone at sunset to their very own sheltering tree. Anne lay wide awake because she was picturing them there where they would surely go first thing tomorrow morning.

Night after night while John was away, she'd lived and relived being there with him under the great tree, lost in their special kind of silence. In none of her imaginings had they spoken one word. The tree, in his absence, had meant only *holding* with no need for words. But John was back now, in a spare bed in Mr. Browne's quarters on the first floor of the old Cannon cottage, and tomorrow—*tomorrow,* they would go first thing after breakfast and nothing would need to be said at all. In a way they couldn't in the bustle of Savannah, they would simply stand there and be together.

Once alone with him, she would know for always that they would never, never be apart again. She really knew it now. From the moment she'd rushed into his arms on the Savannah wharf, time had folded in on itself, almost as though John had never left her. He was as ardent as ever and, even after such a long separation, as gentle as she'd remembered him. But except for that first embrace when the *Neptune* had docked, there had been no chance to feel his arms around her. Not even tonight, back at Cannon's Point, because dear Papa had ignored Mama's urgings that they retire early. Papa, bless him, simply enjoyed John's company so much, he seemed unable to stop talking.

She pounded her bolster and turned over, trying to find a cozy, warm place so that she could fall asleep in order to bring the morning faster. Even if she found no time to scribble one more line in her diary, she had already written down the dates so that they could be checked off one day at a time until February first. One and then two and then three and then four, until the whole seventeen remaining days finally passed, so that at long last she would be able to know his arms without a scratchy woolen jacket.

Her dream of what those first close moments might be like was formless, indefinite, still buried in mystery, but each time she allowed herself to think of what ecstasy could be waiting when she actually felt John's skin against hers, the now too familiar ache rushed through her and she tried to stop imagining.

Once, just once during the long year past, she had asked Eve what it was like when two lovers were that close. Eve had infuriated her by laughing. "You some older than me," the feisty girl had said, "but ain't no way you gonna know it all till you try it."

For the remainder of that day, Eve had acted so superior, Anne could have smacked her. Finally, knowing, as always, when it was to her own advantage to back down a little, Eve had said, "I be glad to tell you what it really be like, but ain't no way you gonna know till you do it wif him yo'self. I be glad for you, Miss Anne, when your fancy white ways make it so you *can* know."

Being white and of a good family carried enormous rewards, but Anne slipped into sleep this night wishing that she, like Eve, did not have to wait for a proper, dragged-out wedding ceremony.

At breakfast the next morning, Anne's heart sank when she realized that Papa was all set to ride with John and his brother, William—just the three men—to the Lawrence land adjoining Cannon's Point. Mama came to her rescue by reminding her father that he'd promised James he'd ride down to inspect the new drainage system at Hamilton Plantation the very first day they were back from Savannah.

"But Becca, we came home early," Papa argued. "As far as our son knows, we're all still away."

"We have no way of knowing James might not ride up here for supplies of some kind today, Jock. Or to ask driver Tom's advice about something. He's been depending so much on Tom since he took on that heavy responsibility at Hamilton. Do you think you three just *have* to see the Lawrence land on our first day home?"

"Excuse me, Mr. Couper," John said affably, "but you can't possibly be depending on either William or me for any kind of knowledgeable opinion of the land, now, can you?"

"You'll find, sir," William put in, "that no two men ever lived with such superior ignorance of farming as do my brother and I."

"William's right, Papa," Anne agreed quickly. "They don't know anything about St. Simons land."

Her father flashed his disarming smile. "I apologize, Daughter, and John. Even with my wise wife right here at the table, doing her best to bring me to my senses, I still barged ahead. One might think I know nothing whatever of the needs of two young lovers. That's just not true. I remember well, and, if you'll forgive me, dear Annie, I promise not to steal John away from you until I have your consent."

Over her father's head, Anne saw Eve in the doorway to the dining room, grinning and clapping her hands soundlessly. Even if Papa had lapsed temporarily, Mama and Eve certainly hadn't.

Eve is quite superior, Anne thought as, at long last, she and John asked to be excused and headed out of the house toward the sandy river path that led to their tree.

Standing together once more under the gnarled, wide, sheltering branches, he kissed her deeply—their first real kiss in nearly a year. Almost instantly, the now familiar ache swept over her with such force that only John's arms about her seemed strong enough to keep her standing.

"Anne, Anne," he murmured, after the long, searching kiss, "can you believe I'm really here? That we're really back here under our tree?"

"Now, I do," she gasped. "I believe it now that you kissed me like that. Please kiss me again. . . ."

He held her to him and this kiss was so intense she almost cried out.

Eve had given her no reason to anticipate this. But Eve had been right in one thing—no one else could describe it. *"Ain't no way you gonna know it all till you try it!"*

"John, how can we wait through sixteen more days and nights?"

As though she were a child instead of the sudden woman she had just become, he grasped her shoulders and held her away from him far enough to look at her with an expression on his dear face she vowed she'd never forget.

"I don't know how we can wait," he whispered, "but we can and we will. We have our whole lifetimes ahead of us for loving. Wherever we are, two long lifetimes stretch ahead for us to fill—with each other."

"But, John—"

When he laid one hand gently over her lips, she knew he hadn't finished. "We can wait because we have to. For one thing, I have to take a boat over to Brunswick on the mainland for a marriage license. Your father's going with me for that. He's also kindly offered to arrange for our ceremony with the Reverend Matthews, your rector. Your father, Anne, has come to be very important to me. Not only because he's your father. I revere him as a man. He actually seems to accept me in a way I never felt my own father did. William was his favorite."

"You only imagined that."

"No, I didn't imagine it. And I'm happy to say that knowing the truth has in no way come between my brother and me. I just feel as though your father seems genuinely to like me—for myself." He smiled a little. "He likes me every bit as much as he likes William. I mean to keep it that way."

"Could you kiss me again, please?"

"I mean to do that, too, every chance we have, even before February first finally arrives. But, Anne, I also mean to give your father's plan for our future a fair hearing. In spite of the fact that I despise farming and I don't think I could ever learn to be successful at it."

"John, what kind of plan has Papa thought up? And when have you two been alone without me long enough to talk plans?"

He laughed. "At the Minises the one day I dined there. After dinner, he and Mr. Minis, William, and I went to the parlor for brandy, remember? Your father wants us to settle down here on St. Simons, to make us a wedding gift of his idle property called Lawrence."

Anne's heart leapt for joy. Had Papa been there, she would have hugged him! Not once had she really faced the fact that marrying John might also mean leaving St. Simons forever. Now, dear Papa had come to her rescue. Wherever John was, there she would be, because without him there was no life at all, but she'd disallowed any thought of leaving St. Simons because such an idea was just too painful. Her world had always revolved around Cannon's Point oaks and pines and hickories and gums and magnolias. Of course, John could learn how to manage Lawrence. He'd be a kind, considerate master to any new people Papa might have to buy at the Savannah market, and he would make a magnificent planter. The child in her longed to run to her father in sheer exuberance, but John still had his hands on her shoulders and the look on his face told her that his mind was far from settled.

"Could you talk fast, please? I think you have more to say," Anne blurted. "But I'm so excited at the idea that you and I might live right next door to Cannon's Point, I'm going to have to kiss you again just as soon as you're finished."

"Does it really mean so much to you that we live here?"

"Oh, yes! John, it would make me so happy, I'm not sure I could bear it. Not that I won't be wherever you are, my beloved, for as long as I live, but—"

He let his hands drop from her shoulders. "I—I see."

"What do you see? What are you thinking?"

"Only that I know now more than ever that I must spend time with your father very soon and, if possible, with a completely open mind."

A prickle of fear ran through her. "Can you keep your mind open to learning a whole new kind of work? Away from the military? I know I fell in love with you in your handsome Royal Marine uniform. I know how much you love being with the others in your unit. I want you to be sure that I know all that. It's just that no woman wants the man she loves to—to put himself, of his own free will, in such danger. John, I—I couldn't live if anything happened to you!"

In response, he only frowned and kicked absently at a fallen pinecone.

"Almost as much as the terror I feel that you might get shot again, I feel a kind of terror at the thought of your gentle self—*killing.*" She grasped his arm. "It's far, far more than just my love of St. Simons Island, dearest. Do you believe me? John, do you?"

For what seemed a millennium to Anne, they stood there in a strange, entirely new kind of hollow silence.

"It's—it's suddenly all different, isn't it?" she asked. "Not more than a minute or two ago everything was perfect."

"Yes. But don't forget, you and I have never had a real chance to talk together about daily things like where we might live. What I might do for a living. We still have so much to learn about each other in the daily round."

"What if you don't love me very much when I'm being—daily?"

This time, his response was an almost desperate kiss. She pulled away from him only long enough to breathe, "Will we ever have enough time for all there is, John?"

After a moment, he saved them both with a soft, adoring laugh. A close, intimate, cadence of laughter that seemed to Anne to be overflowing with secrets. "I'll never have enough days or nights for kissing you, beautiful Anne. But before our wedding, there's something I must do. In fairness, I must at least have a straightforward talk with your father about Lawrence."

"Before our wedding?"

"Yes."

She felt suddenly afraid. Then thought to herself, *no,* I'm not afraid. We're going to be married and once we are, everything will depend on my trusting him. I might just as well begin practicing now. If I can't trust John and Papa together, who can I trust?

"Anne, I'm just trying to do the next right thing. We have to take one step at a time. Are you worried about my talking man-to-man with your father?"

This time, she pulled his face down to hers and kissed him. "Try me, husband."

"Husband?"

"That's what I said. All the palaver of a wedding isn't going to make you my husband. You already are, and no, I'm not a bit worried about you and Papa or Lawrence. You came back to me and for now that's absolutely all that matters."

Chapter 27

Wearing her mother's white silk wedding gown, its full, floor-length skirt embroidered from the long, fitted bodice to the hem with grape clusters of pearls, Anne stood waiting at the top of the Cannon's Point staircase with Anna Matilda, her maid of honor.

"You look as beautiful in that pale blue gown as I feel," Anne said, and they both giggled, then caught themselves and stood, shoulders back, in what they hoped were mature, fashionable postures.

"You're the most radiant bride ever," Anna whispered. Then asked, "We'll go on being best friends, won't we, Anne?"

"Forever! I swear it."

"We *are* supposed to wait right here until Mama begins the music on your pianoforte, aren't we?"

"Yes, we are and calm yourself, Anna Matilda. She'll start any minute now, I'm sure. Did Eve get my curls long enough in back where they show through my veil?"

"They're perfect. I think Eve's more excited than either one of us. She's watching you like a hawk. I can see her, all dressed up in her good blue skirt and striped shirtwaist, standing down there in the hall just outside the parlor. And June's standing there with her! Did you tell her he could come too?"

"Of course, I did. They both fully understand about—love."

At that moment Mrs. Page struck the first chords of "Deck Thyself, My Soul, with Gladness," and Anne began to follow her maid of honor slowly, regally, down the wide stair. When they reached the first landing, she could see dear Papa, every inch the elegant country squire in his gray knee breeches, white stockings, his best dark-green tailcoat over a bright yellow vest. Tears stood in his blue eyes when they'd said good night, but he was beaming now, happy and hopeful, because he and John had come to a loose, rather perplexing compromise on John's future: The newlyweds would spend their first month at Cannon's Point, Papa explaining his widely admired botanical methods. Then the Frasers would sail for England, where, after a wedding trip, John could inquire further about his chances of rejoining his regiment. They would stay for the remainder of the year at the Fraser home in London because Father James Fraser had urged it, and a definite decision could be made later about where they would finally settle. It all sounded vague to Anne, but, today, there was only peace and beauty.

For her, descending the stair to the hall where John waited with William at his side, only one thing mattered: just minutes from now, they would be joined "together this man and this woman in holy matrimony. . . ."

As though lifting the exact words from inside Anne's head, Reverend Edmund Matthews was reading them now from his leather-bound book into the hushed, polished, camellia-bowered parlor. Seated about the room were James Hamilton, Mama, Anne's childhood tutor, angular William Browne, the James Goulds, the Thomas Spaldings, and Major Page. The pro-British Wyllys had come with all their children, including pretty four-year-old Caroline, who seemed to adore James Hamilton, and the "fey gir-rl," as Papa always called dreamy, otherworldly Heriot, maybe eight by now. The Wylly boys, John, ten, looking especially handsome, sat with his somewhat older brother, Alexander William, on straight dining room chairs because the parlor seats were all taken. Anne would have liked to have all her St. Simons friends there, but the parents of most had been strong American Patriots during the Revolution and might not appreciate that John had so recently been an enemy of the United States. At least it was good to see blond, green-eyed Frances Anne Wylly, nearly Anne's age, as striking-looking as ever, witty and always ready for a laugh at almost anything. At this moment, though, even Frances Anne looked quite solemn, taking in every word Reverend Matthews was saying, undoubtedly dreaming of the day when she could stand where Anne stood beside the man she would marry.

". . . to join together this man and this woman in holy matrimony. . . ." Reverend Matthews's clear, gentle voice made each word as magical as it really was. Surely a miracle was taking place this day, February 1, 1816, in the familiar, spacious parlor at Cannon's Point. "Into this holy estate these two persons present come now to be joined."

She and John stole glances at each other. Yes! Oh, yes. *They* were the two persons present and they were being joined forever . . . forever.

"Wilt thou have this woman to thy wedded wife, to live together after God's ordinance in the holy estate of matrimony? Wilt thou love her, comfort her, honor, and keep her in sickness and in health; and, forsaking all others, keep thee only unto her, so long as ye both shall live?"

John looked straight at Anne and said with all his heart, "I will."

When Reverend Matthews asked the same, beautiful, eternally serious question of her, she said "I will" so firmly, so quickly, the rector couldn't help smiling a little.

After Papa had declared that it was indeed he who was giving Anne "to be married to this man," John once more gazed intently at the priest in order not to miss uttering one single word: "I, John Fraser, take thee, Anne Couper, to my wedded wife, to have and to hold from this day forward, for better for worse, for richer for poorer, in sickness and in health, to love and to cherish, till death us do part, according to God's holy ordinance; and thereto I plight thee my troth."

Then it was Anne's turn. She listened to Reverend Matthews but looked only at John. When, on the final line, she was instructed to say, "I give thee my troth," she found herself foolishly wondering why she said "give" and John said "plight." What difference did it make? To them both, whatever the word *troth* really meant, they had entirely, for always and always, given *themselves.*

There was a lot more of the ceremony . . . the part when John placed his mother's plain gold ring on her finger, then too many more words, but every word was directed at them and at the others in the room because of them. The months of waiting, of holding inside herself almost all of what had meaning for her, were over. She and John could now shout to the world that they were one, one, *one*!

After a fleeting thought that William Fraser and Frances Anne Wylly would make a rather attractive couple, she turned to do what was expected of her as the bride. Standing with John, she accepted and gave hugs to the ladies present, steeled herself for the old man's kiss she knew dear Captain Wylly would insist on giving her, and hugged her mother gratefully when she urged the newlyweds to slip upstairs to their room to freshen up a bit before Sans Foix's lavish wedding feast captured everyone's attention.

When John followed her into what had been only her own familiar room and closed the door, the strangeness took her completely by surprise. From the moment of their first meeting in Mrs. Shaw's dining room at Dungeness over a year ago, she had always been able to think of something to say to him. Standing there, a full ten feet away from him now, she couldn't speak one word.

Being in his arms had always fixed everything. She rushed into them now. Still with the strange silence all about them, his hard arms around her, he kissed her eyelids, her neck, her chin, her mouth. He had kissed and kissed her under the sheltering tree—hard, man-kisses that hurt her mouth—but never like this.

And then, he let her go so abruptly, she felt herself sway. He was still there, still close, but now he was smiling down at her with the expression of a shamefaced boy.

"I couldn't help that," he said lamely. "I've waited so long! I know we have only a few minutes up here. I'm well aware of Sans Foix's prestige in the household. I know we dare not keep him waiting. Forgive me?"

"I wouldn't know how. Forgive you for what? But, John, I —I was afraid just now."

"Of me?"

"No. Of myself. Of what I felt!" Then she was able to smile back at him. "You rescued me, though, by bringing up Sans Foix's prestige. I'll be all right now, I promise, as soon as I get my breath."

Through the closed door from downstairs, they could hear the wedding guests gathering in the dining room. Anne couldn't understand a word Papa was saying, but she could tell that he was making one of his proper, merry, welcoming speeches.

"We must go," he said, pulling her to him again.

"Don't be my lover now, please! Or I can't go downstairs and say pleasant things—" He was kissing her. She was kissing him. And pleading between kisses, "John, just—just be my sweet friend! Just help me a little while longer."

He let his arms drop to his side, reached her dressing table in a few strides, used her brush to put his thick, dark hair in shape, and turned to say in a ridiculously friendly voice, "Look here, milady, is it true that Sans Foix can completely bone a roasted turkey so that it looks whole and untouched when it reaches the table? I say, how does he manage that?"

At the looking glass herself now, she swiped at one or two of her curls with the same brush he'd used and caught his adoring eyes in the mirror. "It's a deep dark secret how Sans Foix does it. No one knows. He always works at his turkeys *under* a huge white, clean tablecloth in the kitchen. Even Johnson has no inkling of exactly how it's done."

Arm in arm, they slowly descended the stair. "I do thank you for turning so skillfully into my sweet friend," she said, giving him her most ingenuous public smile. "You are as deft as Sans Foix any day."

"I have to be deft, beautiful Anne. I'm the man who just married you, remember?"

As they headed toward the crowded dining room, Anne heard Eve's "Ps-s-t" from the rear of the downstairs hall.

"Oh, Eve!" she called. "Eve, did you see the wedding? Did you stay in the hall and watch as you promised?"

"Hello, Eve," John said. "I certainly hope you didn't miss the most important event of the decade."

Beaming, Eve curtsied—not to Anne but to John—and said, "I was right there, Mausa John. I had to make sure Miss Anne she do it all right. Took me long enough to fix them curls."

"And did she conduct herself to your liking?" he asked.

"June, he be right there wif me. He thought she done good, too. So did you, Mausa John." Now she turned to Anne, the impish grin on her pretty face. "You better git on in there, if you knows what's good for you, Miss Anne. An' don't be shakin' 'bout later. I kin promise you it's gonna be

—windy an' *perfeck*—tonight! Me an' June we kin bof promise you dat."

At the doorway to the dining room, John grinned at Anne. "Windy and perfect! Did you hear what Eve said, Mrs. Fraser?"

She clung to him, feeling helpless again and almost afraid. He was teasing her, she knew, only because he felt helpless, too.

When he asked her again if she heard what Eve had just said, she was smiling up at him, but barely able to whisper, "I heard. But, dear God in heaven, do you think dinner will *ever* end?"

Chapter 28

Papa had always been known for his colorful toasts, but until after her wedding dinner, Anne had no idea that he knew so many! The ceremony took place at noon, dinner went on—Sans Foix making countless visits to the dining room to receive plaudits—until after four, when the Pages and the Goulds and the Spaldings left, but Papa evidently wanted the wedding merriment to go on still longer.

Wine glasses in hand, they had all trooped outside for one final toast to the departing guests, led, of course, by Papa, who stood in the front lane, his neighbors about him, glass lifted in the afternoon sunlight: "May we keep these few friends rather than a thousand acquaintances!"

All day long, each embrace, good wish, and fond kiss had touched Anne deeply, but by the time her punctual brother, James Hamilton, finally left the parlor, every nerve in her body seemed tied in knots. Even James had behaved in what, for him, was a most ebullient manner. Mama's cherished heirloom clock, said to have stood over two hundred years ago in the great hall of Caerlaverock, the Maxwell family castle near Dumfries, Scotland, was striking eight by the time James and William Browne announced that they were retiring to their rooms to read. Anne felt only gratitude toward her brother and her girlhood tutor, but growing annoyance with John. Didn't he also long to escape the festivities and go upstairs where they could finally be alone? Wasn't it his wedding night, too?

"May we eat our bread with joy and drink our wine with merry hearts," Papa toasted when they and the Wyllys had all sat back down in the parlor.

"I think we've already eaten our bread," Mama said

pointedly, "and unless I'm mistaken, Jock, we've also drunk our wine."

"Aye, Becca," Papa replied, laughing. "So we have!"

Anne loved seeing Papa enjoy himself, but each time she caught John's eye, she felt more and more impatient to be excused. She could tell Mama knew. For the past hour, she'd exchanged looks with Anne, shaking her head, giving her an impatient little smile at Papa's insistence that the party go on.

Finally, though, Captain Wylly dispatched Johnson to send for their carriage and slowly, one by one, the Wylly family donned wraps and began to say their affectionate farewells. Eve brought in the cloaks and shawls so quickly that Anne knew she understood her nervousness. She also caught Eve's tactless pointing toward the front door where John's brother, Dr. William Fraser, and Frances Anne Wylly stood together, deep in conversation, both smiling. Anne gave Eve a nod. She had noticed, too.

On his feet, Papa made what she fervently hoped was his final toast of the day: "May we all live in pleasure and die out of debt!"

Dear Papa. Dear, maddening Papa, so happy today, so delighted to be the master and host of his beloved Cannon's Point. And if the intensity of their talk through the evening had been an indication, so genuinely fond of John, who must be, if he loved her as he claimed, as eager as she to make an escape. Still, she was learning that her husband was also a social person. No one could doubt that John Fraser reveled in company and laughter and good talk every bit as much as Papa did.

If I didn't know better, Anne thought, I'd be worried because John isn't helping at all to get rid of the Wyllys. If he suggests one more toast from Papa, I think I'll die!

"It's been such a glorious day," John said, when the Wyllys were finally in their carriage, "could we have one more of your brilliant toasts, Mr. Couper? For luck?"

As though even he were finally running out, Papa scratched his head a moment, then lifted his voice: "Well, how about this one, son? 'Here's to our absent friends and kin—God bless them!' "

"Splendid, sir," John laughed. "Thank you!"

From his window upstairs, even James Hamilton called

down into the unusually pleasant February night, "Drive safely, neighbors. And God speed you on your way!"

James can prolong it all with no thought of me because he's already doing exactly what he wants to do, Anne thought, hands on hips, not caring much by now who noticed her impatience. James Hamilton will never have to go through what I'm going through right now. If he ever marries, he'll have made a note of the exact time he and his bride will depart to be alone and that will be that. Maybe John and I don't know each other's quirks very well yet, but at least I know he certainly isn't what anyone could call punctual!

Back inside at last, before Papa could suggest that they all return to the parlor, Mama said quickly, "Goodnight, bride and groom!" She spoke the words firmly, as though she'd just given a servant an order. "You have both overstayed your welcome, Mr. and Mrs. Fraser. Isn't that right, Jock?"

The look of surprise on Papa's face turned quickly to shame. "Oh, Annie, darlin'," he said, "Annie and John, can you both forgive a happy old man who allowed his own joy in this beautiful occasion to drown his common sense?" He clapped his hands sharply. "Now, go! Both of you, scoot! Dinna' make me fleech!"

As they climbed the stair arm in arm, Anne heard herself say, because she couldn't think of anything else, that she was glad John was a Scotsman, too, and knew the meaning of the word *fleech.*

"I do indeed," he said, laughing.

Inside her room at last, the door closed, his eyes glowing and triumphant, he took her in his arms.

"We really had to work our way up here, didn't we?" she asked.

"Aye, we did," he said, keeping his voice down as much as possible in his deliriously happy state. "But didn't your father enjoy himself? And what a generous heart! I'm still reeling that he wants to *give* me all of Lawrence right now."

Lawrence had nothing whatever to do with tonight. In desperation, she took his face in her hands and kissed him on the mouth. The ache in her grew almost unbearable when his hands began touching her, pulling her closer, all the while murmuring her name.

Then, he did one of his abrupt things—he stepped back

away from her. "Answer me this, Annie, don't you know the meaning of the word *fleech*?"

"Of course, I know."

"Then, dinna' make me fleech, Annie Couper Fraser. I'm in no mood to coax you out of that fancy wedding gown!"

Until this minute, the actual act of taking off her dress, her underclothes, had not occurred to her. She had lived through endless months for this moment, but not once had she thought of the fact that she would have to undress before him.

Plainly reading her thoughts, he was laughing again. "I'm *not* laughing at you," he vowed, holding her again, "but I am beginning to understand more about you and to like what I —understand. But I'll let go of you, Annie, just long enough."

"Long enough for what?" she asked in a weak voice.

"Long enough to hide myself completely—all the way behind that drapery at the window—while you make yourself ready for me."

"Would you? Is that what you're really going to do?"

"Aye, Annie."

"Then, please do it, and I'll hurry. Eve's left warm water right there by the dressing table for me. Get all the way behind the drapery, John, promise!"

She certainly needed Eve to unfasten the side hooks of her wedding gown, but in near panic she managed them herself and rushed through a splash bath. She made a mental note to thank Eve for having opened the tiny, delicate pearl buttons on the new filmy nightgown Eve's mother had lovingly made and embroidered for her.

His dear voice eager, muffled behind the heavy drapery, John called, "Ready?"

"If you don't care that these pearl buttons aren't fastened," she called back.

In one leap, she was in the carefully turned-down, fragrantly clean bed and was sitting up straight when John stepped from his hiding place, clad only in the tight-fitting drawers of his winter underwear. He had removed the tops so that his wide, muscled shoulders, deep chest, and arms were bare. For what seemed an eternity, he just stood there beside the bed, looking down into her eyes. Anna Matilda's mother had played their song, "Drink to Me Only with Thine Eyes," after the ceremony. John was drinking her eyes with his now, her throat, her form under the covers, his gaze not lingering so long as to embarrass her—but already unmistakably making love to her.

And then the room was dark, as dark as the moonless night outside . . . as dark as were the trees drained of their color because the sun was gone. Almost soundlessly, he had snuffed out the candles on the bedside table, and with only the urgency of his breathing, he slipped into bed.

At long last, she knew what Eve had meant.

"Annie, oh, Annie," he murmured, his dear hands learning her, his mouth learning the throat he'd tried and tried to tell her was the most elegant in all creation.

"When did you decide to begin calling me Annie?"

"When I first heard your father call you that. I—I like the sound of it."

Tomorrow she might be able to think about why it was that she had always loved storms—had, almost as soon as she could walk, adored, reveled in, marching around the porch with Papa when the thunder rolled, the wind blew, the lightning flashed and stabbed.

Now, with this storm crashing, not outside around her but through her, she knew at least one reason why she and Papa had marched, why she had never been able to bear just watching a storm from inside.

Her first thought when she saw bright island sun filling the room was that it could not be morning already. The storm and the wind and the glory were still too close, too clear. Had it really stormed outside last night, too? No. Had she actually slept? Yes! John was still sleeping beside her. They had both slept.

When his arm reached for her, his noble eyelids still shut, she could feel that he was as refreshed as she by their loving and by their long, dreamless sleep.

"Good morning, wife," he said, opening his eyes.

She snuggled against him. "I *am* your wife now. And you're my husband."

The first kiss of their first full day of married life was tender, almost playful. They would be lovers in the daily round, too. To Anne, the kiss proved it.

"Are you—all right, Annie?"

"Can't you tell?"

"I just thought I'd better make sure." Up on his elbow,

looking down at her, dark hair tousled, he smiled his most arrogant smile. "You see, Mrs. Fraser, I'm going to leave you for a while today. I thought I'd better make certain you're in the mood to agree with great, good humor."

"You're one of those people who wake right up, aren't you? You're definitely not a cozy-er."

He laughed. "A cozy-er?"

"I had a big rag doll once and she was a wonderful cozy-er. I was hoping you'd be, too."

He swung his legs over the side of the bed. "Tomorrow, I vow to prove I'm the very best, but today I'm going to inspect the Lawrence land with your father and William and maybe James, if he doesn't have to ride right back down to his new domain at Hamilton."

"Wait! Not so fast, sir."

"Don't you know by now that breakfast is at eight o'clock in this house, milady? I plan to be there on time."

She reached for his hand. "I have the same plans, sir. Besides, I'm hungry as a bear." She hoped her voice showed no trace of the anxiety any mention of Lawrence brought rushing back. Papa just must not trap John into a corner! She would adore living in the old tabby house at Lawrence, so near Cannon's Point. With Mama's help, she could turn it into a dream house, but not unless John wanted to be a plantation master.

From his perch on the side of the bed, he studied her face. "Everything isn't all right, is it?"

"I don't think either of us can know that yet. Papa is always in such a hurry, always so full of big, wild ideas he's sure will work. I know him a lot better than you do, don't forget. I also know pretty well how to handle him when he's riding one of his spirited notions."

John leaned down to kiss her. "I'm sure you do, but can there be any harm in my seeing the land again with him? He tells me there's so much yet to explain about its potential."

"No harm at all unless you fall prey to his charm and agree to do something you'll regret later. Everyone who knows me knows I adore my father, but I'm married to you now and I don't know you as well as I know Papa."

"I'm not a bit complicated." He held wide his arms. "I'm just a plain, open book."

"You are not an open book! There's that secret, military man down inside you and I don't know him at all. I don't understand him. I'm not sure I ever will, but I respect him because he's part of you. John, after last night, I revere everything that's a part of you."

He caught her in his arms and held her tenderly for a long time before saying another word. Waiting, head against his chest, she planted kisses on the silky patch of curly hair growing there.

Finally, in a voice so solemn and sincere she felt almost in awe of him, John said, "I know the part of me that feels fulfilled and at home only in the military disturbs you, Annie. I'm not ready to talk about it yet, but for months you've deserved some kind of explanation. You made yourself clear how you feel in that one letter that I almost memorized. I gave you no real response when I wrote back. I want you to know I'm aware of that. I also want you to know that I know it puzzles you that I'm even considering trying to learn some day to operate your father's valuable property."

"Dearest, are you considering it?"

"I wouldn't give the old gentleman false hope by even riding over there again with him if I weren't at least trying to be open to it. Anne, I have no certain way of supporting you if I don't find some means of getting back my marine commission!"

For a fleeting instant, she felt ashamed that until this very moment she'd refused even to think about that. Papa had always stood for everything she needed or wanted. She had, until John wrote of his intense loyalty to the Royal Marines, simply expected that Papa would have some kind of important work for whomever she married. Well-to-do fathers usually made opportunity and land available to a newly married daughter's husband. That was the whole idea of a dowry. Papa's expectations about Lawrence hadn't particularly surprised her. She wouldn't have given it a second thought had not John let her know that he honestly believed himself to be first and foremost an officer in the British Royal Marines.

"Do you hate the idea of agriculture?" she asked.

"Hate it?" He smiled crookedly. "What little I learned about farming as a boy certainly never bedazzled me."

"Promise me one thing?"

He looked directly into her eyes. "If I can do it—honestly."

"You can. 'Whither thou goest, I will go,' dearest John,

but you must promise me that you won't allow my beguiling father to push you. There is absolutely no hurry. After all, we're going to England to visit your father, then the wonderful wedding trip you say he insists on giving us—maybe even a visit to Mama's Maxwell family castle in Scotland."

Laughing now, he said, "I guarantee we'll see the Maxwell's Caerlaverock Castle. It's right at Dumfries and my father doesn't make gifts of wedding trips without strings attached. He's so Scottish, he'll expect us to make the entire trip right in Scotland."

"Don't change the subject. I'm not finished with Papa and Lawrence. You must not let Papa rush you. Promise?"

The smile he gave her was so warm, so relieved, so expressive of his joy in her, there wasn't a hint of the elegant arrogance Anna Matilda kept noticing. "I promise on my honor, beautiful Annie," he said, "that even your persuasive father won't cause me to feel pushed or trapped. The land has lain there since he bought it in 1801. I guess another year or so can't matter."

Chapter 29

When breakfast was over, as soon as horses could be saddled, John, his brother, William, Mr. Couper, and James Hamilton waved good-bye to the ladies and rode off down Couper Road. Amused, as always, by Anne's brother, the punctilious James Hamilton Couper, John was in no way surprised to learn that young Couper would ride with them only as far as the road to Lawrence, since his duties at Hopeton on the mainland and at Hamilton Plantation on the south end of St. Simons obviously occupied him totally these days.

John had spoken with James as they waited for their horses and, mounted and trotting along later, still marveled at the succinct, carefully worded survey given him of young Couper's schedule for the remainder of this day. "I should reach Hamilton a few minutes past eleven," James had said, "giving me twenty minutes to inspect the cotton barn after its cleaning. I allow myself one hour to read and study the work I'm doing on plantation ditching. Another hour and a half for study of Greek and Latin, then one hour is devoted to poetry in winter when my people are busy repairing tools and harness. In the spring, when planting is in progress, the poetry hour will be spent riding from field to field in conference with my driver. I dine at four and by a quarter to five, if I have no guests, I am back at my managerial duties and records." When John had interrupted long enough to ask how long James allowed himself to dine should guests be present, the tall, severely handsome young man answered, "Oh, I then permit myself an extra fifteen minutes."

The narrow, tree-lined lane, this morning striped by sharp, angular shadows, was wide enough for only two horsemen to ride abreast, so John and William waved Couper father and son on ahead since neither knew the way to Lawrence. The semitropical early February sun turned the fallow fields beyond the stand of trees into sheer magic, because dry stalks of old cotton and corn caught light shafts that caused them almost to sparkle.

"Even winter looks lush on this enchanted island," William called to John as they rode along, far enough behind the Coupers so that they would not be overheard.

"Look up, William," John said, his own head thrown back to watch the ghostly strands of thick gray moss in the giant trees seeming to float on the tidal breeze.

"I'm looking," his brother called back. "Can you believe that one single order from old Cockburn to capture St. Simons Island was going to bring such breathtaking beauty as all this—and Miss Anne too? It seemed just another command at the time."

"I wish our father could see it. The old gentleman might thaw some under these sun-warmed trees. William, have you noticed the ferns growing right on these wide oak branches? I saw them on Cumberland, too, but somehow here on St. Simons they're even more spectacular. They look dead, Anne told me, when it hasn't showered for a time, but an hour or so of good, soaking rain and up they spring."

"Aye. I even know what they're called—resurrection ferns," William said. "One of Miss Anne's close and quite fetching friends told me at the wedding feast."

"Oh? Which one, pray? No, let me guess. Anna Matilda Page."

"I'll give you one more guess."

"I was not the most observant man present, Brother," John laughed. "I had eyes for only the most bewitching young lady. I give up. Who told you the name of those magical ferns?"

"Miss Frances Anne Wylly from the plantation called St. Clair. Not far from where we're going, I understand, but I suppose too far for a casual visit today."

Up ahead, the two Coupers had slowed their horses and were walking them to one side of the narrow lane. The Frasers followed, but still allowed a moment's privacy for their hosts.

"The lane branches nearby, I see," John said. "I'm sure

the Old Gentleman, Anne's brother, is taking his leave of us. Duty calls, you know."

"I take it you mean young James Hamilton Couper when you speak of the Old Gentleman."

"Oh, certainly," John said. "Anne and her father have always called him by that name. Right to his face, too. He seems impervious to teasing."

"Gentlemen who are absolutely certain of their own wisdom and rightness are seldom rewarding to tease."

They both laughed softly. Then, John, walking his mount closer to where William's mare stood munching at some dry grass, said in a very quiet voice, "I do have some influence with the Old Gentleman's sister. I'm sure a call on the Wyllys could be arranged in a day or so."

As was his habit, William answered only with a pleased grin, then changed the subject.

They saw the two Coupers exchange a warm handshake. James trotted back to bid the Frasers adieu, then galloped off in the direction of Frederica Road to take up his planned schedule with obvious vigor.

After another enthusiastic wave, the elder Couper turned to them, looking, John thought, for all the world like an impish boy just freed from the classroom. A big grin spread across his jovial face, Couper called out, "All right, gentlemen, now it's our turn for some fun! It's not far to Lawrence, but far enough to give our horses' legs a good stretch. Follow me!"

After a short, hard canter, John knew from only one brief visit that they'd reached Lawrence Plantation. Unlike Cannon's Point, its fields had gone to forest—sweet gums, their leaves still clinging, some even showing a few brave spots of pink and bright red; a few live oaks, their sturdy, stretching branches thick with the same ferns John so admired, their gray bark coral and pale green with lichen; cedars and more cedars. Of course, there were pines and pines, what looked to be hickories—bare of leaves—and scattered sassafras bushes. Most of the trees were reasonably young compared with the stands along the island roads. After all, the Lawrence property had not been planted in cotton, corn, or any other crop that John knew of in at least fifteen years.

"Wasted land," John Couper declared, reining his horse at one side of the overgrown Lawrence lane, beneath the largest live oak. "A sad site, though with its own kind of wild beauty. At times I wish I could afford to own enormous tracts of land allowed to go entirely to woods. The island heals itself swiftly after man's plows have wounded it. It seems no time at all that those trees you see now were mere saplings."

"Is there some reason you haven't planted this land, sir?" William asked.

"Indeed there is. Look out toward the ocean to the east. Do you see the small tract bare of trees? Not the grassy area. I still graze some cattle there, but beyond it—beyond that sturdy little tabby house at the edge of the marsh."

"Yes, sir," John said. "We see the area you mean."

"I had those trees cleared to plant corn, field peas, green peas, and yams. I must have cleared fifteen acres or more. I'm a staunch believer in plantations supplying their own household tables and those of their people. Too many planters squander cash, an always scarce commodity, in purchases of foodstuffs when, with the help of their hands, they could simply grow their own."

"But you didn't get that fifteen acres planted?" William asked.

"Only ready to plant. Some seed was even in the ground in late February a year ago." The look on Couper's face was half embarrassed, half sorrowful. "If you gentlemen remember, that was about the time I lost sixty of my people. A goodly number were my most productive farmers."

John looked at William, then looked away.

"Yes, Mr. Couper, we both remember," John said, in genuine sympathy. "Some of our unit thought you and Mr. Spalding greedy to go to such lengths to get your slaves back. We're not accustomed to slavery, but my brother and I understood why you did."

"Aye," Couper said, shaking off his momentary emotion. "You went out of your way, John, I've since learned, to try to persuade my people to stay. I'm grateful, most grateful." Looking flustered, Couper went on. "Now, there's another reason I haven't found it feasible to plant Lawrence, to turn it into the productive land it cries out to be. I haven't found the right man to manage it for me." He swept his long arm toward the sturdy, not unattractive though run-down, tabby cottage. "That little story-and-a-half house is soundly built. Lawrence, one of the first Englishmen who came over with

Oglethorpe when he colonized Georgia, built it, and except for where the mice have chewed some woodwork and a patch of flooring here and there, it needs little more than a good coat of paint on its trim."

"Tabby must make a fine building material," William said, looking in the direction of the house nestled in a grove of cedars and oaks beside an expanse of sunlit marsh. "I can see lots of possibilities for that little place, all right. A marvelous setting for children to play in. Look, John, at all those thick grapevines to climb. Even now, they make me want to try it."

Hoping to keep Mr. Couper from jumping right into the good prospects for his own future at Lawrence, John said, "You see, sir, my brother met a young lady yesterday who seems to have captured his fancy, to a degree at least. I—I had no idea he was already thinking of children!"

Enjoying the tease, William merely said, "My brother, Mr. Couper, has an untamed imagination."

"If that's true, then imagine yourself as master of these fertile acres, John, my boy," Couper said with enthusiasm. "Imagine you and our beloved Annie at home in that newly repaired, freshly painted little tabby house, welcoming visitors, inhaling the pungent smell of our marsh mud at low tide, reveling in the sunrise across the marsh and the Lawrence River—exclaiming each time the island sun picks out the glint and sparkle of the ocean in the distance beyond Little St. Simons. I also own another small farm called Longview, adjoining Lawrence to the south. Bought it for the view. On a good day from Longview, the larger Hampton River gives way directly into the sea." He stopped only long enough to rub his nose and consider for a moment. "I could, of course, throw in Longview, so your prospects for profit on the combined acreages would be considerable."

When John looked the other way, pretending to concentrate on the potential, William filled in. "I say, Mr. Couper, that's a magnificent offer, but any owner might well go bankrupt while waiting for either Fraser brother to master what must be the complicated intricacies of planting, of actually managing slaves."

Alert to any change of expression on John Couper's face, wanting desperately not to say the wrong thing, John was glad to see that William's comment had amused their host.

"Now, cast your eyes down about a hundred yards beyond

the little tabby house, both of you," Couper went on. "Do you see those gleaming, dark-green leaves?"

"Yes," John said. "They seem almost to be lit from inside."

"That's the way of our singular island light," Couper exclaimed. "Every visitor to St. Simons is smitten with the light. I'm told that nowhere on earth, save perhaps the south of France, is the light so magical. But, if you'll turn your horses and follow me, we'll ride over there for a firsthand look."

Again trotting side by side along the overgrown lane, the brothers exchanged looks. No words, because neither wanted to dampen Couper's obvious enjoyment of their expedition. But suddenly, despite the glorious island day, the fact that Anne was all his now, and despite her father's obvious faith in him, John felt himself overcome with homesickness for his regiment. Of all times, at the very moment he and William were riding to inspect a particular grove of gleaming dark-leafed trees, his thoughts had fled to the one adventurous life with which he felt familiar. Did William guess? That he knew, John had no doubt, even though his brother appeared perfectly adjusted out of the marines. William had always been able to take or leave the coordinated, colorful, and to John, prestigious, proud role of officer in His Majesty's service. Because Anne so adored her father and St. Simons Island, the moment was not only precarious but important. They were nearing the grove of trees Couper seemed bent on showing them, and almost helplessly, John reminded himself of his vow to keep an open mind.

He reined his horse next to where Couper and William had stopped. The groves on which the almost otherworldly light glinted were obviously orange trees. Couper dismounted, as did John and William.

"Do orange trees require much attention, sir?" William asked.

"A bit more than olives," Couper said eagerly. "But I've been personally acquainted with these sour orange trees, both on other St. Simons plantations and over on our neighboring Jekyll Island, for more than thirty-five years now and believe many to have been planted even before that. Few planters seem to have faith in sour oranges, but then," he added pleasantly, "planters are like the remainder of the human race—spotty in judgment at times. I, for one, mean to do well with them. No fruit on earth makes up into tastier marmalade than sour oranges, when plenty of sugar is used. And that brings me to another experiment that I need help with, John. Sugar cane will, I'm convinced, do well here."

Hoping to deter his gracious host from a lecture on the subject, John asked, "Don't your orange trees freeze when a period of extreme cold strikes, such as that during our stay on Cumberland? Wouldn't a planter's losses be great in that case?"

"That remains to be seen. We were cold here, too, during your 'stay,' as you call it." He swept a hand around the grove. "Look for yourself, son. The fruit was nipped—some lost—but aside from a few drooping branches, the trees stood strong. Like the sour orange, olive trees also withstand our rare cold spells. It's as though these trees possess a sturdier strain of life within them." The older man stood looking about him for a time, his bright blue eyes seeming to caress the grove tree by tree. Then he said, "Now, I have date palms, too, but dates are far more fragile, far more apt to shrink from that icy wind off the water."

"Your date palms at Cannon's Point look fine to me, sir," William said. "I noticed them first thing in your magnificent garden between your house and the river."

"But a year ago, they appeared to have literally melted in the chill. I'm a stubborn Scot, though. I didn't give up on them and they rewarded me, as you saw." Couper turned to face the cleared land where a few of his cattle had moved into sight. "Another dream I have for Lawrence is rutabagas."

"Rutabagas, Mr. Couper?" John asked.

"They're far superior to turnips. Turnips are watery by comparison. Of course, I'd consider them a hobby, but I thrive on experiment and feel sure that with adequate help and proper training of my fieldhands, this acreage where you can now see a few of my cattle could be turned into double-crop land—rutabagas and corn. You see, I now plant my corn in rows five feet apart, land well plowed by oxen in the spring. By the way, I feel almost certain that one day I'll be entirely convinced that oxen are superior on a farm to any horse or mule. Corn planted as I plant it is entirely attended during the summer by a small cultivator harrow of three teeth and a light mule—no bed required for the corn. Through August and into September, say to the fifteenth,

I've found to be our best St. Simons season. During this time the corn is stripped of leaves and tops cut. A furrow is drawn between the rows with a shovel-plow and two bushel baskets of manure dropped into each row. A furrow is made on each side with a bar-share and—"

As soon as Couper had launched into his lecture on how he planted corn, John knew their host had lost not only him but William, as well. When Couper stopped abruptly in the middle of a sentence about furrows and bar-shares, before he got back to rutabagas, it was plain that Couper knew it, too.

"In the name of heaven," the older man said on a slightly embarrassed laugh, "I should have allowed Anne to ride along with us! Either Annie or her mother would have called a halt to my blathering minutes ago. I've done a selfish thing, but at least I realized I'm boring you."

"We're not at all bored, sir," William said.

"Only because you're both gentlemen, Dr. Fraser. I've been known to bore my numerous houseguests painfully by my obsession with agricultural theories. Sincerely, I tell you that I did not mean to do it today. In fact, I warned myself on the ride over here. Even my son warned me before he rode off to Hamilton. He and I, of course, have been known to turn everyone glassy-eyed with our discussions of experimental farming. You're the last men I wanted to see turn numb with listening."

"Oh, Mr. Couper," John said, perhaps a bit too eagerly, "not at all! If my brother and I look numb, it's only because we're both ignorant of such a complicated subject. True, we did grow up on a small farm just outside Dumfries, both forced to pretend at farming. Neither of us took to it, I'm afraid."

"I knew that, John. Dr. William told me and I hope you'll forgive an old man who lives day and night for his family *and* his land and what fine surprises the Almighty has tucked into what the average man calls plain old dirt. I do beg your pardon." Looking at John, he asked, "Have I completely wrecked my own cause, son? Am I a little like a fighting man who oversells his strategy?"

John laughed. "Far from it, sir! I did ride out here today determined to keep an open mind. It's still fairly open. You see, I happen to love my own profession the way you love yours."

"But an intelligent young man like you can do anything he sets his head to do. There's a vast difference between mere enforced farming and the high adventure of agricultural experimentation. And that, I swear to you, is my final argument for the day. Remount, gentlemen, and we'll engage in an activity far more pleasing to you both. You, John, are free to ride back to your bride, while we, Dr. William, will enjoy a brisk gallop to St. Clair, to give you a chance to pay your respects to Miss Frances Anne Wylly. I will gladly visit with her dear parents." In a remarkably agile manner, Couper remounted. Then turning to John, he said, "Ride to Annie, son, and put your mind at rest about your new father-in-law. He has said his piece and throughout the remaining weeks of your stay at Cannon's Point, he vows to keep his foolish but irrepressible dream to himself. And, your new father-in-law will also continue to remind himself that when and if you and Anne return to St. Simons to live must lie entirely with the two of you."

As John galloped alone back over the sun-shot lane to Cannon's Point, he again marveled in the wild beauty around him, the energy and even gait of Anne's horse, Gentleman; but he also worried some, despite the graceful way John Couper had cut off his learned talk on agriculture. That the man held a cherished dream for him and Anne he had no doubt. But that he himself ached, longed, even on the very day after his own wedding, for the freedom and adventure of his old life with the Royal Marines he also had no doubt. Except for the still-glowing distraction of the hours spent loving her last night, sharp longings for his regiment stayed with him. A glance down at his plain gray sleeve, where for years he'd seen the dark-blue and bright yellow braid of his officer's jacket, only sharpened the pain. Until the third failed attempt for a renewal of his commission just last month, he had deluded himself into believing that life would offer him both Anne as his wife *and* a return to the marines.

Well, three failed attempts were not a lifetime. In a little more than a month, he and Anne would sail from Savannah to Liverpool and from there back to London, where his father lived alone and lonely in the fine old house he'd bought on George Street a few years before John's mother died.

He longed to show London to Anne. Equally he dreaded

facing his father's deep sense of failure. Soon, maybe even tonight after they were alone in the room he still thought of as Anne's, he would have to tell her that James Fraser was not particularly successful with his wine business in London.

Anne was excited at the prospect of seeing London and of meeting his father, so he'd seen no reason to dampen her spirits before the wedding. Now, though, they were man and wife. The daily round was upon them. Between their two fathers, they would have to tread softly and carefully: Neither must trammel Anne's father's bright hopes too soon. Neither must misinterpret his father's usual gloomy mood as disapproval of them. The dour, short-spoken James Fraser had seemed pleased, at least, that John had finally settled on one Scottish lass. As pleased as Papa ever allowed himself to be. With cheerful, warmhearted John Couper for a father, Anne might be taken by surprise the first time she heard James Fraser merely grunt good morning.

John knew that his father wanted neither of his sons back in the Royal Marines, and William did seem almost indifferent, quite philosophical, about their rejections. After all, he could practice medicine anywhere and neither had been rejected for want of ability. Both had excellent military records. Britain's wars had simply come to an end. They were no longer needed. As always, John envied William his composure, his quiet acceptance, his contentment with his chosen profession. William would be happy to serve again were he needed. If not, he could as easily decide to stay in Georgia. Clearly, William was as drawn to John Couper as he was, as taken with the always changing St. Simons light and great oaks and winter-flowering camellias with which Mrs. Couper had filled the house for the wedding. Unlike John, William had also saved a little money. To John, youth was the time to enjoy the act of living fully. He had saved almost nothing. Barely enough for his fare back to Georgia and to take Anne to London.

In sight of the Cannon's Point big house now, he turned away his troubling thoughts, a trick he'd learned long ago simply by replacing them with more appealing ones. Appealing thoughts in all ways embodied Anne. And Anne was waiting for his return.

He now believed that her father was not going to trap him with generosity, was not going to go on urging John to accept the excellent opportunity at Lawrence. He trusted John

Couper's sense of timing and his taste. The older man had caught himself going overboard back at Lawrence not half an hour ago. Couper did not strike John as the kind of man who repeated mistakes.

His own father? Slowing his horse at the huge Cannon's Point stable, he prepared his mind and his spirit for greeting Anne and put Papa's heartbreak and gloom to one side.

The sight of her, blue skirt flying as she ran to meet him, reminded him in a flash as bright and blinding as the sunrise over Hampton River that he, John Fraser, was, of all men in the whole world, the most blessed.

Part Three

March 30, 1816–August 1816

Chapter 30

Because John Couper had business in Savannah, only William Fraser accompanied him there on Saturday, March 30, when the newlyweds, almost a month later than planned, sailed finally for Liverpool.

"I did the best I could when I told Annie good-bye," Couper said as he and William climbed slowly up the steps from the Savannah waterfront after they'd watched the Liverpool schooner out of sight and around the bend in the Savannah River. "Actually, I feel quite cruel for having persuaded them to stay longer when I knew how eager they were to be on their way. Do you think I'm showing my age, Dr. William?"

"Not at all, sir. No parent looks forward to saying good-bye to either a son or a daughter, I'm sure. And I'm not so certain Miss Anne was quite as eager to go as she led my brother to believe."

"Oh, I think she was," Couper said firmly. "And she should have been. She belongs to John Fraser now. Not just legally but spiritually, emotionally, bodily. Until you're married, William, you may not be able to understand that, but all of life changes from the moment of those vows. They were both pampering Anne's old father by staying on. I'm helped some in my loneliness, though, by remembering how joyous your father will be to see them once they reach London. Do you resemble James Fraser? Or does John?"

"John *looks* a lot like him. He isn't at all like our father, but they both have the same long, handsome face. Papa is minus the cleft in his chin, though. I've always envied John that cleft because it seems the fair sex is more than a little attracted to it."

Couper had some business to attend to at his factor's on Commerce Row, next door to the countinghouse of Mackay and young Mark Browning, so they headed east on Bay. "Our boat back to Sapelo Island won't be sailing for hours," Couper said. "I'll need time with Mr. Habersham. Would you enjoy dropping in on Browning for a talk? The Mackays seem to feel he's a remarkable young man. Of course, you're more than welcome to accompany me to see my factor. Unless the whole idea of operating a plantation stultifies you as it seems to stultify your brother."

"Do you really think John has no interest at all in learning how to be a planter, Mr. Couper?"

"He tries, bless him, and the Almighty certainly knows I long for him to show some genuine interest, but—"

"But he can't seem to settle into anything until he knows for certain that there's no hope of rejoining the Royal Marines."

"You don't have that obsession, do you, William?"

"No. I rather enjoyed my time in the military. Believed I was contributing with my medical services, but unfortunately for you and your dreams for Anne's future, I'm the Fraser who would welcome such a magnificent opportunity as you're offering my brother. I've always loved the study of science. Being a successful agriculturist is plainly a science."

Couper laughed. "I agree, of course. That's one reason my son, James Hamilton, is going to ring bells all over the world with the progressive steps he'll take once he has a few years of planting experience behind him. He's already made great strides at Hopeton and at my old friend Hamilton's island place. Such strides that this very week Hamilton is having final papers drawn up in Philadelphia for the total transfer of his St. Simons plantation to James."

"He's a lucky young man."

"He's earned it by being James Hamilton Couper."

"I'm sure he has. How he manages to operate a huge holding like Hamilton, along with the other, even larger plantation you and Mr. Hamilton own on the mainland, I can't imagine."

Again, Couper laughed. "You've met my son. Fancying his capabilities shouldn't surprise an intelligent gentleman like you." A departing ship's bell clanged above the shouts of stevedores, then Couper said, with such sorrow William wanted to comfort him, "Can you believe even Savannah seems lonely and empty to me without Anne?"

"Yes, sir. I have no trouble at all believing you miss her even up here in this busy city. Mr. Couper? If it's really all right with you, I think I'd like to tag along when you transact your business with your factor. If you're sure I won't be butting in."

"On the contrary. I'm only doing what every planter does at this time of year—arranging my annual loan. A larger one than usual, of course, after my losses. And, I've known Habersham for so long, without you to fortify me I just might break down and bawl over losing Anne."

More than ever now, William felt a need to comfort this worthy gentleman. But how could anyone short of Anne herself do that? "I can't believe I'll be of any help, sir, but I'm so grateful for your invitation to stay on as a guest at Cannon's Point for as long as I like, I'll certainly do my best. I'll always be a doctor, but I find I'm quite interested in all that goes on in coastal Georgia planting."

Grinning, Couper asked as they turned in at Commerce Row, "And does the vivacious Miss Frances Anne Wylly have anything to do with your attachment to the coast?"

Before William opened the door, he looked directly at the older man and said, "Yes, sir, she has a lot to do with it, but so do you."

Chapter 31

In the cubbyhole aboard ship, which Anne refused to dignify by calling a stateroom, she and John sat facing each other on Saturday of their sixth full week at sea. Anne, as usual, took refuge from the sickening movement of the plunging ship by sitting on the hard bed suspended from the ceiling by ropes, while John straddled a straight chair, bracing himself with his legs each time the ship slid up and then down the great swells outside. They could not hope to reach Liverpool for another day or two, but at least the huge square-rigger was modern enough to provide a private room. For years women passengers had been forced to travel separately from the men, but now any time they chose, which was almost every minute, the newlyweds could be alone together. Once they'd pitched in with buckets and brushes to clean up the cramped quarters, which measured all of six by five feet, they had been alone and, except for walks on deck and at mealtimes, without prying eyes.

Of course, John had laughed at her clumsy efforts with a scrub brush, since Anne had never tried to clean anything, but although this was her first voyage farther from home than school in Charleston, she had proved herself a good sailor. He praised her for that. His praise helped, but not enough to keep back the gnawing homesickness for Cannon's Point. She missed her parents and James, worried about her baby sister, little Belle, missed Anna Matilda, and at almost every turn, missed Eve. Certainly she missed Eve each time she had to wash in cold water, which was every day. She had never gotten up a single morning in her life without fresh underwear laid out, and by now, her knuckles were ugly and red from the miserable chore of washing her own clothes and John's.

The stuffy cabin added to her homesickness for the openness of Cannon's Point, but after nearly ten days of stormy weather, at least the sea had calmed enough for them to walk the deck this morning under a low, heavy sky. That helped, but the missing had become synonymous with suffocation. Oh, she tried to give thanks for every minute spent alone with John, but only last night she'd actually dreamed of the freedom and the mild, soft air of St. Simons. Laughing with John lessened some of the ache for the sound of Papa's voice, but she was sick unto death of being forced to eat every ghastly, greasy, tasteless meal with the seven other passengers, all strangers and all as dull as dishwater.

John praised her also for not complaining before the two dreary men and the five women passengers, all of whom struck Anne by now as being interested in nothing but their own discomforts, railing against the hard beds, the lumpy pillows, and the never-ending groan of the ship's wooden hull plunging through the waters, the incessant creaking of its masts. Anne had always thought square-riggers the handsomest of all sailing vessels, but there must have been a thousand sails, and up on deck the crew never seemed satisfied that they weren't in need of being changed—raised or lowered, furled or unfurled.

From his perch on what must be the world's most uncomfortable wooden chair, John gave her a warm grin. "If by a stroke of luck, Annie, we dock sometime tomorrow or the next day, we'll then have fewer than three days by stagecoach from Liverpool to London. I promise a good meal in Liverpool. For someone who grew up eating Sans Foix's delicacies, I must say you've faced those shipboard concoctions by poor Mrs. Johnson with great, good humor. Your father would be proud of you choking down all that stringy chicken and overfried fish. At least, we have the memories of the succulent ham and beef stew he provided as our contribution to the early meals at sea. Believe me, after gnawing my way through Mrs. Johnson's pullets, I cherish those memories." He moved their one candle close enough for a better look at her face. "Poor Annie. Is anything wrong beyond the suffocation you must feel shut up in this stuffy cubicle, darling?"

"Are you absolutely sure your father is going to like me?"

she asked, caressing his fingers one by one as she talked. "I want the truth. When you've known me longer you'll find I can shake off dark moods a lot more quickly with a little warning of what might be up ahead. I don't do well at all with sudden disappointments. Will he think I'm terribly spoiled and helpless?"

"My dearest girl, I've lived all these years as my father's son and the times I've guessed correctly what his reactions might be are far fewer than I care to admit. William would be the person to ask. Not I."

"But William isn't a bit like your father. You told me that long ago. How would he know more than you?"

"Because he's always been the old boy's favorite son."

"I still don't believe that!"

"Of course you don't believe it because you're so hopelessly in love with me."

"Be serious."

"I am serious. I strongly resemble my father in looks and, if I hadn't found you, would surely have grown old with his grumpy, stern countenance. I did find you, though, and so I intend to remain only dashing and pleasing until I'm an old, old man." He moved to sit beside her on the bed, took her in his arms and said quite solemnly, "Can you forgive me for teasing when you so plainly dread meeting my father? But, Annie, how does a man prepare his wife for an encounter even he can't imagine? My remaining parent is not predictable. He should adore you. After all, he's a man of excellent taste, but he did lose my mother and neither William nor I have seen any sign that he won't live out his lonely life in bitterness because it was *his* wife who died."

"Have you tried putting yourself in his place? Wouldn't that help you to understand what might happen even to your sunny nature if you experienced such grief? How long has he lived alone in the house on George Street?"

"My mother died over nine years ago, before I went into the Royal Marines at barely sixteen. Anne, I've never found it easy to see my father's point of view."

"I don't mean to preach, but now that you love me, you must have some idea of how he misses her."

The candlelight on John's face showed her that he had withdrawn. She couldn't bear that. "I am preaching, aren't I?"

"No."

"Is that all you can say? Just—no?"

"You'll meet Father soon enough. I honestly think you have a better chance than anyone else to break through his stony exterior. The old fellow can't have a hard heart or he wouldn't have adored my mother as he did."

"It helps for you to tell me even that much."

"Look here, I knew we had to have this talk sooner or later. I was just hoping for later. He is my father and I probably care about him far more than I've ever been able to admit."

"Why couldn't you admit it?"

"I didn't think he'd care one way or another."

"But he isn't the only person to consider."

She saw his perfect eyebrows pull together in a frown, and then he said, "I'm afraid I don't know what you mean by that."

"When you keep your—your guard up about someone as important as your own father, don't you think it affects other people too? Like me?"

The frown vanished and in its place came a look of pure adoration. Then he laughed. "You never stop surprising me. How do you happen to be so wise at nineteen?"

"It has nothing to do with being wise. I'm just here in this smothering cabin with you and I plan to be wherever you are for the remainder of my life and I'm not happy if I think anything's troubling you."

He kissed her. "I'm no more troubled over my father now than I was the afternoon my unit pounded on the door of Mrs. Shaw's big mansion on Cumberland Island and took you captive."

"But I didn't love you then the way I love you now," she said. "I thought you were gorgeous, but I didn't know I'd ever care about every single thing that might bother you. And what about William? I wonder if it's fair to William for you to hold some sort of boyhood grudge against your father just because it always seemed to you that he favored William."

John got up abruptly and did his best to pace the cabin. With his long legs, there really wasn't room and Anne couldn't help smiling.

"Did that help?" she asked gently when he sat down on the bed beside her.

Now he smiled, too. "No, of course, it didn't help. I'm

every bit as splendid as you think I am, but any grown man should know better than to try to pace in a box! Did I look as silly as I felt?"

"Yes, but isn't it wonderful that we can both laugh? Let's always laugh when we need to."

"I promise, milady. And I insist that you believe me when I say none of my alienation from Father has ever come between William and me. Why, he can even tease me about it."

"Good. For now, that's all I need to know—except, do we have to take a stage from Liverpool to London? I guess we do or we wouldn't be doing it. I hope they're not as bad in England as they are in Georgia! I hate being slammed around by every rut we hit in the road. All those smelly people packed in with us. I'll hate that even more than aching muscles, won't you?"

"Yes, I will and yes, we have to take the stage. I don't have funds enough for another long water voyage. I'm sorry, but we'll have to let the stage do its worst. I'll be right there to hold on to you."

Both arms around his neck, she whispered, "Always be! Oh, John, always be right here to hold me."

Chapter 32

"It doesn't look like it here," John said as their crowded, rank-smelling but sleek-appearing stage stopped finally at the Lad Lane, Wood Street coach stop, "but London is lovely in the spring. Did you notice the name of the stop on that sign over there?"

"No," Anne said, too mystified by all the noise and confusion and crowds of people actually to see much of anything. Then, she looked at the sign and laughed merrily. "John, how marvelous! Like something made up in an English novel—Swan with Two Necks. Where do the English find these quaint names?"

"Never mind where they find them, they just do," he said, whistling for a hackney cab. "Swan with Two Necks happens to be the nearest stop to Portman Square and Number 2 George Street. There! Look over that way beyond that line of hacks and you'll see an entire clump of London trees dressing themselves for spring, Annie."

It was the sixth of May and indeed the tender green was doing its best in the dust and racket to soften the harshness of what must be the world's noisiest, busiest city. Anne had been enchanted with almost every tiny, quiet, English countryside town through which their stage had passed, had been loath to leave a few of the towns after a brief stop. But John's promise that they would soon spend time in the country consoled her now. She needed that because just the thought of a week, maybe a month, spent in the confusion of London brought the homesickness rushing back.

Sitting bolt upright in the one-horse hack John hired to take them to his father's house near Portman Square, Anne was glad that finally they were alone again, even though the springs stuck up through the cracked leather seat and their excess baggage slid and bumped around where they sat side by side, John's arm around her, steadying her as he'd promised. Over the two hundred miles or so from Liverpool, not one full minute had passed without laughter, grumbling, or raucous shouts among the other passengers. One foppishly dressed, freckled young man, too full of ale, had never tired of shouting derisively in the direction of every knot of country folk gathered to watch the London-bound stage pound past.

"I really must be a country girl," she said, "because I'm already wondering if there's ever any real silence in London."

"Aye, there is—in the still of some nights. Poor little Annie is missing Cannon's Point again. I miss it, too—the shady lanes, the winding, shadowy roads lined with great oaks and cedars, the Spanish moss plumes waving in a wind off the water. Can you bear that it will be different here, my darling? Different in all ways except my love for you. With all my heart, I'll try to make up for some of what you're missing."

The best response seemed to be a smile, a pat on his hand. They had reached a wide thoroughfare that John said was London's famous Oxford Street. Traffic would move a bit more freely than through the just-passed, drab, rackety streets, where every carrier's cart sounded as though it was about to lose a wheel or collapse completely. Few vehicles even slowed for tradesmen on foot, and the hawkers' cries didn't strike her as being nearly as colorful or romantic as English novels had led her to believe.

"I'll take you to see the Tower of London, Westminster, the famous London Docks, Covent Garden Theater—" He looked out the cab window. "Actually, we can visit a spot that should interest you as a resident of St. Simons Island. Did you ever hear of London's Wesley Chapel? John Wesley and his brother, Charles, you know, went over back in 1733 with General James Oglethorpe to help found the colony of Georgia itself. I've heard it said that the Wesleys preached right out under some of those glorious live oaks at Frederica."

Anne took a deep breath, not exactly a sigh, but she had known forever about Oglethorpe and the Wesleys. "Give me a history lesson later, darling, please? I'm too nervous now.

I'm beginning to shake all over at the thought of finally meeting your father. Anyway, how can I concentrate on a tour of London in all this noise?"

She'd already realized that the hideous grinding sound that seemed never to let up was the noise of iron-shod wheels on the stone setts of London streets—iron-shod wheels *and* horses on stone. To her ears, accustomed only to the muffled thud and creaky, homey rattle of horses and wagons and carriages over St. Simons' sandy roads and lanes, the incessant din of the city was unnerving. She would have to find a way to ignore it and she would or die trying. Wherever John was, there she meant somehow to try to be content.

After they'd ridden for what seemed a long time on Oxford Street, she said, "You know my father's place at Cannon's Point so well, and I'm getting awfully nervous at the thought of actually being in the very house you and your father and William call home. I've really tried to be such a good traveler for all these weeks, but now I don't think I can wait much longer."

"You've been a superior traveler," he said, "and I could count on one hand the times you've come even close to losing your temper without Eve to help you. I'm proud of you."

"I don't like being without her, though, one bit."

"Why should you? You've had her for most of your life."

"Won't it be heavenly to have a real bath? Does your father have good servants? I dream of the moment someone fills a tub for me with luscious hot water!"

He laughed. "I'll do it this very afternoon, I promise."

"*You* will do it?"

"Annie, blessed Annie, there aren't many slaves in England. Only a few blackamoors brought home by Empire plantation owners for a visit. Slavery's frowned on in England. Haven't you heard?"

"Of course, I know that, smarty! But I'm serious. Londoners do have white servants—lots of them. All the novels say so and you told me you were a sort of Radical who'd even like to be fighting for the rights of the working class. Your father must have wonderfully obedient servants."

"My father has a charwoman twice a week, one combination cook and housekeeper who lives in, and that's it. We all know exactly how to heat water and fill tubs."

"One woman cooks *and* keeps house?"

"Aye, and she is an amazing woman, too. Her name is Flora McLeod, proud to be pure Scottish, therefore quite disdainful of the English, and I must give you one word of warning. In Flora's mind, she not only owns the George Street house, she also owns my father and William and especially me."

"Oh, dear. Will she like me? Do I need to be careful with her?"

"The answer to both questions is yes. She'll feel you're beautiful enough for me right off and eventually let you know she does. Even Flora won't be able to resist your charms. At first, though, a bit of caution might be best."

"Caution? Is she bossy?"

"Completely. And possessive, but also quite wise in her way. Unlike with my father, I'm Flora's favorite of his two sons."

She turned to look at him. "Everything's so—different. I'm scared. Should I be?"

"No."

"You do that a lot."

"What?"

"Answer in just one word without explaining anything."

He laughed. "Maybe I have a touch of the dour Scot in me after all. My father, much of the time, is the epitome of the dour Scot."

"All Scottish people are not dour!"

"With a father like yours and such a gracious, pleasant mother, I can certainly understand your saying that. My mother wasn't dour, either. Far from it."

"You've said so little about her. Was she pretty?"

"Aye. To me, she was. Unlike your tall, slender mother, mine was short, a little plump, but even on her deathbed—her face waxen and tortured with pain—to me, she was hauntingly beautiful. To my poor father, a veritable goddess."

"I'm glad you were at home when she died. I'm sure she was glad, too."

"William and I were both there." He sighed. "Our mother was all gentleness and patience. A thinking lady. A great reader and student. William is like her in his ways."

"Have you always been aware that William and your mother were alike?"

"Since I've been old enough to notice things like that, I suppose. Why?"

"Then, could William's being like her have anything to do with your father's acting as though he favors him?"

"You are wise, Annie."

Grinning impishly, she said, "I knew you'd discover that sooner or later. Does your father know we're likely to arrive this week?"

With a mock frown, he mused, "Now, that must be about the twelfth time you've asked. Yes, and I guarantee Flora has had our room made up for days and redusts it every day at least once."

"Are the London squares anything like Savannah's squares?"

"In the area where we live, rather. Laid out in grids. They're generally larger, though, in London. But with trees and shrubbery and in season, flowers. My father's house is not right on Portman Square. Just nearby. It's a good house. Built about twenty years ago by Huguenot craftsmen before the Regency architects began to smear buildings with stucco and tack on false turrets. It's honey-colored brick with white stone facing and a brown front door. Four stories, center entrance hall." He chuckled. "By the way, there are thirty-some George Streets in London. I believe Father's address is considered one of the better ones. Like all London houses, I'm sure you'll think it dark and shadowy. You may feel smothered at first after Cannon's Point."

"Does your home have a porch?"

"No, my dear, not on George Street! You won't have a single chance to march in an English thunderstorm. It's a terrace house, flush with the street, with such a tiny court-yard in back, you'd never honor it as a yard at all. It's even brick-paved. Not a blade of grass. Only a few scrawny plants. Unlike your father, mine has no hint of a green thumb. Nothing blooms for the man."

"Oh, I'm sorry for him!"

"Please don't be. He wouldn't like that at all. He simply ignores the fact that, as you can see, everything blooms in London for everyone else. Pretends he doesn't care for plants and gardens. Although he used to buy flowers on the streets for Mother."

"How old is he?"

"Almost exactly your father's age, fifty-seven and a few months."

"That isn't old."

"In John Couper, no, it certainly isn't."

"Are you purposely trying not to get my hopes too high that Mr. Fraser and I will get along with each other? If you look so much like him, he has to be handsome and I plan to love him right off."

He turned to face her. "Take a look at me and add thirty or more years to what you see. My father and I both have the same long, horse face. When I was quite young, I began to realize that I had to cultivate a sunny disposition, to act cheerful whether I felt like it or not, to entertain people, to laugh a lot. A sour look on a face like this is frightening!" His quick laughter came. "So, you see why I fell immediately in love with you? You make me so happy, it's my one guarantee that I'll never turn into a sullen old man."

"Does your father have a dimple in his chin like yours?"

"No. And I resist the word *dimple.* Can't you call it a cleft?"

In response and to keep him amused, she sang a snatch of a lilting Scottish ballad Papa had taught her as a child: " 'He wore a blue bonnet, blue bonnet, blue bonnet—he wore a blue bonnet, a dimple in his chin. . . .' "

The hack driver had passed Portman Square while she was singing and was turning, not too carefully, into George Street when John, in broad daylight, swept her into his arms. "We're about there and it's going to be all right, Annie. My father will learn to adore you before this evening is over. And I do have real affection for the man. I've only been trying to prepare you for someone different in almost every way from your own beloved father."

"I know and I'll remember. If you'll remember that, except when he first left Scotland at sixteen and sailed alone to America as an indentured clerk, my father has, so far as I know, never, never been lonely. Remember your own father's terrible loneliness, please."

"Yes, ma'am. His one letter to me at Cannon's Point seemed to show that he's rather pleased we're coming, that I have taken a wife at last. After all, he's offered to pay for our wedding trip—*if* we choose Scotland. We're also welcome to live at 2 George Street for as long as we like. And

Anne, oh, Anne, best of all—no matter what happens, we're together."

Anne supposed the sun must be setting behind them, out of sight in back of the buildings, as the rattly hack stopped before the Fraser house. The excitement at actually being in a foreign city and about to meet John's father almost overcame her. She felt suddenly in need of air as John helped her down onto the brick sidewalk smack in front of the handsome but flat-faced house, its front steps leading straight up to the dark front door.

The Cannon's Point big house faced east, and the view out over Hampton River and Little St. Simons, to the sea, was as familiar to her as breathing. Watching each morning for a different sunrise, and each afternoon for a different afterglow when the sun set on the leeward side of the island, had been as much a part of her life as the urgent calls and shouts of Papa's people the minute any one of them sighted a visiting plantation boat heading for the Couper dock. To her there was no view on George Street. The wide front door of John's father's house was closed. Across the street, a white-aproned nanny, leading a child, walked past other flat-faced brick and stucco houses, but there was no sign of life at the Fraser home. Not even a curtain stirred at a single window of any of the four stories.

"Well, we're here," John was saying, his voice strained. "I'll pay the driver and give him a hand with our trunks and valises. Wait right where you are, darling. Enjoy the sunset. It's what we have here in London."

That was it! That was the cause of her queasy, empty feeling. She was right in the big, bustling, famous city of London—"the very ground of all our Anglo-Saxon roots," Papa always said—but there were no helpful people to welcome them, to carry things, and John had to leave her standing there alone. She felt desolate, missing the familiar ceremony of coming home. John was right about the sky, too. The pale lemon, smoky London sunset flattened her spirit, even with John so near making his little jokes with the paid hackman as the two piled valise on top of trunk, box on box, right in the street in front of the silent, closed house. Who would carry it all inside? Father Fraser had only one Scottish woman who did everything, but no woman could be expected to take care of all that luggage.

She looked up again at the silent windows, the closed door, then went to the edge of the sidewalk and peered up at the sky, straining to give the sad London sunset a better chance. Perhaps she couldn't see the entire sunset because of all the buildings, one pushed up against another, and the tall city trees, naked, without one strand of moss. Maybe the weak, watery light around her was only part of what the English sky had to offer. No one could see an entire sunset from Cannon's Point, either, but she'd always known when the huge, vermilion sun ball began to sink in the west, because the warm, coppery reflection from it picked out tree trunks and lit banners of gray moss. People always knew, unless it was raining, that another day was ending so that the stars could have their turn.

Back home, had she just arrived, Eve would already have run to greet her, to round up a dozen or so others to help June carry out Eve's orders—exactly how to handle each box and where to place each valise. By the time she'd hugged Papa and Mama and said hello to whoever happened to be visiting Cannon's Point at the moment, Eve would have prepared her bath upstairs in Anne's room and laid out the correct clothing, all hooks unfastened, an assortment of shawls or fichus to choose from, depending on the weather.

There was at least less noise here on George Street than at the Swan with Two Necks coach stop, but nothing gave the least hint of real silence except the still-closed house. Then a dog barked sharply, a vendor cried his wares, and four carriages rattled and careened past over the cobblestones. But there wasn't a single note of music! Her ears ached for just one rhythmic shout from the throats of Papa's oarsmen. One welcoming peal of laughter, one of Papa's jokes, no matter how feeble, would have helped soothe her flailing heart. John told her as he labored past and up the steps, arms loaded, that their hackney driver would give him a hand as far as the front hall. Other than that, no one said anything.

She clung for dear life to the fact that he had said while they were still in the hack, "No matter what happens, we're together."

They were, but John seemed completely at home in this stark, alien setting and Anne was on the verge of failing him —even before she'd met his father.

* * *

Arms folded over her ample, apron-covered bosom, Flora McLeod stood watching the whole scene from a crack in the fresh, white muslin parlor curtains she'd just ironed and hung yesterday so that the room would look light and welcoming for her laddie, Johnnie. Comin' home, he was, just like in the olden days from school, but this time him a grown mon with shoulders wide as a mountain and his dear face so handsome, givin' cheer to the dark old house. Her laddie, strong enough to carry such a load—the load his new bride had forced on him!

Flora missed nothing of John's manliness even though he was dressed in plain civilian clothes now—caught every grin as he talked with the hackman—but she'd also kept an eagle eye on *her* standin' all by herself on George Street, no doubt givin' the house the up and down. Bless them trees, she thought, fer dressin' theirselves in all that new green. She longed daily for Scotland, but the city, she guessed, had its beauty too, in the spring of the year. Her laddie had written that in all his life he never saw trees and gardens and beauty as rich as in Georgia, where *she* come from. Well, he'd be takin' her to Scotland for their weddin' trip and then her eyes could bug right outa that purty face at true beauty.

Flora's laddie's new wife did look to be as purty as any oil painting. Tired and wrinkled and mussed as she was from weeks on the ocean, then from jostlin' over miles and miles of rough road in a stage, the dark-haired girl stood there regal like a queen. She would have given a week's pay to read the girl's thoughts standin' there by herself in a strange land. She could hear Johnnie and the hackman bumping boxes and bundles against the front door, but her laddie hadn't knocked yet. She'd wait. Then wait still longer for his highness to make his way from his home office at the back of the first-floor hall to where she stood now, smoothing her best striped long skirt, wanting, as always, to look as good as a portly woman of fifty-three could look for company.

"I wonder if she's as purty inside as out," Flora muttered to herself, still thinking of her laddie's bride out on the sidewalk. She hoped Mister Fraser hadn't heard, because he was against her talking to herself at all times, a habit she'd come to enjoy since he was so closemouthed. "Well," she muttered, "if he heard, he heard."

He did. He was shuffling down the hall now as if it was no

more than a neighbor rapping on the front door. Heart pounding with sheer joy, Flora kept her place just outside the parlor door while his highness took his time about unlatching the door to Johnnie and his new wife.

"Thank the good Lord he's here safe," she said, addressing herself now to John's father as he swung open the door.

"Father!" She heard Johnnie call out in the same dear voice that had always put her in mind of music. "Father, we're here! Both tired and travel-worn, but we're here. It's good to see you again."

At once, Flora busied herself directing the driver where to pile the valises, hauling one and then another trunk herself to the far side of the hall. Then she stood waiting to be introduced to the dazed-appearing, bonnie lass her laddie had married.

"Father," Johnnie was saying, "may I present my wife, Anne Couper Fraser? Anne, this is my father."

All present had to have heard Flora draw in her breath as she stood waiting to see just how the stern-faced master of the house would conduct himself. Neither Flora McLeod nor Johnnie had ever been able to read him the way William could.

Flora jumped a little and pursed her lips when Anne Fraser stepped quickly forward and planted a kiss right on his highness's cheek!

"Yes," the new wife said cheerfully, "I'm Anne, Father Fraser. I'll look a lot better after a bath and some fresh clothes, but I hope you're glad we're here. With all my heart, I hope you're going to like me."

"And how do you do, Miss Anne?" James Fraser said, one hand touching his cheek where she'd kissed him. Flora sensed the poor, befuddled, dumbfounded man didn't realize his hand had flown there. She'd just surprised him so by the kiss. "I'm sure you're exhausted and—and—" Before he managed to get out one more word, Flora saw the first genuine smile on his face she'd seen in weeks.

"And what, Father?" her laddie asked a bit uneasily, but straight out with it, as always.

"And I'm sure I am going to like you very-ry much, young lady."

When Anne turned immediately to Flora, standing ramrod straight, Johnnie presented Anne to her, calling Flora McLeod his best friend on earth.

"Flora knows all about baths," Johnnie laughed, teasing. "She scrubbed both William and me when we were infants until it's a wonder there's an inch of skin left on either of us. Isn't that right, Flora? And I predict the two of you will be good friends in no time at all."

Her laddie shouldn't have said that. It was too swift. Too soon. Too soon for a body to know any such thing.

When Flora curtsied, a quick, dutiful bob, as any good servant would, Anne held out her hand to her.

"You did that quite gracefully, Miss McLeod," she said, "but I'd like it far better if you shook my hand or gave me a hug. John loves and respects you so much, I find I do, too. More than ever now that we've met."

Giving the strong, refined little hand a quick fingertip squeeze, Flora curtsied again from habit and said, "Thank you, mum. I do thank you. And I'm pleased to mak' your acquaintance." Then, she turned at once to the two men. Her very look ordered their help in carrying the pile of luggage upstairs to the room she'd had ready for days. "Once all this is where it belongs, I'll heat some water," she said. "When it's scalding, Mr. Fraser and Johnnie can carry it up for your baths. I'll bring the cool m'self."

Chapter 33

Since her fine-threaded white linen had been packed for so long in a trunk, it was mussed, but Anne bathed and dressed for a late dinner as presentably as she could, then struggled with her hair. In Coventry last night, she had washed it in three big bowls, much to the annoyance of two grumbling women with whom she'd had to share a room. Their remarks, which she was unable to ignore, had caused her to hurry through the rinsing, so her dark hair had no shine, felt stiff, and certainly needed to be washed again.

When John stooped behind where she sat before the looking glass to brush his own short hair, she envied his not having to fuss with curls. She also missed Eve so much it was all she could do to muster a smile.

"Missing Eve?" He grinned down at her, then kissed the back of her neck.

"More than I have any intention of admitting, even to you," she said. "Do I look all right? I know Flora's going to be inspecting me head to foot. She doesn't think I'm good enough for you."

"Flora wouldn't approve if I married the *grande dame* of the London theater, Sarah Siddons! But, who cares? I approve. And I'm proud of you always."

At their bedroom door, still closed to the upstairs hallway, she whispered, "I marvel at Flora McLeod. Who serves the meal after she cooks it?"

"Flora."

"Doesn't your father feel the need of a butler? What does she do when there's company in the house? When more than two extra people come for dinner?"

"They don't. So far as I know, Father hasn't had anyone

but William and me for dinner in years. We had four servants until Mother died. He let them all go but Flora—at her insistence. What you must try to understand is that by Flora's standards, the good woman has a marvelous life. She's the ruling hand. She alone is the symbol of Father's long-ago, happy days. Hard to believe now, I know, but he was once a most contented man. Now he depends entirely on Flora McLeod, and the harder she works, the more she enjoys being a martyr. That he hires a charwoman two days a week is, to Flora, proof that he esteems her too highly to expect her to do plain cleaning. For her, that's paradise. For Father, I fear, it's a necessary economy."

Anne frowned. "But John, this is a fine house. Surely he doesn't have to economize to that extent."

He reached for the doorknob. "I—I think he does."

"You *think* he does? Don't you know? I thought wine merchants did very well."

"Generally, they do. Father did for much of my lifetime. I'm honestly not sure now. Neither William nor I ever quite understood the whole picture. You'll discover Father can be secretive as well as stubborn. Even now, it may take me weeks to find out the true state of his finances. I may never know. But I've learned to keep my peace and hope for the best. His affairs could have improved some while I was in Georgia. Or he may be worse off. One thing I do know and that is Flora does not tolerate serving cold food, so let's go on down to dinner."

Feeling as though she'd stepped into the pages of a Jane Austen or a Walter Scott novel, where almost nothing seemed familiar or predictable, Anne gave him her most adoring smile, took his arm, and held tight as they started down the stairs—both of them, she knew, hoping for the best.

He and Anne were halfway down the flight of steps when John could tell from the dry sound of his father's cough that he was already waiting in the first-floor dining room. What had been their cheerful family parlor to the rear was now James Fraser's office, and the thought that they would be sitting after dinner in the huge, dark, ornate company parlor, where conversation for John had always been difficult, made him apprehensive. Just after his mother died, Father had emptied the cozy family parlor and moved his library and big walnut desk into it. As John and Anne passed the room now, the door was closed, as usual, whether the room was occupied or not. Were grief and isolation and financial worry lessened, he wondered, behind a closed door? Was his father still as lonely as Anne thought, as worried about his wine-importing business as John suspected?

In the gloomy first-floor hall, Anne stopped to peer through the shadows at what John's father had always called his mother's masterpiece—the Fraser family crest—meticulously stitched in petit point and framed by Father with great care in a polished shadow box.

"Is that your family's coat of arms?" she asked.

"Aye," John said softly, as always careful not to allow Father to overhear him poke the slightest fun at the cherished family symbol. "The noble buck's head of the Fraser clan. See that you pay it the proper respect, lass."

"It's beautiful! And what perfect stitching!"

"You'll do splendidly with Father, have no fear. He's absolutely pompous about my mother's handiwork and his frame. *And* the motto that swells his chest and head with pride. See it there? *'I am ready.'* Remember that, my love. For hundreds of years, the Frasers have been—ready!"

"Stop making fun, John. I just thought of something. As far as I know, Papa's Couper family didn't have a special crest, but Mama's Maxwells certainly did."

"You can be sure of that, beautiful Annie. Even Papa wouldn't claim higher birth than a genuine Maxwell. Don't forget I grew up alongside Caerlaverock Castle outside of Dumfries. William too."

"But something else is even more amazing," she said, plainly excited. "Your crest is a buck's head and the Maxwell crest is a whole stag! They're so similar. Papa always joked about it. Called it 'a dauntless stag lodged in front of a holly bush proper.' Papa respects Mama's ancient Scottish heritage—he's very proud of it, in fact—but he also enjoys laughing about what he calls his own unadorned family. Loves to tease Mama about her family motto—*'I flourish again.'* "

John's smile was wistful. He'd give almost anything if sunny-natured John Couper could join them for dinner right now. His father-in-law would know exactly how to cheer James Fraser, not only would give the man's spirits a lift but would light up even the depressing shadows inside the house on George Street.

If I find myself steadily contrasting both the house here and my father with Cannon's Point and John Couper, he thought, what must my poor Anne be going through? She's not only quite helpless without Eve, she must be wondering how she can survive away from the light and space of Cannon's Point and the sheer joy everyone finds in her father.

Did he dare hope that Flora might sense Anne's needs and understand? Would he be able to find a way to ease the strain at the dinner table without William there to help?

His father's impatient cough jerked him back to the moment as he and Anne entered the chilly dining room, where even Flora's extra Bouilotte gas lamp didn't seem to thin the darkness much. John girded himself, determined somehow to brighten the atmosphere. Flora would come any moment with their entrée and if he raved enough about her cooking, that would help. The suitable time to have begun his commendation would have been with his first whiff from the kitchen of rosemary and roast lamb, his favorite. No surprise that Flora had chosen it for their first meal at home, bless her. But he said nothing. He was still too surprised that Father had been there, already seated before anyone else. Father's usual way would have been to enter at what to John had always seemed a calculated one minute late, allowing time for the long-familiar, odd silence to fall around the table while he and William waited. Small wonder that the memory of Mother's warm, sparkling smile grew more and more important to both boys as the years went by.

"Well, Papa," he said, starting right off on the wrong foot because James Fraser demanded to be called Father. "You must be hungry to have made your way so early to your place at table. Oh, I—I hope you'll forgive me, sir. I haven't slipped and called you Papa in years."

"Blame me for that, Mr. Fraser," Anne said sweetly. "In America, we Southerners call our fathers papa. John's heard it over and over."

As though Anne hadn't said a word, the older man cleared his throat, then declared, "I have never purposely been late to dinner for our good Flora's sake. At times," he went on, addressing himself at least partly to Anne, "I suppose I have been known to be a minute or so tardy, but only when there was one more important business matter to be attended to in my office."

As always, John thought, his parent's explanation told no one anything. An awkward silence hung over the table while Father sat scrutinizing Anne's expectant face. Then, just when John was beginning to squirm, his father said with only the semblance of a smile, "You are welcome at our humble board, Miss Anne."

"Oh, thank you, Father Fraser," Anne said so hopefully that John longed to rescue her from the whole ordeal. "I'm ever so grateful for your hospitality and I'm sure I'm going to enjoy everything. Certainly, if the aroma from your kitchen downstairs is any indication. From what John has told me about your Flora McLeod, I can scarcely wait to taste the first bite!" From her chair at James Fraser's right, Anne reached in her spontaneous way to give him an affectionate touch on the back of his aging hand. "You're indeed fortunate to have Miss McLeod, aren't you?"

Seated across from Anne, at his parent's left, John could scarcely believe what he saw on his father's normally stern face. The man was smiling, almost delightedly, at Anne. As usual, he kept Anne waiting for his verbal response, but he actually went right on smiling.

"Fortunate, Miss Anne? Perhaps. Flora McLeod's been with us for twenty-six years, a part of our now diminished family." John then heard the crackly sound he remembered from the old days as his father's laugh. "I'd say at times," his father went on, "that Flora might be called the head of the family."

"My father's chef has been with us for all of my nineteen years and longer," Anne was saying eagerly. "He's from Santo Domingo and his name is Cassamene Sans Foix. Our home at Cannon's Point is actually famous for his superior cooking, too, as I'm sure yours is. Sans Foix delights in his role, chats with our guests, and certainly acts much of the time as though he's head of our household. Papa seems to enjoy that very much, doesn't he, John?"

Before he could answer, his father asked bluntly, "And is this man a slave?"

John looked quickly at Anne, fearing a bombshell had been fired, intentionally or otherwise.

"Oh, no," Anne answered easily. "Sans Foix is a free person of color. My father pays him for his expertise.

They're good friends. Papa often goes to Sans Foix for advice. But actually, you would have to know my father to understand, sir, that among his—his people who are slaves, he's revered. Papa's really friends with some of them, especially our butler, Johnson, whom we usually call Johnny."

Hoping his relief didn't show, John felt his taut jaw relax and leaned back in his chair. Anne, unlike many of the Couper neighbors he'd met on St. Simons, had taken no offense whatever to the use of the word *slave.* He'd certainly never heard Anne use it, but her new father-in-law's abrupt question had seemed not to faze her.

"I'm sure, as a Scot myself, Mr. Fraser, you'll be interested that in order to please my father, our butler, Johnson, blew and squeaked and labored until he actually learned how to play the bagpipes."

James Fraser was leaning toward Anne now, almost eagerly. "Indeed! Remarkable, I'd say. An African playing the pipes!"

"He's really quite skillful now and when he isn't playing his fiddle for dancing if our house is full of guests, as it frequently is, Johnny entertains nobly on the pipes. Papa's quite proud of him."

"Never did get the knack of pipes," Fraser said. "Flora's brother was born with it. Piped as soon as he was old enough to bear the weight of the drone. Flora, tell our charming guest that I'm right."

John had heard Flora's familiar, lumbering step on the steep stair that led up from her basement kitchen. He knew she was on her way bearing the heavy silver platter of roast lamb, but his father's amazingly warm talk with Anne had so occupied him that he had missed the woman's actual entrance into the dining room. Missed his big chance to create a little more warmth and merriment by exclaiming as he'd always done when she first appeared.

"Aye," Flora said on a grunt, settling the enormous platter before John's father for carving. "You're correct, Mr. Fraser, if piping is the topic of impor-rtance this minute."

Flora's feelings were wounded. Bagpipes, indeed! John could almost hear her thinking as she stepped back from the table, hands on wide hips, her longed-for moment of entrance already past.

"Flora, I'm speechless," John said, lying only a little. "I haven't been able to utter a word since I saw you walk through that door with what must be the most toothsome leg of lamb even *you* have ever baked. Papa, pick up your carving knife and begin, please! Do you realize how long it's been since I've tasted Flora's lamb?"

His father, making no move toward the carving set, slowly turned his head to look at John. "That, m'boy, marks the second time since your return to this house that you've addressed me as—Papa. Is this a custom you've adopted?"

"Sorry, Father," John said. "I—I—"

"It's my fault, remember, sir?" Anne put in quickly. "John's heard me refer so often to my own father as papa, I'm sure he said it without thinking. Please understand how excited and happy we both are to be here with you—and Miss Flora. And forgive us both! When you meet my father someday, and I do hope you will, you'll understand exactly why he's called Papa. Papa is a—a bouncy word, a cheery word. He's—he's like that. . . ."

Anne, John knew, almost never stammered or even hesitated when she spoke. She slowed to a halt now, plainly aware that his father could well take her words about John Couper's bouncy, cheerful nature as a criticism of his own. Not so. While John was casting about for a soothing remark, his father's crackly laughter surprised him again.

"So, your papa's as buoyant and good natured as both my sons claim, eh, lassie?"

"Oh, yes, sir! In fact, my brother, James Hamilton, although brilliant and scholarly, is often quite shocked at Papa and me."

"Oh, and how's that, Miss Anne?"

"Couldn't you just call me Anne or—Daughter? After all," she said, touching his hand again, "I am your daughter now."

A rather obvious amount of throat clearing preceded his father's guarded response. "Uh—aye. Aye, I can call you Daughter, with pleasure. And from now on, I mean to do just that. But tell me, why is it your brother, James Hamilton, is—how did you put it—shocked at you and your father?"

"We're all as close as a family can be, but James is just totally unable to understand why it is that Papa and I find something funny in almost everything."

"Oh—ho, ho." The dry laugh decided John to jump right into the conversation with Anne.

"You may not believe this, Father, but a good, roaring, wild storm never hits St. Simons Island but it sends Anne and Mr. John Couper, hand in hand, outside to the big, wide verandas—to march in it."

There was more throat clearing and then, "March, eh? Both marching, you say?"

"Marching! And laughing and reveling in every wet, windy gust that drenches them."

"Indeed! And your mother, Anne? Does your mother march, too?"

Anne laughed. "No, Father Fraser, Mama doesn't march. When James Hamilton becomes unusually critical of Papa and me, she rather sedately agrees with him, but she secretly understands that when a storm's wild enough and loud enough, the lightning bright enough, everyone should be marching."

Flora, John noticed, had stopped behind Anne's chair, stopped in her tracks, holding a steaming bowl of potatoes not yet served. Just stood there, staring down at Anne's head, quite aghast, desperate, John knew, to say something, but undecided just what it would be.

Finally, she asked, "You're not fidgin' for a sip of that gude white Bordeaux set before ya' in our best wine glass, Mr. Fraser?" Knowing that her employer always had exactly two good sips of white wine before he took even one bite of anything, poor Flora had resorted to tradition in order to break up the oddly happy talk between Anne and John's father. "Tis the very bo'tle you ordered me to open, sir. The ver-ry stuff you claim to be in its finest year. Impor-rted by you alone. Guaranteed by yourself!"

James Fraser, as though to brush Flora off, ordered her to serve the potatoes and bring up the English peas and hot bread and to mind the steep steps because of her rheumatism. After adding that there would be no more mention of the wine business, he turned back to Anne.

"Try the Bordeaux, Daughter," he said, almost, John thought, as though he and Flora weren't even in the room.

After lifting her glass to her father-in-law, Anne sipped and then gave him an appreciative, melting smile. "Father Fraser," she exclaimed, her voice almost reverent, "Papa would give five acres of good cotton land for a supply of this! It's pure nectar. Would it be possible to find another bottle to equal it? I'd so love to surprise him. His first taste would bond the two of you into a lasting friendship even before you've met."

With a snort, Flora had flounced out of the room and was thumping back down the steps for the English peas and hot rolls. John and Anne exchanged a smile, his sent across the table to reassure her that she was doing extraordinarily well with his father. Her smile said "thank you" and also that "there's really nothing to it. Can't you see your father and I already like each other?"

Back upstairs later, making ready for bed, Anne tried not to show how perplexed she felt at John's odd silence now that they were alone with the door closed. He had kissed her when they first entered the room but then had held her in his arms for a long, long time without a word.

Finally, as though he knew she'd begin to fidget any minute, he whispered, "You never cease to amaze me, Anne Couper Fraser. I can't imagine that you ever will."

And then he had gone about undressing slowly, carefully folding the clean white shirt Eve had ironed for him before they left Cannon's Point. "Don't let him wear an' muss this one til your first night under his pa's roof when you'll bof be wantin' to put on airs," Eve had said. The memory of Eve's low, authoritative voice, the memory of Eve herself brought a lump to Anne's throat. How she missed her! How she needed her! How careful she'd been on the entire, long trip to obey Eve's instructions. Twice en route, John had absently taken out the fine white shirt and unbuttoned it for wearing. Twice, Anne had made him refold it and put it back in his trunk. She hadn't offered to refold it for him because she had never learned how to fold, and he did it deftly and perfectly from years of practice as a marine. She watched him now, secretly marveling, envying his dexterity as she tried and tried, then gave up on folding her own linen dress and hung it on a peg in the big walnut wardrobe.

Slipping into a nightgown, she stood looking across the shadowy room at John's broad, muscled back under his nightshirt, the strong, lithe legs below it. For a reason even she didn't quite understand, Anne had been relieved on their wedding night to find that his legs weren't very hairy. Oddly, at this minute, when she hadn't thought once all day about his love for the military, she pictured those handsome legs back in the white breeches of his Royal Marine officer's uniform, encased in black Hessian boots, polished until they gleamed.

He would have preferred, even at dinner tonight, she thought, to wear that beloved red Royal Marine jacket with its white turnbacks and blue lapels. He loved the crimson sash encircling his waist, his sword with its knot of crimson and gold—all of which he could no longer wear. In a way, even for her, it seemed unnatural to see John in a regular dark-gray top hat; she knew how he fancied the sight of himself in his marine hat with its red-and-white cockade.

"What are you thinking?" she asked, now in bed, watching him as he stood by a front window, his back to the room —to her—looking out over gas-lighted George Street. Its iron-wheeled carriages and buggies and phaetons were still rumbling past, the people in them still laughing and calling out at ten o'clock at night.

"I'm thinking about you," he said, after an unnaturally long silence. "You made a miracle with my father at dinner. You know that, don't you?"

Relieved that he hadn't been thinking about how much he missed the marines, she said a bit too eagerly, "I think you really mean that."

He crossed the room and stood looking down at her. He wasn't smiling. "Is it so strange for me to say something I— mean?"

"No. But I hadn't thought one way or another about a miracle. I didn't try for one."

Crawling under the covers beside her, he turned on his back. "I know you didn't. You just can't help performing miracles, though. I hadn't heard Father laugh in such a long time, I'd forgotten he could."

"He'll do better, too. You wait and see. It isn't your father who concerns me. He and I are going to do just fine together."

"It's poor old Flora, isn't it?"

"She worships you. In her mind, I have no right to you whatever. But, oh, John, she's so well-meaning. I'm really going to try to melt her."

For another minute or so, he was silent. Then he said, "I don't believe I'd try too hard. I'd let time take its course. Flora's always been impossible to budge if she thinks someone is trying to budge her."

"I feel so sorry for her I could weep."

Up on his elbow, he stared down at her. "You feel *sorry* for Flora McLeod?"

"Yes. She does six women's work. Can you explain to me why the English and the Scots are so against—slavery—when they demand worse than slavery from their own white working people?"

"No, I can't explain that and I should hang my head in shame, too, because politically, I'm on the side of our working class."

She took a deep breath. "I—I guess it's unavoidable, but I don't think I like having classes at all. Shouldn't I have an answer to the problem, though, before I disapprove? I don't have. Shouldn't the British have an answer to how Papa could operate a huge plantation like Cannon's Point or Hopeton or Lawrence without his people before they proclaim from the rooftops how sinful it is to own other human beings? Isn't it all silly? Your father, I'm sure, would consider Papa a member of the upper class because he has vast land holdings in three plantations and between Hopeton and Cannon's Point over two hundred people and lives in a big house. My father has no formal education, and yet, he'd be considered of the upper class—the landed gentry."

"John Couper's one of the most erudite, most widely read, most truly educated men I've ever known."

"But he educated himself! He came to America indentured to a Scottish businessman already in business in Georgia and Florida. He had to come indentured because his father was a poor parson who didn't have enough money for his fare over. What does make a person a member of the upper class?"

John pulled her to him. "Do we have to think such profound thoughts tonight? Aren't you tired from all our travel? Didn't you miss me last night in that second-rate Coventry hotel when we had to take separate rooms?"

A long kiss right on his mouth answered his question, but they were both so exhausted, the very next thing either of them knew was the glare around the curtains of full daylight, which meant John's father had already gone to his business.

Chapter 34

No one knew better than John that indeed it did take Anne forever to bathe and dress every morning, no matter how earnestly she tried to hurry. His daily visits to Flora downstairs in her kitchen, while both waited for Anne, were beginning to seem endless, although he knew it pleased Flora to have him all to herself. Much of the time their little talks went well, especially when Flora indulged in what she called thinkin' back. Thinking back meant talking of the old days in Dumfries, sharing their love for his mother—remembering her happy nature, her patience with Father, with John and William.

"You're full of her kind of patience, too," Flora said after he and Anne had been in London for a fortnight. "Look at you! Still waitin' for your breakfast and utterin' no word of complaint. You've always been too good-hearted."

Both hands around a kitchen mug of hot, strong tea, John laughed. "And isn't that why I've always been your favorite? Down deep, Flora McLeod, under all that stern, Scottish efficiency, you love goodness. You're partial to me because of what you complain is my good heart."

Never one to stop whatever she was doing merely for conversation, Flora kneaded a big wad of yeast dough so hard she made her knuckles crack. "It's just that so much has changed, Laddie," she said. "Even you."

"I've changed? How?"

"Ah, at times 'tis like you don't remember how long Flora's done for you. Aye, 'tis sure you're a mon now—no longer a laddie—big and strong an' bristly, never needin' Flora to wipe away your tears no more. But 'twould help to know if your path ahead lays smooth." She stopped pummeling the dough long enough to look squarely at him. "I know you been a soldier—the bravest of all—in far places of the world, without Flora to do for you, but you're here in my kitchen now an' e'en though I know about big lads, none of them is my Johnnie. My Johnnie who's changed so much he don't tell Flora no more what's naggin' at 'im."

Her uncanny way of seeing all the way down inside him, no matter how he swaggered or pretended, had not changed. Flora's solutions to his problems had not always been the wisest or the most acceptable, but she had always known when something troubled him. "Nothing is bothering me today," he said a little too firmly, "and I intend to keep it that way throughout the entire trip to Scotland with my bride. You must not go on borrowing trouble, Flora. I certainly don't intend to."

"It's the path ahead that wur-ries me," she mumbled.

"What path?"

"Yours, Lad! Does Flora McLeod care about another body on the face of this green earth the way she cares about you?"

"Yes."

"Who?"

"Father."

She snorted. "Him!"

"Aye, him. Do the two of you ever talk anymore?"

"Who else is in the house but the two of us?"

John thought for a moment. "Father looks so much older. But I think he's brightened up remarkably with Anne, don't you?"

"Aye, some." She spit the words, but she did add, " 'Tis plain that he would. She's right bonnie."

"She is, isn't she? And, Flora, Anne really needs you."

The woman whirled around to glare at him. "Me?"

"You. On the Georgia island where she was born, Anne had friends galore. She grew up with the Couper house filled with guests and laughter and festivity. I know she's happy with me. I trust her love for me utterly. She wouldn't want to be anywhere else but where I am, but I worry that she'll be lonely over here, not really at home in the noise and clatter and rudeness of the London streets. I know she misses the quiet and peace on St. Simons Island."

"Whoever heard tell of a house full of company being quiet?"

"It's a different kind of quiet. Where she lived with her parents, there were no city streets, no grinding iron wheels on stone, no raucous young lords showing their ill manners and wealth by galloping shiny black steeds into crowds of playing children, scaring older people half to death."

"Young lords will be young lords. She might as well get used to it."

"Have you and Anne ever talked—like this?"

Flora slapped the ball of dough into a big bowl to rise. "You know me work in this house! When do I have time to talk?" A half-smile flickered at the corners of her tiny mouth, lips almost lost between fat cheeks. Then she straightened herself as though preparing for something she simply had to do. "There's nothin' left but to ask, Laddie, *What takes her so long of a morning?* Your poor stomach must be grown to your backbone waitin' all this time day in an' day out to eat your breakfast."

John decided to laugh. "Why, she's dressing. I'm taking her to Westminster Abbey today." What he had just said would not, he knew, satisfy Flora. He took the plunge, daring once more to trust the older woman's understanding, but without much hope of receiving it. "The truth is," he went on, "Anne is in the process of learning how to bathe and dress herself and arrange her hair. She's doing her level best, Flora, she really is, but my wife has always had a personal maid. A nurse as a child, then a bright, capable, highly skilled Negro girl who looks after her every need now that they're both grown women. Her name is Eve. Anne misses Eve terribly. She didn't want anyone along on our wedding trip and so left her at home. That's the unvarnished truth of it. Please try to be patient with her. Will you try, Flora? For me?"

Flora was standing stock-still in the middle of her kitchen, obviously having a time of it inside her own head. John knew she was aware of London's aristocratic ladies who couldn't raise a finger without the help of a servant, but her own London life belowstairs had been spent in the service of the Fraser family, where the lady of the house had grown up back in Scotland knowing how to do everything from fancywork to baking bread, even to ironing her husband's shirts when Flora and the other servants left wrinkles or were too busy with more urgent chores.

The deep frown Flora had been wearing faded a little,

and after a time, she said, "You should've told me before, Laddie. I'll do me best with her."

"Flora? I have to ask you something now."

"Anything, Johnnie."

"Is my father worried about his business?"

She tramped across the kitchen to heat his tea. When Flora tramped, the china invariably rattled a bit. After she'd filled his cup, she returned the teapot to the fire, then faced him. "Is it him makin' your path rough, Johnnie?"

"What path?" He forced a short laugh. "Does the Almighty promise any man or woman a totally smooth path through life?" When she only stood, hands on hips, peering at him, he went on. "My father is worried more than usual about his wine business, isn't he? Haven't those sharp ears of yours caught anything that might give us a hint about why Father carries such a burden? I know I'm not just imagining it. Does anyone ever dine here?"

"Nobody sets foot inside that door upstairs but Lettie twice a week to polish the door brass."

"No one, Flora?"

"Not since you an' William when you come home from the war last year. Y'er father still pines for *her,* Laddie. He moves about through his days, but the mon will ne'er get over your gentle mither. It's like she took his soul away with hers to heaven when she went. He misses her and Sco'land. He shoulda' never come to London. Even with this fine house, too big, the good Lord knows, he shoulda' never come to London to settle."

"But he had my mother and both sons when he made that decision to go into the wine-importing business back then." John finished his tea. "Flora, do you ever see anyone aside from Father?"

"The butcher brings the meat, the green grocer comes."

"Poor, dear old Flora."

She straightened to her full height. "Don't you pity me, Laddie! They never was a position in any household where the hired help was to be entertained."

"Shame on you! You're far more than hired help in this family and you know it. Tell me, is Father stingier than usual with the money he doles out to you to run the house? Does he ever hint at being short of funds—anything like that?"

"I only know his highness is giving you and your wife money to take a weddin' trip. That's all I know. He tol' me that because he was so pleased with hisself that you agreed to go only to Sco'land with her. First to Dumfries, where we all used to live. Not one other mention of money, be it plenty or short."

As they talked, Flora had been polishing the already spotless silver tureen in which she served her scrumptious, creamy porridge for breakfast. "Sometimes, when I was in far-off Georgia with the Royal Marines, I dreamed about that gleaming tureen you've always used."

She gave him a crinkly smile. "Not a dream of my porridge itself?"

"Oh, I didn't dare! I might literally have died with longing for just one spoonful."

Her pleased chuckle made him happier than even Flora suspected, because Anne was on her way this minute and he needed Flora's goodwill. He'd heard Anne's footsteps on the stair and felt rather proud to have ended the talk with Flora on a good note—a compliment to her cooking. With all his heart, he wanted Flora and Anne to like each other.

After another good-morning kiss in the first-floor hallway outside the dining room, John seated Anne at the table and hoped for the best. Since by the time Anne appeared, his father was already at his city office, John had almost come to dread Anne's earnest attempts to break through Flora's chill toward her. By the time Flora puffed into the room this morning bearing the tureen, he hoped his smile didn't look as anxious as he felt.

Eyes shining, dressed in her becoming white Indian-twill muslin for their sightseeing today, her dark cap of curls a bit askew on her head, Anne greeted Flora warmly. "I hope you're well this morning, Miss Flora, and that I haven't kept you waiting too long."

With only a glance in Anne's direction, Flora said, "I'm fit, milady, and 'twas the porridge that was kept waitin'. It thickens, you know."

"Oh, I like it thick. Our cook back home serves it good and thick. Papa likes his oatmeal that way too. We all do in my family."

"Then 'tis of no matter that you took so unmercifully long," Flora said.

"Flora, shame on you!"

"Don't scold her, John. Miss Flora's right." Anne was so

blunt and so direct, John looked up from sweetening his porridge, quite surprised because until now she'd obviously been trying hard to pretend things were peaceful between her and Flora. "I'm sure you wonder how I manage to take so long to sponge-bathe and dress, Miss Flora. Well, I'll tell you. I take so long because I'm utterly helpless without my maid servant at home. I'm the one who should be ashamed."

John saw Flora actually jump, and the deft woman committed what to her was an unpardonable sin. She slopped cream out of the pitcher she was handing to John.

"I'm going to learn, though," Anne went on, seemingly unmindful that two big tears had slipped from her eyes. "I vow to you both that if you'll just try to be patient, I'll learn how to take care of myself soon. Getting these curls to sit straight on my head is the hardest part for me. Mama tried to tell me I was wrong not to bring Eve, but, Miss Flora, you do understand, don't you, that all I could think of was being alone every minute with my husband? I'd waited so long. Please tell me you understand!"

"Of course she does," John said, longing to help her somehow. "And of course, you'll learn."

"I want Miss Flora to tell me herself."

Covering her confusion by wiping up the spilled cream from her snowy tablecloth with the flaxen towel she carried at all times, Flora cleared her throat unnecessarily, then stood very straight. "You'll find, milady, that I don't often speak out of turn. I know my place. I spoke out of turn just now. It weren't my place to say one word about you takin' so long. Anybody can notice, but it's not right to voice it." Flora's full, rosy face told John nothing of what she was really thinking until she broke into a wide grin and then her rare, abrupt laugh—almost a shout.

As though he were still a small boy, his heart leaped when the faithful Scottish woman, who had been so much a part of his life, went to stand beside Anne, curtsied and said, "M'laddie Johnnie knows I b'lieve in the healin' power of a good laugh and—"

"Oh, so do I!" Anne interrupted, clapping her hands. "All the Coupers believe in laughing. Well, except maybe my serious brother, James Hamilton. Only the oddest things make him laugh, but then Papa and I have always called

James the Old Gentleman because he's so proper and tends toward stiffness. I don't. John can tell you that."

"Aye," Flora said, her face almost straight again. "I'm sur-re he could, but he needn't. You've done it yourself, milady. An' keep that smile on your bonnie face, d'ya hear?" She reached to wipe away a tear still on Anne's cheek. "There, that's better. Now, eat your oat groats, the both of you. Otherwise, I'll have to trudge belowstairs again to reheat."

Face shining, Anne asked, "Miss Flora, could you call me Anne instead of milady? At least Miss Anne? Wouldn't that mean we're really friends?"

John saw Flora's smile vanish. Proper demeanor as a servant was like a religion with Flora. Anne had successfully caught her off guard. "Well, I—I guess I could try, Miss Anne."

Chapter 35

An hour or so later, Anne, her short black velvet spencer beside her in case the sun should go behind the clouds looming to the west, sat beside John in the bargain-priced carriage he'd hired for their daily visits to as many of the famous London sites as they had time to see. In a week, they would be leaving for the long-awaited wedding trip in Scotland—alone. Her heart felt light as a feather, not only at the thought of being alone again with John but because he had assured her that she had truly won Flora's respect.

"I don't know what I did to win it," she said, perched now on the edge of the carriage seat, trying, as always, to see everything at once. "I just told Miss Flora the truth. I am slow every day because I'm all thumbs without Eve, but—oh, John, I just thought of something funny."

"What now?"

"I just pictured Miss Flora and Eve shut up in the same room together."

He laughed. "Feathers would fly in all directions!"

Leaning toward the side window, she asked, "Are we passing Hyde Park? I think I'm beginning to get my directions straight in London. Am I?"

"No doubt about it. Does Hyde Park interest you today?"

"Everything interests me, even though I do pity the poor, naked English trees without moss and those little hardworking leaves trying to come out in this smoky city air. Don't forget I've been reading about London all my life, and Mama's friend Mrs. Mackay, in Savannah, talks a lot about when she and her husband lived here. They did, you know, until"—she gave him her most flirtatious smile—"until just before the war that ended up making me your captive."

"You see? Not everything about the military is bad. But today is not the time to talk about any of that. Besides, I think I've just had a bright idea."

"Tell me!"

"I'd planned to show you Westminster Abbey. I can't let you miss seeing what the guidebooks call the most breathtaking old English architecture anywhere, but I have a strong feeling that you need to see trees." He pointed out the window. "We're almost to Park Lane. It runs along Hyde Park. Why don't we give you some medicine for that chronic homesickness of yours? Your husband senses that you're in need of open spaces and stands and stands of trees."

"Yes! Oh yes, I am, but could I ask a question? Do *you* ever find yourself thinking about the beauty and the sky and the woods and the soft, clean air on St. Simons?"

He laughed. "I married a clever girl. Do you hope I miss coastal Georgia, too?"

"Of course I hope you miss it! Remember all those bluebirds we saw between Cannon's Point and Lawrence just before we left?"

"Every single one of them and I never forget that your father's generous offer still stands. But for today, my strategy for pleasing you is a drive through Hyde Park. And will you promise just for today that you'll at least be open to its beauty?"

The now familiar strain did not loom between them this time as it had with almost every other mention of Papa's offer. Both beaming, both lighthearted, they shook hands formally, sealed the promise between them, and John ordered the driver to take them slowly along the carriage trail through Hyde Park.

For a time, they just rode in silence, holding hands. Then, with rare solemnity for him, John said, "For all of your life, Annie, I mean to see that your deep-down longings are met if it's anywhere within my power to do it. I know that sounds as wordy and florid as one of your Walter Scott novels, but I mean it. I hate it that you're so homesick for Georgia, that daily life is so hard for you without Eve. Time is on our side, though, and with all my heart, I want to give you everything that makes your life only beautiful."

She reached a lace-gloved hand to touch his face. "Thank you, for being exactly as you are. For loving me even though

I'm spoiled, helpless, and at times terribly homesick. What can I do to let you know how I love you, John Fraser?"

He grinned. "Just keep me. And try to keep a light hand on my reins. To me, that's the only plan we need now and for always. I promise to hold you lightly too."

"And live one day at a time."

"That's right. I've always thought that my mother, gentle and sweet-tempered though she was, worried herself to death because poor Father was working so hard he grew distracted during the years in London. A man tries to be exactly what his wife wants and needs, but men are men and women are women and if even one of them holds the other too tightly, distance can come. Oh, Anne, I'm a fairly independent man, but I couldn't face a day of my life now without you. I need us to be even closer than we are this minute, if that's possible."

As the carriage driver took them over what must have been every inch of Hyde Park, Anne listened to John's explanation of its history. At least she meant to be listening, even to the part where he told her at length that the present-day park was once a portion of the ancient manor of Hyde, which belonged to the monastery of St. Peter's at Westminster until in the reign of Henry VIII, it became the property of the Crown. That it was once much larger and contained Kensington Gardens, but that grants had been given for various tracts on which to build houses. He spoke glowingly of the beauty of the Serpentine River at the western end, as though he cared deeply that Anne learn to love some of the natural beauty of London, too. She listened, but inwardly she smiled at his earnest efforts, every word of which only made her adore him more than ever.

Passing the handsome stands of ancient trees was pure joy for her, but trees of all kinds would go on looking strange without banners of moss adorning their limbs. Pines back on St. Simons didn't attract moss often, but even some of them bore its softening caress. John's Hyde Park trees *were* a picture and what she missed or skipped over in his lecture, she filled in by feeling closer and closer to him for wanting so much to ease her longing for St. Simons. She honestly couldn't remember that she'd mentioned being homesick often in the time they'd been in London, but that he knew anyway only made her love him more.

"I think it was back in 1730," John went on, "that Queen Caroline heightened the beauty of the Serpentine River by having its bed enlarged. The river begins to the north of Bayswater on the Uxbridge Road, winds its way through Kensington Gardens and Hyde Park, and falls finally into the Thames."

None of that mattered much to Anne, but it seemed to interest him, and she was fascinated when he told her that during severe English winters when the river was frozen over, as many as six thousand people could be counted ice skating there. In the warmth of this mild, now sunny mid-May morning, she shivered at the thought of weather so cold that an entire river could freeze deep enough to hold the weight of six thousand persons.

They were passing now beneath a splendid grove of giant oaks and elms on a steep rise John said was called Buckden Hill, and Anne had no trouble exclaiming at the fresh green of their reaching branches. "John, this *is* breathtaking, isn't it? And aren't the tree branches straight?"

He chuckled at that, remembering, she knew, the wide, gnarled, reaching branches of their live oak tree by the Hampton River at home.

"You're dear," she said, hooking her arm in his, "to show me so many trees. It does make breathing easier. Some days we have seen a lot of buildings."

"Aye, 'tis a pity, but cities do have buildings," he teased.

"Does Scotland have a lot?"

"In its cities, I'm afraid it does. You're used to living in your very own city, darling. There are buildings at Cannon's Point, too, but at least you know your father caused them all to be put there."

"A plantation is a village, I guess," she mused.

"A village on an island of other villages. Don't forget, England too is an island."

"I know and don't try so hard, dearest. I'm really loving all this. Do take me to Westminster Abbey tomorrow? Mrs. Mackay would never forgive me if I missed seeing such a famous example of her adored English architecture."

"Mrs. Mackay told me how she loves London, but she's lived much of her life in a city," John sighed. "What I wonder is whether you could ever be happy living even in a rather small city like Savannah."

"With you, yes! But is that the right subject for today? Did you forget our agreement?"

The smile that could brighten even sunshine lit his face. "Indeed not, wife. One day at a time, light hand on the reins. I promise to take you to Westminster tomorrow, but oh, my beautiful, elegant Annie, before that we have tonight."

Chapter 36

On the day before John and Anne were to leave by stage for Scotland, Father Fraser surprised Anne by reaching the George Street house an hour earlier than his usual four o'clock. Anne, writing a letter home at a small kneehole desk by the window in their room upstairs, saw the neatly dressed older man clipping along from the direction of Portman Square, laid aside her quill, and hurried down to meet him.

When James Fraser, top hat carefully in place, umbrella hooked over one arm, started up the front steps, Anne was waiting in the open door. The two greeted each other warmly, always a confirmation to Anne that he had fully accepted her as the daughter he'd never had.

When he stopped halfway up the steps to doff his hat and bow, she called out, "What a happy surprise, Father Fraser! You look very well, so I know nothing is wrong, but I'm about to pop with curiosity. You have a secret reason for coming home early, haven't you?"

"Indeed I do have and 'twill make you happy, Daughter." He stepped briskly inside, shifted umbrella and hat to his left hand, and began fishing in a pocket. "Here! A letter from Georgia! I had business near your favorite mail coach stop—Swan with Two Necks on Lad Lane—and couldna' wait to give it to you in person."

Anne took the letter and threw both arms around his neck. Then, looking at the address, she began to laugh and cry. "However can I thank you? It's my blessed papa's script and you brought it just in time—before John and I leave tomorrow." The man looked so ill at ease and so delighted all at once, she gave her eyes two quick swipes and hugged him again. "John gets uncomfortable, too, when I cry," she explained, "but I'm not crying for any bad reason. I'm crying and laughing for joy and a woman has a perfect right to do both. Especially if she's blessed enough to have a thoughtful father-in-law like you." She took him by the hand. "You and I will open it this minute and I'll read every word aloud to you. John's off with a load of our baggage to whatever coach stop we leave from tomorrow and he can't possibly come back for another hour, so—"

"Bull and Mouth," Father Fraser interrupted. "You two will leave for your eventual destination in Dumfries from the Bull and Mouth."

"Where *do* the English get these funny names? Well, wherever it is, you and I are going to share my letter from Papa—just the two of us. Come on!"

"You don't think John will object?" he asked, hanging his hat and umbrella on the hall tree. "And wouldn't you prefer to read it alone first?"

"No, I would not. And you really must get to know your son better. He's pleased that you and I love each other. Now, hurry. I can't wait to know how everything is at Cannon's Point. It's been so long!"

Fraser followed her into the company parlor, where they took chairs quite close together. Settled in his, legs crossed, ready to listen, but obviously still thinking about what she'd just said about John. "So, you think I don't know my son, lass?"

"Oh, I was only joking. Almost anything is just fine with John. He's really the most agreeable of men."

"More like your father than his own, eh?"

"Pooh! It's so dark in here, I can't see your face very well, but you *are* smiling, aren't you?"

"Aye, as I've fallen into the habit of doing since you came. Go on, lass. Break the seal and read. Remembering that I'll gladly sit here and wait should you care to scan it first in silence."

"I'm going to read it aloud to you, and no more argument, do you hear?" she announced, breaking the dark-red sealing wax. "Now then, when did Papa write this? He's dated it 12 April. Oh my, he and William must have stayed longer than he planned in Savannah after they put John and me on the boat for Liverpool. I was beginning to worry."

"Perhaps he explains," Father Fraser said.

"Ready? 'My Dearest Annie, With all my heart, I hope I have not caused you distress for having waited so long to write these lines. Daily, your mother has agitated for me to write, too busy herself, and finally, with the good news for which we've prayed, I now can tell you that your baby sister, Isabella, is quite recovered from a strange malady that had us both worried and anxious.' Oh, dear!" Anne exclaimed. "Isabella is my only little sister, not yet a year old. Poor Papa and Mama must have been nearly sick with worry themselves!"

"I'm truly sorry, child," Father Fraser said, "but thankful that the infant is improved."

" 'Little Belle seems cheerful now,' " Anne went on, " 'fever gone and gurgling away again at all of life at Cannon's Point, except when she sleeps or is fussily occupied with Eve's forcing spoonfuls of gruel down her helpless little throat.' "

Anne sat up abruptly. *"Eve?* Eve feeding the baby? I'm mystified. I'd never in a million years imagine Eve feeding a baby! Why do you suppose she's taken over that job? I wonder if something's wrong with our old nurse, Liz? She's Johnson's wife. Johnson is our butler, and Liz has always taken charge of children—ours and those of any guests who may be visiting us. Oh, I certainly hope Papa explains about Eve and just doesn't jump to another subject. Wait, let's find out. 'Baby Belle has never had the appetite you had, beloved Annie, but I declare the little one eats now in self-defense against Eve's feeding attacks.' "

"I see what John meant when he said your father is a man of great, good humor." He grinned a little. "And what you meant when you said he was 'bouncy' like the sound of the word *papa.* The mon would undoubtedly find me quite dull and morbid."

"Don't be ridiculous. I've got to find out if he tells us why on earth Eve has become a baby nurse! I'd think Eve would be quite impatient with babies. 'In case you haven't recovered, dearest Annie, from the surprise that Eve has changed specialties since you left, let me assure you that it is not a permanent arrangement, a fact for which we are all grateful. You see, Liz fell and injured her back, the poor thing forced to lie on her cabin floor until Johnson returned home from a fiddling concert during our last entertainment before Isabella became ill. Liz, thanks to the skillful ministrations of

Dr. William Fraser, is much improved and will, I feel, be entirely well by the time your careful mother allows her to return to her duties as a nurse.' Oh," Anne said, relieved, "that explains it. Poor, good Liz. How dreadful she had to lie there on the floor until Johnson came to help her."

"Oh, I beg your pardon, Daughter, but does your family hold all the—the servants in such high regard as this letter seems to indicate? As your own concern indicates?" He cleared his throat again. "One—one hears such ugly stories of cruelty to slaves in the southern United States. The more so in the past several years here in Britain."

Anne looked surprised. "I—I guess I hadn't thought much about that since we've been in London," she said in her straightforward way. If anyone knew how the British felt about American slavery, Anne did after they'd stolen so many of the St. Simons people. "Do you think Southerners who own their servants are all evil people?"

She could see that her blunt question had left him almost speechless. "What? Why, no. Mainly, I suppose, because John has convinced me otherwise. He thinks planters—slave masters in the southern states—are trapped."

She looked right at him. "John has never used that word *trapped* with me, but I—I think I know what he means." Then, fearful of allowing anything so difficult to come between them, she blurted, "Father Fraser, I don't know what I think about owning people. I've grown up with them all around me. Papa allows no whipping at Cannon's Point. That's not true just across a creek on a neighboring plantation called Hampton. But I just try not to think about what might be the bad part of it. My father is a considerate master. Families just do need servants when they own a lot of land and live in a big house."

He was silent for a time and then, after elaborately clearing his throat again, said, "I'm a rude old man, lass. That's not a subject about which you ever need to bother your bonnie head. I—I pray it never brings heartache of any kind into your life. The world needs your sunniness."

Relieved, she smiled. "Now I'll read more of Papa's letter. He says, 'Your brother is seldom at home these days. His dual responsibilities at both Hopeton Plantation on the mainland and down the island at Hamilton keep him feeling as successful and important as we've always been convinced he is. He was here last week to show me and to boast about his meticulous sketches of the new crop rotation plans he's drawn up for Hopeton. Only your erudite brother would take the pains to be artistic over commonplace fields.' "

"Your brother must be an impressive young gentleman."

"He is." She laughed lightheartedly. "I wouldn't want a husband like James Hamilton, but he's certainly high-principled. But then, I already have the only husband I want or will ever need." She looked at her thin gold watch on its chain around her neck. "John should be home soon, I'd think. But there's a little more of Papa's letter. Where was I? Oh yes. 'Your lovely mother wants to add a note, and I am past due in my own fields and will be considered derelict by our punctual driver, Tom, if I do not bring this to an end. But before I do, I must tell you—only for your amusement, John and Anne—that since five of my carpenters are without much to do at present, I have, for my own enjoyment, set them to work on the leaking roof of the sturdy little tabby house overlooking the marshes at Lawrence. I have done this with the full knowledge that you, John, have not yet made up your mind to accept my gift of the fertile, valuable land.' "

"What's this about my son's not being able to make up his mind?" Father Fraser was sitting up straight in his chair. "I've never known John to be anything but impetuous and headstrong. Is he going against your father's wishes in some matter about which I know nothing?"

"John hasn't told you that Papa longs to give us the plantation he owns adjoining Cannon's Point? A beautiful place called Lawrence?"

"Dinna' be surprised, Daughter. The boy's a big talker, but only when the subject suits him. If he refuses such a generous offer, how is it he expects to take care of you and a family some day? Surely he knows his own father has limited means."

Anne knew John suspected Father Fraser's financial troubles, but obviously the two had not really talked to each other. She did love her father-in-law, from the start had been eager for him to like her, but somehow before she could answer, she had to find a way to swallow a heavy wave of homesickness for Papa. Papa, she thought, I need you! I need you even to tell me what to say to him this minute.

And then, with no intention whatever of bringing up such an issue when they were leaving on their wedding trip tomorrow, she heard herself say, "John loves the military! More than anything in the whole world, he wants back his Royal Marines commission."

"But the wars are over now. The boy's not stupid. They've told him there's no place for him. Told him that before he went back to Georgia to claim you. Told him and William both."

"Am I terribly selfish to wish that John felt as William does about rejoining his unit? William has fallen in love with coastal Georgia. He may be falling in love with one of my longtime friends, Frances Anne Wylly, too, but he'll be perfectly satisfied if they never need him again to be a part of war and killing. How can John be so tender, so full of laughter and goodness, and still want to—kill?"

"I doubt the lad even thinks of killing," Father Fraser said absently, his mind not on defending John. "It's just that my son William is more a philosopher. The excitement and adventure of life in the military never especially appealed to him. He's a doctor and they happened to need his skills. William enlisted for that reason. John, I fear, likes the handsome uniform, the snapping flags, the drum rolls and bugles. Wanderlust, too. He's always had it. Ask Flora, who heard even his mother remark on it."

A new panic seized her. "Father Fraser, do you mean that John will never want to make a home anywhere? I can't imagine not wanting one special place that means more than any other spot on earth!"

He turned his face away. "Dinna' press me for an answer to such a question, lass. I can't answer it. My elder son is a good mon. Never in serious trouble. There just are men who take to the uniform and the ceremony like fishes to water. I expect he's lost without that life. I dinna' have to agree with him in order to see he's lost."

"But, he has me now!"

"Aye, and he loves you with all his heart. 'Tis plain he does."

"Should I feel young and selfish for hating the thought of being put in competition with—with parades and guns?"

"Young you are, Daughter, but selfish—no. Give the boy time. I never understood John, but it could be all he needs to get over his fancy for the uniform is a bit more time. A bit clearer conviction that in you, he's already found the only thing that can fill any man's emptiness." She'd patted his hand often, but for the very first time, he reached for Anne's hand. "Look here, lassie, I spoke out of turn. The ver-ry last thing on earth I'd ever mean to do would be to cause you heartache. Wise or unwise, you and my son John love each other. Love is strong enough to overpower a whole army of snappin' flags." He gave her hand a quick little squeeze, as though he wanted very much for her to look at him. He was smiling more naturally, more warmly, than she'd ever known him to smile. "Stay the course, Anne Fraser. And you *are* Anne Fraser now, no longer sheltered Anne Couper of Cannon's Point. Flora McLeod's Johnnie will come through his obstacles all right."

"Flora McLeod's Johnnie? Don't you ever call him Johnnie yourself?"

He shook his head sadly. "Never have. Never understood the lad, but he's my fine, strong son. 'Tis dark and gloomy today and I've saddened you unintentionally, but by tomorrow morning when the two of you leave on your wedding trip, the sun will shine in all ways—maybe even in smoky, cluttered London."

She laid aside her letter and got up to give him a hug. "Have I thanked you properly for giving us our longed-for wedding trip?"

He looked pleased. "There were st-r-rings, remember. I managed the feeble gesture only if you'd agree to go to Sco'land. 'Tis still my r-real home, lass. I can never feel at home in any other place but Dumfries. There's a sense of place in Dumfries. Even Bobby Burns chose it for himself. I'm counting on John's feeling *his* need of a place once he's back there—with you. Especially when you see your own mother's ancestral castle, Caerlaverock. I'm counting on the wedding trip to make my elder lad homesick to settle in one spot, wherever that may be. John even promised he'd pack my Fraser plaid kilt, though I doubt he'll wear it once. Now, you haven't been given a chance to read a line of what your dear mother wrote. Or would you prefer to read that without a meddlesome old man?"

She grabbed up the letter. "No, no! I want you to hear it all. I guess I haven't even read to the end of what Papa wrote. Let me find my place. The last thing I read got us talking about John. It was where Papa just sneaked in, as only he can do, that for his own enjoyment he was fixing up the roof on the Lawrence house. Then he says, 'We all beg to be remembered with the deepest love to the two of you and to John's father. That love comes from your mother, little Belle, James Hamilton, Will Browne, Johnson, Liz, Sans Foix, Eve, and everyone else who calls Cannon's Point home. Yr affectionate father, John Couper, whose lonely life sags sadly without you both.' " She turned over the page. "Mama wrote only a few lines: 'My dear Anne and John . . . With your father's permission, I have read what he said to you above and plead with you both to pay him no mind. By that I mean John must not, in any way, feel a further burden or obligation to hurry back to become a gentleman farmer at Lawrence! You know your dear, generous father, Anne, always dreaming and usually sure that he knows not only the best but the happiest direction for everyone to take. You also know that he never holds a grudge and never makes it unpleasant for a single one of his cherished "victims" of those big dreams of his. Belle is truly fine now, and although we all miss you, we wish for our newlyweds only bliss, interesting travels, and joy. I pray you can visit the Maxwell castle, Caerlaverock. God watch over you and keep you both safe and well. Somehow I have no doubts at all about your happiness. Your loving mother, Rebecca Maxwell Couper.' " When Anne looked up at Father Fraser, she saw tears in his deep, gray eyes—eyes so like John's. "My mother," she said softly, "is the most beautiful woman I ever saw. . . . Did something she wrote make you feel sad, sir?"

"Aye. Rebecca Maxwell, like my departed wife, Margaret, must be far more than beautiful. The Maxwells are true aristocrats, but I can also tell she—discerns. I long every day for John's mother. Margaret could always discern even John, but never scoffed at me because I couldna' get the hang of it." He looked down at the carpet. "My son John has in some manner always seemed a stranger to me. I believe in a young man's serving his country, but not placing himself at the mercy of that country's old men who, safely seated around their long tables, too often try to settle problems by violence. Like you, I—I also dinna' believe in violence, Daughter."

She waited, then asked, "And do you honestly think John believes in it, Father Fraser?"

"Can't say that I do. That's the exact spot where my elder son loses me. He's a truly gentle, grown mon. Was a truly gentle, merry boy. Far more colorful than William, but William's thoughtful. Thr-rives on spending the entire evening with a book in his hands."

"So do I, but it's John I love. Can real love ever be explained or even understood?"

With all her heart, she longed to tell Father Fraser that John loved him deeply, too, but also felt a stranger with him. While she was trying to decide what to say, to draw on whatever wisdom she may have inherited from Mama, he reached again for her hand.

"No, lass, love cannot be explained or understood. I'm a selfish old man to have upset you on the very evening before your wedding trip. I can tell John loves you sincerely, that you love him. Just promise me you won't allow my son to charm you into a life *you* don't want. Nothing would make me happier than to have you both settle right here with me in London. But the same is true of your papa, who wants you both to live in Georgia. Only you and John must decide where you'll spend your remaining years. Just don't let John talk you into anything that goes against your nature."

Hoping to lighten the moment, she smiled. "Don't worry, Father Fraser. I have a mind of my own."

"Aye," he said, returning her smile. "I believe that, lass. But so has my son John. And you love him as he is. Oh, how you do love that boy!"

Chapter 37

"Wasn't it gracious of that man traveling alone to let you sit here with me?" Anne asked as their stagecoach, packed inside and out with men, women, children, boxes, bags, and bundles, rolled north through the London streets. "And isn't this a handsome coach? I know I fuss about the noise and clatter in London, but it *was* exciting when we finally pulled out of the Bull and Mouth, wasn't it?"

Beaming down at her on the crowded seat, squeezed in so tight he could barely move his elbows, John readily agreed. "I think only a few things are more exciting than a strong, clean, well-built stage just ready to start. For your sake, I'm glad we drew such a cared-for contraption. Good horses, too. English horses live a lot better than do many English laborers, believe me. A fine modern achievement, these coaches. The very latest thing. Do you realize that once out of the city, we'll be traveling as fast as seven or eight miles an hour? Our coachman impresses me, too. Bright young buck. He seemed to enjoy taking up the reins and the whip. Did you hear him shout 'Away we go!'? I liked that. Like to see a man thrive on his job."

Anne's thoughts went uneasily back to her talk with Father Fraser yesterday. Her lips were sealed fast against even a mention of John's love of the Royal Marines, but she felt she had found an ally of sorts in his father.

"We did indeed draw a splendid coach," John went on, not really expecting her to say anything, enjoying as always voicing his own thoughts aloud to her. "Did you notice the harness, how all the gear matches—breast collar, girth? All clean too."

She laughed and pushed against him. "No, darling, I'm

too excited to look at anything so commonplace as harness. Will we be out of London any time soon?"

"Very soon. Why?" Returning the pressure of her shoulder with his, he answered his own question. "My beautiful wife is longing again for the countryside."

"Well, I can't help it if I love those dear little English hamlets and towns. But, you know, even when our coach went through some of the sleepiest villages on our first trip to London, I felt a kind of—a kind of—"

"What?"

"I don't know exactly what to call it. Maybe a kind of rowdiness. Am I wrong about that? Everyone in England under fifty strikes me as being on a lark, determined to make all the noise possible."

He laughed. "Oh, England's roaring now that the old King's ill and the Regent is ruling. Your favorite hamlets are likely at this time of year to be even more raucous with tent shows and fairs. Who knows, we may pass a good fight in a prize ring." He tried and failed to find room to stretch his long legs. "And, of course, in the city and out, there are always peddlers and mumpers galore."

"What's a mumper?"

"You didn't learn that from Walter Scott's books? A mumper's a beggar."

"Oh. There are so many beggars right here on the streets of London, I know it must have made Papa very sad when he came here as a boy. It makes me sad. Is begging the only way they get something to eat?"

"Ever notice how many mumpers are very old or very young?"

"I guess I have. Why is that?"

"The public takes pity on the young and the old beggars. Their take is apt to be bigger."

"But what about the sons and daughters of the elderly? Do they work while their parents shuffle around begging?"

"Some do. Some just stay home and drink. The same with the parents of young mumpers. Annie, there are a thousand racehorses in England that live like royalty compared with the alms-seekers. Most live far better than their equestrian slaves do."

"Their groomsmen, you mean?"

"No, slaves. This is surely the age of the blooded horse. The noblest friend of man, he's called, and I can agree with that, but the fine horse's burnished coat is due to its diet, which is far above that of the ignorant two-legged lad who cares for all his needs. Look some time at a picture of one of these pampered beasts, docked of tail, healthy, richly caparisoned. Do you wonder that they call me a Radical because I resent that? The boy whose every effort goes toward the grooming and care of his four-legged 'lord,' the horse, will never know how to read one word on a printed page."

"The really poor people aren't as important as horses. Is that what you're saying?"

"I'm afraid so." Outside London, the road grew bumpier, causing everyone to bounce around more. "I know what you're thinking, Anne," John said after a while.

"You do?"

"That there aren't any mumpers on St. Simons Island. Even the African slaves eat better than London's beggars do."

She frowned. "If I say just one serious thing that's on my mind, could we then talk about only happy things?"

"Try me."

"Were you so—so understanding about not robbing Papa of his people because you saw with your own eyes that they live better than the English poor?"

"Aye," he answered quickly.

"Is that all you're going to say? Just 'aye'?"

"I thought you didn't want to go on talking about serious subjects."

"I don't. I just—well, it's just important to me to know that *you* don't really believe all those stories your father said are told here about how—how cruel Southern planters are to their people."

He gave her a curious look. "You and Father have done a lot of talking since we reached George Street, haven't you?"

She grinned a little. "We're friends, if that's what you mean."

"You'd also like to know if I could ever become a slave owner myself, wouldn't you?"

She took his hand. "Never mind what Papa wrote about fixing the Lawrence roof. We are not going to discuss any of that. This is our wedding trip. We made a pact."

"That's right, we did. And I fully intend to abide by it."

* * *

In bed on the third night of their stage journey north toward Scotland, almost at the Border in the English town of Carlisle, Anne grew drowsy while John explained that poor Mary, Queen of Scots, had once been imprisoned there. She asked sleepily, "Do you love Scotland more than any other place you've ever been? Are you excited that tomorrow we'll roll onto actual Scottish soil?"

John laughed a little. "More than any other place? Oh, dearest, I've lived, since I joined the marines as a boy, in so many parts of the world, I honestly don't know what I feel about one single spot by now. Any full-blooded Scot loves Scotland, no matter where else he's been, I suppose. Your father still speaks tenderly of the 'wine-black moors in the time of heather,' but the man obviously loves the Georgia coast above any other place. He's nearing sixty and he's never once returned to Scotland, has he?"

"No," Anne said, "and I think Mama feels puzzled by that. She's always longed to see Scotland, especially the part we're visiting tomorrow, even though her grandfather got a land grant in Georgia at Midway, right on the Georgia coast, and she was born there. The Maxwells moved down to Georgia from Pennsylvania, I guess about sixty or seventy years ago. But if Father Fraser ever visits us at Cannon's Point, Mama will probably wear him out with questions about the old Maxwell castle at Dumfriesshire."

"Well, I guarantee *you* will see it. You can write all about it to your mother. Caerlaverock Castle is a ruin, but the present laird is in residence there in small quarters about three months out of the year, or was, the last William heard. That part of it must still be quite livable. Between the Romans and the English, the old place has stood amazingly strong."

"Maybe we can see Caerlaverock our first day in Dumfries!"

"That will be up to you, my dear," he said. "I'll have to arrange for a contraption to take us across the old stone bridge. Caerlaverock is a few miles from Dumfries over the River Nith." He slipped his arm around her. "Every day ahead is ours, that's all that matters. Just ours, beautiful Anne."

"Does William long for Scotland? I've heard Mr. Thomas Spalding talk to Papa for hours about Scotland, plying Papa with questions about his boyhood days. I know your father has missed it every minute he's lived in London."

"He proved that, I'd think, by limiting us to travel in Scotland or no wedding trip. As for William, like me, he's lived so many other places. Did you know he was surgeon-in-chief to the East India forces under his friend Hastings and lived in Calcutta?"

"William?" she asked.

"You sound surprised, but that's William. Never talks much about himself. My brother speaks Hindustani like a native."

"You talk a lot more than William does, but never much about yourself. For me, far too little. Where, in all the places you lived with your unit, do you wish you could settle down and stay?"

He laughed. "Nowhere. I haven't seen nearly enough of any one place, nor enough places."

Father Fraser had frightened her by saying John was stricken with wanderlust. Well, he didn't actually use the word *stricken*, but he did say Flora and John's late mother worried a lot about it. Was Father Fraser hoping John might discover a latent longing for Scotland, so that she and he would settle there—Father Fraser with them? She was thinking so hard, understanding so little right now in her exhaustion from the day's travel, she didn't notice how long she'd lain there beside him without saying a word. John could and did answer often with just one word, but she'd learned that her silences upset him.

"If we're going to sleep, let's do it," he said, not unkindly but with an impatient edge in his voice. "Or are you planning to keep on trying to urge me to wax poetic about Sco'land? I can, you know. I grew up knowing how, because it kept Flora happy when I rattled on about the Scottish roads flinging themselves around the shoulders of her hills, or the stark silence of the Scottish countryside with no sound outside the bleating of sheep, the wind blowing, the black crows flying from the tops of the bonnie Dumfriesshire hills low into the valleys beneath." He laughed again. "You see, I do know how to turn a phrase aboot Sco'land, well enough to please even Flora McLeod. How the woman does love the Border country. Flora even loves the painfully built stone walls holding ownership to its stubborn soil." He sighed. "Father loves those old stone walls, too, I suppose."

"You only suppose?"

"Hasn't the mon lauded Robert Burns's worship of the Border country through all those hours you two spent together while I made my fruitless trips to branch headquarters or to the post office, where there was never a scrap of good news of my restored commission?"

John had always been such a skillful actor, she thought she was hearing for the very first time an undercurrent of bitterness in his voice that his unit no longer needed him. He then said something flippant about hoping someday one of his old officers might put in a good word for him. She said nothing because she honestly didn't know what to say. Touching had always helped. She moved closer to him in the sagging bed. "Remember our pact," she whispered. "We promised not even to mention your commission or anything else that might come between us. I wish you were a little bit eager to be reaching Dumfries tomorrow, though. You were born there. Can't you be a little excited for my sake? What kind of country will we be traveling through after we get into Scotland?"

"Wilderness. A wide and persistent wilderness. Border country is almost devoid of humankind. Only the ghosts of the ancient Celts sitting in the heather on their brown moorland, listening to their bees, waiting for honey-wine time and another excuse to roar into battle."

"You're teasing me." On impulse, Anne sat up. Because John would have to pay extra in the morning if they burned more than one candle, the room was pitch-black. "I like it when you tease," she said, "but this is different. Is it so strange to you that I need to know about *some* place in the world that makes you happy? I've never hidden from you the way I love Cannon's Point—all of St. Simons Island. I'm going to love Scotland, too, I know. I'm Scottish all the way through. But it doesn't have to be Scotland *or* St. Simons Island, if I only knew you're even hoping to find the one place for—for us to be at home."

When he just lay there, making no move to pull her back down beside him, she felt afraid. "Does anything I've said make sense to you, my darling?" she asked.

"Yes. I'm just not sure what kind of sense. One place is about as good as another, I guess. I just hope you aren't manipulating me."

"Oh, dear," she gasped.

"What does that mean?"

"I'm—I'm not sure. I'm kind of scared because I don't seem to feel sure of anything, except that I love you! You just went so far away from me. Don't do that, John. Not here in a strange place where we don't know a soul and—"

"And—little sheltered Anne is thousands and thousands of miles away from home?"

The sarcastic edge in his voice cut. "All right," she said. "Yes. I love being with you, but we are so far away from St. Simons. I like it even less when *you* go far away right here in the same bed with me!" Her throat tightened, but she steeled herself not to cry.

"I doubt any two people stay very close when they're on the verge of an argument. But, over what, Anne? Why are you trying to trick me into saying something I can't honestly say?"

"I'm not! I'm not a manipulating woman. I hate women who play tricks, so I'm not one of them."

"Then, what do you want me to say?"

If he had no intention of reaching to pull her back down beside him, then she'd take charge herself. "I don't want you to *say* anything." Close against him again, she spoke so near his face, she could feel his breath. "I—I think what's happening is we're getting to know each other. I don't think there are any barriers at all between us. Almost from the first time I danced with you at Dungeness, I—I've been like a silly girl about believing that you and I, if we ever saw each other again, would be the only perfect, trouble-free lovers in the whole world! I have been homesick since we've been gone—a lot of the time. I've tried hard not to be. But John, I'm just me and I don't know how to be anyone else. I thought because you fell in love with me, you'd want me to be just me."

For the first time, he made no move to caress or even to reassure her. "And I'm just me, too," he said, his voice almost flat.

"A while ago, were you joking about how Father Fraser loves Scotland—just because you can't bring yourself to feel close to your own father?" Her head was on his shoulder, but still he seemed far away, his mind not meeting hers. "I wish I could see your face!" she said, sounding both annoyed and scared. "For all I know, you're laughing at me."

"Far from it, lass," he answered, as though she were ten

years old and he her uncle. "And I'm not far away from you. I—I can't bear the thought of that either. But we're going to quarrel at times, you know."

"Why? Why do we, of all people, have to quarrel—ever?"

"Because we're human beings." Now he did laugh, but dryly. "And, also because we're both Scots. Fighting is in the blood of every Scot. An ancient Roman once said of us, 'They are moved by chance remarks to wordy disputes. They're boasters and threateners and given to bombastic self-dramatization!' "

She laughed a little and nestled still closer to his warm body. "We *are* both Scots. What can we do about it?"

Now he pulled her to him in the thick darkness and held her long and passionately, showing his need of her—every bit as deep as her need of him. He, too, was trembling. This was not the time for her to say one single word. So, she clung to him, intensely aware of their oneness and of their separateness. John's uniqueness. Hers. But together.

They just lay there for what, to Anne, seemed a long, long time. When he finally spoke—no edge in his voice—he said, "I'm not far away from you, Annie. I'm right here with you where I belong tonight. Even if I don't feel especially at home in any *place,* I am at home with you. That I don't seem to revere being a Scot doesn't mean I ignore it." His hand began gently, reassuringly, to smooth her back. "Sleep now, darling. Our firing's stopped. No more ancient Celtic frays between us, and tomorrow night we'll be side by side in another bed in good old Dumfries, just across the River Nith from Caerlaverock Castle. Did you know *Caerlaverock* means 'lark's nest'?"

She did know. Mama had told her many times, but he seemed so pleased to have told her, too, she answered only, "What a beautiful, poetic idea! Caerlaverock . . . lark's nest . . . don't you love the sound of it?"

Now he laughed like John—gently—and lapsed into a light Scottish burr. "Aye, I do love the sound of it, lass. And if milady's hair can be made to please her on our first full day in Dumfries, I'll take her to see the lark's nest. Who knows? We might even spy an ancestral ghost—a wraith of a Maxwell woman almost as beautiful as you. I'll know her at once, if we do, because her head will be sittin' upon her lovely neck giving me 'the look' that won me old heart at fir-rst glance."

Chapter 38

The only timetable they followed on their wedding trip was determined by the limit of the money Father Fraser had given John, so during the full week of steady rain that prevented their leaving Carlisle as planned, Anne wrote letters and did her best to calm John, who seemed even more disappointed than she that they had not yet been able to make it to the Borderland and Caerlaverock Castle.

Would she ever learn to anticipate his mercurial mood changes? Or was she only imagining that, thwarted by the not unusual delay, he seemed abruptly eager to show her Dumfriesshire? The travel interruption was certainly not unheard of. Even a further delay of three or four days, through which they would surely have to wait for the road into the Scottish Borderland to dry out, was common. Anne needed Papa to laugh with her because after all these days in Carlisle, their whole waterlogged journey was beginning to strike her funny.

"Evidently, my father made no allowance for our being stranded by rain with all this unexpected room-and-board expense," he complained at breakfast on the first truly sunny morning. "If anyone should know about the foul Scottish weather, he should. You realize, I'm sure, that this long stay in Carlisle will cut short our wedding trip." When Anne only looked at him, then began to laugh, he smiled. "I deserved that laugh, didn't I? Forgive me. The old fellow meant well. I just feel so sorry for your sake."

"Well, you needn't feel sorry for me, because I'm all caught up with my letter writing, and best of all, I'm with you. Does it matter that much where we are?"

"No. And I say, after all this time and all my wandering

alone around Carlisle while you wrote your never-ending letters home, I've just had a bright thought. We'd better not spend money for a rented carriage, but if the sun stays in place this afternoon, I have a plan. Right here in Carlisle is the very cathedral where Walter Scott, your literary hero, and his wife were married in 1797."

Of course, she'd love to see the cathedral, but what mattered most was the return of John's sunny smile. "I'd like that very much," she said, "but it doesn't have to be today. It will take even that bright sun a few days to dry all the deep mud on our road, won't it?"

"Yes, but I think the sun will hold and I won't feel such a failure if I can show you one site that pleases you."

"You spoil me," she said, "but don't stop. I want you to know I'm perfectly aware that you're not one bit interested in seeing an old cathedral."

"I'm interested in anything that makes you happy, Annie. Don't forget, this is all 'for better or for worse.' " He reached across the narrow table for her hand. "The days pass, don't they? And passing days always mean nights come again. No man could ask for more than our nights, could he? Certainly not this man, who has the superior good fortune of climbing into that rickety, iron bed with thee."

Two days after they visited the cathedral, still another sunny morning set them to packing the few belongings they'd unpacked for the surprisingly long stay in Carlisle. Of course, John finished first and was downstairs checking on the roads. Anne stood alone at the tall front window of their long, narrow room—feeling proud that she'd managed by herself to pack her clothing and even to close the portmanteau without John's help—when he burst through the door.

"Good news!" John shouted. "I just learned from the owner of this dreary establishment that we can take a stage out this very morning for Dumfries. And, Mrs. Fraser, I must say you've been splendid during our imprisonment in Carlisle." Glancing at her stack of belongings, he laughed. "You're more than splendid. You're all packed and you did it without me."

Both arms around him, she planted a kiss on his cheek. "I'm proud of me, too, and dearest, I haven't minded being here at all. You'll laugh at me when I tell you, but I can still see the sheer beauty of that fourteenth-century glass in the great East Window of Carlisle Cathedral. John, I loved seeing where Walter Scott was married."

For an instant, he looked down at her. "I believe you really did. At least, I think that's about the eighth time you've said as much."

Finally on their way to Dumfries, both in great, good humor, John entertained her over the thirtysome miles of rutted, mud-caked road with the one thing he remembered from his youth about Gretna Green, the first Scottish town they'd pass.

" 'Tis the perfect place for lovers," he declared. "A tiny village, but its old streets stream with young English couples hunting the quickest possible way to get married."

"To get married?"

"English laws are strict, but just across the Border at Gretna, all a couple has to do is declare their intentions to a blacksmith and be married."

"By a blacksmith?"

"By a blacksmith, a candlemaker, any handy tradesman."

"You're making that up!"

"I'm not, I swear. If we weren't already married, I'd prove it to you." He took her hand. "Annie," he said earnestly, "you were so sweet-tempered through all that rotten weather. I'm somehow embarrassed, although I'm not sure why. Mostly I'm grateful and I vow that from now on, you won't have the added burden of trying to keep me in a good mood."

He proved it several hours later when they reached the outskirts of Dumfries, because rain was falling again in such sheets, they could have been lurching through a rain cloud itself.

"Did you ever feel wetter rain?" he asked, tightening his arm about her to steady her. "And don't remind me again that you love getting wet, because I won't believe it. We will sleep in Dumfries tonight, though, and we'll soon be at our inn there. I know the quixotic Dumfries weather well enough to know a Borderland rain can all but vanish into a blaze of sunlight. There's a good chance it will, because we are, by now, into June, so dinna' wor-ry, dear-rie."

Smiling up at him, she squeezed rainwater from her bonnet ribbons and told him how much she loved it when he lapsed into a bit of Scottish brogue. "You and Papa both tend to do it when you're either happy or annoyed. Oh, dearest, can you believe we're finally in Scotland? I wrote a long letter to Cannon's Point just before we left London. They'll know in a few weeks at least where we were headed all those days ago. Mama and Papa must both be wondering where we are."

"And where we are would be nearly in the magnificent town of Dumfries, my bir-rthplace, lass," he said cheerfully. "Dumfries and a room at the old Globe Inn, known the world over because of the great bard Robert Burns. Oh, I know you're a Walter Scott devotee, but does anyone ever call him Wally as they call Robert Burns Bobby? Burns was an earthy human being—just one of the neighbors who dr-rank Scotch bear with him."

"What on earth is Scotch bear?"

"You mean to tell me your father never recited the immortal Burns paen known as 'Scotch Drink'?" Ignoring the other passengers, he proclaimed, as though they were quite alone:

"Let other poets raise a fracas
'Bout vines, an' wines, an' drunken Bacchus,
An' crabbit names an' stories wrack us,
An' grate our lug—
I sing the juice Scotch bear can mak' us,
In glass or jug. . . ."

Then John said, "Plainly, darlin' Annie, Scotch bear is whuskey, 'cause any gude Scotch whuskey is made from barley. Bear is barley."

Anne was laughing with him, delighted because he actually seemed happy to be back in Scotland.

"I'm excited, John," she said, "and glad Father Fraser insisted that we travel to Scotland and no place else."

He gave her a quizzical look. "Could it be, lass, that even with your hair sopping wet and your bonnet limp, you're allowing Sco'land to equal St. Simons Island in your heart?"

"No, silly. I'm just happy that some *one place* seems to have this kind of meaning for you."

His heart sank a little. Without mentioning their future, she had nevertheless brought it up. Still, he had spent his adult life mastering the art of avoiding unpleasant subjects by the use of lighthearted teasing. Right now, he would act delighted at being back in Scotland because he meant to create nothing but joy around Anne, come what may.

"I'm as capable as the next mon of loving a place, lass, despite Father's diagnosis of wanderlust." And then he quoted lines from Walter Scott:

"Breathes there the man, with soul so dead,
Who never to himself hath said,
This is my own, my native land!
Whose heart hath ne'er within him burn'd,
As home his footsteps he hath turn'd,
From wandering on a foreign strand!"

He added, "Do ye tak' to my recitin' poetry, ma'am?"

"Oh, John," she said, inching still closer on the wet carriage seat, "I take to you in every way! That was from Scott's 'Lay of the Last Minstrel,' wasn't it?"

"Aye."

"I love you and I love being here in the pouring Scottish rain in this jolting old mail coach exactly as we are this minute. I can also not wait to see Dumfries, the very town where you were born, and the Maxwell castle and—"

"Then hold your horses, milady, because as soon as we've passed the cattle market up ahead, our coach-and-four will turn into High Street and you'll see the most memorable site—our temporary Dumfries home, the Globe Inn. To this day, twenty years after his untimely death, it's a shrine to Sco'land's pride and joy, Bobby Burns!"

"Did Burns actually live at the Globe Inn?"

John laughed. "No, he was too poor for that, but he drank there and, I've always been told, with magnificent capacity. 'Tis said he composed the immortal poem 'Scotch Drink' on a morning after."

At the very moment the muddy coach slowed and stopped before a two-story building with a swinging wooden sign that said The Globe Inn, the sky lit up and every clinging raindrop glistened with sudden sunlight. "Are you always so right about everything?" Anne asked. "Even the weather?"

"Aye, always," he laughed, reaching to help her down from the high seat.

"You're being awfully cocky, sir," Anne said, her soaking-wet feet touching Scottish ground for the first time. "What if there's no room for us at the Globe?"

"I'm not only right most of the time, I'm also well connected. I can guarantee a good room because I've known the McDonalds, the owners, for generations."

"You're not that old!"

"Well, I've known them all my life."

When John took her arm to help her through the puddles toward the double front doors, she gave him a puzzled look. "Why do you suppose Father Fraser didn't talk to me about your family's long friendship with the owners of the very inn Robert Burns made famous?"

"I've never known him to say enough on any subject," John answered as they stepped inside the inn's entrance hall, candlelight gleaming off the wine-dark Spanish-mahogany-paneled walls. "Look around you, Annie," he said softly. "The bard himself—could he ride back here today through the chill and the wind, notebooks under his arm, nag in a lather—would find this spot exactly as he left it twenty years ago. 'Tis said Burns drank so heartily on his final night here, he stumbled out the door, slipped on the icy steps, and lay sprawled there until found the next morning. His final illness. Only thirty-seven, Bobby Burns died soon after of the consequences of that last, carefree night of debauchery."

John certainly doesn't sound as though he's teasing when he speaks of Burns, Anne thought, waiting to one side of the Globe doors while he went to claim their bags. She felt sure he shared every Dumfries man's adoration of the poet. While they were still perched on top of the coach with the rain coming down, he had informed her firmly that Shakespeare was not revered at Stratford-upon-Avon by Englishmen as was Robert Burns in Dumfries, adding that an Englishman would rather choose the genius of even another Scotsman, Walter Scott, over that of Robert Burns.

What, she wondered, caused the English to look down on Robert Burns? His lack of money? His penchant for drink? Papa had recited Burns's wonderfully rhythmic poem "The Cotter's Saturday Night" to her almost every time the two of them had marched in any good St. Simons rainstorm. Looking around now at the high-ceilinged room, she felt awe to be standing in the very place Bobby Burns loved, in which he had reveled up to his final illness.

The rain was over, as John had promised, and a tall, heavyset older man—probably the owner, Mr. McDonald—came from behind his receiving counter to douse the candles no longer needed because golden sunlight gleamed from the polished panels.

A shiver of delight ran through her, and standing there alone, she laughed at herself because suddenly *she* felt at home. Actually, it all seemed so familiar, she almost went to greet Mr. McDonald before John had come back inside to introduce them properly.

I know John finds it strange, she thought, that Father Fraser and I have grown so close in such a short time, but I don't. The old gentleman knew exactly what he was doing when he put strings on his gift of our wedding trip—all Scottish strings. Right now, this minute, since we're so far from St. Simons, even I wouldn't want to be anywhere else but in Dumfries.

When she saw John and a pudgy red-haired boy push their way through the front doors, both loaded with luggage and boxes, she hurried happily to meet them.

Arms still loaded, John called a pleasant greeting to Mr. McDonald, now back behind his counter, then lowered his load to the floor and turned briefly toward the carrot-haired boy. "See to her ladyship, lad. She's a royal personage—wet, stringy hair, soaked bonnet, and all. So, see to her safety while I speak to Mr. McDonald. You'll get your ha'pennies once I've settled on a room and once you've given me a hand upstairs with all this."

Left standing with the lad, Anne said pleasantly, "Why not rest your arms, young man? Go ahead. It's all right to put that down for now. You're quite strong for your age, aren't you?"

"Aye, ma'am," the boy said, letting their bags drop with a thud, but giving her a most comical smile, the corners of his mouth pointing suddenly up like arrows to his blue eyes. "You're a English *royal personage,* ma'am?"

She laughed a bit too loud and denied any relationship to the English throne. "You mustn't take my husband seriously, no matter what he tells you. He teases a lot."

Still grinning at her, the boy asked, "Ya' mean I get no ha'pennies lik' 'e said?"

"No, not that. You'll get your money for helping us. Do you live here in Dumfries? And what's your name?"

"Me name's Bob, ma'am. An' me ma's piggin lies across river a bit off from town toward Maxwell's castle."

Her eyes lit up. "Do you know much about Caerlaverock, the old Maxwell castle?"

"Aye. I walk across the bridge and along the River Nith home every day. Me ma she works for the Maxwell laird hisself. When he's home to Dumfries, he still lives in part of the castle. Me ma's proud to work there." He puffed up his fat chest. "The Maxwells is everything aroun' all of Dumfriesshire!"

"Is that so? I'm not a royal personage at all, Bob, but would you believe me if I told you that my own mother's name was Rebecca Maxwell before she married my father?"

His mouth fell open. *"The self-same Maxwells?"*

"Yes. All my life Mama has talked to me about the stories she heard from her parents of the ancient Maxwells of Dumfriesshire and about Caerlaverock Castle. Will your mother be working there tomorrow? How long does it take to get there in a carriage?"

"You wanna know 'bout me ma first or how long to get there?"

Anne laughed. "Your mother. Will she be there tomorrow? My husband and I are going to Caerlaverock Castle in the morning."

"When the laird ain' home, only three servants works two days a week, but not tomorrow." He flashed the impudent grin. "How long it tak' depend on when the mud dries. 'Tis aboot seven or eight kilometers from Dumfries."

She could hear John's quick laughter across the big room as he shook hands with Mr. McDonald, made a joke, then strode back, triumphantly holding up a huge door key.

"The best room in all the Globe Inn," he declared. "The largest corner room with windows aplenty. Now then, lad, if you and her royal highness can put an end to your conversation, I'll be much obliged for some help with our belongings. One flight up."

"Can't be no more," the boy said. "Only two stories to the Globe."

When they reached their pleasant room and after John had counted out some ha'pennies for the puffing boy, who had dumped his load in the middle of their room as carelessly as he'd dropped it downstairs, John said, "You've been a big help, son, and didn't I tell you the lady here is a royal personage?"

Scuffing a knot in the bare wooden floor with the stubby toe of his boot, the boy said, "She tol' me you josh a lot, but she's e'en better—she's a *Maxwell* an' roun' Dumfriesshire, the Maxwells is everything! Has been for near eight hundred years."

Dinner, which they ate in the alcove adjoining the public room, where Robert Burns's favorite chair had been boarded over to prevent other customers from using it, was surprisingly inviting. At least to Anne, who hadn't found anything interesting to eat since she and John had left Flora McLeod's cooking.

When two steaming bowls of thick, aromatic Scotch broth were placed before them, Anne took one sniff and exclaimed, "John! You didn't tell me we'd find anything to compare with the way this Scotch broth smells. When it cools down enough to taste, it just could compare with the barley broth Sans Foix makes."

"I love it when you're surprised," he said, spooning and tasting. "Didn't I mention that old McDonald's wife herself creates this genuine Scottish concoction?"

"Did you ever eat the Scotch broth Sans Foix makes?"

"Afraid I missed out on that, but if it's in a class with Mrs. McDonald's before us now, undoubtedly your father explained the secret as the Lowlanders meant Scotch broth to be."

"Oh, I doubt that Papa knows how to boil water. If anyone instructed Sans Foix, it was Mama. Remember, lad, me mother is a full Scot, too. With a real ancestral *cahstle*, which we will actually see tomorrow morning. Oh, dearest, I can't believe I'll be seeing Caerlaverock with my own eyes after all this time. It's like a dream!"

"Far better than a dream is that hearty broth before ye, lass, if you'll only pick up your spoon."

"It's too hot. I can tell. I like things cooled off so that I can really taste without burning my tongue."

"Aye, beautiful Annie," he said, his voice tender, already so filled with promise for tonight, the familiar ache swept over her right there in the dining room before a half dozen other customers. "I wouldn't want anything to happen to those lips. Unless, of course, they're against mine."

"That isn't fair! It's not a bit fair, John Fraser, to say a thing like that in a public place."

"All's fair in love and war—at the old Globe Inn, darlin' gir-rl. The Globe's certainly seen loves other than ours, and the Almighty knows it's been here long enough to have endured a few of the Border wars your Walter Scott writes of. One spoonful of broth? Surely, even those tender lips can touch it now."

She dipped her spoon, took all of it into her mouth, and closed her eyes in sheer bliss. After a moment, with John beaming across the narrow table at her, she said, "Heaven! Even at Cannon's Point there was never Scotch broth like this, and don't you dare ever tell either my parents or Sans Foix I said that."

For a few moments they ate in silence, devouring the aromatic cabbage and turnips and carrots, barley and succulent pieces of lamb flank—each exchanged look, each unspoken caress, each half-smile, hurtling them toward the finish of their satisfying meal. Toward a polite, swift exchange of greetings with the McDonalds, the flight upstairs and to bed at the earliest possible moment—both eager to create their own storm even if outside the sun was free of clouds now and about to set.

Chapter 39

Before dawn broke the next morning, Anne was up, bathed, dressed, and trying to arrange her hair by candlelight when John came awake.

"Good morning, lass," he said sleepily, sitting up in the bed. "I order ye to lay aside that comb and come hither, bride!"

"Hush," she said, brow furrowed as she concentrated on the always difficult job of combing out and setting her cap of curls just right—if possible, exactly in the center. "Can't you see I'm busy?"

"But I haven't had a single good-morning kiss and I demand three or four."

"Sh!"

"I've heard tell of a lady's needing a handmaiden to comb her hair, but never a demand for silence. Why can't I at least talk to you while you labor?"

"Because, without Eve, I'll do something wrong."

"I think you're improving greatly. Back in London, you wouldn't allow me even to stay in the room while you did that."

"I wish you weren't here now. You make me nervous. Don't you think I want to kiss you, too?" Sticking a last bone hairpin in at what felt like the right angle, she turned to look at him. "Well? Am I all right? Are my curls piled straight or do I only look rakish?"

At that very moment, before he could even answer, the pin fell out and a curly mass of dark hair cascaded forward over her eyes.

Her first impulse was to burst into tears. She could taste their salt, but she also sensed John's suppressed laughter.

So, she laughed, too, crossed the room, and threw herself onto the bed into his reaching arms.

For minutes on end, they kissed and laughed and tumbled about and not until John began to tickle her did she pull away, leap to the floor trying to smooth the wrinkles from her long, yellow walking skirt. Still laughing, she sat back down before the heavy, dark dressing table. When she peered into the looking glass, her shoulders sagged. "I look like a frizzled chicken," she said, no longer smiling.

"We may *need* you to look like a frizzled chicken," he said, swinging his long, bare legs over the side of the bed. "Who knows how many Maxwell ghosts are still in the old castle?"

"You don't even know what a frizzled chicken is or what it's used for," she snapped.

"Oh, yes, I do know all about frizzled chickens."

"Who told you?"

"Eve's June."

"When did you ever talk to June?"

"Back in the days when I first came to St. Simons from Cumberland. While you were still my captive and I could actually command you. June and I talked often in those early days. I could tell he had influence on the other slaves. I wanted him to know the truth about the British promises."

"You don't sound very loyal to your vaunted Royal Marines when you remind me of what you did to protect Papa's *people.*"

"Excuse me, ma'am," he apologized, half teasing. "I forgot and called them slaves, didn't I. I know you don't approve of that."

"It has nothing to do with whether I approve or not. I've just been taught better." Struggling again with the large bone pin, she asked, "What did June tell you about a frizzled chicken?"

"The truth, I'm sure. He seemed to think some of our enlisted men had laid down conjures on your father's people so they'd believe all the lies about the Queen of England being black and life with the British in Nova Scotia being all roses and ease, so he told me about the value of a frizzled chicken." She could tell John was making fun of the whole idea. "You don't mean to tell me you've lived all your life on St. Simons Island, milady, without finding out that a frizzled chicken in the yard will invariably dig up any kind of conjure laid down on any person?"

Wonder of wonders, her curls by now looked fairly straight and the pin was holding. "Of course, I know! I grew up with frizzled chickens. Why do you think I said I looked like one? And why did you say it might be a good thing if we had a frizzled chicken when we reach Caerlaverock—*if* we ever do!"

"Ah-ha," he said, on his feet now, pouring water for shaving into a big china bowl. "On the haunts of Caerlaverock, I can inform *you,* lass. Unless, that is, your Maxwell mother has already told you of the two-natured Cynthia, who roams the castle ramparts at full moon, walking up and down, up and down, discovering for herself which of her natures will walk that night."

"Two-natured Cynthia? I never heard of her! Does she walk only at night? And what good would a frizzled chicken do to protect anyone from a ghost?"

"Aye, Cynthia walks at night, but also, depending on which nature comes to her on the ramparts, at times she's seen in broad daylight. Exactly how a frizzled chicken might affect her I haven't quite decided."

When John returned from the hall outside their room, bearing a steaming pitcher of hot water left at their door, he poured it into the half-filled bowl of cold, then turned to look at her. "What's wrong, lass? Why are you standing there hands on hips glaring at me like Caerlaverock Cynthia?"

"I don't believe a word you just told me. I think you made Cynthia up out of whole cloth and also I doubt that you and June know each other so well."

One hand raised, he said, "I swear on my honor that I made up absolutely none of it, certainly not two-natured Cynthia, the ghost of your family castle, which we will never reach today if I don't shave."

With every fiber of her being, Anne wanted to see the Maxwell castle. For as long as she could remember, she'd plied Mama with questions about it, laughed with Papa when he teased Mama because, unlike his average Scottish ancestry, the family name of Maxwell had for centuries been linked with truly famous clans—Douglas, Stewart, Campbell, Murray, Cameron. Anne's lifelong vision of Caerlaverock was colored with imaginings of feudal knights, the splendid castle itself under siege time and again by the hated English with battering rams, slings, and hundreds of men clad in metal armor galloping about on frothing steeds —her ancestors charging up and down stone stairs by way of secret passages known only to a true Maxwell. Caerlaverock, in Anne's imagination, had always been shrouded in a blowing Scottish fog. Bright with victories in the name of freedom, mist-shrouded by defeats and stained with the blood Maxwells shed. And yet, despite the mounting excitement because this very day she would at long last see Caerlaverock herself, she felt trapped in her own secret passage darker and more mysterious than any stair she and John might search out once they got there. Would John ever feel at home in any one place? And if he did, could she be at home there too?

"Did I ever tell you that among my own distinguished forefathers were those who fought right with your highborn Maxwells in one of the old sieges of Caerlaverock?"

Her heart leaped. "Frasers fought with Maxwells for Scottish independence? John, I could smack you!"

He only chuckled, fully concentrating now on razor strokes along his strong, prominent chin line. "You'd get a handful of lather if you did, lass. What did I say to deserve a smack?"

"Again, it's what you didn't say. You talk and talk to me, but always with those huge, gaping craters of so much left out. Why didn't you tell me long ago that our ancestors fought together? You complain because Father Fraser leaves out so much, but I don't think he's any worse than you." Abruptly, the comb she'd been trying to insert slid directly into place. Watching closely in the mirror, she slowly, cautiously removed both hands and waited. The crown of curls held, and wonder of wonders, it was also where it belonged, smack in the middle of her head.

In the looking glass she could see him watching her, a proud grin on his splendid face, lighting it, erasing the arrogance, pricking her heart. "Success?" he asked, then leaned over the bowl of water to splash his shaved face.

"Success," she breathed. "Oh, John, I'm so happy to be going to Caerlaverock with you today. And look, the sun is out. I even have faith to believe my hair won't fall down once."

"Then, I also have faith enough to run downstairs and try

to hire something on wheels hitched to something on four legs that will hold together long enough to get us there." He smothered his words toweling off his face, strode to where she sat, and kissed her. "Is my lightweight green jacket warm enough, do you think, bride? I do find it a nuisance not to be simply donning a uniform every day from habit." When she said nothing, he caught her eyes in the mirror and smiled. "Sorry. That slipped out. I'm sure the sun will make my light jacket just right, even if we stay at Caerlaverock until late afternoon."

He had merely had a slip of the tongue, she decided. Both were holding to their pact. Anyone could say something without thinking. Today, of all days, she was not going to allow herself even one thought that John could well be hiding deep inside him a dread of ever learning how to live away from his beloved Royal Marines. "You're terribly handsome in that green jacket, darling," she said. Then she took his face in her hands and kissed him tenderly. "We all forget and say things we don't mean to say. Today is today and I love you."

"Aye, today is today in all ways," he whispered, "and I love you more than even you think I do."

Within half an hour, John was helping her up into the sturdy McDonald buggy, feeling proud because Anne seemed delighted with the arrangement he'd made for their drive to Caerlaverock Castle across the River Nith. Almost since the night he'd captured her at Dungeness, she'd made it plain that nothing he could ever do would please her as much as being absolutely alone with him. No matter how she had struggled without Eve, she had never once voiced a single wish that any other human being be present but John himself. As a consequence, he felt a sense of invincibility as strong as any he'd ever felt as a marine. Snapping the reins over the broad, brown rump of McDonald's horse, he gave a playful shout and away they trotted through the streets of Dumfries en route at last to nearby Maxwelltown, where loomed the ancient ruins of her family's famous castle.

"Happy, Mrs. Fraser?"

"Ecstatic!" she exclaimed, pushing still closer to him on the buggy seat. "We'll have to do something nice to show our gratitude to Mr. McDonald for the generous loan of his horse and buggy. Oh, John, isn't it marvelous that you're the driver and we don't have to be proper or careful about anything we do or say?" She giggled. "We're even saving Father Fraser a little money. If you and Mr. McDonald were not such friends, you'd have had to rent something and you know we wouldn't have ended up with such a good buggy as this. Even with only two wheels, it's really quite comfortable, isn't it?"

"English buggies have only two wheels," he explained. "You've probably only ridden in American-made four-wheelers. They may be a bit safer. We could tip over if I don't keep a deft hand on the reins, but"—he leaned to kiss her nose—"I wouldna' wor-r-ry, Annie. You're quite safe with me."

"Look, we're passing the cattle market again. I remember it from yesterday when we got here after all that pouring rain. We cross the River Nith, don't we?"

"Aye, over a quite magnificent arched stone bridge built in the thirteenth century by the widowed Queen Devorguila. On the next bonnie day I can borrow McDonald's conveyance again, I'll take you to Sweetheart Abbey, where she lies buried."

To John, Anne looked all of ten years old when she caught her first glimpse of the River Nith, its brown waters flowing under all of Queen Devorguila's ancient, stone arches. "There," he said. "Look, Annie—up ahead. The queen's bridge and we're headed right for it!"

In response, she only beamed up at him—too excited, he knew, too expectant, too filled with her singular kind of imaginings, for mere words. One of her hands rested lightly on his gray-clad knee, the touch telling her thoughts in ways far clearer than words ever sat together in a sentence. His own joy mounted. He had wooed and won this beauty of a Scottish girl. It was he, John Fraser, who had brought her to this very country road on this very day in the early summer of the year 1816. It was he who was taking her now, in the comfortable two-wheeler, nearer and nearer to the ancient ruins of Caerlaverock, a place grown familiar to him from his Dumfries boyhood, the symbol of what he now knew had always been one of Anne's brightest, most cherished dreams.

Caerlaverock Castle. He had already told her that while most believed the ancient Celtic word *caer* means "fort," there were also Dumfries natives who swore that *Caerlaver-*

ock truly means "lark's nest." Of course, hating anything to do with war, Anne demanded that it mean lark's nest. Undoubtedly, she'd remind him of that before this day was over. No one knew better than he that Anne hated even the word *fort.* To her, a fort stood only for battles and bloodshed, never for much-needed security. He took a deep breath, a resigned sigh, actually. For today, the famous ruin would be a lark's nest. For today, what mattered was that they were going there together—together and alone—and as magnificent as Caerlaverock was as a fortress, he too would try to think of it as a lark's nest.

"Was that a sigh, John?"

"Not a bad kind," he said. "I was simply filling me lungs with this clean, moorland air."

What he'd just said was only a tiny white lie. Time later to face the truth that Anne wanted him never to be a marine again. That the only thing she truly wanted was for them to go back to St. Simons Island and live at Lawrence Plantation. She would agree to whatever he decided, he knew, but nothing so difficult had to be considered today. Today, he meant to protect her from even one single dark thought.

Chapter 40

Rebecca and Jock were on the front porch when Ebo June rode up the lane on Couper's own horse and dismounted beside the front steps of Cannon's Point. Rebecca jumped up from her chair and went to meet him.

"You got it right, Missus," June called, hurrying up the steps waving a letter. "Mister Abbott say it be from Miss Anne! Womens knows, don't they, Mausa Couper? How she so sure I got a letter from Miss Anne right here in my han'? You see her git right up an' reach for it?"

"Never mind, June," Rebecca said. "I didn't know. It was simply past time for us to be hearing from our daughter. Way past time."

"You see, June?" Couper asked. "We've a tough battle to fight, we men, when we try to understand a woman's instinct. I agree with you. She did know. I only hoped."

"My Eve she be like that, too. Specially 'bout Miss Anne. What that you say she got, Mausa Couper?"

"*Instinct,* June. A woman's instinct is both useful and at times treacherous."

June's smile, which didn't come unless he felt utterly comfortable, lit his dark eyes. "Bof good an' bad?"

"That's right. Both good and bad."

"An' you say, sir, it called instink?"

"That's close, June," Jock said. "And it doesn't surprise me at all that Eve's instinct is sharp. She's a sharp woman."

" 'Scuse me, Mausa Couper, but is womens always right?"

"No," Rebecca said, a little annoyed. "Women are not always right! Just most of the time. We do thank you for riding to Frederica for our mail. That's all, June. You may go."

"Not quite yet," Couper said. "Eve and our daughter Anne are so close, I'd be inclined to trust Eve's hunches about her. I'm sure she has one. I need June to tell me if Eve's worried or happy over whatever her latest instinct is telling her about Anne."

"Jock, that's enough. You and June can discuss Eve's current premonition later." Rebecca sat back down in her porch chair. "I need to read Anne's letter in peace and quiet."

Pleasantly ignoring her, Couper prodded. "June? Is Eve happy or worried?"

"Aw, Eve be happy, sir! An' her instink yestidy tell her it be good news 'bout bof yo' ladyfolks."

"What's that?" Rebecca asked.

"Eve's new instink be 'bout bof you an' Miss Anne, ma'am."

"What on earth are you saying, June?" she asked.

Amused, June shook his head. "How would I know, ma'am? You know Eve. She don't axe nobody's opinion no more than she tell her own when she got one ob her instinks. She stay as mum as her gran'maum, ol' Sofy, when she done seen a ghost."

"You may go now," Couper said, winking at his skillful cooper. "Glad to see you've learned a new word."

"Yes, sir! Wait til I tell Eve I know 'bout her instink!"

When June rode off toward the horse barn, Couper laughed admiringly, watching the broad-shouldered, quick-witted Ebo round the curve in the lane that led past the new row of olive trees he and June had planted right after Anne and John left. "I'm mighty proud of that fellow, Becca. He does build the finest barrels I've ever seen, but I've just about decided to turn him into my main botanist. I can train him to plant and prune and nurture growing things with the best of them."

"That's a splendid idea, dear," she said, the seal already broken on Anne's letter, their first since she went away. "If you'd prefer to ponder future plans for June, I can read this to myself and I'm starting right now. Hush. Anne wrote it from London, 2 George Street, back in May. 'Dear Everyone at my most blessed Cannon's Point,' she begins. And Jock, that means only one thing—Anne is dreadfully homesick!"

"Gude," he said, lapsing into a bit of his Scottish brogue. " 'Tis gude to hear, that is, unless it makes her sad."

"We'll find out if you think you can be quiet long enough. 'As I write this from an apologetic heart for not having done so sooner, John has taken most of our luggage to the coach stop from which we will leave tomorrow on our wedding trip to Scotland. Father Fraser is still at business and I should have ample time for trying, at least, to tell you all how happy I am, how much I have come to like John's father, and that John vows I've won the thoroughly Scottish heart of the Fraser housekeeper, Miss Flora McLeod. Much of the time, though, in spite of how dutiful John has been about showing London's sites to me, I seem always to be gasping for breath. The kind of clean, easy breath everyone draws on St. Simons. Londoners must each burn a ton of coal a day because the air is always smoky and everything feels gritty and shut-in. Father Fraser is a man of some means if the house here is any indication. It is four stories but flush with the street, and unlike my beloved father, the dear man seems unable to make anything grow.' "

"What? Surely, a man of his means would have a gardener of sorts," Jock blurted. "But then I haven't been in London in more than forty years. Ways change." He chuckled. "I certainly have no thought of sending June to rescue him."

"It just could be that Mr. Fraser doesn't like gardening, so spends very little time on it," Rebecca said, amused that her husband appeared genuinely pleased that John's father did not have a green thumb. " 'Our voyage over was not an easy one, or so John says. He is the experienced sailor, of course, and I am a novice on the high seas, but I was not seasick and we did experience more than a week of stormy weather. The seven other passengers, all from Savannah, none known to me, were dreary, and the one chosen to do our cooking quite evidently prefers the taste of sawdust to real food. That is behind us, though, and I will someday have a lot to tell dear Miss Eliza Mackay of my tours of London. We saw the Tower, the palaces, Westminster, Covent Garden Theater, and, it seemed, at least a thousand other buildings, all splendid but still all *buildings.* My most favorite day was spent in a carriage driving through Hyde Park, where there are trees galore and space.' "

"The gir-rl's homesick!" Jock exulted. "She's downright lonely for Cannon's Point, do ya' think, Becca?"

"I do indeed, but don't forget they're undoubtedly in Scotland by now or nearly so. I can't wait for her first letter from Dumfries! How I wish my dear father could know she's actually going to be there so near Caerlaverock."

Jock grinned. "The old fellow would do verbal battle with Cromwell all over again, if you could tell him. I never saw your ancestral castle meself, Becca, but after the destruction of the first one, it took old Cromwell's cannon plus the Covenanters to demolish the second." He reached to pat her knee. "The third splendid Caerlaverock, I'm told, still stands, its ruins as laudable as any in all of Britain. Gives even Anne's aging father a chill to think our gir-rl will be able to see it with her own Druid eyes."

"You can laugh all you want at my family castle. At me for my lifelong fascination with anything Celtic—all our hot-blooded clan chieftains and—"

"—every hand twitching to battle at the first imagined hint of insult . . . Ah, Becca, down under your admirable gentility, especially when one of our people rubs you the wrong way, methinks I detect a bit of the auld Maxwell Caerlaverock swagger, your own graceful hand twitching at the sword hilt."

"Am I to finish reading our daughter's letter or would you prefer tweaking me for having not one drop more Scottish blood than you do, Jock?"

"Aye, the Coupers are full-blooded, wi'out more than a drap of aristocracy. Me humble father, the strong-headed kirk parson, displaying his own fire only by thumps on the Bible of a Sabbath morning and a strop to me buttocks." They exchanged playful smiles, then Jock began to twiddle his thumbs. "How long will you keep me waiting to hear more of my own daughter, Becca?"

"Only as long as it takes to find my place again after your interruptions. There's very little letter left, actually. And she's drawn a line across the page denoting, I suppose, a time lapse as she was writing. After the line, Anne wrote: 'Father Fraser came home early, disturbing this letter, but bringing the most glorious gift—a letter from my adored parents! I read it aloud to him and it led John's father and me to our most treasured and informative talk yet. How I pray that he may someday meet you both. He is not a happy man, but I am pleased to say that he does, in his most typical, Scottish, reserved manner, seem to be genuinely fond of me.' "

"Now, there's a contradiction," Jock broke in again. "A typical Scot is reserved and of few words, eh? Odd no one has ever accused me of that, and my native hamlet, Lochwinnoch, was still in Scotland the last I heard of it."

"You cannot be called typical of anything, dearest Jock. You are one of a kind and unlike anyone else. Anne had to end her letter rather abruptly, it seems. Perhaps John came home or she talked too long with her father-in-law. I hope neither of us wrote anything in our letter that may have made Anne wish she hadn't read it aloud to Mr. Fraser, don't you?"

"What could we write to Annie that couldn't be shouted from the housetops?"

"Nothing, except it is possible, you know, that John hadn't yet told his father that you are trying to force Lawrence plantation on the boy."

"Nonsense."

"You are, aren't you?"

"Aye, but with the most benevolent intentions. He can't go on with no profession of any description, Becca. Not with Annie depending on him. She sends love to everyone by name, I'm sure, eh?"

"She does and especially to Eve. Being Anne, she wouldn't admit it to me, but unless she has hidden talents I've never even suspected, the child must be beside herself without Eve. I wonder every morning how her hair looks. Anne is all thumbs with a comb and brush."

"I'll tell you how she looks—beautiful. Now, give me the letter, if you please. You know I have to read her dear writing myself—probably several times."

Rebecca handed it over, then leaned her head against the high wooden back of the porch rocker. "I wonder what on earth June meant by Eve's excitement over her premonition about both Anne and me? Most days I just ignore our people when they work spells or have premonitions. With Eve, I can't help wondering. Jock, was Eve born with a caul over her face?"

"Only Fanny could tell you that, I suppose," he said, still poring over Anne's letter. "Or old Sofy, Fanny's crazy mother."

"I don't think Sofy's crazy at all. Bossy, hardheaded, can lay down a conjure, but not crazy. What made you say that?"

He looked up from his reading. "Have you seen Sofy lately?"

"No, not in a month or so, I suppose. She does most of her weaving in her cabin. Why?"

"The woman's been here at Cannon's Point from the first week you and I moved into the little old Cannon house, and peculiar as she's always been, I never saw her wear the kind of bangles she's wearing this week. Oh, she's always had that cherished pair of gold hoops in her ears, but many African women wear those. Along with her hoops, she now has two broken bits of looking glass on a string across the top of her head. She must have made a flour paste because each piece is stuck to her temples so that she glints in the sunlight."

"That's just something African, Jock. Most of our people wear peculiar items on cords around their necks or carry dried animal feet to ward off evil. I seldom even notice. As long as Sofy sews and weaves so well, she's fine with me exactly as she is."

"Not when she's scaring my good, dependable Big Boy the way she's doing these days."

"What on earth is she doing to Big Boy?"

"He told me today she's out by the river every single morning waiting for him to untie his boat to do his fishing, threatening him with every kind of conjure if he doesn't get her three eel skins—all three caught within one hour! I don't mind their superstitions. Sometimes I think they may be wiser by far in some areas than we who call ourselves civilized, but I don't like her upsetting Big Boy. A man doesn't fish successfully if he's nervous. Today, Big Boy was on the verge of tears."

"But why? What made him so nervous? Surely he knows old Sofy's ways."

"Oh, he knows she puts down conjures. Believes with all his great, simple heart that her conjures can cause a person to sicken and die. I'd say Big Boy's afraid she might be going to lay one down on him."

"What could Sofy possibly have against our utterly child-like fisherman? It sounds to me as though she just thinks she needs those eel skins to make some kind of potion and knows she can trust Big Boy to get them for her. Jock, you don't believe in Sofy's conjures, do you?"

"Never been able to make up my mind," he said quite seriously. "I've given it as little thought as possible. It's nothing to me one way or another as a rule. I only know I respect the wisdom of most of our people. Especially the older ones, all of whom have been very well behaved."

"I—I suppose I quite agree. But, Jock, you don't think Sofy's new project has anything to do with Eve's premonition about Anne and me, do you? Anne always told me that Eve was able to foretell events that actually came to pass."

"You're letting your Druid fancy get the better of you, Becca," he said lightly. "Ever since we've owned the woman, Sofy has been partial to both you and our daughter. A conjure laid on someone only occurs when the conjurer wants to lay another human being low. Make someone sick. Sometimes, they tell me, sick enough to die." He chuckled. "I know Sofy's a prickly old woman, but I never heard a thing about her despising anyone but Roswell King enough even to think about a conjure. We're making a mountain out of a molehill."

"You brought it up, Jock."

"I did?"

"When you began wondering about those bits of broken mirror and her demand for eel skins."

After a time, he looked up from Anne's letter. "Sofy surely knows the nonsense about King's being Eve's natural father. But why, after all these years, would she suddenly decide to put down a conjure on the man?"

"My guess would be that Sofy is simply repulsed all over again by Eve's white blood. She and Eve, especially now that Eve and June have their own cabin, are not close. But my 'instink' tells me that if Sofy is planning a conjure, it probably has nothing to do with Eve. Or her premonitions about Anne and me."

"You brought that up, Becca."

"I know, but I've changed my mind."

"That's a woman's privilege, too."

"I remember I did take Sofy some salve Dr. Tunno left with us when baby Belle was so ill. Sofy's rheumatism was bothering her, and the salve we had rubbed on the baby's chest was left over. Even knowing Sofy prefers her own remedies, I walked over with it one day a few weeks ago. I found her mumbling furiously about Mr. King's forcing Flora, his oldest woman, to keep earning her way by walking a goose on a string rain or shine. Old Flora is too decrepit to do any kind of work. Too ancient and too ill. Mr. King, according to Sofy, threatened to whip her if she didn't walk that goose. I know you were only guessing, but it could well be that Sofy is working on a conjure to put down on our neighbor because of old Flora. Roswell King has certainly begun to fail, and he must be only fifty or so."

Chapter 41

Always friendly enough when plantation business caused them to meet, Jock's neighbor Roswell King, Sr., never crossed Jones Creek to Cannon's Point except on the occasion of some mutual problem. That afternoon Couper watched King limp along the path from the creek, looking a hundred years old. The man was thin and stooped and walked with the help of a sturdy cane.

Out of human compassion, John Couper got up from the back step of Sans Foix's kitchen, where he'd been reading a letter from his old friend James Hamilton in Philadelphia, and hurried to greet the man. King, obviously, was in pain.

"A good afternoon to you, Couper," King said unsmilingly, "but I'm not here for a friendly visit. I come with a demand that must, of necessity, as you can see for yourself, be met at once!"

"I can certainly see how crippled up you are on this fine, sunny day, but I've missed the point of your demand. What is it, neighbor?"

"That you keep that miserable old wench of yours on this side of the creek under penalty of a flogging! She's laid a conjure on me and I don't intend to let it go unpunished."

"And which old wench of mine would that be, Mr. King?"

"Why, the witch, who else? Sofy! I had to send my son, young Roswell, on important business over on Butler Island because my own body was not up to the trip even by water. Over three hundred acres of dikes and tidal gates need work on Major Butler's other plantation and my niggers don't have any more sense about repairing them than they had in building them in the first place. Somebody with a brain has to be there. My boy's 20 now, but he's forced to oversee the entire project alone because your old witch has kept at it until she's got me in this pitiful fix I'm in. I demand, one gentleman to another, that you punish her at once and put an end to this shriveling and weakening of my poor legs. Understood?"

"I certainly understand that you're in a bad way, Mr. King, but even if I permitted my people to be flogged, which you know I do not, I have no proof at all that Sofy is in any way responsible for the fact that you have a bad spell of rheumatism."

"It was your slow-witted Big Boy caught the eels for her potion! I've got proof of that. Even keeping them on my side of the creek doesn't prevent my niggers from knowing that old Sofy conjures anybody she hates. The old hag has hated me for years."

"I acquiesce to no man's demands, sir," Couper said firmly. "I do have an excellent doctor living at my place now, though. My son-in-law's brother, Dr. William Fraser. Sofy gets no whipping, but before the sun sets, I guarantee to send Dr. Fraser to examine you and prescribe for what ails you." He bowed, tried not to smile and failed. "I wish you a speedy recovery, Mr. King. I will provide you with a doctor, but neither Sofy nor I take one ounce of responsibility for the shape you're in. Good day, sir."

Couper had turned back toward his house when an incensed King shouted furiously after him, "It doesn't stop with me, sir! My wife overheard another of my nigger women say plain as day that your Sofy's granddaughter, that smark-aleck Eve, has prophecies about both Mrs. Couper and your older daughter, Anne, off there across the water."

"I've heard about that, too, but both of Eve's prophecies, as you call them, are supposed to be very fine ones—promising only benefit for both Mrs. Couper and Anne. Good day again, King."

Walking slowly back toward the big house at Cannon's Point, Couper felt a bit guilty, but not much. He admired his overseeing but still didn't like Roswell King, Sr., or his son. Oh, it was a pity about the older King's poor legs, but that bullheaded son of his should be taking over more and more of the man's heavy responsibilities anyway. It would do the boy good to put in a long day's work at Butler Island on Major Butler's rice land, and he certainly had no intention of punishing or even scolding either Sofy or Eve for anything. Just before he reached the house, he stopped briefly to pinch off some dead petunia blossoms from a flower bed he'd had June plant last spring. The petunias were flourishing and he liked it that June seemed to enjoy keeping the fresh pink-and-white blooms in the cabin Couper had had built for him and Eve. He felt unusually contented with his people. While they all waited for Anne and her new husband, John Fraser, to make up their minds about when or if they'd ever live on St. Simons Island again, he was pleased not only with the repairs being done on the Lawrence house he'd offered them. This year's crops looked good, and he was delighted that Becca thought Eve had become an excellent seamstress. Eve left no doubt about hating to sew, but she was doing it and Becca was not one to praise unless praise was due.

He had almost reached the Cannon's Point kitchen for his daily talk with Sans Foix when through an open window he heard quick footsteps cross the downstairs hall. Footsteps so swift, so sure, they could only be Eve's. Good. He had something to ask the girl.

Still as slender and graceful as ever, the light-skinned young woman sailed out the kitchen door, nodded pleasantly, said good morning, and headed through the wooded shortcut toward her grandmother's cabin in the quarters.

"Not so fast, Eve," he called. "I need to have a word with you."

When she hurried back to where he waited, a hopeful smile lit her face. "You done hear from Miss Anne?" she asked eagerly.

"Yes, just today. They're off on their wedding trip, but Mrs. Couper will tell you about the letter. I need to talk to you about a brief, quite surly visit I just had with Mr. Roswell King, Sr."

The smile vanished from Eve's face. "Oh, him!"

"Aye, Eve, him."

"Them pore niggers over there," she muttered. "He be worse than any dog!"

"That's not true and you know it and I didn't call you back to insult our neighbor. Mr. King came to see me just now because somehow he's gotten the idea that your grandmother, Sofy, has laid a conjure on him."

Eve only smiled.

"Don't you have anything to say?" Couper asked. "Does that smile mean you already know about this?"

"Mausa Couper, everybody know 'bout Butler's pore ol' sick Flora havin' to chill an' soak herself even on cold, rainy days by walkin' his goose up an' down, up an' down. That old woman half-dead from it. King deserve whatever he get."

He thought a minute, not at all surprised at what Eve had just said. Actually, he agreed that the frail, aged Flora shouldn't be forced to walk that goose. Still, unsure as he was about the nonsense of conjures, it was up to him somehow to put a stop to Sofy's mischief in case she was working against Roswell King. "Very well, Eve. You may go now, but I'd consider it a great favor if you'd speak a word or two to Sofy. If you're afraid to do so, tell me and I'll speak to her myself. You may feel free to tell her I asked you to urge her to stop her conjure."

"My gran'maum make me mad, too, but I ain' messin' wif no conjure, unless you say I have to do it." She took a step or two toward where he stood. "Oh, Mausa Couper, it do look like Miss Anne she come home soon! Ain't nothin' been right 'roun' here since they went away. Ain't she wrote one word 'bout comin' home to us?"

John Couper knew Anne and Eve were friends, but in his wildest imaginings he'd never dreamed that Eve was still grieving over Anne's absence. The girl *was* grieving. Tears filled her dark, liquid eyes, and Eve, as usual, was not looking at the ground or off into the distance as his other people almost invariably did when addressing him. Eve was looking directly at him, demanding some comforting words, words he simply did not have for her. "I'm sure there's no need for you to worry about Miss Anne," he said weakly. "I know you do worry. The Almighty knows I do too! But when she comes to mind, Eve, try to do what I do. Try hard to think of how happy she is because she's where she most wants to be —with John every minute of every day."

"You think I don' do that, Mausa Couper? I love June more'n my own life, so if anybody know how happy Miss Anne be, Eve know. That don' help my eyes to ketch even one glimpse ob her, though. I spected the time to be long wif'out her here, but not this long!"

For perhaps a full minute, Eve stood there, still looking at him. Finally, she said, "You get mad effen I axe you somepin', Mausa Couper?"

"Why no, Eve, of course not. I only hope I can answer."

"I axe you to make a bargain wif me."

"A bargain?"

"Effen I does my best to stop my gran's conjure, will you promise I kin go on takin' care of Miss Anne when she an' her man comes back to S'n Simons to live?"

Relieved, Couper let out a big sigh. "I certainly will promise that, Eve! There's no possible chance that I'd ever stand in the way of your and Miss Anne's being together—if she, if they, decide to come back to our island to live. That's the only hitch that could occur. She and John Fraser could well make up their minds to stay abroad, especially if he's able to get back in the Royal Marines."

Beaming now, Eve said, her velvety voice really quite feisty, "Oh, don' you worry none 'bout that, Mausa Couper. I can only vow to do the bes' I can with Gran'maum Sofy, but Eve already workin' on Miss Anne. I know I got June, but he be just *almost* all I need. I need her to go 'long wif June. So, I been workin' on bringin' her back since the firs' minute she lef' our dock!"

Chapter 42

Mr. McDonald had assured John that the borrowed horse knew the way to Caerlaverock. He was glad, because it freed him to watch Anne's pure delight in the round backs of the Scottish hills, the sun-shadowed stretch of valleys gathering themselves at their feet, valleys and glens whose greening depths fed countless sheep. The Borderlands around Dumfries were known for Cheviot sheep and half-bred lambs grazing the meadows and the slopes. Although Anne gave him tender, appreciative looks when he explained that the movements of ancient glaciers had formed those hills, she'd said little and he realized that to her, such practical knowledge, at this enchanted moment, was an intrusion. She was happily lost in her own world of childhood fantasy spun long ago around anything having to do with Caerlaverock Castle.

He did mention that half-bred lambs, which brought such a high price at the English markets, were a cross between Cheviot and Border Leicester sheep and always grazed on the richer pastures of the Solway plain.

"Where is the Solway Firth?" she asked. "Mama always told me she was sure the firth could be seen from Caerlaverock—off in the distance." Her mother's grandfather would spend entire evenings around the fire at his Plum Orchard Plantation in Midway, telling tall tales of the ancient Scots—all those wars for independence and the sieges of Caerlaverock itself by the hated English. "I guess all that was so long ago, most Scots have forgotten about hating the English. Mama says, though, that there were so many sieges around the Maxwell castle, it was once really destroyed, so whatever is still standing must have been rebuilt only a few centuries ago. Have the people here in the Border country forgotten about despising the English?"

"I think I can safely say that not all of them have. My father was, like William, quite philosophical about it, but he had definite qualms when both his sons entered the *British* Royal Marines. For all I know, he may still hold it against me because I was so bent on joining."

Their buggy was now rolling across an enormous meadow, and John remembered that only a bend or two in the narrow country road to Maxwelltown lay between them and Anne's first glimpse of the Caerlaverock ruins. The horse required no actual driving. John could treat himself to watching Anne's face when first she saw the great, triangular-shaped old fortress.

"John, look! There's a windmill! Is it a very old one? Oh, I've always wanted to see a real windmill. Does it still work?"

He laughed. "I doubt it, but it did once. Sorry to say it isn't as old as most other buildings around here. It never belonged to the Maxwells as far as I know. I think it became a museum about twenty-five years ago. But it does serve one very important function for you and me today."

Up on the edge of her seat now, she asked, "What? *What?*"

"It tells us that just around that little shady bend ahead you'll get your first glimpse of Caerlaverock!"

The soft little sound she made was somewhere between a gasp and a breathless exclamation. Then, holding tight to his arm, she whispered, "I—I think I might die of joy. Can't our horse go any faster?"

"I expect so," he said, snapping the reins so that their sturdy two-wheeler rounded the last curve at a good clip, and there it was—its three great towers looming darkly, at least twelve or thirteen huge stone chimneys reaching out of embattled antiquity up, up into the clear, cloudless Borderland sky. Because one great section had fallen into ruins, some exposed interior stone walls were bathed in sunlight. It was true that John had seen Caerlaverock not long before his mother died, but he hadn't remembered the ruins as being so entire, the unique triangular shape still capable of vaulting a modern mind back to the thirteenth century or before.

As boys, he and William had climbed up and over the

ancient stone piles, through one great arched doorway onto the shadow-blackened stone staircases, pretending they were medieval knights bent on discovering the mystery of the exact location of a legendary secret entrance to one of the guardrooms. The first Captain Maxwell of Terragles, his father's old friend, had allowed the Fraser boys to roam to their hearts' content, even ordering the servants to welcome them when the captain was away. They had climbed and climbed, searched and searched, but never did either boy find the slightest trace of an entrance in the thick stone walls.

So much of the old castle was still standing, John made a silent vow that once more—today—he and Anne would make another search. Maybe she would bring him better luck.

Over and over, as the buggy took them through the thick groves of trees and patches of wildflowers now growing in the old meadow, ever closer to Caerlaverock itself, Anne breathed, "John. John, oh, John. Don't let me die on our wedding trip! It's all so—so surprisingly beautiful I—I think I might die. Do you suppose I'm dreaming?"

"No, dearest Annie, you're wide awake. I see it all too. You and I are close, but no matter how close, no two people can dream the same dream at the exact same time."

"But those look like real trees—good-sized young trees and grass and flowers of all kinds growing up there on top of the towers. Do you see them too? Trees and flowers growing way up there on the turrets against the sky?"

He smiled down at her and reined the horse so that she could look from where the buggy stood on the Dumfries side of the old moat, far enough away from the ruins for her to drink in the whole of her childhood fantasy castle become real—because they loved each other. The joy John felt in her this moment was proud joy. Little had ever meant so much to him. After all, she was looking at Caerlaverock this instant because he had brought her there.

"Look," she murmured, her voice filled with awe. "There are real flowers and honest-to-goodness trees growing on top of the castle, John. Why?"

"I expect because it's all been here so long." He laughed. "Somehow I'm fairly sure no one planted them way up there."

"You mean they're—gentle bushes? They just grew of their own accord?"

"An Irishman would call them gentle bushes and yes. The long, long passage of time has given the crumbling stone and such leaves as have been blown there plenty of time to turn to earth. 'Gentle' bushes would be close enough. My father might call them volunteers."

"Or a thousand birds could have flown past and dropped seeds down on the towers."

The buggy still stopped, he leaned to kiss her hair. "Dear, tender, imaginative Annie," he murmured. "How I love thee!"

"How I love all this—and you," she breathed. "Oh, thank you, John, for bringing me all the way to Caerlaverock! It's —it's almost too beautiful, isn't it?"

Out of the clear, blue day and into his mind flew a stanza of a Burns poem, "A Red, Red Rose." He began to recite it, surprisingly hopeful that she knew it, too.

"As fair art thou, my bonnie lass,
So deep in luve am I;
And I will luve thee still, my dear,
Till a' the seas gang dry."

A smile of recognition lit her face and she recited the next verse.

"Till a' the seas gang dry, my dear,
And the rocks melt wi' the sun;
And I will luve thee still, my dear,
While the sands o' life shall run."

After a long, lingering kiss, Anne, clinging to him now, her woman heart and body responding, said, "I will love you, John Fraser, until Solway Firth, wherever it is, is dry and until all the stones of Caerlaverock 'melt wi' the sun'—and even beyond that. . . ."

Plainly in no hurry at all, savoring every mysterious moment that may lie ahead, every new and ancient discovery, Anne closed her eyes and leaned her head against his shoulder. "We can drive closer any time now, only I'm really loving that actually going inside Caerlaverock is still a few minutes away. Dreams are all-important, you know. Sometimes they're better than getting there." She sat up abruptly, laughing. "That sounded very pretty, but I didn't really mean it. I'm ready to go! I'm more than ready! How do we get across the moat once we reach it?"

He laughed. "I doubt the absent Maxwell laird was expecting a siege during his absence. Anyway, the old drawbridge is no longer there. 'Twas made into a permanent bridge long ago. William and I always walked right across it over the moat."

He started the horse again at a brisk trot, and in minutes he glimpsed the delight on Anne's face when she first heard the moat ducks quacking.

"Ducks?" she asked, as excited as though she hadn't grown up surrounded by Cannon's Point ducks.

"Ducks, Annie. The old moat's a duck pond now. And when we're a little closer, you'll see also that it's a lily pool as well. In London, I nearly stifled you with buildings. Not here."

"No," she breathed, "there are no buildings here. . . . My childhood Caerlaverock Castle isn't a regular building. It's a lark's nest. Fairies fly through it. Druids march the turrets at night when there's no moon!"

"Did your mother tell you a' that?"

"No," she laughed. "I made it up this minute."

"Nevertheless, I'm sure 'tis true—every word."

For a distance of a quarter of a mile or so, across the flower-strewn meadow, they drove in silence. There was no need to speak. Caerlaverock and every living thing in and near it kept up a steady conversation, all welcoming: Ducks quacked in comical, rhythmless spurts; a blackbird sang far more sweetly, he knew, than any redwing Anne had ever heard back home; what sounded like a distant pack of dogs on the trail of a fox yelped and howled through the brightness around them; some chickens clucked because a rooster had crowed; and tucked within one short beat of quiet, one and then two sheep bleated. They knew—because the red-haired lad, whose mother worked at Caerlaverock two days a week, had told them yesterday—that no one would be there today with the laird away, but they were still being welcomed. John felt it and then, as so often happened, Anne spoke the exact words he had been thinking.

"We're being welcomed to Caerlaverock," she gasped. "Listen!"

"I know," he said. "The same as by the Maxwells themselves. Don't forget, around here, in all of Dumfriesshire, in the whole of the Borderland, in fact, 'the Maxwells is everything!' "

She gave him a quick, sweet smile. "I must remember to write that to Mama," she said. "Papa, of course, will take it right up and worry the poor woman half sick with it."

"I can hear him now. 'Aye, Becca, you must always do exactly as you please, because around here the Maxwells is everything!' "

"He'll mean it too—part of the time." Anne reached for his hand. "How can I ever thank you for—for seeing Papa exactly as he is?"

"Flattery will get you anywhere you're a mind to go, lass," he joked, kissing the palm of her hand. "Of all men, I'd be the most honored if I could really believe I understood such a man as John Couper of Cannon's Point."

Her eyes taking in the beauty of every mass of roadside bluebells, daisies, yellow cups, along with the ever-looming shape of the castle up ahead, Anne asked softly and with great earnestness, "Is ancestry important to you, John? I mean, is it really important? I'm covered with goose bumps at the thought that in only minutes now, I'll actually be walking on the very stone floors where ancient Maxwells walked and strode about, but Mama has always told me that one must keep ancestors in true perspective. Respect them, remember them, even honor them if they did anything worthy of honor. But then, she'd always add, 'Remember, your father's father was a simple, hard-working country parson, born of no one great family, of no appreciable wealth, and look at your papa, Anne! John Couper would be a well-known, well-loved, enormously revered man regardless of whether he had been born of a shoemaker or the laird of a baronial castle far grander than Caerlaverock.' "

"You have a wise mother, Anne. I hope I honor my own ancestors exactly as she suggests. Actually, I should, I guess, give them a bit more thought. Father has told me the tales. William, too, of course. William, I'm sure, pays in his heart, at least, the proper homage. I've always been on a private lark of my own, unmindful of much that perhaps *should* matter." A finger under her chin, he turned her face to him. "Until I found you, that is. Until I made you my adorable captive forever."

She surprised him by frowning. "Wait a minute for my answer, if there is one to that long, impressive speech."

"It wasn't just a speech! Every word was true. I never took the Frasers or anyone seriously enough until I loved you."

"I'm not doubting one word. I just have to sort it all out, because I don't think you answered my question about how important ancestors really are at all! You're very, very skillful at dodging. Did you know that?"

He forced her to tear her gaze away from the castle again. "I swear to you, Anne Couper Fraser, that I, John Fraser, dodged nothing. I like to talk to you. Maybe I even enjoy the sound of my own speeches, but I don't really ever dodge answering you. At least, I don't mean to."

"Hush, I'm still sorting," she said. "You did say a lot, a lot of what I wanted to hear—especially about loving me—but something else is dawning on me right when I should be giving my undivided attention to Caerlaverock. It's just becoming clear to me that with all the hours and hours we've talked, you've told me almost nothing about your own family. I know Mama's right that we're not to worship ancestors, and because Papa's always made exaggerated jokes about his, I never gave it much thought. But except for your father, your mother, and William, you've never said a word about anyone else!"

In the buggy at the edge of the wide meadow, almost at the foot of the ancient moat bridge, he reined the horse again, threw back his head, and really laughed—loud and with abandon.

"What's so funny?"

"Me, I think. There is no way I've found—and I do try now and then—to get ahead of you, is there?"

"Ahead of me? Make sense! Why are you laughing?"

"Because you're as entertaining and dumbfounding as you are ravishing. Actually, I think I'm laughing at myself because you just read my mind—horned in on a secret plan I had held back all this time to spring on you at one certain place on one certain moldy old staircase once we're inside the castle."

"And—I spoiled your secret plan? How could I when I don't know what you're talking about?"

"As usual, I'm talking about us."

"Us?"

"Family history has never been my forte. It's William's.

Father's discussion of the Frasers' involvement in all those struggles for Scottish independence has never much interested me. I've always found my own world quite enough, but because I thought it might please you, I did hatch a little surprise for you once we managed to find one particular turn in those ancient stairs where I always felt—*our side won.*" There was no need to force her to look at him now. In fact, the expression on her face was so curious, so concerned, he made conscious use of what he knew was his best smile. "Annie! Annie, lovely one, this isn't the time for even a shadow of a worry. Today is today and it's all ours and we're about to cross the bridge over the old moat to Caerlaverock. Forgive me for laughing. I was laughing at myself and your uncanny way of picking even my foolish secret plans right out of my brain! A smile, ma'am? Please, ma'am?"

She didn't merely smile, she also blushed. "Now you've made me feel dumb," she said. "But it's only because I love you so much. Do you think I love you too much? Am I—touchy? I loathe touchy women! And you don't need to tell me a single thing about your family history. I don't care anyway. I certainly did not fall in love with your family. And, I didn't mean to spoil the surprise."

"You didn't really," he said, snapping the reins again. "You didn't spoil it." When the horse and buggy clattered out over the heavy planks that led to the old moat bridge, the ducks in the water below quacked so loud that all he tried to add was, "You'll see, you'll see just as soon as we find that one boot-trammeled stair—if I remember the old place as I hope I do."

Chapter 43

For at least half an hour after John had tethered the horse near a stand of daisy-spattered spring grass, the two walked slowly arm in arm about the grounds of Caerlaverock, John mostly watching Anne, who seemed unable to absorb enough of anything, even from outside the massive ruins. He had never known her to be silent for such a long time and felt he would give almost anything to know her thoughts.

Most amazing, in spite of her awe at the expanse of sturdy, stone walls, the high, recessed archway rising above where they stood, she gave him no reason to think that she was not steadily aware of him, too. She had clung to his arm from the moment he lifted her to the ground, her pale blue goddess eyes storing forever the memory of her first sight of the real Caerlaverock, now no longer a romanticized childhood fantasy.

William had always accused John of being an incurable romantic. Perhaps he was, but so was Anne and even she still had no idea how deeply he had longed to bring her here.

When they'd first begun to roam the grounds, John had called a loud, echoing halloo into the bright, sun-dappled day, causing Anne to laugh that he would bother when they'd been told not only that the present Maxwell laird was away, but that today there would be no servants.

"If the present Lord Herries still visits here two or three months out of every year, where do you suppose he lives?" Anne asked. "Oh, look! I see an herb garden over there beside that corner section. And curtains at the windows! That means there's a kitchen close by. Could that be the present Lord Herries's apartment? Our baggage boy's mother probably tends that garden. I don't suppose we can see inside the still-livable part, do you?"

"I'm sure it's locked and barred. Does that disappoint you?"

She shrugged. "I don't care one way or another. It's the ancient Maxwells I know about anyway. I don't even know their names, but I think most of what her grandfather told Mama took place centuries ago."

"Are you ready to explore inside yet?" he asked, growing eager to share that special secret he'd so carefully kept from her ever since Mrs. Couper had told him well over a year ago that her family were of the Dumfriesshire Maxwells.

"Inside?" She repeated his question dreamily, as though her mind had already raced back to childhood visions of vast banquet rooms, lavish furnishings, and great, gilded mirrors; to giant mastiffs waiting under long, food-laden tables gleaming with silver and crystal as in all her books about medieval aristocratic living. "I'm working on going inside," she said. "I do have to work some at realizing that Caerlaverock is mostly in ruins, that the rooms will be empty of everything except my—fantasies."

John smiled to himself. He was learning her. He'd guessed almost exactly what she was thinking.

Would he love Anne as completely, he wondered, had she been born of equally worthy English or French or Spanish parents? His own adult life from age sixteen had been lived among Irish, Scottish, Welsh, and English soldiers in such a variety of foreign cultures, the question seemed unanswerable, almost irrelevant. Had Papa insisted that they travel only in Scotland or do without a wedding trip because he hoped to arouse in John some now faded strain of Scottish loyalty, which Papa thought he'd lost from the long years of serving the Crown of England? If so, what a foolish old man's scheme! The bloodshed over Scottish independence was no more. John had happily served the entire kingdom of Great Britain, which happened to include his native Scotland. Oh, he still loved the taste of haggis, felt pure boyish joy when his ears were assailed by the sudden skirl of bagpipes. John Couper had taught his slave butler, Johnson, to play the pipes, so he obviously needed his ears assailed now and then, too. Did Anne? Did Anne love the wild, plunging sound?

She stood there now beside him, her incredibly lovely face still filled with awe as she looked and looked, trying to take in every split and cracked ancient stone, every column, her eyes lingering on the stained walls that had once sheltered her mother's own people.

He made no move toward her, but remembered no moment of high ecstasy with her that in any way compared with the strange oneness he felt now in the deep, silent way a man feels his own blood.

His own totally Scottish blood.

The fantasies from boyhood when he and William had crossed the River Nith from his father's farm near Dumfries to spend hours exploring Caerlaverock were beginning to rush back . . . to flood John's being so that he felt he could not wait a minute longer to take Anne inside the high, thick walls, into the very rooms that held her beginnings. For his own sake, as well as to surprise her, he *had* to find the one turn on the one stone staircase where the Frasers and the Maxwells had met and fought together in the ringing, clashing, blood-soaked battle to hold Caerlaverock under Robert Bruce against the English. The vast stretch of years between that thirteenth-century siege by bow and arrow, sword, sling, and battering ram squeezed now into a sliver of time no more remote to John than the still-vivid memory of his own action in the Peninsular War in Spain at the old coastal city of La Coruña. A deep thrill tore through him. He still hated the idea of shooting a wild rabbit or a deer, but he loved the daring of battle; and long ago, a young, virile Fraser had indeed saved a Maxwell's life by bounding up that old stone stair, sword unsheathed.

"Annie!" He meant his voice to sound tender. It was urgent, almost sharp. He had startled her. "Forgive me for breaking into your thoughts," he said, "but will you *ever* be ready to go inside with me? I do have a fine secret surprise I've been keeping all this time! Are you afraid you'll be disappointed once we step inside this massive archway?"

She had been as lost in her own thoughts as he. "I wish there were someone here who could tell us how old this all is," she mused. "Mama always said there had been three great houses. Isn't there anything left of the first two? How could such enormous castles just vanish? Were they torn down?"

"Aye," he answered, "torn down one way or another." He

pointed toward the meadow they'd just crossed. "Look over there beside that stand of trees. Do you see that curving rise in the land? A long, irregular mound? If a man dug into it, he'd likely find ancient stones from what was the first Maxwell castle. Now, in the opposite direction, toward Solway Firth, you'll see traces of the second Caerlaverock foundation, just the general outline."

Straining to see, Anne gasped, "Oh, John, don't you wonder how those two old ones looked?"

"Yes, but today, we have this one—the grand one all to ourselves! This Caerlaverock, I think, was built about the year 1371. I should have asked Father again before we left London."

"That's over four hundred years ago! How can so much of it still be here?"

"Oh, your mother's family had to repair and refortify it sometime in the sixteen hundreds. Even after that, the Brits and the Scottish Covenanters battled all over it still again."

For whatever length of time they'd stayed outside, John had kept both hands in his jacket pockets. Now, he turned her to him. "Aren't you at all curious about the inside of your lark's nest? Aren't you the least bit eager to know about the special secret I've kept all this time?"

"Of course I'm curious! I—I just needed time to get myself ready for something as overwhelming and scary as actually being *in* Caerlaverock after hearing Mama talk about it for so long."

He grinned down at her. "Should I be jealous of Caerlaverock?"

"No! And I don't think this is the time for teasing. Come on. Take my hand and let's go inside—all the way inside. Suddenly, I can't wait. Hurry! I've never kissed you in a lark's nest."

Inside the cavernous receiving hall, they kissed, then hand in hand, examined the first-floor guardrooms on either side. John pointed out in the thick stone the grooves cut for the heavy iron portcullis, one at each end of the archway through which they'd just walked—grooves in the ancient stones to accommodate the impenetrable iron gratings designed and forged to keep out a marauding enemy. Anne tried hard to listen while he explained that even on a distant signal that an attack might be coming, these rooms would fill with guards, full-plate medieval armor in place to protect both head and body should close combat ensue.

Oh, dear, I can't follow all that military talk, she thought. He's being so detailed and—and too excited. I don't want you to love that kind of thing, John! It shuts me out. She said nothing.

"Just think of it," he went on. "Your own ancestors, Anne—young, vigorous boys eager to prove themselves in battle, and older men, equally eager, gathered in these very guardrooms and waited in silence for a whistle or the squeal of a thin reed pipe, their signal to be on the ready to defend Caerlaverock! Can you picture them?" His voice was almost ringing with what to her seemed foolish urgency.

And then, he leaped from one corner of a guardroom to another, peering into the shadows, crouching, pretend sword drawn—reveling in his game of playing war.

"John, stop that!"

"But, Anne, your very own forebears crouched here, like this, as alive and red-blooded as I am today, with no fear, no panic in the hand that gripped the bow, the string primed to let fly an arrow that could cut an enemy's heart in two!"

"Stop it!"

He was on his feet now, back in two long strides to where she stood at the guardroom entrance. "Anne, I was just enjoying myself. What's wrong?"

Wide-eyed, she looked up at him. "I don't want to stay in this ugly old room all day. It scares me. *You* scare me. . . ."

John laughed. "I do? Then, that must mean I haven't forgotten after all this time how to be a soldier."

On impulse, she threw both arms around him. "You—you *were* just playacting, weren't you?" she gasped.

"Playacting? Of course! And by the look on your face, I must be quite good at it."

"Maybe—maybe your new profession should be on the stage at Covent Garden or Drury Lane," she said. "You'd make a magnificent Henry the Fifth! I'm only teasing. Is there a law that says *I can't tease you*?"

A hint of the old arrogance—at least, what Anna Matilda would call arrogance—crossed his face. "I don't think you were only teasing," he said. "Sometimes I honestly believe you'd rather be married to a chimney sweep than to a soldier."

From somewhere in her, what Papa called the Maxwell

spirit flared. "If you don't know me well enough by now to recognize a simple thing like teasing, I—I—" She forced herself to stop, just stood there reaching toward him, unable to think how to ease the strain that stretched between them.

John made no move toward her, so she dropped her outstretched hand. Then, after what seemed an eternity, he said in a low, firm voice, "You're really frightened of my love of the military, aren't you, Annie?"

At least he called her Annie, the name he never used except in moments of tender closeness. She grabbed at that. "You called me Annie," she whispered.

The short, elegant laugh he often made use of when other people were around certainly didn't help now. It helped not at all when he said glibly, "Don't I frequently call you Annie? You always seemed to like it because your father uses it so much." When she least expected him to touch her, he took her hand in both of his. "Today is *not* the day to discuss the forbidden subject of my officer's commission."

"That sounds like an order," she said.

"Not at all. I'm merely keeping our pact of silence on the subject of my future. It's far too early for us to speak one way or another of it anyway. I'm plainly more gifted than I thought. I think I really frightened you crouching there in my make-believe armor waiting for the chance to best a Maxwell enemy! Perhaps instead of fumbling about trying to help Father untangle his business affairs when we return to London, I should consider acting lessons under the great Sarah Siddons. Would that please you?"

Without stopping, he had leaped from almost gentle logic to teasing to something near sarcasm. In as worldly a manner as she knew how, she parried, "All I know is that wherever you are, whatever you decide to do, I'll be there with you." Then, giving him a quizzical look, she asked, "Are you as tricky as I sometimes think?"

Now his laughter was *his* laughter, free and abandoned and merry enough to rouse an echo in the vaulted, stone entrance hall. "Aye, I can be tricky. Perhaps even more than you sometimes think, beloved Annie." Grabbing her hand, he led her eagerly through an archway out into what had once been Caerlaverock's open courtyard. "To allay your suspicions of me, though, I shall proceed now to dazzle you more and more with the sight of your ancestral castle. I don't wonder you're suspicious. I've always heard the Maxwells were a suspicious lot."

"Have you really always heard that? My mother surely isn't." Looking around at the great, overgrown, deserted courtyard, she breathed, "Oh, how sad. How dreadfully sad."

"Anything so deserted is bound to be sad," he said as they began to walk slowly across the courtyard, John careful not to let her stumble over the scattered fragments of weather-worn stones littering the old paving blocks.

Then, high above their heads, yet wheeling lower than the tallest tower, Anne saw a buzzard, its wide, dark wings spread as the huge, ugly bird tilted gracefully on the wind.

"Does the sight of a buzzard make you sad?" he asked.

"No. The poor courtyard does, though. I've always loved buzzards. We have lots of them on St. Simons. God's scavengers, Papa calls them. They keep wild places from smelling bad when something dies. I guess I am glad the big towers kept it from casting a shadow, though. Eve vows that if a flying buzzard throws a moving shadow, someone is going to die. You didn't see a moving shadow when the buzzard flew over, did you?"

"Now you're worried someone will die! I've always heard the Maxwells were worriers, too. I'm teasing again, Annie. I swear I never heard that the Maxwells were either worriers or suspicious. If it isn't the wheeling bird up there, why so sad?"

"I told you. It's the way this empty, silent courtyard *feels.* Did you ever feel such desolation anywhere? Isn't it—forlorn?"

He looked around at the surrounding castle walls, up at the clear, nearly cloudless Borderland sky, across the open center of the courtyard at the remains of what he and William always thought must have been a once-handsome fountain. "Forlorn? Not if I picture what once took place out here during both peace and war."

"Can't you say two words without mentioning *war*?"

Still holding her hand, John waited. Then, quite gently, he asked, "You didn't really mean to say that, did you?"

"No! It's the last thing I meant to say." When he grinned, she whispered, "Thank you."

"You're welcome, milady. Look—over there in that far

corner up toward the overhanging cornice near the entrance."

"What?"

"You're not looking high enough. See that arched window in the old wall? The cornice above it with some sort of carving cut into it?"

"Yes! Oh, I see it now—a bird's nest! A wren's nest."

"How can you be so sure?"

"Because all my life I've known how wrens build and that's a perfect spot for her to pick out. See? It's sheltered and has a good, firm base below that cornice and—there, there's the mama wren."

"You have good eyes."

"She's out of sight now, but I just saw her hop around the side of the cornice with a twig of sedge. She'll be back to weave in another piece. There. See her?"

"Aye, and you're right. 'Tis a house wren."

"A castle wren," Anne corrected him.

"Your friend the buzzard is still circling. He seems puzzled to find us here, or maybe there's something juicy and dead nearby."

"I hope not," she said. "It breaks my heart to see a dead animal or bird. Ever since my little dog, Lovey, died when I was about ten, I can't bear to find dead things."

"You haven't told me about Lovey. What killed him?"

"Lovey was a girl. A rattlesnake bit her and we couldn't save her. Papa and Johnson really tried. They cut her front leg where the rattler struck, then sucked her blood to get the poison out, but hard as she tried not to leave me—she did."

"And your father didn't find you another pet?"

She shuddered. "I couldn't bear the thought of being untrue to Lovey. Oh, I'm fond of Papa's hunting dogs, but Lovey was mine. She slept on my bed at night. Eve was just a little girl too then, and Mama let her sleep on a pallet in my room, hoping it might help me sleep better after Lovey died. It didn't. I cried every morning when I woke up because Lovey wasn't there." She took his hand. "I have you now, though, when I wake up. You'll always be there, won't you?"

" 'Till a' the seas gang dry, my dear . . . till a' the seas gang dry.' "

"Do you think Robert Burns ever came over here to Caerlaverock?"

"Oh, he must have. The mon was a rotten farmer, but he was a true poet. How could a poet stay away from all this?" John swept his free hand around the desolate, rubble-strewn courtyard. " 'Tis a lonesome place now, but Burns tended toward the ribald and I'm sure he pictured the riotous festivities that must have taken place here in ancient times, especially following a stout victory. Any Scot knows how to celebrate the same as he knows how to fight." He kissed the palm of her hand. "I need a smile, Annie. And some sign that you're curious to know the Caerlaverock surprise I've been keeping since your mother first told me she was a Maxwell."

"Oh, I am curious, darling. It's just that I'm so excited about everything we're seeing! Like that big, thick clump of honeysuckle over there—look!" Pulling John along, she began to run across the rough pavement blocks for a better whiff of the heavy-scented flowers.

"Watch out for bees," he laughed, "and look back near the old guardroom door. We were almost standing in a patch of blue ragged robin and didn't even notice. How did we miss those flowers?"

Clapping her hands, she announced they'd just have to come back often because no one could take in all there was to see at Caerlaverock in one visit. "And suddenly, I can't wait a minute longer to go inside, so you can show me your surprise. I'm longing to see the banquet hall, too. I've always had my own picture of what it looked like."

As they hurried along now toward the entrance to the highest tower, John reminded her that they were exploring a ruin. "The banquet hall and the state apartment where the Maxwells actually lived are both gone, but unless another wall has fallen in since I was here, you can still tell how grand they once were. The important thing, though, is that I can't wait a minute longer to show you the spot where the Maxwells and the Frasers made a minor bit of history together!"

She stared at him, surprise and delight on her eager face. "Your family and mine—made history? John, how wonderful! It just proves we were meant for each other."

He laughed. "But didn't we already know that? Hush, now. No more talk, because we're on our way inside the entrance to that tallest tower—and eventually to my long-held revelation."

Puffing along beside him as they climbed the steep, stone stair treads worn into valleys by the tramp of ancient iron-heeled boots, Anne not only felt her blood race, her whole body tingled with John's shared excitement. She'd seen him in varying states of anticipation, of exuberance, but even he had never shown her the side of himself capable of the sheer elation he seemed to feel this moment. His strong hand was taking her along so deftly, she felt she needn't bother to move her own feet and legs. With John, she could fly to whatever surprise, whatever shiny secret, he'd been keeping for her, hidden all these months deep in the always surprising mystery that was the man John Fraser, himself.

"Darling," she gasped, out of breath, laughing, "how much farther do we have to climb? Where does that door lead?"

"Down to the dungeon."

"I hate the word *dungeon,* but look at the thickness of that wall! Over there, where another wall broke away. It must be five feet thick!"

"Six," he said as proudly as though he were a Maxwell. "No Maxwell would trust an Englishman to stay within a mere five feet."

"You sound as proud as one of Papa's peacocks and he sometimes says Mama's family should have a peacock in their coat of arms."

"Less difference than you'd think between the Frasers and the Maxwells," he said over his shoulder as he kept her climbing too fast.

"If you've waited all this time, why do we have to hurry so now? I want to look out there over that big, rubble-filled empty space. What was that in the old days?"

Now he did stop to give her a moment to take in the vastness of what he explained had been the banqueting hall and the state apartment. Mammoth broken columns had fallen in on huge piles of stones and bricks, all open now to the sky and swatches of wildflowers, as though to remind any modern man or woman seeing it in the year 1816 that grandeur and beauty once filled the sad vacuum where a real family once gathered to feed their warm, living bodies . . . to make their children grow and the adults strong enough to dance and make love and rally for the wars that, to Anne, seemed to have been as commonplace as coming together for love's sake.

"The size of the banquet hall always overawed William and me when we came here as boys. Wouldn't you say it's more than a hundred feet?"

"And poor Papa thinks he built a gigantic dining room at Cannon's Point!"

"He did. I never ate more excellent cuisine in such an exceptional room anywhere," John said defensively. "But all of St. Simons would not have held the vastness of the holdings of the Maxwells of Caerlaverock. Over six thousand acres right around the castle. They were far, far richer than any man in all of the United States, I'm sure." And then, as on a signal, they chanted together: "*'And the Maxwells is everything!'* "

A thick, sturdy section of one apartment wall still stood well within safe jumping distance. Holding his hand, Anne followed him in one leap onto it. From there they could see across the duck- and lily-filled old moat, out over the meadow they'd crossed earlier, to the lovely green valley of Nithsdale and to their left, a wide morass that stretched away to the dazzling blue waters of Solway Firth.

"How blue Solway is," she breathed. "Is it only the sky today that makes it so blue?"

"Perhaps," he mused. "I never gave its color much thought, I guess. But turn around to our right for a real view." He swept his arm toward the circle of great hills shutting in the sweet, green valley of the River Nith. "Feast your eyes, Annie. Over there is old Criffel, said to be almost two thousand feet above sea level. And over there is Beacon Hill, where for more than two hundred years, the Maxwells kept constant watch by day and by night."

"Do you mean Mama's family kept someone always out on that hill—watching for the English?"

"Aye. Always. And on the smaller Wardlow, the hill overlooking the castle itself, legend has it that when a Maxwell saw smoke rise by day or a fire by night, every mon saddled up, armed himself, and rallied for war."

As though thinking aloud, Anne asked, "*Why,* John, with such a fierce family behind me, do I so hate the thought of war—the hideous noise and killing of it?" Involuntarily, she touched his sleeve. "I was so afraid when they—shot you, dearest. I hated it!"

She'd brought up soldiering again and could have bitten off her tongue.

This time, though, John said nothing. Rather, he circled her waist with the still-scarred arm, as though to prove how completely well it was now. Then he sighed. "You—you can't help yourself, Annie. Most women can't help feeling as you do about war."

"I'm not just 'most women' and that's all I'm going to say because I'd rather draw my last breath right here on this crumbling old wall with your arm around me than to say anything else that might come between us."

"Then, let's jump back to that solid hallway. Ready?"

"Ready!"

Again, they leaped across the empty air that could have landed them in the courtyard rubble had they missed and, arm in arm, made their way along the dim, shadowy, debris-cluttered passageways between and through the remaining shapes of small upper bedrooms, admiring huge old fireplaces and the fragments of carved stone above them.

"My big secret surprise has waited far too long already, but—" he laid a hand over her eyes. "Don't peep! I'm going to give you a test. What, my elegant, wellborn wife, was the first Maxwell motto?"

"That's easy. 'I bid ye fair.' Papa thought of using it when he built our big house at Cannon's Point."

"Correct, and now, another test: After the castle was burned, pillaged, and destroyed twice, what was the Maxwell motto changed to when the vanquished family finally returned to build this one?"

"*Revivisco* in Latin, and it means 'I will flourish again!' "

He took his hand away from her eyes and gave her a congratulatory hug. "Bravo! And both mottoes are carved right up there above that fireplace—the first almost too dim to read, but the second plain as day." After a light kiss, he whispered, "How true the second one is. If the Maxwells had done nothing more than form your lovely beginnings, they would have flourished again indeed."

A dog barked somewhere on the far side of the castle. "That dog must belong to one of the servants," she said. "He sounds just like Lovey. I wonder who feeds him on the days when no one comes?"

"Would you like it if I found you another dog one day when we're settled somewhere?" John asked.

"I've always thought I couldn't bear any other dog in Lovey's place, but yes, I would!" She refrained from saying all she longed to say, that yes, she would love it if John gave her a dog to live with them at Lawrence in the dear tabby house Papa was repairing.

Chapter 44

For the time it took John to go back down to the buggy for their picnic basket, Anne stood alone by the irregular shape of what had once been an upstairs bedroom window, wishing as she'd never wished since she left Cannon's Point, for her mother. She had missed Papa every day they'd been gone, but today, right here in an ancient Maxwell bedroom, looking out at the meadow, it was Mama she missed. How Mama would love standing where Anne stood now! So much of the old castle was still there, it was not hard at all to guess which small and large rooms had been bedrooms. John had even pointed out a few secret chambers from which he swore arrows could have been shot, so that the Maxwells were able to ward off enemies not only from the outside but from the inside, too. How creepy it must have been, she thought, trying to sleep in one of these rooms knowing that somewhere, in the thick stone walls, was an aperture through which an arrow could find its mark!

In every tale of medieval knights she'd ever read, there had been long, hair-raising passages about thick, outer gates broken down, courtyards captured, ancient staircases stormed. Thank God no one was trying to capture the courtyard of Caerlaverock today. Today, at least, John was safe down there.

In no time at all, his steady footsteps echoed as he reclimbed the worn, stone stairs on his way back to her with their basket of food. The ample breakfast eaten hours ago had shrunk to nothing more than a memory. They'd both felt so stuffed after a big meal of herring, eggs, and porridge, they insisted that Mr. McDonald pack only some cold mutton, bread, and fruit. Longing for Mama switched into longing for a huge plate filled with Sans Foix's ham and grits and sweet potatoes and English peas straight from Liz's garden right outside the Cannon's Point kitchen. This part of Scotland had a simple, bewitching beauty, but it wasn't St. Simons Island. She was actually standing in the ruins of an ancient medieval castle, but it wasn't Cannon's Point.

Dear God in heaven, she breathed as John's steps came closer, please let him long, too, for some tiny, unimpressive caerlaverock of our own! A house that belongs only to John and me. A place where our children can grow up feeling as safe as I've always felt—at home by the river. Without meaning to, she said aloud, "Please, God, please!"

And then John was standing right beside her, lunch basket in one hand, a bottle of wine in the other. "Please God, what?" he asked. "Are you so hungry you're actually praying for food?"

"Yes! Yes, dearest, you guessed it." It was only a half-lie.

They spread a blue tablecloth from the basket on the floor and began to gobble the food, washing it down with wine, making it last with periodic kisses and stories from John about how long and painstakingly he and William had searched without success for the one secret entrance said to connect a hidden stairway with the guardroom below the very room in which they chose to eat their picnic.

"You mean you and William never did find the secret entrance?"

"Neither of us believes it to this day, but we failed utterly. And there *is* one somewhere in one of these old walls, because the castle guards had to be able to pass from one guardroom to another without being seen in the main hallway." He grinned at her. "Shall we give ourselves the challenge today? Are you game?"

Anne jumped to her feet. "Try me! But don't forget to show me the secret you're being so mean about."

"I'm not being mean. Your own mother made me promise I'd keep it from you until just the right moment."

Holding hands, they climbed up and then down one dark, shadowy staircase after another, hunting, tapping stone walls, picking at bits of broken mortar.

"People always talk about Papa's sense of humor," Anne said, "but Mama has one too. She just lets Papa show off, I've always thought. Are any houses ever built like Caerlaverock today?" she asked, when finally they sat down to rest on the top step of a landing, its tiny high window giving out to only a glimpse of Beacon Hill.

"Even the great country houses don't need to be fortified now. These days, battles are fought on planned battlefields or from the decks of ships. I know you prefer to call this lark's nest, but Caerlaverock was a fortress, built to ward off Maxwell enemies. We're not going to find that secret entrance either, Annie." He looked up toward the window. "And the sun is no longer high, so I think the time has come to spring my long-held surprise. I'd think—your mother thought, too—that you'd be holding your breath to learn what I have to tell you about the spot where a real Fraser once saved the life of a real Maxwell!" He pulled her to her feet.

After another kiss, he hurried her along the dim passageway toward still another stair and when they'd climbed it halfway, he counted the steps down from the top and stopped. Then, he moved her deftly to one side of the stair so that her back was against the rough stone wall.

"There! Exactly where you stand at this very moment, milady, once stood another Maxwell—a valiant, heroic, medieval knight of old, his back to that same wall, pinned, primed for the moment of his death at the hands of a brutal Englishman—when up this stair, out of the shadows, a Fraser appeared! An equally valiant, noble Fraser, *my ancestor,* probably named Simon the Younger. With one sweep of his broadsword, Simon Fraser beheaded the hated enemy so that Caerlaverock was, from that day to this, *saved*!"

Wide-eyed, she stared back at John. "I'm sure you're at least partially teasing me, but your forebear Simon Fraser the Younger was really here at my family's castle, on whatever day that was? A Fraser was actually fighting alongside a Maxwell?"

"Aye, lass, a Fraser saved a Maxwell's life! For all we know, the life that was saved that day may have been the last living male Maxwell in that century. I choose to believe, because my ancestor saved your ancestor's life, that very date was the true moment when you and I began to find each other!"

Wondering which would please him more—for her to laugh at his tale of high drama or to kiss him with all her might and say nothing—Anne just stood there, longing to believe every word of what he'd just told her in spite of the bloody beheading.

Nothing could ever be wasted by kissing him and so that's what she did, holding his face between her hands, hoping, with all her heart, he'd give her at least one clue to the truth or half-truth of his long-held secret surprise.

Instead, he only kissed her back, again and again, holding her against him there on the staircase that led to the top floor of the old tower. He belonged to her, but sometimes he did mix her up. It was always easy to tell when Papa was teasing. Not so with John.

Finally, he gave her a melting look. "I didn't just make up that story, Annie. I've heard all my life that a Fraser helped save not only a Maxwell, but Caerlaverock itself. Retelling through the years may have added a bit of color, but I know that you and I began to be *us* the very day that Englishman's severed head rolled down those stairs right there all the way to the Maxwell courtyard!"

After another kiss, they were both laughing.

"Well," John went on, "maybe it didn't roll all the way to the courtyard, but it proves the Fraser clan motto is true." He stood to his full height and announced: "I am ready!"

"Ready for what?"

"To take you back to Bobby Burns's favorite watering place, Ye Olde Globe Inn. Are you ready, milady?"

"That's a splendid family motto—'I am ready.' "

"Je suis prêt."

"Your motto is in French?"

"Aye—*oui.* Take your choice. The Frasers way back are of French origin. Does that impress or disgust you?"

"Neither. It simply accounts for a lot."

"Accounts for a lot about me?"

"Aye," she said, giggling as they hurried back down the storied stone stair toward the courtyard. "Or, if you prefer, *monsieur, oui.* I think it tells me quite a lot."

Jiggling along in the borrowed buggy toward the great stone bridge that would take them back across the River Nith to Dumfries and the privacy of their own room, John held the reins loosely with one hand, the other holding both of Anne's hands. She seemed contented now, but his mind flew back to one moment in the Caerlaverock tower when, as though she didn't quite know whether or not he was teasing about the Frasers and the Maxwells, she'd simply grabbed his face and kissed him. Did he conduct himself in too sophisticated a way—too worldly—for a girl who had lived such a closely sheltered life? Most of the time she managed to keep up, to "give him," as his father always said, "as good as he sent." The last thing he wanted to do, though, was to embarrass her in any way or cause her to feel ill at ease in the midst of one of his fanciful, exaggerated stories.

She did seem quite contented now, riding along beside him, her straw bonnet a bit askew, one dear, fragrant curl a little limp as it fell forward over her haughty forehead. Haughty? Anne did have a certain haughtiness about her, which to him only heightened her beauty. Especially the way she carried her amazing head.

"Where are we going tomorrow?" she asked, when the buggy was just reaching the Dumfries side of the River Nith.

"Anywhere you like," he said. "Frankly, I'm already beginning to think about tonight. Tonight comes first. As for tomorrow, how about walking a little way out of town to the house where I was born?" He smiled his devilish smile. "Not quite as splendid as your lark's nest, of course. Not splendid at all, actually. But hallowed because the man Anne Couper picked to be her husband was born there."

She turned quickly to look at him. "You're being flippant again, and this time I definitely don't approve because wherever you were born *is* hallowed and I want to see it right away. In fact, I demand to see it tomorrow." Scrunching closer to him, she added a bit shyly, "Tonight is on my mind, too. Oh, John, how wonderful that you were born! How wonderful that we were both born."

Chapter 45

At breakfast the next morning, Anne felt as excited to be seeing the house where John was born as before their visit yesterday to Caerlaverock.

"Dinna' get your hopes too high, lass," he warned. "The old Fraser place is like most other small farmhouses. A plain, whitewashed, stone box—two stories and a roof. Set on a narrow creek that bubbles over in the spring right through Father's grazing land. If it could be called grazing land, that is. How the man located the rockiest, poorest soil in all of Dumfriesshire I don't know, except that he bought it sight unseen from Glasgow, where my parents lived, a year before I was born."

"I didn't even know Father Fraser had ever been a farmer! You're both so secretive."

John laughed a little. "He wasn't a real one. Oh, the man labored at his work for love of Mother—for sheer stubbornness, she often said—but he had no gift for growing things then any more than now. And he never recovered from missing the cultural life of Glasgow."

She put down her muffin and studied his face, but said nothing. She just sat there stunned that again John had been able to keep something from her. She loved most of his surprises; understood why he'd told Mama about a Fraser's saving a Maxwell's life centuries ago on a stone staircase in Caerlaverock and kept it from her until the time was right, but not this. Unless it was something humiliating, people on St. Simons shared things with each other. Maybe Father Fraser's failure as a farmer did humiliate John.

"Isn't it as plain as the adorable nose on your pretty face why I didn't tell you?" he asked.

"No, it is not."

He leaned toward her across the narrow table. "You and I fell in love in a world all our own. At least, it struck me that way. I still like the idea that I *captured* you. We weren't brought together through any family connection. From the first sight of you, I wanted you all to myself—in a world that belonged only to us. It was very clear to me how close you were to your family. I wanted to woo you my way. Make all my own bonds with you, having nothing to do with fathers or mothers or grandparents." After a moment, eyebrow cocked, he asked, "You've twisted it all around and now think me cruel, don't you?"

"No, not cruel. I'm just trying not to feel cheated that you kept such a thing from me all this time. I like being in our own world as much as you do! But how can we live our whole lifetimes without letting our families in too? How did Father Fraser happen to decide to be a farmer?"

"I honestly don't remember. Anne, dearest, why does any of it matter so much?"

"I don't know. It isn't *why* you kept a secret from me, it's *that* you kept one. Could I ask you something?"

"My life is an open book, what there is of it."

"Don't be glib. I just need to know how you can seem so sweet and open most of the time and still keep such important, family things from me. I don't want you to be a puzzle. I love open books."

He grinned. "And here I thought you adored mystery."

Not often, but at times, he fell into a way of talking that more than puzzled her. Most of the time he was tender, gentle, loving—her tender, gentle, loving John, with whom she would spend all the remainder of her life—but in a second he could change so that he seemed almost to delight in fooling her. At the outset he'd acted as though he didn't have a brother, when all the time after they first met on Cumberland Island, William had been less than a mile away on his hospital ship!

"Are you thinking as hard as you seem to be?" he asked.

"Yes."

"And you don't like me very well right now, do you?" When she didn't answer immediately, he went on. "We need more time to get to know each other, Annie. We met out of totally different worlds. I'm trying very hard to get into yours because I know you've had no experience in mine.

We're both Scots, both brought up to revere not only families but clans, tartans—hearts trained to leap at the sound of bagpipes—and yet my own life seemed to begin only when I joined my unit. I'm doing my best to remember my Scottish roots, but Scots are so inventive, I wonder at times if they don't fool themselves by overquoting Burns, by boasting of Walter Scott's novels, by clinging so doggedly to their burrs."

What he'd been telling her was important, she knew, but all she could think to ask was, "Is it—is it like a game when you keep things as important as family affairs from me?"

He reached across the table for her hand. "Are you too put out with me, even after last night, to care about seeing the piggin where I was born?"

"Oh, John, I'm not put out!"

"What are you then?"

"Puzzled. Maybe kind of hurt. Which only proves what an innocent I am. As you say, 'how sheltered.' Forgive me? I think I'm learning how to take you."

"Am I so difficult? Have I traveled too much, lived in too many parts of the world—been too frivolous and reckless?"

"Why did you say 'reckless'? I never think of you that way."

"Uh-oh, wrong word. Anne, I really can't help being older than my nearly twenty-five years. I know I've just handed you another splendid chance to disapprove of my attachment to the worldly life of a British officer. Aren't you going to take advantage of it?" He cocked his head like a quizzical robin. "I did go too far that time, didn't I? It's just that I so long for you to love me exactly as I am."

"And do you think I don't?"

His melting smile flashed. "On the contrary, after last night, I think you do."

She sank back against the straight coffee house chair as though a big job had just been finished. He had rescued them again, with that smile and a mere mention of the wonder of last night.

"How far do we have to walk to see where you were born?" she asked eagerly. "Should we take another picnic basket today?"

"No, it isn't that far. My mother often walked into town to market and back. I think she found our farm on the edge of town lonely at times. Going to town gave her a chance to see her Dumfries friends. She also thought it kept her from getting any plumper."

"Your mother . . . Margaret Thompson Fraser," Anne said dreamily. "I wish I'd known her."

"So do I," he said, helping her into the short, pale blue silk spencer she wore over a white dress. As they stood to go, he said, "Your eyes and your jacket are almost the same color."

Outside, they strolled slowly along High Street, then stopped to look at the cattle market, where Anne pitied the sheep and lambs and calves, all helplessly trying to move around inside cramped wooden pens.

"But you adore a leg of lamb, as I remember," he joked. "Especially if Sans Foix has worked his magic with it. Do you really pity those lambs waiting to delight someone like you?"

"There isn't anyone like me," she said, determined to try to match his banter from now on. "If there were, you'd be in love with her and not me. Yes, I do pity all those poor, penned-up creatures. Do you think they know death will come—either here or in far-off London or Edinburgh or Glasgow?"

"I honestly hadn't thought much about it," he said. "Haven't dared give it any thought, because when I was a boy of about eight or nine, I had a pet lamb I loved the way most boys love their dogs. He followed me everywhere. Father sold him as soon as the market was right, of course. I cried for a week."

"Show me, when we get there, just where you and your lamb went together on Father Fraser's farm, will you?"

He laughed. "I'd have to show you every foot of it and I have no intention of doing that. I hated it all. Loathed stumbling along behind our old workhorse trying to plow a straight furrow in a barley field. It was bearable only because my lamb, Malcolm, trotted along right beside me all the way."

"Your lamb plowed with you? That's the dearest thing you've ever told me."

" 'Twas dear to me then. I vowed, even to writing it down in my own blood in a copybook, that if Father sold Malcolm, I'd die before I'd ever plow another row."

"You're teasing me again."

"I swear to you, I'm not. Of course, he sold Malcolm, and

of course, I plowed again. I despised it, but not as much as Father's willow switch."

For a time they walked through the rutted streets of Dumfries, Anne only half listening as John pointed out where the old shops once stood, showed surprise to see the same butcher shop still there at the edge of town, talked of his mother's haggis—how he relished the dish to this day while William disliked even the smell of it.

They were out in the Dumfriesshire countryside, where the land rose to the mountains, sloped into rich tablelands back toward the town and off in the direction of the Solway Firth. Anne was thankful that she and John were learning to be quiet together. She was thankful once again to feel close to him as they walked briskly past green meadows dotted with sheep and lambs still free of the market pens. Splashes of daisies and bluebells and buttercups grew everywhere, and along the edge of the roadway an occasional determined late violet still braved the June sun.

The look of Borderland Scotland brought her favorite author, Walter Scott, to mind. "Scott writes a lot about moors and bogs and heather and—"

"—and the reek of peat on the air and around the family hearth," John finished for her. "We aren't really seeing true moors right now, but wait until we cover another half mile or so and you'll see a real moor in what was once poor Father's acreage—not rich and loamy and green like these meadows and hillsides."

"Maybe Father Fraser was just unlucky."

"I know you're fond of the old man, dearest, but it's time you realize he does not have a reputation for careful decisions. As when he picked us up and moved us to London to venture into the wine import business on the word of a young, inexperienced Glasgow man Father happened to like. It was still another absurd young gentleman who earlier had vowed by letter that our Dumfries farm was of the best soil. Dumfriesshire is rich land almost everywhere except where we lived."

"Do you suppose you still hold that against your father?"

He forced a short laugh. "I'm too much like him for grudging the man his opportunity to err, I think. I was only a boy during Father's farming gamble. Children believe, true or not, that their parents know best. They seldom question.

I grumbled, but I didn't question. You believe your father can do no wrong, don't you?"

She thought a minute. Only once had she known Papa to confess a wrongdoing, and that was the scary, stormy night thirteen years ago when he told his family that he and Mr. Thomas Spalding had broken Georgia law by importing that ill-fated cargo of Ebos. Through the years, though, when she had thought about it, Papa's honesty that night had only made her admire him more. "Finding out that someone has made a mistake in judgment shouldn't have anything to do with loving," she said carefully.

"I hope you mean that, Annie. I know I'm fairly handsome, quite dashing, in fact, in my officer's uniform, but I do make mistakes in judgment." He laughed lightly. "Not many, of course, but I've made a few." Then, he pointed up ahead. "There! See? Up there around that bend in the road, almost hidden now behind that big old stand of hawthorne trees? That's it. That's the 'castle' where I first saw the sun come up in the morning from behind old Beacon Hill, where the Maxwells once watched for a signal to rally them to the fray. Can you see the box of a farmhouse?"

"Yes! Yes, I see it, and it must be empty. There's still a Scottish chill in the air, as Papa always says when it's winter on St. Simons. Wouldn't smoke be rising from at least one chimney if a family cooked breakfast?"

"If the old stone pile isn't empty, I fervently hope there are no boys in the family who hate farming as much as I hated it!"

She was beginning to see another reason, aside from loving his unit, why John seemed unable to bring himself to accept Papa's offer of Lawrence Plantation. To Anne, living at Lawrence, so near her own family, would mean the ultimate fulfillment of her dearest dream. But she had carefully not mentioned it to him because she believed his love of his unit was the reason he hadn't agreed. She now knew he also hated even the idea of farming. Not one but two huge obstacles loomed. The passing of time, the coming of children of their own someday, might eventually dim his attachment to his regiment, but could John ever learn to love the St. Simons land as Papa and James Hamilton loved it? Didn't John understand that owning a plantation in Georgia had nothing to do with plowing or feeding livestock? Hadn't he realized that Papa would find a way for him to own people to do all that?

They had reached the overgrown path that led to the two-story box, as John called the stone house where he was born, and for what seemed an awkwardly long time, he just stood there in the road looking at the weather- and vine-stained shape of it. The house *was* boxlike, but sturdy and well built, she thought. It was also somehow sorrowful, because no one called it home any longer. No curtains hung at its windows, their crooked shutters closed, probably nailed shut as was the front door through which John had run as a boy. Unevenly cut boards had been hammered across it. She was looking at his birthplace, but there seemed no chance to step inside even to sample the feel of the rooms in which he'd been a squirming infant, then a toddler, and finally a rebellious lad old enough for school and to grip the handles of a plow.

"I know at least some of what you're thinking," he said after a while, "and I should be man enough to admit how ashamed I am not to have grown up sufficiently to let go of my feelings against poor Father for the idiocy of buying a farm."

"You do still hold it against him, don't you?"

"I probably do, when I think of it. Oh, I've been commended for courage under fire, for being a leader of men, but the truth is that, standing here, I see myself as still a boy, still furious at those barren fields out there. I broke a toe once kicking a clod out of my way because I hated the land so. You deserve a real man, Annie, a grown man with courage, a man able to buckle down to a daily round of some kind without benefit of a well-tailored officer's uniform."

John had never, ever talked like that before. She didn't move a muscle, but her whole body tingled with dread—dread and downright confusion. Even fear of saying the wrong thing. Had he only been making use of what he called his worldly humor, when again and again he'd agreed with her that indeed he was not only handsome, but dashing and brave and altogether desirable as a husband? Had he made up out of whole cloth the notion that Father Fraser favored William in order to hide the fact that John really still felt young and helpless?

"Any other man as much in love as I am with you would jump at the chance your father is offering me," he said.

"Not I. As always, I hedge, stalling for a bit more time to find a way out that appeals to *me.* If time hasn't sweetened my attitude toward farming in twenty-five years, I doubt it ever can."

"John, we have much, much more than time on our side."

He was standing there, hands deep in his pockets, glaring at the deserted stone house, as empty as the rocky fields of pale heather stretching around it, of any living person, of a single cow or sheep, and worst of all, empty of happy memories for John. Anne squeezed her eyes shut to hold back tears. He needed her and she felt as young and helpless as he, because she could think of nothing at all to say and nothing to do except to throw both arms around him right there in the road.

"I want to kiss you," she whispered. "I want your arms around me."

John gave her his abruptly playful look, eyebrow again cocked. Then, he looked both ways up and down the vacant country road and murmured, *"Je suis prêt.* Whatever I'm not, I'm a Fraser, which means I'm always ready to hold you."

In his arms, hers encircling his neck, she said, "Yes! You're always ready to hold me, to kiss me, aren't you? Oh, my darling, always be—always be! Always be close enough for me to reach out and find you. That's really all we ever need, isn't it?"

Once more, his humor—worldly or not—had rescued them, she thought, although nothing had been solved. He was still doing battle with himself over his longing to get back into the familiar world of an officer. She still hated the whole idea that this glorious man with the tender heart could bear to kill. Maybe Father Fraser was right when he said the military to John had nothing to do with killing, only with adventure, the camaraderie of his fellow officers, the bond he'd known with them in the thick of battle. A bond she could never even expect to share. The only way she had ever known how to enter a man's world was by trailing along after Papa on her horse, as interested as he in watching for the progress of his olive trees and sprouting cotton plants. She had never tired of a single Cannon's Point field or a single plant in it. John hated farming.

Too much was coming clear standing there in the lonely road beside him, looking at the deserted, plain house where he was born. With all her heart, she longed for John to want to live and work beside her, with her trailing him through their well-tended fields at Lawrence. He didn't want that and maybe never would.

No wonder she was frightened!

Still, Mama had always tried to tell her that once things come clear, unpleasant as they may seem at the moment, it was only then that a woman knew which step to take next. Only then was there real hope. Such adult advice had only sailed over her head until this minute. Standing in an empty road in Dumfriesshire, Scotland, where the Maxwells were still everything, her mother's wisdom began to free her a little. Nothing had changed except that she saw clearly that he had far more than love of his unit to conquer before they could return to St. Simons to stay.

Things were coming clear. They were also worse than she had thought, but he was holding her and there was an odd kind of brightness somewhere down inside her where she lived. Because of the nameless brightness, vague as it was, she knew she could wait.

In a moment John released her, held her away just far enough to look into her eyes. "You know you didn't get a bargain in me, Annie. I have a long way to climb and many walls to scale. But you do have me. Oh, Annie, such as I am, you do have me! No matter what happens tomorrow and tomorrow, we're in it all—together. Can you find it in your heart to be patient until I'm no longer such an indecisive mess?"

"Hush! I'm not at all good at patience, but even though I'm a Maxwell and a Couper, I'm also a Fraser, so everything for us will somehow be all right because *Je suis prête.* The truth is, I'm mostly a Fraser now, darling, and I really am ready . . . ready to be with you wherever you are."

Chapter 46

For another fortnight they spent almost every minute together, riding in borrowed or rented buggies, or walking for miles about the gentle Dumfriesshire countryside. For the fourth time, with another picnic meal, they rode to Caerlaverock, then walked the two miles or so to the shore. From an old, grizzled gamekeeper he met one night in the Globe public room, John ordered a stout pair of walking shoes made for Anne, and wonder of wonders, they were comfortable from the first day she wore them. And so, day after day, they walked and walked and laughed and talked and held hands and embraced at every opportunity. She vowed never to forget the special tenderness of the kiss he gave her standing on the beach beside the noisy waters of the Solway Firth. John's kisses, even those rough with passion, had always held *their* kind of tenderness, but that kiss caused her to believe that for as long as she lived, the love they had found would, like the waves rolling in from the Irish Sea, never end, would always be coming toward them.

They spent still more of John's dwindling money supply for a drive to the tiny village of Alloway, near Ayr, to see the plain, poor clay piggin where Burns was born, but aside from Caerlaverock, nothing they saw struck Anne as did their visit to Sweetheart Abbey. Astride rented horses, they rode the seven miles from Dumfries to New Abbey, then along a winding road through a cathedral of trees until they came in sight of the vine-grown, roofless red ruin called, for such a sweet reason, Sweetheart Abbey. At length, John had told her of the undying love of Queen Devorguila de Baliol, wife, then widow of John de Baliol, in whose memory she not only helped to found Balliol College, Oxford, but built the unforgettable Sweetheart Abbey. So wholly did Devorguila love her John that when he died, she had his heart embalmed and carried it with her wherever she went until her own death.

"I did tell you, didn't I," John whispered as they knelt together before Devorguila's grave near the high altar of Sweetheart Abbey, "that she's buried here with his heart laid on hers?"

For a long time Anne knelt there beside him, unable to answer. Finally, when they stood, choking back tears, she whispered, "Yes, you told me."

"Seems like a rather primitive idea," he went on, "in the year 1816, but—"

"No, it doesn't, John! I—I understand her." Then, even though three more visitors to the shrine stood only a few yards away, Anne blurted, "I love you that way. I love *you* more than I love Cannon's Point! If you can find a way to get back your commission, do it. I'll follow you anywhere or wait for you to sail back home to me from wherever they send you. Dearest John, I'll wait forever if I have to. . . ."

"Sh!" he whispered, pulling her to him. "Hush, Annie. None of that. You're just borrowing poor old Devorguila's grief because her John died. I'm not even considering death, nor am I thinking about the marines today. I swear it!" For an emotion-packed moment, they stood there until the other visitors straggled outside. "Anne, beautiful Anne," he said, his voice helpless, "I wish I could change me. I would if I could. I don't know how to do it."

"Don't try! I married you exactly as you are and I'm learning more about you every day." She tried to smile, but couldn't. "It just overwhelmed me to realize all over again that I do love you more than I knew I could ever love anyone."

They were alone now and he took her fully in his arms. Then, not in the cocky, teasing way she had come to expect, but helpless and as trapped as the young boy stumbling along behind Father Fraser's plow, he said, "I'd be a rotten farmer, Anne! How could I bear to fail both you and your lovable, generous father?" When she didn't answer, he grinned almost sheepishly. "Do you know I miss him, too? Sometimes, many times a day since we've been away from Cannon's Point, I've missed Mr. Couper more than I ever missed my own father!"

Why those almost pathetic words, which seemed to tumble of their own weight from his dear, embattled heart, should have transformed that moment before the ruins of the high altar at Sweetheart Abbey from distress to sudden expectation, she could not have explained to anyone. She simply knew and somehow would always know that from now on, she would understand how to see John more and more clearly, would know him better and better, learning him with a part of her woman self she hadn't discovered was there.

He had brought her today to pay homage to Queen Devorguila de Baliol's continuing love for *her* John, but this minute, as though she had been the one to bring him, she took his arm and led him gently outside to the ash tree where they'd tethered their rented mounts.

Nearly a week later, John confessed that their money was almost gone.

Walking beside her along High Street at teatime on Wednesday of their third week in Dumfries, he did his best to make light of the shortage. "You'll be proud to learn, milady, that your frugal husband has managed to keep back enough to pay Mr. McDonald's charges and to take us by stage and the cheapest possible hack all the way to Number Two George Street. But not unless we leave almost at once."

"We'll be together, won't we? Staying or leaving," she said lightly.

"And we can always come back, or take another trip anywhere you like, once I've found a way to earn more than the half pay I'm on now. I've done some hard thinking this week and feel quite hopeful, actually, that Father will see fit to allow me to help out with his business. Your husband, dear Annie, can talk his way into almost any situation." His laugh was brittle. "Except, of course, at marine headquarters."

"You don't seem to talk much at all with Father Fraser, though. Will you have trouble convincing him to let you go to work in his wine business?"

"Unless I'm very mistaken, he'll be relieved. Not that the old gentleman will permit himself to show *me* his relief, but I've already told you I'm sure his clients have dwindled in number. He's managed to learn the importing business and ranks among the best importers in London, but working alone, he simply doesn't have the time to make new contacts and handle his accounts. He deals with so many wineries on the Continent."

"If Father Fraser agrees, you'd be going about London finding new customers, leaving him time at his office. Is that it?"

"That's exactly what I have in mind and I'm sure I can increase his business. I knew as soon as we reached London —even before—that he was in trouble. I can always tell, even though he doesn't confide in me. He never talked to me or to my mother when things weren't going well. As a typical Scot, he boasts when they are, of course. Oh, now and then, he used to confide some in William, but we've both known for a long time which signs to look for in Father's manner, seldom in his words."

"This makes me very happy," she said, walking along briskly beside him. "It's the perfect chance to make everything right—the way you always wanted it—between you and Father Fraser, isn't it?"

When they reached the entrance to the Globe, he grinned down at her. "It's the way *you* have always wanted it, but don't get your hopes too high. I've simply decided to try to carry my weight once we're back in London. Unless rain slows us again, we'll find out soon enough if Father agrees. Are you sure you're not too disappointed that we don't have the funds to travel beyond Dumfriesshire, the exciting spot where I was born?"

"I'm not a bit disappointed. I'm only proud of you and I like the idea of going home to George Street. You miss my papa, so let me miss Father Fraser, too."

Inside the inn, they greeted Mr. McDonald warmly.

"Home in time for tea, eh?" the hearty Scotsman asked. "And where did you roam today, pray?"

"Nowhere in particular," John said, "nowhere and everywhere. We just roamed. Mrs. Fraser's not only radiant to look upon, sir, she's a fine long-distance walker."

"I hope your stay's still being a felicitous one, Mrs. Fraser," McDonald said to Anne as he handed John the key to their airy corner room.

"Oh, it's been as nearly perfect as a visit could be," she said merrily.

"And I'm reluctant to tell you, Mr. McDonald, but it looks as though we'll be having to leave for London tomorrow. Tonight will be our last night spent with you." Showing no sign whatever of embarrassment, John added, "Funds do run out, you know, so if you'll tally up our accounts by tomorrow morning, we'll be leaving."

"You be gang awa' hame tae England so soon? With a night or two of lodging at no char-rge, ya' hae to stay at least until Saturday, John Fraser! The word hasn't reached you yet? The big news aboot Satiday's festive day at Caerlaverock?"

"What about Saturday at Caerlaverock?" Anne wanted to know.

"Hisself is back in his quar-rters over there. Laird Herries is openin' the auld castle to a' his friends from Dumfries and the county aboot. Nothin' fancy, but ever'thin aplenty! The laird has already hear-rd you're both here and has left this for you—hand-delivered."

"Lord Herries himself left an invitation for *us?*" John asked, reaching for the elegant folded writing paper bearing an elaborate seal. "Wouldn't this be a great moment for your mother, Anne? A handwritten invitation from a titled descendant of the ancient chiefs of the Maxwell clan!"

"Let me see it! Oh, yes. Mama would appear only genteel and quietly pleased, but she will never recover from our having received this." Breaking the heavy, dark-red seal, Anne read aloud: " 'The esteemed presence of Lieutenant and Mrs. John Fraser is requested at an outdoor fete in the courtyard at the Maxwell Castle, Caerlaverock, on Saturday, the twenty-ninth of June, 1816, from nine in the morning until three in the afternoon. Signed, The Second William Maxwell, Lord of the Barony of Herries.' Oh, John! I'll send this to Mama just as soon as we've had time to show it to Father Fraser!"

John laughed. "And to Flora McLeod."

A look of surprise on his face, McDonald asked, "Flora McLeod, is it? Don' tell me old Flora McLeod still serves yer father-r, sir, off in smoky London!"

"Aye, she not only still serves us, but bosses us all and never loses her homesickness for the Borderland and Dumfriesshire."

"I'll hate to see ya' go, the both of ya'," McDonald said, "and I refuse straight out to watch ya' walk through that door until Sunday or Monday. Four nights welcome lodging I offer and, if ya' care to stay longer, send the balance at some later date." He chuckled. "Me honor lies at stake. Ya' see, I pr-romised Lord Herries I'd guarantee yer presence and 'twill be an event you'll never for-r-get. A' the spit-roasted lamb you kin eat, a' the salmon and grouse an' when the laird hisself is openin' the courtyard, ever'body an' his uncle turns out!"

Chapter 47

Saturday, the twenty-ninth of June, dawned brighter than any day Anne could remember since they came to Dumfries. Her sense of excitement as she and John once more crossed the River Nith and came in sight of Caerlaverock's ancient bulk against the luminous blue sky reminded her of the way she felt on the early January day last year when she and Mama and James Hamilton waved good-bye to Papa at the Cannon's Point dock and headed in the *Lady Love* to attend Louisa Shaw's Cumberland house party.

Sitting beside John now in the McDonald buggy, drawn by the same steady brown horse, Anne chattered happily about how certain she'd been on that Georgia January day that the great adventure of her life was about to take place. "And it did and the big adventure was you and I absolutely adore the way you look in Father Fraser's kilt! Isn't it marvelous that the dear man made you pack it? And I love that borrowed blue bonnet! Oh, John, buy a red, blue, and green Fraser plaid kilt just as soon as we're back in London, do you hear me? You're even handsomer in a kilt than in your officer's uniform. Most men have such ugly, bony legs and yours are downright enticing and you're tall and no one could possibly be anything but awed if the kilt draws attention to you!"

He was laughing at her again, and as they rolled and rattled along, the horse moving at a brisk trot, she felt she couldn't wait for the festive day to begin, couldn't even wait through the next two or three minutes while the buggy passed under the last stand of beeches into the now familiar big Caerlaverock meadow. The meadow, she knew, would be singing today with a riot of color—daisies, yellow tansy, bluebells.

"I can see meself striding about the streets of London, especially in Father's fashionable area, clad in a kilt."

"Pooh! I've seen gentlemen in kilts right in Portman Square." She scooted nearer him on the buggy seat and held his arm in both of hers. "Are you glad I wore what we decided is my Maxwell dress? The print in it does look quite a lot like little sprigs of ash, don't you think?"

"With a bit of imagination, aye," he said, his laugh still running like a brook under the musical voice. Then, with no warning, John yelled, "Whoa!" He reined the horse to one side of the winding road and jumped out.

"What on earth is wrong?" Anne demanded.

"Not a thing, lass," he called over his shoulder, running into the meadow to a clump of evergreen and willow trees. He broke off a sprig of yew, tucked it under the band of his blue bonnet, ran back, and hopped up beside her again, beaming proudly. "Now, how do I look sporting a sprig of me own clan's plant?"

"The Fraser plant is a yew? As usual, you didn't tell me, but it does make you look handsomer than ever, especially in that blue bonnet. Father Fraser would call it a tam-o'-shanter. Why haven't you worn a bonnet before?"

"I'm just feeling quite Scottish today, lass. Hadn't you noticed me bur-rish Bor-r-der speech?"

"I noticed," she said. "Are you feeling Scottish because we're visiting a descendant of a real Maxwell chieftain?"

"Aye, but a tr-rue Fraser bonnet would have a tassel at the back, unlike this borrowed one."

As the buggy rocked across the old meadow road, she began to sing in her clear, lilting voice a snatch of the song that, to her, was now her song for John: " 'He wears a blue bonnet, blue bonnet, blue bonnet. He wears a blue bonnet, a dimple in his chin!' "

Then, as they neared the bridge spanning the ancient moat, together they began to sing what would always be only their song, "Drink to Me Only with Thine Eyes," finishing it as the horse slowed before the massive entrance to Caerlaverock, where today wagons, buggies, even rickety drays, were drawn up everywhere.

"Isn't it different?" she asked, still clinging to his arm.

"Aye, but we can't have it all to ourselves every time. And today could be ver-ry special, me darlin'."

"To me, it already is."

"Before I lift you down from this fine contraption, lass, I want you to know how happy I am that old McDonald's generosity permitted us to stay over to attend the laird's annual affair. I'm sure there've been Frasers imbibing and gorging in the Caerlaverock courtyard often over the eight hundred years past, but today, *I* am the Fraser who's here to listen to the pipers." He kissed the palm of her hand. "And I'm here because I'm married to the most beautiful Maxwell of them all and with a sprig of Maxwell clan flowering ash printed right into her gown!"

This time, because they both felt familiar with Caerlaverock, they hurried arm in arm beneath the massive archway and along the echoing, empty passages beside the guardrooms in the direction of the open courtyard. Unlike the day of their first visit, the courtyard was anything but desolate. Standing like wide-eyed children, they could see seventy-five to a hundred people milling about, the younger ones chasing and shouting, playing hide-and-seek among the huge old pillars.

"What do you think of all this, Annie?" he asked. "It's exactly as McDonald said: 'When the laird returns, activity explodes.' Look over there! See that huge group of young men flexing their arms for the caber toss? I once tried it."

"I'm sure you'd still do yourself proud," she said. "You're strong enough to hurl those heavy timbers if anyone is!"

"I wonder which of the distinguished-looking gentlemen sporting kilts there by the lamb spits is the laird hisself?"

"Let's try to guess," she said, almost shouting over the laughter and hilarity. "After all, he's a Maxwell. Maybe I can find him by the Maxwell plaid. It can't be the fat old gentleman. He doesn't resemble a Maxwell at all, according to Mama, who vows her tall, slender figure is inherited."

"What about the lanky fellow with hair as red as your father's?"

"By his kilt, I suppose he could be a Maxwell, but Mama also swears she never heard of red hair in her family. There are branches and branches of the clan, though. Look!" She nodded in the general direction of a pleasant-looking, middle-aged gentleman in conversation with one of the grizzled workmen tending the fires that burned under perfect control beneath roasting lamb carcasses.

"Ah-ha," John agreed. "He's certainly wearing the Maxwell tartan—red, blue, and heavy green plaid."

"Somehow I'm sure that's Lord Herries."

"Then, shall we present ourselves to him and see how close you came to recognizing a real Maxwell?"

John had led her only a few steps in the direction of the row of lamb spits before the skirl of bagpipes nearly stopped them in their tracks. He glanced at Anne, saw that she was as pleased as he, then began to look for the source of the piping. "There!" he shouted over the din. "Up there—see? There come the pipers!"

From the high-ceilinged, covered passageway that ran alongside the courtyard streamed a formation of kilted Scots of all sizes and shapes, left elbows keeping the bass of their drones going while giving prominence to the wild, blood-tingling melody as their deft fingers moved on the reeded pipe, the chanter.

"Oh, John—listen!" she cried.

"How can I do anything else?" As though repelled by the sound, he held a forefinger in each ear, but only for a moment. He was anything but repelled. As always, his blood was racing as it had raced each time the familiar skirl had reached him anywhere on the face of the earth from pipers attached to the marines, all the way to this very Border country where he first felt the weight of the bag under his own left arm as a boy struggling to master the difficult art of piping.

"Do you realize they're playing the 'Maxwell March'?" she demanded.

"You know it, eh?"

"Of course I know it! I grew up hearing Johnson play the 'Maxwell March.' Papa had him play and play it for Mama."

And then, John spotted the slender gentleman wearing the Maxwell tartan coming toward where they stood, both transfixed by the excellence of the pipers of Caerlaverock. On the lean, patrician face of the man Anne had picked out as the Lord of Herries himself was a warm, welcoming smile that seemed almost to be one of recognition.

"I bid ye fair, sir," John said amiably, his hand out.

"Aye and I bid *ye* fair," the trim gentleman called over the piping. "You are connected with the Maxwells, sir? You did greet me with the old motto."

"I certainly am connected," John said. "I'm Lieutenant John Fraser of London and this is Mrs. Fraser of Georgia, U.S.A., who is indeed one of your Maxwell clan."

"Fortunate for me," the impressive gentleman said, bowing over Anne's hand. "I'm Herries, William Maxwell, present laird of this ancient pile and I confess I'm pleased that my research proved correct. You were a Maxwell before you married this distinguished gentleman, ma'am?"

"Well, my father, John Couper, married Rebecca Maxwell, who reared me on fairy tales and ghost stories and legends about Caerlaverock. My husband and I are deeply honored to have been invited to such a marvelous event."

"And neither of us can quite believe the magic you've worked in the courtyard in such a few days," John said. "You see, Lord Herries, we've come several times from our lodgings in Dumfries to allow my wife a chance to wander among the mysteries of her family castle."

"Sorry I was not at home to welcome you," Herries said. "Isn't my collection of local pipers excellent? Or do you find pipe music to your liking?"

"We love it!" Anne exclaimed.

"More than that, I'm restraining meself," John laughed, "because what I really want to do is—march!"

Looking extremely pleased, Maxwell, Lord Herries, with the most unobtrusive signal in the direction of the pipers, ended the "Maxwell March" and began an even livelier, more martial tune, which brought John to attention as though a command had just been shouted. Beaming his delight, he gave Herries a smart salute, which, with a mischievous grin, Lord Herries returned. Then, without another word, blue bonnet riding at a rakish angle, John turned on his heel and began a brisk march around the courtyard alone. The obvious fact of Herries's sophistication, his foresight in preparing his pipers to play John's own beloved "Fraser of Lovat's Salute," freed his spirit in a way it hadn't been freed since the day he left home to be sworn into the Royal Marines! Pleased as he was that his host had bothered to find out his own clan march, the foolish, carefree abandon John felt came even more directly from the very presence of even one other man of the world who would know exactly why he dared to enjoy making a fool of himself. Herries, he knew, understood and would in no way think him odd or objectionable to be behaving in such a boyish, show-off manner.

Not that Anne would disapprove. She wouldn't. She might be a bit surprised at first, then she would laugh, too, and tell him how graceful and handsome he looked marching about in Father's old kilt, the blue bonnet jaunty on his head. Within her stirred all the makings of a truly sophisticated lady. It simply took a bit of time for any sheltered butterfly to find the way out of its cocoon.

At the far corner of the courtyard, where the neighborhood men who would take part in the hammer throw were assembling, John turned sharply right, his dormant marching skills still keen, and for the first time since boyhood, seemed to feel fresh, invigorating ties with Father *and* his dead mother and a surprising sense of pride in his own Dumfriesshire roots.

Marching across the north corner of the courtyard, where still another gang of men were tying the last bundles of hay for the sheaf toss still to come, he looked back toward where he'd left Anne. Once, over the shouts of small boys and the barking of neighborhood dogs brought to the fete by farmers and shopkeepers of Dumfriesshire, he thought he heard her calling his name, but couldn't be sure. He'd go back to her, of course, very soon now and what she would have to say about his aberrant behavior should be good for a real laugh, or she wasn't truly John Couper's daughter. In the meantime, though, he could see her deep in conversation with William Maxwell, Lord Herries, and at this point he certainly had no notion of giving up one step of his brisk and enjoyable march.

"I do apologize for the lack of furniture in Caerlaverock's courtyard, Mrs. Fraser," Lord Herries said as he and Anne stood together, both delighted by her husband's antics. "Would you care to sit down on that broken column over there? I could have a blanket spread for you."

"Oh no, thank you. I'm having a most pleasant time. In fact," she added, dropping all effort to speak in a socially proper way, "this is the most fun I've had for a long time!"

"My local spies inform me that you're on your wedding trip, so you could pay me no finer compliment. Somehow I sense that you and the lieutenant have liked your stay in Dumfriesshire immensely, Mrs. Fraser."

"Oh, we have, Lord Herries! Every minute with my husband is the best minute of my entire life and since he grew up here, he knows all the interesting places to take me." She looked up at him. "However distant, you and I are blood relatives. Can't you call me Anne? I'd feel ever so much more comfortable."

"If you'll call me William. Better still, Willy. My real friends and most of what family I have still alive in Scotland call me Willy. Anne and Willy from now on?"

"By all means, I'd like that."

Herries could see she was trying again to get a glimpse of her marching husband making his way around and through the clumps of people. "I admire you greatly, Anne," he said simply.

"Thank you, Willy. I'm as susceptible to flattery as any woman, but was there a special reason to say that now? Do you admire me for not being embarrassed at the spectacle my husband is making of himself?"

Lord Herries grinned. "Actually, I didn't expect you to be at all embarrassed, although many English ladies would be. I paid you that quite truthful compliment just now because I'm impressed with how drawn you seem to be to the warring, reveling, confusing history of our antecedents, the Maxwells. Unlike many ladies of breeding, your mind is extremely perceptive, especially for one making her very first visit to Scotland."

"I've had excellent tutoring on my Scottish roots from my mother, my father back in America—and from my husband. I'm not sure, though, that I have all the centuries straight in which Caerlaverock has been stormed or destroyed, or even by which English kings. I don't really care about all that. I do know both our Maxwell mottoes and that we, as a family, did flourish again. That's what matters. Now, I also know you and that matters a great deal. Obviously, you've won Mr. Fraser, too, by ordering your pipers to play the 'Fraser of Lovat's Salute' in his honor. I can tell, even with him off marching, that you've made him deliriously happy. That means more than anything to me." She looked up at him, her lovely face almost troubled, her mind plainly turning over something of importance. "You *are* as trustworthy as you seem, aren't you, Willy?"

"The most trustworthy Maxwell of them all, Anne. Why?"

"I'm not sure. Yes, I am. I sense that you know what Fraser's Salute is doing right now for my husband. You see, he misses life in his Royal Marine unit painfully."

"And they no longer need him, is that it? I'm acquainted socially with Admiral Cockburn, under whom he served. Frankly, I inquired of Cockburn about Lieutenant Fraser. With a record for valor like his, I'd think they'd make room for your husband somewhere. After all, Britain doesn't stay long out of war for one reason or another."

"Forgive me if I'm imposing, but if there's a chance today, could you—would you find a way to talk alone with John for a few minutes? I'm just so sure you can say something to help him."

His fetching, distant American cousin was, Willy thought, a most surprising woman. He was not at all sure he understood why, but her abrupt request appealed to him. In the brief moments they'd shared before he'd gone marching off around the courtyard, Willy had felt an unusual affinity for Fraser. Because he himself had always been able only to respond to, never act on, impulse, he admired the kind of abandon John Fraser showed.

To Anne, he said, "When he completes his march, we'll circulate among my guests for a time, then I promise to make an opportunity for your husband and me to take a walk together. I really can't imagine, though, what help I might be to a man so obviously in charge of himself."

Chapter 48

While his guests gorged themselves from the plentiful feast spread on enormous plank tables about the courtyard, Willy Maxwell watched Anne make friends with another distant Maxwell cousin, a maiden lady, Middy Maxwell, who had come with him from Terragles to visit in his small quarters at Caerlaverock. He observed Anne with interest, knowing two things full well: She seemed, at least, to be enjoying her talk with Cousin Middy and, at the same time, was offering him the perfect chance to invite her husband for a walk along the moat.

Cousin Middy would, when they returned to Terragles, take with her endless gossip to entrance other Maxwells there about the charms and social skills of their heretofore unknown American kin.

Lieutenant Fraser not only had eaten heartily of roast lamb, salmon, and grouse, the tall, energetic young man had indulged in not one but two helpings of plum pudding. That this guest was reveling in the Caerlaverock fete no one could doubt.

An hour later as Lord Herries and John ambled across the heavy wooden bridge above the moat and set out to walk off their excessive feast, young Fraser threw both arms in the air and exclaimed to the sun-filled day, to any nearby listening bird, to the moat ducks, and almost incidentally to his host, "If a man could measure his life in divided sections of unsurpassed pleasure, I would have to label this one as nearly perfect, Lord Herries."

"No host could be more pleased than I to know that, Lieutenant."

"Splendid," Fraser rejoined quickly, then lapsed into a brogue as thick as a stout Scottish fir:

> *"As fair art thou, my bonnie lass,*
> *So deep in luve am I;*
> *And I will luve thee still, my dear,*
> *Till a' the seas gang dry."*

"I don't need to ask the bonnie object of that burst of Burnsiana," Herries said, "but are you a Burns worshiper?"

"Aye, what Scot isn't, if he's honest, on a day like this when his stomach is filled with excellent grouse and rare Scotch bear juice?"

Fraser had imbibed a drink or two of Scotch bear, but his gay mood was due, Herries felt sure, to far more than gude Scotch whuskey. "You turn me greener than the slopes of yonder Criffel," Herries said, "to be so much in luve! But, having met your wife, Anne, I understand. How could you not be almost beside yourself with love for her? I feel a special kind of pride in laying claim to such a beautiful, though distant, cousin as your Anne. While you were off marching, we became quite well acquainted. What a surprisingly direct, yet subtle beauty she is!"

Fraser looked at him, the long, proud face abruptly troubled. "She deserves more than she got in me, Lord Herries," he said in a solemn voice. "You called her surprisingly direct. She is, but Anne is also contained."

"Contained? I found her altogether natural, open, trusting, as though confidences come easily to her."

"Aye, they do. She's lived her life in an atmosphere of total safety. A decidedly sheltered life, under the graceful care of your Maxwell cousin, her mother, and the benevolent watchfulness of her excellent father, John Couper, master of Cannon's Point Plantation, but she's strong and knows how to keep her counsel." Herries saw a deep frown worry the young brow, a brow high and noble enough, he thought, to be a Fraser of Lovat. "I say, Herries, did Anne mention her father's generous offer to me?"

There was no need to feign surprise. Herries *was* surprised. Not once had she mentioned such a thing. "Why, no. She didn't speak of her father at all."

"That's odd."

"Odd?"

"Until she met me, the man was at the very center of her life."

Lord Herries was amused at such unselfconscious acceptance that Fraser was, indeed, now at the center of Anne's life. And yet, the boy only *looked* haughty at times. There seemed to be no haughtiness in his manner or in his speech. In a measure, of course, all Scots were a bit haughty. "I know her father's name, John Couper, the son of a Presbyterian parson, I believe," Herries went on. "According to my family research before I returned to Caerlaverock, frankly hoping you'd both still be in Dumfries, I learned that Rebecca Maxwell of a village in Georgia called Midway had married a John Couper. I learned nothing more, I'm afraid, about the Coupers of Scotland."

Fraser's bright smile returned. "That would indeed make my good father-in-law burst into laughter. He vows he can't trace one Couper chieftain anywhere in antiquity, regardless of what most Scots would have the world believe. But he is a chieftain now in the finest sense of the word. A respected, beloved chieftain to his slaves and to his family and to every neighbor who lives on the tiny coastal Georgia island called St. Simons." Then, Fraser repeated the statement that had so startled Herries earlier. "Anne deserves far more than she got when she married me. That's why I say she is contained, poised. Most of the time she conducts herself, even seems to conduct her very thoughts, as though my restless, often unreliable nature, my failure so far to accept the generous Couper offer that would assure her future security, were not driving her almost to distraction."

Herries stopped walking to look at him. "Anne Couper Fraser is—distracted? Forgive me. I truly can't conceive of that."

"Could we sit down over there on that mossy log?"

"Of course."

For quite some time they just sat there, Fraser's face buried in his hands, as though thinking through what he evidently felt compelled to say. Herries waited, fingering a pale pink moss blossom growing on the log. Innate good manners kept him from breaking the silence.

From a distance, the yells, commands, shouts, and laughter inside the courtyard told him that the games were beginning. As host, he should be there, would be expected to judge the victors in the caber toss, as well as in the hammer throw and the sheaf toss among the younger boys not yet strong enough to heave a caber. But he chose not to mention his duty as host to his obviously troubled new friend. He would wait.

A lark let fall a melody from the sky somewhere over their heads, one bolt of melody and then two. On the third lilting peal as the bird soared directly above them, Fraser asked softly, "Have you always heard that Caerlaverock in ancient Gaelic means lark's nest?"

Herries chuckled. "Aye, I've heard it all my life. The old pile was really a fortress, though."

"That's what I told Anne, but she will have none of it. Much prefers lark's nest over even the thought of a fortress. She hates the military in at least most of its aspects. Its only redeeming grace, according to her, is that had I not been an officer in the Royal Marines when the British captured an American island near her home island of St. Simons, she and I would never have met." He grinned impishly. "I captured her, you know—in all ways."

"You captured her literally?"

"In all ways," he repeated. "She and her Maxwell mother, her brother, and a young lady friend from St. Simons were attending a house party on Cumberland. Our contingent of marines under Admiral Cockburn took over the area, made our headquarters in the very mansion where she was being entertained. It is indeed the story of a miracle. Not that we captured the area. All the military action was simple for us. The miracle is that she goes on loving me as though I hadn't this restless, headstrong side to my nature. As though I had the courage to give genuine thought to accepting her father's generous offer."

Lord Herries waited a moment, then said, "I must admit your romance is most unusual and—real. As for your restless nature or even the nature of Mr. Couper's offer to you, I'm in total darkness, therefore mum. And, Fraser, it's against my nature to pry."

"You didn't pry. I brought up the entire subject, but aren't you the least bit curious?"

"Only if you feel strongly that you need to tell me."

"Excuse me, but somehow I didn't judge you to be such a reserved Britisher," Fraser said, thwarted. "I felt as giddy as a schoolboy let out at term's end marching about your courtyard, feeling certain that you were worldly enough not to stand on formality. Not to withdraw if I felt like opening up to you."

"I'm here, Fraser, and I'm listening."

The younger man studied him for a moment. "Did I only imagine a kind of reserve just went up between us? Am I touchy on the subject? Have I been among my outspoken, rowdy fellow officers too long? Did I misjudge you, Lord Herries, when I marched like a frisky calf in a meadow because I felt your signal for 'Fraser of Lovat's Salute' was also a signal to me?" After a moment, Fraser, somewhat flustered, grinned. "I feel very immature right now, but my instinct was that you'd understand why I feel lost and almost desperate—as though no one needs me anymore for my own sake. Except Anne, of course. I always know about Anne. Do you understand at all why I'm lost away from my regiment? I need a gentleman friend with some sense of the real world—a friend nearer my own age and kind."

"You've had no one with whom to talk about the decision you have to make? Or is it actually a decision? Do you have a choice about regaining your commission?"

John Fraser fell silent, then picked up a chunk of fallen bark and threw it. "Not a choice at the moment about my commission, it seems. I'm no longer needed in the Royal Marines, but I don't know how to live any other life. I do have a choice whether to accept or refuse a three-hundred-acre plantation on St. Simons Island and a house—as an outright gift. Of course, I've spoken with John Couper. The man's closer to me, far closer than my own father. But it is he who has made the magnanimous offer."

"*If* you'll bring Anne back to Georgia."

Fraser gave him a quick, almost startled look. "Aye."

"Couper may not boast about a distinguished clan behind him, but he's a canny Scot."

Fraser looked as though the thought had never crossed his mind. "Canny? I suppose he is, but can you believe me when I swear to you that he doesn't make me feel as though he's tricking me into accepting?"

"Having sensed Anne's directness, I think I can believe that. Do you know how to plant cotton, Fraser?"

His young friend clapped both hands to his head. "I know nothing whatever about planting cotton or corn or—or Dumfriesshire barley for that matter. Years ago, my own father tried to operate a farm only a few miles from here.

He tried desperately to make farmers out of my brother and me. My brother, William, is of a more philosophical bent than I. He maneuvered his way through boyhood holding his tongue, until he could begin medical training. I rebelled and only stopped rebelling when he and I became Royal Marines, he as a surgeon, I as a career officer. It's of no import whatever to William now that the country has no more need of our services, but the very foundations of my world have crumbled. My foundations are far less stable than all the ruins of Caerlaverock."

Herries was watching the well-shaped hands of the young man beside him as Fraser talked. The strong fingers made and unmade themselves into fists, not fists to do damage, rather showing the damage being done inside the man himself. Anyone could sense, could actually see, conflict in the clenching hands. Some shame, too, Herries felt sure, because much of John Fraser's vital self seemed taken up joyfully with the seldom-granted bliss of having found the one woman he loved, the incredibly spirited and intelligent woman who loved him with all her heart. What could he possibly say to Fraser? Anne had already startled him by being so sure that he could help her husband. Willy Maxwell had never fancied himself a counselor of any description, had only just met Fraser and felt unsure of his ground except to know in a surprisingly positive way that he liked both husband and wife immensely.

"I think first of all," he said haltingly, "that I'd like you to know how deeply I already regard you and Anne. She and I were quite comfortable talking to each other while you were giving us your marching demonstration."

"I hope I didn't embarrass you, sir. Somehow I thought you'd accept the performance for what it was—sheer horseplay."

"The truth is that in spite of Anne's spirited company, I longed to be marching with you, although I doubt my middle-aged legs would have allowed it. I'm already in my forties, Lieutenant, and I'd give almost anything I own if I could honestly say I'm devoted to even one interest equal to yours in the marines. I've spent my life in a fair amount of inherited luxury, but envying every man I've met with a passion for his work."

"You've never thought of farming the vast acreage around Caerlaverock?"

"Not really. I'm sentimental about every ancient kilometer of it," he said, looking about him beyond the moat in the direction of the road that led to the Solway Firth. "There have been offers from others to farm it, but I already own so much Dumfriesshire land, I see no reason to detract from the romance of Caerlaverock's setting, do you?"

John laughed a little. "I'm afraid I seldom, if ever, think of despoiling any acres with a plow. Love changes many things, though. At least, loving Anne as I do has brought my very first deeply personal battle. She will stay beside me wherever I decide to work, but I'm beginning to see that half the joy of loving is in making the loved one happy. Though sheltered, my wife is a highly intelligent woman. True intelligence, my father always says, can be measured by how flexible a human being can be under all circumstances." John's short laugh was almost a snort. "The old man's theory doesn't apply to him, though, because I know him to be a gentleman of high intelligence, with fine taste in wines, art, architecture, a constant reader, but he's about as flexible as a ramrod."

"A wine merchant in London, isn't he?"

"You did quite a lot of research on the family, didn't you, sir?"

"My friends call me Willy. Anne is obliging me. I hope you will."

"My pleasure, Willy," John said easily. "Do you make your permanent home in Scotland? Down the road at Terragles?"

"Not at Terragles, no. When I'm not knocking about the world, I live some of the year in smoky old Londontown. I really can't think why I haven't met up with your father socially. He is still active in wine importing, isn't he?"

"Oh, yes, he goes to business every day and works very hard and conscientiously, but the man is in need of help from someone who can get around London more easily than he, seeking out new clients who have the means to purchase only the best French, Italian, German, and Spanish wines. My father finds it impossible to admit, but I sense he needs help. A younger man. I have no real hopes of making a difference for him. He and I have never spoken of it once since Anne and I came over from Georgia, but I—I need to feel useful to someone."

"Are you and your father close?"

Fraser looked directly at him and with no hesitation said simply, "No. We've never been. My brother, William, now in love with a St. Simons girl and probably making his permanent home there, has always been Father's favorite."

"If my questions grow too personal, feel no need to answer, but is there no chance your father will become dependent on you and think of as canny a way as Mr. Couper's offer of a plantation in order to keep you in London?"

"That, Willy, is the last thing about which I need to worry! Father is devoted to Anne. She's made him smile, even laugh, for the first time since my mother died some ten years ago, but it's Anne he depends on, not her husband."

"I must say you surprise me, Lieutenant. There's certainly nothing in your manner or your extraordinarily striking appearance to indicate that you hold yourself in such low esteem."

Fraser got slowly to his feet and stood looking down at Herries, his face genuinely perplexed. "Low esteem?" The short laugh held no mirth in it. "I've been called arrogant, even cocky, but have never before been accused of lacking self-esteem!"

On his feet, too, now, Herries again laid his hand on John's arm. "I say, I'm sorry! I've gone too far, but I want you to know that I haven't missed the point of what you've been telling me. You are faced with finding a totally different means of earning your livelihood, isn't that it? Yet the only thing you want to do is to return to your marine unit."

The tall young man turned to look back toward the valley that stretched north in the direction of old Criffel. "Thank you for being astute, sir, and believe me, that isn't sarcasm. God knows my beloved Anne is painfully aware that rejoining my unit is all I really want, but—"

"—but it helps when an almost total stranger senses it too," Herries finished for him. "It's more than having a sense of your dilemma, Lieutenant. You see, out of the morass of superficiality and pretense that clog the social life I live, I meet few people as honest and direct as you and Anne. I can't think of one right now and almost no gentleman who even cares whether or not he's found work he loves. Unless there's inherited money, the men I know only work at all in order to live beyond their means. Oh, there is one who shows almost unceasing devotion to his work—a writer, actually. Walter Scott earns good money in the practice of law, but the man lives these days to write his books and is like a child in letting it be known near and far that he thrives on it, both financially and emotionally."

"Willy, are you really a friend of the famous poet-novelist Walter Scott?"

"Walter and I've been friends for years. We knew each other as boys right here in the old Borderlands. The young Walter Scott was unflagging in his effort to overcome his lameness at his grandfather's farm near Kelso and thought little of fifty-mile walks to Dumfries with a strong, young servant in tow. You know, in his novel *Guy Mannering,* he patterned his old castle Ellangowan after Caerlaverock. Walter loves this place still."

"I say!" Young Fraser's dazzling smile revealed his sheer delight. "You've just given me an amazing gift, Willy, my new friend! Anne will be beside herself with joy when I tell her. She's done most of her reading under an Oxford-trained tutor who swears by Walter Scott's work. Oh, he worships first at the shrine of Shakespeare, of course, but Anne reads Walter Scott regularly." He shook his head. "It's beyond me, but she even likes that heavy-booted *Lady of the Lake."*

"Then, we'll surprise her. I doubt that a copy of Walter's *Guy Mannering,* just published late last year, has made its way to her remote Georgia island yet, but I have one with me. The old boy even autographed it. I'll give it to the lovely Anne this very evening before you head back for Dumfries."

Chapter 49

They had been back in London for well over a month before John found enough courage to invite his father to join him for a glass of wine after an important business meeting that afternoon, which John knew would take Father Fraser to a part of town near London Bridge.

"You've been paying more attention than I thought, son," his father said at breakfast on the muggy, early August morning as Flora McLeod hovered over them, seeing to their every need. "I had no idea you'd remember my meeting today at the Vintners' Company."

"We always pay attention when you tell us something that's important to you, Father Fraser," Anne said brightly. "Don't we, John?" John saw her reach to pat her father-in-law's slender, brown-spotted hand. "This meeting certainly sounds important."

"Well," Father Fraser mused, his long, thin face almost pleasant, "at least my son is aware of what part of London my business takes me today. And if you like, John, I'll gladly meet you at my favorite wine house near there. If this day's encounters are as harrowing as I expect them to be, I'll be ready for a drop."

"And John's already told me he wants to take you there," Anne said. "I can't think of its name, but it's wonderfully English and the place is old and mostly left untouched for two centuries or more."

"Aye, Anne, dear," Father Fraser said in the affectionate tone he reserved only for her. " 'Tis owned by my old friend Sprague, a free vintner. Called the Olde Wine Shades." He folded his napkin and got to his feet. "Four o'clock, son?"

"Fine, Father," John said, rising too. "Can I do anything, run some errand for you before we meet?"

"Nothing, thank you," his father said before kissing Anne's hand gallantly. "I trust you won't mind taking tea this afternoon without us, my dear."

"Of course, I'll mind! I'll miss you both, but Flora McLeod and I will do just fine, won't we, Flora?"

"Aye, Miss Anne."

"Gude," John's father said, nodding to Flora as he headed for the entrance hall to pick up his top hat.

"Don't forget your umbrella, sir," Flora called after him. "It can come down in buckets on any August day and we don't allow sneezes in this house."

When they heard the front door close, John said to Flora and Anne, irony in his voice, "You see, my father has great need of me." Then, he made himself smile, the smile that never failed to work with Flora and almost never with Anne. "I trust the two of you can fare without me, because I've waited as long as I dare to pay another visit to my headquarters today. You have your novel *Guy Mannering,* anyway, Annie, and I know this is Flora's baking day."

"Is there a special reason to go all the way to headquarters?" Anne asked.

"Aye, lass," he said, helping her to her feet. "I'm a bit worried. It isn't at all like the unit paymaster to be late with even my enormous half pay. Frankly, I need it today if I'm to host Father at the Olde Wine Shades this afternoon."

"Wasn't last month's pay here when we got home from Scotland?" Anne asked.

"Think back. Have I taken you for one carriage ride since we reached London? Have we done anything that cost even a shilling?"

" 'Tis a rotten shame," Flora grumbled from the doorway, holding a tray of dishes she'd just removed from the table. "Nearly ten long years of your life you gave to that precious unit of yours, Johnnie! That's the English for ya', carin' naught but for carousin' an' ridin' their mighty steeds an' sailin' their warships. Ten long years of your gude, st-r-rong, young life an' them a' holdin' back your pitiful pay like this!"

"Oh, Flora, I'm sure there's just been an error somewhere," Anne said. "Please go right on, dearest. Flora McLeod and I will be fine. You're right, I'll read my wonderful Scott novel and Flora will create her scrumptious bread and—"

John saw the blood drain from Anne's face as she clutched the back of her chair. "Flora—she looks so pale! Is something wrong, Annie?"

"No! Absolutely nothing. I—I'm sure I just tried to stand up too quickly. I'm fine. I want both of you to go about your business."

His arm around Anne's waist, John told Flora he supposed they'd just have to believe her. Flora only shook her head and made a clicking sound with her tongue as she headed downstairs.

"I won't be gone long," he said to Anne, still supporting her. "I promise. I'll simply file my late complaint and ask if Captain Menzies is in the London office this week. If he's there, I'm sure he can expedite matters. I'll try very hard to come back here before time to meet Father at four."

"Please go, darling. It would be foolish for you to come all the way back across town. I'll be fine and you know without my telling you that I'll be right here waiting."

"Anne, I wouldn't be going at all if it weren't so important. I need my money. Are you sure you aren't ill? Here, let me help you into the parlor. Isn't that where you left *Guy Mannering* last night when we went upstairs?"

He could feel her struggling to laugh normally. "Yes. Yes, I left *Guy* in the parlor. And will you kindly oblige me by going so you can come back?"

He led her to the little parlor armchair, its rose and green colors faded with the years since his mother had worked its needlepoint cover. It was the one chair Anne had made her own, much to his father's pleasure. "There," he said. "Better?"

"Of course," Anne answered. "I'll be better still if you'll hand *Guy* to me. Walter Scott has really made his Ellangowan castle a lot like Caerlaverock."

John handed her the book, even opened it to the place she had marked with a piece of scarlet ribbon. "You know I wouldn't leave you if I didn't have to."

"Yes, yes, I know." She took a deep, heavy breath. "I know how important it is to you."

"To us, dearest," he whispered, leaning down to kiss her housecap, then her forehead. "Please be all right, Annie, please!"

"I'm fine. I really am. I think I just ate too much breakfast. Blame Flora. I shouldn't have had two muffins, but they tasted so good with honey. I can't seem to eat enough sweet things. Will you still love me when I'm fat?"

From the parlor, Anne heard Flora's affectionate, curt admonitions to John about the look of rain in the sky and his teasing assurances that he loved rain; then, within seconds, Flora was standing beside Anne's chair. Without looking up from her book, she knew the big woman stood as straight as a pine. She also knew that Flora wouldn't say a word until Anne spoke to her.

"I did feel queasy," she said, "but it's your fault. No one can bake muffins to compare with yours. I ate too many."

"That's twaddle, Miss Anne, and you ken it is. I watched. You ate no more than any other day and you near scared my boy out of his wits by your color drainin' out the way it did. Look up here at me."

Anne obeyed. "See? I'm fine. I just ate too much and then got up too fast."

"I might swallow such talk if you was about fifty years older than you are. Young girls don't get dauncy from standin' up too quick. An' I know you still feel queasy this minute. Nobody ever gained ought by fibbin' to Flora McLeod. How many months have you missed?"

Not only did Anne feel queasy again, she felt downright sick and with all her heart she wished Flora would go back downstairs to her kitchen. She would also be scared half out of her skin if the woman left her. John had warned her that Flora had a sixth sense about when she was being lied to, even in jest, so why not reach for the help she so desperately needed? The whole room was whirling.

" 'Tis plain as the nose on your face you're more than dauncy," Flora was saying again in her Flora way, which was both tender and cross. "Only you know, Miss Anne, how many times you missed."

"Two, Flora—*two,*" Anne gasped.

The big woman sighed with relief. "Then what's wrong with you ain't bad. 'Tis *the blessing* for you and mi'laddie. What you need is a cold cloth." From the door, Flora commanded, "Bend over and hold your head between your knees till I get back up them stairs."

In desperation, Anne did as she was told and tried to

think only of the words Flora had used—" 'Tis *the blessing* for you and mi'laddie."

What made no sense to Anne, sitting there with her head hanging between her knees, was that she was thinking of Flora's muffins and honey. This dreadful sickness would surely pass if their first baby was causing it. Praying not to make a mess on the carpet, she would have laughed had she been able to because at this precarious moment, she actually wanted more muffins and honey! Was this the way Mama felt the day she and James Hamilton and Anne and Anna Matilda had to pile into Papa's big plantation boat at Cumberland and head over that heavy, heaving water all the way back to their own dock at Cannon's Point? If Mama felt like this that morning, all Anne could think now was how selfish and preoccupied with her own thoughts she'd been, concerned only about why John hadn't come to tell her good-bye.

The heavy, rapid clump of Flora's shoes on the stairs was making glorious music when almost as quickly as the morning sickness had come, it began to fade. Her head cleared a little, then a little more, and when Flora huffed and puffed into the parlor, the clean, cold cloth applied under Anne's chin took care of what surely must be the last wave of nausea.

"Oh-h, thank you, dear Flora McLeod! How can I ever thank you? Please tell me what I can do for you. If John gets his pay today, can you think of anything we could buy for you the next time we go for a walk?" Holding the wet cloth under her own chin now, she was not only sitting straight up in the chair, she had grasped Flora's hand in one of her wet ones. "I'm sure he'll be paid today, so anything—just anything to show you my gratitude—not only for the cold cloth but for knowing *why* I felt so sick!"

Standing as though at attention, Flora snorted, "Pooh! 'Twasn't nothing I did. 'Tis the good Lord that's sent the blessing. He tends to all the other bad mornings, too, you'll see. They'll come, but they'll also pass."

"The other ones?"

"Seven months' time holds a heap of mornings, Miss Anne. Ain't you watched your own ma through the birth of your baby sister, Isabella?"

"Yes, but I—I guess she mostly stayed in her room. I do remember having breakfast alone with my tutor and Papa a lot. But, can't you think of anything, even some little gift we could get for you when John gets paid?"

"Laddie needs his money, but that ain't his main reason for hightailing it to his headquarters and you'll find the work of bringin' a new life into the worl' a mite easier if you face up to things the very way they are, child. That man of yours, my Johnnie, really ain't gonna rest none till he knows if they do or if they don't want his dear self back in them Royal Marines."

"Do—do we have to talk about that now?"

"No'm, but do ya' ken what I mean?"

"Yes. I was just trying to get you talking about something else."

Flora came close to a real laugh. "One thing my laddie don't have to fret over is you not tellin' him the blunt truth. I like that in you, Miss Anne. Lets a body know where she stands. Lets Johnnie know where he stands too. Never was anything to cause him more trouble in his heart than not knowin' somethin' he was itchin' to find out. His ma knowed that about the boy. His father was always too stubborn to learn it."

Anne held Flora's hand to her own cheek. "My heart wants very much to say thank you with something you can use or just keep to remember the morning you helped me through such a scary and wonderful time!"

Flora took Anne's hand just long enough to give it an affectionate smack. "The best giftie you kin ever make Flora McLeod, Miss Anne, is to give mi'laddie a fine, healthy baby —a lass or a lad. You do that and anything I kin ever do to help you will be pur-re pleasure for me."

"Oh, I want to give John the healthiest, most beautiful baby in the whole world! I hadn't thought much about it yet, but now that you and I have had our time together, now that I know I'm carrying his child, I want to be the best mother who ever lived anywhere, in any century in all of human history!"

Now Flora did permit herself a real chuckle. " 'Tain't no wonder you an' mi'laddie is a good match the way you do both carry on."

"Flora, I told a white lie just now. I have been thinking a lot about giving John a child, but I guess you already knew that."

"Aye. 'Tis only nachural. An' you're as scared as you are

happy. The Almighty saw fit not to give me bairns meself, but Laddie's ma, Miss Margaret, felt free every day of her life with me. I ken. Mi'laddie's going to be a handful when he finds out. 'Twould be best for you, ma'am, not to shut yourself off from me. I'm here. 'Tis my job and my sun rises every day for Johnnie. Now, for you, too. You might as well start leanin' on Flora McLeod. Your own ma bein' way off in Georgia lak she is."

"Flora, thank you! I do need my mother and I am afraid, but far less now because you know too. What we have to think about, though, is John's meeting this afternoon with Father Fraser. I feel much better and I'll try not to worry about myself. John and I have a pact that we're going to take everything one day at a time. I'll tell him the minute he gets home about our baby, but the important thing is that he and Father Fraser will find a way to talk to each other. I mean really talk."

At the hall door, Flora stopped to look back at her. "I say hallelujah, ma'am! You may have been born in Georgia on the other side of the water, but your pure Scottish blood is showin' when you speak such wisdom as that."

Chapter 50

By half past three that afternoon, John was waiting in the dark, low-ceilinged public room of Sprague's Olde Wine Shades in Martin Lane. He felt both nervous and expansive. He had been paid at the barnlike London headquarters of his marine unit two hours ago. Father would be his guest and he'd already ordered good French Burgundy, a crock of soft cheese, and a basket of crusty rolls. Wine could be bought by the drink, and James Fraser would undoubtedly have approved the frugality, but John hated halfway measures and so had ordered a full bottle, which stood uncorked now on the narrow, age-blackened wooden table. No connoisseur would even taste wine that had not been allowed to breathe before pouring. His father was a man of excellent taste. It was pompous, actually, to have dared select a wine until he got there. John had done it deliberately. For a man almost twenty-five to go on struggling for his father's approval was ridiculous.

Fingers drumming nervously on the scarred, old table, both the wine and the cheese untouched, he made no effort to prepare himself for the meeting, which, so far as he knew, had only one purpose—to offer his inexperienced services in the family business. Father, of course, would open their visit by asking point-blank if John had been given any hope at headquarters today of being needed again in the marines. He had not. The young officer did apologize for the lateness of his pay, and John had loitered around the building for well over an hour, hoping for even a chance meeting with other inactive officer friends, for some kind of contact with almost anyone who might be of help to him. No luck. The room where it was possible to inquire about future reinstatement was closed and locked. From the pay officer he had learned that Lieutenant Basil Hall, whose family Father knew from the old days when, as a young man, he was courting young Margaret Thompson at her family home in Prestonpans near Edinburgh, was still in service. Hall was off exploring this very month for the Navy somewhere in the China Seas. A surge of envy caused John to rub both hands over his face as though to wipe away even the thought of how much he would like to be standing today in Lieutenant Basil Hall's boots.

British need for exploration went on, of course, because it was necessary to the expansion of the Empire, which appeared at least not to have need anytime soon of a man with John's battle experience.

He took out his watch. Father, prompt to a fault, would not think of walking through the door at the Olde Wine Shades one minute before the appointed time of four o'clock. Fifteen minutes left to wait, and as always, when he felt restless or anxious, his thoughts flew to Anne.

Anne.

What was she doing back at 2 George Street this minute? How did she feel? Perhaps she'd caught a summer cold. Had she and Flora had one of their woman talks? Were they discussing him? He could be thankful at least that Flora made no bones about being genuinely fond of Anne. Flora McLeod was the nearest to a mother he had now and what Flora thought of his wife mattered. That Anne returned Flora's affections was plain. As plain as was his father's seemingly total devotion to her. Father does approve my choice of a life's partner, he thought.

The expression *life's partner* set the conflict stirring again. He could not imagine one day of all the remainder of his life without Anne at the heart of it. How could a man survive for long being split down the middle? Did the part of him agitating even now to return to his unit care nothing about Anne's peace of mind? A wife could not live aboard ship with her officer husband!

The straight, high-backed wooden bench in the shadowy corner pen he'd selected began to close in on him. There was barely room for his knees under the table. Sprague's Olde Wine Shades was almost two centuries old, but hadn't men always needed room to stretch their legs? Even the walls moved in toward him, crowding him, their smoky oil paintings and sketches too close.

He could *not* have Anne and the work he craved too! The only way he could support her, be with her and the family he longed for, as a member of the Royal Marines would be by squeezing himself into an office at headquarters for the remainder of his days. He loathed the thought of that and probably would turn it down even if an offer came.

Of course, such a job would put him once more back in uniform, would give him a chance to take part in an occasional parade. He would again be welcomed into the camaraderie and revelry of the old Officers Club as an active member. While working daily—going to business much as Father had always done—with a headquarters commission, he could also come home to Anne at night. At least until the chance came to go to sea again.

Turning on the wooden bench, he looked beyond the few customers toward the narrow, inconspicuous front door for his father. To his relief, relief that made him feel a bit ashamed, there was no sign of him. Another check of his watch and he saw that there would undoubtedly be no sign of him for at least five more minutes.

In the cozy, shadowy old room, overwhelming the bouquet from huge barrels of tawny port over the wine bar, the fresh, flower scent of Anne wafted about him. Even when they were apart, many times a day, without warning, the essence of her came to him and for those moments, all conflict lessened. As a younger man, he had surely thrived in the marines, but now he also needed Anne.

The two lives he wanted did not mesh. How, he wondered, do other officers manage to live for such long stretches of time away from their wives, their children? He longed for children but had no idea how a man could learn to be a good father when lengthy absences kept him away during the years in which a son or daughter was growing up.

"Lieutenant!" The quiet but somewhat urgent voice of the bartender broke his reverie. "Your father's here, sir."

John jumped to his feet and made use of his best public smile as he held out his hand. "Father! I figured you'd be right on time. It's so hot outside, did the walk from the Vintners' Company seem long? Sit down, sit down."

His father returned John's handshake, sat opposite him, and before he answered, picked up the Burgundy and examined the label—making note, John knew, of the year, the French winery, and, of course, the British importer.

"You must be thirsty," Father Fraser said. "No man needs all this wine on a steamy summer afternoon. But you made an excellent choice. Have you waited long? You did say four o'clock."

"Not long at all," John said, half filling both their glasses. "Did your meeting at the Vintners' Company go well, sir?"

"No, but as well as I had any right to expect, considering the heedless way in which most men conduct business these days. How did it go with you at headquarters? Did they pay you?"

"Oh, yes, sir. The delay was some sort of clerical error, I believe. You're my guest, Father, so I hope you'll drink hearty, and do help yourself to those delicious-looking buns and cheese. I ordered sharp cheddar. I thought you might approve."

"You knew, of course, that I would. My favorite. Did you receive any hope of being taken back into your unit?"

John caught his breath sharply, then fell back on the smile and forced himself to wait a few seconds before answering. Father had always needed careful handling. It was far from easy to lounge casually against a straight-backed bench, but he tried. "To answer your question, sir, no. The officer in charge was not even in the building today. But that isn't why I asked you to meet me. I am trying to accept the handwriting on the wall at headquarters. In spite of my considerable record, His Highness simply does not need fighting men right now."

After raising his glass briefly to John, the older man took a critical sip, nodded satisfaction, and then asked as though it were no more than a question about the weather, "And does that mean you've given up on this foolishness about gaining back your commission?"

"Given up, Father? I—I don't think so."

"I see."

"What is it exactly that you see?"

"Do you mean beyond my chagrin that you intend to go on torturing Anne?"

He had in no way expected an easy meeting. John had invited his father today for the express purpose of offering, even in some small way, to help out in the business, to show his appreciation for the older man's hospitality. But after being accused of torturing Anne, he could only stare at his parent and try not to drown in despair at ever being able to converse with this man free of barbs and sparring.

The elder Fraser broke one of the large buns, slowly spread it with cheddar, took a bite, chewed carefully, then—looking straight at John as he seldom did—asked, "Is your clumsy silence due to some lack of mine or simply that, however unbelievable it may be, you hadn't given a thought to the pain you cause Anne by refusing to settle down and make something of your life?"

As though by a sudden time warp, John was shot like an arrow back to boyhood. He sat there in a heap of childlike helplessness, desperate for one gentle, understanding word from the father who not only had always favored William but was now attacking him out of what appeared to be deep concern for Anne.

Struggling to right himself, he thought, well, if he's never going to like me, at least he's doggedly loyal to my wife, who *does.*

"Son? Were you not listening to my question?"

"Uh—yes, sir. I—I heard it all too clearly." As far back as he could remember, John had never tried outright honesty with his father. Neither had he been consciously dishonest. He had only tried to charm or manipulate his way through every tangled, stilted talk they'd ever had. As thwarted as he felt this moment, as downright fearful of the stern man across the table, he decided to say exactly what he was thinking, nothing more and nothing less.

But before he could speak, his father pressed his question. "Then, son, if you heard it all clearly, could you bring yourself to honor me with an answer?"

"Yes, sir. I know William has always been your favorite. Now, before you attempt to deny that," John said, holding up one hand to make sure his father didn't interrupt, "I also have to be sure you know that your preferring William has in no way ever—not once—come between my brother and me. In fact, right up until he and Mr. Couper waved Anne and me off on our voyage over here, he and I were able to discuss the whole situation freely. He knows it's true and he knows that I know you're partial to him over me."

"Since you're being blunt, I'll be blunt too. I'm glad that's been the case. Glad you and William have stayed close. I have wondered about it often. I wondered aloud, in fact, many times to your dear mother."

Something resembling a tiny ray of hope moved in John. His father still spoke in his dour, formal manner, but he was going to believe that what Father had just said was not only true, but that saying it had somehow been of help to the older man, too. At least, it gave John the courage to go on with what had to be said. He had come to make himself available to his father—and even if James Fraser turned him down, he meant to do it.

After clearing his throat a bit more than necessary, John said, "Thank you, Father, for telling me that you spoke to Mother about your concern over me. Even if I do seem to be unwilling to settle down, as you say, and make something of my life, I am a grown man and I find I have to be sure you'll listen to what I have to say as coming, not from a boy who has always managed to charm or talk or wiggle his way through any difficult predicament, but from what I believe myself to be—a grown man."

After another long, maddening pause during which he spread a second crust of bun with cheese, then took his time eating it, his father said, "I promise to listen to a grown man, John. A grown man whose military record has made me feel proud, in spite of my own conviction that war is futile."

Such frankness, from the man whose deepest self had always been a mystery, emboldened him. "I say!" John exclaimed. "I'm more pleased than you might believe that you were proud of my record! And I've always known you don't believe a country needs to defend itself with arms."

"I believe in necessary defense but not attack. And most of all, I expect diplomatic negotiation can accomplish more in the long run. Not that I have any reason to think that *our* nattering old diplomats know what they're doing."

"It's—it's good to be able to discuss such things with you, Father," John said a bit impatiently. "We've done little enough of it in the past, but I do want to answer your question about Anne—about my causing her pain. Surely you know that's the last thing I'd ever do willingly."

"If you're questioning my belief about your love for her, stop. I know you love her, John. And since your mother left me, there isn't a man on earth more aware of the enveloping necessity of love. Real, enduring, self-sacrificing love. You do love Anne Couper Fraser. The question is, with what kind of love? Love that considers Anne? Or love that inflates your pride and gives *you* happiness?"

"Did Anne put you up to this?" John blurted. He could have bitten off his tongue! He could not have said a worse thing, so braced himself for the tirade he had every right to expect.

Nothing came. Twirling the dark-red liquid in his glass, the older man sat there quietly, giving him a curious but definitely unaccusing look.

There will now ensue another of his maddening silences, John thought, feeling himself snap shut like a clam in its shell. Just when hope seemed almost palpable, just when he was almost convinced that maybe, after all these years, they were going to be able to talk to each other, Father was pulling one of his tricks. What the man intended the trick to accomplish he had no idea, so decided to wait him out. He could be just as canny. After all, he was James Fraser's son.

Let him sit there, let him take all the time he needs to cut me down to size, the shrinking-boy size that has always given him the upper hand but won't this time. If I'm to prove my manhood to him, now is the moment. I can fall silent, too. I'm as stubborn as he is. To my own satisfaction, I've proved myself during the past ten years in the service to be as sly as he or any other Scot!

The silence went on for such a long time, John began to feel blood pounding in his head. All but two other patrons had left the dimly lit winehouse, so that, except for an occasional clink of glass from the counter in front of the rows of casks, a bit of laughter from somewhere across the room, the place was quiet. Quiet, that is, until the wine tender, working halfheartedly at the end of his wide counter nearest their table, asked casually, "Is business going well, Mr. Fraser? I've heard nothing but praise from our patrons who've sampled your latest shipment of Bordeaux. Your ties must be as close as ever with the vineyards there. The Moselle, too, for that matter."

"Aye, I have good cooperation in France," his father answered, somewhat annoyed. " 'Twould be still better could I but trust the young Londoners who work on a part-time basis for me. By the way, has one of them been by lately to check your port casks?"

"Not since last month, sir. They're past due for checking."

"Very well. Thank you for telling me," Father Fraser said, the terse tone in his voice dismissing the wine tender as surely as though he'd said "Enough, now leave us."

Still, John waited. The Olde Wine Shades employee had given him the perfect opening by which to make his offer to help out should his father have need of him, but he said nothing, determined that his parent would make the next gesture toward him.

More time went by. John drained his glass, then refilled it. Still without a word, he held out the bottle toward his father, who made no move beyond placing his hand over his own partially emptied glass.

Finally, James Fraser said the last thing John expected. "I thought I was giving your mother the kind of unselfish love I hope you can learn to show Anne. I now see I dinna' even know its meaning."

Stunned, John simply didn't know what to say. "I'm afraid I have no idea how to respond to that, Father."

"You were a relatively young boy, as was William, when I allowed myself to be persuaded to sell our house and land in Dumfriesshire, give up the moderately lucrative wine business I conducted on the side there, along with farming, and drag my entire family, poor Flora McLeod included, to London. There's no good excuse for what I did, except that man-to-man, John, I can now admit that I was a rotten farmer but still young enough to hold big ambitions. The weak condition these days of my London importing firm, I can also admit, is my own fault. Somehow I failed as a father to influence either of my sons to learn importing *or* farming along with me. I understand the purchase of fine wines, get along well with my London clients, but I'm needed in my office to handle the business correspondence, keep accounts, and so on. Unless I can find a younger man willing and able to obtain new business for me, I may have to give up."

Never in his years as James Fraser's son had John seen his father appear powerless, but the man sat now with both palms up and out on the table, as close as his pride would let him come to crying for help.

"Have you wondered why I asked you here today, Father?"

"Aye, almost constantly since this morning."

"In view of what you've just told me—which I'd already

suspected—in plain view of what I know to be your opinion of me as a possible businessman, I want to offer my services to you at no salary. Your kindness to Anne and me has not gone unnoticed. My paltry half pay will cover our personal needs." Then, surprising even himself, John managed his disarming public smile, the one he used when he felt helpless. "Is your financial crisis desperate enough to accept me, Father? To give me a chance? If charm sells wine, if perseverance strengthens dealer contacts for an importer, I'm not afraid to match mine against any man's. I'm downright scared of business, of ever grasping its essence, but I'm afraid of no man when it comes to convincing him of"—he laughed a little—"of almost anything."

When his father finally spoke again, it was as though John had said nothing at all. "Your mother did everything her wise, mild character allowed in order to convince me not to move my family away from Dumfriesshire. As you know, I plunged ahead. After that, not once did she even hint that she did not hold complete confidence in my plans. She loved me with an unselfish love. I did not love her that way, but believe me, Son, I *thought* I did."

John could only stare across the narrow table at the inscrutable, aging face, giving his father all the time he needed to speak of his love for Margaret Thompson Fraser, the warmest, merriest, dearest mother a man ever had. In fact, hearing Father speak of her to him, as he knew he'd spoken often to William, caused John to long for him to go on.

Not one more word was said of her. In a quiet, oddly trusting, now almost affectionate tone, his father said, "Aye, Son, I accept your generous offer."

"You do?"

"On one condition. I'm not yet totally depleted financially. You will be paid a modest salary so that you will not be humiliated with blessed Anne. Am I to assume you've discussed this with her?"

"No. No, I haven't—well, not specifically."

"I see."

"Again, I have to ask—what is it you see? Anne is so fond of you. She'll be quite happy for us to stay on here in London with you until I can—can find a way of my own to support her. To support her and the children I hope for someday."

"One thing I see is that you made this offer without fully

consulting her. You're still very young in many ways, Son. I also see that perhaps only the passing of years, or with men as stubborn as I am, only crushing grief, has the power to mature a man's love. Trouble or great joy or, again as with me, shattering loss can turn a man's love for a woman from mere glowing romance to God's kind of oneness."

Such talk about the quality of John's love for Anne frightened him far more than anything else his stern, surprising parent had ever said or left unsaid. When his father looked at his watch, John searched for a way to keep him talking. So much seemed left dangling.

"But I—I love Anne with all my heart, sir!"

His father nodded. "I know you think you do. I did too. And I want you to know I'm rather looking forward to working with you. Giving it a try won't prevent your reentering the service should the opportunity arise. I also want you to know that. We'll just do what we can to salvage some accounts for as long as we have."

His parent took one more sip and began to slide himself stiffly toward the end of the wooden bench. They were going to leave. John *had* to hold him there.

"Father, do you question the—the true nature of my love for Anne because I still long so to return to my unit? Is that why you consider me selfish?"

"I don't question the nature of your love for her. I understand it. I just don't want you to wait too long to begin to think first of Anne, then of yourself. I want to save you the unbearable pain of finding out when it's too late." James Fraser got to his feet. "Don't try to pay for our refreshment, John. Sprague and I have an arrangement."

"I did get paid today, sir," John protested, feeling a bit demeaned since it was he who had invited his father. But he also felt so relieved that, at least temporarily, he could tell Anne he had work, he tried to be gracious, adding pleasantly that had he known he would be the guest, he'd certainly not have ordered a full bottle of wine.

As the two climbed into a hackney cab, his father asked, "Would I be interfering to inquire about this plantation on St. Simons Island, which Anne's father has offered you as a wedding present?"

John had certainly not expected that, but he kept his voice casual. "What would you like to know, beyond the fact that it's a fertile, quite beautiful piece of land with a good, small house and a marsh view? The place is called Lawrence. It adjoins Cannon's Point."

"And has Couper given you a time limit in which to make up your mind or to learn once and for all if you'll ever be allowed to recapture your commission?"

"No, sir. There's no time limit. Mr. Couper is the most affable of men. In spite of my having told him repeatedly that I'd be the world's worst planter and slave manager, he simply made the offer and told me to take all the time I needed to think it through. Mr. Couper lost slaves to the British, but he vows he and his son can spare some for me to use. Whether or not I could become a slave owner I honestly don't know."

"You don't feel as warmly about coastal Georgia as William does, I take it."

"Oh, but I do! Father, especially if William is successful in marrying Miss Frances Anne Wylly, you must visit. The mild weather is bound to help your rheumatism. You walk well, but I couldn't help noticing the trouble you had climbing up into this chariot."

They rode for a time in silence. Finally, his father said out of what must have been much thought, "There's no chance for me to visit anywhere right now, John. I've tried to keep it from you and Anne, but unless you and I find a way to rescue it, I'm going to lose my importing business."

"It's that bad?"

"Aye, and as usual, I've failed to thank you properly for offering to help."

John turned on the cab seat to stare at him. "I'm the one to be grateful, sir!"

"I see no reason why we need to tell Anne or Flora the true state of things, though, do you? I don't plan to write William."

Even more amazed, John asked, "You *don't*?"

"If the boy has found the young lady blessed enough to become his wife, I have no intention of allowing my troubles to worry him. Of course, there's never been any thought of his coming into business with me. Even on a temporary basis of the kind you and I have agreed on. William is a physician. He's never had any question in his mind about his profession. And John, I know you have no question either. By some freak of nature, unfortunately, you seem born to be an officer."

John said nothing because no words could possibly let his father know, not only the extent of his gratitude for such unexpected understanding, but his downright surprise. And relief. It was as though the Red Sea had opened before him, as though a smooth, unobstructed new road lay ahead. Where it would lead he had no notion. At this moment, the relief and joy he felt were too great for thought.

"Odd," his father said with just the hint of a wry smile, "for you, of all men, to be at a loss for words, but I accept it. I also accept your love of your unit. I don't approve of, or believe in, such a life, but at long last I find I can accept it. Do you mean to begin collecting, taking new orders for the firm tomorrow, Son?"

"Oh, yes, sir! Any time you say."

"And you agree that dear Anne need not know of the severity of *our* money crisis?"

"If you say so, but Anne is strong. And so devoted to you. I'm sure she'd want to know."

"I'm also sure I don't want her to know right now. Not until you and I have had time to find out what we can do to save the business. I can't offer you an officer's commission, John, but I can offer you a place to live and enough money to care for your wife." He held out his hand. "And also my gratitude for your good sense in realizing how much I needed help."

"Father," John said, "I'm the one to thank you and I do—oh, I do! In fact, I can't wait for this hack to pull up at the house so that I can tell Anne I now have work to do."

Chapter 51

After tea that afternoon, so that she would look her very best for the still almost unbelievable news she would tell John the minute he reached home, Anne went upstairs to their room to bathe and change into the cool, pale pink lawn dress Flora had washed and ironed.

As always, when she was fussing with her hair, or sometimes out of the blue, Anne's thoughts went to Eve. Today, in spite of the warmth and understanding Flora had offered when Anne knew for certain that she was carrying John's child, she missed Eve more than ever. Mama hadn't mentioned one word about Eve's having given June a baby and until she had become sure about her own today, Anne hadn't given a thought to whether Eve and June might now be parents. Actually, as she was seated at her dressing table having some of the same old Eve-less trouble with her hair, the idea of Eve with a child still struck her as peculiar. To Anne, Eve somehow, although blindly, wholly in love with June, had always been complete in herself. Eve's slender, perfectly formed body bulging with a baby just did not fit her impression of Eve.

Oh dear, she thought. I'm going to bulge, too! What on earth will I do so far away from home without Fanny to make new dresses for me? One thing I know is that unless John begins to get his pay, I'll soon have to write Papa for money for new clothes!

That caused her to remember the letter she'd received last week from Louisa Shaw, enclosing money and asking Anne to buy a certain kind of British corset to send to her on Cumberland. She'd have to ask Flora how to find the right London shop. It was true that they had stayed close to

2 George Street since their return from Scotland. Anne did not know London shops. Poor, dear, embarrassed John! Anything was easier than seeing him humiliated by lack of funds, even though he managed to make light of it.

She heard the front door close downstairs and John's excited voice calling up to her. "Annie! Annie, where are you? I'm home!"

On her feet, leaning down to be sure her curls were in place securely enough not to have to wear a housecap, because he liked her best without one, she smoothed the long, pink skirt. Hands pausing inquiringly over her still-slender figure, she smiled at her image in the looking glass and thought, he'll love me anyway—even when I bulge!

Then, she raced out into the upstairs hall. He was talking to Flora in a low, impatient voice and Flora, obviously not wanting to be overheard, was whispering some sort of nervous admonition to John.

"Nonsense, Flora," he answered, not caring that he could be overheard. "I'm simply bringing my wife flowers because I have wonderful news to tell her and I don't want to hear a single one of your old Celtic superstitions about bad luck. I'm lucky to have found a street vendor with English daisies still perky enough to sell in this hot August weather."

Leaning over the banister upstairs, Anne saw him plant a kiss on Flora's cheek, flip her housecap askew in his usual teasing way, and bound up the stairs, bearing a handful of pink-edged white English daisies as though he were bringing Anne a diamond necklace.

"I'm here, John," she called. "Hurry!"

Taking the steps two at a time, he rushed to where she stood in the hall and took her in his arms for such a long moment one would think they'd been apart for a week.

"I thought you'd never get back," she breathed, returning his eager kisses, using her handkerchief to wipe the perspiration off his brow. "Oh, what pretty, pretty daisies! Isn't it awfully late for them to be blooming?"

"Pleasing you is my specialty," he boasted, holding out the flowers. "I know you like them. Remember the masses we saw in the fields in Scotland? And that's all I ever need to know—in season or out. If my girl wants something, she shall have it!"

Taking him by the hand, she led him into their bedroom. "Right now, sir, I want another kiss from you—in the privacy of our own room." After he released her, she said, still holding the daisies, "You are strutting about something, John Fraser. Did you get paid? How was the time with your father? Didn't he come home with you?"

"No, because he had another business stop to make. Yes, I was paid—and I do have wonderful news!"

Fearing the worst—and to Anne, the recovery of his military commission would be the worst—she caught her breath but carefully kept on smiling. "You're a—lieutenant again!"

She saw his smile fade and then relight his face. "No," he laughed, "I'm not back in the marines, ma'am. Maybe though, in a way, what happened is even better. For now anyway."

"What, *what*?"

"James Fraser and his son John had what struck me as their first real talk in all the years I've been on this earth!" He whirled her around. "I'm going to try my hand at working with Father in his importing business."

"Darling, that's wonderful news. What will you be doing?"

"Probably all the wrong things, but Annie, he agreed almost at once."

"Do you—do you really want to work in his business, John?"

He crossed the room and stood looking out onto George Street. "If I'm truthful, no. But I do intend to support my wife. Half pay as an erstwhile Royal Marine officer won't do that."

"Then, why are you so excited?"

Without turning around, he said, "Because Father seemed almost pleased that I offered. Even though I'm not William. I mean always to take care of you and, someday, our children, Annie. If I have to work at something not to my liking, so be it." He turned back to her, smiling tenderly again. "My agreement with Father is strictly on a temporary basis. Maybe the man knows me better than I thought. For whatever time I'm available, I'll be calling on his customers, expounding the merits of Bordeaux, claret—"

"Claret! Papa is famous for his stock of claret."

"And I fully intend to send him a supply of the best I can find."

"Be careful, darling, or you'll give away all your profits.

And I need to run downstairs and put my daisies in a vase of water."

He strode back from the window to take her in his arms again. "I think you really like them. Do you?"

"I love them! Look at those dear little pink edges on each petal." Then, surprising herself, she felt tears fill her eyes. "Oh, John, I'm so glad you're in a good mood, so happy you brought me flowers, happier than I could possibly tell you that you and dear Father Fraser got along so well, because—" Her voice choked off.

"Because what, Annie?" He wiped away a tear slipping down her cheek. "Is—is this what women mean when they say they cry when they're happy? Or have I been talking so much you haven't had a chance to get a word in edgewise? How do you feel? Is anything wrong?"

"No."

He made her look at him. "Something is wrong!"

"Flora and I—"

"You and Flora—what?"

Daisies still clutched in one hand, she threw both arms around his neck. "I'm—I'm—*you* are going to be a father, my darling! Does that make you happy or does it—scare you?" He waited so long to answer, he frightened her. "John?"

"Oh, my dearest, it makes me happy and proud and more determined than ever to earn a decent living," he said. "But, you told Flora before you told me?"

"Remember, I didn't feel well this morning? Flora just *knew*. I didn't tell her. She told me! But the baby can't get here until sometime early next year, so please don't feel pushed to—to earn money—or anything. Please, John?"

"I'm human, Anne. Any man wants to provide for his family." He went on holding her, even tighter now. Then, abruptly, he took the daisies, rushed across the room to where the tapestry servant pull hung against the wall and gave it a yank. As quickly, he rushed back to Anne, took her arm, and led her as though she were made of spun glass, to the bed. "You must lie down at once. We can't take any chances! None at all. Thank God for Flora," he mumbled, half to himself.

"But, dearest, I'm all right! Don't run poor Flora all the way up the stairs for nothing. I can go down for a vase and water for my beautiful flowers."

"You'll do no such thing. Now, of all times, I'm going to see that you do absolutely nothing but take care of you and our child. If you don't lie down, I'm going to pick you up and put you on the bed myself!"

"Darling, handsome husband, we can't live this way for seven more months. I won't hear of it."

"Sh! Not another word," he ordered, picking her up, then easing her down onto the coverlet, lifting her feet, slippers and all, up onto the bed.

When she realized how deadly serious he was, she began to laugh, to pull him down beside her. "I love it when you pamper me, but I'm perfectly all right. I did have some morning sickness earlier today, but I'm fine now. I won't even have to begin staying indoors for at least two or three months, Flora says. You have to take me to all the London sites we didn't have time to see before we left for Scotland. John Fraser, I demand to be allowed to get up. If you don't stop blocking me, I'll crawl over and out the other side of the bed."

Abruptly, his face solemn, he got up, stepped back from her, and said in a voice so strange, so puzzling, Anne stopped laughing. "There won't be much time for sightseeing from now on, wife," he said grimly. "Have you forgotten? Your husband will have to go to business every day of the week. Don't make it harder for me. Our lives just changed suddenly a few moments ago. Surely you realize that."

"Yes, of course I realize it, but more than anything else, the way you're acting, I'm scared. I'm going to take care of myself. I long to give you a perfect child, but everything goes wrong for me if I think I've added to your already heavy burdens."

"That's a silly thing to say. Any woman, it seems to me, who loves a man the way I believe you love me, would give the fellow a few minutes to adjust to such a new, totally unfamiliar future."

Her heart tightened. Telling him about their baby had seemed to make him happy at first. Now her sunny, lighthearted lover, who almost always found a playful, easy way to cope with any knotty situation, was a man flailing about in a heavy sea—still strong, still determined to be responsible, but he had almost turned into a stranger. This big, muscular, laughing man had found all the courage and daring he needed in battle after battle, had been honored for that courage, but now he stood there in the middle of the floor looking like a scared little boy. Poor darling had probably not yet found it possible to believe that his father had finally accepted him. To have to absorb the new truth that within a few months, he'd be carrying all the responsibility of becoming a father himself must be far too much—too quickly.

Dear God, she breathed, show me how to help him. To convince him that in no time he'll feel like himself again, eager and excited, even with everything so changed. For that matter, Lord, help *me* too. John was never any more carefree than I, never leaned on his superior officers any more than I leaned on Mama and Papa. We're both babes together and part of me wants to stay that way, too.

"Annie, I'm sorry," he said, coming to sit beside her on the bed. "I guess some part of me wants to stay young and reckless, the way I always felt in my unit. Can you forgive me?"

"No, because there's nothing to forgive. Did you know you are a mind reader?"

"I am?" The familiar, almost sunny smile was back on his face. He was trying.

"Yes, because I was just telling God that part of me wanted to stay Papa's daughter in the safety and comfort and luxury of Cannon's Point, with someone always there to make everything right and familiar again."

He had taken her in his arms and was kissing her when Flora's knock sounded at their door. He leaped up, grabbed the daisies, threw open the door, and asked for a vase and water as breezily as though nothing at all unusual had just turned both their lives upside down.

When Flora left, puffing and complaining about how spoiled her laddie was, he stood looking down at Anne, still stretched on the bed. Then he began to laugh—the carefree, musical laugh that had always saved them.

It saved them again.

Part Four

November 1816–August 15, 1817

Chapter 52

Breakfast at Cannon's Point on an unusually cold, dark, mid-November morning found Rebecca and Jock alone in the big dining room, a lighted candelabra on one end of the table.

Normally the two chatted freely, but today Rebecca kept an eye on her husband, hoping he felt all right because for John Couper, he was unusually silent. Oh, now and then as Johnson brought and removed dishes, they exchanged smiles. Smiling at Jock was as natural for Rebecca as breathing. Perhaps, she thought, it's only this gray, chilly day, a sudden change from the warmth and sun of yesterday. Perhaps, too, as he grew older, dear Jock felt more and more in need of having people in the house. After all, it was no secret to her that he missed Anne painfully, that the passing weeks and months of the year 1816, now nearing its end with Anne and John still abroad, had taxed even her ebullient husband's cheerful disposition.

Of course, hearing that, at last, he was to become a grandfather had worked wonders for him, but if Rebecca wasn't careful, she herself worried too much at being so far away with Anne's first baby due in February. For the past two weeks she had almost sewed her fingers to the bone in her effort to stay creatively occupied on her new project with Eve. She liked to think that what the two were doing was brightening Eve's life, too, giving it the purpose it had seemed to lack since the day Anne went away.

"It be different wif Miss Anne an' me," Eve had said again and again as she worked at her newfound drawing skill. "Miss Anne, she be at my weddin' wif June an' she an' me went right on here together same as always. I be at her weddin' to her man an' she leave me! It be different, Miss Becca." And then, Eve would look back down at the quite striking tree she happened to be drawing freehand right on the fine piece of canvas where Rebecca planned to work her needlepoint as a get-well gift for dear old Mrs. Ann Armstrong. Poor Margaret Wylly's aging mother had failed rapidly all year.

"You and Eve spending the day again with the muse, Becca?" Jock asked, breaking their long silence while Johnson poured fresh coffee.

"I'm sure we will be," she answered. "That is, unless you and Johnson here have other plans for Eve. Do you think Sans Foix has need of her in the kitchen? He told me yesterday that Eve has learned how to make piecrust that almost satisfies his high standards. Is that really true? Or was Sans Foix just trying to horn in on my new interest in Eve? She does continue to amaze me, you know. How did we have her right here in the house for all those years without knowing the girl had a remarkable talent for drawing? Jock, she not only has done three magnificent, matching live oak trees as patterns for me to work for poor Mrs. Armstrong's coverlet, I caught her last week drawing Anne's favorite big red-crested woodpecker!"

"Annie's Lord God Bird?" he asked, brightening more than at any time since they'd sat down at the table. "And will you work your needlepoint magic on that, too?"

"Not that I know of. Eve was drawing it with a quill and ink right on a large piece of wood. A quite valuable piece of finished hickory I think it was. I didn't ask where she'd gotten it. I presume June finished it off for her. Should I have asked?"

"Knowing Eve, I doubt that it would have done any good, but I'll lay a wager that she's making a present for me to send Anne. Probably thinks that new grandchild of ours will need to learn right off what a coastal Georgia pileated woodpecker really looks like. What do you think?"

"I only know she's making her own bright-red dye for coloring the cockade. Who ever really knows what Eve has in her mind? I'm afraid I paid very little attention when Anne used to tell me that no one would ever really know what Eve was thinking. I'm beginning to catch on to what Anne meant now that I'm also spending time with Eve. She does talk quite a lot about our hopes for the new grandchild sometime in February of next year, though. Eve is very excited that Anne will . . . will . . ." Unable to finish, she tried hard to give Jock a smile. Then, dabbing at quick tears with a handkerchief, she said, "Forgive me, Jock. It's—it's just very hard for a mother to be away from her daughter at a time like this. It's not only hard, it's unnatural!"

He was on his feet, bending over her chair, his arms around her, and that was the worst thing he could have done because she broke into silly, uncontrollable sobs the second Johnson left the dining room.

"Cry, Becca, go on, let it all out," he soothed. "Of course, it's much harder on a mother being away from a daughter at a time like our Annie's having now. The Almighty knows it's hard enough on her papa, but—"

"I—I'm so sorry, Jock," she sobbed, leaning on his broad chest. "I know you hate it when I cry. I—I honestly didn't have any idea I'd start blubbering. Anne is doing fine. She even had John write to us so we'd really believe that she's having a quite normal time of it. It's just that—" Again she broke off. This time, to listen. Her ears, noticeably sharper than Jock's these days, had caught the thud of a galloping horse outside in their lane. "Oh, dear! I must stop this foolishness. Someone's coming, Jock."

"It must be Dr. William. Big Boy told me before he went fishing early this morning that the good doctor had stayed at the Wyllys' place all last night. I fully meant to tell you first thing when you came downstairs that old Mrs. Armstrong must be worse or William wouldn't have stayed right there to watch over her."

Rebecca was standing, too, wiping her eyes, poking a stray wisp of dark hair back in place, when the front door opened and closed and William Fraser stood in the dining room doorway.

"You look as though you've seen a ghost, William," Jock said, going to the slender young man. "You haven't slept a wink, have you, son? Come in, come in and have some breakfast with us. How did you leave poor Mrs. Armstrong?"

"Do sit down, William," Rebecca urged. "I think I already know how you left your patient."

"Yes," William said, sinking gratefully into the chair Jock settled under him. "She's dead, Mrs. Couper. I did all I could possibly do. Frances Anne helped me all night long with her grandmother. I—I feel the loss too. She was a dear, spirited old lady. I'd come to care deeply for Mrs. Armstrong myself."

"I'm sure you did all anyone could have done, son," Jock was saying, while ringing the bell for Johnson. "Any man who looks as exhausted as you certainly did more than he could be expected to do. Johnson will be here directly with your breakfast. I'm sure he heard you ride up. He and Sans Foix are preparing it this minute, I'll wager." Jock seated Rebecca again, reached for one of her hands, then one of William's, bowed his own head, and said to God as though the two had already had much conversation that morning, "Almighty God, Thou knowest I'm a Presbyterian at heart, even though a member of the vestry of an Episcopal Church, where they believe in praying for the souls of those who have gone before us. Presbyterians, dear Lord, believe a loved one departed steps right into Your presence. At times like this, I'm probably a bit more Presbyterian than Episcopalian. But Thou knowest which is right. We simply place our dear departed Mrs. Armstrong into Thy loving hands by means of whichever doctrine turns out to be the correct one. And we thank Thee for receiving her according to Your grace. One thing more, Lord. Here is Dr. William and we are asking that he be rested by the kind of peace that does pass all human understanding. Amen."

"Thank you, Jock," Rebecca whispered.

"Yes, sir, I certainly thank you, too. I hope you'll both remember Frances Anne in your prayers too. She and her grandmother were very, very close toward the end. They hadn't always been, you know, so losing the old lady right now is quite hard for her."

"We'll go on remembering each one of the Wyllys, son," Jock said, "and particularly your intended. She is your intended, isn't she? You did get that settled some time ago, I believe?"

For the first time, Rebecca saw William manage a half-smile. "Aye, Mr. Couper. As God is my witness, we're intended. Finding the people of St. Simons Island, even in the rude way we British were forced to make our discovery, was certainly the best day of our lives for both my brother and me. A man can't be in two places at once, of course, but many times I wish I could be in London to help Anne these days."

The mere mention of Anne, along with William's tender thought of her at a time like this, brought tears again to Rebecca's eyes. Before she made a further spectacle of herself, she got up with the hurried excuse that she really must let Eve know that they didn't get their needlepoint pieces finished quite in time for dear Mrs. Armstrong to enjoy the coverlet on her sickbed.

Couper, ignoring his third cup of coffee, sat with William while he picked at fresh-caught, crisp-fried trout, biscuits, and grits and heard himself plunge directly into the one subject he vowed to avoid today of all days: Anne and John.

"Anne's mother is beside herself with worry that she can't be with Anne when her first child arrives and I sit here selfishly hectoring a tired man like you on the subject of John Fraser's future! Am I getting old, William? I'm breaking promises even to myself. I promised myself not to mention John's future plans one more time—especially to you, who are as helpless as I to influence the boy. You're the doctor. Is such weakness in me a sign of old age?"

Toying with a biscuit and a bit of Liz's wild dewberry jam, William said, "Mrs. Armstrong was eighty-two. She was very old. You, my dear sir, are not only in excellent health, you have years to go before you're old. As for my brother—" He held out both hands helplessly. "Who has ever known what John may ultimately decide? What trouble he must cause himself because of his enormous talent to charm!"

"To charm, William?"

"Surely you, of all people, know that John finds it so easy to charm even those he loves most that at times, he must deceive himself. Now, wait, sir. I saw that frown cloud your face. I don't mean to imply that John is in any way deceiving Anne. I merely mean that it's so important to him to create a happy atmosphere and so easy for him to do it, sometimes even he must wonder if things are really as splendid as he convinces others that they are, if things are actually as splendid for him working with Father as he's persuaded himself to believe. I've spoken that plainly to him often through the years, so I'm not denigrating him in his absence. John knows this about himself. Charm simply comes so handily to him, I don't think he realizes it most of the time."

For a moment Couper sat thinking, stirring fresh, thick cream into his coffee. "I should be shot at dawn for putting you through all this after the long, hard night you've had, Doctor. I've come to need you as a friend and I know it's an imposition today. With my old companion James Hamilton gone forever to Philadelphia to live, I'm left with only one other close gentleman friend on St. Simons with whom I can unburden my heart—James Gould—who still lives, until his new place is finished, all the way south near his lighthouse."

"Your considering me a friend, sir, is far from an imposition. It's one of the real honors of my life. But, it's growing harder and harder for you to wait for John to make up his mind now that the time is so close for Anne to have her baby, isn't it?"

"Aye," Couper said on a heavy sigh. "Oh, not as hard for me, mind you, as for poor Rebecca. Something deep gnaws inside a woman at a time like this when her only grown daughter needs her and her alone." He tried to give a convincing chuckle. "Of course, I could say that my restlessness where John's future is concerned also has to do with the fact that except for one more coat of paint on its trim, their good little house at Lawrence is ready for the happy family to take possession."

"And it looks handsome, I must say. Frances Anne and I rode to Lawrence one day last week. I wish I thought I could ever give her a home that made her eyes dance the way they danced when she saw the amazing transformation in the Lawrence house! You know, sir, Frances Anne is almost as outspoken and frank as your daughter, Anne. Certainly she was far less tactful than you were a moment ago when she tried to pin me down as to the future intentions of my esteemed brother, John."

"Tried to pin you down, eh?"

"The way your scientific son, James, pins his magnificent butterflies to that impressive specimen board! I had no better explanation for her than I had for you. John declares, and so does our father, that indeed he has been a big help in Father's importing business. It seems my brother has obtained several new accounts, although actually collecting, Father says, is not much easier for him than it was for the others."

"Parting a man from his money is never easy," Couper said. "I'm proud of the way John has stuck with it, though. Anne writes that the boy is out working most of every weekday, even Saturdays."

"And he despises every minute of it, I'm sure," William said. "Even when our forces were occupying your island here, John's work allowed time with Anne. Some mornings, I can feel his heartache at leaving her every day, especially now."

Couper stared into space. "Will he ever be able to do anything except marine duty and *not* despise it, William?"

"I wish I could answer that." William Fraser set down his cup, fished through both jacket pockets, then took out a crumpled letter. "This seems as good a time as any to let you read this latest word from John, sir. Your stakes in his future are high, I know. I also know the uncertainty he's putting you through. I am, by now, quite aware of how you long for Anne to be free to come home. Being here has taught me more about real living than have all the books I've ever studied." He held out the letter. "Read my brother's latest letter to me."

Couper took it, put on his spectacles, and began to read silently. "Father seems better than at any time since our mother's death and it is plain to see that his mostly good spirits are because of Anne. I beg you to excuse such a hasty note, but I'm due over near London Bridge in a little less than an hour and wanted you to know that I may be on the right track at last where retrieving my commission is concerned. Anne doesn't know this yet, nor does Father, of course, but I will probably be taking the stage down to Portsmouth before the week is over. I have learned that there may be need of an additional officer or two on Captain Basil Hall's crew, now doing scientific exploration near Korea. My past fighting experience does not specifically qualify me, but our mutual friend, Captain Menzies, believes I could adapt quickly and it is he who wrote concerning the chance that a personal interview in Portsmouth might be of value. The need to return to regular pay and some semblance of future stability weighs heavily upon me now that Anne's time is so close. Can you believe that within three months your old brother will be a proud father? And you an uncle? I awaken in the night filled with wonder and sure in my bones that something will occur for me soon that will, by some means, fill my every need. Write to me more and more about the state of your own romance with Frances Anne and assure her that daily my prayers ascend that you will, in your adventure together, find half as much pure happiness as Anne and I are finding in ours. I admit news of the first child gave me quite a jolt at first, but now it is all joy and only heightens my zest to be an enormous success in life as both a husband and a father. Anne has never been lovelier than now. Should I be fortunate enough to find Father receptive to my going to Portsmouth before Christmas, I will write you from there. I am atingle with anticipation and feel sure that a turning for the best is just ahead. Yr Affectionate Bro., John Fraser."

When Couper finished reading, he looked at William for a long time, then said quietly, "How I wish I could help the boy."

"Help him, Mr. Couper? You've been a gracious host to me for nearly a year. He and Anne have a home waiting, a well-renovated, beautifully situated home on a fertile acreage. James Hamilton tells me that among the three plantations, the two of you can spare John enough slaves to get by until he's making a profit and can buy more. I'm sure that's true, since you've been able to borrow, shift tasks, and plant here in spite of your losses to the British. You've offered John the means for a lucrative career and your rare friendship. What more could you possibly do? I haven't said this before, because my regard for my brother runs deep, but it seems to me that John needs to grow up and offer to help *you.*"

John Couper got slowly to his feet, as did William, so that no response to what the weary young doctor had just said was necessary.

"It's your bedtime, Doctor. I insist and I'll see that none of our people are allowed to disturb you." Jock laid an arm around the shorter man's shoulders. "Your brother, my well-intentioned son-in-law, owes me nothing. He has filled Anne's world, and even with our new child, little Isabella, to adore and to watch grow and flower, nothing will ever be more important to me than that Anne's world be bright. I'm her father, but I'm also her captive and will ever be."

Chapter 53

Early in the second week of December, the very week John was due back from Portsmouth, Anne was startled awake at first light by the familiar but still-frightening nightmare in which June and his Ebo friends had jumped from a slave ship into Dunbar Creek back on St. Simons. The Ebos who had drowned were still, to Anne, after all these years, *not* really June's tribal members and friends. The flailing, drowning Negroes in the black water that stormy night when Anne was only six were just that—separate and beyond help—one with a bloody stump because an alligator had bitten off his leg.

Minutes after she woke up, still terrified, she sat in her nightdress on the side of the bed—without John—without anyone to run to for comfort. Both hands held her now misshapen body where their baby lived, kicking and struggling this morning more than ever, impatient to get out, to see life from the outside, in the sunlight. Perhaps her baby was as filled with longing as was she for the sight of St. Simons pine trees tall against the sky—not pointed, short-needled pine trees, not Scotch firs. Only majestic, rounded, long-needled, plumed Georgia coastal pines would do for her baby, because only they would have done for Anne this minute.

"John! John, come back to me. . . . You promised to be back two days ago. I don't even know what it means that you didn't get here. I waited—the baby and Flora and Father Fraser waited the night you promised to come home until nearly midnight! Even then, Father Fraser had to take me by the hand and lead me upstairs into this huge, empty, lonely room."

She tried to jump to her feet, then remembered that even getting out of bed these days without John's strong, warm hand to help her was a struggle. All of life was a struggle without his hands, his arms, his laughter. The big brick house on George Street was gloomy without him, its fine old furniture almost ugly, and all of it making shadows she'd never even noticed until he went away more than two weeks ago. Even when Flora and dear Father Fraser went about lighting lamps, it made no difference, helped not at all. Anne and John together had brought what cheer and brightness there'd been in the four-story, flat-faced house with no stretching lawns and no tempting pathways outside leading to the river. No paths leading into the welcoming woods in which she'd spent her girlhood walking and running and stooping to enjoy white starflowers or to seek out shy, tiny blooms half-hidden in a thick, green cushion of moss after a rain. Why was it bad form for a woman to roam London streets when it was perfectly all right on St. Simons? Life here was like being in a cage! Why couldn't women live as free as men did?

Again, she tried to hoist herself up from the side of the bed but sank back down. Flora, she supposed, was down all those stairs in her kitchen making breakfast. Father Fraser would be in his study, doing whatever he did until Flora pulled her warning cord on the kitchen wall to tell him she'd be up any minute with a loaded breakfast tray. They were both dear to her, dear and necessary and more and more dependent, it seemed to her, on Anne herself for their dispositions.

Without John, there was no cheer and she felt exhausted, not only from the old nightmare but from trying to be buoyant and confident for the sake of the only two people in the whole city of London who loved her when John was not there.

This time, one hand firmly on the corner of the night table beside their bed, she heaved and pushed her heavy body until she was standing, not too steadily, on both feet. A shudder ran through her when she realized that again she would have to fix her own hair in order to look good for Father Fraser's close inspection at breakfast. She also knew that she had no choice but to pick out another of those hideous, tent-sized sacque dresses to slip over her head.

As on all the other mornings with John away, she had

settled grimly for a cold sponge bath on weekdays, not wanting poor overworked Flora to carry hot water up so many stairs. There was just no way to measure the way she went on missing Eve! Still, so much had happened here that was good. The thrill of seeing and actually living in the famous foreign city about which she'd heard and read all her life seldom left her. She'd actually seen Mama's Caerlaverock with her own eyes, had kissed and held and listened to John in every nook and cranny of the ancient ruins, except that one secret passage that even they hadn't been able to find. Now, her body, which she'd always taken for granted was beautiful, agile, willing to do anything—including wild horseback rides in the woods, long swims in the Hampton River, tree climbing, wide and exciting swings on heavy old grapevines—was only a burden because John was nowhere in the house on this cold December morning.

The simple act of going up and down stairs had, in the past few days, become an ordeal to dread. If Eve were here, she could have breakfast in bed, a hot bath, and the least ugly of all her four sacque dresses would already be laid out. Even one of their sharp exchanges would seem like heaven, if only Eve weren't all the way across the ocean at Cannon's Point.

Dumfries and Caerlaverock were a part of Anne's heritage as well as of John's; she had come to care deeply for Father Fraser, loved watching him bloom in her company, felt grateful that she might have had, as John insisted, a part in easing the old man's burdens, in lifting his spirit. She was devoted to Flora and now, with the baby so close, more dependent on her than ever, although unlike in her life with Eve, she had to try hard not to *act* dependent on Flora. Did the fact that Flora's skin was white cause her to behave differently with the only regular servant in Father Fraser's house? Definitely not. At home she was Eve's responsibility and it made Eve furious not to be needed for everything. If Anne forgot and selected a dress she'd like to wear to some special function or to receive certain guests, Eve hit the ceiling. Eve knew best. Anne had grown up believing Eve knew best. Most of the time, she did. Eve was Eve!

Splashes of cold, soapy water, more splashes of even colder rinse water from a second bowl, helped some. As she pulled on her warm cotton stockings and dropped a pale green sacque dress over her head before tackling her curls, she felt a little brighter, dreaded the laborious trip down the stairs a bit less. The nearer her time came, the more Father Fraser seemed to intensify peering at her. The coming of his first grandchild filled his life these days, but the peering somehow made Anne's load heavier and heavier. The doctor said she was fine, but both Father Fraser and Flora kept such close watch, Anne found herself struggling some days not to give in to sudden impulses to run out the front door and up George Street by herself.

All of the heaviness in her spirit today, even the painful need of Eve, was because John was still gone. When at last he walked through that wide front door downstairs, everything would right itself. Especially the dreadful, debilitating, almost endless bouts with homesickness! Through the long days since he left, she had been fairly successful at keeping even the word out of her mind. That she would experience periods of homesickness had seemed to haunt John. For the first few months of their time abroad, he had almost made a nuisance of himself by asking. Not lately, though, because even though he had frightened her by his earlier response to the news that he was going to become a father, daily she had seen his near rebellion at the idea that their lives would never be the same again begin to dim. He was not only happy when he left, he seemed oddly relieved. Over and over he told her that knowing new responsibility lay ahead for him helped explain him to himself in a way nothing else had ever done.

The need to explain herself to herself had never once occurred to Anne. She was simply Anne Couper, then Anne Couper Fraser, the most loved and adored woman in the whole world, the most blessed to have a man like John to love, to be loved by him. To be the one woman who was almost ready to give him his first child.

She had finished dressing and was far enough down the first flight of stairs on her careful way to breakfast to be able to hear Father Fraser's voice unnaturally raised. He didn't sound angry exactly, but somehow balky, thwarted, and he was taking it out on Flora. Anne stopped to listen, hating the whole idea but needing to know what she might have to face once she walked into the large, dimly lit dining room.

"You'll take his side, Flora McLeod," Father Fraser was saying, his voice all edges. "I never expect anything else from you, but if you'd use some of that tongue of yours on

John when he does deign to come home from his wild-goose chase to Portsmouth, it might drive some sense into his hard head!"

"I'm tellin' you again to hush," Flora barked in a perfectly audible stage whisper. "That little thing'll be traipsin' down them stairs any minute an' this is no time for you to be causin' a stushie of any kind!"

Anne gripped the railing. She'd promised John to be ever so careful on the stairs while he was gone. If she fell, the baby would fall too. Heart pounding, she felt for a few seconds as though she might be taking leave of her senses, not only because of what Father Fraser had said but because standing stock-still there on the staircase, she thought she could *see* as plain as day the big old wild holly tree at the corner of Papa's house. It *was* that very tree, and although she knew perfectly well that it was December in London, bees swarmed over every branch she was seeing because every branch held clumps of tiny white holly blooms! The bees swarmed slowly, up and down, round and round the almost invisible clumps, but they had to be blossoms or bees wouldn't be there. One other morning, long before John took the stage alone to Portsmouth, she had told him in detail about a half-dream in which she had not only *seen* a clapper rail scurrying along the edge of the narrow strip of marsh along Jones Creek, across which the Hampton Point people dared not come, she had heard the bird's spurt of wild, insistent clucking. John, of course, had made a joke of it and a funny remark about Anne's being the rare person who could allow the shy, seldom-seen rail freedom to show himself.

John wasn't here now to fix anything, so she blinked her eyes fast and hard, still holding to the stair rail. The holly tree faded away, taking the honeybees with it. She was left standing, waiting nervously for Father Fraser to say something more about John's wild-goose chase to Portsmouth.

"The boy's got no right to treat her this way with her time so near," he was declaring, his voice a little lower but still sounding almost angry. "And you'll see, he'll come swinging back through our front door tonight or tomorrow, his face longer than mine, lip down to his chin, because he was turned down again. I ken he's not content to be helping his old father in business."

"But Laddie has helped you, ain't he?" Flora insisted.

"You told me yourself your firm meets accounts better than ever before Johnnie come aboard with you."

"Aye," Father Fraser agreed halfheartedly. " 'Twould seem that might be enough for him at least for now, but one whiff of hope that he might—might, mind you—be able to retr-rieve his commission and off he goes at a gallop, hoping to be sent heaven knows where in the China Seas. Away from blessed Anne and the baby!"

Flora snorted. "But he'd be earnin' enough money to feed and clothe them both and put a roof over their blessed heads."

Slowly, carefully, Anne began to move down a step at a time, trying as always, for John's sake and the baby's, to be careful, but dreading more than ever the moment when she would have to face Flora and Father Fraser and their smothering attention.

Her "Good morning" from the doorway brought them both scurrying to her, each taking an arm, leading her as though she were feeble and crippled to her familiar chair at the table.

"Flora and I were just saying," Father Fraser lied boldly, "that this could be the happy day for our Annie when the proud father of her child could well come through our front door."

"Aye," Flora lied too, "we was just sayin' that, dearie. Now, how about a nice, hot bowl of Flora's gude por-r-idge, saved steamin' for ya' in the chafing dish?"

"Yes, thank you," Anne said, hearing the strained sound of her own voice. "I have to eat for two now, you know, just as you always tell me, Flora."

"Take plenty of sugar and cream, Anne," Father Fraser said, putting the pitcher and bowl where she could reach them. "It could be tonight the boy will return, you know. Are you ready, lass, for whatever he has to tell us?"

She gave him her dazzling smile and said, "Oh, I am. Nothing really matters except that John gets home safely."

They had both told white lies. She saw no reason not to join them and through her mind flashed one of dear Papa's little speeches on his flimsy belief that God looked on white lies while judging their motives. They had all told whoppers to one another today for what she felt could safely be called love's sake, at least in mutual effort to keep the peace until John got there to make everything right.

After she'd sugared and creamed her oat porridge and praised Flora for its deliciousness, she surprised herself by blurting: "Do you both hope they'll turn John down at his unit headquarters in Portsmouth? I told you a white lie a minute ago. It does matter to me what John finds out. It matters dreadfully! I want him to be happy in whatever work he does. I know he's a proud man who wants to be able to support our baby and me all by himself, but—oh, Father Fraser, Flora—I guess I'm through with that awful morning sickness, but nothing seems to stop my homesickness! I'm so lonely for Papa and Mama and baby Isabella and Eve today. For my brother, James, too, of course, but I'd give almost anything to hear Papa laugh. I—I had a dream about home, about being at home with them all one stormy night at Cannon's Point back when I was just a little girl and—and sometimes I think I'm actually seeing certain trees in our yard, actually hearing the birds, watching the sun come up over the Georgia side of the Atlantic and the Hampton River in front of our house. Is it just dreadful of me to feel so homesick when you're both terribly good and kind to me? I don't want to hurt anyone. But, all of a sudden I realized how long it's been since I wrote to my best friend on St. Simons. I don't think I've written to Anna Matilda Page but twice since John and I reached London the first time! Do—do you think it would help me be better company for both of you if I wrote to her after I've had my breakfast?" She was weeping now, unable not to, although she tried to laugh through it. "I know you'll be going to business soon, Father Fraser, and I know this is the day you'll start the hard work of preparing for your fine, fancy Scottish New Year's spicy fruit and nut cake, Flora. But I do need some kind of touch with home, with someone on St. Simons Island."

Flora hurried to stand behind Anne's chair, big hands smoothing her shoulders. "There, there, dearie. 'Twould be the ver-ry best thing of all for you to write a letter to your little friend at home. A nice long one. 'Twill help heaps. But, do finish your por-ridge, girl. You need your st-r-ren'th for whatever time is left to wait for Laddie to get here."

"Aye, lass." Father Fraser joined Flora in trying to comfort her, leaning toward her at the table, patting one of her hands. "I never heard of a better idea for a way to spend—maybe the whole mor-rning. The lad must this minute be rocking along the road from Portsmouth toward our ver-ry house."

For the time it took her to stop the helpless tears from flowing, Anne waited, then said, "I wasn't eavesdropping. I want you to know that, but I was making my way slowly down the stairs and I couldn't help overhearing what you were both saying. You don't want John ever to go back in his beloved Royal Marines, do you, Father Fraser?"

She felt Flora's wide, warm hands jerk away from her shoulders and knew the woman was in her ramrod posture behind her. "The-r-re, sir! Didn't I tell you she'd likely overhear your bombast before she got here to the table? Shame be upon you! The gir-rl dinna' deserve such!"

After a long silence, Father Fraser, resembling a whipped dog with its tail between its legs, got up from the table without a word, went into the hall, picked up his heavy coat and top hat, and left the house.

Upstairs in her room again, Anne felt so ashamed of herself for having talked too much, told too much, made such a ruckus at breakfast, that she sat in a crumpled, wretched heap on the big, empty bed and tried not to think about what she'd done. She did think about it, though, and longed to run after Father Fraser and ask his forgiveness. She dared not. She was too big and clumsy, too far along, to be seen on a London Street—especially in an upper-class neighborhood so near Portman Square, where only ladies dressed for walking or calling were ever seen outdoors. She would humiliate both Father Fraser and John were she to expose herself in her condition!

Almost all her life she'd heard of women doing what was called lying-in. There were even lying-in hospitals in London for women unable to afford a doctor at home. Of course, women in the Coupers' class didn't appear in public on St. Simons Island, either, after they began to show, but were she carrying her baby at Cannon's Point, there would be nothing to stop her from going outside except the weather, and that was mostly good. There had been times, and this was one of them, when she would have given almost anything to be able to march, Papa's strong arm to steady her and the baby, up and down and around the wide Cannon's Point porches. A woman's surroundings while she carried a baby were supposed to be awfully important. Babies could be marked by events that took place, even by the mother's thoughts while the infant was still inside! How was she marking her child? The tiny boy or girl would be here soon, and because only she could control her feelings and mind, she'd better busy herself right now by doing something.

What might I be doing if I were at home, she wondered, as she heaved herself off the bed and moved slowly and carefully across the big, shadowy room to the pretty, old kneehole desk, lit a half-burned candle, and sat down to write the long-overdue letter to Anna Matilda. If I were safely at home with Mama and Papa and Eve and all the other people to help me now, I know at least I wouldn't have to dread making my bed or taking my own chamber pot downstairs before the morning is over. Maybe George Street is in an elegant section of a famous city, but life is anything but easy and pleasant without willing or even unwilling hands to help! Anna Matilda would never believe the things Anne had to do for herself these days, all because John's mother was dead and Father Fraser had dismissed three house servants when she died, wanting only Flora because she understood his black grief.

A clean sheet of paper before her on the desk, she dipped the quill John sharpened before he left for Portsmouth and began to write.

9 December 1816
2 George Street, London

Dearest Anna Matilda,

I am writing this from a contrite heart, ashamed that so much time has gone by since my last. Do forgive me and do keep any confidences I may, on this somewhat melancholy morning, set down here. I fully trust you since you were so mature and sensitive as to keep my secret when I was waiting for John to come to St. Simons for our wedding. When I allow myself to remember how true and trustworthy you were, my pleas for forgiveness for my long silences grow louder. I need you now. Only the good Lord knows how much I need you. We are supposed to be grown women, but today especially, I am not finding it easy to be grown-up or even one bit mature. Anna, dear friend, I am so homesick for the sight of Cannon's Point, my parents' faces, Eve's face, your face, I could die, but, of course, I won't, because my greatly beloved John could, at any moment, walk through the front door—back from a trip to Portsmouth, where he had another chance to regain his commission.

Oh, there is so much to write! So much to confess to you in our old, familiar, safe way of showing each other the very contents of our hearts! First, I confess to being scared. I'm told by our housekeeper, Flora McLeod, the Scottish lady who not only cooks but manages this big house and all of us in it as a benevolent general manages his troops, that it is all right for me to feel scared since the baby crowding me this minute as I write, is my first. Flora vows that once I've had the first, I will never again be as frightened and uneasy, and I suppose, even though she is a spinster, Flora is right. Dr. Mauldin comes twice a week to examine me and will be on hand to deliver my child because neither Father Fraser nor John will hear to my entering what Londoners and New Yorkers call a lying-in hospital. I am sure it will all be terribly expensive for poor Father Fraser and I know that unless John regains his commission, he will have very little money to help out. He has done well at finding new accounts for his father's wine-importing firm and does receive a small salary for his work, which, even when he is in London, takes him away from me all day long. I am just going to write this and then not bring it up again—but if I am any judge of myself, I believe what is wrong with me this morning is far more than my fear of having my first baby. It is the gnawing fear that John might be needed in his unit again and be ordered to ship far, far away to some foreign port! Loving and needing the presence of one man and one only can bring more joy than you will believe until it happens to you, but it can also bring sharp, agonizing pain! John has been away more than two weeks and I am bereft. Our bed is so empty, this room we share so huge and forlorn, the entire house so stifling, I have one of my headaches and I sometimes fear for my sanity.

I'm sure Mama would ask, if she were aware of my

dark state of mind today, how long and how fervently I have prayed about it all. I'll tell *you*—I've prayed until I'm exhausted. In your latest letter you asked if John ever shows any sign of interest in our coming back to live at Lawrence. My answer will madden you as it maddens me—yes and no. He adores Papa. Our time spent in Scotland gave me great hope that his childhood memories of Dumfries, his obvious love of all things Scottish, from the skirl of bagpipes to his hard-to-believe love of that dreadful dish haggis, might cause him to announce any day after our return to London that we were sailing for Savannah and home. Instead, he offered his services on a temporary basis to Father Fraser and here we are. Here I am—alone—with John once more in pursuit of his precious commission! Of course, you've already sensed that I'll hate his getting it back since that will close the door forever to our returning to St. Simons except for a visit during one of his leaves.

Life here is precious to me in many ways and not all is gloom, because I truly love Father Fraser and Flora McLeod, but how I miss an occasional house full of pleasant guests! My sweet John knows this and he has vowed that when he returns from Portsmouth, we will again, once the baby is born, see London sights and begin to accept social invitations. You see, he felt the need to devote most of his time to pleasing Father Fraser, who, John has always believed, favored William over him. This had to be worked out, and although Father Fraser now seems to show pride in John's hard work at obtaining so many new accounts for the firm, it is temporary. Actually, after an especially close talk I had with the dear old fellow the other day, I feel he'd like to sell his firm and move with us to Georgia! Don't get your hopes up that anything so wonderful is going to happen soon, dear Anna Matilda, but if it were in Father Fraser's hands instead of John's, I believe it could. Some of my agony at having my first child away from my own beloved parents is eased because I know how happy it makes Father Fraser that the baby, also his first grandchild, will be born here in his very own house. As he said, the only thing that could make him any happier would be that this house stood on its foundation somewhere in his native Scotland.

I find I tire rather easily these days. There is *so much* of me to carry around! I have sat here thinking and writing my thoughts to you for most of the morning, and although I can only get loathsome sacque dresses over my bulk by now, I must try to make myself more presentable in case anything so marvelous as John's coming home might take place before this day is over. How I miss Eve! Do you know I sponge in cold water, comb and pin my own hair, take down my chamber pot each day, and that I even packed for our trip to Scotland alone? Without any help?

I have asked you to keep the particular confidences of this letter, but only because my mood is so dark today. Do let my sweet parents know that I am often homesick and would give almost anything to be able to take just one carefree walk beside the river! I used to worry about you in letters to John because you were down there at Retreat, forced to take walks along the ocean alone. Count your blessings, because you can go outside—even alone—any time you feel the urge. Of course, I can't. I'm too big and ugly. And women live indoors over here. But Flora swears only beauty and joy will come out of it and I do feel deep within me that my blessed John will come home today.

At that very moment, with the ink not yet dry on the page, she heard the front door close downstairs and his voice calling her name.

With a mighty heave, she was on her feet, hurrying, not even trying to be careful, out into the upstairs hall. "John! Oh, John, my dearest—I'm up here in our room. Hurry! Please, please hurry!"

Anne could hear Flora stomping up her kitchen steps, but not in time to greet her laddie first because he had dropped his heavy valise in the front hall, was taking the stairs two at a time, and in seconds was holding her again as hard against him and as close as the baby would allow. Then they just stood there kissing and holding and murmuring each other's names, over and over and over.

Finally, he looked down at her and said in what, if she'd given it any thought, was a carefully rehearsed way, "You can let your heart rest, Annie, my beloved. I'm home—I'm home to stay!"

"You—they didn't—need you on Lieutenant Basil Hall's exploration?"

She had seldom seen such a show of effort, but he went on smiling and answered almost flippantly, "No, ma'am. My vast experience, it was decided, while laudable, is not appropriate. They don't need me, but you do!" He kissed her again. "You do need me and that I know right well. And that, beloved Annie, is all that matters to me."

He was fibbing and so convincingly she almost believed him. Fibbing to her for love's sake. For her sake. She could almost hear him reasoning with himself as the hackney cab rattled him toward George Street: Anne needs me to be buoyant, my most charming best. With our first child so close, she needs her husband to be strong and sure.

Oh, John, she thought, clinging to him as they both still stood in the upstairs hall. Don't make me do battle with the work you love so much! I know you. I know how much you love me, but I also know that it frightens you to the marrow of your big, strong bones even to think you might have to learn how to live again for always—out of uniform.

In the indefinably short space of time in which thoughts come tumbling, she thought all of that. What she said before lifting her mouth to his for another welcome kiss was, "Dearest one, for this minute and this minute is what we have, I'm the most blessed woman in the whole wide world—because you're close enough for me to touch again. . . ."

Chapter 54

Through the Christmas holidays and into January of the new year 1817, everyone at 2 George Street, including Anne, enjoyed, but felt surfeited with, Flora's rich Scottish New Year baking. Mostly though, her state of mind swung from high anticipation and joy that her first child would be born early in February, to fear of the pain of the birth, to nerve-wracking fidgets at her confinement to the house while John was off working. Flora and Father Fraser did their best to reassure her of Dr. Mauldin's expertise, that the baby would be fine and healthy, and that once it was here, all of life would be good.

By now, Anne and Flora were more than close. Exchanged looks between them had come to mean even more than words, and although Flora and Father Fraser hovered too much, their love and devotion sustained her. Mama's letters, more frequent now, kept Anne so aware that she, of all people, should be only grateful that the secret guilt, because she went on worrying, grew even heavier than her awkward body. Some of the secret worry eased when Mama sent money enough to hire a nanny for at least a full year, but only Anne knew that the prospect of actually caring for a tiny, helpless baby loomed ahead almost like a storm cloud. Nothing in her entire life had prepared her for such responsibility.

At home, there would have been no shortage of eager, skillful dark hands to look after an infant's every need. Even a warmhearted, trusted black woman to breast-feed her child for her. What did an English nanny really do for a baby? How much would be expected of Anne herself? The joy didn't lessen, no matter how her secret worries mounted, but it seemed to have to do mostly with the happiness she hoped to give to John. Flora, by telling her of the happiness Anne would know in holding a soft, cuddly little body and in feeling so needed, helped. Oh, how it helped, but as the days moved toward the end of January, Anne found it more and more difficult to keep her feelings of inadequacy from John.

There was no doubt that he felt vast relief and gratitude when Mama sent more than enough money for a good nanny, but could an English girl know more than Anne about guarding the very life of her baby? And how would Flora get along with a strange young woman in the house when she had always been the "head"? Anne also worried about John and his father. The more helpless she felt in her obligation to keep them from stewing, the more she herself stewed and even rebelled at feeling she had to look after their foibles too. John was relieved when he found a highly recommended nanny, but his moods seemed to swing as wildly as Anne's. And Father Fraser went on prodding Anne in his overly attentive way to assure him that her parents did not think *him* a slacker for being unable to afford more than the services of capable, middle-aged Dr. Mauldin.

"You just must believe me," she begged John's father, "when I tell you that my parents are only happy that they can help even in such an impersonal way as paying for a nanny. Either one of them would change places with you in a minute. You'll be here, right with me. You'll know everything that happens and I'm—I'm almost too tired of all this waiting to make even one more effort to convince you that you're terribly important to me these days."

Far more care was needed to help John make his giant leaps from mountaintops of excitement because he would finally be the father of a child—to sudden low moments of what to her appeared to be downright fear.

Upstairs in their room after breakfast early in February, Anne watched him struggle into a proper stiff collar for business. Morning after morning, she did her best to send him off for the day in a happy frame of mind. Today he was frowning, irritated, she felt sure, to have to be dressing once more in the dull, gray business clothes he so disliked.

"Some day," she said, "there will come a time when you can afford a whole new wardrobe. You'd make a devastating dandy in ruffles and rings." Then, she sighed. "Some day, even I'll be able to make myself beautiful for you again. All of life will be so much better when—"

He turned abruptly from the mirror. "When what, Anne?"

"When the baby comes," she said, her voice sounding more as though she were asking a question than stating a fact. "You—you are as eager as I am, aren't you, dearest?"

Unsmiling but looking directly at her, he said, "Yes! I—I long to know whether I'll be the father of a boy or a girl even half as beautiful as her mother. But, I guess most of all, I wonder if I'll ever learn how to be a father at all! I'd give anything to know something to *do* for you to help you through these final days. The truth is, Annie, I'm doing well to—to get through them myself. None of this is easy, is it?"

A hot flare of self-defense shot through her. "At least it doesn't make you lumpy or keep you in the house from morning to night!"

When his dear, troubled face flushed, then buried itself in his hands, she knew what a dreadful, shrewish thing she'd just said. "John, oh John, I'm so sorry." Helpless tears filled her eyes—tears that came so often these days, it was downright humiliating. "I'm sorry I'm lumpy and I'm even sorrier I said that! I don't feel a bit cross. I just feel scared too and helpless. If you wonder how you'll learn to be a father, think about me! I'll be worse trying to be a mother without our people to help me than I've been fixing my hair without Eve. But—but you're here with me. I'm just so relieved *you're here* where I can look at you at least every morning and every night."

He wiped away her tears and held her carefully and tenderly. "Your mother is helping you, all the way from Cannon's Point, darling. The nanny, Katy, will do fine. I'm sure there won't be any more for you to do here than if you were back in Georgia." He managed a half-laugh. "I guess your mother knows how naive we both are at this sort of thing—how much it's going to change all of life for us."

Anne caught her breath. He'd said almost the same thing the very first time she told him about the baby! *Having a child would change everything.* "If I'm truthful, I'm worried about that too," she whispered. "I'm worried because our life has been so perfect. And, John, it was perfect because we were almost always—alone. Just the two of us, and that will be gone."

She could feel his relief. "Oh, Annie, you do understand!"

"Yes! Oh, yes, I do."

"Our baby won't come between us, will it?" he asked. "Do you know enough about things like this to be able to answer such a crazy question?"

"No, because I have to think Katy is going to be fine. And you and I can try hard to keep Flora from resenting her. Anyway, if I do what's expected of me—if I give you a happy, healthy child—we won't let it do anything but bring us closer."

"And we'll be as free as ever in no time," he vowed, struggling, she knew, to convince himself along with her, "to see more of London, attend the theater, concerts—get you out of this dark, old house."

"It's time for you to go now," she said, clinging to him. "But if you don't hold me and kiss me several times, I might not make it through even this day." Her weak giggle was not convincing, but she tried. "That is, hold me as close as my lumpiness allows!"

For an hour or so after John left, she sat at the small desk in their room. Her time was so close, some kind of letter to Mama and Papa had to be written today. The talk with John had helped. She was the lumpy one, she was the one who was shut up in the house, but at least they held the same fears along with the same hopes. And he had met her in them. She felt she had also met him. She was far less afraid, far less lonely. No less homesick. Everything would be better, easier, if she and John were only back at Cannon's Point, but they lived in London now and they were together. With a burst of determination, she began to write in as cheerful a vein as possible.

3 February 1817
George Street, London

Dear Mama and Papa and Everybody,

Since kind, skillful Dr. Mauldin thinks my baby could be born some time next week, this may be the last letter until the joyful announcement from John. He has promised to write to you the minute our blessed baby is here. In my last letter I told you he was not able to regain his commission as a member of Lieutenant Basil Hall's exploration crew, and knowing, as I surely do, of his abiding attachment to the military, I am happy to report that he seems cheerful in spite of what must have been a deep disappointment. My husband is a courageous and persevering man, who lets me know daily that he now places our baby and me foremost in his pursuits. We are so close, I know how hard this must be for him, but mostly he remains lighthearted and keeps us laughing, and that is important not only for the infant I carry but for me. I miss you, Papa, so much at times, I think I might die without the sound of your laughter, your funny stories, your delicious humor, but John is certainly a fair substitute and his devotion to you as a friend is touching. Mama, dear Mama, there is no substitute for your steady grace and support when I need you most. Have I told you that my admiration for you has multiplied since our visits to the Maxwells's Caerlaverock? How proud I am to be the daughter of two such superior and adorable persons!

I miss you both, my brother, James, blessed little Isabella, and do tell Eve how I continue to miss her—every day. We have retained a red-haired nanny named Katy Higgins, who moves early next week into the house with us. Flora McLeod has no use for her, of course, but I like her because, in her cockney, independent way, she somehow reminds me of Eve. Until the glorious day when you two dear ones become grandparents, I send my love to all and my prayers.

Yr Affectionate daughter,
Anne Couper Fraser

P.S. Tell Eve I'm terribly excited that she has discovered her talent for drawing and expect to show everyone I see over here whatever it is she is making as a gift for me. I know I shall boast extravagantly.

Chapter 55

Just after dawn on the morning of February 11, James Fraser sat eating his breakfast, head pounding with worry, stomach rejecting the creamy porridge set before him. Flora had all but slammed the tureen of oat porridge on the table, scooted the sugar bowl and cream pitcher close enough for him to reach, and clumped noisily out of the room. Such rare, churlish behavior had sharpened his anxiety. He'd sent John hurrying for Dr. Mauldin nearly an hour ago and wasn't surprised that Flora was banging about in her haste to get upstairs to where poor little Anne lay on her bed, alone except for the new, untried girl, Katy. Anne, suffering God knew how much pain and fear at what lay ahead for her this day.

Where could John be? Dr. Lester Mauldin had always come as promptly as his driver could bring him from either his office in Oxford Street or his home near Grosvenor Square. John had leaped, half-dressed, down their front steps early this morning when Anne, afraid and in pain, wakened him.

Letting his spoon fall into the barely touched porridge, Fraser got up from the table and hurried to the foot of the stairs in the front hall to listen. Until now, in spite of the stark silence in the house, he had heard nothing from the front bedroom, which Anne and John shared. Flora had been up there—he looked at his watch—more than half an hour. It seemed far longer.

How would John conduct himself while Anne labored upstairs to bring forth the first fruit of what his elder son believed to be his one great love? Believed to be? That, he told himself, was an irrational return of his lifelong doubts about the true character of his firstborn son. It was and had always been an irrational doubt. He knew that now because he and John had made so much progress toward breaking down the wall between them. He must be strong for John.

I can afford the best medical services for my beloved Anne now, Fraser reminded himself, back again at the table. Even if John had not come to my rescue, by hook or by crook I would have found the money for the best possible care for Annie.

He sniffled, swiped with his linen napkin at his eyes. Anne was the daughter he'd never had. She'd brought life back into his house, dispelling the years of grief over Margaret, his beloved. The last thing he remembered before sleep finally overtook him last night was a prod of hope that soon his arms would be cradling the warm, soft, tender body of a grandchild.

I'll just listen at the foot of the steps again, he thought. He could tell by the tone of Flora's voice whether the faithful woman was worried or in charge, working hard and fast, irritated with the new girl, or merely waiting for the next thing to happen. He listened. There wasn't a sound.

When at last James Fraser heard John pound up the outside stone steps that led to their entrance, heard the door burst open and his son's low, anxious voice directing Dr. Mauldin upstairs, his heart began to thump harder than ever—to thump and skip in the way he'd felt it skip fairly often lately. Breathing deep, he willed his head to stop whirling when he got quickly to his feet. His head usually did calm when he willed it. It calmed now and he walked steadily into the hall, where John stood gazing after Mauldin, who by now would have reached Anne's room.

"I thought you'd never get him here, John," he said.

"So did I, Father. Drays and wagons are thicker and slower than ever so early in the day. I had no idea how reckless those cockney drivers can be when they feel they own every street in London because it's too early for gentlemen to be out."

"Not spoken like the true Radical you claim to be, Son," he said. "Never mind, though. A man in your boots is entitled to conduct himself in any way he feels necessary to get him through this trying day." He laid his hand on John's

wide shoulder. "No thought of work for either of us. I need you with me right here."

John's attempted laugh was tight, nervous. "Don't worry, Father. Even at the risk of your fury, wild horses could not drag me out of this house today!"

"I don't own a single wild horse," Fraser said, noticing how feeble his humor had become. John, when things were normal, especially with Anne in the room, laughed often—almost as often as the boy and his mother had laughed together during the years in Dumfries and even toward the end, after they'd moved to London. With all his flailing heart, James Fraser wished he could engage John in some kindly, humorous way. Laughter had always seemed this son's best outlet for his great, virile energy—never reserved like William, and, of course, James Fraser had always found William more companionable.

"You've been through this twice with our mother," John said after they'd both taken chairs in the dark, shadowy parlor. "A man does get through it, doesn't he?"

"Aye, Son. A woman gets through it too. You'll see."

Leaping to his feet after no more than a minute in the high-backed chair, John demanded, "But how? I know Anne needs me to be up there with her. I—I *caused* all this! It's my fault, Father, and I can't even be there to hold her, to beg her forgiveness."

Remembering his own brooding years ago, he said softly, "Aye. You're the very first person I've ever told, John, but I also felt the need for your mother's forgiveness. Especially when she finally cried out for someone to help her seconds before you came kicking into the world to be our firstborn son."

"You—you felt at fault?"

"I felt at fault."

John, his face pale and taut, only stared at him. He said absolutely nothing. He didn't need to say anything, because his father knew that he was witnessing his son's first, stark realization that the warm, fragrant, spirited loved one he'd chosen was enduring for him, too.

Finally, Fraser cleared his throat and said, "Someday, maybe not too far from now, I plan to ask the Father above about this whole, odd, seemingly unfair arrangement. A mon is taught from babyhood to shelter and protect and care for a woman. A mon has it dr-rilled into him as a small boy that men don't show weakness, don't cry, don't even acknowledge when they've been hurt. 'Tis bred into a mon to protect, to shield a woman and yet, 'tis the woman who must alone be torn by pain and anguish in order to bring what is called blessed into the world. Aye, I plan someday to discuss the whole arrangement with the Almighty, *in person.*"

He watched his tall, fine-appearing son stride from window to window, pulling back Flora's heavy, green winter curtains as though hoping for a sign of some nameless help. The boy was feeling too scared and nervous even to recognize help if he saw it. And anyway, the only two people best suited to help Anne now—Dr. Mauldin and dear, no-nonsense Flora—were both upstairs already doing their best.

"I know it sounds ridiculous, John," he said after a time, "but you'll need your strength later. Anne will need your strength. I don't suppose you could eat a little breakfast, drink a spot of tea? I'm sure I can figure out how to heat up the porridge. I know perfectly well how to brew tea. You left this morning without a bite of anything."

John kept pacing the long, dark room. The clatter of traffic was heavier in the street. Still, the slow, unceasing clomp of workhorses pulling loaded drays to market, iron-bound wheels grinding by, did not mask what sounded like the rumble of thunder outside. Thunder in the dead of winter? A thunderstorm coming on a cold, knifing February morning? Stranger things had happened, of course. Margaret had left him forever.

James Fraser buried his head in both hands and willed the dizziness away again, willed his jarring heart back into rhythm. Willed his wild thoughts back to the necessity of today. In that necessity lay his own obligation to John, his firstborn son, who needed a father and was struggling not to show that need.

"Stop it, Johnnie!" Not in his own memory had James Fraser ever called him Johnnie before. That was Margaret's name for the boy. It surely had always been Flora's. Johnnie or Laddie. "Laddie," he heard himself say, his old-man voice almost wailing the word. "Dinna' try so hard to carry it all yourself! I'm here—I'm here to help."

John stopped pacing and stood staring down at him where he sat on the edge of his favorite, deep leather chair, willing himself for once to be a real father to John. The kind of father he had always found it easy to be to William.

Just then, before either had said another word, a door opened upstairs and down the two flights came Flora. It could be no one else but Flora, her always aching feet pounding hard, but faster and faster as she hurried across the second-floor landing and headed down the final flight to where they both waited—father and son standing in the parlor doorway staring up at her.

"Flora!" John gasped. "Flora? *Flora?*"

"That was my name the last time I heard, Laddie," she snapped, the flat tone of her voice telling them almost nothing beyond the obvious fact that she was upset and on some vital mission.

"Anne? Is—is everything going all right, Flora McLeod?" the older man croaked nervously.

" 'Tain't time, yet. 'Tain't her time yet an' I let us run out of sweet balm. I come down for it." She whirled to face them from the top of her stairs to the kitchen. "You two had enough breakfast?"

"I—I can't swallow," John said. "Flora, please tell me! I'm begging you to tell me she's doing all right. How long will it be? Will it take all day?"

"I told ya', Laddie. I come down for more sweet oil!"

"Why didn't you send Katy?"

"Cause *she* don't know where I keep my balm! It ain't Miss Anne's time yet. She's doin' her level best to go with it, not to fight, not to strain herself. Nothin' more to tell, Laddie. Now, I'm in a hurry. Both of you eat!"

When Flora disappeared down her kitchen stairs, John turned to his father. "What's the good of sweet oil?"

"To calm Anne. Flora's a great believer in soothing oil rubbed over the body to help quiet the straining muscles, to calm fears, and—your mother always said later, laughing about it—to help the struggling mother to pass the time until the waters begin to flow."

"Until the *waters begin to flow*?"

"You've got it all to learn, haven't you, Son?" Fraser said, leading John back toward the parlor. "I want you out of sight by the time Flora comes up those stairs again. She'll not want to be slowed by any more mon questions."

Back at the corner parlor window again, John asked, "Did

you say Mother *laughed* later when she told you about Flora rubbing her body with sweet balm?"

"Aye."

"They—they really laugh again later on?"

"Yes, they do, Son. That's another part of God's odd arrangement. One of the better parts of it. A woman can go through the torments of the damned for hours and hours, and later on, with the squirming, dependent little bundle in her arms, she'll laugh every time and act for all the world as though she's forgotten the whole thing!"

Chapter 56

It was nearly four o'clock when, huddled on the top step of the third-floor landing just outside Anne's room—as close as his father and Flora would allow—John heard her frantic screams for help. For more than help. He knew it was Anne's voice crying out, but the screams were those of a wild creature, shrieks of desperation—a helpless, terrified animal caught in a trap—surprised that there could be so much pain anywhere in the world.

For an instant he sat gripping the stair with both hands—his brain, his body, his very spirit, straining also for a way to escape his own torture. Then, he found himself at the door to their bedroom—one ear against the wood panel—trying to hear what Flora might be saying, Dr. Mauldin, even Katy. Was Katy really needed in there? Had Father Fraser been right to order Flora to let the girl stay? Had John been right to agree that since she had been hired to take care of the baby, she had every right to begin once the baby had come?

He hated upsetting Flora, but this minute he hated his own helplessness more and fell back quickly on the man's trick of shutting out the foolishness of all women—all women but Anne. Even to him on this nerve-shattering day, it made no difference one way or another whether Flora's jealousy over having another servant in the house caused trouble. There could be no more trouble anywhere than to be forced to stand there and hear Anne's cries of anguish. Anguish he had caused her to bear simply by loving her, by needing her as he'd needed her again and again—back in Georgia, on board ship months ago headed for Liverpool, in London in the very room where she was suffering now, in Scotland on their wedding trip when each of them was so convinced that beauty and beauty alone would follow them all the days of their lives.

Without deciding to do it, he ran blindly down the stairs and stood in the parlor doorway staring at his father, who stood gripping his chair, staring back at John.

Breathing hard, seeming to struggle in order to form even one word, Father whispered, "Steady. Steady, John. It must be almost—over."

And then an odd silence engulfed them. Only the drum of cold rain falling outside the parlor windows reached him in this blank moment of what seemed to be almost nothing. He, John Fraser, knew nothing of what was happening to his very life upstairs. His father's drawn face was blank, too. Father knew no more than he.

"What will happen now?" John asked in a hoarse whisper. "What happens next, Father?"

Loosening his grip on the chair back, the older man eased around it to where John stood. "Anne is quiet now. It's over. Any minute now, the baby will—"

A thin, reedy, struggling cry interrupted them. His child was no longer hidden out of sight in Anne's body, no longer forced to be silent. Another helpless human being had lunged its tiny way into the idyll that had been and would never again be the bright realm of only John and Anne. The infant's second cry was even more piercing, more insistent—to John, more desperate.

"The baby's not right, Father! There's something dreadfully wrong with your grandchild!"

"No! Oh, no, Son. That's a normal cry if I ever heard one. And Anne's agony is past."

"But the baby's in some kind of terrible pain! I've heard men cry out like that the second after a bullet tears into their chest."

Both arms around John, Father Fraser stood there trying for the first time in his life to rock his big, scared son. In his own chaotic state of mind, it came to John that the man had never even attempted such a thing before—ever. He stiffened, then let his muscles relax. Arms at his sides, head on his father's shoulder, he sobbed, relieved that his father had been right: Anne was no longer crying out.

Nor was the baby! The thought jerked John back to his full height, to resistance at being forced to feel so helpless, so ignorant of what might happen next—unprepared for whatever was going to happen next. Typically, his father wasn't telling him anything. The man was just trying to comfort him as though he thought such a babyish thing could help a grown man with no idea at all what it was going to be like to accept the responsibility of another human life to care for. A man with no money, no profession, no strength.

He disengaged his father's arms gently and slumped into the small armchair Anne had chosen as her own, the one covered by the tiny, exquisite stitches of his mother's needlepoint flowers. In a minute or two, he realized why he'd never sat in that tiny chair, also why Anne liked it. The chair was so small!

A light sound of slippers on the stairs brought him to his feet. Father rushed ahead of him to the parlor door. Someone—Flora or Katy—was coming carefully, steadily, down the stairs.

"Katy!" Father's greeting was nearer a scold, as though he'd found it impossible to believe that anyone but Flora had been allowed to bring down the new baby. Indeed, Katy, red curly hair a bit mussed, was proudly bearing a tiny, invisible bundle wrapped in a blanket.

John felt uneasy, too, but for another reason. If the physician's work was ended—the baby safely born and Anne all right—why had Dr. Mauldin sent Katy downstairs? Why hadn't he come first, so that John's fears for Anne could really be calmed?

"Katy," Father Fraser repeated. "You're beginning at once to be the infant's nurse, eh?" He sounded a touch more pleasant now, perhaps, John thought, merely ill at ease with a new woman around his place. "Careful, lass. Mind where you step now! You'r-re bear'rin' my fir'rst grandchild! A boy, is it? Or a gir-rl?" Already holding out his arms, lapsing in his eagerness into a thick burr, Father asked outright, "How in blazes did you manage to get past Flora with the wee bairn?"

John was waiting, too, standing almost at attention, digging uncertainly through his mind trying to remember whether he'd hoped for a son or a daughter. A daughter. If their nearly perfect romance was to be changed overnight into the long-heralded, fulfilling adult life of fond parents, he'd just about made up his mind that a tiny daughter, who looked exactly like Anne, would make the leap possible for him. He could adore a little girl, could watch every day for signs that she was indeed more and more like Annie. He hadn't talked it over with his Annie yet, but unless she objected, he would name her Anne—and would also call her Annie.

"I say it again, Katy," Father repeated insistently, "how did you get past Flora with the wee bairn? And give us a look! Do I have a grandson or a granddaughter?"

Smiling as though she'd already accomplished something quite special, Katy, still holding the edge of the blanket over the tiny face, teased, "Guess, sir! I ain't one of them nannies that don't take pride in their work. Not on your life! I'm one that prides herself on pitchin' right in the minute the baby shows a sign of life. That minute, my work begins and my first job was to bathe the blood away, wrap the little thing good and warm, an' tote the big surprise down to show its father. Not its *grand*father, sir, its father!"

"It's all right, Katy," John heard himself say, needing somehow to show gratitude because his father had tried so hard to help him. "It's all right to show the—the baby to Mr. Fraser Senior first."

Katy held the bundle resolutely in her arms, not at all willing to do as John asked. "I dare not, sir! Oh, I dare not begin by disobeying my madam. Madam's first words after—after all 'er screamin' was done—was 'take the baby down to show me 'usband.' Madam, you see, is my main employer. I reports to Madam."

"I see," John said. He had only half heard the girl's prattle, but what stuck in his mind was that she had told them a moment ago that she had first washed the baby of blood. Whose blood? Anne's? Dear God, no one had mentioned that there would be blood spilled! He swallowed hard, then said, "Very well, Katy. I'm waiting to see—my first child. . . ."

"Aye," Father mumbled, half apologetically. "Forgive an excited old man, Son."

Katy, who had been standing on the very bottom tread of the stairs, took one final step down into the hall and, as though unveiling a masterpiece, lifted the blanket and held out the wriggling bundle for John to see—held it out quite grandly, lifted up to make it, John sensed, somehow easier for him to reach with his own hands. He didn't reach for it, though. Not yet. He just stood there peering down into the tiny, red, wrinkled, seemingly unformed face—at the miniature fists made of fingers too weak and too small for any use.

"Can you tell, John?" Father Fraser asked in an awed whisper. "Can you tell by looking at that little face whether it's a gir-rl or a boy?"

John looked at his father, then back at the baby. He glanced also at Katy, whose bright, proud smile announced that she was taking full credit.

"Shall I pull back the blanket, sir, for you to inspect? Or can you guess which it is?"

Dazed, John asked, "What? Oh, no, it's chilly in the hall here. Can't you—just tell us whether it's a boy or a girl?"

Unlike John, his father held out his arms while Katy deposited the blanketed bundle carefully into them and stepped back a little.

For a long, long time, the older man feasted his eyes on his grandchild, poked one of his fingers into the clutching, tiny hands, and wonder of wonders, John saw the baby grasp the old finger and hold on as for dear life. The little fingers were *not* too small to do anything. They were holding his father's huge finger.

Then Father Fraser began to speak to the baby as though they hadn't been interrupted in a long conversation begun eons ago. "You're a little girl, aren't you, Baby? A beautiful little lady just like your lovely, lovely mother, Anne. Did you know your mother's name is Anne? And did you know this big, tall, wide-shouldered, uneasy, excited man is your father—standing right here beside us now? I'll bet you didn't know his name is John Fraser. Well, it is. Your mother and father are called John and Anne Fraser by people in this big old world you've just entered. What's your name, little lady? Do you have a name yet?"

A strange but somehow knowing sound that resembled a gurgle came from the bundle of wriggling life in his father's arms.

"Oh, is that so?" Father asked, sounding both silly and more lovable than John had ever known him to sound. "You don't yet have a name? Well, you will have one. Your old grandfather promises you a name. But, right now, he has to ask to be excused, if you please, young lady, so that you can find out before another minute passes what your very own father's arms feel like." He held out the child. "Here, Son, I present you with your—daughter."

For an instant, but only for an instant, John couldn't move at all. He'd always assumed, when he'd thought about it, that Anne would someday present him with their first child. But here he stood beside Katy in the strange, awkward moment with his father offering him the first touch of the child born of the deeply personal, private love he owned with Anne. With Anne and no one else—until now.

"Gentlemen, in particular, have trouble inchin' theirselves toward that first samplin' of the warm, cuddly feel of a new baby, Mr. John," Katy piped. "I take it I'm free to address you, sir, as Mr. John, since y'er 'andsome father 'ere's got the same last name. I might git misunderstood now, mightn' I, was I to call you both Mr. Fraser. Go on, sir, an' take y'er pretty new daughter."

Frowning suddenly, John asked, "Are you quite sure, Katy, that—that Mrs. Fraser is all right up there? Is there any reason Dr. Mauldin and Flora are still with her behind a closed door?"

"None, Mr. John. Madam is tuckered out, but when I left her, she was smilin' that angel smile. Dr. Mauldin is givin' 'er 'is instructions, I'm sure, as to how to care for herself an' the little girl." Then Katy plainly snorted. "As for 'er, Miss Flora McLeod, I'm a'mind to guess she's poutin' good by now. She nursed both you an' y'er brother, Mr. William, I'm told—by *'er,* of course. She's got 'er nose out of joint that I'm 'ere to nurse the baby. Ain't no cause to worry none about my beautiful madam upstairs. She's havin' the ol' pickle-puss 'elp 'er fix 'er 'air, wash her face, dab on a little scent for when you go up to tell Madam how good she done. But first, Mr. John, you better try that baby on f'er size right in her father's arms!"

"Oh, oh, of course, Katy. And then, may I see your madam?"

"Aye, John, aye," his father said on a rare chuckle. "But Katy's right." He held out the baby. "Here, she's your treasure, Son."

His heart thumping far harder than in the thick of any battle on land or sea, John reached for the infant, so slowly, so carefully, he knew Father saw his hands tremble.

"I—I hope I know how to do this," he muttered as he felt, for the first time, that touch of warmth, of softness, of tender, tiny, somehow clinging weight in his own hands. "Good day, little one," he said stiffly. "Good day, little Miss

Fraser. I'm—I'm your—father." He glanced briefly up at his father, trying one of his casual, offhand smiles. "I—I want you to know right off that I'm going to try hard to be the kind of father you need me to be. I—I've always been fairly adept at making people laugh. Your mother firmly believes I can sing, I tend to show off and to boast some. I'm planning to do the major portion of my bragging from now on about you, Little Annie."

"Son! Did you just name her *Annie?*"

Giving his father an almost shy smile, he said, "I—I guess I did, didn't I? Yes, I just named her Annie."

"Strike me blind!" Katy exclaimed. "The mother names a new baby, or leastways 'as a 'and in it, Mr. John. But"—she beamed up into John's face—"if I'm any judge a' women, Madam will not be one to cross you, you hankerin' to call 'er by 'er very own name like that."

As though not hearing Katy, John said, "I've just named you Annie because your eyes, if you ever deign to open them, are hooded just like your beautiful mother's enchanted eyes. When do you plan to let me see their color, Little Annie girl? Can you tell your father when?" He glanced at Katy. "When can I see my wife?"

He saw Katy's own eyes roll helplessly. "That's up to *'er,* old pickle-puss, Mr. John. I knows my limits. She'd best stick to 'ers, though. I'm the one in charge of the baby!"

"Watch your lip, lass," Father Fraser said. "Flora McLeod's been a part of my family for more than a quarter of a century. The woman's to be respected, isn't she, John? Fully respected."

John grinned at the nanny. "If my advice means anything, Katy, yes. I'd suggest you tread softly when your work takes you to Flora's kitchen."

Katy took the baby from John, curtsied briefly, and headed back upstairs. "I know you mean only the best, Mr. John, but in my position, I does nothin' but what's best for this baby, and since I'm the nanny, that's for me to say. My ma always said I'm born to nannyhood!"

Left alone at the foot of the stairs, John waited until the girl was out of hearing, then smiled broadly at his father. "Well, sir, we tried, didn't we?"

"Aye, we tried. Flora McLeod's not used to sharing authority. The charwoman's all right twice a week, but with Katy we'd best brace ourselves, Son."

"When do you think Flora will let me see my wife?"

"As soon as Anne herself sends for you. Flora's wrapped around your wife's finger. Give Anne time to make herself presentable. They always want to do that first, you know."

Chapter 57

When Flora gave John a brisk nod from the parlor doorway almost half an hour later, he leaped to his feet and headed for the stairs.

"Don't you go bullin' it into her room now," Flora scolded, working hard, John thought, not to look too happy. "That little thing's all tuckered out, but her highness, Queen Katy, is out an' gone. I tended to that. Nobody but the baby with Miss Anne and they're waitin' for you to get there."

In his excitement, racing up two flights of stairs, he forgot and burst into the room, then remembered and closed the door softly. Anne's one free arm was reaching for him, the infant sleeping on the other.

"Darling," he breathed, kneeling by their bed. "Was it—dreadful?" Gathering them both in his arms, he persisted. "Are you sure you're all right? Are you sure Dr. Mauldin told me the truth when he said you were both fine? Am I holding you too hard? Don't let me hurt you! You've been hurt more than enough! Can you ever forgive me? I promise it will never happen again! Never."

She was doing her best to laugh at him as Father said she would, but her eyes were more convincing than her laugh. They were full of mischief.

"That's the most ridiculous thing you've ever said—even you, John Fraser," she said, pulling him closer. "If I thought we could never have another child, I'd—I'd want to die this minute, but you'd have to promise to bury me back on St. Simons."

How totally she knew him! Anne knew better than anyone else on earth that humor—their kind of humor—would quiet him, reassure him. She was all right. Anne was not going to die and leave him, and becoming a mother hadn't seemed to change her one bit. She was still Anne—tired, weak, but the spirit, her dear spirit, more shining than ever. They could still play and laugh together and he'd certainly started life as a father in the worst possible way, by lying to her! To promise she'd never have to endure giving birth again would mean that they could never fly and soar through another of their own special storms together and that *was* sheer nonsense, even for him.

"Tell me you're sorry," she said, holding his head against her breast. "I demand an apology. I want more babies! It—it was all just a different kind of storm, John. Look at her! She's going to be beautiful enough to be your daughter. I know she's all squinched up still, but you wait. Just wait even a day or so, Flora says, and she'll begin to unfold and then you'll see what real beauty is." Her smile was already freer, proud, contented. "She's asleep. I—I guess she's awfully tired, too, don't you imagine?"

"I suppose so. I hadn't thought about it, but I'm sure being born is—is a kind of battle for the baby. Father vows he's going to confront God with the whole arrangement one day. Anne?"

"What?"

"Father and I have never been as close as now. The old fellow was quite remarkable with me during the whole thing. Even though he's been through it twice, it was still hard on him. I never thought of Father's having an unanswered question. He has lots of them I now know."

"Where is he?"

"Downstairs in his office. Resting a little. Watching for the post to come, I'm sure." He tried to smile. "That's his best way of checking up on how well I've done my work of collecting past-due accounts, you know."

"Aren't you forgetting a promise you made to me about a month or so ago, dearest?" she asked.

He leaped to his feet. "The letter to your parents! Yes. I had forgotten all about it." Kneeling beside her again, he touched her cheek, then the baby's. "Anne, I'll write that letter before Flora can get our tea ready, I promise, but—" She interrupted him with a kiss, laughing. She was still Anne. Quick, funny—*his.* "I know our daughter has eyes exactly the color of yours!"

"Babies don't keep their eyes open during the first few

hours long enough for you to know that," she chided. "Katy told me they don't. I think I remember Mama's saying that when Isabella was born, too."

"Well, our daughter is unlike all others, Madam," he said, imitating Katy. "I'm sure I glimpsed 'er eyes with me own eyes an' there's not nothin' can ever convince me they ain't goin' to be the eyes of my first goddess! Now, I have two goddesses with luminous, wondrous eyes."

Anne's smile, though brief, told him she had caught and fully appreciated his skillful rendition of Katy's cockney dialect, but the smile vanished when she asked, "You love our baby already, don't you, John?"

"Love her? She's the delight of my heart! I could take right off marching again if I had Lord Herries's pipers to accompany me."

"We have to give her a name before you write to my parents. Papa always wants to know what a new child will be called so he can begin, as he says, 'to imagine a face to go with that particular name.'" She laughed. "I know that doesn't make a lot of sense, but then Papa often doesn't."

"She already has a name. *Her* father gave it to her when she took her first ride downstairs in Katy's arms. By the way, Katy vows it's going to bring her, Katy, good luck because she was the first to carry our daughter down a flight of stairs. She's going to need it, if I know Flora McLeod."

"Oh, busy as I was having a baby, I could tell that! Mama always said I showed signs of knowing how to handle servants. I think we're going to find out when I attempt to handle those two. But, darling, the baby's name! Don't you think her mother should have a little something to say about that?"

"Ah, that's the beautiful part of it! You've had everything to say about it already. Her name, my lovely Annie, is Annie."

The evanescent light, which could somehow change Anne's eyes from merely pale blue loveliness to an otherworldly beauty, glowed. "Annie?" she whispered.

"Yes. If you now held a tiny son in your arms, don't you think you'd want to call him John? For me? And for your dear father?"

"I can't win with you, can I? No. That's wrong. I can't do anything *but* win with a lover like you. Yes, oh, yes. If I'd given you a son, his name would be John—absolutely!"

"Then, her name's Annie. Anne, if we have to be proper for christening and things like that, but it's been Annie now for almost an hour." He laid his hand on the child's silky, dark hair. "Ever since her father had his first glimpse of her."

"All right," she whispered, kissing his hand. "But you're being dismissed. You must write that letter to St. Simons. John, it has to go out in the post before five today or it won't make the next boat to America."

Early in March on what St. Simons islanders knew as a full-blown spring day—spring having begun its magic touch long before February ended—John Couper and Dr. William Fraser rode together down Frederica Road. They were en route to visit James Hamilton, who had written that he would go to Hamilton Plantation from Hopeton on the mainland that day.

As their mounts trotted side by side, neither in a hurry, Couper said, "A man is better off to make a firm appointment with his own son when that son's name is James Hamilton Couper."

"You did make this trip twice lately, missing him both times, didn't you?" William asked. "One thing we all know by now, though, is that if he says he'll be on St. Simons at Hamilton today, he'll be there."

"Aye. I wonder at times about my son," Couper said. "He's never given me a moment's real worry. But I do wonder at him. Unlike his father, everything he touches succeeds. Still, can a man find happiness in business and scientific study alone? There seems no end to the boy's need to experiment with everything from methods of drainage to new means of fertilization. Here he is running two huge plantations, managing and guiding his people with such skill he can spare hands for Cannon's Point—but with no wife. No family. Who comforts him at day's end? William, where does he find the warmth and fulfillment needed by every man?"

"Afraid I have no answer to that, sir. You know I'm aware of how much a man needs a wife. I wonder about James, too, but somehow I feel the expertise he shows in every other way will serve him well when it comes to choosing a wife. Does he ever mention marriage to you when the two of you are alone?"

"Only that he'll know when the time is right. My son always does the correct thing, you know. Unlike his impulsive father."

"Sir, I know you're anxious over the birth of Anne's first child, especially now that we're sure Mrs. Couper is honoring *you* with another baby in the late summer. My latest letter from Father assures me Anne's doing fine, though. And, it's significant that the man is more lighthearted than I've known him to be since he lost my mother—all because Anne is there and because he's going to be on hand when his first grandchild comes. My guess is that the baby's already born. Wasn't it due about mid-February?"

"Aye," Couper said wearily. "Such a long wait, though, for the letter John promised to write the minute he knew the child and its mother were safe. Spalding told me he once received a letter from Liverpool in a little over a month, but we don't get that kind of service from London."

"Undoubtedly, your new grandchild is nearly a month old by now! I'm sure John wrote. His letter should reach St. Simons in another few days."

"I've been trying to remember about our little Isabella during her first weeks of life. Always such a merry, well-behaved baby. Not like our other daughter, Anne."

William laughed. "Anne misbehaved?"

"Well, not in her father's opinion, but I've heard Rebecca say often that from almost day one, Anne knew exactly what she wanted and exactly when. I swear those beautiful, pale blue eyes of hers were following light and shadow within a month! If her nurse, Liz, happened to turn her away from the light, a real racket broke loose." He chuckled. "Anne was walking before she was fifteen months old."

"You're a blessed man, Mr. Couper."

"Aye. Almost as blessed as your father, who can simply move to another part of his own house when he's overwhelmed as am I for a glimpse of his first grandchild."

James Hamilton Couper enjoyed the trip by water from Hopeton Plantation on the mainland, north of Brunswick, to Hamilton on St. Simons. If his estimate was correct—the careful estimate made while he ate his solitary breakfast at dawn in the Hopeton dining room—he could expect to reach his new dock on St. Simons in plenty of time to attend to a few duties in his Hamilton office and be free to meet his father no later than ten minutes past 10 A.M. He was right on schedule.

The work just finished at his Hamilton desk, he looked at his watch. With seven minutes to spare, he decided to inspect the planting in progress in at least one cotton field near the Frederica River before taking a brisk ride to the end of the lane along which his father would arrive. Older people, he thought, relish being met. He had made it a point always to meet his father, who never failed to act surprised.

Never had James found it difficult to revere or honor his colorful parent, but always he had been keenly aware that within reason, he, James Hamilton Couper, must reverse their roles—must stay ever-watchful of his buoyant parent's generous impulses, his sometimes impractical new ideas. For that matter, he had kept records of every Negro purchase his father had made in the past decade or so, meticulous records, too, of every dollar borrowed from their Savannah factor, of every penny spent on the rather extravagant refurbishing of the small, well-built tabby house at Lawrence.

That James Hamilton thought the latter undertaking foolish and highly unrealistic was well known to his parent. Papa, being Papa, had gone right ahead with the work. They had not argued once about the project so dear to John Couper's heart. James had simply kept accounts in case it would be he who might be left with the full responsibility of deciding at some future time what would indeed be done with the three hundred or so fertile acres now lying fallow at Lawrence Plantation on St. Simons Island. If James had sized up his sister's charming husband, John Fraser, correctly, Father's dream that the newly married couple might soon agree to leave England behind and return to Georgia was little more than a dream.

Actually, James hoped Papa would ride up alone within the next five minutes. Waiting annoyed him.

In exactly nine minutes, he heard what was surely the galloping of two horses. Father had not come alone. The man's lifelong enjoyment of people went on puzzling James Hamilton. When the two riders came into sight around a shrub-choked bend in the lane that led to his well-built plantation house, James felt a measure of relief that Papa's companion was Dr. William Fraser. At least, the younger brother of Anne's husband was thoughtful, definitely not impetuous beyond having decided rather quickly that he wanted to marry Frances Anne Wylly, and would be sensitive enough to give James time alone for a discussion of family matters with his father.

In his own busy day, he had allowed three-quarters of an hour for dining, but dinner was more than two hours away, so he decided to have his talk with Papa first. Knowing that every dollar earned from occasional medical services counted for Fraser, he could, of course, pay him modestly for examining some of his ailing people. Then James and Papa could talk.

That decision made, he greeted his visitors warmly, pointed the way to the small slave hospital he'd built since he took over Hamilton, thanked Fraser, and turned the horses over to young Job, who had been standing in his shy, backward way behind a clump of wild yellow jasmine until needed.

"It's splendid to see you, Papa," James said as he and the older Couper headed alone for James's office on the river side of the Hamilton house. "And certainly, we have a splendid spring day for our visit. Is Mama well? And little Isabella?"

"All fine as fiddles, son," his father said, striding along briskly beside him. "Your mother's an amazing woman. She's almost forty-two and she's carrying our unborn child like a gir-rl of twenty! Never a complaint, at least not in my hearing. She vows that she's suffered that infernal morning sickness only once or twice with this one. She had many bad mornings on Cumberland while she was carrying Isabella." His somewhat solemn tone dissolved into laughter. "By the time this baby arrives—probably in August of this year, Dr. William says—I can guarantee Isabella will be lyrical with excitement."

"How old is my little sister now?" James asked, opening the front door for his father.

"She'll be two in September. Walks everywhere, sometimes where she doesn't mean to, but never willfully. She is so docile, merry. I find my old brain toying often with the amazing fact of how different two little girls can be—both born of the same parents. When Annie was a year and a half, she not only walked in the wrong places, she ran—a bit tipped forward—but that was because she'd made up her independent mind to reach something always a bit ahead of her physical ability to get there. Annie never walked when she could run! Isabella is going to be a proper young lady. Unlike her sister, she's far more submissive already." The hint of laughter left him. "If only we'd hear from John! I'm in a lather to know your sister and the baby came through the ordeal."

Seated at his plantation desk, after pulling out a comfortable chair for his parent, James Hamilton went straight to his main reason for their meeting today. "I feel the time has come, Papa, for me to ask if you also expect any definite response from Lieutenant Fraser about his plans to return to St. Simons in order to take over at Lawrence. Or is he still wasting time hoping to regain his military commission? Surely you gave him a limited period in which to come to his senses?"

His father said nothing, but sat there seeming to study James's face.

"By your own admission, Father," James went on, uneasy under the scrutiny, "the man has tried more than once to be accepted again and failed. Do you think it's quite fair to the Couper interests for that good, rich land to lie there in its unproductive state?"

Still in no hurry, the older man said slowly, carefully, "It's been there totally unproductive for years now, Son. Is there some new reason why you're in such a hurry to have John claim my offer?"

"One highly important reason, Papa. *You.*"

"Me?"

"I dislike intensely seeing you so humiliated—your generous offer spurned in such a high-handed fashion! I revere you, sir. I've always revered you. Any new obligation you've ever asked of me I've tried my utmost to fulfill. Anne's husband is not equipped to follow any other profession but soldiering. Can you go on holding any measure of respect for him if he persists in procrastinating like this?"

"I wasn't aware that he's procrastinating. The boy's working hard, traveling about London all day every day helping his own father save his wine-importing business. There's no more difficult job anywhere than collecting monies from reluctant men. You're right, though. You have put your shoulder to every wheel that's come your way. You're destined to be an influential, highly prominent coastal planter—you are already—while still in your twenties. But James, no two human beings are alike. God did not make molds and pour us into them. I don't mean to disagree with you. And I'm not arguing. I simply hope that some word of mine might serve as a warning to you."

Unable to believe his ears, James demanded, "A—warning, sir?"

"Aye. You have a long life ahead. I'm in my fifty-eighth year. Give me credit for having learned a thing or two along the way. If you go on expecting even a few people to be as brilliant, as responsible, as energetic, as ambitious, as you prove yourself to be every day, you'll wake up someday a sadly disillusioned old man. Even a bitter old man. There is no young gentleman anywhere exactly like you. That makes you neither better nor worse. It just proves that you're—you. I could not be more proud to be your father, and Son, I am your pr-roud father, but I'm not much like you. You're not much like me. 'Twould be a relief to us both could we but accept each other as we are. And John Fraser as he is."

"Have you finished, Father?"

"Aye. For now."

"Then, with your indulgence, I'd like to thank you for sharing your wisdom and I'll give all you've said to me much thought when I find free time in my schedule. You are correct, of course, that no two men are exactly alike. I must remind you, however, that I am sharply aware of your need, not only of someone younger, but a bit less burdened than you with family and home duties, to travel in your behalf—"

"Ah, there you've hit it, Son! No man relishes being at home more than I! I'm blessed indeed that my trustworthy, brainy son is young and able and willing to traipse about the country in my behalf. The older I get, the more like bad medicine it becomes each time anything drags me away from my beloved Cannon's Point. Why, if I weren't such a homebody, I'd surely be taking your dear mother to Newport to have her next child, now, wouldn't I? She'd find Newport far cooler, far more comfortable in all ways."

"Should my own business responsibilities here and at Hopeton permit, I'll gladly escort Mother to Rhode Island come summer," James said. "All of which brings me straight back to the purpose of our meeting—John Fraser's stubborn refusal to accept your magnanimous offer. If he would only bring my sister home where she belongs, take full advantage of learning how to run a plantation under your expertise and mine, he could be of immense help to us both. I'm sure Anne would enjoy a trip to Newport with Mother. Impossible, of course, if my poor sister is still stuck in crowded, filthy London because she chose to marry such an obstinate buck. John Fraser isn't stupid, you know. He's just spoiled. Headstrong, irresponsible, determined to do only what *he* chooses to do!"

" 'Tis always good to hear your opinion, James," his father said in a quiet, calm voice. "Having you free to speak so frankly to me is worth the ride down here. I expect the favor of also speaking frankly to you now."

"By all means, Father."

"Gude. When your sister Anne married John Fraser, she and he became, in the sight of God, as one person. Anne does not belong to me any longer, or to her mother, or to you."

"But I'm as certain as that we're sitting here in my office, Papa, that she's longing for even one glimpse of a Cannon's Point sunrise—a clean, fresh breeze off the river. Anne's roots are here on St. Simons Island, not across the Atlantic in faraway England among foreigners. Those two gave no sane, careful thought to what life might be like once they'd married. Their entire romance must rank among the most irrational, precipitate courtships anywhere. I would stake my life that Anne gave no forethought whatever to how he might support her or a family!"

"In that respect, she's quite like your own father. I also offered your mother nothing beyond my determination to succeed and my eternal love for her. I was barely beginning to get a foothold when you came along, James."

"Before you remind me again, sir, that no two of us are alike, let me hasten to say that you, at least, had the drive to succeed. I see no indication of that in John Fraser. He's infatuated with the uniform and the adventure of life in the Royal Marines—nothing more."

"Have you been corresponding with him, James?"

"Why, no. No, of course not. My own growing correspondence among the increasing number of scientists and planters and engineers, both here and abroad, preclude any such thing. Mama assures me the two of you keep my sister aware of my continuing devotion to her. I simply need to be sure that you know her young man not only is making a fool of himself by refusing your kind offer, he's making a—a bit of a fool of you, too."

His father laughed. " 'Tis no big piece of work making a fool of me, Son. Were he still alive, I'd recommend your asking my own straitlaced father, your grandfather, who arranged my passage as a brash boy of sixteen all the way to America for the good of Scotland!"

James had heard his father say that a hundred times. It still somehow annoyed him.

"One thing more, Son, before the good doctor rejoins us for dinner. If you had any notion of pressing me to put a time limit on my love offering of Lawrence to John and Anne, forget it immediately! It is my land and it is I who am free to do with it as I see fit. I'm sure you'd hoped I'd force John to accept this year, work under my supervision until he learns how to manage a big plantation, help me pay off my vast debt incurred by the loss of my people, perhaps then begin to give you a hand here with Hamilton in the near future. A laudable plan but not one I necessarily intend to follow." James saw the slightly faded blue eyes brim with quick tears. "The Almighty knows I'd give this right arm of mine for one look at my cherished daughter Anne. He also knows I'd give as much to hold my grandchild in my arms, but I've won the battle with myself where they're concerned. It's not been easy, still I've done it. The Frasers know the Lawrence house is repaired, painted, and ready for them. They also know that only they can make the final decision. Your mother and I simply wait out every letter, watching between every line for some word of hope that they might come home soon. So far, nothing. Such a decision on John's part will not be simple. Aside from his love of the military, the boy also hates farming! Shows no signs of having been born with a leaning toward it. Running a huge plantation, learning how to make use of the quirks and talents of the people we own, is hard enough at best, even when a mon th-r-rives on it. Have I made myself clear, James?"

"Quite clear, Papa. I simply would have felt remiss not to have tried, at least, to persuade you to urge them back here where opportunities are limitless for John Fraser."

"I ken, son. I ken your good intentions." Couper got to

his feet. "I've lectured long enough and I hear Dr. William talking to one of your people outside that open window. Like me, I'm sure he's hungry as a bear. Isn't it time you served us dinner?"

Chapter 58

May, even in sooty old London, was, to Anne's beauty-starved spirit, lovely. Every available space seemed crowded with bright blossoms, except, of course, poor Father Fraser's neglected back courtyard. In places where the earth was covered with houses and paving blocks, geraniums and vining begonias overflowed window boxes and hanging baskets. Fewer fires burned because the weather was no longer so cold, and above the normal layer of smoke from factories and smelters, the sky shone clear and blue.

Aware that she had every reason to be lighthearted, Anne found herself actually feeling guilty when a dark mood struck. Her baby, almost fourteen weeks old, was healthy and for nearly a fortnight had been responding to her mother's soft murmurings and smiles. Little Annie, John swore, the night he left once more for Portsmouth, had actually laughed at one of his jokes. Anne now nursed her only three or four times a day and yesterday, attempting to avoid still another fuss between Flora and Katy, had humored Flora by trying the infant on two spoonfuls of thin porridge, which Little Annie swallowed with remarkable relish.

Days and nights with John away were in themselves hard. Equally as hard was the constant need Anne felt to walk on eggshells when Flora and Katy chanced to be in the same room with the child. Instead of adjusting to another servant in the house, Flora seemed more rankled by the hour that perky, opinionated, skillful Katy had come tripping into her domain.

Just a few minutes ago as Anne was about to begin a letter to Anna Matilda—her first since the baby's birth—

shrill, raised voices from across the upstairs hall stopped her.

"Your kitchen is yours to do in as you please," Katy was declaring, "but this upstairs room belongs to my charge, Annie Fraser, and *to me,* Miss Flora! I'll thank you to keep yourself downstairs in your own bailiwick. Do I make myself clear?"

"An' I'll thank you, Missy, to remember that you was nothing more than a pukin' baby yourself, all red and squinch-faced, while I was feedin' an' changin' an' carin' for this baby's father! I fed him an' Dr. William both me thin porridge and if you can find a healthier specimen of a grown man than my laddie today, 'twould be a fine idea to print it in the papers."

Anne, leaving her desk, had crossed the hall to settle the dispute. Little Annie had now eaten two more bites of gruel, Flora was back downstairs in her domain, Katy and the baby were in theirs, and maybe, Anne thought, writing to Anna Matilda will help quiet *me.*

For a long time, she sat toying with the quill John had once more remembered to sharpen for her before he left. No woman ever had a more thoughtful husband. Not once in the year and three months they'd been married had John ever been unaware of her small desires or needs. She smiled a little sadly, dipped the quill, but as she wrote the date, thought how desperately she longed for him to fulfill her greatest need—to be together again—back on St. Simons Island.

15 May 1817
2 George Street, London

My Dearest Anna Matilda,

I am writing to you at last as a full-fledged mother and I wish I really knew all of what that means! I'm sure Papa sent Big Boy riding to Retreat to tell you the good news as soon as John's letter reached Cannon's Point. I don't feel too guilty for my long silence because Mama and Papa have told me of your happiness in my behalf. Thank you. And they have also told me at length of your amazing maturity! I am duly impressed by all you have learned about managing a huge plantation. Some days when trying to keep my equilibrium inside one London house, I have grave doubts that I would ever learn how to direct Negroes and business the way you do. You'll say that is my native air and the Lord above knows St. Simons is where I long, night and day, to be. I'm at sixes and sevens today because again, my beloved John is off in a stagecoach, having heard that if he reports this month at Portsmouth, there might be a chance for him to regain his commission. If this letter skips about and makes less than usual sense, his absence is the reason. That and my own panic that at some point, he may be successful in regaining it.

Oh, Anna, my dear friend, although I am most comfortably situated and have come to love my father-in-law deeply, I fear my longing to be at Cannon's Point may have marked my beautiful new daughter! Perhaps the most wrenching part of this homesickness of mine is that I cannot talk about it freely to anyone. I love John and Father Fraser too much—even Flora McLeod, the housekeeper—and don't want them to think I'm ungrateful. Am I being kind to them or just plain false?

Mama, bless her, sent ample money for a nanny—a girl named Katy with fiery red hair, who not only is very good with my child, but is extremely aware of her own ability and so does a lot of bossing. She'd rather die than take even a suggestion from Flora, who nursed both John and William. To give you an example: Last week, Katy, vowing that Little Annie's bottom is still too round for her to be able to keep her balance on it in her crib, supported her all around with pillows. Flora happened to see this and began to preach against it, saying it would weaken the child's back muscles. I am always put in the pickle of being peacemaker (truly impossible!) and so, bowing to Flora's age and experience, I ordered Katy to remove the cushions. At which moment, Katy flared that I always gave in to Flora. As indeed, minutes before beginning this letter, I gave in again in another fracas that had to do with porridge! Except to feed and play with her, I am, of course, helpless and clumsy with a new baby.

But Little Annie is a beautiful child—a soft cap of

dark hair and, John swears, odd, blue eyes exactly like mine. Oh, Anna, am I getting old? Is it old-woman-like of me to worry and fret and stew that I might become so entwined in these petty household uprisings that John will find me unattractive and dull? Except when invited formally, we go out so seldom, and in such a noisy, dirty, smelly city, I admit to you that even taking walks is not a refreshing experience. I fear this has been one long complaint from the start, and there you are caring for sick Negroes, riding the fields with your father's overseer, and, Mama wrote, ordering lumber to build a new and fine slave hospital—even beginning the building while your father is away! Of course, I keep telling myself that you do not have a child or a husband to care for—then I long for the day when you have both—and then I go back to longing to be in your shoes on St. Simons doing all you do there!

When John finally comes home, we will be seeing something of one of Mama's very distant cousins, the present Lord Herries, who, as I wrote while we were in Scotland, lives three months out of the year in the old Maxwell castle, Caerlaverock, and at other times in London. John and I both find him excellent company and so, after some social life when he reaches London, I'm sure my next letter will be more interesting. I'm ashamed of this one and feel most inadequate saying that I count myself blessed.

She added her love to Anna Matilda's parents, to all their St. Simons friends, and especially to Frances Anne Wylly, now known far and wide to be deeply attached to John's brother, William.

After addressing and sealing the letter, she went to stand at the window overlooking George Street and tried to imagine what on earth she would find to do if John came home a week or so from now with the news that he would have to leave again because indeed he had been accepted back into his unit.

She had never been one to endure even the thought of sameness because, except for the long months of waiting for John to come for her on St. Simons and for Annie's birth, there had been so little sameness to endure. The mere thought made her feel empty and frightened. At least, if one were at home at Cannon's Point, there was someone to talk to—Eve or Mama or Papa. She had only to whistle for Big Boy and after a brisk gallop, she could be down at Retreat, where Anna Matilda was always ready for gossip and laughter and dreaming. An even shorter gallop would take her to St. Clair, where the Wyllys lived in the old house beside the great oak tree they called Old England. For that matter, at home there was actually no need to turn to people for company. There was always some new flower blooming or a bird nesting or a lamb or puppies or rabbits or calves being born.

At home there were so few, if any, problems to sort out. No Katy to heckle a Flora McLeod. No Flora to boss Katy. No roles to play. Although her heart invariably melted with love when she spent time with Little Annie, she didn't yet feel natural as a mother. Having to be on hand so many times a day for nursing was all joy in one way, but had she been at Cannon's Point, there would have been one or more of Papa's people who would have vied for the sheer privilege and honor of nursing and singing to Miss Anne's baby.

With John gone, I'm lost, she thought, sinking down in the little wooden rocker, where she had begun to spend so many lonely hours.

One thought tortured her—how would she act, what would she say, if indeed he came home this time, face beaming because he had finally found it possible to return to his regiment?

"I'll want to die," she said in a half-whisper. "And I dare not even want to do that! I'm not free to die. I have an adorable, helpless little girl depending on me now."

With all her heart she longed for Papa, who for every day of her life had always been able to fix anything that troubled her. Papa was on the other side of the ocean this minute with the full and perfect solution to all that tore at her today. The dear little house at Lawrence was repaired and waiting. Her parents were waiting—both as starkly helpless as she because there was John. There would always be John, and what John wanted she would have to choose, and none of what he wanted could ever possibly work out.

"If I really love him—and I do—dare I pray that there will never, never, *never* be a commission open to him in his beloved regiment again? Do You hear selfish prayers like that, God? Do You?"

Chapter 59

The first of June came and went, with Flora still making a daily inspection to be sure Katy had not sneaked pillows around Little Annie when she tried to sit up in her crib. Of course, the pillows were always there and Flora knifed at Katy in her sharpest Borderland brogue.

To offer Anne a respite in her long day, dear Father Fraser had begun to hire a hack home for dinner, then back to finish out the day at his office, longer days than usual because John was still in Portsmouth. Because Father Fraser agreed so thoroughly with her, hoped as fervently as she did that John would find an interest outside the military, Anne had begun to look forward to dinnertime spent with her father-in-law. She not only enjoyed his company, his presence invariably calmed Flora a bit, and at least while Flora was busy downstairs with dinner, Anne knew the baby was not being exposed to a spat. Mama had always declared that even a baby a few months old—and Little Annie was now nearly four months—sensed trouble among adults whose anger and harsh words invaded the world in which the child was just learning to live.

"Are you worried about John, Father Fraser?" Anne asked when they had bragged on Flora for the delicious loin of pork and new potatoes she had served them. "He's been away over three weeks! I know I've had one loving letter, but I keep thinking about something downright weird and maybe if I tell you, I'll stop worrying about it."

"You haven't mentioned it to Flora?" he asked.

"No and I worry about that too. Flora and I have always been close enough for me to tell her many things, but the poor woman is so annoyed with having Katy in the house,

I'm afraid I no longer confide in her. Do you remember John wrote in that letter about seeing a longtime marine friend named Lieutenant Griffith?"

"Aye, I recall that. The boy seemed most pleased to see him again. We both know John misses the camaraderie of men his own age, but everything is bound to be more pleasant once he's home again and the two of you can begin accepting invitations. The evening you spent at the theater with Captain Menzies and his wife before he left London seemed to lift John's spirits for a week or so afterward. Of course, Captain Menzies was also a friend from his service days in the marines."

"Oh, Father Fraser, that's the trouble! Except when he's alone with Little Annie and me, John seems to work at being genial. This is such a hard interim for him. Morning to night I try to think of ways to ease his restlessness, but he's so skillful at fooling you and me. No one could say John is bad-tempered or sullen. If I didn't know my own father so well, I'd think maybe *he* was acting sometimes, too, because Papa is known by everyone for his sunny disposition. He and John are a lot alike, really. Except that I'm never as sure John really *feels* cheerful. Maybe I've always believed too much in my father's good humor, but I don't think so. He's a contented man."

Giving her a forlorn smile, Father Fraser said, "I'm not so sure of that these days, Anne. Mr. Couper misses you too much. It's in every line he writes, no matter how he tries to keep you free from worry about him. And to think he's never laid eyes on that adorable grandchild of his! I pity the man. I pray for him. But, what worries you especially about John's mention of Lieutenant Griffith?"

"I don't know. I honestly don't know. He didn't stay this long the last time he went to Portsmouth. I—I can't help wondering if this Lieutenant Griffith has heard of another opening in the marines John might fill. Am I—am I being silly about all this?"

"My dear lass, the boy has placed you in an untenable position. I confess there are times when I feel I should ask your forgiveness."

"Father Fraser, *why*?"

"Simply because he's my son. I sired him. Somewhere in his character is a terrible flaw. I know I've failed John as a father, but how does a father remedy that when the son's now a grown man with a mind of his own?"

Anne's eyes flashed blue fire—half anger and half panic. "Don't ever say such a thing to me again, do you hear? Don't criticize yourself to me and don't criticize John! I love you both too much."

For a long time, they just sat at the table sipping tea, the silence growing more and more awkward. Finally, Father Fraser set down his cup, cleared his throat firmly, and said, "The only solution I see that will make you happy and guarantee that our precious Little Annie grows up in healthy surroundings is for John to be man enough to accept your father's generous offer of that St. Simons Island plantation. 'Twill tear the heart out of me to see you go—taking my granddaughter away from me—and until this minute, so help me God, I haven't myself found the courage to voice it, but that is the only solution, Anne. So, put whatever concern you're imagining about Lieutenant Griffith out of your mind and determine once and for all to tell John the truth. Tell him the only thing you really want is to go home—home to your parents, where there will be productive, full-time, responsible work for your husband. I want to hear you say it, Anne. I need to hear you say you'll do it. Wouldn't most of your fears slip away if John would only take you—home?"

Anne stared at him, her eyes stinging with tears, not only because what Father Fraser had just said was true, true, but because she knew he would again sink into his long-faced, hopeless old age if they did leave. She could never force John to take her home. Far better to try to change the subject.

"Did I ever tell you about the odd thing the mother of my best St. Simons friend, Anna Matilda Page, once said to Anna and me?"

"I don't recollect that you did," he said.

"Well, dear Mrs. Page, although she's happily married to a handsome, prosperous, kind man, once said, 'Girls, if you both knew what was good for you, neither of you would ever, ever marry!' "

She could feel him studying her. "But you did marry, lass. You married my complicated son. And would you change that fact were it in your power?"

"Oh, never! If I could be sure such a thing could ever make John as happy as it would make me, I'd have told you straight out a moment ago that yes, what I really want is for him to take over the management of Lawrence. When I think of living so near Cannon's Point, all that comes to me is that then everything would again be all right. But that could be because I was young, awfully young, when I remember life being so tranquil and cozy back home. That was before the pure magic of loving John filled my days and nights. That was also before I was Annie's mother. Before I was even a real woman. John is honest enough to admit that part of him wants to stay young. Part of me does, too, but for me, John will always come first. Now, don't tell me I'm being noble. I'm not! I'm as scared of growing up, of being responsible for guiding Annie, as John is. It's—it's just simpler for me. Not easier, *simpler.* I don't go around half-dead inside because I now live in London instead of in the safety of my father's house. Father Fraser, John does go around half-dead inside without his regiment. I'd do almost anything you asked except put myself first, ahead of John."

"I'm to ignore, then, that he puts himself ahead of you?"

His voice was so flat and toneless, she felt a chill even on such a mild summer day. From her first meeting with Father Fraser, Anne had set her heart on bringing him back to feeling the goodness and warmth of living—even without his beloved Margaret. She was not going to allow her own longing for home to spoil that after all this time.

"Anyway," she said quite brightly, "if John did decide he really wanted to own Lawrence Plantation, you'd have to go with us. I can't bear the thought of ever leaving you."

"Nor I of seeing you go, lass. The light would go out again for me." His struggle to hide the sorrow in his voice was so evident and so futile, she felt she'd never loved him so much as this minute. "I expect," he went on, "that as soon as I could dispose of my business, I'd be hightailing it across the ocean to make my home, for what years are left to me, with William and his intended, Miss Frances Anne Wylly."

Anne brightened because the whole idea was so unexpected and so glorious. "What makes you think I'd allow you to live with William and Frances Anne when John and I would have a house in which you'd always have a room of your very own?"

"What makes me think that?" he mused. "To be realistic, with the years coming on, I yearn for peace and I'd be more peaceful with William. No one knows that better than John, but I'd likely be close by and it's a lovely dream for us both to dwell on, isn't it? Even if it's only a dream, lass, what do you say we agree on it and see what happens?" He reached to lay his hand on hers. "From now on, in secret, you and I will dwell only on our private dream. Don't you think that will help ease us both into whatever comes next? My son will come bursting back into this house any day now, as full of himself as he's always been, and whether he's acting—pretending—or telling us the truth, we'll ride it out together. Just remember, I'll always be on hand to listen to you, Anne, to try to understand, to do my best to smooth your way."

With the birth of her own child less than three months away, Rebecca Couper found herself spending more and more time with Eve, who was so caught up in her newly discovered talent for drawing, the hours with her seemed to fly past. For Rebecca, waiting had always been the hardest part of bearing a child and Eve certainly kept her occupied.

"Do you realize, Eve," she said one June morning, "that you've already made more new needlepoint designs than I'll ever find time to work? Look at that stack of canvas pieces!"

"They don't be all for you to work, ma'am. Miss Anne, she good too wif a needle."

"You're making all these patterns for Anne to do? Heaven knows she doesn't write often, but I know her husband's due back from Portsmouth again any day now and she fully expects, with her own baby doing so well, that they'll be leading a busy social life. How do you know she'll want all this needlework to do?"

"Oh, I don' know that. What I know is Miss Anne's comin' home!"

Rebecca stared at the dark head bent over a brand new design in which two more of Anne's favorite birds—male and female painted buntings—were taking shape under Eve's long, skillful fingers. "You *know* Anne's coming home? Back here to Cannon's Point?"

"No'm. Oh, she stay here jus' til I get things fix in her own house. But Miss Anne an' her man, they *be comin' back here to Lawrence to live*!"

Rebecca's heart leaped. Eve had known before anyone else that both Rebecca and Anne would be having new babies. Before anyone at Cannon's Point knew of either event, Eve was absolutely certain. Dare she hope that the girl's foreknowledge was working again? For that matter, had she ever really believed, even when the facts were known, that Eve actually did know about both babies ahead of time? There would, for Rebecca—for any white mistress, she felt sure—always be a mysterious veil between the mistress and her Negro servant because such so-called secret knowledge was a way of life for the servant.

So far as she and Jock could tell, Anne's return to live on St. Simons Island seemed less and less likely. Yet, Eve's certainty was there. The bright, talented girl had not even stopped working at her drawing when she simply announced that Anne would indeed be back in plenty of time to work all those needlepoint patterns.

"You don' need to b'lieve, Miss Becca, for what I say to be true. Eve's heart too light. Eben you doubtin' my word don' make it heaby. In one way, I belong to June, an' they neber be a better man than June. But Miss Anne she come along before June come to love me. I be a better wife to June when she git here, Lord knows. Half my heart been dead since Miss Anne leave me."

Eve's almost casual certainty had so startled Rebecca, she fell silent for a time. As awkward as a real conversation could be with a servant, long silences that would trouble or annoy another white person seemed not to matter to them. Finally, because the silence bothered her, Rebecca said, "I know you still miss Anne."

"I done said half my heart be dead."

"Eve, have you told June or your mother, Fanny, or anyone else about your premonition that my daughter and her husband and little girl are coming home?"

"Not June. Not Mama. But my gran'maum, Sofy, she know."

"You told Sofy and not your own mother?"

"No'm I ain' tol' nobody. Gran'maum, she just know, same as me."

Remembering the trouble Jock had gone through with Sofy over the conjure she had silently laid down on poor Mr. Roswell King, Rebecca shuddered. The long-standing trouble with Roswell King, Sr., over Sofy's supposed magic, had not lessened. Despite Jock's insistence that Sofy remove her conjure and let the man's legs get well, he grew only more lame. More and more, Roswell King, Jr., made the boat trips to Butler's Island, rode the cotton fields at Hampton.

But as odd and puzzling as his father had always been, the heavyset young man was even more overbearing. If there was a remote chance that something as uncanny as a conjure could influence anyone, Rebecca would give almost anything to find a way to force Sofy to lift it. "Eve, I don't want you to turn out to be like Sofy, do you hear me?"

Eve sighed her annoyance loudly. "You think I axed to be born wif' a caul over my face? Kin I help knowin' things once I know 'em, Miss Becca?"

If Eve was annoyed, so was Rebecca. "I simply don't want you to turn out to be a witch, Eve! Miss Anne and her father and I have always felt you were above that kind of thing. I've come to enjoy our work together since we learned of your talent for drawing and I'll be quite put out if our feeling for each other changes in any way. Is that clear?"

Eve looked up—looked directly at her. "Yes, ma'am, it be half-clear anyway."

"Half-clear?"

"My half-white blood—which I hates—cause me to half trade places sometimes wif you, Miss Becca. I don' hate you, though. How could I? You be Miss Anne's mama."

"Eve, since you and your grandmother are so much alike—in certain ways—can't you use your powerful mind to overrule hers? Can't you persuade her to lift her conjure from poor old Mr. King? For Master Couper's sake? Mr. King's disposition is growing more and more burdensome for my husband."

After drawing painstakingly the details of the tree branch where her two painted buntings were perched, Eve looked up. "I don' put down conjures, Miss Becca. I don' cross my gran'maum, neither. I just knows certain things ahead—like the pure truth that Miss Anne, she be comin' home. Not *when*. Lord, I wish I knowed when. But sure as the moon come over the big water, Miss Anne, she comin' home to stay!"

"You know how far along I am with my own child, Eve! You know this is a dreadful time for you to upset me like this. I've been counting on you to help me. More, obviously, than I should have. There *is* something different about you that makes me understand, in a way I never understood before, why Anne cares so much for you. I beg you not to make me more apprehensive than I am. I'm forty-two years old and I'm going to have a child in less than three months now!"

Eve dropped the quill she'd been using, jumped up and ran to where Rebecca sat in the shady corner of the Cannon's Point porch. "You oughta thank me, Miss Becca!"

"Thank you for what? For raising my hopes when I know perfectly well they'll be dashed by the very next letter from Anne?"

"But she might not *know* yet that she be comin' home to raise the rest ob her chillurn. Dat don't keep her from comin' jus' the same. You mark Eve's word, Miss Becca. Miss Anne an' her man ain' gonna' hab eben one more baby 'fore they bof be right down the lane there in their own place at Lawrence. She be there—an' me right wif' her! Me an' June go too. You make me a promise, Miss Becca?"

Rebecca stared up at her. "A—promise, Eve? You want me to promise that Mr. Couper will allow you and June to live at Lawrence with Anne and John Fraser? You know I can't do that!"

"No such thing! Dat man he walk his fiel's on his hands if you tell him to." Eve stood to her full height, actually peering *down* at her mistress, sitting helpless and bulgy in her rocking chair. "You don' tell him to let me work for Miss Anne, I sell my drawin's an' earn the money to buy bof' June an' me in the name of Mr. John Fraser!"

What came to her would be an insensitive thing to say, but the girl had made Rebecca feel so distraught, she said it anyway. "I believe my husband would have to agree. He is the master."

Eve threw back her proud head and laughed. "You take it all wrong! An' here, nex' to Miss Anne, I think you be the smartest lady on S'n Simons Islan'!"

"You—you were teasing me, Eve?"

"No'm, not teasin'. Just makin' it plain as the nose on my face that I means to pick right up takin' care of Miss Anne when she git home. Makin' it plain that I'm tired luggin' roun' a half-dead heart."

With no warning, Rebecca began to weep. "Oh, Eve, I'm tired of it too! If you promise not to tell anyone—not even June and certainly not your master, Mr. Couper—I'll confess to you that even with my precious little Belle and my own new baby on the way, my heart is also half-dead without Anne."

Chapter 60

Anne thanked her lucky stars that Katy knew how to help fix her hair, so that she was already bathed and wearing John's favorite yellow lawn day dress when she heard a brisk knock at the front door downstairs. No one knew for certain that he would be home today, but she could hope. She could even believe. All thumbs in her excitement, she made a clumsy half-bow of her sash, sent Katy back to Little Annie, and hurried downstairs, heart pounding. It had to be John! After all, since their first meeting on Cumberland, he'd been using a similar brisk, playful knock.

Flora, she knew, would be halfway up her stairs from the kitchen by now, but being Flora, she'd wait on the landing and only listen until Anne and John had met again after such a long, painful separation. Father Fraser had gone out early, so nothing would stop her from welcoming him—alone.

She reached the downstairs hall as the playful knock came again. Already feeling his arms, she flung wide the door to Willy Maxwell, Lord Herries—top hat in hand, a big smile on his pleasant, open face.

"I bid you good morning, Cousin Anne," he said, bowing. "And my apologies for not having written first that I would reach London in time to call on you and John today."

Maybe this is the first time I've ever been struck dumb, Anne thought wildly, but I am! Finally, she said, "It's—it's all right, Willy. It's quite all right that you didn't send a note. At least, I—I think it's all right. I mean—well, to be frank with you, I was sure you were John, back from Portsmouth."

"Dear Anne," Willy said, clapping a hand to his forehead.

"I am so, so sorry! How dreadful for you. Can you ever forgive me for not being the dashing lieutenant?"

"Thank you," she said, still standing there in the entrance staring at Herries.

"For what, Cousin?"

"For being the same, easy person you were when we saw you in Scotland, I guess. It has been a long time, almost a year. I'm—I'm even a mother!"

Still smooth as silk, Willy took charge of the awkward situation by showing little or no surprise at her announcement. "A mother, eh? Anne, is it an inconvenient time for me to come in—just for a few moments? I want to know all about your child, of course, and I also believe I have a rather brilliant idea to share with you."

Anne felt color rise in her face, thought her mumbled plea for forgiveness at leaving him standing outside was the most awkward she'd ever imagined, and so pulled him into the hall, laughing. Laughter with Willy Maxwell was still easy. Everything with him was easy. "Tea? Could I ring for tea? Is there anything I can do to make up for my flustered behavior?"

"You can agree that indeed I did come with a brilliant idea," he said pleasantly, following her into the parlor. "You can also tell me John will be back by June fifth. Otherwise, he'll miss the benefit of my surprise."

Anne tried hard to think what date this was—remembered it was Monday, June 2—and said fervently that she hoped with all her heart to have John home by June 5. "But, why?" she asked, offering him Father Fraser's big leather armchair, taking her favorite rocker. "Is something special happening on the fifth of June?"

"To me something extraordinary, but first I have to hear all about your becoming a mother!"

As though they'd been talking only yesterday, Anne poured out her heart about Little Annie, about John's pride in the child, about her own growing dependence on the beautiful infant, and only slowed a little when Willy interrupted to ask why and how she had become so dependent on an infant who couldn't even talk yet!

"I don't think I should be leaning on her like this, Willy. Not when I have John, who loves me as he does, and especially when Little Annie needs to depend on me now, but—but—" From their first meeting in the Caerlaverock courtyard, it had seemed natural to confide in her cousin. It was now, so without even asking if John had given him any hint of how deeply he longed to regain his marine commission, she explained how scared she was at this moment because John had been in Portsmouth so long.

The tone of Willy's voice told her how often he'd thought about John Fraser and his grief over the loss of his officer's rank, leaving no doubt in her mind that John had told Willy a lot the day she'd maneuvered them into private conversation.

"He never told me a word of what you two talked about," she said. "Only that he liked you so much."

"But he is in Portsmouth trying again to get back into the marines?"

"Yes. Oh, I am embarrassed to be so rattled. I'll ring for tea."

"I wish you wouldn't. I really can't stay. My luggage is on its way to my London flat on Upper Baker Street. Quite nearby, actually, so I do have but a short time to stay this morning. I feel stupid barging in on you like this. And, if it weren't that I must arrange for tickets today should my brilliant idea please you, I wouldn't have come so early."

"I've done nothing but talk about John and Little Annie and me since you got here. Do tell me about your idea, Willy. I long to know what you have planned. I'm ever so glad you're in town! I doubt if you can know, really, how glad and relieved I am."

"And if the lieutenant isn't home in time, will you go, Cousin?"

She frowned. "I—I don't know how to answer that. What if he came home while we're out taking advantage of your brilliant idea? Can't you tell me what it is first?"

"Of course!" He laughed. "On our private walk that day at Caerlaverock, John told me you love the theater, and, Anne, on June 5, none other than the great Madam Sarah Siddons will be coming out of virtual retirement to play Lady Macbeth for the benefit of her younger brother, Charles Kemble, who manages to keep his beloved Covent Garden Theater in the worst possible financial straits."

On the edge of her chair, Anne clasped her hands in delight. "Oh, Willy, yes! With all my heart I want to see her! My best friend back on St. Simons Island and I have dreamed our wildest, most improbable dreams while reading the play, trying to imagine Madam Sarah Siddons's incomparable voice bringing Lady Macbeth to life. Oh, yes! If John's home by then, yes!"

Looking a bit crestfallen, Willy asked, "But not unless he's back, eh?"

"We'll make a pact, you and I. We'll begin as of this minute to believe that he will be back. And he could be, he *will* be at almost any minute."

"Then I'll send for tickets. It's worth the gamble, even for one who fears gambling as I do. We'll not only see Sarah Siddons, at whose feet I've lived my life, but there's almost as much talk around London, I hear, because her niece, the talented eight-year-old daughter of Charles Kemble, is slated to make a brief appearance, too, between acts. It's said that little Frances Anne Kemble, known as Fanny, has inherited the magnificent, deep, dark eyes of the Great One, her aunt, Madam Siddons, and is already the subject of London gossip for being a bit of a hoyden."

"A hoyden?"

He chuckled. "You're wondering right now what manner of child *your* little girl will be, aren't you?"

"Oh, all the time, but I must say she shows no signs yet of being anything but sweet-tempered. Already, she laughs a lot—much like her father. She also knows how to get her way."

"Is John's disposition always sunny, Anne?"

"Sunnier than any woman has a right to expect."

"And does he pretend for your sake?"

"Did you see another side of John that day at Caerlaverock when he apparently unburdened his heart to you? Oh, Cousin, if you did, I beg you to tell me! In one way, I'm sure everything will be perfect again the minute he walks back in this house. In another way, I'm . . ."

"Your husband is very human, Anne, and when a human being is torn in two, he hurts. John Fraser—even with you beside him and now with a child to love and support—is often a man in pain. You see, I believe he knows what he should do in order to be the kind of husband and father he expects himself to be, but he can't let go of what, to him, has always been his very life. Life lived among *his* kind of people —men who see things his way, who thrill to the same drummer, who march to the same pipes, who often laugh when most might cry, who cry when others might find it natural to laugh."

Anne sat staring at Herries, too many confusing thoughts crossing and crisscrossing her mind for words. Up to this moment, she had been struggling to understand John as a part of *her,* as much a part of her as she felt of him. Now that her cousin Willy, almost a stranger, had somehow opened the windows of the secret room in which she'd been confining John, she could think of nothing to say. Two people in love were still separate people, no matter how close they were. What Willy had said with such certainty had thrown her off balance, but he had also given her hope that she could right herself. At least, for better or for worse, she was seeing John far more clearly. Herself, too. They were surely *one,* but they were also—two.

"I must sound ridiculous, dear Anne, lecturing you on the nature of the man who loves you beyond reason. I—a hopeless bachelor by choice—but I care, Cousin. And I do, by some quirk of fate, seem to understand why John finds himself in a muddle. He even told me of your father's generous offer of an entire plantation. But I feel I know *why,* in spite of seeming to have everything life could possibly offer, the man remains restless."

"Is—is John afraid, Willy?" she asked.

"Does he act afraid to you?"

"Not really, but he is so skillful and he does love me."

"And you love him with all your heart."

"With all of *me.*"

"I know. A woman has to love a man in rare fashion not to see him as diminished in her eyes simply because he's afraid. Yes, I believe John is afraid. Not all men are really brave, you know. They act masterful because men have been taught to act that way. Walter Scott and I confessed once to each other, when we were thirteen or fourteen, that both of us were riddled with fears of one kind or another. The confession rather sealed our friendship, it seemed, even though we see each other so seldom as grown men."

"John took me to the Carlisle Cathedral, where he was married. Is Walter Scott happy in his marriage?" she asked.

"He'd been married to Charlotte for years the last time I saw him. I can honestly say I sensed no ripple of anything but devotion and good humor between them. She's an interesting, patient soul. She has to be. Scott's a man who's never satisfied with the daily round. He'll be changing the plans and adding rooms—whole wings—to his dream castle at Abbotsford until the day he dies, I'm sure. Charlotte, though of French ancestry, takes it all in a gracious, rather absentminded, philosophical stride. You see, neither of them grew up in the countryside. Both were city-bred—Edinburgh—until his endless trips through the wilds on foot in order to strengthen his lame leg caused him to fall in love with open spaces. If ever a man made a complete change in his way of living, it's your favorite author, Walter Scott. His wit, his spirit, his need to be excitingly involved in whatever he does, are all quite like your John's qualities, actually." Willy took her hand. "I've stayed too long," he said, getting to his feet.

"No! I wish you wouldn't go yet." She forced a slightly embarrassed laugh. "On second thought, maybe you should go. You've given me so much to think through. But, dear Willy, please come back very, very soon. Tomorrow? John could be home tomorrow—even this evening! How did you get to be this wise?"

He grinned. "In self-defense, I think. You see, until I met you and John, I wasn't even wise enough, or brave enough, to admit that I'm a lonely, lonely man."

Chapter 61

The next day, Tuesday, Willy came again, for tea, and more than ever Anne found him to be like part of the family. She had never known Father Fraser to act so responsive, from the very moment she'd introduced them. On Wednesday Willy was back, and that night, alone in her bed, still with no word from John, she lay thinking about all the romantic lore Mama had ever told her of the Maxwells. Her mother had been such an integral part of life, Anne found herself wondering if she'd ever truly appreciated her as she had now begun to do. Because of Mama's stories, Caerlaverock had cast an almost mystical enchantment over her childhood, but now that Anne had been there, her own memories of the ancient castle had her thinking of Rebecca Maxwell Couper in a whole new light—as a highly romantic woman in whose very blood flowed the essence of a centuries-old clan still revered in the Scottish Borderland, in all of Scotland.

I must have been blind as a bat about Mama, she told herself, only half hearing the rattle of carriages rolling by outside on George Street, each sending up to her open window the typical sounds of upper-class Regency revelry. I had to be blind, or just plain young, not to have realized what an unusual mother I have. Of course, no one could miss her breeding, the fact that she's more cultured than are most wives of St. Simons planters, but Mama has within her far more than I recognized and I think I've just realized she never forced any of her woman secrets on me. Why didn't you, Mama? I could use some woman secrets now. Did Papa ever go away on wild-goose chases and leave you at home just wondering?

Anne thought not. So far as she knew, he had made only water trips to Savannah on business with Major Page, Mr. Spalding, or Mr. Wylly. Of course, when the British stole their people, Papa had gone all the way to Bermuda to try to get them back. Surely one thing Mama didn't know about was the desolation of being left alone for weeks with no word of when the emptiness might end.

All that day, June 4, she had been truly agitated, unable to hide it even while playing with Little Annie. Would Anne really go to Covent Garden with Willy if John didn't come home in time? With all her heart she longed to attend, and somehow the thought of Madam Siddons's little niece performing too only made her want to go more than ever. As sleep seemed about to overtake her, she thought about the young Kemble girl, called Fanny. What must it be like, she wondered, to be an eight-year-old girl in an overpowering family of famous theatrical personages, most of them honored and praised all over the English-speaking world? She supposed the child would recite some short piece between acts of *Macbeth* and knew how much John would adore watching and listening. But could she bear to go without him? And would it hurt Willy if she refused? Sleep overtook her in the midst of trying to remember what life had been like without John in the center of everything she did or thought.

How long she had slept when the unmistakable click of the big lock and the familiar sound of brass on brass as the latch slid back on the front door downstairs roused her, Anne had no idea. Still groggy, she found herself at the window, peering out into the dim light of the gas lamps on George Street. Except for one passing carriage crowded with merrymakers and an old, rickety cab stopped in front of their house, she could see nothing. The street was deserted and there was no sound of any kind inside the house until a heavy object thumped against something in the downstairs hall.

She fumbled for her chemise in the dark room, pulled it on, and stood listening. Now, she could hear Flora's slow, heavy steps descending from her own room on the top floor. Flora had heard the door, too, and was on her way downstairs to investigate.

No! Not to investigate. Flora knew, as Anne now did, that

John was in the entrance hall, trying to ease his way into the silent house without waking anyone.

Hand trembling, Anne opened the bedroom door, then stopped. No one had more right than she to greet him first, but she'd learned long ago of Flora's need always to be the first to "do for Laddie" in an emergency of any kind, and so she waited in the shadows for Flora to pass. Waited and listened.

"Laddie?" Flora, having read in the papers too about the spate of robberies near Portman Square, was making sure. "That you, Laddie?"

"Yes, Flora," she heard John whisper. "It's I—creeping in at this ungodly hour. Get right back to bed, please!"

"With you always hungry? All week long I've had oatmeal cookies an' shortbread waitin' for whatever time you come home. Got 'em in a tin with a good tight lid. I reckon they're still fit to eat. You gonna just stand there?"

Anne heard John's low laugh. "No, but I'm too tired to eat. Could I save that shortbread until tomorrow? The one thing I want is to go up to bed. I suppose my wife's sound asleep."

"The way she's drooped around without you here, I'd be the most surprised if she's not wide awake waitin'. I'll fix for the both of ya'."

With Flora in the downstairs hall, Anne had been creeping down, one step at a time, and was now on the second-floor landing, from where she could see Flora grab John's valise and set it in a corner. Then, without another word, the woman vanished down her stairs to the kitchen.

In what seemed only one or two giant leaps, John reached the shadowy landing and literally bumped into Anne, who all but fell into his arms. Over and over she gasped his name as he whispered hers—and kissed her so many times they both began to laugh.

"At least we have this minute alone," she said, both arms around his neck. "And I'm hungry, even if you're not, so we'll humor Flora and eat her shortbread and then—oh, John!"

"I know, beautiful Anne, but wait till you hear my marvelous news!"

The old panic rushed back. He'd gotten his commission! This time, she could already hear him boast that perseverance paid off. He was an officer in the marines again, and

before I was to leave. I stayed on just to hear him talk of the endless opportunities for a man at the Cape. I could eventually own my own ship or make a fortune in the prospering fisheries business there. More and more English are migrating to that unspoiled region and in families—women, children, grandparents. All are reveling in far more than the excellent weather—the Cape social life is superb! And maybe best of all, now that I'm something of an expert on wines, a huge quantity of South African wine is being shipped this way to supplement the fine European wines Father and I sell, and even more than that—"

"John!"

In what appeared to be pure boyish glee, he threw back his head and laughed. "Annie, forgive me! I'm rolling over you like a huge wave, aren't I? But, dearest, the potential is absolutely—"

"—absolutely insane!" That was too strong and she knew it. "Please forgive me," she murmured, "but it is the middle of the night. I was so sound asleep when I heard you turn the lock on the front door and—could we just go to bed now and be close? Could we talk first thing tomorrow morning about your new dream?"

She felt more than saw him wilt. "Of course, we can. I'm a brute to be blurting out all this Good Hope talk when all you know is that I went to Portsmouth for still another try to regain my lost commission." He leaned wearily back in his chair. "I didn't get it, Anne. I'm sure that relieves you. I also know it will relieve Father. It nearly destroyed me until I saw old Griffith and listened to him tell me about life at the Cape of Good Hope. Just think—*Good Hope.* If ever a man needed good hope, I do!"

He got to his feet, almost lifted her out of her chair, and pulled her close. "Want me to carry you upstairs to our very own room? I can, you know. And what I really need is to love you. What I really need tonight and always is to know you love me—enough."

"Oh, I do, John! I do love you—enough."

Moments later, in their bed, her body feeling the warmth and silkiness of his skin against hers, they discovered almost at the same instant that they were both too weary for passion.

"Just let me hold you," he whispered, "let me hold you and you hold me until morning, blessed Annie."

One kind of loving between the two of us, she thought, is as perfect as another. For now, at least, even the threat of the Cape of Good Hope faded away. She felt safe. She could wait to tell him that Lord Herries was in London and that tomorrow night, the three of them would actually see Madam Sarah Siddons perform Lady Macbeth!

During the moment while she was drifting off to sleep, a fragment of something Father Fraser had read to her by William Hazlitt moved into her mind: "As Lady Macbeth, Madam Siddons was something above nature . . . almost as if a being of a superior world had dropped from a higher sphere to awe the world. . . ."

Maybe, she thought, she should at least tell John that Willy Maxwell was in town. No. He was already asleep.

Chapter 62

By the time Anne awoke the next morning, the sun was so high it was throwing bright streaks from behind the shutters across the foot of her bed and onto the wide floor boards. It had to be very late, she thought, feeling for John beside her. He wasn't there!

Something must be terribly wrong. Even on the mornings when he had an early appointment at Father Fraser's business, he had never once slipped away without kissing her good morning.

Still wearing her nightcap, she hurried out into the hall to listen down the stairs. She heard nothing. Even Little Annie had been bathed and was sleeping, because there wasn't a sound anywhere. Katy was probably down in Flora's kitchen emptying the bathwater.

No woman ever bathed and dressed more quickly. Within minutes, Anne was hurrying down to the dining room. John just might be there waiting for her.

She burst into the room to find Father Fraser still at the table, reading the paper. "I'm so sorry," she gasped. "I must have overslept. Where's John?"

His face solemn, Father Fraser said, "Out and gone. We had breakfast together early. He was hoping you'd go on sleeping, Anne. Better ring for Flora before you sit down. She told me to tell you she'd hold your breakfast."

"I don't care about breakfast. Why did John go so early? I know it's nearly nine o'clock, but you're still here—"

"I was waiting for you, lass. My son and I both knew you must be exhausted, having your sleep broken into as he broke into it last night with his ranting and raving about his latest ridiculous scheme."

She sank into her chair at her father-in-law's right. All she said was, "Oh."

"And what does that mean, my dear?"

"He must have told you about the Cape of Good Hope." She could hear her own voice. It was as toneless as Father's.

"Aye, he told me. At least, we know he did *not* get his commission."

"I'm as relieved as you about that," she said. "But, Father Fraser, what do you suppose will happen?"

"Right now, I think you'd better ring for Flora or she'll feel hurt. Flora would as soon cut off her hand as for one of us to go without porridge and muffins at the start of every day."

Back at the table from the bellpull in the corner, Anne took his hand. "What did you say to John about the Cape of Good Hope?"

"As little as possible, but I did remind him that he had not only a father to whom he owed loyalty and consideration, but a father-in-law as well."

"You brought up Papa's offer of Lawrence?"

"Aye. And John's warmth took me by surprise when I did."

"Don't be so mysterious! What did he say?"

"That he had forgotten neither John Couper's kindness and generosity, nor the fact that I've given him work to do until he can find his own way—whatever that turns out to be."

It had been so long since John had even mentioned Lawrence to her, Anne was afraid to hope. "Well, do you think he's even still considering that we might someday actually go back to St. Simons to live?"

"He's considering far more than I gave him credit for even remembering. I've made mistakes with the boy since the day he was born, Anne, and I was on the verge of making another mistake with him this morning. I was just about to tell him he'd taken leave of his senses even to think of dragging you and Little Annie all the way to South Africa and that I certainly would *not* pay for the trip!"

"You stopped yourself?"

"Aye," Fraser said dryly. "By changing the subject to our good friend Lord Herries."

"Did you tell John that Willy Maxwell is in London? I

wanted to tell him last night, but he went to sleep too fast. You do like Cousin Willy, don't you?"

"Like him fine. Evidently, so does John." He took a deep breath. "Your husband, Anne, is visiting Lord Herries this very minute. He walked over to his flat on Upper Baker Street almost an hour ago. It seems Herries told him the location of his London quarters when they first met at Caerlaverock Castle."

"Oh, dear!"

Anne could feel him studying her. "You sound distressed, lass. Did I say something wrong?"

"No, not you. I—I just hope John doesn't do anything foolish."

"No need to try to explain your distress about his mission to Maxwell," the older man said. "I already know what's bothering you. It bothers me, too."

On the morning he chose to sleep late, Willy Maxwell had just begun to yawn and stretch in his bed when he heard a brisk knock from downstairs.

Expecting no one to call so early, he considered turning over, pretending not to have heard. But the knock came again with urgency and with it the wild thought that it just could be that Anne needed him. That she had walked out alone, inquired of passersby the number of his leased flat, and was now waiting downstairs on the narrow stoop for him to answer. The mantel clock struck ten. Past time anyway for a man to be about his business—that is, if Lord Herries of Terragles had any business. Willy had none, but yawning again, he got to his feet, put on slippers, wrapped himself in a gray silk robe, brushed his thinning, tousled coppery hair, and headed down to the narrow front hall and the door where the brass knocker was by now making a dreadful racket.

Even though he'd forgotten to splash his eyes, sleep vanished when, the minute he cracked the front door, he stared at a beaming John Fraser.

After greeting John, Herries begged his pardon for his disheveled appearance and the lack of a houseman during his London stay, then led the way up to his second-floor quarters. In the parlor, he began at once to open the heavy silk curtains.

"I recommend that chair with the high, winged back,

John," he said, making the usual polite talk as sunlight flooded the elegantly furnished, though small, room. Willy sat down and looked at his guest with curiosity. "Now, the proper thing for me to ask next is—when did you get into town?"

"Late last night," John said, his manner even more irrepressible than Willy remembered. "In the middle of the night, I fear. I know I roused poor Anne and my father's housekeeper from a sound sleep."

Herries glanced at him quizzically, then said that he supposed John was there so bright and early out of sheer delight that the three of them would be attending Covent Garden tonight for a rare performance by the immortal Sarah Siddons.

"We—you and Anne and I—are attending the theater tonight?" he asked.

"Anne hasn't told you yet?"

"I'm afraid I'm specializing these days in disturbing those dear to me as they attempt to get their rest," John said, ignoring Willy's question, overtalking a bit and appearing to be aware of it. "Look here, Willy, old man, I do owe you an apology. It never occurred to me that you'd be forced to answer my knock yourself."

"If you know where I can hire a good temporary man to handle my flat here and my bachelor needs for a few months, I'd be most grateful. I manage, however, and I can even brew a wicked pot of tea if you'll excuse me for a few minutes."

"No, no thank you—but I'm sure I pounded you out of bed. You must need a spot of something yourself, so I'll get right to the point of such an early morning call." Smiling a bit sheepishly, John added, "I did slip out without rousing Anne. Left her sleeping, and if I'm to keep my happy home, I should get right back over to George Street."

"What's on your mind, John?"

"Bluntly, I have need of a bit of capital. You see, while I was in Portsmouth trying vainly to regain my marine commission a few days ago, I met an old officer friend, James Griffith, who raised my hopes amazingly with his story of having moved his wife and children to what sounds like a pleasure and business paradise—the Cape of Good Hope. Jim has found a splendid opportunity there, and, of course, more than anything on earth, I want to find a place for myself where I can not only work hard without dying of boredom as now, but most important, provide for my beloved Anne and our little girl—without the worry of trying each month on my half pay to make ends meet." He studied his hands for a moment, then looked up, grinning. "Why weigh you down with a long tale, Willy? I need money to make an exploratory trip to South Africa in order to look things over, find a position in the relatively new British colony before I move my little family."

"I see. You'd like to borrow money from me, eh?"

"I wasn't looking forward to asking outright."

"But have you tried your father?"

"I know my father's accounts, Willy. His good property on George Street is no indication of his wealth. His business does not really prosper. I can't get the money from him, so could we say no more about that?"

For a long time Herries sat there thinking. Indeed he did like John Fraser, felt quite at ease with him. Not only was he distantly related to Fraser's wife, in an unexpected way he had come to love her. Until now, he'd barely admitted it to himself, but Willy had come to care for Anne in a way quite unlike the affection distant cousins might hold for one another. He'd already dreamed of her three times! In fact, this very minute, with her husband waiting uneasily for his answer, he knew that he did love Anne—too much. Too much, certainly, to give John money for such a wild-goose chase. A partial lie, if well worded and gentle, had never bothered Willy Maxwell. It didn't bother him now.

"I'd really have to give that some thought, John," he said at last. "I'd need to consult my barrister, my bankers. I live well, but much of what I own is tied up in my various estates, some of it in farmland I've never even seen. Afraid, old man, I can't give you an answer now—or much hope."

John stood up. "Well, there's no big rush, Willy. And, of course, should we work something out, it would be on a purely business basis. I—I simply felt that I could trust you not to embarrass me further by mentioning my request to anyone. Certainly not to Anne or my father, who seems, for him, unusually free to express his high regard for you." He held out his hand. "We're seeing each other at the theater tonight, then?"

Going with him to the front door, Herries hoped that he had conducted the difficult interview with no more than gentlemanly friendliness, under usual circumstances quite easy for him. This was not easy. John Fraser would be hard to fool and Willy knew that he could easily afford to help. He simply had no intention of doing it—for Anne's sake. Nor could he bear the thought of her living so far from the British Isles. At the door, he said, rather too effusively, "This very night, friend, we will feast our eyes and ears on the still-superb Madam Siddons—'power seated on her brow, passion emanating from her as from a shrine.' You've experienced the magnificent woman before, of course."

"Indeed I have," John said, "but that was back before I entered His Majesty's service. I fear I was too young to grasp her greatness. Certainly, in those days I'd cultivated little admiration for the immortal Shakespeare. My dear parents soared on air for a week, though, after seeing Madam Siddons perform Lady Macbeth."

"I regret that I couldn't get four tickets so we might have given your father the pleasure, too," Willy said. "For Anne's sake, I'm relieved that you reached London in time. She wasn't going without you, you know."

John laughed easily. "How like her! Well, until tonight, Willy."

"Until tonight," he said, giving a farewell salute as John hurried down the front steps.

Looking after him as he strode along Baker Street, Herries could not hold back the thought that John Fraser took Anne too much for granted. Either that or, as Anne truly believed, the man simply knew, as men rarely do, that no matter what he did or did not do, nothing would ever diminish her love for him.

Chapter 63

Minutes before Willy's carriage arrived that evening, Flora and Katy stood together in Little Annie's room smiling their approval at the way Anne looked in a still-fashionable shell-pink high-waisted crepe worn over a darker pink slip. Katy even agreed when Flora told Anne how "gude Laddie's late ma's gold brooch went" with the gown. After their first few weeks in London last year, Anne had not found many opportunities to wear the brooch. John's enthusiasm for the Cape of Good Hope had already come between them in a way that frightened her, but he would be pleased that she was wearing his gift. Actually, Anne had said very little as he'd talked and talked of future opportunities for him on the other side of the world. She had simply tried to smile a lot, to recount Little Annie's latest accomplishments, and now hoped he'd notice the brooch when he came to tell their daughter good night.

Relieved that not one glare had been exchanged between Flora and Katy, Anne leaned above her daughter's cradle. "Did I tell you I'm going to see the world's greatest actress tonight, Little Annie?" The child responded with a gurgle of delight. "And do you know her small niece, Fanny, will do a recitation some time between acts of the play Mama and Papa are going to see with Cousin Willy Maxwell? It won't be long until you're grown up enough to memorize and recite Shakespeare, too. Do you know that?"

When John walked in a moment later, Little Annie seemed to turn herself inside out with delight at the sight of her tall, striking father dressed in his double-breasted gray-blue cutaway, yellow vest, and black-and-white striped cravat.

"Good night, my little princess," he said gaily, leaning over her crib so that, at once, she began to reach for the gleaming watch fob on its chain across John's ample rib cage. "Your mother's right. We're going to see the magnificent Sarah Siddons and her little niece, but neither, I vow, will be able to match my little girl's beauty! Be good to both Katy and Flora now and Mama and Papa will see you first thing in the morning. Then who knows? Your old father just may have some splendid news to tell you!"

Anne's heart squeezed. Not one word had been mentioned all day about the possibility of Willy's financing John's exploratory trip to Africa, but she knew, without being told, why he had gone so early today to call on her cousin.

Descending the stair now, arm linked with John's, she smiled at him. Part of her wanted to shake him. From childhood, patience had not been one of Anne's virtues. With all the practice John had given her since their first meeting, she still resented waiting. Why on earth couldn't something good happen, she wondered, that would bring an end to all of this uncertainty? Life at Cannon's Point had always been right there, out in the open, waiting for *her*. The security and shelter and joy she'd known being the elder daughter of John and Rebecca Couper had not in any way prepared her to wait. Certainly not to wait for something about which she knew absolutely nothing. If Willy Maxwell did let John borrow the money to make that long, long sea voyage to the Cape of Good Hope, the waiting up to now could seem like nothing at all. Only heaven knew how long he might be away.

Willy's brisk tap with the brass door knocker came just as they were both looking in the parlor for Father Fraser.

"I'd hoped we could at least tell the old fellow good night," John said. "How he did love going to Covent Garden with Mother in the old days. I wanted him to see you wearing Mother's brooch, too. Still, we're Willy's guests. We dare not keep him waiting."

"I'll see to Willy," Anne said quickly. "Please do tell your father good-bye."

John laughed. "Not on your beautiful life, my dear. You're not allowed to be out of my sight this evening, not for a minute."

Was he only teasing? she wondered and felt a bit guilty for

hoping he might leave her alone for one minute with Willy. He didn't. Exchanging affectionate good-byes had not yet become a habit with John and his father.

After greeting Willy, the three left the house and headed in his carriage along Orchard toward Oxford Street for the drive to the rebuilt Covent Garden theater, now operated, not too successfully, Willy informed them, by the great Siddons's younger brother, Charles Kemble.

"Charles himself is a skillful actor but evidently not a businessman," Willy said as they rolled along in the evening flow of fine carriages bearing other elite Londoners. " 'Tis said his wife, Marie Therèse De Camp, the colorful French lady, who also once acted, is really the one who keeps Covent Garden open."

"Do you know the Charles Kembles, Willy?" Anne asked. "And is it their little daughter who will do a recitation at some point in the performance tonight? Thrilled as I am at the thought that I'm actually going to see Madam Siddons, I find I'm also eager to hear that little girl. Doesn't it take a great deal of nerve for a child of eight to appear on the same stage with such a famous aunt?"

"For the average little girl, I suppose so," Willy laughed. "Yes, I know the Charles Kemble family well enough to know their daughter Fanny is no average girl. At least two years ago at a Bath school, she was called *diable de Kemble* by her teacher."

"But why?" Anne asked. "Is she a bad child?"

"Not bad, just rather bumptious—a really free spirit. What interests you so in her?" Willy asked. "Your own new role as adoring mother?"

"I guess so," she said. "I told Little Annie, John, just before you came to her room to say good-bye, that someday she'd be daring enough to recite Shakespeare. Oh, I do wish my old tutor, Mr. William Browne, were with us tonight! He all but worships Shakespeare and how well he knows it—line after line after line."

"You think often of everyone at home, don't you, Anne?" Willy asked, studying her face from the seat opposite where she and John were sitting. "You're young to be adjusting to life in big, old, noisy, sooty London, but—"

"But doesn't she manage it well and with grace?" John interrupted, rather insistently, Anne thought, as though determined not to be left out of the conversation. "The truth is, I think a lot about Cannon's Point, too," John went on. "Our old Borderland around Dumfries has its charm, Willy, and heaven knows I've seen quite a bit of the world in general, but I must say there's something almost mystical about St. Simons Island. Anne's parents' home is built in the most favorable spot imaginable. Actually, the weather is quite like the weather must be at the Cape of Good Hope—mild, sunny days, soaking afternoon showers, and then sunsets that take your breath away!"

Such a long time had passed since John had even mentioned St. Simons Island, Anne gave his arm a hug. "Do you really think about coastal Georgia, darling? I mean, we never talk about it, so I just supposed you had almost forgotten St. Simons. Except, of course, that we were married there and—and—" She had shown too much enthusiasm for what was probably only a passing remark.

"Yes, my darling," John said tenderly. "We certainly were married there and that alone makes it the most enchanted island anywhere on earth. The truth is, I've thought often about it lately. In fact, ever since I met my old friend Lieutenant Griffith in Portsmouth. You see, Willy, Griffith was never what anyone could call a romantic, but the man waxed eloquent over the balmy, soft weather at Good Hope. Into my mind flashed my own pleasant, even ecstatic, memories of St. Simons Island. Especially its light. I knew at once that Anne would be right at home in every way at the Cape of Good Hope!"

Anne exchanged glances with Willy. John had without doubt—that very morning—asked her cousin for a loan to make the South African voyage! She believed that Willy knew she knew. Dear Willy. If only he lived year-round in London, her aching homesickness might somehow lessen. He was not only a very dear man, he was Mama's kind of Maxwell.

As though unable to endure another minute of the silence into which she and Willy had lapsed, John repeated, "Yes, sir, Willy, not only would Anne feel at home down there in the thriving new British colony, I think her father would like it too." Forcing a short laugh, he added, "I believe even you would like it, Lord Herries of Terragles. From what I hear, you wouldn't be the first titled Scot to take to the place."

"Ah-ha," Willy said, sounding relieved that they had turned into Bow Street and were in sight of Covent Garden

—patterned almost garishly after the Temple of Minerva. "What a glorious time of day to have reached our destination." Giving John what could only be called a polite smile, he said, "I really know nothing of Good Hope, my friend, but there is good hope for our splendid evening if that milling throng out there is any indication. I know the house is sold out, and Madam Siddons is always at her best when her idolaters are forced to stand for lack of seating. This will be excellent for her brother Charles's poor, deflated purse, too. I'm told, though, that she's refused to see anyone backstage after tonight's performance, because even in this newly built theater, it's cramped and stuffy back there."

"I remember how disappointed I was with everything backstage," John said, "when Father and Mother took William and me there as boys. Of course, that was the old theater before it burned. I dare say all the expected magic will be here tonight, though, because Madam herself will create it!"

Their carriage had pulled over and her two escorts all but wafted Anne down to the street. Theatergoers thronged the entrance and the grand lobby, so there would be too much laughter and conversation for more than cursory talk among the three of them from now on. Anne was relieved. There had been two meanings to almost every word John had spoken during the entire carriage ride. His dear, venturesome heart seemed dead set on the Cape of Good Hope, and the whole idea was almost more than she could bear.

The curtain would go up in less than twenty minutes and the tragic story of Macbeth and his lady would come flooding back to her. She and Anna Matilda had memorized long passages at Mr. Browne's insistence, and although she'd never been quite sure of Anna Matilda's feelings about it, the play had always held a strong fascination for Anne. Already, the prospect of actually seeing the powerful tragedy played out before her own eyes was giving her goose bumps. She did know every line of act 1, scene 1: "When shall we three meet again / In thunder, lightning, or in rain? / When the hurly-burly's done, / When the battle's lost and won. . . ." One day, somehow, by some means, she thought, her hurly-burly would also be done, her own battles won.

As they settled into the best seats in the Grand Circle on the first floor next to the orchestra, near enough to the stage for her to see the dark, arresting eyes of Madam Sarah Siddons, Anne vowed to concentrate only on the world's most fabled actress. She also relished the thought that, had Anna Matilda any way of knowing Anne was at Covent Garden in Cousin Willy's splendid box, her best friend would swoon with envy!

Seated between John and her cousin, Anne was enthralled through the first four scenes of act 1, and then the golden moment was upon them: scene 5, she knew, would bring the thrilling entrance of Sarah Siddons herself.

When the great actress appeared, now a bit thick of girth and stiff of joint, but still magnificent, Anne clapped until her hands felt numb, as did Willy and John. She glanced often at Willy, who was invariably looking at her, his gray eyes soft, wondering. Was he wondering, too, what John was really thinking, even while doing his best to enter into their excitement?

The applause died at last and the memorable voice of Sarah Siddons's first soliloquy was filling the great auditorium with a kind of thrall that held everyone in the packed house. The soliloquy was, for Anne, too short, too quickly ended; the messenger entered and took his exit. Then Macbeth himself was there, on stage with his wife, in the scene that Anne remembered now as though William Browne had just heard her recitation of it. All too soon, scene 5 ended with Lady Macbeth's lines:

"Only look up clear;
To alter favour ever is to fear.
Leave all the rest to me."

For a suspended moment, there was silence and then again, wave after wave of applause resounded through the great gold and white hall as the heavy brocade curtain slowly closed. Anne sat, eyes wide, still applauding, but believing—oh, truly believing that somehow she could now also "look up clear."

Of course, she was taking the three words *look up clear* out of the context of the play, but somewhere, sometime, somehow, John would find his way to being a success as a complete man, not only as a "mighty warrior." Until then, Anne must look up clear. Nothing had changed. John was, she knew, still bent on making his mad voyage to South Africa and the thought chilled her. Yet those three words, *look up clear,* trumpeted in her heart. To her, at this moment, the trickery of both Lady Macbeth and her once mighty warrior husband had nothing to do with what Anne was beginning to realize. As the applause roared on, she reminded herself that John was *not* an evil man as Macbeth turned out to be once he tried to live his life away from the battlefield. John was simply lost without a superior officer to make decisions for him and needed more time to sort things out as they really were for him and Anne. And unless she looked up clear, she would fail her husband.

Papa would say I'm allowing my romantic imagination to run away with me, she told herself as along with the theater audience, she settled back for the unfolding of the treachery, the evil plotting, the play's ultimate, bitter taste left in the mouth. Her own life with John was going to be saved from a bitter taste! She was, after all, only watching a play, and Mr. Browne always contended that William Shakespeare was, when he wrote *Macbeth,* in the depths of his own lack of belief in all of life.

As the play moved on, the one word *selfishness* began to loom in Anne's private thoughts running alongside her absorption in the play. Could she be realizing for the very first time that even her life with John could also be choked by despair brought on by selfishness in them both? Being truthful with oneself was far harder than being truthful with others, she thought, and then tried to stop thinking. Wasn't one only supposed to enjoy such a special night at the theater?

Life for Anne had, in the main, brimmed with the confidence and the blessed safety of being loved, of loving in return those who lived their lives about her . . . Mama, Papa, her little sister, Isabella, her brother, James Hamilton, Eve, faithful, tenderhearted Big Boy, Anna Matilda, the Wylly girls, especially Frances Anne, so adored now by William Fraser. And John! Love, for her, now began and would end in John. Until this minute she would have fought even the suggestion that either of them had a trace of selfishness!

She looked over at his face. He appeared to be giving rapt attention to the play. Now in act 4, scene 1, the stage had become a gloomy cave where the three witches crouched and a boiling caldron steamed. "Thrice the brinded cat hath mew'd. / Thrice, and once the hedge-pig whin'd. / Harpier cries; 'tis time, 'tis time. / Round about the caldron go; / In the poison'd entrails throw. / Toad, that under cold stone . . . / Double, double, toil and trouble; / Fire burn and caldron bubble. . . ."

Anne shuddered. John looked down at her. He was smiling as though it had been a long time since anything had so amused him. His face beamed love and tenderness, and then a gentle nudge with his shoulder against hers, in the silence around them, seemed to assure her of his special kind of insouciance, as though he had spoken the words, "All is really very well, blessed Annie. There's nothing to fear, you know. This is only a play—and to me, a rather overacted one at that."

Had she ever truly known what John was thinking in his secret heart? In his most personal, private, secret thoughts?

Look up clear, she reminded herself. Don't let your own private thoughts get cluttered. Dear Willy Maxwell is here in London now and somehow I know he understands. Even Father Fraser understands.

Anne realized she had not thought of Father Fraser moments ago while mulling over those who loved her, those she loved. She did love John's father, though. He had, of course, not come to her mind, nor had Flora or Willy, simply because they had never lived on St. Simons Island.

Would she have to live the remainder of her life loving only at a distance, longing only for the sight and voices and familiar ways of those who knew, and were at home on, her island? Her one place on earth to be?

This is all silly, she thought to herself. I'm actually sitting here watching the great Sarah Siddons act and pining to be back at Cannon's Point. Why had John grinned at Shakespeare's terrifying use of the supernatural in the scene with the witches? Had she only amused him when she told him that Eve's grandmother, old Sofy, was keeping a conjure on Papa's neighbor Mr. Roswell King, Sr.? When she had told John about Sofy's conjures, he had smiled the same, merely amused smile. Did he hope she would outgrow her own uneasiness about the powers of Papa's superstitious people? Even her attachment to them?.

Was she allowing her first sight of the seemingly endless murders in *Macbeth* to sicken her? Reading the play had not sickened her at all. Actually seeing the actors lift and lower their daggers—killing—was altogether different. Could

John do that in battle? Then, at last, the final scene unfolded with Macduff bearing the bloody, severed head of the tragic Macbeth. The heavy curtain fell to even more applause, more lusty shouts of approval. Anne felt only relief. Relief and exhaustion from sheer wonder at the acting skills she had witnessed, but also from trying too hard to think.

When Sarah Siddons appeared to receive the crowd's roaring accolade, Anne grabbed again at the one hopeful line the great woman had spoken. The line Anne had taken for herself, even if it was out of context: "Only look up clear . . ." As though Siddons had called out the line directly to her, Anne vowed that it would be, from now on, her very own motto to repeat and repeat in her heart—no matter that she didn't understand all the line meant in the play, no matter what John decided for their future.

On her feet, applauding with the others—especially when little Fanny Kemble, memorable as a small, poignant Juliet in her moment alone on the great stage, appeared again to bow and to receive flowers with the same presence and grace as did her famous aunt—Anne vowed to herself that she would, if God gave her strength, continue to look up clear.

She could even face moving to South Africa, should it turn out that nothing else would make John happy.

Once back in their carriage, Willy again seated across from them, Anne gave him a warm, grateful smile. "I'll never live long enough to thank you, Cousin Willy, for such a magical evening! I know it sounds odd because *Macbeth* is almost pure tragedy, but I feel—"

Leaning toward her, his face eager in the light from the gas lamps along Oxford Street, John interrupted. "You—you feel what, dearest Annie? Willy and I both long to know exactly how it all struck you."

"Yes," Willy agreed quickly. "You don't seem depressed by it. I always am! Are you merely being socially correct? Don't be. Tell us the truth."

Sitting up very straight on the tufted carriage seat, looking at neither of them, Anne said with the merest hint of Madam Siddons's cadence and eloquence, "I feel surprisingly strong, thank you both. I also feel ready."

"Ready?" John asked hopefully. "You feel ready for what, Annie?"

"For life," she answered. "And don't laugh, either of you! I know how young and foolish that sounds, but from this evening on, no matter what lies ahead, I intend to 'look up clear'!" She sensed, more than saw, the two men exchanging tolerant smiles. "No one needs to tell me that you're both more worldly-wise than I've ever thought of being, but just give me time. Years from now, you can both think back on tonight and know in your bones that I meant it. And that's absolutely all I'm going to say."

Chapter 64

Over the next weeks, with and without Willy, they attended concerts and other performances at both Covent Garden and Drury Lane, Anne enjoying all of it. But alone in the daytime hours while John went doggedly about his work for Father Fraser, she could feel the slow, steady change taking place in herself. John was still at the center of her universe, but in a way she couldn't have explained, she was learning how to keep her own balance when there seemed simply no means of understanding what he was thinking. Perhaps, she thought more and more often, she was finally beginning to accept him as he was, without the exhausting effort of having to understand everything he thought, did, or did not do. At any rate, even in the now familiar, shut-away daytime world at 2 George Street, the revelations seemed to go on, and what they showed her was that life grew better in every way each time she was able *not* to pin down either John or herself.

One rainy morning early in July while writing a letter to her parents, she was struck with a longing to try, at least, to put into words something of what having Willy Maxwell, Mama's distant relative, in London meant to her. She also tried to set down something of how foolish she felt now thinking back to the days on St. Simons while waiting for John to return for their wedding—the period when she'd been so sure she had already grown up, had felt altogether ready for whatever a loving, faithful wife would ever need in the years ahead.

How wrong she had been! Still, the bright shaft of hope she had somehow grasped back in June as she watched Sarah Siddons weave her spell in, of all things, a bitter tragedy, lasted to this day. Each morning, Anne renewed her real though almost formless vow to "look up clear." Could she trust her parents not to fret because she felt forced to cling to that challenge? Surely, she could trust Mama's discerning good sense. Papa might be another matter. The darling man was growing more and more impatient for her and John to bring his only grandchild to Cannon's Point at least for a good, long visit.

"I have no plans now ever to return to my native Scotland," he'd written last week, "so at my advanced age, I fail to see how you can go on depriving me of time in the company of the little girl who makes John think of my own beloved Annie. I confess that I flatter myself in hoping that perhaps, just perhaps, all the loving work our people have done on the little tabby house at Lawrence might extend a mere visit to a gloriously happy future—all of us together here on St. Simons Island." Anne dared not reread that portion of Papa's letter often and when she'd read it to John the day it came, even he got big tears in his eyes.

"Do you think me a brute?" he had asked, not joking.

"No, no," she'd insisted. "Of course I don't, but I do want you to know that I'm painfully aware of the turmoil in you these days. Of your terrible restlessness."

"Give me a few more weeks, blessed Annie. Time to find out if it's going to be possible to raise enough funds for a voyage to South Africa. Can you stall your parents for just a few more weeks?"

Still seated at the desk in their room upstairs, she felt suddenly convinced that she should write her parents about John's apparent determination to move them to the Cape of Good Hope. Even if it worried them, it was not fair to keep it a secret any longer. "I wasn't going to write this, dear ones, but beloved John, in his desperation to end what he terms his 'idle life' even as he works all day every day for Father Fraser, has his heart set on making a voyage to the Cape of Good Hope with the idea of moving Little Annie and me there should he find the kind of golden opportunity he believes awaits him. I am certain, Mama, that in his eagerness, he has not only asked our cousin, Willy Maxwell, for the loan of monies for his initial voyage, he is stubbornly certain that eventually Willy will give it to him! Part of me feels a traitor to John for sharing this with you—I am sure it would embarrass my husband—but I am swimming in uncertainty. As do I, John also longs to visit you at Cannon's Point. In fact, he never speaks of the St. Simons beauty in any but glowing terms, but the man just has no confidence that he could ever learn how to plant! And except for planting, there is, of course, nothing for him on St. Simons. I may as well tell you, also, that in England there is much criticism, some of it rather harsh, about our institution of slavery. I know you don't like me to use that word, but I have grown accustomed to hearing it here. John, I feel sure, although he hasn't said as much, worries also about how he would reconcile himself to becoming a slave owner, or that he could ever be strict enough to get productive work from them.

"Now, can you both understand a bit better why it is that we, at present, can make no firm decisions? Many mornings, after he has gone valiantly to his dull business duties, I am nearly swamped alone in my room by heavy waves of homesickness. Some days I allow myself to weep, trying to imagine exactly what you're all doing back there beside the river, picturing which birds are showing themselves in the bright-dark glooms of the Cannon's Point woods, seeing that line of light on the ocean's horizon. Thinking of it all in the rain, the trees clouded with mist. My beloved husband is wasting the prime of his life—at what he considers nothing. He despises business. Still, as bewildered as I am over our future, I wouldn't change my lot for anything in all this world. Dear Mrs. Page once told Anna Matilda and me that if we knew what was good for us, we would never marry! I cannot and do not agree. I have been Mrs. John Fraser for almost one year and a half now and can only swear to you that John does all in his power to make me and Little Annie happy, comfortable. Every day I count the hours, then the minutes, until it is time for him to come home to me. I will never love anyone but John and would not want to live even one second without him.

"We are dining tonight with Willy at the London apartment of one of John's old Royal Marine friends, Captain Menzies. Perhaps I will gather my courage and ask Willy outright if John can expect to borrow money from him. I pray all this has not upset you too much and that you will accept my telling you as a sign of my admiration and love for you both. Always taking into consideration, of course, that now and forever, only one thing rules my life and that is my love for John."

Assuring them that Little Annie was fine and healthy, and promising to pray for her mother's health so close to the time for still another baby, she ended the letter, as usual, with love for everyone by name, then added this postscript: "I can still hear Lady Macbeth's line in act 1, in which she says, 'Only look up clear'! The words stay with me. I shall never forget Sarah Siddons's superb delivery. Did I tell you that her eight-year-old niece, Fanny Kemble, made almost equal magic between acts with her rendition of a passage from *Romeo and Juliet*? I vow to you both that I will always remember that child's amazing stage presence! She wasn't even nervous to be appearing on the same bill with her fabulous aunt, before whom every knee doth bow!"

That night, after a pleasant meal at the Menzies home, Anne did find time for a brief talk with Willy while John was again cornering Captain Menzies in the hope that he may have heard of a chance for John to regain his officer's commission.

"Are you sure that's what your husband and Menzies are discussing, Anne?" Willy asked as the two waited in Willy's carriage alone outside.

"Yes, because I know my husband."

"Sometimes I wonder if I know the man at all, Cousin," Willy said on a light sigh. "In conversation with me—anytime, anywhere—all he seems to be interested in is money for that voyage to the Cape of Good Hope! Anne, you don't want him to go, do you?"

"No. No, I surely do not, but I can't tell John that. I'd die first. He has to do only what *he* needs. You both laughed at me after we saw Madam Siddons as Lady Macbeth, but I did learn a lesson of some kind that night. One I still don't fully understand, but its meaning lies somewhere in three words —look up clear. Willy, do you think I only thought that line held a message for me in the midst of all John's turmoil, or was it Siddons's magic that fooled me?"

He turned on the seat to look straight into her eyes. "Only you know that, lovely Anne, just as only I know this—if *you* don't want John to go to South Africa, then I cannot let him borrow the money for his fare."

An alarm bell went off in her mind. "Willy! Don't let the fact that I want to go home to St. Simons force you to do something that might harm or hurt John!"

"Do you think I want *you* harmed or hurt? I've gone unscathed through most of my life, not worrying too much about how deeply anyone gets hurt, including myself." He grasped her hand. "I find I care deeply about you, Anne. So, it's settled. I'll tell John tomorrow. He whispered at dinner that he's dropping by my place first thing in the morning. Most of my money *is* tied up in property. I can tell him almost truthfully there's none available for a loan of that size." He dropped her hand. "Smile! Here he comes striding toward us. And I think, from the disappointed look on that handsome face, Captain Menzies had no good news for him about his commission."

She forced back tears. "Oh, Willy—Willy! What *am* I going to do?"

Chapter 65

When Anne's letter reached St. Simons on August 15, John Couper first read it alone because Rebecca, so near her time, was resting upstairs. Seated in his favorite rocker on the big, empty porch of the Cannon's Point house, Couper broke the seal, hoping that much of the bad taste left from even the brief contact with young Roswell King, who had been neighborly enough to bring the letter, would vanish as he perused Anne's familiar, spidery script. The King son had said nothing today, but Couper was convinced that at almost any time, his old neighbor Roswell King, Sr., was going to turn over both of Major Butler's plantations to his son. Well, so be it, he thought. The management of Butler's vast holdings was certainly none of his business, but he did find overweight, cocky, young Roswell King still harder to abide than his father.

Couper took his time with the letter because Becca had promised to obey his order never, in this final stage of her pregnancy, to go up or down the stairs without someone there to support her. Anne had written a lengthy, newsy letter this time and she'd been gone so long, he fully intended to make it last.

Slowly, savoring each word, he read the first of the four pages, in which Anne confessed far more concern for her mother's condition now than when Becca was carrying dear little Isabella. Anne admitted she'd been too wrapped up in her own new romance back then to be properly sympathetic. Couper smiled at his daughter's straightforward honesty. He'd always counted on that with Anne.

When he came to the part where she told them how fond she was of Rebecca's middle-aged cousin, Willy Maxwell,

Lord Herries, Couper's smile vanished. Why hadn't he written to invite Herries to visit them on St. Simons Island? The man was well-off, lived on the income from vast land holdings and his barony. He could easily afford both the time and the fare.

But then, on the next page, Anne had exploded the bombshell about her John, newly smitten with the altogether crazy notion of making the long sea voyage to the new British colony, the Cape of Good Hope! Couper's first thought was that young Fraser should be turned over his father's knee. Needed a good walloping for his seeming determination to stay out of step with the rest of the world. The thought was short-lived. John Couper truly cared about his son-in-law, and somehow, as wild as the new notion sounded to him, it didn't seem quite as absurd as the boy's stubborn, unending efforts to regain his military commission.

On his feet, pacing the porch, batting at deerflies so thick and relentless in August they'd bite a man even under his spectacles, he tried to think his way through what must be causing Anne real despair. Being Anne, she had written carefully of her own worry, but close as they had always been, he could read real misery between the lines. His new, precious grandchild did not need parents who were forced to pretend all was right in her little world. Little Annie needed confident, lighthearted parents—ready to surmount the normal woes of daily living. Couper was also humiliated to the soles of his feet that John Fraser had dared to beg money from Lord Herries.

Up and down the long, wide porch, where he and Anne had marched through so many nor'easters, he kept pacing—up and down, up and down, trying to think. There simply had to be something he could do that would convince his son-in-law to bring both Annes back to him!

He was still walking the porch when a woman's scream from inside nearly scared him out of his skin. It wasn't Becca—it was a black woman's voice—but just the same, it meant trouble. It was not a shriek of laughter. Then, there were running footsteps. The same voice that had screamed was now yelling his name. In two strides, he reached the open front door and saw, hurrying toward him along the wide entrance hall, the plump, driving figure of Johnson's wife, Liz.

"It comin', Mausa Couper," the woman cried. "The baby it comin' ahead ob time! Rhyna be wif' Miss Becca, but Lord have mercy, Mausa Couper, it comin' ahead ob time!"

"Liz," he ordered, "get hold of yourself! Is Mrs. Couper all right? I mean, is everything—as usual? There's nothing bad wrong, is there?"

"You lak eber other man God eber made, sir! If a woman ain' dyin', she *all right*! Co'se Miss Becca's doin' 'er bes'. If you don' know dat by now, ain' no hope fer you nohow, but git a nigger to saddle up a horse! Dr. William, he be ober at the Wyllys. Rhyna think Miss Becca, she might need a doctah!" Liz slapped her hands together at him sharply. "Git! You heah me? You gonna git yo'sef outa' hearin' distance anyway effen Miss Becca, she scream—so make yo'sef useful an' git de doctah!"

Within minutes after Couper rode to the Wyllys's farmhouse at St. Clair Plantation, William Fraser and Frances Anne, who went along to help out, were riding hard for Cannon's Point. Both rushed right to Rebecca. The aloneness Couper felt, standing in the suffocating August heat under the ancient live oak the Wyllys called Old England, was somehow heightened by the nearly black shade of the mighty tree.

Liz is as right as rain, he thought. I do run like a scared boy when my Becca gives birth! I rode nearly five miles from our little house up at Sunbury when James Hamilton was born and when my beloved Anne came, I walked and walked until I thought I'd drop. When Isabella was arriving, I hightailed it all the way down to James Gould's lighthouse. I, who pride myself on staying in control most of the time, can't face the sound of Becca's suffering. I turn to jelly!

The birth would take a while, perhaps hours or longer. What would he do this time? Alexander Wylly was away. Where to go? James Gould had been steady and understanding while Couper waited out Becca's ordeal with Isabella. Why not try to find Gould? Besides the shock of Becca's going into labor ahead of time was the unexpected jolt of Anne's letter. His stomach and head ached.

Annoyed with himself for having left the unfinished letter lying on his rocking chair back on the front porch and feeling utterly helpless, he strode rapidly toward the hitching post, making his escape before Mrs. Wylly came out of the house and attempted to comfort him. He loosed Anne's horse, Gentleman, from the old iron post, swung into the saddle, and galloped out the tree-lined, shadow-cut lane toward Frederica Road. Galloping his daughter's horse was calming him a little, but something had to be done for Anne off there in London, and as always, he was sure he was the only person who could do it.

By the time he reached the recently purchased Gould property on Frederica Road, now called New St. Clair, he had decided to turn off onto Gould's freshly made lane leading to the big new house his friend was building. There was a good chance he'd find James there since, in his prudent, New England way, he worked right along with the men he'd hired to build his long-dreamed-of home.

As Couper rode up, he realized he'd have to find a way to convince his enigmatic friend that in the future, he was the master. Gould would never be able to handle a gang of fieldhands if he pitched in and helped them as he was doing now, hauling a load of two-by-fours with a block and tackle up to the second-floor level of the handsomely framed structure.

"I know you've been a builder all your life, Gould," he called, as he looped the horse's reins around a scrub oak sapling, "but you'd better get over working yourself so hard before you try to manage the people you're planning to buy one of these days."

Gould didn't answer but finished the block-and-tackle job, then ambled up to where Couper stood admiring the perfect symmetry of the house.

"It's as plain as the nose on your face that some worry has brought you here, Jock," James Gould said. "Need to talk?"

"Do I look that glum?"

"You do. Sit down on that stump there and catch your breath. You're wringing wet, too." Gould pulled up a toolbox and sat across from him.

"Rebecca's baby is coming today—a week or so before anyone expected," Couper said, "but don't give me that same sermon you preached when Isabella was born. I still remember it and I do have faith in the Almighty."

"Thanks to my Janie," Gould said dryly, "so do I. Much more so than when I preached to you before. Is there something else bothering you?"

Couper managed a feeble laugh. "For a man who talks so

little, you sense a lot, don't you? What I'm enduring over my dear wife today comes to all men, I know. What I'm enduring for having read only part of a troubling letter from my daughter Anne, before I rode off, is harder to explain."

But he did explain as much as he'd had time to read in Anne's letter of her husband's irrational scheme. "I go to pieces over Anne worse than I do when Becca's having a baby, James! I've got to do something to help the girl. To help John, too, for that matter. I'm as fond of the boy, in spite of his bullheadedness over my Lawrence offer, as a father-in-law can be. It also kills me that I've got a granddaughter I've never laid eyes on! I—I did think of one possibility. It's fairly farfetched, but—"

"That's why we're sitting here, Jock. For you to confide in me."

Couper wiped his perspiring brow with a handkerchief, stuffed it back into his sleeve, and tried to smile. "You're a good, patient friend, Gould. My idea is pretty farfetched, but there's a middle-aged fellow distantly related to my wife's ancient Scottish family, by the name of Willy Maxwell, Lord Herries, the Second or Third, I forget which. Anyway, Anne seems to like him. He's been more than kind to her and John. Lives part of the year in London, travels to and from his home in Terragles, Scotland, even spends a few months in a small remodeled apartment at the ruins of the Maxwell family castle near Dumfries. John and Anne met him there on their wedding trip. I've thought of inviting Herries to visit at Cannon's Point on the chance that he just might bring Anne and her family with him. Anne told her mother right after she and John made friends with Herries that he seemed quite taken with the sound of our island here. If I don't buy any more hands at the Savannah market this year, my cotton crop will bring me enough money for the Frasers to make the voyage with Maxwell. Of course, I need to get Becca's opinion—later. What do you think?"

"I know perfectly well that you're counting on John Fraser's taking up your offer of Lawrence once they're back here, so I'd go slow. Hate to see you let down even more."

Couper buried his head in his hands. "No, I'm not counting on it, James. At least, I hope I'm not. Sometimes I get almost a vision of the kind of agony John might be under trying to run a three-hundred-acre plantation even with me right next door looking over his shoulder. The boy simply has no idea how to go about living what we think of as an average life. He's worse than a fish out of water away from a regimented routine!" He looked at Gould. "He puts on a good act, I'm sure, but the whole idea of running Lawrence must scare him more than either of us can realize."

"I think maybe I understand it a little," Gould said. "I've never run a plantation before either. All new to me. Never did anything but build houses and trim lighthouse lamps."

"I know that, but no two men are alike. You'll make a good planter. Planting requires thinking ahead, planning crops much as you make plans for a house." He brightened a little. "But Gould, you may just be able to help my son-in-law more than anyone else can. By the time they could see to John's father's needs, arrange to leave London, then get all the way over here, you'll have bought at least some of your people, have your fields cleared and ready for planting. A man like you could inspire young Fraser!"

James Gould's normally stoic face broke into something like a tight grin. "You're several miles ahead of me, Jock, as usual. You're even ahead of yourself, I think. Could we just agree to let Mrs. Couper and her new baby recover from today and see what your wife thinks of the whole idea? I know how you want everything decided yesterday, but I doubt you have any choice beyond letting a bit more time go by. And while you wait, at least you'll have something to turn around in that busy mind of yours. I thought the time would never come when I'd finally be free to build my lighthouse. I was past middle-age before my St. Simons light was commissioned. Remember? I began drawing plans for it back when I was just a boy. Time does pass, Jock. And, most always, it's shaping a man's dreams as it passes. I hope you can hold on to that fact."

Part Five

September 1817–October 1817

Chapter 66

Willy Maxwell had not planned to stay in London into the fall, much preferring the changing colors in the rich wooded country north of Edinburgh, but he'd found a good servant, so as September wore on, he was still living on Upper Baker Street. He saw Anne almost daily and spent pleasant evenings with the Frasers as they made calls together, dined out, or spent time in his own apartment. There were days when Willy felt he'd overstayed his welcome, but had sensed nothing in their manner to indicate that he had, so stayed on. When he had finally told John outright that he could not let him borrow money for a voyage to the Cape of Good Hope, the young man reacted with unrestrained charm. To Willy, it was truly a performance.

"In no way will this damage our splendid friendship," Fraser had declared, making use of his most effective smile. "My wife and I are so devoted to you, the least I can do is accept your refusal gracefully and beg you not to give it another thought, Willy, old man. Something will turn up for me. It always does."

That was over six weeks ago. So far as he knew, nothing had turned up and Willy Maxwell found himself planning some manner of entertainment for the three of them nearly every day. He himself needed to be busy. He'd begun to spend most of his private time in unaccustomed gloom over Anne. Not because he hadn't known from the start that such a love was utterly hopeless. He had known it and had gone on enjoying, in secret, his own emotional indulgence. Now in his mid-forties, he had believed since his thirtieth birthday that real romance would never touch his life. It had, though, and there was no denying it. Instead of fighting the way he felt about his distant cousin, he had rather appalled himself by welcoming it. He simply set about learning to live with both the futility and his feelings by doing all in his power to be Anne's true friend, to think of more and more ways to cause her amazing, pale blue eyes to shine.

The way they had shone just yesterday as the two of them took tea alone at 2 George Street, when Anne shared the short, elated letter from her adored father in Georgia telling of the new son her mother had presented to him on August 15. In general, after that letter, he thought Anne had seemed less nervous, less preoccupied. For weeks now, she had made no bones about telling Willy of the debilitating homesickness she carried through every hour of every day. With all his heart, he yearned to ease it for her, especially when she painted her glowing word pictures of the beauties of the faraway coastal island called St. Simons.

Willy longed to see the place himself, to such an extent that he'd barely stopped short of urging her and John to surprise her parents by taking their little girl—with Willy—to Georgia, all at his expense. But he had not asked because it seemed soon to be making such a generous offer after having refused John money for his venture. No matter how Anne longed for her home and family, such a decision was Fraser's to make and his alone. John Fraser unfailingly showed Anne the utmost kindness but seemed to take for granted, as did most men, that where they settled was entirely up to him. Evidently, he had no other source of funds for the voyage to the Cape of Good Hope, but only last week at dinner in the house on George Street, John had again regaled them all with seemingly undiminished fervor about the possibilities in the new British colony.

Was her husband the enigma to Anne that he seemed to Willy? If so, loving him must be more than maddening. He could tell that Anne had grasped at one vague and puzzling sentence in her father's letter announcing the birth of her new baby brother. "I will be praying, John," Mr. Couper had written, "that you won't be off to the Cape of Good Hope before my next letter arrives. I am trying to work out a surprise for Anne." Couper had written nothing more, except that it would require a few weeks to work out details. Young Fraser had merely lifted an eyebrow and grinned. It was Anne who seemed to cling to her father's curious hint. A "surprise" could be anything from a visit by her parents to

London once Mrs. Couper was able to travel, to a sizable amount of money with which Anne would be free to shop in London for a new wardrobe. To Willy, she was always the most arresting woman anywhere, but Anne certainly did need new gowns.

Right then and there, he thought of a happy surprise of his own for her! For John too, he hoped, but one that would surely make Anne glow.

Mind made up, Willy rushed to his desk and began a letter to his longtime friend Walter Scott, Anne's favorite novelist, who was now living with his wife and four children in the partially finished section of his dream castle near Selkirk, Scotland. As he dashed off a note to Walter asking if the early part of October would be a convenient time for the three of them to visit, Willy could almost see Anne's elation. His happy-natured friend Scott was known to keep the latchstring out at his country place almost any time of the year when he was not, as Scott said, "earning a bit of honest money at the law in Edinburgh." Willy felt sure an invitation would be not only quickly forthcoming but eager. "With every new book I publish," Walter had written in his most recent letter, "I am adding rooms and wings and turrets to this dream sanctuary for my imagination, so when are you arriving, dear Willy, to feast your eyes upon the wonder I now call Abbotsford?"

The scenery around Selkirk, especially on the River Tweed, beside which Scott was building the extravagant place he insisted on labeling a "mere cottage," was surely not Scotland's loveliest. Still, Walter, his writer's imagination steeped in the lore of ancient Scotland, had "eternally fallen in love with heather" and was convinced that God had never created such beauty as that which lay in the rolling hills and vales and streams where he would undoubtedly still be "building and settling" for years to come.

His own blood racing, not because visiting his old friend was more than a pleasant interlude to him, but because of Anne, Willy finished the note, set his seal with a flourish, and hurried out into the soft, golden September day to post it at once.

Under the same September sun, James Fraser, with firm resolve, made a point of reaching his house on George Street well ahead of his son. The time had come, was long past, in fact, for a face-to-face talk with Anne. For weeks he'd known that the girl had been carrying far too heavy a load, especially since, like John, she insisted at all times that everything was fine. Still, the headaches she'd told him she had suffered since girlhood came now more and more frequently. She could become physically quite ill, he was convinced, if the uncertainty and insecurity of her life were allowed to go on. He, James Fraser, meant to break up whatever logjam was so plainly blocking communications between his son and Anne. All summer, in spite of their perpetual pretense at good humor, he had been more and more aware that both were trying too hard, were undoubtedly no longer able really to talk to each other.

Anne, he knew, was upstairs at this hour with her child—playing, laughing, giving Little Annie her special kind of unrestrained love. Exactly what any baby needs at all times from both parents, he thought, hanging his top hat and umbrella on the hall rack, then listening down the kitchen stairs for Flora. He could hear her rattling pans, so went to his home office to wait for her. Of course, she'd heard him unlock the front door and could be counted on to check on him at any moment. Sure enough, in no time, here she came, out of breath.

"Kindly send Miss Anne to me here in my office, will you, Flora? I need to speak with her without disturbance."

"But what if Laddie comes home for dinner?"

"I believe I said without disturbance and that means from anyone. The boy knows better than to barge into my private quarters."

Frowning, as though Fraser himself had done something wrong, Flora turned on her heel and left the small, book-lined room.

When Anne knocked at his office door, he called for her to come right in, then showed her to his seldom-used visitor's chair at one end of the desk. "Don't look so alarmed, my dear," he said, seated again in his own chair. "I've asked to speak to you here for privacy's sake. I trust my pretty granddaughter wasn't too upset having your time with her shortened."

Anne gave him an uncertain smile. He had alarmed her. He must plunge immediately into the awkward task at hand. "I flatter myself, dear Anne, that you think of me first as your warm, trusted friend."

"Oh, yes," she said, her voice unsteady. "I'd—I'd never make it here in London without you."

Fraser cleared his throat. "I'm quite aware of all you just —left unsaid, my dear." He was careful to speak softly. "Living in London in our dirt and stench and noise is not and will never be your native air. You've tried. God above knows you've tried to find your place in it. Except in my Margaret, I've never seen more spirit in a woman. You do love my undeserving son with all your great, generous, strong little heart, don't you?"

She had been looking at the worn oriental carpet on his office floor. Now, she jerked up her head, and the unusual, light, light eyes shot fire. "Of course I love him! He's my *life.* Maybe a good mother shouldn't say this, but even our baby has to make room for her father with me. So, don't ever, ever let me hear you call John *undeserving* again. Do you hear me? If I'm being discourteous for flaring up at you like this, I'm sorry. But anyone who looks at my husband *clearly,* as I believe I do, knows that he's not only the most loving, tender man on earth, he's—he's deserving of far more than I can ever give him!"

At first, her sharp words cut him, then an overwhelming wave of understanding and admiration and affection for this loyal young woman swept over him. She did truly believe that she was seeing his son clearly. The troubled girl was still clinging to whatever it was she'd thought she learned from that one line of Shakespeare's *Macbeth.* Bless her, he thought. She is honestly still trying to "look up clear" at my difficult son John. Oh, bless this lovely, struggling child!

He knew Madam Siddons had used one of her stage tricks to grab Anne's attention with those three words. The girl was still deceiving herself with them. She was not seeing John clearly. His son was all the things she'd said he was—except deserving. Almost daily, with his useless prattle about the Cape of Good Hope, the futile attempts to regain his commission, John was pushing his adored wife to the edge.

"Did you hear what I said, Father Fraser?"

"Aye, Anne. I heard. To me, you sound only homesick for fresh air and sky and the freedom to be in or outside at will. Except when you two go out with Lord Herries, you're penned up in this musty old house, growing more homesick for your parents and the life you and John could be sharing in Georgia. I'm sorry I called John undeserving. I've never known how to be with my elder son, and obviously, I don't even know how to discuss him without putting my foot in my mouth. But I sent for you today to tell you one thing. I love you with all the heart I have left. I also believe you and I want much the same thing for John. We both—"

"I'm not sure we do want the same thing for him," she broke in. "We know what we don't want, but what *do* we want for him? For him—not for me—for him!"

"I have never been very generous with John."

She jumped up from her chair and threw both arms around his neck. "Oh, Father Fraser, I should spank you for not seeing John's real worth, for not giving him time to find his own way in what has to be a totally strange world out of uniform, but I also love you, love you, love you for being so honest."

He gave her a quick hug and a pat, then released her. When she didn't sit back down, he got to his feet. "Anne? I sent for you today hoping to find out if there's anything an old man can do to help you. I was planning, true to form, to try to shame John into choosing whatever it is *you* want most. I meant to tell you little more than—if going back to Georgia is your real heart's desire, then not one thought must be given by either of you to leaving me here alone. I got along before you came. I can do it again."

"How did you know I was already worrying about how we might hurt you if, by any chance, John ever makes up his mind to accept my father's offer on St. Simons? I *was* worrying. I've come to care about you—so much." Her sudden smile lit the dim office. "Aren't you and I funny?" she asked.

"Funny? Perhaps we are. Surely, we're helpless to change John."

"I don't want him changed!"

The stark truth of what she'd just said struck him silent and set him trying desperately to turn things around in his own mind, so that he, too, for Anne's sake, could tell her that he didn't want his son changed either. All he managed to say was, "You—you really don't want him changed, do you?"

"No. I just want to change enough myself so I'll know better how to be with him."

"Can you and John talk to each other, Anne?"

"Oh, yes! We talk and talk and much more. You've simply got to get it through your head, Father Fraser, that John and I are almost one person. No two people could be closer than we are—most of the time."

"Do you always know what the boy's thinking behind that charm of his?"

"Not always, but can anyone read another person's most secret thoughts?"

"I guess not, but John is just not being fair with your generous father, Anne."

"John is being—John. He's the only person who can decide about his—our future. Papa might not like the final decision, but I know he expects John to make it. Being a plantation owner is far from easy. If John never finds in himself the real desire to be one, then even he would fail at it. Something has to happen to help him make that discovery for himself. He loathes farming, you know."

"He blames me for that, too. I forced him to farm as a boy."

Still standing there facing him, she took his hand. "Dear Father Fraser, has it ever occurred to you that no one is to blame for anything? What possible good can it do any of us to pin blame anywhere on anyone? We're all just living our lives and Mama has always warned me that mere living, no matter how beautiful it seems much of the time, is full of rough patches. John is in one of those now. We just have to be patient with him and I'm dreadful at patience! So are you."

"Aye, lass. I'm perfectly dreadful at it. Always have been. Want people to see things my way and none other. My Margaret told me that a hundred times."

"She—she actually told you that?"

"And much more. I needed her frankness. Don't you tell John what you really think of him?"

"Most of the time, I do, but because I believe this is such an important time for him, I try very hard not to shake his confidence. Thank you for this little talk, though. I'm going to give all of it a lot of thought. I'm trying to learn to do that. I'm trying to *look up clear.* You know, I want to hurry back to St. Simons with Little Annie—to move into the good house Papa has all remodeled and repaired and waiting for us, but—"

"—but you don't tell John any of this?"

"He already knows."

"Did he tell you that?"

"No, he didn't need to."

Feeling like an old fool, Fraser said, "You'll laugh, I suppose, when I tell you my real reason for sending for you today. If you don't laugh at me, you should. I—I thought maybe between us we could come up with a way to get you and John headed down the same path, so to speak. A way to stop him from circling all around the important issue. Anne, so help me, I was dumb enough to think you and John weren't really talking to each other."

"Look at me. You see? I'm not laughing and I love you even more for what you meant to do. We are talking to each other—as freely as I believe John is able to talk until he knows deep inside himself what it is he truly wants to do."

"And you're willing to wait until that nebulous something happens—to wake the boy up? Without infinite patience, Anne, how can you possibly do that?"

Her smile came again. "I might not be able to do it. I simply love him enough, Father Fraser, to try."

Chapter 67

Off and on, all morning, with a late-September rain falling outside his parlor windows, Willy Maxwell had tried to concentrate on the new copy of *Guy Mannering* his friend Walter Scott had sent him to replace the one he'd given to Anne months ago at Caerlaverock. An ardent admirer of Scott's work, he should be devouring the novel, in which the old Maxwell castle had served as a setting, especially since he'd given Anne his own first edition on impulse without having read it. Instead he paced the room far more than he read. There had been plenty of time for a reply from Scott to reach him in London, and his own desire to please Anne by giving her a visit to Scott's country place had grown all out of proportion.

At a tall, front window, staring unseeing out at the falling rain making puddles on Upper Baker Street, he laughed dryly. He would tell Scott, when they got there, that he'd been too impatient for his letter to concentrate on his fine novel, and his old friend Walter would laugh. The man's humor could always be counted on when needed. Often, when not needed.

When he heard the rapid footsteps of his good, young house servant, Freddie, Willy was certain he was bringing the post and that in it would be Scott's invitation.

With only a hasty thank-you, he grabbed the mail from the silver tray the servant held out to him. It was there. Right on top of the small stack of bills and other letters, Freddie had purposely placed the one from Scott. Leaving the other mail untouched, he broke Walter Scott's blobby, elegant seal even before he sat down in a chair near a lamp.

Thousands of readers all over the English-speaking world would have paid good money for a single handwritten sheet from the now famous author. To Willy, the quickly scrawled note was worth far more than money. The thought of the sunny, impetuous, almost cherubic face of his boyhood friend had always made him smile. He was smiling now as he began to read.

22 September 1817
Abbotsford, Heaven on Earth

My dear old friend, Willy, the Laird of Herries,

I have contained myself until now, hoping against hope that today's mail would not bring me word that I would be forced to leave my beloved Abbotsford and hie me to Edinburgh to pretend at the law should court convene this week. I am a free man. My summons did not come and so rooms for you and your traveling companions, the Frasers, are this day, under the expert guidance of my wife, being readied for your arrival—I hope, no later than a few days hence. You will, of course, take the stage to Carlisle, then on to Selkirk, where you will find no difficulty in hiring a chaise for the glorious ride to Abbotsford, where all the Scotts will be waiting to greet you with open arms and shared dreams and good talk and more food than anyone needs, to be washed down with more wine and brandy than any man should consume. The turreted second story of my unpretentious cottage is now in place, and as you will see upon entering, I am collecting for myself a veritable museum of ancient relics, all the way from complete medieval suits of armor to jail keys, to executioners' swords, to battle-axes. That you will be bringing Mrs. Anne Fraser, an ardent admirer of my yarn spinning, is an added inducement to me to cry "Welcome!" all the way down to smoky, cluttered, clattering old Londontown. I shall hope to feast my eager eyes on the three of you no later than a week or ten days hence!

Your old friend and Borderland ruffian,
Walter Scott

The letter was almost word for word as Willy knew it would be, but now he faced the chance that for some reason,

Anne and John might refuse to make the journey. His rapport with Fraser's father was strong enough, he felt sure, to enlist the older man's approval. It was young John Fraser who gave him concern. Anne would, he knew, thrill at the whole idea.

Dressing in subdued clothes, old enough not to be damaged by the rain, he wrapped himself in a dark-gray cape, raced downstairs and out the front door. It would only waste time to send Freddie for a hackney cab. The walk to George Street was not long, and anyway, the very activity of striding along, while dodging puddles, would help vent some of his excitement and suspense.

Young Fraser himself swung open the front door of his father's house, with his usual open smile.

"What a pleasant surprise," Fraser said heartily, taking Willy's arm and steering him inside out of the rain. "This must be an important visit to bring you out on such a wet day, Willy. Come into the parlor. Flora has a small fire going to keep down mildew, she says. Anne is upstairs with our daughter, busily giving her a bath despite Katy's objections that no one but Katy can do it correctly."

Standing with his back to the tiny, sizzling coal fire in the grate, Willy asked, "Will Anne be down anytime soon? I think my visit *is* important and I want her to know as soon as possible what a fine treat I've planned for you both."

"She should be here in a few minutes," John said, glancing at the mantel clock. "Our Little Annie goes off to sleep about one o'clock. Won't you sit down?"

"Thank you," Willy said. "Flora's fire feels good. There's a chill outside today, as you know."

"Indeed I do know," John said emphatically. "I couldn't find a hack, so walked nearly seventeen blocks in that soupy chill."

"My old friend Walter Scott would insist on calling it mere Scottish mist."

"Do tell Anne that when she comes down," John said. "She hangs on every word you tell her about her favorite author, you know."

"What is it Willy's supposed to tell me?" Anne called, hurrying down the stair and into the parlor, hand out to Willy. "I thought I heard your voice, Cousin, so I relented and let Katy put Annie to bed." After giving Willy a quick hug, she took a small chair near John. "What brings you out in all this rain?"

Her lack of response when he told them of the planned trip to visit Scott at his Abbotsford estate almost made his heart stop. He had been so certain she would dance with joy. Instead, she said not one word, did nothing but look silently toward John.

"I thought it might do wonders for Anne," Willy heard himself saying nervously—not to her—to John. "Because she's lived most of her life on a river that empties into the ocean, where the sky is never murky with black smoke, I thought a fine journey to where she could walk the moors to her heart's content might—"

Face beaming with boyish delight, John interrupted. "Enough, Lord Herries! It's quite the loveliest, best plan a man ever hatched! Of course we'll go. It so happens that my end of Father's business is a bit slow at present, and Katy and Flora can fight to their heart's content over who does what for Little Annie while the three of us trek merrily off to Scotland and the fulfillment of one of Anne's most cherished dreams. Isn't it a marvelous idea, darling?"

Anne's eyes had lit with joy the minute she heard John say, "Of course we'll go." She jumped up from her little rocker now and gave Willy a huge hug.

"So, you do want to go along with John and me, Anne?" Willy teased.

Evidently his facetious question had not sounded facetious to Anne because, hands clasped together, she said in as solemn a voice as her eagerness would allow, "More than almost anything I can think of, dear Willy! It's going to take me a minute before I can actually believe I'll really get to meet Walter Scott and hear his voice—really see him face-to-face—but oh, yes! You are the world's very, very dearest cousin and I'm going to write at once to my best friend, Anna Matilda Page, who will turn not just green with envy but green with bright yellow spots!"

"Did you have a departure date in mind, Willy?" John asked. "I can leave as soon as the day after tomorrow."

"Can't think of a better time, John," Willy said. "I'll scribble off a note to Walter this afternoon. In his brief letter welcoming us, he informed me that his wife, Charlotte, and the servants were already preparing our rooms. Shall we say the day after tomorrow then, John? Your father will approve?"

"Oh, yes!" Anne answered for him. "I know he will. Father Fraser will revel in the whole idea."

John laughed. "As nearly as my staid, Scottish father ever revels," he joked. "I'll let him know, though, just as soon as he comes home from business today. I'm sure he'll agree and undoubtedly welcome having his granddaughter all to himself. The truth is, Willy, my father agrees to anything—so long as he thinks it's what Anne wants."

"It's like old times being on the road again, isn't it, beautiful Annie?" John asked, taking her in his arms the minute they'd said good night to Willy and closed the door to their room in the far better inn in Manchester than the one they'd been able to afford on their wedding trip. "I feel almost as though we're newly married, do you?"

She reached up to kiss him, the ache to be nearer deep within her already. "Yes, oh, yes," she breathed. "I always have the same glorious feeling—even back at 2 George Street—when at the end of any day, we're finally alone."

"Do you? Do you really always feel that way?"

His voice was so earnest, so in need of her, so desperately in need of so much, she thought, how can I answer him in just the right way? "I not only always feel that way after a day of just usual things with you out of my sight, I think of you almost every minute while you're off working. I haven't changed, John. Have you?"

He tried to laugh naturally. "No, of course not. I—I go on loving you, wanting you through thick and thin, as Flora says—and for me, these days, thick and thin is the hideous monotony of going from one dreary wine dealer to another. Thick and thin for me, lately, is admitting to myself that with a little effort I can turn into one of the world's most magnificent failures."

"John, no!"

"Hold me, Anne. Come as close to me as you can! For some reason I'm very eager about this trip we're taking with good old Willy, but I'm lost. Darling, I feel so lost! How can I feel excited and lost, too, both at the same time?"

In that moment, holding him as tight as she could, Anne tried to shelter him, longed to say just the right words to reassure him. She knew so well by now that words meant more to John than to most people—words and the tone of her voice. Through almost every prickly moment, he had guarded the tone of his voice with her. If she allowed herself to sound as terrified now as his word *lost* made her feel, she could easily change the whole course of their lives. Of Little Annie's life.

"You're *not lost,* John," she said at last. "You just haven't decided yet—which way to go. You can do so many things, you have to give yourself time to choose. Most men are limited to following one dreary path. You have choices!"

"Anne, I've tried telling myself that. The truth is, the only two things I know how to do aren't possible. I haven't the funds to explore South Africa, and my old unit doesn't need me anymore."

The small-boy brokenness in his voice tore at her. "Well, at least you know two ways you can't go. Don't you see? You're not lost. You're making full use of your manhood."

He released her with a scoffing laugh. "Manhood?"

"Yes! It seems to me it may be just as important to know which roads *not* to take. Only a mature man could admit that."

Abruptly, John did something very unlike him. He turned and walked away from her toward the window that opened onto the noisy Manchester street, along which people were heading home in buggies, on foot, a few on horseback. He often grew distracted, but it was unlike John to turn away from her! She almost stopped breathing and then slowly began to sense that maybe, for the very first time, he was daring to be himself with her—stripped of his charming manners, all his practiced courtesies, all the winning ways he'd used so long they'd become a part of their communication.

He isn't turning away from *me,* she told herself firmly. He does feel lost, but he isn't. All I have to do is just stay with him, give him time to realize on his own that he's finally begun to face things as they really are. For some reason she couldn't think through now, her mind went to her mother. She was being quite like Mama, as Mama would be this minute if Papa were standing there confused and helpless, suffering the shame of it—the utterly false shame men suffer when they don't have all the answers.

The strength and steadiness of her own voice, when she did speak, surprised her. "You're probably at the very best moment of your whole life, John, right now. You're always so—so in charge of yourself—"

"I'm always pretending to be! I'm good at that."

"Women too sometimes have to pretend to be in control when they're not. We don't always weep and wait for someone else to help us, you know! I don't want to hear any argument when I say this, but I know for certain that you're on the verge of being able to *look up clear*!"

Now he whirled around. "Anne, what in the devil are you talking about? I know you latched on to that line of Madam Siddons's the night we were out accepting Willy's charity as usual at Covent Garden, but what in the name of common sense does it mean?"

"I don't know exactly what it means—I surely don't know all it means—but I do know that God doesn't clutter things up for us. We're the clutterers. Can't a person know something without being able to explain *how*? It's a fact, dearest, that for all of us—for me and for you—there is a clear way. Our part is to dare to take it."

The sound he made wasn't a laugh. It was almost a snort. "I've always thought of myself as daring. Plainly, I'm not! I'm embarrassed to have admitted it, even to you."

"That's only because you're so in love with me, John Fraser."

Now he smiled a little. "I am—really?"

"Yes, you are and I'm in love with you, so I know what I'm talking about. A lot of times people so hopelessly in love as we are torture themselves by trying to be what they think the loved one expects, or deserves. People like us can get almost to the point of dishonesty with each other and not know it at all."

He was looking straight at her now, studying her intensely. *He had heard her.* John had listened and heard the surprising things she'd just said—things she wasn't aware she knew until now. Maybe he'd never thought, until this minute, of lovers pretending. She certainly hadn't.

Still across the room near the window, he said, so simply that he brought tears to her eyes, "I have spent my life—pretending. Even in the marines, where I felt more at home than at any other time, I took on stupidly dangerous missions because I wanted my superiors to think I was the bravest man in the unit. I went through with every mission, too, because I've never stopped trying to convince myself of my own skills. The truth is, Anne, I think I was born scared. That's probably one of the reasons Father always favored William. He doesn't put on airs. I'm still scared. I'm terrified of failing. Now I'm a married man, the father of the sweetest-tempered, prettiest little girl in the world, and I dare not stay scared."

Some secret voice told her to say nothing. To wait.

"More than anything, I want to take care of you and Little Annie," he said, his voice husky. "One road only is open to me and I do love St. Simons Island. I've seen enough of the world to know that. I think I miss it almost as much as you do. Very little stirred in me when we were in the old Borderland, where I lived as a boy. At least not to compare with the strange, almost eerie longing I feel when I allow myself to think of the island light glancing off the leaves of our gnarled, old oak tree out by the river. Do you remember our tree, dearest?"

Struggling not to overwhelm him with her joyous relief, she said in what she hoped was a controlled, loving voice, "Oh, yes! John, how could I ever forget our tree? You—you kissed me a hundred times under its blessed old branches. . . ."

His smile was genuine now—definitely not his public smile but his Anne smile. He crossed the cramped room, his very being illuminating the shadows. The sun was almost gone outside.

Taking her in his arms, he said with just a touch of mischief, "Something tells me there's going to be a storm tonight. Anne, I am thinking about all you've said to me. If I weren't a skeptic, I'd believe such wisdom a miracle. I'm grateful to you, but at least for this night I'm going to stop thinking—shut out every thought. Every thought, that is, except that with all my ridiculous, mixed-up, would-be brave heart, I need you. . . ."

Chapter 68

A violent late-afternoon thunderstorm jolted and drenched the lurching stage on which Willy, John, and Anne were riding. Within a few miles of Selkirk, the rain came in such torrents, not only they but every passenger aboard could not have found a dry stitch.

Willy sat hunched and miserable in the far corner of the outside seat shared with Anne and John, and for the first time since they'd left London to visit his old friend Walter Scott, he could gladly have choked them both. They were laughing—Anne in particular—taking pure pleasure in the rain, yelling at Willy, trying to tell him above the roar of thunder and wind across the ghostly, wet moors, how all her life she'd loved marching on their veranda back home in Georgia with her father through every storm—the wilder, the better. The whole idea of being soaked to the skin, of being slowed by the mud so near the end of their tedious journey, did not amuse Willy, but part of him could not resist Anne's delight. There was also no resisting or escaping John's over-dramatized chanting of the old Scottish ballads Walter Scott had gathered for his book *Minstrelsy of the Scottish Border.* John, who had spent much of his life among the British in far-off foreign places, still affected a thick Scottish brogue here in the Border country. He also knew Scott far better than he'd bothered to admit, "not being," Fraser insisted, "a ver-ry bookish kind of mon."

" 'About the dead hour of the night,' " John was shouting into the falling rain, " 'she hear-rd the br-ridles ring. Oh, there was horsing, horsing in haste, and cr-racking of whips and o'er the lee—r-revenge!' " Anne shrieked her delight.

And then, to Willy's surprise, through the thunder, the

young man began to sing the old Ben Jonson verse set to music—"Drink to Me Only with Thine Eyes." And sing he did! At no other time had Willy even guessed that the fellow might own such an amazing voice. Neither shrilly tenor nor exactly baritone—toned more like a clear horn. Unmindful that there was even one other passenger aboard except Anne, John sang all the way through the poignant song, his wet, dark hair plastered to his hatless head as though storms belonged only to the two of them.

The rain had lessened some by the time John finished the song, and the man was sitting up straight, attention fixed on Anne, making a joke of steadying her against the jerking stage. Why, Willy wondered, had young Fraser chosen such an intimate, romantic ballad right after having shouted Scott's nearly savage-sounding Borderland chant? Why, indeed, he scoffed to himself. Why not? The lovely Anne, breathtakingly desirable even soaking wet, hair dripping beneath a limp bonnet, *belonged* to this colorful, unpredictable, seemingly rudderless young gentleman with the silvery voice.

"Don't look so scrunched up and wretched, Willy," Anne scolded, turning to smile at him. "We can't be far from Selkirk and tomorrow—oh, tomorrow, thanks to you, my blessed cousin, I'll actually meet Mr. Walter Scott! We'll all dry out. Do try to be happy! I know John and I are acting like idiots, but think of what you're doing for us both by giving us this fantasy journey."

Even Willy's offer of a generous bribe could not get them private rooms at the ancient Selkirk Inn that night. He and John had to share a room with two other men, while poor Anne was forced to get along quartered with three strange women—two decidedly fat, the other bone-thin.

But morning came at last and a clear sky with it. Having what passed as breakfast in the low, peeling public room of the tavern downstairs, Anne and John's soaring mood seemed to perk up Willy's own flagging spirit, so that he felt oddly pleased with himself as he made arrangements for a chaise and horse to take them the remaining two or three miles to Abbotsford, where Walter Scott was undoubtedly making preparations this very minute to give them his typical rousing welcome.

"I will rise before the sun on the day you hope to arrive,

dear Willy," Scott had written in a second note urging them to come. "I publish a book, you know, and then build another wing and turret onto Abbotsford, so the writing must come first, but I shall finish for the day in ample time to show you the wonders of my meager cottage. Me auld heart leaps with joy at the thought of meeting the young lady, Anne, with such excellent taste as to find me her favorite author!"

A decent chaise and horse were available, but no driver, and since John insisted that he liked to drive, he helped load their belongings, settled his passengers, then cracked the whip. Off they went rattling along the road toward Abbotsford with Willy wondering what chaos and good humor and half-finished lodgings awaited them in Scott's beloved Abbotsford "still abuilding."

"You seem to have forgotten all about our soaking of yesterday, Willy," John joked as he maneuvered the rented horse through deep ruts and puddles. "Methinks you're looking forward almost as much as Anne to seeing your friend. Tell us about him. We embarrassed you enough yesterday with our raucous behavior in the storm before those other passengers. We do promise to be on our best behavior today, don't we, Annie?"

Sitting between them on the hard, wooden chaise seat, she said gaily, "Cross my heart and hope to die! I'm really too full of awe to misbehave. Oh, Willy, you're a sweet man to make all this possible. Do you think Mr. Scott will actually talk to me about the writing of *Guy Mannering*?"

"The man seldom lets a silent moment go by," Willy said. "He's never happier than in the presence of a devoted reader—or to have the chance to show anyone what he is now calling the wonders of Abbotsford. Our evenings should be pleasant, too, I'd think, now that I know John is such a talented singer. You see, Walter's quiet, almost shy daughter Sophia—about seventeen or eighteen—is a superb harpsichordist and also sings in what her father calls a sweet, Scottish, heathery voice."

"Does his wife enjoy company as much as her husband does?" Anne asked.

"Charlotte has always been rather an enigma to me, I'm afraid," Willy said. "I'm fond of her and must say she has the soul of a saint to put up with Walter's untiring activities. The man has changed the plans for Abbotsford five times already. Some changes came after certain rooms and alcoves were finished, so they had to be torn down and rebuilt—all of which meant moving furniture, buying new pieces. She seems content, though, well occupied in her own rather private world, allowing Scott and all his ebbs and flows to bubble past undisturbed by wifely nagging. The man is, to me at least, a great teller of tales. Sophia and her younger brother, Charles, pay their father rapt attention, no matter how often they've heard his stories. They certainly laugh at him more than Charlotte does." Willy himself laughed now, remembering one dinner taken at Abbotsford while the Scotts still lived in a small cottage on the grounds. "Charlotte, I fear, does not always listen when her husband talks. He was telling a sad tale one night about the laird of Macnab. At one point Scott remarked, 'Macnab, poor fellow, is now dead and gone.' At which moment Charlotte Scott interrupted, 'Why, Mr. Scott, Macnab's not dead, is he?' 'Faith, my dear Charlotte, if he's not dead, they've done him a great injustice—for they've buried the man!' "

"Did Mrs. Scott laugh?" Anne asked.

"Not at all. Scott was rewarded, though, because his children's tutor, dining with them, was just raising a cup to his lips when, in a great snort of laughter, he sprayed tea all over the table. Actually Charlotte found none of it funny." Willy looked out over the green hollows to the friendly hills. "Scott will surely want you to accompany him on one of his famous and very long walks, John," Willy went on. "He'll invite me also, but I'm already mulling over a plausible excuse. He's really quite crippled, you know. Walks, and has since boyhood, with a decided limp—always with a stout stick—but it slows him not at all. So be on guard, friend, and don't say you haven't been warned."

"You mean I can't go too?" Anne asked.

"I'm serious when I say the man takes *long* walks, Anne. Anyway, I'm sure Charlotte and Sophia and Anne, the other daughter, will want to show you Dryburgh Abbey. Really quite picturesque ruins there. She may even want to drive you to Melrose Abbey. Young Charles Scott is the official family guide to Melrose. A courteous chap, who loves to show his father's houseguests the old place."

"Will we impose if we stay two or three days?" John asked.

"We'll not be permitted a day less." Willy leaned forward

to look at John, holding the reins in both hands now over an especially rutted stretch of road. "You appear more interested in spending time with Scott than I expected, John."

"You know, I think you're right, Willy," Anne declared. "And all this time he's pooh-poohed me for burying my nose in Mr. Scott's novels!"

"Where," John wanted to know, "is it written that a man can't look forward to meeting an author without ever having swooned over a single one of his books? Writers of books are just people, after all." John glanced guiltily at Anne. "But—all right, I admit it. I am anticipating the great Walter Scott. Not because he's a famous writer, though."

"Then, why, darling?" Anne asked.

John shrugged his big shoulders. "I honestly have no idea. But we must be getting close to his place by now, and in no time, I'll have a chance to find out."

Chapter 69

Their welcome at Abbotsford in the late morning was exactly as Willy had expected. With a rabble of small, yelping dogs and Hamlet, the black greyhound, circling him, Walter Scott, clad in an old green shooting coat, brown pantaloons, and a shapeless white hat, came hobbling vigorously through the high entrance of an unfinished section of a great gabled house.

"Come, Laird of Herries," Scott shouted in the general direction of the chaise as John drew up and stopped. "Ye're just in time for breakfast and afterward we will divide ourselves amongst ourselves and show you the wonders of Abbotsford!"

With everyone in great, good humor, John jumped down to hitch the horse while Willy helped Anne to the ground, which was strewn like a quarry with huge cut and half-cut stones.

After returning Scott's hearty embrace, Willy introduced them and did his best to convince Scott that they had already had breakfast in Selkirk.

"Hoot mon," Scott exclaimed, "a ride in the morning through the keen air of the Scottish hills is warrant enough for a second one!"

So, without more useless protest, they were whirled by their host into the dining room and quickly seated at a long table, surrounded by Scott's family—his wife, Charlotte; Sophia, a slight and blue-eyed girl; dark-haired Anne; young Walter, gangly tall though only sixteen; and Charles, a lively eleven-year-old, obviously with his father's zest for life.

After a few rapid questions concerning the nature of their journey, Scott turned to Anne. "You, dear lady, must be the creature of such superb taste as to choose me as your favorite novelist!"

Appearing far less awed than Willy had expected, Anne said firmly, "Oh, yes, Mr. Scott. I finished *Guy Mannering* only a short time ago and have devoured every other book of yours available to me. You see, my Oxford-trained tutor at my father's home on St. Simons Island, Georgia, is a devotee of yours *and* of Shakespeare's. So, I feel as though I grew up with most of your books."

"And which of us do you prefer, Mrs. Fraser," Scott asked, "the bard of Avon or the laird of Abbotsford?"

Scott and Anne laughed together quite spontaneously, Willy thought, and felt proud of her poise. Walter Scott had been known to take far more worldly-wise women completely off guard.

"Oh, I prefer your work, sir," Anne said, eyes dancing, "if for no other reason than that I'd much rather read than attend the theater."

"Words chosen carefully and with flawless tact," Scott vowed, with a wave of his hand. "I am not at all surprised to see you've captured such a dashing husband." Now he turned to John, who, Willy observed, was wholly delighted with their host. Of course, John had made it plain that day outside the Caerlaverock courtyard that he missed the company of sophisticated men. Scott, though smitten with his obsession to be a country squire now, was indeed a man of sophisticated humor, who could converse as easily with the Prince Regent himself as with a stone mason or a common chicken farmer.

"Actually, Mr. Scott," John was saying, "I captured my wife in all ways. I'm afraid she had very little choice in the matter."

And then, for ten or twenty minutes, young Fraser held the family and Scott spellbound with the story of how, under British Admiral Cockburn, he and the other Royal Marines had taken over a mansion on Cumberland Island in Georgia, capturing every person in it, including Anne Couper, who happened to be attending a house party at the very mansion the British forces chose as their headquarters.

Perhaps, Willy mused, Charlotte Scott often did not listen to her own husband, but without doubt, she was listening attentively to the story of what both John and Anne called their bright captivity.

"I take it, Mrs. Fraser," Charlotte said when John had finished, "that the bright captivity goes on. I've scarcely seen two married people so carefree and happy as you and your husband!"

"Happy, oh yes, Mrs. Scott," John answered for Anne. "But since we all feel so compatible together, I can tell you honestly that my wife has not found married life with me to be quite carefree. Far from it, eh, Anne?"

Willy thought Anne looked a bit stricken, certainly taken completely by surprise because John so seldom committed a social blunder. To Willy, he'd committed more than a blunder—such a question in public was almost cruel. With all his heart, Willy longed to help Anne.

His impulse was futile, since she responded promptly with her most enchanting smile. "We are happy beyond all reason, Mrs. Scott. I've never loved anyone else in my entire life but John Fraser. I never will."

Scott cleared his throat rather noisily. "In my humble, dogmatic opinion," he said with a half-grin, peering at Fraser, "your charming wife handles awkward moments to perfection, eh, young man?"

"She does indeed, sir," John said, his own smile a touch sheepish. "I took an ungentlemanly liberty and I apologize, but I think I'll blame the remarkable atmosphere of your castle, Mr. Scott. You see, I've not recovered from my first sight of its splendor and here we all are at your very table feeling quite at ease together. Were these delicious fish caught right out there in your own River Tweed?"

"Aye," Scott said, "only this morning. So, my simple cottage has already cast its aura of freedom and naturalness over you! Good."

"Oh, yes, sir. In all my travels," John went on, "to many parts of the world, only one other house has ever caused me to feel so free of foolish restrictions."

"And what place might that have been?" Scott wanted to know.

"My wife's father's plantation on an enchanted little American coastal island in Georgia. Another house beside another river. The entire estate is so welcoming, the laird, John Couper, so easy and natural as to cause any man or woman to shed unnecessary formalities. 'Tis called Cannon's Point, and although not such a large or ornate edifice as yours, there's a strong resemblance in the way both places make a man feel."

When John compared Abbotsford with Cannon's Point, Willy watched Anne's face light up in a way he'd never seen in all the hours he'd spent looking at her.

In a quiet voice, Anne declared, "Yes, Mrs. Scott, I can assure you that my husband and I are not only totally happy, but at this moment, almost carefree."

That John had caught her double meaning Willy had no doubt.

After ringing for a servant, Scott got to his feet. "Well, that settled, I shall get right on with my plans for your first day at Abbotsford. After you've been shown your rooms in my newly completed turret to our right, my son Charles will escort Mrs. Fraser—my wife and other children, should they feel up to visiting the old spot again—to Melrose Abbey by carriage. You, Willy, have convinced me in the past that you are too city-bound for my kind of activity, so Charles will welcome you on his abbey tour as well." He turned to John. "Fraser and I will limber up my author's stiff muscles with a fine, long walk abroad in this breathtakingly scenic Scottish countryside. Shall we all be about our day?"

Dogs gamboling ahead, Scott, his polished thorn staff thumping rapidly along in support of his quick, lopsided gait, led the way past what John surmised was Scott's private quarry and up into the surrounding hills. John himself strode along briskly, but evidently not a step too fast for his host, who was rattling off story after story of ancient Celtic battles, taking affectionate potshots at Willy's lack of interest in long tramps, allowing that had their ability to "flourish again" depended on Willy, the Maxwell motto might never have come true.

Now and then, between Scott's tall tales, John broke into a Burns poem or raised his voice with abandon in an old Scottish song. After all, both abandon and singing were second nature to him. He'd performed much of his life, until his mother died, for company at home, as well as for his marine comrades through all the years with his unit in distant and familiar lands. That his host admired his voice was obvious, and though the great man's natural ebullience caused him to join in now and then, it was also obvious that Scott's musicianship left much to be desired. To John, what still seemed to matter most was that he himself had spoken the truth at breakfast; it was indeed true that the very atmosphere of Abbotsford brought a man a brand new sense of liberation.

When John began to sing "Drink to Me Only with Thine Eyes," Scott fell silent and listened. John sang through all the verses as their path led farther up toward the top of one gray hill.

At the end of the song, after a long silence, Scott said, "I daresay you sing that very song to your enchanting wife."

"Yes, sir, often. By now, I guess I can say it's our own special ballad."

Almost at the top of the hill, Walter Scott stopped briefly to give John a curious, concerned look. "Is Miss Anne your —first love, too, Fraser? As she declares you to be hers?"

"My first *real* love, Mr. Scott."

"You can't bring yourself to call me Walter? I'm still in my forties, you know."

"I'd like that, sir."

Walter Scott looked out and down over the rock-strewn valley for a time, deep in thought. "Charlotte, my wife, is not my first love," he said. "I lost my first love to another man. I died some over it, but Charlotte has endeared herself to me more with every day. You're blessed by the Almighty Himself if the lovely Anne is truly your first real love, John. I don't believe a man loves that way but once, do you?"

"I only know Anne is my whole world."

"I can believe that. Still, a man needs work in his world, too. Don't you agree?"

"Yes, I do agree. And I have no work now to absorb me."

Starting out again at the same fast clip, Scott said, "The one ambition of my life since boyhood was denied me because of a crippling fever I had as a child."

"Is it too painful to talk about?" John asked. "I'd like very much to know what kind of work you most wanted."

After a deep breath, Scott said, "To be a *real soldier.* And yes, it's too painful to talk about to this day."

Hearing this world-famous author, the respected Edinburgh barrister, confess to hunger for the life of a soldier struck John dumb. He stopped walking to look at his new friend's face. Scott's long upper lip, were he not almost always smiling, surely would have tipped his expression toward a pout, but the honest, intelligent eyes held John's.

"I see I've surprised you, Fraser," Scott said with a wry grin. "Why is that? You were a Royal Marine. Surely you know the thrill and adventure of such an active life. Surely you rejoiced in it."

John's heart leaped. This was why he had felt so uncommonly at ease from their first meeting! "Oh, yes, Walter! Yes. More than anything, except to make Anne happy, I still long to regain my officer's commission. That door is closed to me, though, at the moment at least, as tight as the life of a soldier was shut in your face."

"Because Britain is no longer at war."

"Yes, sir. I'm not needed at all. God knows I've tried. I'll probably keep trying right up to the end."

"The end of what?"

"If I'm truthful, to the end of—peace. I say, Walter, you do force me to say things I've never spoken aloud before. I really don't want to see peace end!"

"And you believe you sincerely want to make the lovely Anne happy?"

"Oh, yes!"

"Obviously, she fell in love with you as a marine officer. How does she feel about it now?"

"That's the box I'm in, sir. Anne hates anything to do with killing."

"You love the military—she hates it," Scott said, pulling himself up a slight incline by a stout ash branch. "The reason, of course, that your Anne could not honestly say she's carefree, isn't it?"

John laughed a little, shaking his head. "I've always believed anyone or any circumstance that made a man look squarely at his real self must be good—at least safe. These days, I'm not so sure," he said, evading the blunt question.

At the peak of the hill, as though they'd been speaking of nothing more serious than his host's romantic attachment to the Abbotsford scenery, Walter Scott swept his arm about, declaring, "These, John, are the Eildon hills and so I tell you that I have brought you, like the pilgrim in *Pilgrim's Progress,* to the top of the Delectable Mountains, that I may show you all the goodly regions hereabout. Compare them, if you will—you a born Scot—with the tiny island in your Anne's America. The Georgia island must fall far short, eh? Yonder is Lammermuir and Smallholm and there you have Galashiels and Torwoodlee and Gala Water." Walter rolled the names of the hills off his Scottish tongue with near reverence. "In that direction you see Teviotdale and the Braes of Yarrow and Ettrick stream, winding along like a silver thread to throw itself into the Tweed. . . ."

For a moment, John stood looking at what to him seemed a quite ordinary Scottish landscape, no more than an unremarkable succession of gray, waving hills, line on line, as far as the eye could see. Even the famed Tweed struck him as a rather naked stream flowing mildly between the hills—heather-covered only in scattered patches. He felt at a loss for words.

In his mind's eye, he was seeing the great, spreading, fern-covered branches of the live oak at Cannon's Point beside the Hampton River, where he and Anne had so often held each other, fleeing even the pleasant company of the Couper family. For an instant, he caught and relished the salty smell of Georgia marsh mud and the pungent scent of Couper's orange grove as he'd experienced them both each time his boatload of fellow marines had docked just below the Cannon's Point house, during his first weeks on St. Simons while all the Coupers were still his captives. And the island light—nowhere was there light to compare with the almost mystical shadow-light on St. Simons.

John liked this eager gentleman so much, he longed to say something favorable about what Willy had told him had come to be known in the area as Scott's View, but what was there to say about the River Tweed, glinting in the flat sunlight, flowing along over its pebbles between bare hills without a tree or a thicket to soften its banks?

Evidently sensing John's dilemma, Scott began to hum a little toneless tune and then defended his favorite view by declaring that to his eyes, the stark beauty of his stern and solitary slopes appealed far more than did the ornamental garden look of the richer scenery around Edinburgh. With a kind of feisty courtesy, Scott said, "I've put you in the same dilemma in which I placed my American friend Washington Irving, who was my guest here last month. Irving wasn't as wise as you, though. He tried to talk his way out of the fact that he obviously preferred the more romantic landscape of his own country. Plainly, I adore this vista!" Then he laughed. "Forgive me. My intention was to prove nothing. I like you, John Fraser, and intended only to give you a way out of what had begun to appear a too personal tangle in our conversation about your wife's aversion to the military."

"I know what you were doing, Walter," John said softly. "But it really wasn't necessary. It's hard to believe I feel so free with you. I was actually enjoying our personal talk. I hadn't admitted, even to myself, how much I needed a sympathetic ear."

"You and the lovely Anne seem fated for each other," Scott said after a while. "I'll never be a soldier because I'm a cripple. I've stopped yearning, I suppose, because I have no other choice. But, do you truly have a choice? Think about it and try to free yourself—much as you've been kind enough to declare that I free you."

John turned to give him an almost stunned look. He felt a torrent of words push up, but all that came out was a boyishly simple question. "Did you say—*free myself,* Walter?"

"Aye. Every man has to do that for one reason or another, sooner or later."

The hard climb up the hill had not winded John, but he was breathing now with difficulty—fast, driving breaths, strong and sharp as though he were forcing off one tight bond after another. Then he began to smile, to laugh—not his well-practiced public laugh but one that gushed up from deep inside. "I say, Walter, you may have just performed a miracle! Probably some manner of Celtic witchcraft. *Free myself,* eh?"

Scott was chuckling, too, his pixie, small-nosed face looking downright impish. "I did make great sense, didn't I?"

"Uncommon sense, sir. And I am drawn to the uncommon."

"I know," Scott said. "I already know that about you and no trait could please me more." Suddenly he gave the ground two thumps with his staff, declaring, "Right now, I insist that you and the lovely Anne put all thought of a short visit out of your heads. I'm not due to return to the dull and malodorous practice of law until November. Charlotte and I want you—and dear, lonely Willy Maxwell, of course—to stay at least a week or more."

The day before Willy, John, and Anne were to take the chaise back to Selkirk, then retrace their stage route through Carlisle and Manchester to London, Charlotte Scott invited Anne for coffee with her after breakfast, to be served in the cozy, now familiar drawing room, which also served as Scott's study and library. It was a livable room snug with Charlotte's chintz chairs and Walter's bookcases stocked with rare and antique volumes. Almost every evening of their visit had been spent in this comfortable room, and Anne was glad to have the time alone today to tell Charlotte Scott how she admired her taste in color and furnishings.

"I dream of the day when I, too, will have a house—almost any kind of house, no matter how simple or how small—to decorate as I please," Anne said. "You've made the dream even more urgent, Charlotte."

Charlotte, who didn't laugh often, seemed to enjoy a good laugh now—at herself. "I do my best," she said. "It isn't always easy to make a house feel like a real home in the midst of Walter's suits of armor, ancient swords and all manner of old weapons, warriors' relics—even bandit paraphernalia. A wall covered with often harsh heraldic blazonries is not exactly conducive to intimacy and beauty, you know."

"I had no idea your husband was so attracted to—to the implements of war, although he does, of course, write vividly of old Scottish battles."

"Oh, he can still grow misty-eyed over his own impossible boyish yearning to be a soldier." Charlotte's expression gave Anne not even a hint of how the woman truly felt. "The world knows he's a highly successful writer—all Edinburgh knows he's a fine lawyer—but I try to keep him content by remembering always that the little boy in him still longs for two good legs fit for long marches under snapping banners, to the beat of drums."

"Is there as much little boy still in him as I think?" Anne asked.

"Probably more, my dear. In your handsome husband, too, I'd guess. I will never, never be able to forget how moved I was by what you two call your bright captivity. It is a rare story, you know."

"Oh, I believe it truly is," Anne said eagerly, on the edge of her chair, balancing her cup and saucer. "I suppose all people in love think that, though."

"No, you're wrong there."

Anne said nothing but couldn't resist a quizzical look. When Charlotte Scott also fell silent, Anne said, "You and your warmhearted, irrepressible husband are surely convinced that what you have together is rare, aren't you?"

With an almost sad smile, Charlotte said, "Yes, I think we are. Not, however, for the reason you and John Fraser are convinced. You see, I'm not my husband's first love. Certainly not his first *real* love."

Anne's heart rushed out to the small, dark-eyed, rather plain but obviously strong woman. "I—I'm sorry," she said lamely.

"Don't be. Walter has always been honest about it with me. The other woman, his real love, married elsewhere. I knew from the start that I was his second choice. Our affection has grown with the passing years, though. It is deep and sure now. Even living my life under this morass of metal armor and closets still packed with ancient bows and arrows, I'm a blessed woman because I do have Walter. You see, he is not only my first but my only love."

Anne put down her cup and saucer and just sat there, hoping her face showed at least some of the unexplainable, strange release she began to feel because of what Charlotte Scott had just told her.

Then, after a long moment, she heard herself say, "I wish I could tell you what such a tender, personal confidence has done—is doing for me, Charlotte. To thank you seems cold and only polite. But my heart thanks you."

"I know, my dear. Otherwise, I wouldn't have told you. I'm as proud as the next woman, but I sensed your need to hear someone tell you face-to-face that no matter what cares you might ever be asked to bear, all that really matters is that you have always been and will always be—first with John Fraser. After his many years in the Royal Marines, you couldn't expect to be the first woman in his life, but any fool can tell you're the first he's ever truly loved. Your little daughter, Annie, will live a blessed life because of it." She reached for Anne's cup and returned it to the ornate silver tray on the table before them. "Walter and I do have a strong, deep partnership. I've watched him cultivate your young husband. I feel strongly that I've actually seen John growing freer and freer of whatever was troubling you both when you first arrived at Abbotsford. Maybe our understanding—yours and mine—will free you, too, my dear. I hope neither of you minds our intrusion too much."

Mama, Anne thought, would have found something sincere and genteel to say to this wise, compassionate lady, who had just renewed the kind of hope Anne had almost relinquished—the radiant, expectant hope that had always been natural to her. "Not all the Coupers are like us, Anne," Papa used to explain. "Some are dour and crotchety, but to you and me, expecting the best comes naturally. Never forget that, lass. Never let it go."

Still, Anne could think of nothing to say that would make sense or even begin to let Charlotte Scott know what she had just done for her, and so she did the impulsive thing. She jumped up, threw both arms around her hostess, and wept.

Chapter 70

Saying good-bye to the Scotts and their children a fortnight later was far from easy. If Willy hadn't seemed so restless, John and Anne so eager to get back to Little Annie, they may have relented when Scott urged them to stay still another week.

In their honor, Walter Scott had broken with daytime custom and dressed in his elegant dinner black for the morning of their departure early in the third week of October. "Just my small, awkward way of saying that I'm in mourning because you're leaving us," the great man had said as he stood waving them farewell, his family gathered around him. "Do come again," he'd called as John climbed into the driver's seat of the chaise. "And do, all of you—Willy included—have a downright unforgettable drive through our breathtaking Scottish countryside!" Scott laughed. "Remember, John, you'll never see its equal again!"

His teasing, warmhearted farewell brought a smile and a hopeless shake of the head from Willy as they started off briskly in the direction of Selkirk.

"I hope I warned you sufficiently about old Scott ahead of time," Willy said, settling on the hard seat, Anne again between him and John. "The man, not his countryside, is unforgettable, wouldn't you say?"

Anne felt John looking down at her even before she smiled up at him. "Yes, Cousin," she said, eyes locked with John's, "my favorite author is surely unforgettable. And so is his Charlotte." She forced her eyes away from the somehow new, almost peaceful adoration on John's face and turned to Willy. "How can we ever let you know what you've done for both of us, dear, dear, Willy?"

Almost solemnly, John said, looking straight ahead now over the trotting horse's rump, "We'll never be able to let you know what the visit did for us, good friend. Actually, I'm not at all sure that I know—yet."

"Oh, I don't either," Anne agreed. "We not only enjoyed every minute of the Scotts' hospitality, I think something brand new has happened! Or is about to happen."

John laughed. "You *think*, Anne?"

"No, I don't just think. I *know*, but I don't know what to call it. All I'm sure of is that I love you both, I love even poor Walter Scott's plain hills and homely little River Tweed, and I'm as sure as that I'm sitting here between you that something wonderful is going to happen—very soon!"

She felt a quick, affectionate pressure from Willy's shoulder, and catching some of what must seem to him their puzzling elation, her cousin began to sing lustily, John joining him.

"Her shirt was o' the grass-green silk,
Her mantle o' the velvet fine:
At ilka tett of her horse's mane
Hung fifty siller bells and nine,
Hung fifty siller bells and nine!"

Obeying Scott's parting instructions, they indeed enjoyed not only the drive into Selkirk, but the topplingly crowded stagecoaches all the way back to London, which they reached some three days later.

It was chilly, but no rain fell and even Katy and Flora looked pleasant as a beaming Father Fraser helped unload the cab when they pulled up, weary but still high-humored, at 2 George Street.

All reports on Little Annie were extravagantly good, and after a light tea and an adoring peep at their sleeping child, John and Anne closed the door at last to their own room and stood looking at each other, both feeling giddy and saying any silly thing that popped into their heads, larding each foolish remark and feeble joke with bursts of laughter.

"I don't understand it at all," he said a few minutes later, when he leaped into bed to take her into his arms as though he hadn't had the chance nearly every single night they'd been away. "Not even one drop of rain fell on us over all those bumpy miles in that overstuffed stage, but tonight, dear Annie," he breathed between kisses, "I predict there's going to be a wonderful—and quite terrible—storm right in this very room."

"I predict it too," she whispered, pulling him closer, her body aching with desire and that still-nameless, wholly unexplained sense of release and anticipation. "Oh, John . . . John, am I crazy? Or did something amazing really change for us?"

"You're not crazy," he said, kissing her throat and shoulders till she was breathless. "And I don't know any more than you know, but yes, something changed and something very truthful and nearly unbearable is about to take place—this moment. Maybe—maybe the windiest, wildest moment in history! Even better than any you and I have ever made happen. Oh, this is good, Anne! This is so good."

Bodies one, souls, minds, and spirits reaching, she gasped, "Then, help me, John! I'm—I'm drowning in goodness. *Your* goodness. I can't hold it all. Help me! Please help me!"

His whole being enfolding her, he groaned, "I'm trying, Annie—God in heaven knows I'm trying. But I need help, too."

When morning came, neither of them was surprised that rain was falling onto George Street. John felt rested and yet was somehow still soaring with the curious, high anticipation they'd both sensed, not only during the last few days at Abbotsford but all the way back to London.

Almost at the same waking instant, they reached for each other. "I know we both long to visit Little Annie now that she's awake and waiting to charm us with those eyes almost as glorious as her mother's," John said, "but tell me first—*how are you* today, Anne?"

Both arms around his neck, she laughed up into his face. "How am I today, my darling? Oh, I couldn't possibly be better," she said in an exaggerated British accent. "And how are you today, John?"

He kissed her nose. "I know that was a dumb question. What I meant was, do you still feel something still more wonderful, if possible, may be going to happen to us? In fact, I think I just had a dream about it!"

She sat up. "You did? What did you dream?"

Rubbing his eyes, he thought a minute. "I don't know exactly. But I know that in my dream stood our great, gnarled, blessed live oak tree—right there by the Hampton River. I could feel the rough bark!"

John could tell he had startled her because she gave what sounded like a little, helpless scream and sank back onto the pillow. "Our—*tree,* John? Don't tease. Did you really have a dream about our oak tree? Please don't joke! I know how silly we've been acting and I still feel that way today—almost. But, don't ever tease about our tree!"

"I wasn't, darling. Honest. Annie, are you scared? You look almost scared."

"I don't think so," she said in the smallest voice. "No. I just—I just nearly choke sometimes because I long so for just one glimpse of our tree. I also know how stupid that sounds." She held his face close to hers. "Our life is so perfect, I don't need a dumb old live oak tree, for goodness' sake! I've had live oak trees all my life, and now I have you and you said right in front of the Scotts that you'd never loved anyone else but me. I don't need anything I don't already have, darling. I don't. I don't!"

A rap at their door, unmistakably Flora's brisk, hard knock, shattered the moment.

"We're awake, Flora," John called, "but just not yet out of bed—not dressed. What is it? Is anything wrong with Little Annie?"

Through the closed door, Flora's Borderland burr, firm and sure, relieved them both when she shouted, "The bairn's as good as gold today. 'Tis just that a package come for Miss Anne! A package that looks like it's been through sixteen shipwrecks—a fair-sized one, the wrappin' most torn off it. You want I should leave it at your door, Laddie?"

"Please, Flora, and thanks so much. You won't need to wait. I know how busy you are fixing breakfast."

On a deep sigh, John sank back onto the pillows. "At least we know Little Annie's fine," he said, then kissed Anne, hopped out of bed and into his worn silk robe.

"Why am I getting a package?" she asked.

"Who else gets packages around this house but you? Hold your horses. I'll find out."

In his bare feet, John padded across the room to open the door, and came back bearing a dog-eared bundle that indeed did look as though it had weathered more than sixteen shipwrecks.

Up on the side of the bed, Anne asked, "Is it from St. Simons?"

"Of course it's from St. Simons! At least, as much of the writing as can still be read. I think whatever it is, it must be in some kind of box under this torn, rumpled paper. Do you want me to unwrap it?"

"Yes! Hurry," Anne ordered.

He fumbled in a drawer for his penknife, cut the half-tattered cord with which someone had securely wrapped whatever was inside, ripped off the paper, jerked the lid from a flat, sturdy box, and took out what appeared to be a thin piece of board with painting on it. A letter, which had once been carefully pasted to the back of the board, fluttered to the floor. Anne leaped up to grab it. John could see her hands shake as she broke the dark-red wax of the seal bearing her father's initials, JC.

"John!" She sank back onto the side of the bed, the single-page letter clutched in both hands. "Oh, John, it's a letter from Eve! Look, darling, Eve wrote this herself! I doubt she's ever tried to write a real letter before in her whole life. I taught her to write a long time ago, but look! No, don't look. Listen and I'll read it aloud."

7 August 1817
St. Simons Island, Georgia

Dear Miss Anne,

This be Lord God Bird I done paint fer you and yer man. Miss Becca an me we done do lots of such fanciework these days. I miss you till my stomack hurt all the time. I would cut off one arm and be glad to do it could I only fix your hair 1 time more. Ain't you eber comin' home to see me? Ain't I took the bes care ob you than anybody else? I hope you like and ain't forgit your favrite Lord God Bird.

Yours sinceer,
Eve

When he saw Anne begin to fight tears spilling down her sleepy face onto the pale pink collar of her nightgown, John could only stand there. With all his heart, he longed to take her in his arms and tell her that it was only natural for her to cry because it had been such a long time since she'd seen Eve. That no one knew better than he how much Anne had missed her and not only Eve, but every person, bird, and leaf at Cannon's Point. To tell her that he knew she was painfully homesick but just too brave and too unselfish to tell him how really lonely she was. Oh, blessed Annie, he thought, still unable to take a step toward her, have you kept such pain bottled up inside you all this time because I'm a selfish, heedless lout?

Anne was hungrily studying every stroke of Eve's painting of the big, red-crested woodpecker John knew she had always loved. She'd told him even while she was his captive on Cumberland Island that her papa's people called the huge woodpecker the Lord God Bird. In Scotland, they'd looked and looked for one. Maybe Lord God Birds lived only on Georgia coastal islands.

"John?"

He found the courage then to go to her. "What, Annie? Oh, what can I do for you?"

That instant, as though the last ounce of courage had drained from her heart, she crumpled away from him onto the bed and sobbed in the uncontrollable, deep, helpless way he'd heard a woman cry only once before in all his life. His mother, the night before she died, had sobbed like that —with the same, mysterious, woman-pain tearing at her because she hated so to leave him and William and Father. Back then, John had stood, able only to watch his mother suffer; had stood hearing the same, helpless agony that tore from Anne now. All those years ago, he could do nothing to help his mother, but *he could help Anne.*

He fell to his knees beside the bed and reached for one of her hands. "Darling, is homesickness this bad?" He honestly hadn't known. "Anne!"

For the first time since they'd loved each other, she didn't answer. Anne always answered. He knew she had always been too careful, too afraid of hurting his feelings ever to fall silent for long with him. She didn't answer now because she couldn't.

A minute or so passed during which he was only half aware that an empty produce wagon was rattling and jolting along George Street, and then, he knew. In a brilliant flash of time, he knew—everything.

"I know what to do, Annie," he said firmly, his voice suddenly strong. Almost as strong as the decision he'd just reached. "Listen to me, darling," he said, still on his knees beside her. "Do you remember how we've been puzzling over what wonderful thing might be up ahead for us both—ever since we left Walter Scott's house in that old chaise?"

"John," she gasped, still sobbing. "John, I'm so sorry to cry like this! Forgive me!"

"I will not forgive you because nothing's been your fault. I won't even ask you to forgive me since all that I've been doing that was stupid and insensitive was because of my blindness. Father told me, but I didn't realize I was causing you so much heartache. Listen, Annie, I'm not going to be that way anymore! I know now, just this minute, what's going to happen for us."

Slowly, she raised her head, then began to pull herself up. She pulled and he pulled until she was sitting on the side of the bed, her tearstreaked face level with his.

"What, John? What's going to happen?" she asked hoarsely. "You sound so certain. All the way from Abbotsford, I believed whatever was up ahead would be—clear and good."

"Yes, oh yes, it's going to be all of that. I didn't know either, dearest, what it was. But I do know now. Oh Anne, I know!"

Puzzled, half-frowning and at the same time trying to smile, she peered at him, eyes still streaming tears. "What? *What?*"

When he began to laugh softly, so did she. At least he could tell she was making a valiant effort. He was trying, too, to find the exact right words to convince her that somehow at Abbotsford they had both begun to be free of all that had been holding them away from one another so that neither had dared to take the happiness that life, through her father, was trying to offer them. The words stuck in his throat. How could he bear to admit that his own selfishness now looked—even to him—only young and stubborn, the way it must have looked all along to her? His frantic efforts to raise funds for South Africa were the efforts of an unthinking madman. His equally frantic, futile attempts to regain his commission could only have forced them apart—

physically apart—when all the time Anne had known that neither of them could live without being able to touch the other.

"Can't you tell me, dearest?" she asked. "I can feel all sorts of hopeful ideas forming in your mind. Please try! I was dreadful to give way to tears like that, but you must know I kept so much locked inside me because I only adore you and—and so much of the time I've been afraid you'd sail off somewhere and leave me!"

As though she'd tightened her fingers around his heart, he felt the certainty. "Anne, no! I'll never leave you. But this minute, I know all about what's going to happen for us and I am trying to put it into words. You've been so long-suffering with me. *I* caused those sobs when you looked at Eve's painting of the Lord God Bird."

"You did not! I'm the one who can't grow up enough to control my silly emotions. Don't you dare blame yourself, do you hear me?"

"I hear you," he said, unable not to smile because suddenly, he could hear them both, was aware of both their struggles. Struggles that each had been too afraid to share with the other.

"You're smiling," she said. "What does that mean?"

"It means your husband is, from this moment on, going to follow a *possible* dream. It's still scary and it took me a while, but even I can be slow. Disgustingly slow to grow up."

"Darling, I know about your dream. I do know the only thing that can make you happy is to wear your gorgeous uniform again. And I've stopped crying. For good. I think I've grown up this morning, too, and it's past time to visit our daughter."

"Hush!"

"Hush?"

He got abruptly to his feet because if he stayed near enough to touch her, he'd never get it said. "I can't think straight or talk straight when I'm close to you, so I intend to stand right here in the middle of the floor until I've set you straight, Mrs. Fraser. I don't think you really believed me when I told you I dreamed last night about our oak tree. Well, I did dream about it and I'm insanely impatient, suddenly, to stand under it again—with you! I think I must have begun to want that at Abbotsford, maybe even during the walk I took with Walter Scott our first day there. Anyway, I know for certain that this man you say you adore is going to live his life—all the remaining days of it—acting like a man. I found you, I captured you on a Georgia coastal island, and as soon as I can arrange to put Father's business in order here, I'm buying a one-way passage to Savannah for us and for Little Annie. John Couper has waited long enough to see his only grandchild."

He had not touched her, but as he talked, he could see the touch of his words on her face, could see her fears begin to fade, could feel understanding begin to free them both. Finally, as she leaped to her feet to reach for him, he recognized her in a new way—the spirited Anne, her dark, elegant head tilted ever so slightly on the perfect throat, offering him with open hands the chance at last to become his own best self.

"Are you quite finished talking?" she asked. "I hope you are, because I need a kiss, desperately!"

Arms around her, he whispered, "Yes, ma'am, I'm finished. Except to say that all my speech making was intended to let you know that my new dream—my real dream—is leading me straight to that snug little house at Lawrence."

Anne could only stare at him.

"Dearest, the whole prospect is still scary, but can't you tell I'm begging you and Little Annie to live beside me on St. Simons Island—for the remainder of my days?"

Afterword

John's decision was firm, and as far as my research has revealed, Father Fraser was eventually able to find a replacement for him. No date is available, but some time after 1819, John, Anne, and Little Annie sailed back to Georgia to begin their life on St. Simons Island—the place I have chosen to live out the remainder of my days.

All the main characters and most of the minor ones in *Bright Captivity* were real persons. As nearly as possible, I have used actual names for the slaves, and if I have come close to capturing the too frequently untapped facets of their often complex personalities, I shall have reached an important personal goal. By accident of birth a member of the white majority, I have felt hesitant at times in the past attempting to write "from inside the head" of a black slave. But more than a year ago an articulate young scholar, Deborah Barnes, began to free me. This is what she said: "You have as much right to characterize a black slave as I have. I'm black but I certainly don't know what it was like to be a slave!" My gratitude to Deborah and to her parents, Hal and Shirley Sieber, who urged me to call her. I'm especially grateful to Hal Sieber for the use of his splendidly researched, unpublished manuscript, *The Igbo Strike of 1803,* which contains the confirmed facts of the often-told St. Simons legend about the Ebos (originally *Igbos*) who drowned themselves in Dunbar Creek rather than submit to slavery. Hal's careful research on St. Simons and in Africa liberated me to use the tragic story in my Prologue.

The books I have devoured are too numerous to list here, but I must mention the latest from my valued friend Malcolm Bell of Savannah, an altogether compelling volume titled *Major Butler's Legacy* (Athens, Ga: University of Georgia Press, 1987). I have never learned more from any single title. Thank you, Malcolm and Muriel Bell, for the superb research you did and for your always encouraging friendship and advice.

I stay too busy to allow myself a wide circle of truly close St. Simons friends, but snug inside the small circle are Tina McElroy Ansa and her talented husband, Jonée Ansa. On the strength of one excellent novel, *Baby of the Family* (New York: Harcourt Brace Jovanovich, 1989), Tina has won her place as an important American writer and has lived in a unique place in my heart and daily life as I worked on *Bright Captivity.* I told her early on how I longed to make my black people "whole." She promised to stick with me through the writing and to be candid about the results. She has done all this and more. Working novelists share an otherwise unshareable world. I wouldn't have missed having Tina in my world for anything! My gratitude runs deep.

As intent as I've been on avoiding stereotypes among my black characters, I have been equally determined not to fall into the same trap with the white slave masters and their families. The social ambience, culture, and neighborliness of St. Simons plantation families were singular. The island is small. Everyone knew everyone else then and so gave one another high standards to uphold both in their planting methods and in the treatment of their slaves. Except at Major Butler's Hampton—during this period run by Roswell King, a conscientious but severely strict overseer for an absentee owner—the actual conditions on St. Simons, despite the deplorable system, were probably above those of many other Southern communities. Malcolm Bell confirmed this in his excellent book on Major Butler. No two masters were alike as no two persons are alike—white or black.

My kind friend Reed Ferguson is writing a biography of Anne's father, the colorful Scot John Couper, and I thank Reed not only for his help with research but for the warm enthusiasm shown me by him and his charming wife, Cornelia. I am deeply indebted also for the friendship and extraordinary insights of W. W. Law, prominent Savannah black historian and founder of the King-Tisdell Cottage Foundation, who keeps me reminded that "both Thomas Spalding and John Couper were highly estimable men—and they are rightly revered to this day."

It took me a while to catch on, but Captain Edwin Fendig, senior bar pilot, in numerous telephone conversations successfully "piloted" me through the winding waters between St. Simons and Cumberland islands. Without him, we would all be lost at sea. My deepest gratitude.

Another friend, Frances Burns, once more gave me invaluable help—first by being Frances and then by being a knowledgeable descendant of the Wylly-Armstrong clan. With her, our friend Sarah Plemmons answered nature questions and gave valuable help in a search of the photo archives at the Coastal Museum on St. Simons.

As with every novel I have written, my closest friend, Joyce Blackburn, with whom I share my home and all meaningful hours, has again devoted her time (months of it!) and astute critical assistance with each line. Anyone who knows me knows not only some of what Joyce means to me, but that it is she who ultimately makes me sound good, if I do. Joyce and I have "lived" with John and Anne for two years in the kind of particular "bright captivity" on which we both thrive. Since she was with me thirty years ago on the day we first discovered the enchantment of St. Simons, we are both glad and relieved to have me working again in the locale of the island we love so much. You know, Joyce, that I've been at this for a long time and that each time I attempt to express in one of these Afterwords even a hint of your value and meaning to me, I feel my own inadequacy with words as at no other time. There simply are no words to reveal my heart.

I have been at the task of putting together eleven long novels for more than a quarter of a century, but never before have I been so aware of the high caliber of what my agent calls Genie's support group. I dare any novelist to lay claim to better or more freely given support, not only by Joyce but by my one-of-a-kind full-time assistant, Eileen Humphlett, who has been with me in all ways—heart, mind, and spirit—through the writing and daily living of each novel since *Margaret's Story* back in 1978. *Stranger in Savannah* is dedicated to her, but she deserves boundless credit for everything I write, including letters. Cleaning up my long, heavily marked, manually typed manuscript pages is almost the least of all Eileen does for me. She and her entire family are at the top of the list of my intimate and fun friends. Best of all, Eileen knows me and loves me anyway.

I dedicated another novel, *Maria,* to the third and equally necessary member of my long-suffering support group, Nancy Goshorn, who not only (along with Joyce and Eileen) keeps me intact but believing in myself. Nancy learned how much I need to believe in myself straight from my late mother, who taught me to believe in the first place. I've lost track of how long Nance and I have known each other, but the important thing is that we do. Almost from our first meeting at Mother's dining room table, I had one of my hunches that Nance would make a superior research woman. Now, she lives in her own house down Frederica Road from mine and has masterfully handled the bulk of the detail and nitty-gritty research that would overload an average mind. As you so quickly learned to "read me," Nance, please read between these lines and know how grateful I am.

Nancy has also tended the all-important connection between my brain and the resourceful minds of the staff of the Glynn-Brunswick Regional Library's expert reference department. My longtime friend Director Jim Darby sat with me at a Friends of the Library dinner recently and therefore knows how I value not only him but his superior staff—in particular, Marcia Hodges and Dorothy Houseal. Nance found them always available, always eager, and—to me, best of all—genuinely interested in my ongoing writer's needs and problems. Along with Marcia and Dorothy, I must thank Diane Jackson, Jane Hildebrand, Stuart Gardner, Betty Ranson, Jim Kammerer, and Jimmy Smith. We also received most helpful materials through Director Al Spivey and Ginny Boyd at the Clara Wood Gould Library of Brunswick College. I have long been interested in the excellent Bryan Lang Historical Library in neighboring Woodbine, Georgia, and the help given so warmly by Librarian John H. Christian is much appreciated. One of the movers and shakers who worked to bring this unique library into being is a dear friend, the historian Eloise Bailey, of St. Marys, Georgia, the most qualified person I know to have helped with the little-known and complex activity on Cumberland Island at the close of the War of 1812. With a heart full of love, I thank you, Eloise.

The third book in my Savannah Quartet, *Before the Darkness Falls,* is dedicated to one of my favorite people anywhere, Barbara Bennett, who stayed with me through the difficult research for the whole quartet as acting director of the fabulous Georgia Historical Society archives in Savannah. Through *Bright Captivity,* when we were struggling for accuracy in Regency London and had other such obscure needs, there was Bobby—now far away in New York City attending Columbia University but still beside me in her heart and brilliant mind. She even came up with an 1806 map of London and a travel guide published in 1817, which John and Anne may well have used! Before she left Savannah, Bobby also "gave" me Anne Smith, now Georgia Historical Library director, and Tracy Bearden, senior archivist, assuring me they could deftly handle me and my oddball requests. Believe me, they did. Tracy, in particular, was always cheerfully and expertly there for me. Nancy and I were also helped at those same invaluable archives by Ryan Johnson, Jan Flores, and Eileen Ielmini. I must thank Carolyn Crowder, library manager of the Ida Hilton Public Library at Darien, Georgia; Marilyn Cunningham at the Midway Museum, Midway, Georgia; and most especially, courtesy of Scott Smith, director of Savannah's Old Fort Jackson, I'm grateful for the time given Nancy and me by Superintendent Joe Thompson at the Wormsloe Historic Site. Joe is an expert, believe it or not, on the highly styled uniforms of John Fraser's beloved Royal Marines in 1812. I deeply thank Shirley O'Dell, too, of Wormsloe, for her welcoming kindness to us. Also in Savannah there is another admirable, perceptive friend, Stephen Bohlen-Davis, of the Juliette Gordon Low Center, who knows so much about nineteenth-century London I have only to call him for enlightened answers to my most peculiar questions—most not to be found in any book. It pays to have Anglophile Savannah friends and I have another, Maryann Wilborn, of E. Shaver's Fine Books. Thank you, dear Maryann, and all those other delightful creatures around you in one of my favorite bookstores.

After the expert help and access to rare materials from our own Coastal Georgia Historical Society archives on St. Simons, I'm prouder than ever to be a charter member! From my heart, I'm grateful for the super cooperation from Director Linda King and Curator Martha Teall. It was here that Nancy Goshorn found a handwritten description of Caerlaverock Castle, and in Fodor's Travel Guide she also discovered that the ancient Maxwell ruins still stand, "noble in decay," and that the site has fortunately been made a National Nature Reserve and thus will remain. Buddy Sullivan, editor of the *Darien News,* and Robert G. Kenan, a perceptive, generous gentleman from Birmingham, Alabama, combined—without knowing each other—to help greatly with research on Mr. Kenan's ancestor, Thomas Spalding. Fraser Ledbetter, one of our earliest island friends, now director emeritus of the St. Simons Public Library, used her usual magic to obtain for me a long-out-of-print copy of *A Seed That Was Planted in the Colony of Georgia* (New York: Neale Publishing Co., 1910), by Charles Spalding Wylly. Present Director Frances Kane, Mary Jean Mullis, Janie Hanneld, and Julie Shelfer (a Gould descendant I've known and loved since the days of the first St. Simons Trilogy) all helped with interest and great willingness.

A friend from our old Chicago days, Lucille Ingebretsen, sent a useful Scottish vocabulary and samples of Scottish ballads, and for all reasons she goes on being dear to Joyce and to me. Mary Burdell, St. Simons historian, whose remarkable husband, Bill Burdell, manages my finances, used her expertise along with that of our mutual friend Dewey Benefield, executive vice president of the Sea Island Company, in finding valued information on Cannon's Point. Once again Anita Raskin and Lonnie Evans at The Book Lady in Savannah were able to unearth old books no one else could or would bother to find for me.

Chuck and Bettie NeSmith at Insty-prints in Brunswick, as always, went the second mile in handling multiple copies of the long manuscript for Eileen and me, and because writers need personal comfort too, I must also thank a warm-hearted young man named Lieutenant Davis, of the Glynn County Fire Department, because he took charge in the most reassuring manner one dark, stormy night during the writing when a bolt of lightning set my woods afire!

Again I called for help and received it from my good friend Dr. Perry Cochran, historian supreme, of Statesboro, Georgia. And here, even though only they will know why their love and loyalty have special meaning for me, I want to thank Easter Straker, Mary Porter, Glenn Smith, Sara Pilcher, Clara Marie Gould, Ruby Wilson, Emma Gibson, Freddie Wright, Cathy Hively, Rosalie Kelly, Bob Summer, Gene Greniker, Rosemary Holton, Fred and Sara Bentley,

Grace Wolff, Ann Hyman, Dena Snodgrass, Faith Brunson, Sarah Bell Edmond, Jimmie Harnsberger, Marian Seidel, my sister-in-law, Millie Price, Cindy and Mike Birdsong and tribe, and a beautiful St. Simons artist, Ana Bel Lee Washington.

One recent, sharp personal loss still leaves me feeling lost. For most of my writing life I have depended on the carefully worded critical commentary of a singular friend named Frances Pitts of Duluth, Minnesota. Along with my beloved Easter Straker, Frances held a rare place in my working heart. She lived long enough to visit us the winter of 1990 on St. Simons and to read about a third of the very rough manuscript. Then she went home to Minnesota and died. I feel cheated without her and can only hope that she approves of what I've done with *Bright Captivity.*

Another enormous heartache still reminds both Joyce and me that our cherished friend Dr. Junius Martin lies now in Christ Churchyard at Frederica. In the research for this book, as always, buoyant, much-loved Junius and his Dot encouraged and cheered me. No one knew as much about the little church as did Junius, who not only wrote extensively of its history but served for many years as its truly Christian and learned rector. For thousands of others, as for us, there will be no end to the missing of this great and liberal-hearted man.

Peggy Buchan and her husband, Danny, live now at what is called Lawrence or Taylor's Fishing Camp, where Danny will take you fishing if you visit St. Simons. Lawrence, of course, adjoins Cannon's Point and I doubt that anyone loves those picturesque woods, marshes, rivers, and ruins as Peggy loves them. Happily, she is our valued friend, and although the Cannon's Point ruins are rightly protected behind a locked gate, through her I have had free access both to Lawrence and to the old Couper Place. Thank you, dear Buchans, for your treasured support, generosity, and kindness. Major Butler's Hampton Plantation, across Jones Creek from Cannon's Point, is now a handsome, affluent suburb called Hampton Point. But the nature-magic is still there, and, of course, for me there is also the tragic memory that the Butler slaves dared not cross that beautiful, treelined little creek. All of Cannon's Point and Lawrence are now owned by the Sea Island Company, and the years have proved that because they are, the land will always be wisely managed.

Two descendants of the Coupers via the brilliant James Hamilton Couper's branch of the family, Ann Fettner and Jo Cauthorn, have become an eternal part of my small circle of truly intimate and trusted friends. Ann Fettner, of Brooklyn, New York, would make even James Hamilton proud because she is as erudite as he and a brilliant professional writer. Ann has not only become my cherished friend, she has freely shared her time helping me understand the Couper family and, from her years of working in Africa among villagers, has taught and guided me in African tribal customs and mores. More than giving such distinct help, she inspirited me by being Ann—full of courage and as undaunted by hard, concentrated, ceaseless work as any truly professional writer must be. Ann, your critical opinion of my work and of me as a human being means far more than you think. Thank you, thank you.

And now to Ann's sister, of Fort Lauderdale, Florida—beautiful, equally erudite Jo Cauthorn, whose real middle name, by the way, is Farley and not Couper, except to me. I wrote Anne Couper Fraser to look quite like a photo of attractive Ann Fettner at about twenty, but there is a lot of Jo in my Anne's makeup. There just may be still more of Jo in a later daughter born to Anne and John, whose nickname was Pete. I already love Pete because with all my heart I love Jo and have dedicated *Bright Captivity* to her. For at least fourteen years, Jo Cauthorn and I have been easy friends because writing and the world of books constitute Jo's native air, too. I loved her from her first letter to me, and when we met a year or so later at the time the family made the invaluable gift of many of John Couper's letters to our Coastal Museum archives, our friendship was sealed. Jo and Joyce Blackburn are also bonded now and that only strengthens all ties. Except for my immediate St. Simons "support group," no one held up my hands throughout the writing with more daring and verve, more steady faith and stimulus, than Jo did. So, with heart-deep thanks for your freeing insights into what I faced in the actual doing, dear Jo, and with all the love there is, *Bright Captivity* is yours.

In the making of this book, I have been vastly rewarded by meeting many Couper descendants—none more knowledgeable, none more generous, than Frances Daugherty of

Marietta, Georgia. Not only has Frances, in her quick, naturally likable way, been right there ready—along with her cousin, Elizabeth Zervas, of California—to help with the often complex genealogy, she came here to discuss my manuscript and then went to London for photographs of the very house at 2 George Street where the Frasers lived. The old house still stands, its entrance remodeled into shops now. If I had not already fallen captive to this story, its writing would be memorable because I have come to know not only the Couper descendants mentioned above but other members of the clan, all of whom I know would make Jock and Becca Couper proud. I must here mention my personal attachment for descendant Julie Couper Beziat, who, like Frances Daugherty, still has never met either Jo or Ann—but will one day—and especially Jo's husband, Robert Cauthorn, himself knowledgeable and admirably patient with my many requests to call Jo in from her mysterious work on the compost pile in their yard.

Almost as long as I've known St. Simons Island, I've known and loved Burnette Vanstory, whose superior book, *Georgia's Land of the Golden Isles* (Athens, Ga.: University of Georgia Press, 1956, 1970), has for years been my research bible. Anyone who knows me knows how much you mean to me, Burney, and I will never forget the golden afternoon at your cozy house on St. Simons when you gave me, from your vast store of research, two or three St. Simons stories from which to choose—the day you and I decided on Anne Couper Fraser as the main character for my new trilogy, laid for the most part in the Golden Isles. You're aware of how long my readers have urged me to return to St. Simons as a setting, but I wouldn't have dared try without consulting you first. By now, you must know how deeply I thank and love you.

There is today something of a proverb in the publishing world that a good agent is harder to find than a publisher. If my mail is any indication, this is true. I am besieged with requests for my agent's address. I simply cannot comply. She remains among the best simply because she refuses to take any more clients than she can manage by her own high standards. Her name is Lila Karpf, and although I recently read in my *Authors Guild Bulletin* that "an agent does not have to be your friend," Lila is my friend all the way. She not only attends expertly to my every need as a writer, no one could convince me that she doesn't care about me as a human being. Lila, for all that only you and I know about, my heart thanks you.

One of Lila's cogent sayings is that "these days in New York publishing, one never knows from Friday to Monday" who will still be working where. I have suffered (and one does suffer) so many abrupt changes through my long years as a published author that I should be far more flexible. At least, I have learned how to compartmentalize my attachments so that after a recent period of heavy losses, I can honestly say my heart has once more rushed out to meet and enfold the new, enthusiastic professionals who have taken the places of my lost co-workers. In a way I believe he already knows, I have taken our new Doubleday president, Steve Rubin, straight into my heart. Steve's secretary, Naomi Fields, and assistant, Renée Zuckerbrot, are more than I dared hope and I am once again having fun with a new book. To say thank you, Steve, for being as you are, is to understate. Filling another loss at Doubleday is my caring new marketing expert, Jayne Schorn, on whom so much depends, and as my new, equally caring art director, I have Whitney Cookman, who supervised the excellence of the *Bright Captivity* jacket. I am lyrical once again to have had access to the catalog and general copy expertise of Jennifer Brehl and to the rare talent of my favorite jacket artist, Pamela Patrick, who not only did the painting on this jacket but that on *Stranger in Savannah* as well. One of the reasons Pamela was able to create such a perfect live oak tree, although she had never seen one, was the fine effort of my new St. Simons photographer, Merriam Bass, who made countless pictures of the island's few remaining live oaks and, with Joyce, Eileen, and Peggy Buchan, climbed about Lawrence and Cannon's Point to give Pamela many of the shots she used to "make her tree." I can honestly say that the jacket *is* the book itself.

My cup runneth over because through another novel, I will have my much-loved publicist, Ellen Archer, whose merry heart, enthusiasm, and fertile brain delight me. Not least among Ellen's values to me is that, as with so many mentioned here, she and her Jeff share my eccentric and (of course) "correct" political views. Thank you, dear Ellen, and all those who help you let it be known that I have a new book. Few readers think of book designers except to bless or chastise them, depending on the readability and appearance of the type on the page. I bless mine, Marysarah Quinn, who has again turned out an artful reading masterpiece. I also toss love and many blessings around this country and in England and Canada to my many skillful sales reps and to every bookseller, large or small, to whom I owe so, so much. For her renowned sales expertise and her long and loyal friendship, I especially thank Bebe Cole at Doubleday.

Here I must again thank Doubleday's new, sensitive president, Steve Rubin, for two more valued gifts to me. Really skillful copy editors, who make authors sound careful and meticulous when we frequently aren't, are hard to find. I have found one in Janet Falcone, and thanks to Steve and Harold Grabau, Janet and I are together again on still another novel. For remaining my friend and booster even during the years your schedule precluded our working together, Janet, thank you and my love. I began publishing books with Doubleday five long novels ago because Carolyn Blakemore was there as senior editor. Again thanks to wise Steve Rubin, Carolyn, though now a busy and successful freelance editor in New York, is, as I write these lines, marking up and touching the *Bright Captivity* manuscript with her special magic. If you know me at all, you already know that Carolyn Blakemore is not only a beloved friend, she is my favorite editor anywhere. Her approval matters to me more than she knows. Even after more than thirty years as a published author, I wait for that first call from Carolyn. This time, she found grace enough to declare *Bright Captivity* my best yet. I am, of course, on cloud thirty-nine because she also considers Anne Couper Fraser my strongest character. Carolyn, you and I *are* friends, but it never gets in the way of our professionalism. I hope I can go on writing novels forever—with you beside me.

For respecting my particularly close relationship with and regard for my readers, one more bit of gratitude to the house of Doubleday. No one there has ever attempted to crowd me for space or content in these Afterwords. As a friend said recently, they are my letters to my readers, who respond to every word in them with far more interest than even I have come to expect. Authors unjustly get most of the credit for a book, but far more people are involved than even my leisurely Afterwords can mention. Indeed, this *is* my letter to my readers and a most inadequate attempt to thank each of you for the loyalty few authors experience.

I can't resist telling you that I, for one, am glad and relieved that we're just getting started with the story of Anne and John Fraser. Two more books follow, so think of me and of all those who help me, because we wouldn't make it if we didn't think daily of you who read.

Eugenia Price
St. Simons Island, Georgia